READERS ARE RAVING ABOUT ALYXANDRA HARVEY!

"Witty, sly, and never disappointing. . . . Fun, funny, and a relief from Twilight wannabes." —*Booklist* on *Hearts at Stake*

"A smart mix of darkness and humor." —*Publishers Weekly* on *Hearts at Stake*

"A highly entertaining and funny book that will be sure to make you smile the entire time through." —*Juciliciousss* on *Hearts at Stake*

"An action-packed story full of intrigue, suspense, and romance with a great cast of characters." —*School Library Journal* on *Blood Feud*

"Will keep readers entertained from start to finish. . . . Fast-paced and engaging." —*VOYA* on *Out for Blood*

Also by Alyxandra Harvey

Haunting Violet

RULING PASSION

INCLUDES

HEARTS AT STAKE

BLOOD FEUD

OUT FOR BLOOD

ALYXANDRA HARVEY

Walker & Company New York

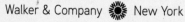

Hearts at Stake first published in the United States of America in January 2010
Blood Feud first published in the United States of America in July 2010
Out for Blood first published in the United States of America in December 2010
by Walker Publishing Company, Inc., a division of Bloomsbury Publishing, Inc.
Ruling Passion published in September 2011
www.bloomsburyteens.com

For information about permission to reproduce selections from this book, write to
Permissions, Walker BFYR, 175 Fifth Avenue, New York, New York 10010

LCCN: 2011931315
ISBN: 978-0-8027-2802-9

Book design by Danielle Delaney and Regina Roff
Typeset by Westchester Book Composition
Printed in the U.S.A. by Quad/Graphics, Fairfield, Pennsylvania
2 4 6 8 10 9 7 5 3 1

All papers used by Bloomsbury Publishing, Inc., are natural, recyclable products
made from wood grown in well-managed forests. The manufacturing processes
conform to the environmental regulations of the country of origin.

HEARTS AT STAKE
Thanks and chocolate kisses to:

My editor, Emily Easton, and everyone at Walker Books/ Bloomsbury, known and unknown, who have helped make this book a reality. You are the cause of many happy dances in my kitchen.

My wonderful agent, Marlene Stringer, who is helping to make my dreams come true.

My parents, who are unfailingly supportive and love me just the way I am, tattoos, pink hair, and all.

My long-time BFF Jess, Google Queen Extraordinaire, for the cheerleading, commiserating, and demands for more books.

My husband, Khayman, who guards my writing time almost as zealously as I do, and who only ever wants me to be me.

All my friends and family, especially Crystal, who regularly drives all the way up to the farmhouse for visits.

BLOOD FEUD
For Pat, who suggested to a bored nine-year-old me: "Why don't you write a story?"

OUT FOR BLOOD
For Anne, from my inner ferret to yours!

THE DRAKE FAMILY TREE

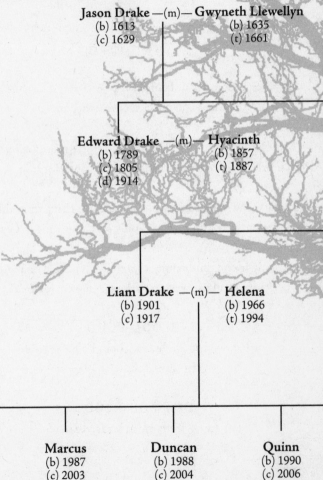

Jason Drake —(m)— **Gwyneth Llewellyn**
(b) 1613   (b) 1635
(c) 1629   (t) 1661

Edward Drake —(m)— **Hyacinth**
(b) 1789   (b) 1857
(c) 1805   (t) 1887
(d) 1914

Liam Drake —(m)— **Helena**
(b) 1901   (b) 1966
(c) 1917   (t) 1994

Sebastian
(b) 1986
(c) 2002

Marcus
(b) 1987
(c) 2003

Duncan
(b) 1988
(c) 2004

Quinn
(b) 1990
(c) 2006

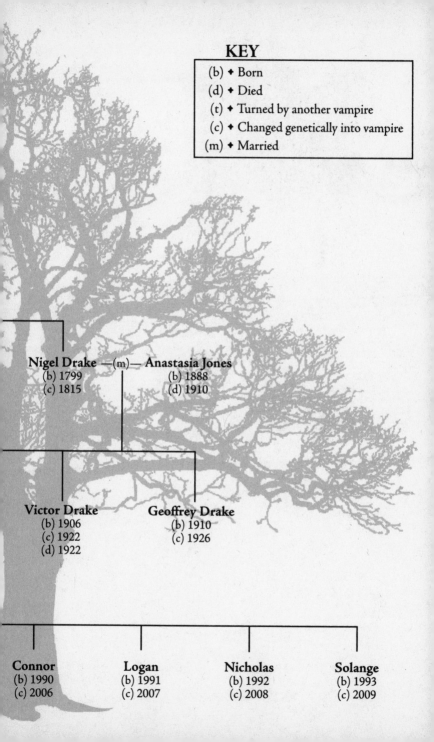

KEY

(b) ✦ Born
(d) ✦ Died
(t) ✦ Turned by another vampire
(c) ✦ Changed genetically into vampire
(m) ✦ Married

Nigel Drake —(m)— **Anastasia Jones**
(b) 1799   (b) 1888
(c) 1815   (d) 1910

Victor Drake   **Geoffrey Drake**
(b) 1906   (b) 1910
(c) 1922   (c) 1926
(d) 1922

Connor   **Logan**   **Nicholas**   **Solange**
(b) 1990   (b) 1991   (b) 1992   (b) 1993
(c) 2006   (c) 2007   (c) 2008   (c) 2009

Hearts at Stake

PROLOGUE

◆

Lucy

Friday, early evening

Normally I wouldn't have been caught dead at a field party.

If you'll pardon the pun.

This was a supreme sacrifice on my part for my best friend, Solange, who was having a really bad day, which was about to turn into a *really* bad week. Her sixteenth birthday was coming up, and we weren't talking a new car and a pink dress for her sweet sixteen. Not in her family.

This wasn't much better though.

She was standing in the middle of a field, trying to drink cheap wine and pretend she didn't want to be anywhere but here. The music was passable but that was about all it had to recommend it. The cars were parked in a wide circle, the sun setting behind the trees with all the colors of a blood orange pulled into pieces. Practically my entire high school was here; there wasn't much else to do on one of the last weekends before school started. People danced and flirted in a sea of baseball caps and faded denim. Someone burped loudly.

"This was *such* a bad idea," I muttered.

Solange smiled softly, abandoning her plastic cup on the hood of someone's rusted truck.

"It was a nice thought."

"It was stupid," I admitted. She just looked so sad lately, I'd hoped a complete change of pace might distract her from all that worrying. Instead it made me want to bare my pitifully human teeth at the rowdies. Someone's shoe nudged my heel, and when I looked back at it, I was greeted with way too much information about the mating habits of my fellow students. I kicked hard at the boot.

"No one needs to see that," I said, turning away quickly before more clothing came off. The couple giggled and went deeper into the corn. I stared at Solange. "What the hell was I thinking?"

She half grinned.

"It is rather unlike you."

Darren, from my math class last year, tripped over his own feet and sprawled in the dirt in front of us before I could answer. His grin was sloppy. He was nice enough usually; in fact, he was the reason I hadn't entirely flunked out of math. But he was drunk and desperate to fit in.

"Hi, Lucy." Apparently beer made him lisp. My name came out as "Loothee"—which was marginally better than my real name, which was Lucky. I had *those* kind of parents, but I'd made everyone at school call me Lucy since the first day of first grade.

"Hi, Darren."

He blinked at Solange. Even in jeans and a tank top she looked dramatic. It was all that pale skin and those pale eyes. Her black bangs were choppy because she trimmed them herself. The rest was long and hung past her shoulders. Mine was plain old brown and cut in a wedged bob to my chin. My glasses were retro—dark rimmed and vaguely cat's-eye shaped. I didn't need them to see the way Darren was drooling over Solange. All guys drooled over her. She was beautiful, end of discussion.

"Who's your friend? She's hot."

"You've met her before." Solange was homeschooled, but I dragged her around when I could. "Sober up, Darren. This isn't a good look for you."

"'Kay." He spat grass out of his mouth.

I slung my arm through hers. "Let's get out of here. The sun's starting to set anyway, and maybe we can salvage the rest of the night."

The wind was soft through the corn, rustling the stalks as we wandered away. The stars were starting to peek out, like animal eyes in the dark. We could still hear the music and the occasional shout of laughter. Twilight was starting to settle like a soft blue veil. We'd walked from my house, which was a half hour away. We'd probably waited too long. We picked up our pace.

And then Solange paused.

"What?" I froze beside her, my shoulders tensing until I was practically wearing them as earmuffs. I was all too aware of what could be out there. I should never have suggested this. I'd just put her into even more danger. I was an idiot.

She held up her hand, her eyes so pale suddenly that they were nearly colorless, a ring of ice around a black lake. And because I was scared, I scowled into the gathering shadows around us. Mom always said bravado was a karmic debt I had to work through. She was basically saying I'd been mouthy and obnoxious for several lifetimes now. But somehow I didn't think this particular situation called for a round of *oms*, which was my mother's favorite way of cleansing karmic baggage. Most babies were sung lullabies; I got "Om Namah Shivaya" when I was really fussy.

"Cops?" I suggested, mostly because they seemed like the better alternative. "They always break up these parties."

She shook her head. She looked delicate and ethereal, as if she were made of lily petals. Few people knew the marble all that softness concealed.

"They're close," she murmured. "Watching."

"Run?" I suggested. "Like, right now?"

She shook her head again, but we did at least start walking.

"If we act like prey, they'll act like predators."

I tried not to hyperventilate, tried to walk quickly but confidently, as if we weren't being stalked. Sometimes I really hated Solange's life. It was totally unfair.

"You're getting angry," she said softly.

"Damn right I am. Those undead bastards think they can do this to you just because—"

"When you're angry, your heart beats faster. It's like the cherry on a hot fudge sundae."

"Oh. Right." I always forgot that little detail. Maybe my mom was right. I needed to take up meditating.

"Lucy, I want you to run."

"Shut up," I said, disbelief making my voice squeaky.

"They'll follow me if I run in the opposite direction."

"That's the worst plan I've ever heard," I grumbled, fighting the urge to look over my shoulder. Stupid creepy cornfields. Stupid creepy stalkers. A cricket sang suddenly from the tall corn and my heart nearly shot straight out of my chest. I actually pressed my hand against my rib cage, half-worried. The cricket went quiet and was replaced by the rumble of car tires on the ground. Cornstalks snapped. A familiar jeep skidded to a dusty halt in front of us.

"Nicholas," Solange breathed, relieved.

"Get in," he snapped.

I was slightly less enamored with her older brother, but I had to admit he had good timing. In his black shirt and dark hair, he blended into the night. Only his eyes gave him away, silver and fierce. He was gorgeous, there was no use in denying it, but he always knew just how to make me want to poke him in the eye with a fork.

Like right now.

"Drive," he said to their brother Logan, who was behind the steering wheel. He didn't even wait for me to get in. Logan lifted his foot off the brake. The car rolled forward.

"Hey!" I shouted.

"Nicholas Drake, you let her in the car right now." Solange leaned forward between the front seats.

"She's fine. We have to get you out of here."

I grabbed on to the half-opened window. Logan slowed down.

"Sorry, Lucy, I thought you were in already," he said.

"Don't you *read?*" I asked Nicholas, disgusted. "If you leave me here now that you've got Solange all safe, they'll grab me to get to her."

Solange opened the back door and I leaped in. The car sped off. Shadows flitted beside us, menacing, hungry. I shivered. Then I smacked the back of Nicholas's head.

"Idiot."

CHAPTER 1

◆

Solange

"I can't believe you were actually going to just leave her there," I grumbled again as Logan pulled into our lane, which was overgrown with hedges. The unnatural glint of unnatural eyes had faded, and there was nothing but ripe blackberries and crickets in the bushes. Not only was our farm well protected, but it was also surrounded by other family farms, with forest surrounding all of them. Drakes have lived in this area since it was considered wild and dangerous, best left to gunslingers and outlaws. Now it was just home.

But dangerous all the same.

"She was fine," Nicholas said testily. "She was safe as soon as we got you away from her." He only ever called her "she," except to her face, when he called her Lucky because it annoyed her so much. They'd been getting on each other's nerves since we were kids. There was a family joke that Lucy's first words were, "Nicholas is bugging me." I couldn't remember ever *not* knowing her. She'd drawn me out of my shell, even when we were little, though it wasn't until my fifth birthday that I'd started calling her my best friend, after she threw a mud ball at Nicholas's head for stealing my chocolate cupcake. We'd learned to ride bikes together and liked the same movies and talked all night whenever we had slumber parties.

"She was *fine*," Nicholas insisted, catching my glare. "Despite being reckless."

"She was just trying to help me."

"She's *human*," he said, as if it were a debilitating disease, as if he wasn't human as well, despite the bloodchange. We aren't undead, like the horror novels say, though we definitely look it during our transformation. That particular stereotype clings so deeply that sometimes it's easier to embrace it. Lucy's mom calls us "differently abled."

"And you're a jerk." I touched his sleeve. "But thanks for coming to get me."

"You're welcome," he muttered. "You know you shouldn't let her talk you into stuff. It never turns out well."

"I know. But you know how Lucy is. And she meant well."

He grunted. Logan grinned.

"She's getting cuter. Especially from behind."

"She is *not*," Nicholas said. "And quit looking at her butt."

I was so totally going to tell Lucy they'd been talking about her butt.

"You're such an old man," Logan said scornfully, turning off the ignition. "We have all this power. We should use it."

"Flirting is not a power," I told him drily.

"It is if you're good at it. And I'm *very* good at it."

"So you keep telling us."

"Being charming's my gift," he said modestly. No one else could have pulled off such an old-fashioned shirt with lace cuffs and such a pretty face. The pheromones that vampires emit like a dangerous perfume keep humans enticed and befuddled with longing, and Logan's are especially well tuned. They don't have an actual smell that can be described, except lately in my case. It's more subliminal than that, with the power to hypnotize. Kind of like the way wild animals can smell each other out in the forest, especially during mating season. If a vampire is particularly strong, humans don't even remember being a meal; they just have a craving for rare steak or spinach. If we drink too much, they become anemic.

The pheromones don't work on other vampires, except, of course, for mine, which are rapidly becoming a beacon for all of vampire kind. I'm special, and not in a good way, if you ask me. Vampires are rarely born, except in certain ancient families ... Exhibit A, me and my seven obnoxious older brothers.

But I'm the only girl.

In about nine hundred years.

And the closer I get to my sixteenth birthday, the more I attract the others to me. It's all very Snow White, except I don't call bluebirds and deer out of the woods—only bloodthirsty vampires who want to kidnap me or kill me. Vampire politics are messy at best, and all Drakes have been exiled from the royal court since the very hour I was born. I'm considered a threat to the current ruler, Lady Natasha, because my genealogy is so impressive and because there's some stupid prophecy from centuries ago that says the vampire tribes will be properly united under the rule of a daughter born to an ancient family.

And Lady Natasha, unlike me, wasn't born into an ancient family—even if she considers herself to be the reigning vampire queen.

As if that's my fault.

Luckily, my family much prefers living in quiet exile in the woods. I'd heard enough rumors about our ruler to be glad we'd never actually met. She feeds off humans and is barely circumspect about it; in fact, she loves the attention and the vampire groupies. She apparently doesn't like pretty young girls; they never seem to survive her mood swings.

Technically, she shouldn't be feeding off humans, and certainly not so nonchalantly. It was becoming an issue, even among her own people. There are royalists who follow her just because she's so powerful, not because they particularly respect her. Fear, as always, is a great motivator.

And lately she's been turning more and more humans into vampires, in order to gather more followers. The council makes her nervous, and I make her nervous, but most of all Leander Montmartre makes her nervous.

He has that affect on all of us.

He's been turning humans for nearly three hundred years now, and he's so violent and careless about it, he's basically created a new breed of vampire. He leaves them half-turned and usually buried under the ground, to conquer the bloodchange on their own without any help at all. The thirst is so strong that it twists them and gives them a double set of fangs instead of just our one retractable pair. The ones that stay loyal to Montmartre are called the Host. The ones who defect call themselves the Cwn Mamau, the Hounds of the Mothers. They were either strong enough to survive alone, or were rescued and trained by other Hounds. Everyone knew they wanted to kill Montmartre, but they were so reclusive they wouldn't accept outside help. They are fiercely independent, live in caves, serve a shamanka (female shaman), and wear bone beads in their hair. They're kind of scary, but nowhere near as scary as the most dangerous of Montmartre's creations called the *Hel-Blar*, who have blue-tinted skin, and teeth that are all fangs, sharpened like needles and unretractable. *Hel-Blar* means "blue death" in some ancient Viking language. Their bite, known as a "kiss," can infect without any blood exchange, and it's rumored they can turn both vampires and humans into *Hel-Blar*. Even Montmartre avoids them as much as possible. He's not big on cleaning up his own mess. And they want him dead even more than the Hounds do—when they're lucid enough to want anything more than blood. The Host and the Hounds managed to stay sane, unlike the *Hel-Blar*. No one can control them, not even Montmartre.

We live peacefully with other humans, and our family is one of the few ancient clans of the Raktapa Council. The council was formed ages ago when the families realized that we weren't like other vampires: our change is genetic. We transform without being bitten, but we need vampire blood to survive that transformation. Afterward, we're nearly immortal, like the others, vulnerable only to a stake through the heart, too much sunlight, or decapitation.

"Do Mom and Dad know about what happened after the party?" I asked, finally getting out of the car and facing the house. The original building had burned down during the Salem witch trials, even though we were nowhere near Salem. The locals had been superstitious and scared of every little thing. The house was rebuilt farther into the sheltering forest. It was simple and a little shabby from the outside, but the pioneer-style log cabin hid a luxurious heart full of velvet couches and stone fireplaces. The rosebushes under the leaded-glass windows were a little scraggly, the oak trees old and stately. I loved every single treated inch of it. Even my mother's pinched and disapproving face behind the glass.

"Busted," Logan murmured.

Moths flung themselves at the lamps. The screen door creaked when I pushed it open.

"Solange Rosamund Drake."

I winced. Behind me, both my brothers did the same. My mother, Helena, was intimidating at the best of times with her long black hair and her pale eyes, and the fact that she can take down someone twice her size with a sword, a stake, or her petite bare hands.

"Ouch—middle name." Logan shot me a sympathetic smile before easing into the living room and out of the crossfire.

"Snitch." I pinched Nicholas. He only raised an eyebrow.

"Nicholas didn't tell us anything." My mom pinned him with a pointed glare. He squirmed a little. I'd known grown men to back away physically from that look. "One of your aunts was patrolling the perimeter and saw your escape."

"Escape." I rolled my eyes. "It was barely anything. They didn't even come out of the cornfields. They were just sniffing me."

"You have to be more careful," my father, Liam, said calmly from his favorite chair. It kind of looked like a medieval throne. No surprise there. He'd only been born in 1901 but he carried himself like a king.

"I feel fine," I said, exasperated. He was drinking brandy. I could smell it across the room, just like I could smell Uncle Geoffrey's cologne, Aunt Hyacinth's pug, and the thick perfume of roses. Just another one of our little gifts. I rubbed my nose so I wouldn't sneeze.

"What's with all the flowers?" I asked, noticing the roses. There were dozens and dozens of them everywhere, in every shade of red, stuffed in crystal vases, teacups, and jam jars.

"From your . . . admirers," my father told me grimly.

"What?" Admirers, ha! They were only coming around because of my pheromones. It's not my fault I smell funny. I shower every day, but apparently I still stink of lilies and warm chocolate and something else no one can accurately describe. Even Lucy commented on it once, and she's nearly immune to us, having practically grown up here. No one else was smelly in such an obvious way; pheromones are usually subtle and mysterious. I really hope it fades once I fully turn.

The prophecy and my family's legacy in the vampire world won't, though.

Sometimes it sucks having a family that's so old and powerful.

"Darling, it's a great compliment, I'm sure," my aunt Hyacinth said. She was technically my great-great-great-aunt. She didn't look much over forty, even though she clung to the fashions of her youth in the privacy of the tribe, like most vampires. Her dress was Victorian in style, with a lace corset and jet beads. "When I was your age I had the best time. There's nothing like the rush of being a debutante. All those men hungering after you." She gave a delicate shiver.

"Hyacinth." Dad grimaced. "You hadn't even been turned then, and this is hardly a debutante's ball. They don't want to waltz, damn it." My great-great-great-uncle Edward had married Aunt Hyacinth in 1853 and turned her in 1877, at her insistence. She was inspired by Queen Victoria's undying love for her own husband and wanted to live for centuries by Edward's side. I'd never met him, though, because he'd died in World War I, shot one night on a spy mission for the Allies because he was determined to do his part. She'd been alone ever since.

I glanced at a thick cream-colored paper card pinned to an enormous bouquet of white roses in a red box and froze.

"Montmartre?" I squeaked. "He sent me flowers?"

Dad flicked the box a baleful glare. "Yes."

"I'm putting them down the incinerator," I said darkly. The last thing I wanted was Montmartre or his Host to know who I was. I was also hoping to slip out while everyone else was distracted. I should have known better.

"You can do that later." Mom pointed to a chair. "Sit."

I dropped onto a velvet settee. Nicholas sat as well, joining my other brothers, who were all watching me grimly.

"Don't you lot have anything better to do?" I asked.

"Than protecting our annoying baby sister?" Quinn drawled. "No."

Being the only girl in a family of boys would have been tough enough to navigate, never mind a family with the rare ability to give birth to mostly male vampires. Even among the Drakes, that ability is rare. Most vampires are "made," not born. My mom, for example, had been human until my dad turned her shortly after I was born and they'd decided they didn't want any more children. He'd been born human too, like my brothers, until his sixteenth birthday—when he'd sickened, the way we all did—and would have died if my aunt hadn't given him her blood to drink.

Family legend has it that the first of our clan was William Drake. No one knows how he was turned. We did know he married Veronique DuBois, a lady-in-waiting to Queen Eleanor of Aquitaine. A year after their wedding, she went into labor with their firstborn. After twenty-seven hours of childbirth, the midwife told William that Veronique was not going to survive the birth. In desperation, William turned her, and their twins were born healthy. By their sixteenth birthday, though, the twins weakened and grew unnaturally sensitive to the sunlight. They were hungry but couldn't eat, thirsty but couldn't drink. Nothing tempted them.

Except blood.

And so the Drake vampire family began.

Veronique, as the oldest surviving Drake, is our family matriarch. William was staked by a hunter during the reign of Henry VIII. Veronique rarely visited, preferring to have us come to her once we'd survived the change and she could afford to get attached. At least she hadn't joined us tonight, which meant it wasn't a formal meeting, just a family ambush. She was scary enough that she probably could have given Lady Natasha a run for her crown if she'd wanted it. Luckily for everyone, she preferred embroidery to court intrigue.

"Solange, are you listening to me?"

I jerked my head up.

"Yes." I'd heard this particular lecture enough times over the last few months to know it intimately. "Nothing happened. You're all overreacting." I did feel guilty; I just knew better than to show it.

"There were at least three of them in that field tonight, maybe more." Nicholas scowled. "You know they don't all send flowers. Most of them just want to grab you and run."

I scowled back. "I could have handled it. It wasn't even full dark yet. Besides, if they were so dangerous, why'd you nearly leave Lucy behind?"

"You were going to leave Lucy there?" my mom sputtered, and Nicholas narrowed his eyes at me. I crossed my eyes smugly. Growing up with so many brothers taught me the fine art of misdirection, self-preservation, and revenge, if nothing else.

"She was *fine*." I knew Nicholas was trying not to slump in his chair. "They weren't after her. And she's not fragile, for God's sake."

"She's under the protection of this family," my father said.

"I know, but she can look after herself. Broke my nose last summer, didn't she?"

"Be that as it may."

"Okay, okay." Nicholas backed down.

"And you, young lady." Dad turned to me. Every single one of my traitor brothers smirked. They look enough alike that people usually assume they're all sets of twins. Only Quinn and Connor are actually twins. Quinn keeps his hair long and Connor, like Sebastian, prefers to fade quietly into the background. Logan is the flamboyant one, and Nicholas spends most of his free time worrying about me. Marcus and Duncan just came home from a road trip. They're all gorgeous; it's like living with a bunch of male models. And it makes girls stupid around them.

"You have to take this seriously."

"I do, Dad," I said quietly. "You know I do."

"What I know is that they're coming for you and soon you'll be weaker than a blind kitten."

"I know." This totally sucked. I was getting in trouble over a party I hadn't wanted to go to in the first place. I *like* being alone and staying on the farm. But I hate being trapped and hovered over.

"Let the girl be," Hyacinth said, drinking delicately from a goblet. It looked like cherry cordial. It wasn't.

"Thank you." I swallowed thickly.

Did I mention?

I was squeamish about blood.

CHAPTER 2

◆

Lucy

"Lucy, is that you?"

I kicked the door shut with my heel, still muttering under my breath. Nicholas was so infuriating. What was wrong with him anyway?

"Lucy?"

"Yeah, it's me," I called out.

"Where have you been? We nearly started without you, kiddo." Dad came out of the kitchen with a bowl of hot popcorn, made from the corn he'd grown in the backyard. It was as close to junk food as my parents came. His long hair was in its usual ponytail, his sleeves rolled up to display his wolf and turtle tattoos. The wolf was his personal totem, and the turtle was our family totem.

"Pick out a movie, honey." Mom looked up from the beads spread out on the coffee table. She was sitting cross-legged in old jeans and a peasant blouse, stringing a hundred and eight rose quartz beads together to make prayer malas. She makes them to give away as gifts at the ashram. My parents went every year, and they were leaving tomorrow morning before dawn. "What's wrong? Is Solange all right?"

"She's fine." Mostly.

"Tell her we've asked the swami to pray for her. Why do you look so grumpy?"

"It's Nicholas. He just makes me so mad sometimes."

"Honey, you know anger poisons your body. You've always been too quick to get mad. Why do you think you have allergies? Your body's always on hyper defense."

"*Mom.*"

"Okay, okay," she said. Dad winked at me and passed the popcorn. "Are you going to be all right here on your own while we're away? I stocked the fridge."

"With tofu?" I grimaced.

"I don't want you gorging on junk food while we're away, young lady."

I rolled my eyes. "Well, I'm not eating weird tofu casseroles for two weeks." My parents had passed on their sense of social justice, even if they chose to fight with sit-ins and I preferred to swing a punch. Call it family rebellion. I felt the same way about tofu as I did about sit-ins. I'm sure they're both good for the soul, but I'd once breathed in a lungful of tear gas when my parents took me to a global warming protest and I swore I'd never lay limp in the road again. One time, Dad was hit by a rubber bullet, and the bruises on his chest had scared me more than any polluting global corporation or vicious dictator could have. Even scarier was the fact that he hadn't gotten angry, had actually lain down for it. When I turned fifteen, I was finally able to convince them to leave me behind when they went on their annual retreat.

"Maybe we should call your aunt to come stay with you," Mom said.

Not that they didn't worry.

"I was fine last year and I'll be fine this year, Mom. Besides, Lucinda's in Vegas with her new girlfriend, remember?" I crunched some popcorn. "Stop fretting, it's bad for your chi."

"She's got you there." Dad grinned.

"I'll probably stay at the Drakes' most nights anyway, just like last year," I assured her. "So, can we just watch the movie now?" I turned up the volume before she could find something else to worry about.

When the movie was over, my parents went to bed and I went back to Solange's. I'd only had my license for a few months, but the car already practically drove itself there. Although I didn't see a single person, I knew I was spotted by various guards and family members before I'd even made it onto the outskirts of the Drake compound. I didn't know why Mom was so worried; she'd already asked Bruno, the Drakes' head bodyguard, to check up on me.

The dogs didn't bother to bark when I got out. There were three of them, big, shaggy gray-black Bouviers, which looked more like bears than dogs. They might have been intimidating if they weren't currently shoving their damp noses in my pockets and whimpering for treats. I had more to fear from the windstorm they might cause with the ferocious wagging of their stubby tails.

The lamps were lit—soft yellow light gleamed through the windows. The light was always soft in the Drake house. I went around to the side, hoping Solange's bedroom window was open. I could have knocked. I usually did. It wasn't as if anyone would be asleep, and they could usually smell my presence anyway. But I didn't know if I was in trouble. I'd apologize if I was, but I hated going in unprepared. Regular parents were bad enough, but vampire parents were in a class all their own. Solange's window was closed, so I texted her. Nothing.

"Lucky."

I yelped like a scalded cat, whirling so fast I made myself dizzy. My phone landed in the bushes. Nicholas smirked at me, easing languidly out of the shadows. His pale eyes gleamed. I gasped for breath, thumping my chest. That was the second time in one night I'd practically choked on my own heart. Nicholas licked his lips. I remembered Solange's warning and tried to calm my pulse.

"What the hell, Nicky!" I muttered. He hated being called that as much as I hated being called Lucky. He stepped closer, totally invading my personal space. I hated that he was so handsome, with his tousled dark hair and his serious expression, like some ancient scholar. There was something else in his expression suddenly, something slightly wicked. I took a step back, wondering why my stomach felt funny. He advanced and I backed away some more, suspicious, until I bumped into the log wall of the house.

I remembered, too late, Solange's simplest warning about vampires: if you ran, they chased. It was just in their nature.

I stopped abruptly and lifted my chin, trying to pretend my shoulder blades weren't pressing into the log wall and I had nowhere to go.

"What?"

He was close enough that his legs practically brushed mine.

He was close enough, in point of fact, to kiss.

I was instantly horrified the thought had even crossed my mind. I tried to comfort myself with the idea that it was probably just those legendary pheromones. I was used to them, but I wasn't completely immune. And the fact was, he was looking at me the way I looked at chocolate fudge.

I bit my lower lip. He blinked, and then his face went impassive again, nearly cold; but I noticed the flare of heat in his eerie eyes.

"That was a stupid thing you did," he said.

And there was the Nicholas I knew. Of course he hadn't been flirting with me. What had I been thinking?

"It was just a party."

"It was reckless." He jerked a hand through his hair, messing it further. "We're trying to protect her. You're not making it any easier."

"You're smothering her." I scowled. "And I was protecting her, too."

"By putting her in needless danger just to flirt with some drunk kid? This isn't a game."

"I know that," I snapped. "But you don't know her like I do. And she's been so stressed out by you and your overbearing baboon brothers, I just wanted to cheer her up."

He paused, and when he spoke again it was quietly. "She can't protect herself if she's worried about protecting you."

Ouch. Direct hit. The indignation whooshed out of me, leaving me feeling deflated and foolish.

"Oh." I really hated it when he was right. "All right. Fine."

I was spared his self-satisfied reply when his cell phone rang discreetly from inside the pocket of his black cargo pants. He barely glanced at me.

"Go home. Now."

He walked away, leaving me staring at his back. I retrieved my phone to text Solange: *I do not like your brother.* I stomped all the way back to the car. The dogs had abandoned me to follow Nicholas, growling low in their throats. I kind of hoped they'd bite him. Right on the ass.

Just as I was reaching for the car door handle, a hand clamped over my shoulder and spun me around. Before I could make a single sound, Nicholas's mouth covered mine completely. He yanked me closer. His eyes were the misty gray of rain. His lips moved, briefly. It wasn't even a whisper but even that sound was hidden under the almost-but-not-quite kiss.

"We're not alone."

I stiffened.

"Shhh." He bent his head. Anyone watching would have assumed he was kissing me and enjoying it. I admit, I was enjoying it too.

A shadow moved near the hedges, too quickly to be natural. The crickets went silent. Knowing the sharpness of vampire hearing, I darted a glance pointedly over Nicholas's left shoulder. He didn't speak, didn't even nod, but I knew he understood. He kept kissing me, his tongue darting out to touch mine. It was totally distracting. He was edging me away from the car, guiding me backward, toward the house.

"Don't run." He nipped my lower lip.

"I know." Afraid I was the only one experiencing all these interesting feelings, I nipped back. His hands tightened. His mouth was on my ear when we reached the porch. By the lower step his palms moved over my waist, my hips. His lips were clever, wicked.

Perfect.

At the front door he stopped and shoved me abruptly into the foyer. I stumbled, knocking over a vase of roses. Glass shards, red petals, and water scattered over the stone floor. My lips felt swollen, tingly. *Focus, Lucy.* The hallway was already full of grim-mouthed Drake boys before I'd even caught my breath. Solange's mom pushed past me, leading them out. Nicholas was a blur between the oak trees. There were the unmistakable sounds of fighting: grunts, hissing, bones snapping.

"Are you okay?" Solange practically leaped on me.

"I'm fine."

She was heading out after her brothers when her father's voice cut through the foyer.

"Solange."

She stopped, looked over her shoulder. "They might need help."

"No."

"Dad."

"No. They're here for you. If you go out there, it will only make things worse."

I knew that look on her face. She was biting her tongue. I knew how much she hated this. Helena was the warrior in the family, had been even when she was winning martial arts competitions as a human, and she'd trained her children well. Even I'd gotten the benefit of a few tricks, but none of it would do us any good tonight. Still, I was really glad I knew how to break someone's kneecap and three ways to incapacitate using only my thumb. And to think I used to worry about midterms.

The foyer was warm and civilized, lit by warmly glowing Tiffany lamps. Liam stood between us and the battle raging in the bedraggled garden. He was nearly tall enough to obscure our vision, but we leaned sideways around him. Part of me didn't want to see what was happening; the rest of me absolutely couldn't handle not knowing. The shadows coalesced, and I watched fangs gleam and bodies jump higher than they should have been able to. The snarls lifted the hair on the back of my neck.

Nicholas was fast and clever but I'd never seen him like this before. His face was hard as he leaped and dodged, sent his boot into the midsection of a vampire not much older than us, with long blond hair. They both tumbled, but only Nicholas landed on his feet. I felt inordinately proud about that.

All of Solange's brothers held their own, but only Quinn appeared to be enjoying himself. He grinned even as a fist, moving so fast it was a flesh-colored blur, broke his nose. Blood trickled down to his lip and he licked it. Helena laughed behind him, somersaulting out of the way of a stake and landing behind her attacker. He disintegrated in a cloud of dust at her feet.

"I want one alive and able to speak," Liam called out. He shook his head at Solange. "Honestly, your mother's worse than the boys. Helena"—he raised his voice slightly—"leave me one, damn it."

"Spoilsport," she muttered before reining herself in. Her flying kick only knocked the vampire into a tree instead of shattering his ribs. Hyacinth made a small sound behind us. The jet beads around her neck caught the light, glimmered.

"That's hardly ladylike," she said disapprovingly. Which was amusing since I'd heard the stories of what she did in her spare time—and it wasn't taking tea and eating cucumber sandwiches.

A vampire fled, disappearing into the woods. One of them shuddered, turned to ash, and drifted into the hedges. The stake tumbled to the ground. Solange's second-oldest brother, Sebastian, wiped his hands off dispassionately and then turned to help his mother drag the half-conscious vampire she'd thrown into the tree toward the house. Connor was speaking quietly into his cell phone to Bruno.

I pressed my back against the wall as a parade of teeth and feral smiles passed me. When they were all gathered in the parlor, I followed. I went to my favorite purple velvet armchair by the fireplace. Solange stood next to me, her eyes never leaving that of the young man currently being tied up. His shirt was torn, his dark reddish brown hair pulled back into a ponytail. His eyelids fluttered but didn't open. I wouldn't have opened them either if all seven Drake brothers were standing around me, glaring. Never mind Helena, who waved them aside with barely a flick of her wrist. She sniffed once, delicately.

"He smells like kith." She whispered but shook her head. "Kind of."

Liam frowned, sniffed as well.

"Something's not right." His gaze narrowed, sharpened. "Left arm."

We all looked even though I didn't know what I was looking at. The tip of a tattoo poked out from under his pushed-up sleeve. It looked like a stylized tribal-style sun but I couldn't be sure.

"Damn," Nicholas muttered. "Helios-Ra."

Everyone looked totally bummed out over such a comic-book name. He stirred. There was a gentle waft of lilies and chocolate, almost right, but not quite. Everyone else was still scenting the air like hunting hounds, nostrils flared.

"What?" I whispered to Solange. "What's with all the sniffing? It's creeping me out."

She didn't have time to answer because he opened his eyes, suddenly, as if he'd been poked with something sharp. His eyes weren't pale, not like every other vampire's I'd ever seen.

They were very black and very hostile.

CHAPTER 3

◆

Solange

"You're . . . m-mortal," I finally stammered. I knew Lucy liked to think all vampires had this suave quality, but I so didn't, and not just because I wasn't technically a vampire yet. She was the one with the beaded velvet scarves, and I was the one with the pottery clay dried on my pants. Plus, I was totally gaping at him. He was a hunter, and he worked for an organization devoted to wiping us out. The sun tattoo was proof enough of that, underscored by his expression: righteous anger.

Great.

"I don't get it," Lucy whispered to me. "Who is he?"

"Not one of us," I whispered back, my gaze never leaving his. I didn't know what I was reading there, but it was complicated, whatever it was. I'd heard of the cologne some hunters wore; it mimicked vampire pheromones, to take a potential enemy off guard. We'd believed it completely out in the garden, until he'd had to fight my mother, who would have killed him if my dad hadn't been so adamant about having someone to question.

Nicholas half stepped in front of us, annoyingly overprotective as always. He didn't like surprises and unanswered questions and we'd just had our fill of both. I'd been trained just like they had, but none of my brothers could get it in their thick heads that I wasn't delicate or defenseless.

The Helios-Ra agent was wearing black nose plugs, which just proved he knew more about us than we knew about him. I reached over and yanked them out.

"What are you doing here?" I could tell he was trying to hold his breath. I could've told him that strategy never worked for long. He glared at me mutinously.

"Tracking," he finally answered on a sharp exhale.

"Let me guess," I said, disgusted. "Because I'm just so beautiful and you don't know why but you just have to be with me?" I was really starting to hate this whole pheromone thing.

He blinked, nearly smiled. "Not exactly."

I blinked back. "Oh." Damn it, he was even more attractive when he didn't seem particularly affected by my questionable charms. "Well, who are you then?"

"Helios-Ra," he answered, his tone clipped.

"Yeah, we got that."

"Your name?" Dad scowled.

"Kieran Black."

"Since when has Helios-Ra been on our trail? Last time I checked, we had a treaty. We don't eat humans, so you don't bother us and we don't bother you."

My mom snorted. She hated the treaty. She preferred fighting, being much more skilled with weapons than tact, but my dad was all about practicality and the long view. He'd made the treaty before my oldest brother was born, determined to give his children a chance. He didn't want us being harassed and followed about by the league just because we're vampires. After all, vampires aren't all good or all bad, any more than humans are. But try telling that to the Helios-Ra. They only recently admitted that being a vampire wasn't a good enough reason to be killed on sight. Still, old traditions die hard with them, almost as hard as with us.

But our family, at least, has a good reputation. We mostly drink animal blood, only resorting to human blood if it's consensual or if we're ill and can't heal without it. If that fails, a quick break-in at the blood bank works well enough. We've never gone feral; the disease has been in our bloodline too many centuries for that, and every generation is born stronger than the last. It's not easy dying, even if you know you're going to wake up afterward. And it's even harder controlling the bloodthirst. Still, hardly any of us go mad anymore during the turning. I had to remind myself of that little fact every time I looked at the calendar to see my birthday edging closer and closer. Lucy nudged me.

"You're looking morose," she said under her breath. "You're thinking about it again."

I turned my attention back to the matter at hand. I couldn't afford to get sidetracked with self-pity—or by the fact that this particular Helios-Ra agent was really good-looking, with his dark eyes and strong cheekbones.

"Things change," he said. "You should know. You broke the treaty."

Mom's eyes narrowed dangerously.

"I beg your pardon?" she said, soft as a mouse near a sleeping cat.

Uh-oh. Mom was big on that whole honor thing.

"Big mistake," Lucy said pleasantly. She was a lot more bloodthirsty than I was, ironically enough. She would have made a better vampire than me. I shot her a look.

"What?" she asked innocently. "He was after you, he deserves it."

Nicholas barely turned his head. "Do you two mind?"

"Yeah, yeah," she muttered.

Mom stepped up close enough that Kieran was sweating a little and breathing as shallowly as he could. Our pheromones when we were distracting mortals to drink was nothing compared with the pheromones when we were angry. His entire body was probably flooding with adrenaline, trying to decide between fight or flight. I couldn't sense it yet, but soon enough I'd be able to taste it on my tongue like champagne bubbles. It wasn't a particularly comforting thought.

"Are you accusing us of breaking an oath?" Mom's voice was like broken glass—glittery and dangerous. Beside her, Sebastian bared his teeth. His fangs were retracted, but still, there was something too sharp about his teeth. He barely spoke, even to us, and his silence was terrifying to those who didn't know him.

"It's common knowledge."

"Is it?"

"Drakes," he spat. "I know better than to trust any of you."

Byron, one of the dogs, growled. Quinn smiled.

"Let me talk to him," he suggested. There was always something slightly violent about his smiles. Dad held up his hand. Quinn subsided, but barely.

"We haven't broken the treaty," Dad said quietly.

"Helios-Ra says you have."

"Then Helios-Ra is misinformed. And I won't have your organization endangering my daughter."

He glanced at me, glanced away.

"If you keep me here, you really will be breaking the treaty." He was breathing through his mouth, as if that would help.

"Actually, since you broke the treaty by coming here in the first place"—Dad's voice was silky—"we really needn't concern ourselves with those rules." Mom actually smirked.

"I . . ."

"How old are you?" Dad asked.

"Eighteen."

Dad shook his head, dismayed. "They're training them younger and younger."

"They need to be able to infiltrate the high schools and colleges to spy on us," Connor pointed out.

"I'm only doing my job. Keeping people safe from monsters like you."

"People like you are the reason my aunt Ruby won't leave her house anymore," I snapped. She'd lost her husband and three sons to hunters and had never really recovered from the loss.

His face went hard. "Monsters like you are the reason my father's dead."

"Oh and we've never lost family members to hunters or Helios?" I shot back even though I felt bad that he'd lost his father.

"And they're not monsters, you bigot," Lucy broke in, incensed. She leaped to her feet. "It's a disease, you ignorant prig. Are people with diabetes or arthritis monsters too?" If secrecy wasn't so important, she would have used her theory in her personal crusade to make the world accept us.

"It's not the same."

"It is *so*."

"My dad's throat was ripped out."

There was silence. Then Dad frowned. "Only the *Hel-Blar* rip out throats, son."

"A vampire's a vampire," Kieran insisted stubbornly. Lucy went red in the face.

"Why are you really here?" Dad pressed before she could explode.

"Because of the bounty," he answered tightly.

Mom went unnaturally still. Her eyes caught the light and reflected it. "What bounty?"

"The bounty on the Drake family."

Someone snarled. The air was so charged I was vaguely surprised it didn't spark and catch fire. Dad stalked toward the phone on the desk. He barked orders into the receiver, not even bothering with a greeting. "Double the patrols. Get word to everyone. Yes, even her. And the council." He switched to the cell phone in his pocket, dialing grimly. His voice muted to a soft murmur I couldn't entirely make out. My hearing wasn't sharp enough. Yet.

"What the hell's the bounty for?" Sebastian demanded.

"I don't know."

Quinn sauntered over, leaned in close. "You'll tell us."

Kieran paled slightly, trying to break eye contact. Quinn's hand closed over his throat. Kieran seemed a little dazed when he finally answered.

"It was posted tonight." He shuddered. Sweat beaded on his upper lip.

"Is this about Solange?"

"I don't know." He choked, tried to swallow. "I don't know," he repeated. "I heard there was a bounty, and I wanted in." Something in his voice made me think it was less about the bounty and more about the chance to stick it to our family specifically.

Quinn eased back, letting his hand drop to his side. "Some agency, attacking a fifteen-year-old girl." He spat. "Cowards."

Kieran took several deep ragged breaths. "We protect the innocent."

"This isn't a comic book, idiot," Lucy muttered crossly.

"If you're going to kill me too, get it over with."

"We don't drink from people like you," Nicholas sneered, making it sound as insulting as he could.

"Do you drink from her?" Kieran nodded at Lucy. "Have you made her your slave?"

"Who, Lucy?" Nicholas snickered.

"Hey!" Lucy snapped. "Shut up."

I wasn't entirely sure which one she was talking to.

"This isn't getting us anywhere," Duncan said quietly. Like Sebastian, he rarely lost his temper or his focus. "Let's not get sidetracked." He tied a black bandana over Kieran's mouth, knotting it securely. Dad nodded approvingly before pointing toward the kitchen.

"Kitchen. Now."

◆

Our kitchen looked like any farm kitchen: a huge wooden table, ladderback chairs, painted cupboards, and a kettle on the stove. There was a basket on the counter full of red apples and pomegranates and even food in the fridge, mostly for me and for Lucy when she stayed over. In fact, she was already pouring herself a glass of cranberry juice. The blood was kept in an old wine cellar, hidden in the wall and locked with three deadbolts and an alarm system. That was a fairly new precaution, ever since one of Logan's ex-girlfriend's brothers had barged in after Logan had broken up with his sister. The guards hadn't stopped him; it would have seemed suspicious to have them swarm out just because someone came to the front door uninvited. The dogs had stopped him though, even before Mom had. He hadn't made it past the front hall. It was only luck that he hadn't seen into the kitchen, with the jug of blood on the counter. Needless to say, we were strongly encouraged not to date humans after that.

Now Quinn paced beside that same counter; Nicholas leaned against the wall, arms crossed. The rest of my brothers sat, though their muscles were tensed for sudden movement. I watched the dark fields on the other side of the glass with suspicion. Dad's phone rang again. Mom glanced at Lucy.

"We should call your parents."

"Can't." She set her glass down. "They're at the ashram for two weeks, remember?" The sun was edging up over the horizon. "And they always leave early to watch the sun rise over the lake."

She sighed. "Of course. You'll stay here then."

"I will? But no one's after me."

"You're part of this family, young lady, and your mother would never forgive me if I left you unprotected, especially now," Mom told Lucy sternly.

"Yes, ma'am." My mother was the only person on the planet who was able to get that meek tone out of Lucy. No one else would have even known it existed. I dropped into the chair next to her and stole a sip of her juice. I tried not to imagine what it would be like to drink blood instead. My stomach tilted.

"This is unacceptable," Aunt Hyacinth fumed. "The Drake family has a good and honorable name. They've no right to do this. We're on the council."

"Let's go straight to the Helios-Ra headquarters," Quinn added, his expression hard. "I can clear this up."

"As if your temper has ever helped us." Logan snorted.

"Careful, little brother."

They were all talking over each other until my mother cleared her throat.

"Boys."

Silence fell, reluctantly but quickly. Dad switched off his

phone. There were lines around his mouth I'd never seen before. "The boy was right. Bounty's been set."

Mom cursed. "Why?" she asked.

"That may take a while to figure out. There've been a few disappearances, rumors that don't make sense. I've got people on it." He leaned down on the counter, his fists clenched. "I've put a call in to Hart and to Lady Natasha."

"Natasha?" Aunt Hyacinth frowned. "Is that wise? She exiled us all."

"I know." Hart was the head of the Helios-Ra and not a fan of Lady Natasha. "Until we know more, no one leaves this property alone. Solange, you don't leave at all."

"Why am I the only one under house arrest? That's so unfair."

"Solange, you know why."

"I know how to take care of myself." I gritted my teeth.

"Yes, you do. But you know as well as I do that you're not at your full strength."

"But I feel *fine*." I was so tired of saying it over and over again. I already felt trapped, smothered. I'd chew off my own foot like an animal caught in a leg trap if they didn't give me some space.

"Sol," Nicholas said softly. "Please."

I hissed out a frustrated breath. When I looked at my mom, I made sure my chin was up, my gaze steady. "I still get to go to my shed." If they tried to keep me from the kiln and my pottery wheel, I'd be insane by my birthday. Mom must have seen my desperation.

"Agreed."

I let out another breath. "Okay."

Dad's phone rang again. He listened quietly before motioning to Sebastian and Connor. "Your uncle Geoffrey is on his way. And your aunt Ruby's arriving; go on and help her inside." The fact that Ruby had been persuaded to leave her house for ours spoke volumes as to the seriousness of the situation. Dad touched Mom's hand, his mouth tight. "We'll figure this out," he promised before sending us all up to our respective bedrooms.

"Are you okay?" Lucy asked me as we got ready for bed. She started by taking off the pounds of silver jewelry she always wore—proving that it's only a myth that vampires can't tolerate silver.

"I'm fine, it's everyone else who's losing it," I muttered.

She snorted. "Big surprise. You're the baby sister and you *know* how your brothers get."

I rolled my eyes. "What's it like being an only child?"

"How would I know? Your brothers harass me just as much as they harass you."

"True."

Lucy waited until we'd changed into our pajamas before speaking again. She wore a long black cotton nightgown that looked like a sundress, and I wore my favorite flannel pj bottoms and a T-shirt. Out of the two of us, she always looked like the one who should be turning into a vampire. I sighed.

"Sol," she said. "I never saw Nicholas's bloodchange, or Logan's. I was banned from the house, remember?"

"I remember," I said softly. I hadn't been kicked out of the house, but I certainly hadn't been welcomed on the third floor, where all my brothers slept. I'd heard the unnatural silence and seen my parents' pale, worried faces as they took shifts sitting with Logan and then Nicholas the next year. With my other brothers I'd been too young to really know what was happening, and my parents had sent me off for slumber parties at Lucy's. Her mother had fussed over me and fed me chocolate, which made Lucy cranky since she only ever got to eat carob. I hadn't really understood it then.

I understood it now.

"So . . . what really happens?" Lucy pressed. "I know you get sick, but is it as bad as all that?"

It really was.

"No, it's fine," I lied as we climbed into our respective beds. "I mean, it's not fun or anything, but you know the Drakes. We love a good overprotective melodrama."

Yup, totally lying.

And I could tell Lucy wasn't really buying it. She opened her mouth to ask me another question. A soft knock at the door interrupted her. She shot me a glare like I'd orchestrated it.

"Sol, it's me," Nicholas murmured from the other side of the door. "Can I come in?"

"Sure," I said as Lucy sat up suddenly and smoothed her hair. I blinked at her. Since when did she care what she looked like for any of my brothers? The door didn't make a sound on its hinges as Nicholas slipped inside. He was wearing his black pants but no shirt, like he'd been interrupted changing. Clearly something was up. Just as clearly, Lucy was trying not to stare at his chest. He flicked her a glance, frowned.

"What?"

She jerked her eyes away. "Nothing." She looked like she might be blushing. I was definitely going to bug her about that later. For now, it would have to wait.

"What's up?" I asked him.

"Someone's downstairs," he said quietly. "He scratched at the window and Dad let him in after Mom threatened to eat his face."

"Ew," Lucy said.

"Vampire."

"Lurking at the windows?" I slid out from under my blanket. "That's not good."

"They're in the library."

We looked at each other, then nodded and hurried out to the hall without another word. The library was one of the only rooms in the house where we could properly eavesdrop. We'd discovered, thanks to a tip from Quinn, that if you lie on the floor in the spare guest room next to mine and pressed your ear to the vent, you could pretty much hear everything that was going on.

We stretched out on the hardwood and wriggled into position. Nicholas was between us, hogging the best listening spot. His face was turned toward Lucy.

"I can't hear—" He pressed his finger to her lips to stop her from saying anything else. My parents would hear us if we whispered right over the vent. There were definite disadvantages to having vampire parents: sneaking around was nearly impossible. At least come my birthday, I wouldn't be the only one clomping around the house deaf to all the intrigue. I'd hear as well as them.

"Is there a single reason why we shouldn't stake you where you stand?" my mom asked pleasantly.

"I'm not here for the bounty," a male voice assured her. It was low and rumbly, as if it came from a really big chest. I couldn't help but imagine a wrestler down in the library. "I would hardly announce my presence, would I?"

"You didn't exactly knock at the front door," Dad said drily.

"There are humans in this house," he said as if that was explanation enough. "I smell at least two, but not here in this room." If we were really lucky, he wouldn't smell Lucy and me over his head before we heard what else he had to say.

"I've come to offer my allegiance to your daughter."

On second thought, I could have done without hearing that.

"Have you?" Mom didn't sound convinced. Dad was probably overjoyed at the thought of negotiating another alliance. I kind of just wanted to go back to bed.

"You're sworn to Lady Natasha," Dad said softly. "You wear the mark of her house."

"I'm sworn to the royal court, yes." It was an important distinction. "But there are those of us who would rather oath to the House of Drake, and I am here representing them."

Crap. That prophecy thing again. Why didn't anyone believe me when I said I didn't want to be a princess or a queen or whatever? I didn't want to be the excuse for a civil war within the tribes. I shuddered.

"We'll keep that in mind. We'd need proof of your loyalty, of course."

"Of course. When the time comes, you'll get your proof." He sounded like he was bowing. "Until then."

I heard the window shut and Mom and Dad moved out of the

library. I sighed and closed my eyes. I'd felt fine all day but now I was exhausted, almost like I had the flu.

"I'm sorry I almost left you behind," Nicholas whispered tightly to Lucy. "I really thought they'd follow us and you'd be safer at the party.

What?" he asked when she didn't immediately respond.

"You've never apologized to me before."

"I said I was sorry the time I used your doll for target practice with the pellet gun."

"Because your mom had you by the ear."

"Well, whatever. Sorry."

"Thanks," she whispered.

"You're welcome," he whispered back.

I suddenly felt like a third wheel. Weird.

Nicholas scrambled to his feet. "We should go."

"She's asleep," Lucy said. I wasn't, but I didn't have the energy to tell her that.

"I've got her," Nicholas said grimly, picking me up and carrying me to my room.

CHAPTER 4

◆

Lucy

Saturday morning

Mornings were always quiet in the Drake household, even with nearly twenty people stuffed into its tiny rooms and narrow halls. Sunlight sparkled at the windows, made of some sort of treated glass. Ancient vampires can stand sunlight though they never really love it, but it dangerously weakens the younger ones, who haven't had a chance to build up an immunity. I never took sunlight for granted now, or my ability to eat every meal with cutlery. Though, aside from the whole blood thing, the Drakes were very civilized. They used glasses and goblets, not plastic blood bags.

Lady Natasha, by all accounts, was *not* civilized. She'd been Montmartre's second-in-command and his lover. When he'd tired of her, she allied herself with a powerful vampire family. She knew the customs of the vampires, the Host, and the Hounds, and she was determined to bring them all together under her leadership. Biases ran deeply though, and so far she hadn't managed to unite them. It wasn't for an altruistic motive like ending what was basically a civil war; it was all about the power for her. And possibly sticking it to Montmartre.

I'd seen the roses with his name on them.

They didn't bode well. He clearly wanted a Drake daughter to give him vampire babies—and the power of the council and the royal courts if Solange really did take them over. He wanted it all.

Lady Natasha, who wanted him as much as she wanted power, wouldn't be too keen on any part of that plan.

If only vampire politics were on high school history exams, I'd be all set.

Solange was still asleep, curled around the sunbeams falling on her pillow. I'd already noticed that she was sleeping later and later. I was starting to get nervous for her. Everyone else seemed to think it was a totally normal part of the change. I pulled a sweater on over my nightgown and added thick socks. It was always freezing in the Drake house, no matter the time of year. I went straight to the kitchen to make myself some tea and toast. No one else was awake. I ate my breakfast and then took my tea with me as I wandered through the house.

In my sleep-dazed state, I'd actually forgotten about Kieran, tied to a sturdy chair in one of the parlors. I froze, cup halfway to my mouth. His eyes were intent, curious, edgy. I might not like his attitude, but I guessed I'd be edgy too if I was tied up in a vampire's house. Especially if I was a brainwashed Helios-Ra agent.

The gag was loose around his neck, lying next to his nose plugs. In daylight I noticed he was wearing black jeans and a black shirt, with bare straps where Helena had removed his weapons.

"You look like you belong in a bad comic book," I told him cheerfully.

He stared at me. "You really aren't bothered by the whole vampire thing, are you?"

I shrugged. "Whatever." It was obvious he didn't know what to make of me. I approached curiously. I'd never actually seen a Helios-Ra agent before. I wondered what the fuss was about. He was barely older than we were. His hands were lashed loosely at the wrists so he could move them a little, but his shoulders were tied tighter to the chair back. He wore steel-toed army boots, also attached tightly at the ankles. "What did the Drakes do that's got you all pissy?"

"Pissy? Did you just call me pissy?"

"I call 'em how I see 'em."

"You are the weirdest girl."

"From the guy who thinks he's a secret agent man."

"You should take the Helios-Ra more seriously," he warned me.

I smiled at him with very little humor. "I don't take direction well." I raised my eyebrows. "So? What's with the vendetta?"

His jaw clenched. "I told you."

"I'm sorry your dad died. But you can't blame all vampires for the actions of one." I tried to sound reasonable, calming. My mom was a natural at that sort of thing. Me? Not so much. "That's called racism."

"They're not human."

"That's so beside the point."

He gaped at me. "What?"

"And besides, the Drakes are human, or were mostly. And they've never gone all rogue and fangy on the general populace. Don't they teach you anything at that hotshot secret academy?"

"How did you know about the academy?" He was trying not to look startled.

"Please. It's kind of obvious."

"You don't understand."

"I understand exactly," I said.

"They've brainwashed you."

"Hey, you're the one in some kind of hunter cult."

He narrowed his eyes. "This isn't a joke, Lucy. The Drakes killed my father."

"They did *not*."

"You don't even know who my father is."

"I know you're an idiot."

He looked at me for a long silent moment as if he was searching for something. Then he looked at my cup.

"Can I have a sip?" he asked. "I haven't had anything to drink all night."

I didn't trust him, obviously. He'd scaled several fences and snuck onto a heavily guarded vampire land with less than polite intentions. Still, it was only tea. How dangerous could that be? I stepped closer. I lifted the cup to his lips and he drank gratefully.

"I'm sorry," he whispered, smiling sadly. He slipped his right hand under his left cuff and there was a small cracking sound and a puff that looked like powdered sugar from a vial sewn into his sleeve. The heavy scents of chocolate and lilies hung between us. It made me want to sneeze.

"I'm pretty much immune to vampire pheromones," I informed him loftily, crossing my arms.

He didn't look disappointed or defeated.

"You're not immune to this blend," he said.

"Yes, I am. I don't know what you think—" The room wavered slightly, like I was seeing it through heat waves coming off asphalt. "What the hell?"

Another puff of powder.

"This is a special blend." He sounded briefly apologetic. "No one can resist it for long."

"You're not going to get away with this." All the colors looked weird, as if they were full of light. The red of the velvet drapes looked as if it were dripping blood. "I'll scream." I opened my mouth.

"You will not scream," he said calmly.

I closed my mouth. The taste of cocoa and flowers made me gag. There was something else laced under the flavors, but I couldn't place it. Licorice, whiskey, something. I felt faint, befuddled. And underneath the vagueness, fiery anger.

"Untie me, Lucy."

My hands fluttered forward.

"No," I whispered, watching them as if they belonged to somebody else. I curled my fingers into my palms. Sweat beaded under my hair, on my face. My glasses slipped down my nose. "No."

"Untie me, Lucy," he demanded, more forcefully. "I'm

impressed. Few people need a repetition. But you can't win against it—you'll only hurt yourself trying."

I fought the compulsion frantically, and lost. The knots loosened, fell free. When his hands were unbound, he wiggled out of the shoulder ropes and then bent down to untie his ankles.

"Stay there, Lucy. Don't make a sound, don't make a move until I'm gone."

I struggled and strained but it was like sticky chains held me tight. The Drakes were going to kill me. I had freed their only advantage, who was now lifting the window open and slipping out into the ragged garden. At least he didn't know about the silent alarms. Still, they weren't enough. I watched him hop the decorative stone wall, run across the field, and slip into the forest. The sun beamed brightly on his head. I heard footsteps, a soft curse, and Nicholas's furious voice.

"What the hell have you done?"

The release was abrupt and total. My muscles felt like water. My vision grayed and I crumpled to the carpet. I didn't pass out but it took me a moment to open my eyes again, a longer moment for all the furniture to settle back down into their proper places. Nicholas was crouched beside me, eyes gleaming.

"You little idiot."

The last of the spiderweb-sticky film of compulsion dissolved. I was eager to reestablish myself, panic running like angry ferrets through me at the thought that the effects might be permanent. The anxiety had me nauseous. I reared up suddenly, as if I'd been poked with a cattle prod. The exhilaration of controlling my limbs again was sweeter than any chocolate.

Nicholas, possibly, didn't agree.

"You have *got* to stop breaking my nose!" he hollered as the rest of the family thundered in. Blood stained his fingers as he cracked his nose back into place.

"Oops," I said, wincing. It was probably a good thing he healed so quickly. I rubbed my forehead where I'd crashed into his nose. My breathing was uneven, as if I'd been underwater too long. Quinn, only half-dressed, glared at the chair with the empty ropes coiled like sleeping snakes. His expression went hot, then cold.

"Where the hell is he?"

"She let him go," Nicholas explained tightly, rising from his crouch. It was then I finally noticed he was wearing only pj bottoms. His chest was bare, roped with slender muscles. My breathing sounded loud, even to me. The combined weight of the Drakes' outraged fury made me cringe. More adrenaline pumped into my bloodstream. Great. I already felt as if I'd drunk a gallon of espresso. I didn't know if I was going to pass out or explode. Solange helped steady me.

"Are you okay?"

"I think so." My teeth were chattering. I fought back tears of frustration and guilt burning behind my eyelids. Nicholas heaved a disgusted sigh before wrapping me roughly in an afghan and shoving me onto the couch.

"You're practically green," he muttered, pushing my head down between my knees. "Breathe."

Helena was at the window, snarling. She shaded her eyes. The glass might make the sunlight safe but their eyes were still pale and sensitive.

"I'm sorry," I said miserably. "I only meant to give him a sip of tea. He said he was thirsty." I could tell Liam was reining in his temper with a formidable amount of willpower. The tendons on his neck stood out in stark relief. His jaw might have been carved out of marble.

"What happened?" he asked very slowly, very precisely.

I wanted to crawl into a hole.

"He blew some sort of powder in my face." I rubbed my chilled arms. I wondered if it was a side effect of the drug or if I was in shock. "I resisted it at first, it was kind of like your pheromones. But the second dose did me in. He told me to untie him." I closed my eyes briefly, irritated with myself. "And I did. I couldn't stop myself."

"Willingly?" Quinn hollered. "On purpose?"

Liam silenced him with a look and came to sit in front of me. I tried to avoid his eyes, gave up. There was mostly hard patience and very little recrimination in his face.

"I'm so sorry. I tried to fight it. It was like being hypnotized or something."

"I need you to tell me everything you remember."

I described the way it tasted, that it tickled my nose, clung to my sweater.

"Hypnos," Liam said coldly. Helene turned from her post. She pointed to the desk, and Connor went to retrieve a little jeweled box from the bottom drawer. Then he used a small brush to collect whatever powdery residue he could from my sweater and the carpet.

"We've never been able to get our hands on any," Liam explained smugly. "We'll have Geoffrey analyze it." Geoffrey taught night classes in biology at the local college. But he also had his own lab and was always running experiments and studying the Drakes' unique gifts.

"But what is it?"

"We're not sure about all the components; certainly it contains one of the zombie herbs. The rest, we don't know enough about, only that it's very powerful. Apparently, we should have searched him more thoroughly."

"It was hidden in his sleeve." I scowled. "If I ever see him again, I'm going to shove it right—"

"Stay away from him," Nicholas interrupted my rant. I ignored him.

"Now what do we do?" I asked.

"Now we go back to bed and get some rest," Liam reminded me gently. "Let us worry about it." Solange yawned wide enough to split her face. The brothers were all paler than usual, dark circles like bruises under their water-colored eyes. They were still young. In fact, Logan had only turned two years ago. He was so exhausted he looked drunk, barely able to stand up by himself. Sebastian propped him up, leading him toward the staircase. Nicholas had been turned even more recently than that, so I assumed only his irritation with me was keeping him upright.

Solange yawned again. "Are you going to be okay?"

I nodded. "Go on back to bed." It was nearly eleven but she was weaving a little on her feet. The rest of the family wandered off to their respective private quarters, Liam and Helena whispering to each other. Liam was already dialing his cell phone. Only Nicholas remained. He was the color of milk.

"Aren't you going up?" I asked.

He stepped closer to me.

"In a minute."

I finally felt warm. The afghan slipped from my shoulders. He was looking at me as if he wanted to peel me open like an orange. I remembered the feel of his mouth on mine. I frowned, nervous for no reason.

"What?"

"I just want to try something." His touch was gentle, skimming my cheek, my arm, down to my wrist. His eyes were like rain in autumn; violent, mysterious, beautiful.

Hypnotizing.

"Stop it," I whispered.

"Stay away from Kieran," he demanded softly. "He's dangerous."

"And you're not?"

"Let's find out." He closed the distance between us before I had time to even blink.

"What are you doing?"

"I have no idea," he admitted. His lips hovered just barely a breath away from mine.

"I thought you were mad at me." I really wanted to lean forward, just ever so slightly.

"I am."

"You're also trying to use your vamp mojo on me."

"It doesn't work on you."

"Remember that." My voice was soft, like whipped cream, and at odds with my smug smirk.

Lucy

We didn't close our eyes, not even when our lips met. I tingled all the way down to my toes. I wasn't remotely chilled anymore; in fact, it felt like the longest, most humid day of summer. His skin was cool. I kind of wanted to nip into him like he was ice cream. When his tongue touched mine, my eyelids finally drifted shut. I gave myself to the moment, all but hurled into it. I wanted it to last for the next year and a half at least. I'd never felt like this before.

It could totally become addictive.

Just imagine if we actually *liked* each other.

CHAPTER 5

◆

Solange

Saturday afternoon

When I woke up, Lucy was muttering to herself. It wasn't unusual, but there was a particularly strident edge to it, even more than was ordinarily the result of her impatience with our slow Internet connection. The several farms comprising the Drake compound were nearly a thousand acres, some without any power source. Our house was lucky to have satellite service even if it meant our connection suffered when it was a cloudy day somewhere else on the continent.

"Stupid satellite."

I'd need a calculator to figure out how many times I'd woken up to her yelling at my computer. Patience was not one of Lucy's finer qualities. I snuggled deeper into the nest of blankets. The sun seemed a little too bright, but I liked the warmth of it on my face. "What time is it?" I yawned.

Lucy flicked me a glance. "Just past two, I think." She scribbled on a piece of paper. "Nose plugs, definitely need those. And a pocket knife, something really pointy. Ooh!" She interrupted herself excitedly. "A stun gun. Think they sell those on eBay?"

I yawned again, pushed myself up on my elbow. I was more tired than usual but I ignored that. "What on earth are you doing now?" I asked.

"Making a list of supplies," she answered grimly. "I have no intention of letting that Helios-Ra jerkface use me to get to you again."

"It wasn't your fault."

She didn't look remotely convinced. "Nicholas thinks it's my fault."

"Since when do you care what he thinks?"

She paused. "Oh. Good point." She clicked the mouse. "Hey, look, they do have stun guns. That one has Hello Kitty on it, I think. Maybe not, it's hard to tell." Her eyes widened comically. "What are they made out of, solid gold and diamonds? I can't afford that on my allowance."

I groaned, letting my head fall back on my pillow. "Lucy, you can't order one of those. Not exactly subtle."

She made a face. "I guess."

"Besides, you know my mom's probably got one in the storeroom."

She swiveled on her chair, eyes shining. "Think she'd give me one?"

"After last time? Not a chance."

"What, come on! That was ages ago."

"No one's forgotten what happened when you convinced her to teach you archery."

"How was I supposed to know I'd have such good aim?"

She'd very nearly skewered Marcus through the heart, which would have killed him, like anyone else. Arrows worked as well as stakes; it didn't matter what the material was, as long as it was pointy and went right through the heart. It was actually fairly difficult to do: rib cages weren't easy to pierce. She frowned at me.

"You're really pale. Are you feeling okay?" she asked.

"God, not you, too." I pulled the pillow over my face. "I'm *fine*."

"You're crabby."

"Because you're bugging me."

She poked me. "I haven't even begun to bug you."

I uncovered one eye. "Go away, Luce. I'm tired." I tried to make my one exposed eye do that cold flare thing my mom was so good at. Lucy tilted her head.

"You're getting better at that."

The one thing about being best friends with someone for so long was that even turning into a vampire didn't really faze her. Her smile softened. Great. My vampire mojo engendered pity, not fear.

"Go back to sleep," she said. The light caught the sequins on her velvet scarf, making me blink. "I'll keep making lists of the painful and very slow ways I can make Kieran suffer."

Kieran.

I closed my eyes, wondering why it was no effort at all to call up the exact shade of his dark eyes, hostile as they were. I should be thinking about the bounty on our heads, not whether or not I'd get to see him again. Because of course I'd get to see him again; he'd probably try and stake one of my brothers, if not me. Hardly a promising start to a relationship.

Relationship?

What the hell was I thinking?

No doubt my impending birthday was making my head fuzzy. There was no other explanation. I just needed more sleep. Because I did feel more tired than usual, as if keeping my eyes open was becoming a ridiculously difficult task, on par with algorithms and Hyacinth's needlepoint. When I woke up again, I was alone in my room. My stomach grumbled loudly. I felt better, rested and clearly hungry. Maybe I'd make myself waffles with blueberry syrup. I couldn't imagine ever not wanting to eat my way through a huge pile of them with whipped cream, even if every single one of my brothers assured me that by this time next week the very thought would make me nauseous. So I'd better eat as much as I could, while I still could.

The house was still quiet. The sun hadn't set yet, my brothers would still be asleep. My dad could stay up all day and could even sit outside under a shady tree. But today, I knew, he'd be on the phone with every operative and vamp he knew, and Mom was probably taking inventory of the weapons. She wasn't very strong during the day yet, but she wouldn't be able to sit still—not after last night.

The kitchen was empty though Lucy had left a pot of coffee warming for me. I poured myself a cup and though it tasted good,

I wasn't in the mood for food anymore. We were out of blueberry syrup anyway. When my parents went shopping for groceries, they tended to bring home bloody steak and anything red: raspberries, cherries, hot peppers. It didn't make cooking easy.

"Darling, try the raspberry mousse. It's fresh."

Neither did Aunt Hyacinth.

I tried to conceal a shudder as I turned on one heel to smile at her. She stood in the doorway, wearing what I called her Victorian bordello dressing gown: all lace and velvet flowers and silk fringe. Her long brown hair was caught in a messy knot. Her pug, Mrs. Brown, sniffled at her feet. If Mrs. Brown was out of Aunt Hyacinth's rooms, then it followed that the other dogs, giant babies that they were, were currently cowering under the dining room table. They feared Mrs. Brown the way I feared reality TV.

"Come up for a chat," Aunt Hyacinth invited after pouring herself a glass of cherry cordial. She liked to experiment with flavoring her blood-laced food and drink.

Which is why I had absolutely no intention of touching the raspberry mousse.

We could technically eat food after the bloodchange, only it had virtually no taste and absolutely no nutritional value for us. Only blood kept us alive and healthy. Gross, gross, gross.

I was so going to have to get over this blood phobia of mine.

And soon.

"Are you coming?" Aunt Hyacinth called from the top of the staircase. I followed her up, Mrs. Brown nipping at my heels enthusiastically. There was a canine whine from the dining room.

Aunt Hyacinth had a suite of rooms on the second floor, as did my parents and I, next to one of the guest rooms. Aunt Hyacinth preferred to live with us instead of building her own house on the Drake compound. She could certainly afford it. Our family had been around long enough to learn how to be comfortably wealthy. At first there was considerable theft involved, which no one ever reported, thanks to the pheromones. But in the last few hundred years, everyone had begun stockpiling coins and decorative pieces, which turned into very valuable antiques with very little effort. In fact, every child born or made in the Drake family had a trust fund begun in their name in the form of a chest full of antique gold locked in the basement safe room. But, wealth notwithstanding, Aunt Hyacinth claimed being alone too much made her maudlin. Her word, not mine; though according to Lucy's school friends I had a weird vocabulary and a weird accent—a hazard of being homeschooled by a family with members born anywhere from the twelfth century on.

Aunt Hyacinth's rooms were pretty much what you'd expect from a lady who still mourned Queen Victoria's death—and the fact that said queen turned down an offer of bloodchange.

I turned my attention back to my surroundings. My own imminent bloodchange not only made me unbearably sleepy, but it also made it really hard to concentrate. Aunt Hyacinth's parlour didn't help. And it was a parlour, not a sitting room or a living room. A *parlour*. I'd learned the difference before I'd learned to spell the word. With the proper British spelling, of course, for Aunt Hyacinth. I'd also learned medieval spelling for words in honor of Veronique—with a French flair in honor of her Aquitaine heritage—and modern English from Mom and Dad. It was a wonder I'd ever learned to spell my own name.

I sat in a brocade-cushioned chaise next to a huge copper urn filled with ferns. Aunt Hyacinth loved ferns; they'd been the fashion when she had her coming-out ball on her eighteenth birthday. She'd worn a white silk gown and made her curtsy to the queen. She'd taught me to curtsy and I'd taught Lucy, who had practiced until she gave herself leg cramps. The parlour had lace tablecloths on every surface and silver candlesticks and painted oil lamps and silhouettes in gilded frames. There was a small dressing room filled with corsets and petticoats and pointy boots. Lucy and I had spent hours playing in there when we were little. Lucy would still play in there, if Aunt Hyacinth would let her.

Aunt Hyacinth reclined dramatically on a velvet fainting couch, drinking her cherry-flavored blood. Mrs. Brown hopped up to curl by her feet, accepting slivers of rare beef as a mid-afternoon snack.

I wondered, not for the first time, if it was possible to be a vegetarian vampire.

"If you keep worrying so much you'll give yourself wrinkles," Aunt Hyacinth scolded me gently.

"I can't help it."

"Darling, your brothers survived the change. As a Drake woman, you are far stronger than they are. Just think, you'll wake up so refreshed. There's no feeling like it." She fanned herself with a silk fan decorated with white feathers. "And meanwhile, you ought to enjoy the courting."

"Courting? Aunt Hyacinth, they're drunk on my particular stink. And they don't care about me, they just want me to give them little fanged babies or whatever. And they want the power of the Drake name. Not exactly romantic."

She fanned harder. "But it can be, if you use it to your advantage."

"No thanks." I loved my aunt but there were certain topics we would never, ever agree on. Case in point: boys. Also: boyfriends, husbands, flirting techniques, and the supposed comfort of steel-boned corsets.

Aunt Hyacinth leaned over to run a hand over my hair. "It amazes me how beautiful you are sometimes, even with that loose, messy hair." Her expression was dark, fierce. I'd have been terrified if I didn't love her so much. "No harm will come to you, Solange, not while any of us live."

And that scared me most of all.

CHAPTER 6

•

Lucy

Saturday afternoon

I left a note on the fridge door and snuck out, keeping the car in neutral until I was clear of the driveway. I knew they would have wanted to send someone with me, but I was incidental and I didn't want Solange to have one single minute of less protection because of me. Besides, I waited until the brightest and sunniest part of the day, and I only needed to make sure the cats had enough water and food. Everything else I needed was in town, in nice public crowded places or right on the Drake compound.

I knew Geoffrey would be in his lab now that he had a sample of the Hypnos powder. It really rankled that I'd been the weak link. Kieran had a lot to answer for, the jerk.

I drove to the last house on the compound and around to the

barn set out back. Geoffrey had been using it as a lab for decades. I knocked on the door before going in. It was a lesson I'd had drilled into me since I was old enough to know that it was okay to ignore certain explosions and black smoke out of this particular barn but that it was never okay not to knock. Geoffrey might hear my heartbeat approaching, but some of his experiments were delicate and dangerous and he wasn't always able to step away from them or close them down for visitor safety. And though I usually preferred Hyacinth's closet for my explorations, Geoffrey had helped me pass my biology exam last year and I was hoping he'd be as helpful today.

"Come in, Lucy," he called out, already sounding distracted. I'd have to make my questions short. The barn was outfitted with the most modern equipment, acres of counters and refrigeration units and at least a dozen fire extinguishers. Geoffrey was standing over a tray of beakers, wearing a creased lab coat.

"Hi. I know you're busy so I'll be quick," I said, wrinkling my nose at the familiar odor of formaldehyde and rubbing alcohol with a tinge of hay. There hadn't been hay stored in this barn for nearly a hundred years, but apparently that dusty smell never really went away. "Any progress with the Hypnos?"

"These things take time, you know that." He added a drop of blue liquid to a slide and slipped it under a microscope. "Just like I know that's not why you're really here."

"I'm sorry I let him get away."

He looked up. "It's hardly your fault—even I would follow orders if I got a mouthful of Hypnos. It's very potent, Lucy."

"I know."

"Now, what can I do for you?"

I bit my lip. "I want to know about the bloodchange."

"You know about the bloodchange."

"No, I don't. I know it's the big bad and everyone's freaked out, but that's it. And every time I ask Solange, she tells me not to worry."

"And she's right."

"Please." Apparently I wasn't above begging. "I just want to understand it so I can help."

He smiled gently. "Unfortunately, there's not much you can do to help, my dear. This is Solange's battle."

"Solange is my best friend," I said stubbornly. "So it's my battle too."

Something in my face must have convinced him I was going to make a nuisance of myself until I got what I wanted, because he finally sighed and said, "All right, Lucy. Have a seat."

I sat quickly, before he could change his mind.

"The bloodchange is still a bit of a mystery," he admitted. "I've been doing research and experiments to better understand our family's special challenge, but with varying degrees of success. It's not strictly scientific, nor is it strictly supernatural, so we have as many questions as answers. There are only a few other families who can procreate like we do. All other vampires are made, not born. Technically, the *Hel-Blar* are made the same way; it's only that they have a more violent transformation, without guidance or mentoring until it's too late."

"Are they as scary as everyone makes them out to be?"

"Yes."

"Do the Hounds get sick too?"

"In a manner of speaking, though not like us. Our change is genetic, you understand. As near as we can explain it, when our young reach puberty, the flux in hormones triggers the change. It's like the body attacks itself and then shuts down—until it is reawakened by drinking vampire blood. Our children need to be very strong to fight through it and win."

I swallowed. "But mostly everyone gets through it, right?"

"Mostly."

"Why do some go crazy? Is that a hormone thing, too? Like permanent PMS?"

He smiled briefly. "Not quite. It's just that some are stronger than others. The bloodchange is so difficult, some just can't hold on to themselves. If they get only just enough blood to survive, the thirst takes them over and it's all they can think about, like the *Hel-Blar*."

"Are you telling me Solange could turn into one of them if she's not strong enough?"

"I wish I knew for sure. The more likely outcome would be that she might simply die and not reawaken."

"This sucks." I scowled. "But Solange is totally strong enough. She won't die for real and she won't go crazy." If I said it enough, it would be true.

"I'm sure you're right," Geoffrey said soothingly. "She has strong genes, which is an asset. Drinking the blood from someone of the same lineage will restore her enough to win the battle. Her body won't attack the new blood, but it can't create its own supply either. At first, she'll need to drink every day to supplement, less as she gets older."

"She's not going to get older." I tried not to dwell on the fact that one day I'd be wrinkled and wearing dentures and she'd still look young enough to be my granddaughter. We had way bigger worries.

"She won't age physically, no. At least not for a few years, after her body completely adjusts to its new form. I'm afraid I don't really understand the science behind this adaptation yet. My theory is that it's another genetic survival mechanism: we reach our optimum age, where we look the strongest. It's a way to scare off predators, like making yourself look bigger to scare off a black bear."

"Oh. And her special pheromone thing is a survival mechanism too, right? How everyone's all obsessed with her?"

"Yes. It's a mating thing. Everyone is wondering if she'll be able to carry a vampire child to term."

"Gross."

"Study your Darwin, my girl."

As if. "One more thing, why are the *Hel-Blar* blue?"

"It's a side effect, like their fangs. Their extra fangs enable them to take their first . . . meals . . . with such violence and greed, it leaves them, in effect, engorged and bruised."

"Oh." I had to learn to stop asking these questions. I never liked the answer. I swallowed. "Thanks. I guess I should let you get back to work."

"Yes, Darwin's going to get a little help when I'm through." He turned back to his microscope and I knew he'd pretty much forgotten I was there by the time I reached the door. I didn't feel better exactly, but at least I didn't feel like I was the only one in the dark anymore.

I drove home, mind racing. My house seemed too quiet somehow, too empty. Mom's Kali statue watched as I put out several bowls of water. It had to last until my parents came back—just in case. It felt melodramatic to think like that, but I needed to be prepared. Solange would have been happy hiding out in some deserted cabin until this was all over, but I wanted to fight. My parents still didn't understand my violent tendencies considering the way I was raised: meditating, eating tofu, and taking long road trips in the middle of the school year to see petroglyphs or observe moose. My mom's rabid tolerance extends not just to people but all species—vampires included. Helena and my mom were best friends in high school but drifted apart when Mom went to college and then traveled around the world to find herself. It was ten years before Mom came back to her hometown. One night she went on one of her full-moon hikes and ran into Helena, who was pregnant with Solange and drinking the blood of a deer Liam had killed to help sate her cravings. Apparently, that kind of thing had only happened when Helena was pregnant with Solange and not any of her seven brothers.

Anyway, no amount of vampire mind control was going to make my vegetarian mom forget that particular sight. Helena couldn't hide from my mom, and their friendship was rekindled, which was how we came to be so close and comfortable with the Drakes. More comfortable than they were with us sometimes—case in point: Nicholas.

Nicholas.

I really wished he'd been a bad kisser. It would have been much easier to forget it ever happened, to not wonder if it might happen again.

"Focus," I told myself sternly, locking our front door, double-checking it. I watched every bush and tree suspiciously on my way back to the safety of my car. The tires squealed, sending up clouds of dust as I sped out of there. The back of my neck didn't relax completely until I'd reached the outskirts of town, with its candy-colored galleries and ice-cream parlors. The area was popular with artists, environmentalists, and homesteaders like my folks. There were few places with so much wilderness all around—dense forests and hidden waterfalls and even wolves, sometimes, singing on cold winter nights. The combination of the untamed countryside and the fact that everyone here was pretty private and accepting of alternative lifestyles made it a perfect place for vampires to live in undiscovered. At least I thought they were undiscovered. If not, no one talked about it. Folks here were far more likely to get heated over conspiracy theories and nuclear waste sites.

First, I stopped by the drugstore for nose plugs and I cleared them out entirely. The cashier didn't even blink. Then I went to the hardware store for hunting and camping supplies, which were big business in town. I felt a little silly, I admit, kind of like the comic book character I'd accused Kieran of emulating. But I was determined, too. If there was anything I'd learned from my parents, besides how to chop wood and prime the water pump, it was that you did what needed doing and you didn't complain about it or pretend it wasn't necessary. Afterward, I felt perfectly justified in rewarding myself with a double-shot cinnamon latte. And since my parents weren't there, I didn't even use soymilk. That was downright rebellious in our family. I nearly snorted—I was going back to a house where blood was sipped like a fine wine and vegetarianism wasn't exactly an option. I'd already made Solange promise she wouldn't drink any bunnies dry.

I was halfway back to my car when I felt the warning prickle. I swallowed, forced myself not to speed up or slow down, to keep my pace even and oblivious. There was a family eating hot dogs on a bench, someone else on a bicycle, two girls walking a tiny teacup Chihuahua. There was something else as well, that indescribable feeling of being watched, followed. I turned the corner, the green lawns of a park on my left, my car farther down on the right. No other pedestrians. The sun was making the sidewalk feel soft under my sandals. Almost definitely not a vampire then, it was too hot and bright.

There was the barest tremble from the hazel thicket. I wouldn't have noticed it at all if I hadn't been so paranoid about every single thing around me. Adrenaline shivered through me. I hoped I still looked like any other distracted girl, sipping my latte and juggling shopping bags. I waited until I was right next to the hazel before I chucked my latte and hollered, launching myself at whoever was skulking around back there. We went down in a tangle of flailing limbs and blistering curses. I saw black cargo pants, black nose plugs, black eyes. His code name was probably Shadow.

Kieran.

CHAPTER 7

◆

Solange

I went out back to my little shed. The sun was soft on the clapboard siding and the kiln tucked into the back. I did need my sunglasses but at least I didn't feel as tired as I had last night. I knew that when it came to me, my entire family went all overprotective and dramatic, so it was hard to know how many symptoms on their long list I could really expect.

I let myself into the studio and closed the door very deliberately. I wouldn't think about it right now. It never helped anyway. What did help was burying my hands in clay and the rhythmic spinning of my pottery wheel. It was dusty and quiet in here, just how I liked it. The long window offered the distraction of the wild fields and forest when I needed them. My tools and chemicals were stored in plastic tubs; the walls were fitted with wooden shelves all but groaning under the weight of bowls and cups and oddly shaped vases. Lucy kept telling me I should take my stuff into the gallery shops by the lake to sell it. It wasn't a bad idea. Though most of them did their business during the daylight hours, Lucy would make deliveries for me if I asked her to. It was something to think about.

If I survived my birthday, of course.

I scowled and attacked the clay. It was cool and obedient under my determined hands. I hated being frightened, almost as much as I hated being coddled. I worked until the sun was dipping slowly behind the trees. Geese flew overhead, honking. I wasn't any closer to figuring out Kieran Black or the bounty or how to give in gracefully to the bloodchange, but at least I was calmer. And possibly hungry again. I wiped my hands clean and went outside, inhaling deeply the fragrance of roses and wild mint. I was thinking so hard I wasn't paying attention to my surroundings.

First mistake.

I might not have super hearing yet, but the arrow whistled so close to my head I could hear the air through the fletchings. It thunked into one of the oak trees, showering splinters. At the same time, someone crashed into me, curling around me like a particularly heavy parka.

"Oof! What—"

"Get down, you ijit!" It was Bruno. He only slipped back into his native Scottish accent when he was really pissed off. "Get in the damn house." He ran me up the porch steps. I felt like president of a small country under attack. All he needed was the ear transmitter and a pair of mirrored sunglasses. And a black suit—but I didn't think he'd ever wear a tie, even for us. He looked just like what he was: an ex-biker with a shaved head to disguise the balding, and tattoos from shoulder to knuckle. He'd been working for us since before I was born. Bruno shoved me inside and slammed the door behind us.

"Stay here," he barked, running back out, shouting orders into a walkie-talkie. The gardens were quiet; even the birds were cheerfully oblivious. My heart was thumping wildly, making me feel dizzy. That arrow had been really close, too close. And only one organization used wooden arrows of that style.

Helios-Ra.

I wondered if it had been Kieran, skulking in the shadows, waiting for me to turn my back. The sun glittered on the gravel drive, the black iron fence. No vampire ancient enough to withstand this kind of a summer day would be able to sneak onto the property. Someone would have scented his pheromones.

Bruno came back, eyeing me grimly. "The tunnels for you from now on, lassie."

"Did you get him?"

"Not even a damned footprint." He rubbed his head. "Get away from the window, Solange. It's not safe."

"This is getting ridiculous," I muttered.

"Agreed," he replied.

"I'm going to the loft," I told him peevishly.

"Use the tunnel," he repeated.

I went down into the basement and used the short passageway that linked the house to the garage. The second floor had been converted into training space complete with floor mats, punching bags, a weight machine, and two treadmills. The back wall was covered with fencing gear and swords. I didn't bother with the uniform or the mask since I was practicing on my own. I just needed the distraction. If pottery wasn't enough to really calm me down, lunging and stabbing an imaginary foe would have to do. I took up my favorite sword, or foil as it was called in fencing.

Out of habit I saluted my pretend opponent and bowed. Then I cross-stepped back and forward a few times to warm up. I lunged, I stabbed, I parried and circular parried and disarmed. I lunged again and again until my thigh muscles ached and sweat spiked my hair. I ducked right, I parried low, I jabbed high. Retreat, riposte, retreat, riposte.

I felt better until I happened to glance out the window and saw Bruno going back into the house, dragging a huge bag full of packages and flowers. I tossed my foil aside and sprinted down the steps, through the tunnel and up to the front hall. I scowled at the open bag, panting and scowling.

"What the hell is that?"

"More gifts, lass," Bruno said. "We're finding them all along the property line."

For some reason, all those presents were really pissing me off. I jabbed my hand inside and pulled out postcards, a clump of daisies, something that looked like a Ziploc bag full of blood.

"That's disgusting." I dropped it immediately. The light glinted off something silver and I pulled it out gingerly. It was an apple, perfectly crafted out of silver, with a leaf dangling from the stem. The delicate leaf was engraved with a name: Montmartre.

I put the apple aside so I could wipe my hands completely clean of Montmartre cooties, and it teetered on the edge of the table. It hit the floor, and the top opened on tiny hinges I hadn't seen. Blood poured out of the opening, thick and red. The coppery smell made me gag but I didn't have time to otherwise react. I was too busy staring out the front window.

"Where's Lucy's car?"

CHAPTER 8

•

Lucy

"You asshole!"

I didn't think, just reacted with all the anger and guilt and worry I'd been carrying around all day. I punched him right in the nose. He reared back, grabbing his face.

"Shit, shit!"

"That's right, you sneaky bastard." I leaped to my feet, panting. "Use me against my best friend, will you?"

He reached into his pocket. I got to mine first, took out the pair of nose plugs I'd stashed there, just in case, and I shoved them in.

"Oh, no you don't," I snapped, smug as a cat with a mouthful of canary feathers. I was going to redeem myself, if I had to punch him ten more times to do it. My knuckles felt bruised, sore. Vindicated.

There was the teeniest, tiniest possibility my mom was right about my temper.

Kieran just blinked at me, bewildered. "Who taught you to punch like that?"

I smiled grimly. "The Drakes." He shifted, as if he was going to get up. "Uh-uh. You stay right there or I'll scream so loud half the town will come running. You might be part of some secret club, but I can still get you arrested for being a creepy stalker." I noticed the way he was trying to look at the back of my neck, and my wrists. "And what the hell are you doing now?"

"You don't have any scars."

"What?"

He pushed himself up so he wasn't sprawled in the dirt. His nose looked sore but I hadn't actually broken it. "Bloodslaves have scars, from the feedings."

"Don't use that word, it's insulting. And it makes me want to kick you. Hard."

He held up his hands, palms out, as he stood up fully. I took a step back, raised a fist. I could see the hilt of a knife in the top of his boot.

"You have to know that vampires murder people." I could tell he was thinking about his father. Sometimes it was a real pain that my own father had encouraged such a strong sense of empathy in me. He couldn't have taught me math?

"Kieran, humans murder all the time. And the Drakes aren't killers. They're not *Hel-Blar*, they know how to control themselves."

"They're all the same."

"Don't make me punch you again. My hand already hurts."

He nearly smiled. "You might be as scary as Helena Drake, one day."

"I intend to be."

"You're well on your way." He wiped blood off his face ruefully. A car passed by on the street.

"Leave them alone, Black."

"It's not that simple."

"It is *too*. Helios-Ra has a treaty or whatever, so stick to it."

"I'm a new agent. I only just turned eighteen. Do you really think I'm in charge over there? I have orders, just like everyone else."

"That's convenient," I sneered, gathering up my bags before turning away. "And totally lame." I stopped at the driver's-side door. "Don't be a lemming, Black."

◆

When I got back to the farm, one of the guards stepped out where I could see him and shook his head disapprovingly. Ooops. I was already flinching when I let myself out of the car and Nicholas opened the screen door. So much for sneaking out and then back in, none the wiser. Nicholas's nostrils actually flared.

"Lucky."

I flared mine back and felt like an idiot.

"Nicky."

I pushed past him, then wished I could go back out onto the porch to fight with him. I'd take that over Solange's pale, worried face any day.

"Lucy, are you okay?"

"I'm fine, Sol. I just needed supplies and to feed the cats." I dropped my bags, felt Nicholas come up behind me. She looked so relieved, it gave the guilt sharper teeth. No one else could make me feel so bad without saying a single word. Bruno was doing a pretty good job though, looking like a disappointed parent before he went out to patrol.

"I'd have fed your bloody cats," Nicholas muttered. He saw my drugstore bags, looked at me incredulously.

"You went to buy lipstick? At a time like this?"

"Yeah, that's right, and an exfoliating mask. Don't be an ass. I went for supplies."

The sun filtered in through the window, and he flinched away, even though it was specially treated glass and he was in no danger. He looked tired enough to fall over. Even the shadows under his eyes had shadows.

"You should be in bed."

"I *was* in bed," he said pointedly. "Until you went shopping."

"I needed nose plugs." I lifted the pair hanging on a string around my neck. "And they've already come in handy."

He narrowed his eyes at me.

"Why?" He grabbed my wrist. "Why, Lucy?"

I tugged back but couldn't break his hold.

"Because." I stopped pulling. I'd only dislocate my own wrist. "I ran into Kieran Black. Literally."

They both stared at me.

"What?" Solange finally squeaked.

Nicholas turned my hand over. His eyes flared, went the color of frost, at the blood on my knuckles. I shrugged sheepishly.

"I nearly broke his nose." I half smiled. "I'll have to try harder next time."

He dropped my hand, stepped back. There was something fierce in his face, even when he smiled faintly.

"I guess I should be glad I'm not the only one you punch."

I made a face at him and dropped into a chair. I was starting to ache in muscles I didn't know I had. There were still roses everywhere, and the smell was overpowering.

"Did he hurt you?" Solange's face was stony.

"No, I'm fine." I watched Nicholas trying not to weave on his feet. He looked as if he were standing on a particularly wave-tossed boat. "Go back to sleep," I said with more gentleness than I'd planned. I paled when something occurred to me. "You didn't tell your parents, did you?"

"No," Solange said. "I only just found your note. I didn't even get a chance to tell Nicholas. He just stumbled out of his room, all freaked out."

We both turned to look at him. I thought he might be blushing—if vampires could blush, that was.

"The house smelled wrong," he muttered. He glared at us. "Shut up." Then he went up the stairs. I raised my eyebrows.

"He's getting weirder."

Solange snorted, pulled out a handful of nose plugs, air freshener sprays, and a bowie knife from my plastic bags.

"So are you."

◆

I waited until we were alone before I hustled Solange into her room.

"What are you doing now?" she muttered when I shut her door

and pressed my ear to the wood for a moment to make sure no one was listening. And by no one, I meant Nicholas.

"Okay, I should totally be a spy." I grinned at her. "All I need is some funky accent and I could be a Bond girl."

She groaned. "What did you do?"

"I stole this from Kieran, right after I punched him." I pulled out a small book from the inside pocket of my jacket. It looked innocuous enough, slender as a poetry chapbook, with a simple font and a sun illustration on the front cover. It was the title that stood out: *A Field Guide to Vampires.*

Solange read it, blinked, read it again, and then stared at me. "*A Field Guide to Vampires?* Is that a joke?"

I laughed out loud. "Nope. Just a little souvenir from the Helios-Ra." We sat on her bed and set the guide on the blanket in front of us. We skimmed the index, snorted at the pompous introduction and the pseudomedieval oath new recruits had to take. There was a bunch of stuff on hunter protocol that could come in useful someday. There was also a whole section on the Drake family, and a page devoted just to Solange, listing her stats, like she was a rare kind of frog one could search for in a swamp.

"It's kind of creepy." She made a face. "I'm starting to feel like the bearded lady at the carnival."

"I would never let you grow a beard," I assured her, trying to lighten the mood. If she hunched her shoulders any tighter, her collarbone would shatter. "I'm way too good a friend for that."

"Gee, thanks."

"All in a day's work."

"I can't believe they study us like that. I mean, did Kieran sit in a classroom and learn that I wear cargo pants and like pottery? And how do they know that anyway? And I'm not solitary, damn it, I just don't like crowds." She paused. "Okay, so maybe I am solitary, so what? And my nickname is *not* 'Princess Solange.' Give me a break."

I tugged the book out of her hands before she could twist it in half. It flipped open. "Hey, no way. I'm in here too."

Her eyes narrowed. "You are not."

"I totally am."

"Okay, that's going too far."

"Apparently, I'm brash and reckless." I snorted. "Better than being a mindless droid to some secret society." I did a double take. "Did you know one of my strengths is annoying Nicholas?"

She laughed despite herself. "Okay, that part's true."

"Shut up, he's the one who annoys me." I tapped the book thoughtfully. "Hmmm."

"Oh, God. That 'hmmm' is never good."

I ignored her and reached for the phone. "They know all about us, shouldn't we know a little about them too?"

"How? You can't just phone up a secret society."

"Maybe not. I mean, Kieran might not have a MySpace page, but he has to live somewhere, doesn't he? He's not like Black Ops or anything, right?"

"I guess not. Wait, what are you doing?" she asked as I dialed 411.

"Shh. Hello? Kieran Black in Violet Hill. Address unknown." I covered the mouthpiece. "I need a pen." She ran to her desk and practically threw one at me. I wrote on the back of the guide. "Thank you," I said before hanging up.

Solange and I smiled at each other, and it felt like the smile of two lionesses about to take down a gazelle.

I pushed each number as if I were squishing a bug. Kieran picked up on the first ring.

"Mom, for the third time, I've got the milk—"

"It's not your mom," I interrupted, smirking at Solange.

"Who is this?" he asked suspiciously.

"It's Lucy."

He made a very gratifying choking sound. "*What?* I never gave you my number."

"You're listed, genius. So you can add that to your little guidebook. I'm not only reckless, I'm resourceful too. And Solange isn't solitary, she just doesn't like you." She had a weird look on her face. "Are you okay?" I whispered to her. "Lie down." I could hear Kieran shuffling the phone, probably searching his pockets.

"You took my guide!"

"Yup. You want it back? Meet us tonight." Solange's eyes widened. I waved away her concern.

"I can get another guidebook," he told me.

"Yeah, but how would it look for a new recruit to have lost it to one of your profiles?" I had him there. "Besides, you owe me, Black." And there.

He sighed, like an old man. "I don't actually owe you, Hamilton."

"Do *so.*"

"Does Solange know you're doing this?"

Interesting. "Yes, she knows. Don't you think she's tired of playing monkey in the middle for you people? Ow, what?" That last part I said into the air since Solange had grabbed the phone from me, scratching me in the process.

"My nickname is not 'Princess,'" she said witheringly. "Fine. After sunset." Her voice hardened. "Come alone."

CHAPTER 9

◆

Solange

Saturday evening, sunset

That night every single one of my brothers was in a foul mood. My parents were worse.

"We have some leads," my father said tightly from where he stood by the fireplace. "Though not nearly as much as I'd like."

My mom was wearing her leather vest, the one with all the hidden compartments. Not a good sign. She only wore it for serious hunting or ass-kicking.

"Your father and I have to follow them, as will Hyacinth and your uncles." Aunt Hyacinth might have been off to track assassins, but she still looked stylish in her riding habit and jet cameo. Her only concession was a pair of pointy granny boots instead of silk dancing slippers. "Geoffrey is in his lab with the Hypnos sample. Ruby is . . . indisposed." Which was a polite way of putting it. "Bruno will patrol with his men." Mom looked at my brothers. "Every single one of you will stay here and look after your sister. Except for Sebastian, who's already left on an errand."

I gaped at her, horrified. "Mom, *no*." My brothers were insufferable enough as it was. Six of them duty bound to follow me would make us all crazy. Lucy cringed sympathetically.

Mom glanced at me. "Solange, you have to take this seriously."

"Mom, I *do*. You know I do. But you don't have brothers, you don't *know*."

Logan contrived to look offended. "We're wonderful brothers."

The others ignored me, nodding solemnly at our parents. I groaned. I was going to have to get Lucy to break all of their noses before the night was through. Good thing she'd had so much practice. It wasn't that I was ungrateful or didn't adore my brothers— it was just that Drake men were arrogant, unbending, and liberally laced with white-knight complexes, especially when it came to their baby sister. I watched my mom strap her scabbard on, the leather strap between her breasts, the sword at her shoulder. It made me feel small, frustrated, useless. I couldn't even Google bounties or Helios-Ra because I'd find nothing but gaming Web sites and bad movie clips. I admit I had already Googled Kieran, but nothing came up.

I followed them to the basement stairs. They'd take the underground tunnels that connected all the farms, with exits in the forest and out near the town, as well as farther into the mountains.

"Maybe you shouldn't go." I wouldn't be able to forgive myself if they were hurt on my account. Dad put his hand on my shoulder. He wasn't tall, but he had the solid, regal bearing of a medieval king.

"We'll be fine," he assured me, and I nearly believed him. I watched them go, feeling utterly wretched when I heard the heavy steel door clang shut. My brothers positioned themselves in a half circle around me, staring.

This was already a disaster.

"All right." Lucy shouldered her way to my side and made a waving motion as if they were annoying flies. "Shoo!" She narrowed her eyes. "I said shoo."

They dispersed, mostly startled into moving. Only Logan remained, leaning casually against the wall.

"Darling, I'm not some insect to be chased away."

"Darling?" She snorted amiably. "You're not ninety years old, either."

He straightened. "I'm charming," he informed her. "And women like endearments."

"Women know you just can't remember their names, but they like your pretty face enough not to care. Now give your sister some space before she short-circuits."

He winked at her before sauntering away. She winked back. I knew they were trying to keep the mood light for my sake.

"Thanks."

"You're welcome. You know how I love to boss your brothers around. Let's go upstairs."

I waited until we were safely ensconced in my room with the stereo playing loudly to cover our voices.

"How are we going to do this?" I asked. "I can't believe Mom and Dad sicced them all on me."

"It's okay, we can totally do this." She started to pace between my desk and the closet door. "We just have to keep them distracted somehow." She paused. "Connor will be on his computer all night. Maybe we could ask him to track Kieran down online, keep him busy."

"That'll definitely work. And maybe you could try convincing the others to watch a movie or something? Make it sound like I'm sulking and just want to be left alone?"

She nodded. "Brilliant. I'll be right back."

She wasn't gone long, and by the time she came back I could hear the sounds of some action movie on the television in the far family room. It was conveniently on the other side of the house from the sunroom, which had a door to the backyard.

"I made it really loud," she informed me proudly. "Logan looked a little suspicious but he's watching it. Connor's online and Nicholas was up in his room, so I thought it was probably safest to leave him there. If he's brooding, it could buy us some time."

I shook my head. "No amount of brooding or distraction will keep him off our trail."

She snorted. "As long as we act suspicious, he'll follow us for a while without saying anything and think it's his idea. Besides, it might be good to have a little vampire instinct on our side."

"You're kind of evil, you know that?" I grinned at her.

"I've been practicing," she shot back with her own grin. "So are you ready to do this?"

I nodded, pulling on a black sweater so I'd blend into the

shadows better. "You know this is definitely one of our dumber ideas?"

"Please, would you rather sit around here and worry?"

"Hell, no. Let's go."

"That's what I thought." She poked her head out the window. "I don't think we can climb down from here."

"Not without you falling on your head." I pulled her away. "I've seen you in gym remember?"

"Hey, you don't even go to my school."

"In that class you had at the park, that time you tripped on your shoelace and took out a row of girls in pink shorts."

"Oh." She made a face. "Right."

"We'll use the back stairs and go through the sunroom."

For some reason we had to stifle giggles as we crept down the stairs. I felt like I was in some bad silent movie. Lucy clutched my hand and we used the movie's car chase to cover our movements. My brothers were still young enough that they shouldn't be able to distinguish our heartbeats over that kind of volume, even if they thought they could.

The backyard was dark—we remembered to avoid the motion-sensor light. We stayed low, moved quickly.

"How do we know we can trust him?" Lucy worried, not sounding quite as confident and cavalier now that we were getting closer to the edge of the forest.

"I think we can." I didn't know why I thought that, I just did.

"Oh man, is it wrong that now I really hope Nicholas is following us?"

I shook my head mutely. I was kind of hoping the same thing.

Vampire hearing would be an advantage right now. We crouched in a thicket and waited. My palms were damp. Lucy fidgeted anxiously. Even the crickets sounded sinister.

The crack of a twig underfoot had us clinging to each other.

"Solange? Lucy?"

Lucy popped up, scowling. "You scared the hell out of me."

Kieran jerked back. "Likewise."

I stood up much more slowly, wondering why I felt shy. This totally wasn't the time. He looked at me for a long moment, then nodded. Lucy stared at him, then at me. If she said anything I was going to kill her. She pursed her lips but mercifully stayed silent, instead staring over his shoulder suspiciously.

"You don't have to do that," he told her. "I'm alone."

"Forgive me if I don't entirely trust your motives," she shot back grimly. "You tried to kill my best friend."

"I did not!" he exclaimed hotly. Lucy had the ability to make most guys revert to being ten years old. That should've been in their stupid field guide. "She wasn't even out in the garden."

"Technicality," Lucy grumbled. "You came for the bounty."

"Yeah. It's my *job*."

"You should get a new one. Your boss sucks."

"Here's your book," I said quietly, handing him the guide before they started to pull each other's hair.

"Thanks." Neither of us said anything else. I was starting to hope Lucy would snap at him again, when he finally glanced away. "Why'd you want to meet?"

"You have to know we didn't break the treaty."

"Look, like I told your mental friend here, I don't make the rules. I just graduated. And anyway, isn't it all part of your coup? To be queen?"

"Is that what they're telling you?"

"You don't *want* to be queen?"

"*No*," I said emphatically. "I don't. Look, I'm the first girl born to the House of Drake. That's all. It's only a big deal because of people like you. I didn't ask for this."

"Then don't let them turn you into a vampire."

"Oh, sure, she'll just die instead," Lucy said waspishly. "Nice plan."

He blinked at me. "You really would? That's not a myth about the ancient families?"

"No, it's not a myth. And I really don't want my family being hunted because of me. Can't you do anything?" I wasn't sure why I was asking him for help; I only knew that we really had no other options. I had to do *something* and this was it. Problem was, he didn't look entirely convinced. "If you really believe we should be hunted down, why don't you just kill me now?" I took a step closer to him, opening my arms.

"Don't be stupid." He took a startled step back, as if I was the one covered in weapons.

"Why not? It's what you do, isn't it?"

"It's not like that. Besides, you're human. Mostly."

"For now. Does that mean you'll kill me after my birthday?"

"No! Maybe. I don't know. I just want to find the one who killed my dad."

"You were so convinced it was one of us." I stepped even closer, could see the way his pupils dilated.

"Solange," Lucy said nervously.

I didn't look away from Kieran. "So go ahead."

"What the hell do you think you're doing?" Nicholas stalked out of the woods, fuming. I was half-surprised smoke wasn't coming out of his ears. Kieran reached for one of the stakes on his belt.

"Don't," I said, stepping in front of him. "Please."

"Solange, get inside," Nicholas ordered through his teeth, forcibly lifting Lucy up off the ground and setting her out of his way when she tried to stop him. She clung to his arm like a monkey.

"We know what we're doing," she insisted, her feet dragging in the long grass. "Stop it, Nicholas."

"We won't bother you again," I told Kieran, and for some reason my voice came out sounding sad. I turned away from him. "Nick, let's go."

I marched across the field knowing Nicholas would follow me, no matter how much he wanted to hang around to punch Kieran.

I didn't look back to see what Kieran was doing.

◆

Logan was in the back garden when we got back to the house.

"I knew something was up with you two," he said, seething.

"They had a secret date with Kieran frigging Black," Nicholas informed him stonily.

"Oh, it wasn't like that," Lucy retorted. "Give me a break."

"What is *wrong* with you?" Logan's mouth dropped open. I pushed past him to go inside and then wished I hadn't. Quinn, Connor, Marcus, and Duncan were waiting in the sunroom, and each of them started yelling at once. Lucy winced, stepping up beside me.

"She's fine," she said. "She's fine!" She yelled at the top of her lungs. My brothers paused. The sudden silence was broken by a bell ringing from the basement. Quinn and Connor took off at a run. By the time we stepped into the hall toward the kitchen, they were already leading someone up the steps.

"London," I said in surprise. She was a distant cousin and we rarely saw her. She was slim and pale and looked just like her name, with black hair so sleek it always looked as if she'd been walking in the rain. There were silver studs in her ears, seventeen at last count, one in her nose, and another in her left eyebrow. She wore tight black clothing, as always. "What are you doing here?" I asked.

"You've been summoned."

"Our parents aren't here," I said.

"I know," she replied. "It's not your parents who've been summoned, only you."

"By who?"

"Madame Veronique."

I stepped back. "I don't want to go."

"You can't exactly refuse."

"Why does she want to see me?" Veronique never saw any of us before the bloodchange. Ever.

"Why do you think?" London's fangs were out, not because she was angry—she was always angry—but because she refused to be anything but what she was. She sneered at Lucy. It was a constant source of irritation that Lucy was mostly immune to her phero-mones. "*That* has to stay here." London didn't approve of Lucy, never had. She thought mortals were too fragile for friendship, for the strength required to carry our secret. And she hated that she'd been every bit as mortal as Lucy before she was turned three years ago.

"As if I want to hang around you for a single second longer than absolutely necessary," Lucy snapped. I knew she was lying; she'd been desperate to get a look at Veronique for years now. Under the bravado and temper she was disappointed. Her pulse must have sped up, because London smirked. Nicholas licked his lips.

Marcus whistled between his teeth. "Bad luck, Sol. Veronique's terrifying."

Lucy stomped on his foot. "You're not helping."

"Why'd she send you?" Quinn frowned at London. "You're still one of Lady Natasha's ladies-in-waiting, aren't you?"

She nodded stiffly. Her divided loyalties were a sore spot with everyone. "I serve Veronique first, like everyone else in our family."

"That doesn't explain why she sent you."

"Because Veronique isn't the only one who's summoned Solange. Lady Natasha has too. Once Veronique heard Solange was being called to the royal court, she wanted the first visit."

"Crap." My eyes widened. "Both of them? Tonight?"

"Solange can't go now," Nicholas said. "It isn't safe."

London quirked an eyebrow. "You know as well as I do that it isn't a request. Just be grateful I was already in the area so Lady Nastasha didn't need to send one of her Araksaka boys." The Araksaka were feared. Every single one of them wore Lady Natasha's royal tattoo on their faces. They were her private army and answered only to her. Ever. And they were utterly ruthless about it; not only killing but torturing as well.

"Hell," Quinn muttered.

"Fine." I wiped my hands off on my pants. "Let's get this over with."

London shook her head. "You are *not* going dressed like that." I blinked down at my T-shirt and cargos, which only had one smear of dried clay on the cuff. "You'd be laughed out of the Hall. And Lady Natasha'd be insulted, having granted you a temporary reprieve from exile. Not to mention what Veronique would do."

"Shouldn't have exiled the Drakes in the first place," Lucy muttered.

"She had to, because of the prophecy. You wouldn't understand."

"Give me a break." Lucy visibly bristled at the disdain in London's voice. "I probably know more about your own history than you do. The prophecy was recorded during the reign of Henry the Eighth, after he cut off Anne Boleyn's head. Some old madwoman in Scotland went into a trance and babbled about a blood-born Drake woman ruling over the tribes, and when Solange was born you all freaked out about it, including Lady Natasha." She looked proud of herself. "See? I totally get it. Although, I don't get why she's not Queen Natasha instead of Lady Natasha? Wouldn't that make more sense?"

"She hasn't had a coronation," Logan explained. "She's technically not queen, because we technically don't have queens. We have autonomous tribes and civil wars and a love of tradition."

"So what's the big deal about Solange stealing her crown then? If it's all semantics?"

"The tribes are letting Lady Natasha play queen because she used to be part of the Host and she knows their ways. And she claimed power back in the twenties, before any of us were even born and a Drake daughter wasn't even an issue. Drake women were discouraged from court but not outright exiled until Solange was born."

"She sounds like a piece of work."

"She's the first to have ties strong enough even to hope to rule. She's kind of our best bet if we want to stop all the infighting and control the *Hel-Blar*."

"Until Solange," Nicholas added grimly.

"Exactly." Logan nodded. "Half the courts would defect to Solange if given the chance. Natasha might be our best bet, but she's also a power-hungry cow and still totally obsessed with Montmartre. Everyone knows that."

"I don't want her stupid crown," I muttered. I hated all this talk of prophecies and politics. As if I even *wanted* to be queen.

"Why didn't she exile *you* too?" Lucy asked London.

"I'm not really a Drake." London looked annoyed at having to answer the question.

"Are so." I frowned at her. She just shrugged.

"It's different for me. Anyway, you should be grateful for the exile. She could have just had Solange killed at birth, you know."

"And make her a martyr?" Connor asked. "Or draw Veronique out and have to deal with her wrath? Or have it look as if she might not believe herself to be the rightful queen after all?"

"She is the rightful queen," London insisted. She turned to me. "But *you're* the only Drake daughter born, not made."

"I know what I am, London."

"Well, then. Start looking the part."

"So now it's a fashion show, too?" I grumbled, following London and Lucy to my room. London went straight to my closet, made a face.

"Solange, honestly."

"What?"

"You can't wear any of this."

"She can wear something of mine," Lucy suggested. "I have better taste."

"Please."

Lucy, notorious for overpacking, pulled a dress out of her bag. It was more like a silk slip with lace on the hem and loops of beaded fringe she'd sewn to the straps. It was the exact color of red wine.

"It'll have to do," London said grudgingly.

I changed quickly, nerves fluttering in my belly. Dressing up like I was going to a high school dance was making me even more anxious. I put on a pair of Chinese slippers and the silver bracelet Hyacinth had given me last year.

My brothers lined up in the foyer, each wearing his best clothes. Sebastian was even wearing a suit. Logan was the only one who hadn't had to change. He was always stylish.

"You're not all coming with us," I said, pausing on the bottom step.

"Damn right we are," Connor said.

"What about Lucy? You heard what Mom said."

"I'll be fine," she said from behind me on the landing. "Don't worry about me."

I glared at my brothers mutinously. "We are not leaving her here alone."

Nicholas pushed away from the wall. "I'm staying."

"You don't have to," Lucy muttered.

"Good," I said, ignoring her. My mouth was dry. "Let's go."

CHAPTER 10

♦

Lucy

The very second the door closed behind them, Nicholas started shouting. I guess I shouldn't have been surprised.

"I can't believe you did that!" he railed. "After the field party, the vamps in the garden. Didn't you hear a single word I said?"

"No, why don't you yell a little louder?"

"This isn't funny, Lucy."

"I never said it was." I crossed my arms and watched him stomping furiously around the foyer. "We did what we had to do. It was worth a try."

"He could have killed her. And you." He slammed his hand down on a side table, dislodging a vase of roses. It fell to the floor, cracking on the marble. Water and rose petals clung to his boots.

"But he didn't." The truth was I was still feeling the adrenaline.

I curled my hands into fists so he wouldn't see the way they were trembling. Maybe I wasn't made for this spy stuff after all. "And anyway, you went out there and fought a bunch of pheromone-crazed vamps and we didn't lecture you."

"It's not the same."

"Right."

"For one thing, I'm a lot harder to kill than you two."

It was hard to argue with that. "Well, whatever," I mumbled lamely.

We glowered at each other for a while longer. For the first time, I could really see the worry etched around his eyes and the way his mouth tightened. He wasn't just pale, he was faintly gray. We must have really scared him. I tried to imagine what he'd felt seeing his baby sister and her best friend in the woods at night with a Helios-Ra hunter. I sighed. "As much fun as it is to stand around here yelling at each other, do you think maybe we could do something else for now?"

He jerked his hand through his hair. "It's pretty late. You could go to bed."

"Are you kidding?" I stared at him. "Like I could sleep."

"It'll be hours before we hear anything."

I bit my lower lip. "Is Veronique really that scary?"

He looked up, nodded once. "There's just something about her."

"She wouldn't hurt Solange, would she?"

"No, she's really big on family and tradition and all that. It's the royal courts I'm worried about."

"Did you reach your parents yet?"

"No."

"Crap."

"Yup."

"Well, we can't sit around here worrying all night. I have to do *something*."

"Why don't you call up another vampire hunter for tea?" he suggested drily. He looked calmer though, less like he was clenching his jaw so hard he'd snap off a fang. "How did you manage that, anyway?"

"I called the operator. His number was listed."

"Seriously?"

"And I picked his pocket." I preened like a peacock.

Nicholas shook his head, grinning that rare crooked grin that made my stomach flutter. "You didn't."

"I totally did. And I found this Helios-Ra handbook guide to vampires. I guess all the recruits get a copy. I was even in it; I'm a Person of Interest. Go me."

I thought he'd get a chuckle out of it, but his face went so cold I had to stop myself from shivering.

"What?" he asked with deadly calm. "Helios-Ra has targeted you?"

I shook my head enthusiastically. "No, nothing like that, don't worry. It's just a profile page. Solange had one too." His jaw clenched again. Oops. Shouldn't have mentioned that. God, maybe he was right. I do have a big mouth. I tried a soothing smile. "Really, it's okay. Anyway, we made photocopies of everything on Sol's printer. And we had Connor doing his computer geek thing before London dropped in to be her usual sunny self." I tilted my head. "Your computer's faster than Solange's laptop. Think we could find something on the bounty or Helios-Ra? Anything?"

He looked thoughtful. "It beats sitting around here waiting. Connor's the one with the Internet mojo though, not me."

I shrugged. "Worth a try." Anything to fill the time, because otherwise I was going to bounce between worrying about my best friend and wondering when her brother got so freaking hot. Neither of those appealed to me as a sane pastime.

We went up to the attic floor, which had been converted into seven bedrooms, two bathrooms, and a sitting room—all without a single window anywhere. Nicholas's room was the smallest; there was space only for a bed, a dresser, and his desk. I had to sit on the edge of the bed since there was no other chair. It was only half-made, with a navy blue blanket. The last time I'd been up here there had been pirate sheets and wooden swords.

I looked around curiously. There was an iPod dock and stacks of music magazines and clothes in a pile in the corner. There was also a small photograph on his nightstand. It was of the two of us on my fifteenth birthday. I was laughing, the light glinting off my glasses and the sequins on my scarf, and Nicholas was turned toward me, with serious eyes and a half grin. I touched the frame.

"I've never seen this picture," I said quietly. I kind of wanted to ask him if I could get a copy, but I didn't want to sound sappy. He looked over his shoulder from where he was booting up his computer.

"It's . . ." He grabbed it, stuffed it into the top drawer of his desk. "It's nothing."

Liar. Still, even though I knew it wasn't nothing, I didn't know what it actually meant, either. It was probably no big deal. I shouldn't read into it. I couldn't help smiling, though.

"Stop that," he muttered, not even looking up from the keyboard. I smiled wider. "I mean it."

"So how do we find and infiltrate the database of a secret society?" I asked.

"I have no idea."

I scooted to the edge of the bed so I could see what he was typing. "Hey, you do have some mojo," I said approvingly. The screen was a garble of HTML codes. "I can't even read that."

"Don't get too excited," he warned me. He typed for a bit, waited, typed some more. I watched, got bored, lay back on the bed, and stared at the ceiling. He put music on, choosing some of my favorite bands. He typed some more. I felt my eyes drifting shut despite myself.

"Think your boyfriend would mind the photo?" he finally asked quietly, so quietly I barely heard him.

That woke me up. "What boyfriend?" I sat up. "I have a boyfriend now?"

"Jett or Julius or whatever his name is."

"Julian?" I blinked, confused. "You're way out of the loop. Julian dumped me during exams. Well, actually, he didn't even really dump me. I just found him with his tongue in Jennifer King's mouth."

"You don't sound torn up about it."

"Please, it was forever ago. I called him names, and then when I got home I realized I didn't actually care. I didn't even bother with the requisite breakup hot fudge sundae."

"Oh."

I didn't know what to do with this Nicholas. It felt like we were about to have a moment. We'd never really had a moment. Okay, we'd had that kiss—make that two kisses. But they weren't real, were they? The first was in the interest of subterfuge, the second a scientific test of my immunity to pheromones. I swallowed, suddenly nervous. I hadn't been expecting a moment.

"Got something."

Which was for the best because I clearly wasn't going to get one. I tried not to feel disappointed.

"What did you find?" I asked, pretending my voice hadn't squeaked.

"I'm not sure yet but it's got more security than I've ever seen." He frowned. "I can't crack this. I'm not even sure Connor can."

"But he has a place to start, right?"

"I guess. For what it's worth." He pushed away from the desk.

"We had to try."

"Yeah." He didn't look pleased. I nudged his foot with my boot.

"Want to crank call Kieran?"

He sat next to me, smiling. "Maybe later. Nothing gets you down, does it?"

"Sure it does." He was close enough that his knee brushed mine. "When this is all over I'll have myself a good cry and a pity-party. Right now, I just don't have the time."

"You're kind of amazing."

I looked at him out of the corner of my eye, flushing. It was odd to get a compliment like that from him. And really nice. "Solange says I'm kind of evil."

"That too."

"Can I ask you a question?"

"Sure," he replied warily.

"Were you scared during your bloodchange?"

He stilled. "Yes."

"Did it hurt?" I couldn't stand the thought of Solange suffering. It wasn't fair. She was too good a person to go through all of this.

"Some. Mostly I just felt weak and exhausted, like I had a really bad fever. By the time I lost consciousness I didn't really care anymore. I was too tired."

I was sorry now that I'd been locked out of the house, that I couldn't have been there for him. I could easily picture him writhing in pain on this bed, soaked in sweat, delirious. "Geoffrey says it's kind of like a battle."

"It is. It feels like you're hallucinating though and even now it's hazy. I'm not sure what was real and what wasn't."

I touched his knee. "I'm sorry I brought it up."

"Don't be."

"Solange is really strong," I said it again. "Stronger than everyone thinks she is."

"I know."

"What got you through?" I whispered. "Do you remember?"

He nodded but wouldn't look at me. When he didn't elaborate, I turned to face him. "What? Is it a secret? Don't I know all the deep dark Drake secrets by now?"

He shifted uncomfortably. "I guess."

"What then?"

"You."

I swallowed, stunned. "Me?"

"Yeah." He stood up and went to the door, where he paused for the barest second. "You got me through."

CHAPTER II

◆

Solange

I was not enjoying this.

We weren't even there yet and I just wanted it to be over.

We didn't take the tunnels to Veronique. Her house outside of Violet Hill was completely independent of the Drake compound and Natasha's royal courts in the caves and pretty much everything else. The house was perched on a hill and painted dark gray, with Victorian gables and stunted thorn trees all around. It was straight out of *Wuthering Heights*.

"I can't believe she came here for this," I muttered as Marcus turned into the lane. It was miles before it wound through the woods and then out onto a clearing with a narrow driveway. "She never comes here."

"You're special," Quinn told me. "She came here for you."

"Great."

We got out of the car and I tried not to compare the slamming of the doors to gunshots. Everything had a dark, final feel here. I shook it off. I was letting the melodrama of the house infect me. This was technically my great-great-several-times-great-grandmother. While I doubted she'd baked me cupcakes, I had to assume she didn't mean me any harm either. Each of my brothers had survived the formal introduction. I would too. I kind of wished Lucy was here; I could have used some of her swagger. I'd just have to find my own.

"Come on, little sister." Duncan nudged me up onto the porch. The door swung open before we could knock. Veronique didn't have guards, but she did have ladies-in-waiting. The one who answered the door didn't betray a flicker of emotion. She was dressed in a suit with a pencil skirt and wore her hair scraped back into a bun. She looked competent and about as warm as winter at the top of a mountain.

"You're expected," she said. "Come in." She stepped aside. "I am Marguerite."

We bustled into the foyer and then just stood there in a hesitant clump. Even Logan wasn't flirting with her. London scowled but looked at the floor. There were chandeliers everywhere, made of jet and crystal drops. Oil lamps burned on wooden chests serving as tables. It smelled vaguely like incense. A shield with the Drake family crest hung on the wall with our motto: "*Nox noctis, nostra domina,*" which translated roughly to "Night, our mistress."

"Only Solange was summoned," Marguerite murmured disapprovingly. "The rest of you may wait here." She pointed to a long church bench. My brothers sat obediently, without a word. That was enough to scare me, even without the whole matriarch thing. "You"—she turned to me—"may follow me."

I took a deep breath and trailed her down the hallway. There were several doors leading into drawing rooms and parlors and a huge dining room. She ignored them all and went straight back to a set of French doors, opened up into a long ballroom with polished parquet floors and tapestries on the wall.

"Madame." Marguerite bowed her head. "She has arrived."

Veronique sat on one of those curved padded benches that were in every medieval movie I'd ever seen. She wore a long blue-gray gown with intricate embroidery along the hem and trailing bell sleeves. Her hair was hazelnut brown, her eyes so pale they were nearly colorless, like water. She was so still, she didn't look real. There was something definitely not-human in her face. I swallowed convulsively. I was so nervous I thought I might throw up on her. When she moved, just an inch, I jumped.

"*Mon Dieu*," she murmured in a voice as distant and mysterious as the northern lights. "Your heart is like a little hummingbird."

"I'm sorry." I wasn't sure why I was apologizing, only that it seemed best. Some instinct inside me trembled, like a rabbit under the shadow of an eagle. For all her porcelain beauty, she was a predator.

"So you are Solange Drake," she said, considering.

"Yes, Madame." I curtsied, putting every detail Hyacinth had painstakingly taught me into it. This was no courtesy bob a la Jane Austen; this was a full court curtsy. I stepped my right foot behind my left and bent my knees out and not forward. I went as low as I could without toppling over or sticking my butt out. I bent my head slightly. I prayed really hard that she'd be impressed.

"Very good," she said. "You may rise."

I stood back up and wobbled only a little. *Thank you, Aunt Hyacinth.*

"I am gratified to know your family has taught you proper etiquette."

"Thank you, Madame." Could she tell I was starting to sweat? It was hard to just stand there under her scrutiny. She was so composed, so hard.

"I understand Lady Natasha has summoned you to her court."

"Yes, Madame."

"She is not to be trusted, that one."

"No, Madame."

"You know the prophecy, of course."

I nodded.

"We've been waiting a long time for a girl to be born to us."

Great, no pressure.

"Your bloodchange is fast approaching. I can smell it on you. Even frightened as you are, your heart beats slower than it ought to."

I wondered if that was why I felt like I might pass out. I lifted my chin. I was not going to embarrass myself or my family.

"I would have you strong enough to survive, little Solange. I may not want the royal courts for my own, but I won't have them taken from our family as if we are nothing."

She picked up a long silver chain from the small table beside her. The vial on the end was clear, capped with silver and held with more silverwork, curled to look like ivy leaves. "Do you know what this is?"

"No, I don't." She held it up. From this angle I could see the vial held a dark red liquid inside. "Oh. It's blood."

"My own, to be precise." She twirled it once. I watched it, mesmerized despite myself. "I do not share my blood lightly—only in extreme circumstances, you understand."

I didn't understand actually. But if she made me drink that, I really would throw up on her.

"I am prepared to give this to you. When your birthday arrives, drink it and it will give you the strength you need to claim your legacy."

This probably wasn't a good time to tell her I didn't want to be queen.

"Your brothers didn't need it; the Drake men have been turning for centuries. But you're different. I am curious to see how this will play out, and precious little incites my curiosity these days."

So maybe being the bearded lady at the carnival wasn't so bad after all.

"You will, of course, have to prove yourself worthy."

"Of . . . course." Because just handing it over would be too easy. "How do I do that?"

"There are skills every Drake woman should know, to honor her heritage. We will begin with embroidery."

My mouth hung open. "Embroidery?" I sucked at embroidery. Aunt Hyacinth had tried to teach me, but we'd both given it up as a lost cause. Lucy, strangely, had picked it up really quickly and embroidered a tapestry of Johnny Depp as Jack Sparrow for my last birthday. Somehow, I didn't think that was going to help me right now. "I'm afraid I'm not very good at embroidery."

Her lips pursed. My palms went damp. Her fangs were out, as pointed and delicate as little bone daggers. "That's disappointing, Solange."

I was going to die because I couldn't embroider roses on a pillow.

"I'm sorry," I whispered.

"Can you draw?"

"A little. I can throw pots. I don't suppose you have a kiln?"

"No, but duly noted." She waved her hand and suddenly Marguerite was back. I hadn't seen her leave, and I hadn't seen her return. She was carrying a small table like it weighed nothing and a chair. She set them down in front of me, then produced a sketchpad and pencils. "Go on," Veronique murmured. "Draw me something."

I wiped my hands and reached for a pencil, eyes racing over my surroundings for a subject. If she asked me to draw her, I might as well kill myself right now. I noticed a clay vase in the corner, holding a bouquet of stakes. I drew vases and pots all the time, getting ideas for my work at the pottery wheel.

I broke the tip of the first pencil. I took another one but had to wait until the tremor in my fingers subsided before trying again. This time I drew lightly, trying to pretend that my future didn't actually depend on it. Veronique glanced at my page.

"Passable."

I let out a breath in a big whoosh. She was like the scariest teacher ever. It made me glad I'd never gone to a regular school.

"And now for music. The harp? Piano?"

The harp? Was she serious? My mother taught me how to avoid hunters, shoot a crossbow, and stake a rabid vampire at twenty paces, not how to play "Greensleeves."

"I . . ."

She rose from her chair with the speed of an ancient vampire and the grace and posture of a prima ballerina.

A prima ballerina who was about to pass judgment on me.

"No music at all?" She did not sound pleased. I stumbled back a step before deciding to hold my ground. I'd been telling Lucy for years not to run because it only made vampires chase you. "Tell me, what *can* you do?"

I felt useless and insignificant. And I couldn't think of a single thing I could do that might impress her. How did you impress a nine-hundred-year-old vampire matriarch?

"Math?" she snapped.

"Yes," I replied, relieved. "I'm good at math."

"History?"

"Yes."

"When was the Battle of Hastings?"

"1066."

"Who was Eleanor of Aquitaine's first son to rule?"

"Richard the Lionheart."

"What year were my twins born?"

"1149."

"Can you fight?"

"Yes."

"With a sword?"

"Yes."

"Show me."

She clapped her hands once and another woman walked in, wearing the traditional white fencing uniform and face guard. I could tell by her eyes, which were light green, that she was a vampire. I had no idea if she was a Drake. And though I was pretty good at fencing, how was I supposed to beat a vampire? I was still human, and it was late enough that I would have been yawning by now if I'd been any less scared. My opponent gave me a mask and a vest and a foil.

"Begin," Veronique demanded before I'd even had a chance to test the balance of the blade in my hand.

We began.

I gave the proper salute, bringing my handle up to eye level and bowing. My opponent did the same. Then she lunged. I cross-stepped backward, blocking her attack. The slender blades scraped together. She lunged again and I used a circular parry, low this time. I didn't touch her, not once. She was too quick, a blur of white. I'd never felt slower. I was at a distinct disadvantage but I kept going.

"*Riposte!*" Veronique hissed, and I obeyed, cross-stepping forward to attack. I blinked sweat out of my eyes.

She blocked me, feinted, and then brought her sword down toward my head. I held up my own sword, parallel to the gleaming floor, and absorbed the power of the blow in my arms. The force of it rang through my bones. I knew if she'd wanted to, she could have cleaved me in half.

"Enough," Veronique called out, sounding satisfied. I lowered my arms, panting. There was the sound of footsteps in the hall and then my brothers all trying to race through the door at the same time.

"Solange!"

"Are you hurt?"

When they realized I was unharmed, they stopped together, mouths snapping shut. Their eyes went from me, to Veronique, and then they bowed in unison.

"*Bien,*" she said to me. "You may go."

I took off my mask and left it with my foil on the floor. I was halfway to the door in my haste to get out of there when she stopped me. "Solange."

I nearly groaned. "Yes, Madame?"

"Don't forget this." She moved so fast I didn't see her, but she was suddenly standing next to me. Even my brothers looked startled. She handed me the vial. I slipped the chain over my head.

"Thank you."

CHAPTER 12

♦

Lucy

Nicholas lounged in that irritating way of his, reading through the photocopy of the field guide. He glanced up, watching me pace back and forth, back and forth. "I had no idea you were so fitness conscious."

I paused. "What?"

"Well, you *are* doing aerobics in the middle of the night."

I hadn't realized my pacing had practically turned into a jog. My breath was a little short, my leg muscles vibrating with tension. He was holding himself very carefully, as if he might break apart. Or as if I might. I made an effort to calm my pulse, dropped onto the sofa, and tried to sprawl as irritatingly as he did, but I couldn't just sit there waiting. I piled kindling in the hearth and lit a fire. It was too warm outside for one, but I needed something to do. Nicholas's fists unclenched.

"I hate this," I said as the flames caught. It wasn't nearly enough to distract me.

"I'd never have noticed. You hide your feelings so well." His grin was crooked. It made him look nearly approachable, warmed by that unearthly beauty. Solange was the only scruffy Drake I'd ever met, and I didn't know if she'd suddenly start wearing dramatic gowns after her birthday.

"Really, *really* hate this," I added. The gardens were dark behind the treated glass. Or so I assumed, since we'd pulled all the curtains shut, just in case. It made everything cozy, romantic. "We should never have let her go," I said.

"Bossy as you are, Solange doesn't take orders from you."

"I can't think why, the Drakes are so malleable." I sat up straight as something occurred to me. "Hey, you have the key to the vault."

"Do I?"

"Yes, you do," I told him pointedly. "And I want a stun gun."

"It's not a department store."

I got up, tugged on his hands. They were cool to the touch. I pulled harder, before letting myself get distracted. "Come on."

He made a big production of sighing like I was crazy, but at least he followed me down the stairs and through the halls, some of which doubled back on themselves, toward the family vault. It was more of a safe really, with a secret-tunnel exit, oxygen, blood supplies, and weapons. I'd never actually been inside before. I bounced on my heels impatiently. He shook his head.

"You're acting like we have Santa locked in there."

I rubbed my hands together.

"This is better than some old fat guy. Now gimmee."

His glance was dry. "You're not even supposed to know where this door is."

"Please. I know every corner of this house, including the dirty magazines Quinn keeps under his bed." I tossed my hair back smugly. "Helios-Ra has nothing on me. Rat bastards." I knew I was starting to babble, even for me, but I had to keep my body from reacting to his closeness. I should have been immune to his pheromones. I must have been more tired than I'd thought.

He unlocked the door, angling his body so I couldn't see if he was using a key or a numeric code. He probably knew that if I actually saw what the key looked like, I'd try and steal it. The door swung open silently, heavily, and he switched on the lights, which flickered briefly before glinting on a wall of steel shelves lined with boxes of arrows and stakes and cases of bullets. Guns were securely hung on a steel rack next to swords and claymores and axes on iron hooks. I let out a reverent breath. Nicholas shook his head at my avarice.

"This was a bad idea."

I lightly touched a wicked-edged blade.

"It's even better than I thought." There were baskets of quarterstaves and fighting clubs and spears. "Where are the stun—oooh. Shiny." I reached for a crossbow, turning to grin at Nicholas. He swung backward, bending to get out of arms' reach in a way that would have snapped a human spine in half. His dark shirt fluttered like wings. I lowered the crossbow, rolling my eyes.

"Stop it."

He straightened. "We all remember what you almost did to Marcus."

"That was two years ago." I grabbed a quiver of wooden arrows that looked more like stakes. "I'm taking this one."

He frowned. "No, you're not. And why?"

I frowned back. "Hello? Bounty hunters? Helios-Ra? The walking undead? Pick one."

"No one's going to hurt you."

"Not with this thing in my possession." I propped the crossbow against my shoulder. It was surprisingly light. He looked as if he wanted to argue but changed his mind. I was instantly suspicious. There was nothing he loved more than to argue with me. We'd been honing our skills on each other for nearly a decade. Instead he opened a carved wooden chest that looked as if it belonged in a pirate movie. He pulled out a silver chain, with thick, old-fashioned links.

"Here, put this on." He tossed it to me.

I caught it seconds before it collided with my nose.

"What is this?" A cameo roughly the size of a dollar coin hung on the chain. It was carved with the Drake family insignia, a dragon with ivy leaves in its mouth, symbols of strength and loyalty, respectively. It was beautiful, accented with a single teardrop jet bead. "How come I've never seen these before?"

"Your parents probably have one, but they've never really needed to use it."

I held it up to the light.

"Why, is it magical or something?" I rattled it gently, waiting for something weird to happen.

He smiled at me. It was kind of unusual for him but not quite the magical event I'd been hoping for.

"Not really." He nudged me to turn around so he could work the clasp. His fingers were light and cool on the back of my neck. For some reason I had to stop a delicate shiver. "There." His voice seemed husky. It tickled my ear. "This will keep you safe. It marks you as one of us. Vampires or the Helios-Ra would recognize this and know that to take you on would be to take on the entire Drake clan."

I touched the pendant briefly. "Thanks."

"Of course, I wouldn't flaunt it until I knew for sure I wasn't dealing with a bounty hunter." He paused. "On second thought, maybe you shouldn't wear it." He held out his hand, as if he wanted me to take it off. I took a step back, clutched it protectively.

"No way." The lights flashed twice. I frowned at them. "Power surge?"

"Silent alarm. Someone's here."

We both rushed toward the door, nearly getting stuck, like some bad sitcom episode.

"Stay behind me," he snapped. His eyes were eerily pale. The weight of the crossbow was reassuring in my hands as we crept up the stairs. "And try not to shoot me in the back with that thing."

"Yeah, yeah."

When we reached the top, he paused, nostrils flaring. The front door shut quietly.

"Uncle Geoffrey." Some of the tension leaked out of his stance. I lowered the crossbow.

"I didn't know your sense of smell was that particular," I said. "I just thought you could tell if it was vampire or not."

"Everyone has a scent. If you're around them long enough, you kind of catalogue it." He didn't look at me. "You smell like a blend of pepper and cherry bubble gum."

"I do?"

Before I could press him further, he stepped out into the foyer, where his uncle was setting down a cardboard box.

"More gifts for Solange," he said drily. "Bruno's been through and scanned the bunch. Careful," he added when we bent for a closer look at the jumble of packages, wrapped in everything from brown paper to silver tissue. The lumpy envelope on top had a brownish stain leaking through. "That one's a cat's heart," Geoffrey said calmly.

"Ew." I recoiled. "What? Ew!"

"A gift." He shrugged, unconcerned. "It's considered a delicacy in some of the more remote tribes."

"Okay, gross . . ."

"That one's a kitten's. A love letter, I imagine."

"A kitten?" I stared for a full ten seconds, my mouth hanging open. I only managed to close it to swallow the threat of bile. "*A kitten?*"

"Uncle Geoffrey." Nicholas winced. The family dogs raced over to see why I was shrieking.

"Sorry. Sometimes I forget she's not fully one of us."

Later, I'd feel flattered by that. Right now I was mad. Way too mad.

"Is there a return address? Who sent that? I'm going to kick his ass." I had to turn my back on the package. "I'm not happy about this. Seriously."

"We got that," Nicholas said. There was something weird about his expression. His jaw was clenched so tightly I wondered why his teeth didn't pop right out.

"What's the matter with you?" I asked.

"Nothing."

"Nicholas, you just bent your ring, you're clenching your fists so hard."

"It smells like candy."

"What does?" I asked, confused. "What are you talking about?"

He glanced at the stained envelope. "It's still covered in blood."

"You are not serious." He nodded once, as if it was the hardest thing he'd ever done. "That's disgusting," I told him. "Seriously."

"I know."

"Okay then."

We went into the huge living room, where his uncle was already busy at the library end, pulling books off the oak shelves. Then he sat down at the table. Lamps burned behind ruby glass. Byron, the oldest Bouvier, licked my fingers, sensing my lingering agitation. Seeing vampires drink blood or snap each other's necks and crumble into dust was different than craving kitten hearts. That was just too much.

"Easy," Nicholas murmured. Geoffrey glanced at us.

"Lucky, sit down, your heart's racing. If it goes much faster, you'll pass out."

"She's still mad."

"She can be mad sitting down."

I sank into one of the chairs, leaning my elbows on the wide table, the same weathered oak as the shelves.

"Has your aunt Hyacinth come home yet?"

Nicholas shook his head. "You're the first."

Geoffrey frowned. "Am I?"

"Why?"

"She's not answering her phone or her pager. Hmm. Well, never mind, I'm sure she's fine." He looked around. "Where's Solange? Is she asleep?"

Nicholas sat next to me. "She's not here. She was summoned by Lady Natasha."

"What?" Geoffrey was on his feet so fast he blurred around the edges. "Why?"

"London wouldn't say, or more likely didn't know. If she *had* known, she'd have bragged about it." Nicholas frowned at his uncle's reaction. "And she wouldn't have come to fetch Solange if there was any real danger."

"She's rather dazzled by royalty, my boy." Geoffrey closed his eyes. "Damn." He reached for his phone. "We know who set the bounty, Nicholas." He pressed a button and the number dialed itself quickly.

"Who?"

"Lady Natasha."

(HAPTER 13

◆

Solange

We left the car just inside the property line of Geoffrey's house and used his tunnel access. The tunnels smelled of damp and smoke from the torches in the lesser-used parts of the corridors. It was very quiet—there were only soft footsteps and my ragged breathing. It was the safest route to Lady Natasha's royal court. She stayed in the mountains during the summer months in a complicated cave system. She traveled the rest of the year between her different holdings, like a medieval queen. Our town is considered her summer retreat, simple and countrified but relaxing enough for the odd week or two. And everyone knew the real reason Lady Natasha had chosen to come here was to keep an eye on our family.

"Are you sure she didn't say anything else?" I asked London.

If Lady Natasha expected me to embroider or dance a waltz, I damn well wanted a little notice this time.

London shook her head. The flickering light glinted off her tight leather pants. "She's a good queen, Solange. You don't have to worry."

"London, in case you failed to notice, there's a bounty on all our heads. Yours included. And our side of the Drake family has been exiled for years."

She shrugged one shoulder negligently, though I did see her hand tighten. "It's not the same for me. I was turned, I wasn't born into the Drake family."

"Your dad married your mom and then he turned you on your twenty-first birthday. I'd say that makes you a Drake."

"Whatever."

"It's no different than our dad turning our mom after Solange was born."

London shrugged again. It was starting to get on my nerves. We couldn't all be as blasé as she was. Some of us were going to be very grounded by morning. And by some of us, I meant me.

"Mom and Dad are going to freak," I muttered, stumbling into Logan. "Oof."

He steadied me. "Careful. You'll wrinkle the velvet."

Connor stopped as well, in the lead. He held up a hand.

"Someone's coming."

"Stay close to me." Logan's fangs elongated, gleaming wetly.

"It's probably just an honor guard," London whispered. "Lady Natasha's big on ceremony."

Quinn shook his head, nostrils flaring. "I don't think that's it."

"You're overreac—"

Vampires raced down the hall toward us, some scuttling on the walls like giant ants. Every hair on the back of my neck stood up. Maybe they weren't *Hel-Blar*, but they were warriors; either sworn to Lady Natasha or seeking the bounty for killing us. Connor, Quinn, and Marcus formed a front line of defense, and Logan and Duncan circled around to guard our backs. London and I stood in the middle. I took the stake she handed me. I didn't have anywhere to keep a weapon in this stupid borrowed dress. I wouldn't make that mistake again. Adrenaline flowed through me, making my fingers tremble slightly.

The hissing rolled over us, crackling like static. One of the vampires caught Marcus on the shoulder. He immediately used the dagger in his wrist sheath to turn his attacker to dust. A battle cry rang through the corridor. One of the vampires broke through the line, leaping down from the ceiling, snarling at me. I kicked high, catching him off guard. London's knife caught him even more off guard. Dust billowed briefly.

"We are so grounded when Mom and Dad find out about this."

"They aren't Araksaka," London said. "This isn't the royal guard."

"How do you know?"

"No tattoos."

"Bounty hunters then," Duncan said with a grunt, catching a fist to the eye. "Ow, damn it."

"No hard feelings." The female attacker grinned, jumping nimbly out of range of his return blow and kicking out at the same time. "But you're going to make us a fortune."

"Bite me, you vulture." Quinn sprawled on the tiles, groaning.

An older man in a pinstripe suit grabbed Quinn's ponytail, yanking him up.

"Hey!" I yelled, leapfrogging Duncan and the girl and elbowing another vampire, who reared up at my passing. "Get off my brother!" I wasn't fast enough or strong enough, not like they were, but I was angry and scared and they'd underestimated me. I broke Quinn's attacker's kneecap and staked him before the others could react. Quinn jumped to his feet, grinning.

"Thanks, little sister."

I grinned back, wiping my hands clean.

"Duck!" he added.

I ducked.

Vampire dust drifted over me like pollen. I sneezed.

One of the vampires, newly turned by the look of him, smiled at me as if we were on a date. "Fancy a shag?" He sniffed the air and licked his lips. "Come on, love." He sauntered over, or would have if he hadn't tripped over Logan's foot.

"Might I suggest you get the hell out of here?" Logan said, yanking on my arm. "Run, you bloody lunatic."

I ran a few steps, stopped when no one followed me. "I'm not leaving you guys here!"

"Just go!"

"No!"

"Solange!" All five of my brothers hollered my name.

"No!" I hollered back. "Come *on*!" I knew it didn't sit well with them not to finish off the last two vampires, and Mom certainly wouldn't approve either. But I just didn't want any more deaths on my hands. In the movies when a vampire dies, there's a puff of dust and everyone cheers because the bad guy's dead. In my world, the vampire might well be one of my brothers. And technically, though the bounty hunters did want me dead, I wasn't sure if they were the bad guys yet. I mean, they were following orders, right? Did they even know that I didn't want anything to do with Lady Natasha or her stupid crown? There were rules to this sort of thing, even if nobody else wanted to play by them. I also had no qualms about using guilt to my advantage.

"Who knows how many others might be out there? You want me to go alone?"

They made a collective chorus of annoyed grunts, knowing full well what I was doing, but they reluctantly came with me, which was all I'd wanted. We tore down the hall, skidding slightly on the tiles. My breath was ragged and hot in my lungs, tearing at my throat. Connor scooped me up over his shoulder, barely pausing to adjust my flailing limbs, and kept running. He was so quick, as were the rest of them, that they seemed more like washes of color around me. My stomach bounced painfully on Connor's shoulder, but we didn't stop until we'd reached a rusty door. It swung open to the moonlight trickling between the trees down onto the forest floor. Connor tossed me to my feet. I rubbed my bruised stomach.

Quinn eased ahead, peering into the undergrowth. Ferns waved their green fingers all around us. We moved quietly behind him. I might not have vampire speed or scent-tracking, but I did have Drake training and I knew how to move without being heard or seen. And I knew the forest as well as anyone, certainly better than

Logan, who preferred the city streets to mud on his expensive boots. The heady scent of pine needles and earth was soothing, cooling my throat. There wasn't a single bird or rabbit or deer. They all knew the smell of a predator, animal or otherwise. The wind tickled the oak trees. Quinn halted, held up a hand. I strained to hear what he was hearing, but all I could make out were ordinary forest sounds: the wind, the river, an owl.

"We're not alone," Logan mouthed to me.

I froze, trying not to breathe, hoping my heart wasn't pulsing like a beacon in the center of the dark woods. I might know how to step so I didn't snap twigs or crush acorns underfoot, but silencing my heartbeat was a trick I wasn't all that keen on learning. We could be as silent as we wanted, but if the vampires were near enough, they'd hear me. Frustration hummed through me. Something rustled, like bat wings.

"Get down," Logan snapped, but I was already hitting the ground. It was so dark and the vampires were so fast, it was as if shadows had collided around me, hissing. Bones shattered and mended; blood sprinkled like rain. Someone grunted. I couldn't see very well—not only was it dark, but I was half sprawled in a thicket of ferns. I scrambled up into a crouch. Logan hurtled past, cursing. The moon silvered the gleam of fangs and eyes. Another vampire rolled past me, landed on his feet.

"I smell her." He looked nearly drunk. "She's here. She's mine."

"Oh, I don't think so," I muttered grimly, reaching for a branch and breaking off the end so it was sharp and splintered. I hadn't been raised to sit around wringing my hands. We'd all known this was coming, even if I was only now truly realizing the scope and magnitude of my bloodchange. Everyone basically thought of me as a vampire broodmare, meant to give birth to lots of little royal vampire babies.

No amount of red roses sent to my door was going to make that okay.

I slammed my heel into the back of his knee as he whirled to attack Marcus. He stumbled, turned. His angry hiss shifted into a grin.

"Solange." He took a step forward. "I'm Pierre."

I lifted the branch threateningly. "Look, this is just a phero-mone thing. Get over it already."

"You're even more beautiful than I thought you'd be."

"Great." The sarcasm in my voice didn't appear to register. "You know, it's been a really long night. Could you be creepy later?"

"I love you."

"Apparently not." I was feeling tired. Incredibly, I felt like yawning, even as someone grunted in pain.

"Incoming!" Quinn yelled. "There are more of them than we thought."

I tilted my head at Pierre, tried a winsome smile. Marcus stared at me.

"Are you going to be sick?"

Brothers.

"Pierre," I said. Would fluttering my eyelashes be overkill? And did I even know how to flutter my eyelashes? "Could you help me?"

"Anything for you, my love." Okay, so maybe this pheromone thing might be useful after all.

"There are bounty hunters coming." I tried to look innocent. Lucy would have fallen over laughing if she could see me now. "They want to kill me and my brothers."

"I will not let that happen," he promised fervently.

"Great." I patted his shoulder. "Go on."

He made a very dramatic departure while Marcus and I watched. Quinn and Logan joined us.

"What's going on?"

"Solange just got some sappy vamp to fight for us."

"Then what are we standing around for?" Connor said. "Let's get the hell out of here."

We ran, leaving behind the sounds of Pierre and his friends battling the bounty hunters. I really hoped he'd win. I didn't like the thought that I might have sent him to his death.

"Slowing down's not exactly the goal here," Logan said.

"Shouldn't we help him?"

"No, run faster."

"But . . ."

"Solange, you're so pale you practically glow. Move it."

I might have argued further but I was feeling very sluggish. I was barely able to push one foot in front of the other, never mind performing heroics to save a vampire who I was probably going to have to stake anyway, if the pheromones had anything to say about it.

"I feel . . . funny."

Connor scooped me up again. I was too exhausted to feel

particularly alarmed, though some part of my brain registered that this was hardly the time for a nap.

"It's just the change," he said. "You're overtired. It's normal."

The yawn was so big it made my eyes water.

"Are you sure?"

I wasn't awake long enough to hear his reassurance.

CHAPTER 14

•

Lucy

"What the bloody hell do you mean Solange went to see Veronique? And Natasha?" Everyone took a healthy step back out of range of Helena's fury. "I specifically said she wasn't to leave the house."

Liam sat in his chair and grimly drank a brandy. Hyacinth's pug was sniffing under the front door and whining. I shifted from foot to foot. The thick miasma of anger and pheromones was starting to make even me light-headed. Liam reached out for his wife's hand.

"They'll be all right," he said darkly. I'd never heard his voice have that particular tone and kind of hoped I'd never hear it again. It made the hairs on the back of my neck shiver.

"Why'd Lady Natasha set a bounty in the first place?" Nicholas asked hotly.

"There's a rumor going around," Sebastian explained. "That Solange really is going to take Lady Natasha's crown as soon as she changes."

We stared at him, all sorts of horrible scenarios unfolding in the spaces between us.

"But Solange would *hate* that," I said.

"But Lady Natasha would never want to be anything else," Helena said. "So she'll never understand that, or trust it. Also, she knows Montmartre is courting Solange, in his own twisted fashion. Even though they haven't been together for a long time, she doesn't share well." She glanced at the window. "Where the bloody hell is Hyacinth? It'll be dawn soon."

"Bruno has his boys out looking for her."

"I should be with them." Sebastian was standing stiffly in the corner, glowering.

"No." Helena narrowed her eyes in his direction.

"Mom."

"I said no, Sebastian. You've done enough tonight."

"What about London?" Nicholas asked. "She's the one who came to get Solange."

Liam sighed. "She's a royalist, like the rest of that side of the family. But I have to believe she didn't know about the danger."

"There's more." Geoffrey tapped his pen on the cover of a leather-bound book. His hair stuck up everywhere; he'd been raking his hand through it constantly since he got here. Liam tilted his head back and briefly closed his eyes.

"Of course there is."

"I've finished analyzing the Hypnos sample."

Liam straightened, his eyes flaring like hot silver.

"Tell me."

"Several zombie drugs, as we'd assumed," Geoffrey said.

"And?"

His expression was hard. He didn't look like a slightly distracted scientist anymore, or like the handsome intellectual who attracted all the divorced women in town.

"It's ancient blood. Ancient enough to be Enheduanna."

The silence fell like a hammer through a glass window. I blinked.

"Who's Enheduanna?" I whispered to Nicholas. No one was speaking. It was kind of creepy, actually. "Hello?"

"An ancient." Geoffrey was the one to answer me, though he didn't glance my way. The fire crackled softly, falling to embers in the grate. "The oldest vampire still alive."

"Oh. Um, and?"

"And her blood has magical effects. Like Hypnos, it takes away your will."

"I remember." I stifled a shiver.

"On vampires too, not just on humans."

"Oh." My eyes widened. "Oh!"

"Indeed," Geoffrey agreed drily. "And now it's in the hands of the Helios-Ra."

"Who are only marginally better than Lady Natasha or her tribes." Helena's black braid lifted into the air as she whirled to kick the leg of a spindly Queen Anne chair. It splintered loudly.

"That was my mother's," Liam murmured.

"This is bad," Nicholas said to me. "The thing about vampires, of any kind, is that we're supposedly immune to each other's pheromones. It's what's stopped us from wiping each other out entirely with clan wars."

"But not anymore," I whispered.

"Not anymore."

"How did they even get it?" Sebastian asked.

"I can assure you I plan on asking Hart that myself," Liam said through his teeth. "He's on his way here."

"Here?" Sebastian gaped at him. "You're not serious."

"He was amenable."

"Amenable to staking each and every one of us in our own home," Sebastian muttered.

"No, we're safest here and we outnumber him. I allowed him only a single companion."

"And a bucket of Hypnos powder."

"Sebastian," Helena snapped. "Your father knows what he's doing."

Liam smiled.

"I'll remind you of that, love."

Nicholas sat down, shaking his head.

"So, the head of the Helios-Ra is coming here for tea, they have Hypnos at their disposal, Solange is possibly in the hands of the vampire queen who set the bounty on her head, and we can't find Aunt Hyacinth. That about cover it?" He looked suddenly young and overwhelmed, like the Nicholas I'd known before he turned. I touched his shoulder. Before I could think of a single helpful thing to say, Liam's cell phone vibrated in his jacket pocket. He glanced at the display.

"Bruno." He and Helena exchanged a grim look. "Hart's here, and Hope." They looked at us.

"Lucy and Nicholas, upstairs."

"Mom!"

"But—"

"Now," Liam insisted. "Lucy, the presence of a human girl will not help our cause at the moment. And Nicholas, you can barely stand."

He was rather wobbly on his feet. Dawn must be filling the garden on the other side of the drapes. We shuffled upstairs, reluctant but obedient.

More or less.

Mom says my temper isn't my only karmic baggage. I have this thing about taking orders, no matter how well meant. And though I completely understood why it might be best to remain out of sight, it hardly followed that I should sit alone in Solange's room and not know what was going on. Just because they shouldn't see me didn't mean I shouldn't see them.

"Lucy?" Nicholas whispered, stopping when he realized I wasn't following. "What are you doing?"

In point of fact I was lying on my stomach at the top of the curving staircase. From this vantage I could see the front door. I couldn't see into the living room, but I heard Helena ask Sebastian if he wanted to retire and his emphatic refusal. He was newly turned—it had only been a few years, after all—but I wouldn't have left either if I were him. No matter how exhausted I was.

I wondered again where Solange was. And if she was okay.

"They can hear your heartbeat, you know." Nicholas stretched out next to me.

"Hey, I'm upstairs. Technically I'm not breaking the rules." I slid him a sidelong glance. "Can they really hear my exact location?"

"Probably not," he admitted. He was very close. I could feel the cool length of his body pressing against mine. His eyes were very pale, his teeth very sharp. If I was immune to his pheromones, then why did I find him so annoyingly attractive?

A knock sounded at the front door. The dogs barreled into the foyer, growling. Mrs. Brown barked from behind Hyacinth's bedroom door. Bruno escorted the heads of Helios-Ra inside, his expression implacable and hard. He considered the Drakes his own family, and Solange an honorary niece.

"Hart and Hope," I muttered. "If you're going to name your kids like that, of course they're going to think they live in a comic book." Although I had to admit Hart was handsome, practically debonair. His hair was threaded with silver and rakishly messy. "Okay, he's totally got that yummy secret agent thing going on."

Nicholas scowled at me. I didn't have to turn my head to look at him to feel his eyes burning.

Hope was short, barely five feet tall, with a cheerful face and a ponytail swinging from the crown of her head. She wore jeans and a thick leather belt hung with stakes under her long sweater, and sandals. Somehow I hadn't expected her to be so perky, in her strappy silver sandals.

"They're going in," I whispered.

"I can see that," Nicholas muttered. His nose twitched.

"You look like a demented bunny," I told him. "What are you doing?"

"You switched to lemon shampoo."

I blinked, thought back to my morning shower, which felt like years ago. He was right. His hands were clenched, but his voice was soft and husky. He turned his head away, was close enough that his hair brushed my cheek.

"Smells good."

CHAPTER 15

◆

Solange

I only woke up because I had a mouthful of mud and a lump of hard dirt as a pillow.

"Ow." I sat up, blinking blearily. "What the hell, you guys?"

"Shh," Connor hissed at me, his hand covering my mouth. "We're not alone." I could barely hear him, he was speaking so softly. I couldn't hear heartbeats or frightened porcupines or twigs snapping under combat boots, but I knew the rest of my brothers could. He drew a sun in the dirt at our feet. I could barely make out the shape in the moonlight falling through the branches. Not just vampires then.

Helios-Ra.

The wind was warm, persistent. The crickets had stopped singing, no doubt sensing predators in every corner of the forest. This was our forest, damn it. The Helios-Ra had no business here.

Shadows flitted between the trees, making an unearthly sigh of displaced air. A vampire screamed and turned to dust, billowing between the leaves. A wooden Helios-Ra stake bit the maple tree behind her as she crumbled. Someone screeched. Connor leaped into the fray before I could stop him. Marcus was fighting, and Quinn, of course, who couldn't be kept from a good fight no matter the circumstances. Logan crouched between me and the worst of it, Duncan was farther behind, guarding our back. It was standard formation, one my mother drilled into us along with our ABCs and why we mustn't tell anyone our parents had fangs and drank blood instead of coffee. For my mother to have been truly proud, we should have had the high ground.

We didn't.

In fact, we weren't even all accounted for. "Where's London?" I asked.

"She took off," Logan answered grimly. "She ran off down some tunnel while you were napping."

"And you didn't go after her?"

"Little busy for a temper tantrum."

"She probably feels bad about dragging me to court."

"Too busy for that, too. She'll be fine," he added. "And anyway, she mentioned something about doing some recon of her own. The royal guard should have been there to protect you if you were such an honored guest. She wants to know what's going on."

"Everything's a sad-ass mess, is what's going on," I muttered. "Doesn't take a genius to figure that out."

I didn't even know how far away from the farm we were, having slept through a good part of the journey. We could be half an hour away or three hours. The stars were faint above us, visible only when there was a particularly violent gust of wind. I studied their patterns, as much as I was able. The moon hung low.

"Nearly dawn," I muttered at Logan. "We have to get out of here."

"You think?" he muttered back, using that tone reserved for only the most annoying of little sisters. I rose to my feet, feeling as if I were moving through water. I was that tired, with my eyes burning and my throat clenched against a yawn. Logan glared at me.

"Get back down."

I shook my head. "We're outnumbered."

"Not the first time," he grunted, ramming a stake into the heart of a vampire Connor flipped toward him. A hiss, a burst of dust.

"I can smell her," someone interrupted, excitement thrumming through his voice. I had no desire whatsoever to meet the owner of that voice. The moon continued to drop behind the horizon. I dove toward Logan, coming up at his side. I yanked stakes out of his back holster.

"Stay down, damn it."

"She's mine." One of the vampires caught my scent and turned sharply away from where he'd been beating Duncan to a pulp. The vampire looked around, distracted. "Solange? I'm here for you, my love."

"If he starts spouting poetry I'm staking him myself," I promised through my teeth. Duncan rolled toward us, a deep gash bleeding profusely on his head. Blood matted his hair to the side of his face. Logan's nostrils flared.

"Cutting it close, aren't you?" he muttered.

"Bastard's stronger than he looks," Duncan muttered back as I propped him up against a tree. I swallowed against the gag reflex when his blood oozed over my fingers.

"Are you okay?"

"I'm fine." He wiped his face with his sleeve. "It's healing already."

The sounds of battle came closer.

Too close.

I heard the snap of a twig. And then Marcus roaring. Not a twig. His arm.

I threw one of my stakes. It didn't hit the vampire's heart but she did stumble back, hissing. Marcus hid himself in the bushes, cradling his injured arm. Quinn laughed even though he was fighting off a vampire and a Helios-Ra agent who were also fighting each other. Fists thudded into flesh. Blood splattered through the air. The darkness was fading slowly to the gray light of predawn, glinting off night-vision equipment. I sat back on my heels, stomach clenching.

"Logan," I said. "There's too many of them."

"We're fine," he insisted.

"Are not," I insisted right back. "You guys have to get out of here."

"We're trying," Duncan grunted.

"I mean right now. Without me."

"Forget it."

"We have you surrounded," a voice announced over some kind of scratchy amplifier. Quinn blinked, midpunch.

"Cops?"

"Worse," the vampire currently ducking hissed. "Helios-Ra."

"Damn it all to hell, they're not even being subtle about it."

"We only want the girl, not the bounty," the amplified voice shouted out. "We're willing to let the rest of you go."

"Bite me," Quinn suggested.

"And me," his new friend agreed.

The sun was hovering on the edge of the horizon. I could see it in my brothers' faces. A fine sweat beaded Logan's forehead, and vampire body temperature was generally much lower than human temperature. To see one sweat was rare. Very rare. His face looked drawn too, nearly gray with fatigue. Duncan's hand shook as he shoved himself to his feet.

We could probably fight our way through the others. After all, they'd have to seek cover soon, just as we would. But even if we did get through them with minor damage, we still had to get through the Helios-Ra, who could lie out in the bright sunlight and just wait for my brothers to sicken and die. My choices were narrowing drastically. I knew what I had to do. I also knew that each and every one of my pig-headed brothers was faster than me. I couldn't hope to outrun them.

But I could take them by surprise.

I let them mutter among themselves, let Logan pull me to my feet. The other vampires scattered, like earwigs under a shifted stone. The leaves barely trembled at their passing. Quinn and Marcus closed in and Connor moved toward us through the undergrowth. An arrow whistled between the trees and hit him in the shoulder. He jerked back, clutching at his bloody arm.

"I'm all right," he told us, jaw clenched in pain.

"A warning shot," an agent called out. "Next time we hit the heart."

My brothers were scowling at each other, dragging Connor to safety.

Now or never.

If I thought about it too long I might wimp out.

Now.

I eased away from Duncan, who was half–turned away to prop up Connor. Only Logan blocked me and he wasn't expecting me to knee him in the kidney and then leapfrog over him as he doubled over.

So that was exactly what I did.

A rain of Helios-Ra arrows flew over me, biting the ground behind me like the ramparts of a castle fort. They protected me from my brothers, who had to halt their forward charge, if only for a moment.

"Your word," I yelled, running even though my legs felt like lead and my lungs burned. "Your word my brothers go free."

"Take her."

They swarmed around me like beetles. I jerked away, all instinct and thrumming adrenaline. They were faceless, eye goggles obscuring their features, and black vests, black pants, black boots.

The sun crested the horizon, dripping softly between the leaves.

"Run, you idiots!" I hollered at my brothers as my arms were seized. I knew they didn't really have any other option. The sun was now bleeding through the trees. They wouldn't even be able to make it home. They'd have to use one of the caves or the secret safe houses, and by house, I really meant hole in the ground.

"Got her."

"This is her?" one of the agents said as they began to march me through the forest. A few of his companions were hobbling, one was being carried. "She's just a kid."

I knew what he saw: a fifteen-year-old girl in a muddy slip dress and scratches all over her arms from running through the woods. His companion shrugged.

"Bounty's the same. And anyway, come her birthday she'll be a monster like the rest of them."

"The Drakes are all right," someone else muttered. "They're on the Raktapa Council, at least. Now, would you stop your damn gossip and hurry the hell up?"

I was so tired I could barely see straight. I shuffled my feet, hardly having the energy to lift them off the ground.

"What's the matter with you?" he snapped. "Are you hurt?"

"I'm *tired*."

"Fresh out of coffee, princess, so move your ass."

The morning continued to unfurl around us in pink misty dampness, as if we sat in the center of a rose after a rain. The leaves shivered above us, so green they nearly glowed. Birds sang cheerfully, oblivious to my predicament. Pine needles crunched under our passage.

"Where are you taking me?" I asked, biting back a yawn.

They didn't answer as they formed a tight circle around me, one I knew I had no hope of breaking through, especially since I felt about as strong as a wet noodle. I squinted at the sunlight, eyes tearing. I hoped my brothers were safe. They'd be nearly defenseless. Each of them was still new enough to the bloodchange that they slept hard, too hard to defend themselves quickly if there was an attack.

We continued to march along until I began to recognize where we were. The mountains were on our right and a small lake glistened in a lower valley. The tunnel ran right underneath us, no one the wiser. I was so close to an escape and it might as well have been on the other side of the planet for all the good it did me. Even if I could get to one of the doorways, which was doubtful, I couldn't afford to give away the secret location to the Helios-Ra. I was thinking so hard I didn't see the shadow leap down from a tall gray aspen, scowling fiercely. He wore unrelieved black like the others and was armed to the teeth. His dark eyes pinned me.

"What the hell is she doing here?"

Kieran Black.

CHAPTER 16

◆

Lucy

Saturday night, very late

I ignored the pleasantries being stiffly exchanged since Nicholas was lying really close to me. It was so wrong that I wanted to snuggle against his side.

It was *Nicholas*.

Byron was a welcome distraction as he ambled up the stairs and lay on my other side. He had kibble breath and was close enough that he drooled on my arm. I nudged him.

"Move over, you big lump." He just gave me that doggy look, the pathetic one I could never resist. "Fine, but at least quit drooling on me. It's gross." I scratched his ear briefly. "Some watchdog you are." I knew the other two Bouviers would be lying down near Hart and Hope, eyeing them hungrily.

"I want to assure you," Hart was saying in the living room, "that I have officially retracted the bounty on the Drake clan, just so there are no more misunderstandings."

"We're glad to hear it," Liam said blandly. I could just imagine what retort Helena was biting back.

"It was an accident," Hart continued, sounding hard. "And one that will be rectified immediately."

"I suggest you keep a closer rein on your organization," Helena said. "Or I will cease to keep such a tight rein on mine."

"Understood. We stand by our treaty," Hope interjected. "This is an internal problem and should never have leaked out."

Their voices dropped slightly. There was the clink of glasses. I squirmed, trying to peer around the stairs into the living room. I could see the edge of a chair and nothing else. There wasn't even anyone sitting in it.

"I'm going to try and get closer," I murmured.

When Nicholas didn't try and stop me, I turned to look at him. He was asleep. His cheek rested on his hand, pale skin gleaming, dark brown hair tousled. His features were sculpted, sensual, and dark. It was totally unfair how beautiful he was. Even if it did sound like he might be snoring a little. Byron snorted and rolled over.

"You two are a lot of help," I said.

And then the quiet shattered.

There was no actual sound of warning, only Hart sailing out of the living room, crashing into the foyer wall and sprawling across the floor in a heap. The chandelier above him rattled alarmingly. At the sound, Nicholas startled awake and flipped himself over me, as if he was protecting me from an airborne missile. He pressed into me, about as yielding as a slab of cold marble. He looked slightly disoriented, not quite fully awake.

"Can't breathe," I croaked.

He shifted slightly but didn't get off me. I could see the thick fringe of his eyelashes, his hair falling over his forehead to tickle mine.

"Foyer," I wheezed. We both craned our necks. Helena marched out, all black leather and motherly fury. Byron raced down the stairs.

"Where is my daughter?" She seethed, her pale eyes practically glowing. Liam flanked her, simmering. I could all but see the leash on his temper straining to release. Hope took a stake from her belt.

"I wouldn't," Bruno advised quietly.

"What the hell was that for?" Hart sat up, his left eye already purpling.

Liam lifted his cell phone. "That was one of my sons, gone to ground because of your blasted league."

"I told you we didn't set the damn bounty," Hart said through his teeth. "I explained."

"Then explain to me, human," Helena sneered, "why my daughter has been taken by your agents."

Hart stared at her. "What?"

Sebastian and Geoffrey joined them from the living room. Boudicca barked once, blocking Hart from doing anything more than sitting up. Nicholas shifted off me, growling low in his throat.

"That's impossible," Hart insisted. He reached for his own cell phone and punched in a number. He barked out questions, swore viciously under his breath at the replies. Sunlight touched the windows on either side of the door.

"Unit's gone rogue," he declared.

Hope paled. "No."

Helena sniffed the air delicately, then nodded at her husband. "He's not lying."

Beside me, Nicholas sniffed as well. He frowned. I frowned back.

"What?"

"It's not a lie, but I smell something else. Something I can't quite place."

"More lemon shampoo?"

"No. Definitely not that."

Bruno signaled to the dogs and they eased back, letting Hart get to his feet.

"We have to shut them down," he said darkly. I wondered if he had a gun strapped inside a shoulder holster under his coat. "Now. Before the damage becomes irrevocable."

"I am forced to agree." Liam held up a hand. "However, we had a treaty, Hart. And it was broken. Under the circumstances, I believe a show of faith is in order."

Hart sighed. "What did you have in mind, Drake?"

"One of you stays here."

"You're taking hostages now?"

"You have our daughter. Her safety must be assured."

"You have our word," Hope said.

Liam raised one eyebrow. "Not nearly good enough."

Hart rubbed his face wearily. "All right. All right," he repeated. "I'll stay."

Hope whirled on him. "No, I'll stay. You know how some of the units still see me as a paper pusher. They'll respond to you quicker and with less posturing if they truly have gone rogue." She squared her shoulders. "So, I'll stay." She narrowed her eyes. "You don't have a dungeon, do you? Because I expect a guest room." She showed her teeth in a bare approximation of a smile. "As a show of good faith, of course."

Hart met Liam's grim gaze, returned it with his own. "I expect her to be safe here."

Liam inclined his head. "As long as our daughter is safe."

Hart barely suppressed a wince. "I'll do my best," he said.

"If your best isn't good enough?" Helena said softly, silkily. "I will personally drain every single person in your league. Understood?"

He nodded stiffly.

"Your mom rocks," I muttered. "You know he's totally shaking under all that suave sophistication."

Bruno showed Hart outside, trailed by the dogs, except for Byron, who kept sniffing suspiciously at Hope. Geoffrey nodded his head at the stairs.

"Your room is this way."

Nicholas and I scrambled to our feet. He pulled me down the hall, his fingers like a vise around mine. We leaped into Solange's room just as Geoffrey led Hope to one of the guest rooms with its own bathroom. He shut the door behind her and locked it, with an ominous click that seemed to reverberate. He paused on the other side of Solange's door, and I half expected him to lock us in as well.

"Get to sleep, you two," he muttered before walking away.

I turned back to Nicholas, who was already stretched out on Solange's bed, his head resting on the Hello Kitty pillow I'd given her for her ninth birthday.

"What do we do now?" I asked. My eyes felt gritty and dry. I'd been awake for nearly twenty-four hours. I felt a little light-headed. Nicholas didn't even open his eyes.

"I have to sleep." His words were slurred. I sat down next to him, touched his forehead. There was an unhealthy pallor to his skin. "Save Solange."

He didn't say anything else for a long time. I poked him once.

"Nicholas?"

Nothing.

It felt wrong to sleep when my best friend was out there at the mercy of rogue vampire hunters. Buffy wouldn't have slept.

Of course, Buffy had supernatural powers.

Me?

Not so much.

"Shut up about Buffy already," Nicholas muttered. I hadn't even realized I'd spoken out loud. He didn't open his eyes, only reached out and yanked my sleeve until I fell over, sprawled next to him. "Go to sleep."

The bed was soft and smelled like vanilla fabric softener. Nicholas was a comforting presence against me. He was already asleep again. He wouldn't notice if I snuggled in just a little bit closer.

For safety's sake, of course. There were bad guys everywhere, after all. One couldn't be too careful.

He shifted midsnore and pulled me closer.

I fell asleep feeling better than I had all week.

CHAPTER 17

◆

Solange

"Get lost, Black, this doesn't concern you." The agent in the lead tensed. His shoulders knotted and his hand strayed to the hilt of his weapon. Sunlight glinted off his night-vision goggles, pushed up on his head. The others exchanged wary glances. There was something in the air, some secret I didn't know about.

"Like hell it doesn't," Kieran said.

"Look, we don't need you, kid. Go home."

"Go to hell," Kieran shot back. "I'm a full agent and deserve a cut."

Whatever was sizzling around us seemed to relax slightly.

"What are you saying, Black?"

"I'm saying the bounty's enough for all of us."

Someone snorted. "Your uncle know you're doing this? Or haven't you heard? Helios called us off."

"What?" I asked. "Then what the hell are you doing with me?"

Kieran ignored me. Black nose plugs hung around his neck and stakes lined the leather strap across his chest.

"Vampire queen's still got a bounty on her, doesn't she? I want in," he repeated.

I hadn't known that, either. I was starting to hate my sixteenth birthday. A poufy white dress and a cake with roses made out of pink icing and awkward dancing with boys in awkward suits was starting to sound like a great alternative. Seriously. Sign me up. I wouldn't even complain.

"You'll have to prove yourself."

Kieran shoved up his sleeve, showing his sun tattoo. "I've proven myself, thanks."

"We're taking out more than one little girl, no matter how freaky she might be."

"Whatever, look, I just want the money." He pushed toward me. The woods seemed to glow so brightly, I shaded my face. My vision was more sensitive than it had ever been. The trees might as well have been carved out of emeralds and filled with sunlight. His eyes were soothingly dark.

And glaring at me pointedly.

I glared back.

He broke contact only long enough to glance to his right, brief as a lightning bug's flash. My glare lost some of its oomph as I tried to figure out what was going on. The agents were spread out slightly on his right. Not enough to make an escape, but almost. Kieran tripped over a tree root, his elbow catching one of the guards in the sternum. He stumbled back. The gap widened. Kieran grabbed my hand and tossed me through the brief opening. I could feel him at my back, pushing me on. Behind us the agents hollered. A shot rang out, pinged bark off a pine tree not a foot from my head. Kieran shoved me. "Run faster."

"Trying," I gasped. Only adrenaline kept me going, and it was starting to make me feel sick. There was nothing quiet or vampiric about the way I was crashing through the woods. A deaf and blind kitten could have followed my trail.

They were closing in.

We'd never be able to outrun them. Especially not since I was already wheezing and stumbling. I tripped over my own foot and went sprawling in the dirt. Kieran reached down to haul me back up.

"Wait, don't," I said. I recognized the nick in the oak near my head, right near the root. At first glance it wouldn't have been noticeable, at second it would have looked like a deer or a coyote had rubbed up against it. But I knew what it was.

Safety notch.

And sure enough, when I clawed through the undergrowth, I found the wooden handle, carved to look like an exposed root covered in moss. The actual door was just a chunk of wood and it was painstakingly covered with mud and leaves that camouflaged it even after it had been opened.

"Are you nuts? Get up!"

Instead I pushed into a crouch and yanked at the handle. It opened to a deep hole with a rope secured to the side and dangling down to the bottom.

"Let's go," I told him, sliding in feetfirst. The rope burned my hands. Kieran followed, the door shutting with a thunk above our heads. Darkness swallowed us as my feet hit the ground. Kieran landed beside me. I reached out tentatively to run my hand over the walls, feeling dirt and roots as thin as hair. The dirt gave way to Kieran's shoulder.

"Um . . . sorry."

I could hear his ragged breathing, and my own breath burned in my lungs. There wasn't much space to maneuver. I shifted away, hit the wall behind me. Shifted again and my hip bumped his. His hand closed over my arm.

"Wait." His voice was husky. I heard him rummaging. I wondered if I should be worried about Hypnos powder. But it didn't make sense for him to drug me after he'd helped me get away.

Unless he wanted the bounty for himself.

I was close enough that I should be able to hit some vital organ with my foot or my fist. If he was unconscious while I was under the effects of the Hypnos, he couldn't take advantage of my hypnotized state. There was a click and I launched myself at him. His arms closed around me, and we hit the wall with enough force to rattle my insides. My teeth cut into the inside of my lip. I tasted blood.

A blue glow from the lightstick he'd broken filled the cramped space.

He hadn't been reaching for Hypnos after all—he'd only been trying to find us a light source in his belt.

"What the hell?" He grunted, rubbing his bruised knee. I was pressed against him, chest to ankle. I struggled, leaning back. I didn't have any strength left. My angry leap had sapped the very last of it. I sagged a little.

"I thought you were going for the Hypnos powder."

His eyes were very dark in the weird blue light. His eyebrows nearly snapped together, he was glowering so deeply.

"I've been *trying* to save your life."

"Um. Thanks?" I tried a smile, then decided on just glowering back. "Look, it was an honest mistake."

"If you say so."

He still hadn't let go of me. When he released his hold, I leaned against the wall, closing my eyes.

"What's the matter with you?" he asked. I could hear the concern in his voice, under all that irritation. "Are you hurt?"

"Bloodchange."

"What . . . right now?" He might have just possibly squeaked.

"In about two days, actually. Happy birthday to me."

"Isn't it supposed to make you get stronger?"

"Sure," I said drily. "If it doesn't kill me first."

"We can't stay here."

"The tunnel leads to another safe room."

"They won't stop searching for us. They'll comb the whole forest."

"I can't run anymore," I said apologetically. "I just can't. Pull that lever there, by your head."

He pulled it down and then leaped back out of the way when a gate swung closed, blocking access to the tunnel.

"This way," I told him, literally dragging my feet. He came up beside me, putting his arm around my waist to help me. "I'm okay," I muttered.

"You're practically green. Except for the lovely bloodshot eyes, of course."

"Oh." My vanity twinged. I knew it was stupid; I had way bigger problems. But I still didn't want to look like a haggard, disgusting mess around him. He was warm against me, and I felt chilled and was trembling with it suddenly. The damp of being underground didn't help. My teeth chattered. I just needed to get to a corner where I could collapse. Kieran half carried me down the passageway. It smelled like mud and green and water, dripping somewhere we couldn't see. The tunnel widened and then we were in a round chamber with flagstones on the ground and a narrow bed in the back corner. There was a chest I knew was filled with blankets, matches, and various other supplies, including a thermos of blood. There was another gate, locked with an alarm system. The red light blinked like an eye. Kieran helped me to the bed, then stared at the alarm as I leaned over to pull blankets out of the metal chest.

"Can you get that open?"

I shook my head. "The grate you closed in the tunnel and that door there are both automatically wired to stay locked until sunset." I raised an eyebrow. "I'm sure I don't have to explain why."

"I had no idea any of this was down here. It's like an old-time war bunker."

"It's been here for at least a hundred years. It helps us get around and stay out of the sun." I leaned back on the blankets, yawning. "And since we're constantly being attacked by snipers and warriors and idiots, I guess it kind of is like war."

"Am I a sniper, a warrior, or an idiot?"

"Don't know yet."

"Well, thanks very much for that." He frowned, glancing around. "If the Helios-Ra find the opening, we'll be trapped in here."

"They won't find it—it's really well camouflaged. And there are ways around the alarm if we really need them. But we don't yet." I tried to call my parents but my cell phone wouldn't work. "Low battery," I muttered. "Figures." I looked at him. "What about your phone?"

"If I turn it on now, Helios will activate the GPS chip." His voice softened. "So I guess we just wait."

My eyelids were so heavy. I had to assume I could trust him not to stake me if I fell asleep, because I wasn't going to be able *not* to fall asleep for much longer. And he'd proven himself trustworthy enough for a nap. I heard him rummaging in the chest and then the scratch and hiss of a match being lit and the wick of a fat candle catching. The artificial blue glow faded to candlelight. The smell of melting wax crowded out the damp.

"Are you scared, Solange?"

My eyes popped open briefly. He was watching me carefully, seated on a folded blanket on top of the chest. The flickering light glinted off the edge of the goggles loose around his neck and the snaps on his cargo pants and the metal under the scraped leather of his combat boots.

"Scared of what?"

"Being a vampire."

I glanced away, glanced back. He was still looking at me, as if there was nothing else worth contemplating in the world.

"Sometimes," I whispered truthfully. "Not so much about being a vampire—that's all I've ever known. More about the change." I shivered. "The last of my brothers to go through it nearly didn't come out the other side."

"I didn't think it was that dangerous."

"It's why they confused it with consumption in the nineteenth century."

"Consumption?"

"Tuberculosis."

"Oh." He paused. "Really?"

"They don't teach you this at the academy?" I couldn't help a very small sneer.

He didn't sneer back. "No."

Now I felt bad for being petty. He had saved my life, after all.

"We have the same symptoms as tuberculosis, especially in the eyes of the Romantic Poets. Pale, tired, coughing up blood."

"That's romantic?"

I had to smile. "Romantic with a capital 'R.' You know, like Byron and Coleridge."

He gave a mock shudder. "Please, stop. I barely passed English Lit."

I snorted. "I didn't have that option. One of my aunts took Byron as a lover."

"Get out."

"Seriously. It makes Lucy insanely jealous."

"That girl is . . ."

"My best friend," I filled in sternly.

"I was only going to say she's unique."

"Okay, then." The room was spinning slowly, the edges blurry. I wouldn't be able to fight the lethargy much longer. "Just so we're clear."

"She's just as protective of you as you are of her, you know." I could hear the smile in his voice.

"I know. I'm worried about her. I think this is going to get really ugly."

"I think you're right."

"Is it true Helios called off the bounty?"

"Yes."

I turned over onto my side so I could see him without having to hold up my head, which now weighed approximately as much as a car. "Then why are they after me?"

His posture changed, as if something that had been holding him up wasn't there any longer. "One of the units has gone rogue. I got a call before, just as they found you and your brothers."

I rested my cheek on my hands. "That really happens? Units going rogue, I mean?"

"It hasn't in nearly two hundred years, but yes, it happens. It's been a bad year for the league. My uncle's in charge, and he's great, he really is, but since his partner was replaced, it hasn't been the same."

"Why not? Who was his partner?"

"My father."

I had to ask. I didn't know what to say. I remembered him saying his father was killed by a vampire. Which made me want to apologize. Which was ridiculous. I hadn't killed him and neither had anyone I knew, so why would I apologize? Would he apologize to me for the Helios-Ra agent who'd killed one of my cousin's girl-friends?

Still. He'd lost his father.

"I'm sorry your father died."

His jaw clenched. "Thank you." His voice was very husky.

"We didn't do it."

Something bloomed right then and there in the small dark space between us. I didn't know what it was, but I knew enough to know it was rare and delicate. And it felt so real I might have been able to reach out and touch it if I tried.

"You can go to sleep," he told me softly. "I'll look after you."

CHAPTER 18

♦

Lucy

Sunday afternoon

I woke up late the next day, smothered by my very own vampire blanket. I shifted experimentally but Nicholas didn't budge. His arms were wrapped around me, pinning me ruthlessly to his chest. That might sound passionate in romance novels, but in real life, it was uncomfortable. My arm was asleep, my nose was mashed against his chest, and I really had to pee.

"Nicholas," I whispered.

Nothing.

I pushed his shoulder.

Still nothing.

None of those same novels had ever made any suggestions as to the extraction of one's self from a superhuman embrace. There were logistical issues. Such as the fact that I could break my own arm trying to squirm away and he'd sleep right through it. I squirmed anyway, just in case.

"Damn it, Nicky, wake up, you undead slug."

It wasn't a good sign when I couldn't even irritate him into a response. There was a narrow window beside Solange's bed. I might just be able to reach it with my toe. I stretched until the arch of my foot and the back of my calf began to cramp painfully.

"This is ridiculous," I huffed, stretching farther. I could feel my face going red with the effort. With my luck, this would be the exact moment he woke up—to find me inches from his head, straining and panting like I was passing a kidney stone.

I finally managed to hook the cord of the blinds with my toes. One yank and a quick release and the blinds snapped up. Late-afternoon sunlight slanted over the bed and across his pale, still face. The glass was treated, of course, so it wasn't dangerous, but Nicholas's young vampire instinct made him recoil from the sudden fall of light. He burrowed under the security of blankets, shifting his arm and throwing it over his head for good measure.

The only problem was that he did it so fast, the momentum shoved me right off the bed and onto the floor. I landed with a squeak and a particularly ungraceful display of flailing limbs, neither of which helped to make my landing any softer.

My elbow tingled and my tailbone throbbed, and I now had intimate knowledge of the dust bunnies under Solange's bed. And the patchwork skirt I thought I'd lost last year, twisted under a storage box covered in stickers. Yes, even little girls with vampire lineage have a sticker phase. I shoved to my feet, grimacing. Nicholas slept on peacefully, looking exactly like a marble carving of a sleeping angel. Hah.

There was nothing angelic about the way he kissed.

When I caught myself snickering, I realized I must be groggier than I thought. I hurried out of the room before I embarrassed myself irrevocably. The house was quiet. Boudicca lay in front of Hope's door. She wagged her tail when she saw me but otherwise didn't move. Liam must have sent her to guard the bedroom. I went to fetch Mrs. Brown and then let her out to terrorize the wildlife in the backyard. One thing I'd learned in my family was that if you had an animal companion, never "pet," who was dependent on you, you lived up to your responsibilities. No excuses. Ever. When I was seven I'd begged my parents for a goldfish because I loved feeding the ones at the Buddhist temple we went to every New Year's Eve. Only I forgot to feed mine, and it floated belly-up one sad Sunday morning. To say that my mother overreacted was to vastly underestimate my mother. We had a funeral, complete with a papier-mâché Viking boat, which she set on fire, sending my goldfish's spirit to Valhalla via Lake Violet.

"Hurry up," I called over to Mrs. Brown, who was wiggling her little pug bottom in joy at finding one of Byron's abandoned beef bones on the edge of the lawn. The sun was soft, like warm honey poured onto the treetops and the roses, glittering over the windows of the farmhouse. It was one of those perfect long summer days just before school starts. Solange and I usually wandered around town, complaining about how bored we were and how much it sucked that I had to go back to school and she had to learn how to pour tea in the precise Victorian way. You know, in case Charlotte Brontë ever dropped by for tea cakes. I would have given anything to be that bored right now.

I wished we knew where Solange was and whether she was all right. We didn't even know if she was still conscious. There were only two days left until her birthday. If someone wasn't there to help her through her bloodchange, she'd be dead before she even got a chance to be sixteen—or else she'd turn into a *Hel-Blar*.

If she wasn't already dead.

"Can't think like that," I muttered, shredding the rose I hadn't realized I'd picked. Torn petals drifted messily to the ground. Mrs. Brown attacked them as if they offended her sense of order. I didn't hear the window slide open over her fierce growls, but I did hear Hope raise her voice.

"Lucky, isn't it?"

"No one calls me that." I looked up, shading my eyes. "There are alarms on the windows, and if you jump, Byron will chase you." I snapped my fingers at the shaggy dog, who slunk over from the porch, head lowered submissively as soon as he saw Mrs. Brown. As a threat, he needed work.

"I'm not going to jump," Hope assured me. "Anyway, I'd break my leg from this distance."

"Good." I didn't know what else to say.

"I can get you away from here," she added softly.

Now I knew exactly what to say.

"Not you, too," I said impatiently. "I'm not a prisoner, and the Drakes aren't monsters. They're family."

"You're not a vampire." Her expression darkened. I wouldn't have thought such a cheerful face could look so angry. "Did they change you?"

"No, of course not." I scowled back. "Wait, how did you know my name?"

"You're Solange's closest friend. Of course we know who you are."

"That stupid field guide, right? Do you also know how creepy you are? Stalking a fifteen-year-old girl in your commando outfits?"

"But drinking blood isn't creepy?"

"No creepier than eating a dead cow."

She shook her head. "Kieran said you wouldn't be interested in detox."

"Detox? From what? My friends?"

"From vampires. From this lifestyle." She waved a hand at the treated glass. "From alarm systems and nightwalkers and sword-fights."

"Okay, first of all, I happen to love swordfighting. And second of all, what, your lifestyle of secret agent assassins is somehow suburban white bread all of a sudden? Please."

"Oh, Lucky, it's not like that."

"It's Lucy," I corrected her through my teeth. "And your people tried to kill my best friend, so you'll forgive me if I'm not overly keen on learning the secret handshake."

She shook her head sadly. "You should be going on dates and hanging out at the mall. Not wearing stakes on your belt."

I shrugged one shoulder. "The mall sucks."

"I can help you."

"Like you helped Solange? No thanks."

"You can have a normal life. It's not too late for you."

I nearly laughed. "You've clearly never met my parents. Normal was never an option." I folded my arms and smiled at her sarcastically. "You could leave the Helios-Ra. We could help you stop trying to kill people just because they have a medical condition that you don't understand."

She sucked in a breath. "It's not like that."

"It's totally like that. *God.*"

"You're so young. You can't see the bigger picture."

"I'm sixteen, I'm not an idiot."

"We could use you." She made it sound like it was something I should be excited about. "There's so much we could teach you. You have the instinct for it, I can tell."

The thought made me shiver. "No."

"The offer stands. If you should change your mind." She looked young, with her ponytail and her round cheeks. Still, her eyes were old, knowing. I was spared further conversation when Bruno came striding out of the wooded area bordering the lawn.

"Are you daft, lass?" he asked, accent thickening with disgust. "It's nearly dusk. Get your arse inside." I hadn't noticed the sky had turned to lavender and pink, the edges burning like tissue paper set on fire. He glowered at Hope. "And you, get inside and close that window. If you run, we have ways of fetching you back. You won't like them."

"I'm not a prisoner," she reminded him gently. "I'm here as a gesture of good faith."

He snorted but didn't answer, preferring instead to nudge me back inside like a great big Scottish bully.

"All right, all right, I'm coming," I muttered. "Someone had to let Mrs. Brown out."

He shut the patio door behind me and locked it. His eyes were smudged with bruises of fatigue. Mrs. Brown chased Byron around the living room until he hid under the library table, whimpering. That, at least, made the night feel more normal. It wasn't long before Liam and Helena came downstairs to join us, followed by Geoffrey, Sebastian, and a rumpled Nicholas. For some reason when he looked at me, I felt myself blushing.

"Still no word from Hyacinth," Helena said grimly and without preamble.

Bruno shook his head, confirming. "We can't track her phone. It's possible she's out of range."

Liam shook his head. "Not likely. I talked to Hart and he claims none of his people came into contact with her."

"And we believe him?" Nicholas asked, leaning back against the mantel and yawning.

Liam's phone rang from the depths of his leather jacket. He answered it, listened, and said only one word. "Good." He looked at his wife. Her shoulders lost some of their tension and then the front door burst open to the rest of the Drake brothers. They rushed in, covered in mud, clothing torn, faces angry.

"Where is she?" Logan asked. "Where's Solange?"

"We don't know," Liam answered him.

Logan closed his eyes briefly, his face pale as lily petals. Quinn swore viciously. Connor punched the wall, denting the plaster.

"Where's your cousin?" Helena frowned, after giving each of her sons the once-over to be sure they were unhurt.

"London took off," Marcus sighed. "She locked one of the grates behind her and just took off."

"What?" Nicholas pushed away from the wall. "You're kidding. She got you into this mess in the first place."

Logan dropped into a chair. "I think she was embarrassed. Or confused. She loves Lady Natasha, you know that."

"And what about Solange?"

"The good news is that Veronique gave her a vial of blood to help her through the change. The bad news is the little idiot gave herself up to the Helios-Ra to save us."

"Not quite," Liam told them starkly. "Your sister gave herself up to a rogue unit currently unrecognized by Helios."

"Well that's just freaking great."

The Drake brothers put a rioting soccer stadium to shame when they got going. And there was nothing like the news that their baby sister had sacrificed herself for them to someone worse than Helios-Ra. The language currently blistering the air would have made the proverbial sailor blush. Helena had to whistle around her thumb and forefinger to make the yelling subside. She was on her feet, her long black braid hanging behind her, her pale eyes like summer lightning.

"Enough. We don't have the time for this." She jabbed a finger at Logan and Nicholas. "You two stay here with Lucy. Sebastian, Geoffrey, your father, and I will find your sister. The rest of you will help Bruno's team find your aunt." She snapped her fingers and it was like a pistol shot. "That's final, not one word out of any of you. Go. *Now*."

The house emptied so fast the silence felt like a slap. I blinked at Nicholas and Logan.

"They don't really think we're going to sit around here and wait, do they?"

"Of course they do," Nicholas replied.

"Look, I'm not sitting around here anymore. Solange needs our help."

"You don't know what you're getting yourself into," Logan said. "You're sixteen and human."

"Shut up."

"I mean it, Lucy. Solange would kill us if we let you put yourself in danger."

"Logan, don't be an ass."

"I have been sleeping in mud. I'm covered in dirt and blood and these were my favorite pants before I landed in raccoon shit."

I bit back a totally inappropriate chuckle. "Raccoon shit?"

"Lucy."

I kissed his cheek, wrinkling my nose. "Why don't you go up and take a shower. If you stop bitching, I'll even wait for you before I figure out what to do next."

He pushed to his feet, groaning like an old man. "I don't think I like you anymore."

I patted his head. "Don't be silly, you love me."

"Try and stay out of trouble in the ten minutes it's going to take me to get clean."

"I can't make any promises," I replied primly.

He shot Nicholas a smirk. "Good luck, little brother."

I scowled at his retreating back.

"What's that supposed to mean?"

CHAPTER 19

♦

Solange

Sunday, sunset

When I opened my eyes, Kieran was crouched next to me, his hand on my shoulder. I jerked back, reflexively. Startled, he did the same.

"Easy," he said. "It's just me."

I blinked, pushing myself up into a sitting position. I felt less like a truck had run over me and then backed up to make sure the job was done properly. Now it felt as if the truck had hit me only once.

"What time is it?" I asked groggily.

"Almost dusk. I tried to wake you earlier but you didn't respond. Scared the crap out of me," he added, muttering as he got to his feet. "I'd rather be well out of here by sundown."

I swung my feet over the edge of the cot.

"Okay, give me a minute." I yawned.

"Whoa." He was staring at me. I resisted the urge to wipe my face to see if there was drool on my cheek or something. "Your eyes."

"What? What?" I scrubbed at them violently, horrified at the thought they might have those gross goopy things at the edges. Or were they even more bloodshot? I'd heard of that happening, where the whites ran with blood.

"I think . . . the color's changing." He paused. "Is that even possible?"

"Is that all? Now you're the one scaring the crap out of me," I muttered back. "Honestly."

"I could have sworn they were darker before you went to sleep."

"They were."

"But they look really blue now."

"They probably are," I replied. "Our eyes get lighter. The really old ones go gray usually."

"Oh."

I shifted uncomfortably. I didn't know how to analyze the way he was looking at me. It made me feel shy and kind of like giggling. And I *so* was not the giggling type.

"Didn't you want to get out of here?" I asked.

"Yeah." He handed me his jacket, which I slipped on over Lucy's dress. It was torn and stiff with mud up one side. "Are you . . . hungry?"

I froze, looked up at him through my eyelashes. He wasn't offering me blood . . . was he? I tried not to gag.

"I just meant..." His ears went red. "Protein bar?" he explained, pulling one out of his vest pocket.

"Oh." I took it from him, my stomach suddenly rumbling. "Thanks."

We chewed quietly while I tried to figure out what to say to the guy who had tried to kidnap me for money and then within the week saved me from a bunch of his armed brethren. I got that he was doing it for his precious Helios-Ra, to stop the rogue unit before it did serious damage to the league's reputation, but still, I couldn't help but feel as if he might care just a little bit about whether or not I lived through my birthday.

"Can you get us out of here?" he asked once we'd finished our mock chocolate bars. It had settled the hunger pangs but made me thirsty as well. My mouth felt chalky. "Or do we really have to wait until the sun sets?"

"It's easier if we wait, but I think I can turn the alarm off." I raised an eyebrow. "You'll have to turn your back."

He turned slowly. The view from the back was just as good as the view from the front. I could practically hear Lucy snickering in the back of my head. I might be the vampire daughter, but she was the one who was a bad influence. No question. I made sure Kieran wasn't peeking and then cupped my hand over my fingertips as I punched in the code. The light went from flashing red to full red. It was bright enough to have me squinting, my eyes tearing.

"Shit."

"'Shit'? What do you mean, 'shit'?"

"It's okay," I rushed to assure him. "I just used an old code. And, um, set the alarm on freak-out."

He whirled. "Can you shut it off?"

"Of course." I sounded confident for someone who really wasn't. I raced to remember the codes. There was a rotation of a minimum of seven codes, which were changed randomly and continuously. I'd been taught them the way most children were taught their phone number. This should be easy.

The second code didn't work either.

Or the third.

"We're not going to get gassed out of here or something, are we?" Kieran asked nervously.

"Of course not." I paused. "I don't think."

I punched the next code in but my fingers were slippery and slid off the last number. I tried again. The light held red, then went green and blinked off. My shoulders released some of their tension.

"See?" I said nonchalantly. "No problem."

The gate unlocked with a resounding click and I pushed it open. Kieran was close at my back. The smell of damp intensified and then faded, tinged with sunlight and grass. The tunnel led us to a ladder. I paused on the lowest rung.

"Ready?"

"Maybe you should let me go first."

"Forget it." I climbed to the next rung. His hand closed around my ankle. I looked down at him. "Relax, Black. I can climb a ladder."

"What happens when we get up there, Solange?"

"We run like hell until we're home safe and sound? It's a basic plan, but it works for me."

"That rogue unit might still be up there."

"Maybe. But we're coming up pretty far away from where we vanished. And are you telling me they'd hang around for an entire day, just in case?"

"I wish I knew."

"Well, we can't stay here all night."

After a moment, his hold on my ankle released. I could still feel the warm imprint of his palm on my skin as I continued to climb. The trapdoor wouldn't open right away. Kieran had to wedge himself between me and the wall, and we both shoved until the door creaked open. A spear of sunlight landed between us. His eyes were the color of earth—the dark, rich kind you just know will grow the best flowers, the best vegetables. He was very close, close enough that I could see the faint stubble of a beard on his chin and the way his sideburns grew long, shaved to a straight line, the way the men in movies like *Pride and Prejudice* always seem to wear them. It gave him the air of a gentleman pirate. The weapons strapped to his chest didn't hurt. He hauled himself up, never breaking eye contact, even as he snuck past me and managed to be the first one out of the tunnel after all.

"Clear," he called down quietly.

He reached down to grip my upper arms and pulled me up and out, onto the forest floor. The sun filtered softly between the leaves, the shadows long and blue over the ferns and fallen pine needles. Birds sang, oblivious to our presence. There were no footprints in the loam. I stood up, brushing my hands on my dress. Kieran pulled a compass from his pocket, turned it this way and that way.

"There," he said, nodding toward and across a valley of ferns and elder bushes. "Your house is that way. Northwest."

"Thanks." I glanced around awkwardly, glanced back. "I guess this is it, then?"

He frowned. "What are you talking about? I'm not leaving you here alone."

I swallowed, tried to smile. "You have your own stuff to deal with."

"Solange, your eyes are changing color."

"So? What does that have to do with anything?"

"Let me put it this way." He moved so fast, I was impressed despite myself. He shoved my shoulder. I stumbled, hit a nearby oak tree, then tumbled into the mud. My shoulder pulsed painfully.

"Ouch! What the hell was that for?"

"Just proving my point," he told me grimly. "You think I don't see how tired you are? How you're getting weaker?"

I frowned, rubbing my arm. "You pushed me."

"I barely touched you," he pointed out. "And you fell over. I guarantee the rogue Helios-Ra unit will be a lot rougher. Not to mention Lady Natasha's bounty hunters."

I hated that he was right.

"I'm taking you home." He looked stubbornly mutinous. I'd seen that particular expression on every single one of my brothers' faces at one time or another. And there was no gracious way for me to turn him down. No logical, intelligent way, either. He had weapons. I didn't. If someone came at me in the woods, the only thing I could do was yawn them to sleep. And this was the girl Lady Natasha, queen of the vampires, was afraid of.

"Are you coming?" Kieran asked impatiently but with half a smile, as if he knew what I was thinking.

"Okay, but if vamps attack, I want you to run away."

"Sure, right after I pirouette in a pink tutu." He stopped, waited for me to catch up. "Come on, already."

The woods were peaceful and quiet, under the chatter of insects and hidden rabbits and porcupines. Frogs sang from some nearby pond, obscured by the green lace of summer leaves. It might have been romantic if I wasn't convinced someone was waiting around the bend to kill us. He slanted me a glance out of the corner of his eye. And another.

"What?" I asked, without turning my head.

"You're squinting. Do your eyes hurt?"

"A little." I hadn't realized how tightly the muscles around my eyes were scrunched until he mentioned it. My eyes did feel more sensitive, as if the sunlight, even faded the way it was, was hurling needles at my face. I used to love sitting out in the sun with Lucy. It made me a little sad to think we wouldn't be able to do that anymore. Kieran handed me a pair of sunglasses. His fingers brushed mine. He really was kind of sweet for an agent of the cult dedicated to wiping out me and my entire family.

"Are you going to grow fangs too?"

I nearly stopped in my tracks. His hand was still holding mine.

"I guess so." I ran my tongue over my teeth.

"Is your boyfriend worried?"

"I don't have a boyfriend." My smile was ironic. "Kind of hard to bring dates home to meet my parents—and my brothers."

"Good point." His palm pressed against mine. "Watch your step."

We crawled over the exposed roots of a tree that must have fallen in the last storm. It wasn't covered in moss yet or those weird ruffled mushrooms. We climbed down into the valley, as the sun set lower and lower behind the horizon, leaving us in thick, cool shadows. The ground under our feet was soft. There was a wide groove, as if something had slid down to the valley floor.

A scrap of lace trailed from a broken branch in the tangled undergrowth.

My heart stuttered. I felt my hands go clammy before I could even form a coherent sentence. I knew that kind of lace.

"No," I gasped, plucking it like it was a tattered black rose. "No."

I tore down the hillside, slipping in the dirt, skinning my shins and my palms. Pebbles flung up at my passing and pinged me in the legs. Branches scratched my bare arms.

"Solange!" Kieran called, hurrying to catch up. "Wait. Where are you going?"

I slipped and slid the last few feet.

"Be careful!" he hollered behind me.

I barely felt any pain, I was so entirely focused on following the body-wide scrape in the rotted leaves and pine needles.

"Oh my God," I said, spotting a ruffle of lace and ribbon. I'd know those black petticoats anywhere, and the silk corset and jet beads. "Aunt Hyacinth," I called out, crawling closer, tearing ferns out of my way. "Aunt Hyacinth, hold on, hold on."

She was lying on her back, her arm thrown over her face. Her arm from elbow to wrist and the entire left side of her face were blistered and raw. Only her age and the thick shadows of the valley had saved her from the full impact of the sun. Even so, she wasn't moving, wasn't responding at all. I hovered over her, not wanting to touch her in case it caused her more pain.

"Is she . . ." Kieran's question trailed off as he came up behind me, panting for breath.

"I think she's still alive so to speak," I said, swallowing the lump of fear and grief forming in my throat. "She's my aunt." I could practically see bone under the ruin of her cheek. Sunlight alone wouldn't have done that kind of damage. I scowled.

"Holy water," I said through my teeth. "Holy water" was what we called the water Helios-Ra used as a weapon. They charged it with UV rays and vitamin D because we were deathly allergic to it in such concentrated form. "Someone threw holy water on her and then pushed her down the hill. The Helios-Ra use holy water, don't they?" I pressed.

"Solange," he said softly, tightly.

"Don't they?" I yelled.

He nodded once, jerkily. "Sometimes."

"Still so sure your league is totally blameless in everything? Look at her!"

"I'm sorry. I know what it's like to lose family. My father was killed by vampires, remember?"

"I haven't lost her yet," I said grimly, pulling the thick chain out from under my dress. The liquid inside was deep, dark.

"What is that?" Kieran demanded.

"Blood," I said, not looking away from Aunt Hyacinth. I'd never seen her look so frail, so still. It wasn't fair. She'd been hunted because of me, because of the damn bounty on my head. She'd have been safely at home drinking Earl Grey tea or critiquing Lucy's curtsy if it wasn't for me.

"Ancient blood," I explained. "From Veronique Dubois, our matriarch. It has healing properties for anyone of her lineage. I'd give her my blood, but it's tainted right now because of the change."

I didn't mention that my vial held only a single dose, meant to give me an edge even if someone was there to help turn me on my birthday. And no one would be.

I'd see to that.

But first I had to save Aunt Hyacinth. I used my thumbnail to lift the lid, the hinge sticking slightly.

"Hold on, Aunt Hyacinth," I pleaded. "Please hold on. Please, please hold on."

I held the vial to her mouth and tipped it slowly. Blood welled over her lips, filling the crease until it trickled through her teeth and down her chin. She was so pale, nearly blue as her veins struggled to accept the only substance that could save her. Her throat moved slowly, spasmodically.

"She swallowed!" I nearly wept with relief. I held the vial over her mouth until she couldn't swallow anymore. She still didn't open her eyes, didn't talk. But she looked less like she was about to turn to dust. "It's all I can do," I said, letting the chain fall from my fingers. "She needs more, but she's too weak to finish the rest right now. I'll leave the vial with her so that someone can use it to keep her alive if they find her soon enough to revive her."

I rifled through her reticule until I found her cell phone. It had turned itself off when she'd fallen and the plastic was cracked, the screen flickering blue when I finally managed to turn it on. I pressed the code to activate the GPS chip. We weren't that far from the farmhouse. Someone would find her in time.

But I couldn't let them find me.

My brothers had nearly been captured and my aunt was hurt, all because of me. I couldn't bear it if she died or my parents were killed fighting to save me. And Lucy would jump in over her head if she thought it would save me. Even Kieran was putting himself in danger for me and going against his training. I couldn't let any of them sacrifice themselves for me. I just couldn't.

They all wanted to save me, but I just wanted to save them.

And there was only one way to do that. I'd always known it, but I'd hoped I was wrong. Kneeling in the forest with my aunt's burned body convinced me I'd been right all along.

I pulled out my own phone and didn't turn it on, only placed it gently on the ground. And then I smashed it repeatedly with a stone until the case cracked open and the insides were dented beyond repair. I looked up at Kieran, knew my face had gone hard by the way he looked back at me.

"I need your help."

CHAPTER 20

•

Lucy

Sunday evening

While Logan cleaned up, I took the dogs out again. The gardens were different at night, scraggly and thick. Crickets sang cheerfully from the fields bordering the forest. The moon was yellow and hung in a tatter of clouds like lace. Nicholas was standing guard by the back door and scowling into the darkness. His eyes gleamed.

"Hurry up," he said.

"I can't make the dogs pee any faster." He didn't look at me, turning sharply when something rustled in the bushes. "You look like secret service. All you need is a black suit and shiny shoes."

"I'm just being careful."

"Bruno's out there and we're barely three feet from the door. Besides, no one's after *me*."

"Says the girl with a row of wooden stakes strapped to her chest." He paused. "And are those pink rhinestones?"

"They are," I said proudly. "Who says you can't vanquish in style? And see this one?" I pointed to the stake next to the one I'd decorated with pink rhinestones. It had a skull and crossbones drawn on with black marker. "Pirate theme." He just shook his head at me. I shrugged and tugged on Mrs. Brown's leash when she wriggled her entire front end into a rosebush. Her bottom wagged furiously. "Get out of there," I told her. "Before you get a thorn up your nose."

It took another tug to convince her I was serious. She waddled backward, covered in pink petals. The light from Hope's window above us made a square of yellow on the grass at my feet. It caught on something hanging from the trellis underneath the ledge. I had to stretch up on my tiptoes to reach it. It was a large bronze sun with jagged rays on a leather thong. I plucked it down, wondering if Hope had lost it when she'd hung out the window, trying to convince me to give up the sordid life of a bloodslave.

"Let's go," Nicholas said, opening the door to let the big dogs inside. Mrs. Brown nipped at their heels, grinning her canine grin when they jumped to get away from her. Nicholas ushered me into the safety of the conservatory, his hand on the small of my back. I could feel the coolness of his touch through my shirt. It was dark here as well, full of lilies and orange trees and rare red orchids. A moth fluttered at the glass ceiling, as if the moon were a candle burning over our heads.

Nicholas didn't say anything, and he didn't move away, either. Instead he dipped his head lower, his mouth brushing the skin under my ear and then trailing down to the side of my neck. My head lolled back. Part of me waited for the scrape of teeth, but there was only his lips and his tongue. I was the one who turned slightly and bit gently on his earlobe. His hand pulled me closer against him. It was a struggle to remember why we hadn't gotten along all these years. I couldn't think of a single thing to bicker about.

I couldn't think at all, actually.

I was all warmth and shivers. Night-blooming jasmine sent out sweet tendrils of scent. If I closed my eyes, I could believe we were somewhere exotic, in the jungle or a secret garden in India. I had just slid my arms around Nicholas's neck when the lights flashed on, then off. We froze.

"Alarm," Nicholas whispered. "Someone's opened the tunnel door in the basement."

We hurried down the hall, just as Logan came running down the stairs, his hair still wet, his shirt half-buttoned. There was a shadow in the doorway to the steps leading downstairs. When it stepped forward, it became London, her fangs out as usual. Her hair, usually so strictly slicked down, was a mess of oil-dark spikes.

"You!" I hollered and launched myself at her. My temper burst like a pie left too long in the oven. Nicholas's arm clamped around my stomach, holding me back. I felt like a cartoon character, punching and kicking at air and cursing. London just stood there, pale and quiet. That had me calming down more than Nicholas's struggles to contain me. I'd never seen London when she wasn't sneering at me or shooting her mouth off. She didn't do meekly repentant. It scared me as much as, if not more than, everything that had happened so far.

"I'm fine," I muttered so Nicholas would let go. I pushed my hair out of my eyes.

"Where the hell have you been?" Logan demanded, advancing on London with the kind of fury I'd never thought to see on his pretty face. "We thought you were dead. Or had betrayed us right into that bitch's hands."

"I didn't know," she said softly, wretchedly. "I swear to you, I didn't know." She lifted her chin, expression hardening so that she looked a little more like herself. "Where's everyone?"

"Trying to find Solange," Logan told her. "Who gave herself up to save us all. You included."

"I didn't know Natasha set the bounty. I've served her for years, loved her like a mother. How was I supposed to know? Or do you not remember that she was there for me when the Drakes weren't?" I hadn't heard about this particular blemish on the Drake family tree. I'd just assumed London was crabby all the time because it was in her biological makeup. "She asked me to bring Solange to her, to put an end to any rumors that might start a civil war. And she thinks Montmartre will take her back when there's no threat to her crown."

"Damn it, London," Nicholas muttered.

"I thought I was helping. And I'm oathed to her service, to the royal court." London whirled on him. "What was I supposed to do?"

"Not hand your own cousin over to that bitch, for a start," Nicholas shot back.

London's eyes narrowed. I assumed she was going to launch into a vicious tirade, but instead she took three steps toward me so fast I bumped into the wall behind me trying to get away from her.

Rage poured out of her. If I wasn't immune to her pheromones, I might have passed out at the onslaught. As it was, it made me vaguely light-headed. Nicholas half stepped in front of me.

"Stop it, London."

"Where did you get that?" she demanded. She grabbed the bronze sun hanging from the strap of stakes between my breasts. Her grip was so hard, the bronze dented. I was trapped between her, Nicholas, and the wall.

"I just found it. Get off of me."

"Do you know what this is?"

"No. I found it under Hope's window."

Her pale eyes went pink at the edges. I'd never seen that before. I leaned back to get away from her even though there was nowhere to go.

"Hope? Hope is here?" She whirled, glared at Logan. "Where is she? Where's the Helios bitch?"

"She's an honorable hostage. She doesn't get hurt, Solange doesn't get hurt." Logan blocked the staircase.

"She's a traitor." She said it so quietly I nearly didn't hear her. I did hear her teeth grinding together, however.

"What are you talking about?" Logan demanded.

"I went back to the court after I left you. I still have friends there despite the bounty, friends that will help the Drakes, should it come to that. Hope is double-crossing Helios. She has her own unit, secretly plotting with Lady Natasha. If Hope helps Lady Natasha get rid of Solange and any Drake threat to her throne, Lady Natasha, in return, helps Hope gain control over the Helios-Ra by refusing to treaty with anyone but her."

"Lady Natasha would never treaty with humans," Logan said quietly. "She's always refused."

"Exactly. It would be quite a coup for Helios. And Lady Natasha gets her own human army, ready to wipe out any vampire who doesn't serve her."

"Well, that's just freaking great." Logan jerked his hand through his hair. He blocked London when she tried to dart around him. "You can't kill her," he insisted. "Solange's safety might just depend on it. It was a fair exchange at the time."

"I'm not worried about Solange right now." London snapped the sun disk from the strap, yanking me forward with the sudden momentum.

"Hey!" I stumbled and then straightened, glowering. "Ouch, damn it."

"Do you know what this is?" London yelled at us, holding up the sun. "Do you have any idea?" She tossed it on the floor and spat on it. "This calls Hope's unit to her. They knew she was here—they've known all along."

"She offered herself," I whispered, glancing at Nicholas. "Remember? Hart said he'd stay, but Hope insisted."

"It's a declaration of war," London continued. "It means they're on their way here right now, to set her free and kill anyone in their way. We have to get out of here."

"We can't just hand the farmhouse compound over to them, even saying they can get past Bruno and his crew," Logan said.

"But someone does have to warn the others," Nicholas argued.

"Call them," London said. "But do it fast. We have to get out of here."

"They're in stealth mode. The phones'll be off," Nicholas said. "And I'd bet anything either Mom or Dad or both of them are on their way to the courts right now. You know Dad'll try and talk his way out of the bounty. He'll be walking right into her hands."

Logan pulled his phone out of his pocket.

"Let's at least warn Bruno." He dialed, waited, his mouth tense. His fangs seemed longer, sharper. He hung up after a moment of quiet, clipped conversation. "Good news and bad news." He started up the stairs, taking them two at a time. When the rest followed, I had to grab the back of Nicholas's shirt to keep up. "They found Aunt Hyacinth. Bruno's gone to get her."

"So, we're on our own," London said grimly.

"Aside from the guards. What's that noise?" Nicholas frowned as we rushed down the hall. Boudicca barked loudly, scratching at Hope's door. It took Logan only one kick to break down the door.

The sound was the whirling of helicopter blades.

And Hope was launching herself out of the window, toward the rope. The trees bent, leaves whipping into the room from the force of the wind. The sound of the engine shook the walls. A painting fell off the wall, glass breaking.

Three vampires and a large dog leaped at Hope and not one of them reached her in time.

She swung out of reach, her blond ponytail and strappy sandals incongruous against the helicopter as the armed agents pulled her inside. Arrows rained through the window once she was safely out of the way. An arrow thudded into the bed, three into the floor, another missed Logan's ear only because London shoved him behind the dresser. I leaped toward Boudicca, grabbing for her collar. I tugged her behind the door, Nicholas pushing us both when we weren't moving fast enough for his liking. He cursed the entire time.

"You lunatic, leave the damn dog."

"Shut up, she's a member of this family, too!"

"And she knows how to get out of the way."

"In your family you drink blood. In mine we look after animals."

Boudicca was growling, straining against my grip, trying to get back to the window.

"If you two are done yelling at each other," Logan said drily. "They're gone."

"But the rest are coming," London said. "Ground crew," she added when we just stared at her. "Do you really think they'll let this opportunity pass them by? They know half the family's scattered, looking for Solange or Hyacinth."

"Well, shit."

"Exactly."

"I'll go," Logan declared.

"You can't," I said, chasing him down the stairs.

"I damn well can." He nodded at Nicholas. "Get her in the safe room and lock her in."

"Bite me, Logan," I shot back hotly. "You can't just go barging into the courts, you idiot. You're a Drake, and every bounty hunter in the country is out for your blood."

"So? We can't just let the rest of them go in blind."

"I know that. I'm suggesting you and London stay here and defend the farm."

"And you?" Nicholas asked silkily, suspiciously. "What exactly do you think you'll be doing?"

"Hope was so keen on having me join up with the Helios-Ra," I said, crouching down to pick up Hope's dented sun pendant. "So why don't I?"

CHAPTER 21

◆

Solange

Sunday evening, later

"You look awful," Kieran said.

I would have glared at him but it was taking all of my concentration just to drag one foot in front of the other.

"Stop saying that," I muttered. I hoped I wasn't slurring my words. Even my tongue was tired. Nighttime helped, my metabolism was already stronger when the sun was down. Come morning though, I just knew I'd pass right out. Passing out didn't worry me so much; it was not knowing if I was going to wake up again.

It was nearly my birthday. No party, obviously; no silver-wrapped presents or cake for me—just blood pudding. Gag. I couldn't help but remember my brothers' desperate fights to survive their bloodchanges. They'd weakened so much so fast, it was almost like they were in a coma. It hadn't lasted long, but it hit hard and heavy. Only the elixir of Veronique's blood would give me a fighting edge.

An elixir I no longer had.

I couldn't think about it. It wouldn't do me any good and, anyway, if I had to do it all over again, I would. I stumbled over a tree root, caught myself on an oak branch, and nearly put my own eye out. Kieran caught my elbow. I had to blink rapidly so there was only one of him, not two dancing blurrily with each other.

"You're getting worse."

"If you tell me I look awful again, I am so going to kick you in the shin." I yawned, swayed slightly. "Tomorrow."

"Just try not to fall asleep before you hit the ground. You're harder to catch that way." I knew he was trying to sound confident, but I could smell the worry on him. I could actually smell it, like burned almonds. Weird. I sniffed harder. He raised his eyebrows at me. "Are you smelling me?"

I smiled sheepishly. "Yeah, sorry." I rubbed my nose. "You're worried about me. It smells like almonds."

"Seriously?"

"Yeah. Weird, right?" I sniffed again, frowned. "And I smell stagnant water or mud or something."

"I smell like an old pond?"

I shook my head slowly while my exhausted synapses finally fired straight. My mother's training flooded me, my brothers' stories heard from the privacy of the stairs leading to the attic.

"Not you," I said suddenly. "*Hel-Blar.*"

Kieran froze, but only briefly. "Out here? Now?"

I tried to make my feet move faster. He grabbed my hand and dragged me. *Hel-Blar* weren't to be trifled with. Faintly blue, smelling of rot, with red-tinged eyes and an insatiable appetite for blood. Animal or human, willing or unwilling.

And quiet as bats.

Still, my hearing must be getting sharper even as I grew weaker, because I could hear them skulking between the trees, trailing us, surrounding us like a pack of rabid dogs.

"They're coming," I whispered. "And I can't outrun them like this."

Kieran nodded grimly, swinging an odd-looking gun out of its harness.

"Holy water," he explained. I made sure I was well out of the trajectory of his modified bullets. "Stay behind me," he said needlessly. I was already behind him, using a maple tree to prop myself up, a bouquet of sharpened stakes in my hand. The smell of rotting vegetation and mushrooms was overpowering to my suddenly sensitive nostrils. I gagged.

"They're here."

Their speed alone was terrifying, along with the animal gleam to their eyes. They practically floated, pale as wraiths, slender to the point of being skeletal. Their fangs were sharp and pointed, but so was every other tooth in their head. One of them licked his lips at me.

"Just a taste, princess," he drawled. "You might like it. What do you say?"

I whipped a stake at his chest and he exploded into dust the color of lichen. All vampires crumbled to ash. If I died during the bloodchange, I'd turn to ash too, but it might take a few hours. Uncle Geoffrey claimed it was a Darwinian safety mechanism, to make sure we were never discovered as a species, even after we died.

And this was so the wrong time to be thinking about it.

The others hissed and snarled and all the hairs on my arms stood up. Kieran fired his gun. Light burst like embers whirling through the air, like a carnival trick. Another scent joined the wet rot: singed flesh, burning hair.

"There are too many of them," Kieran grunted. I just grunted back and threw another stake. It missed its mark and was hurled back at us so quickly it pinned the flared hem of my dress to the trunk. Bark flew off in bits, biting into my legs. I swore and yanked myself free.

"Too close," I murmured, nearly tired enough not to care if I fell over and was eaten.

"Stay with me," Kieran snapped, firing again. A *Hel-Blar* flew like a rag doll, crashed into one of his friends. I was already on my knees. That patch of thick ferns looked so inviting. Kieran hauled me up with one arm, still firing with the other.

"You're supposed to run away," I mumbled through a yawn. "You promised."

"The hell I did." He shoved me behind a massive elm tree. "We have to get out of here. Any of your secret gates around here?"

The moonlight was almost as bright as sunlight, searing my pupils. Everything else was blurry. I squinted, tried to make out the shape of the trees around us, the valleys, the location of the river.

"Over there?" I suggested hesitantly. "On the other side of that valley. Maybe."

He kept firing, to give us some cover, and I concentrated on not passing out. Those jagged rocks looked just as comfortable as the ferns. Just a little nap.

"Don't you dare," Kieran said sharply. "You can't sleep yet."

"But I'm so tired."

"Keep moving."

"Wait. The rocks . . ." I rubbed my eyes. "There's a gate behind those rocks."

"Good, get—*ooof*." A dagger bit into his arm, cut through thick leather and skin. Blood welled like plump raspberries. He gritted his teeth. "Just a cut. Keep moving."

I had to crawl through the undergrowth, feeling through the dead leaves for the handle. The iron was cool under my fingers, the rust rough against my palm.

"Got it."

Kieran kicked out at a *Hel-Blar* who was far too close for comfort. He kicked out again, switched his gun for one that shot little vials. The first one hit the ground and broke open, releasing a cross between mist and powder. It was delicate as lace, hovering in the air. I felt funny, entranced by the way it clung to leaves and the *Hel-Blar*.

Hypnos.

"Stop," Kieran commanded grimly. The *Hel-Blar* paused, confused. They hissed frantically but didn't move. I didn't move either. "You," he said to the vampires straining against invisible chains. "You'll get the hell out of here and you won't come back. You'll keep running until you're clear out of the country. And if you try to drink a single drop from any human, you'll walk straight into the next sunrise."

A howl, a grunt.

"Go." They shuffled away. I lay where I was, unable to move. Kieran crouched beside me, his expression regretful but determined,

"I'm sorry," he said.

"Kier—"

"Shhh," he interrupted. "Don't say anything." The Hypnos powder worked through me, making my limbs heavy, my voice falter. "I have to do this, Solange," he murmured. He brushed a kiss over my forehead, gentle as moth wings. Anger and fear burned through me, betrayal was a conflagration that might burn the entire forest to the ground. When I'd suggested he betray me, I hadn't thought he'd take me literally. I'd been a fool to trust him.

And now it was too late.

CHAPTER 22

♦

Lucy

Sunday evening, later still

"I don't know how I let you talk me into this," Nicholas muttered as we ducked into the corridor. "It's a bad idea."

"It's brilliant," I insisted with more certainty than I actually felt. The corridor was damp and cold and confining and hardly gave us an advantage in a fight. But the only alternative was the woods, which were swarming with renegade Helios agents.

Sometimes my life was just weird.

Nicholas stayed close, his arm stretched behind him so that his hand could grip mine. I tugged experimentally. He tugged back.

"I'm losing feeling in my fingers," I complained. He relaxed his hold, infinitesimally. His eyes caught the glow from the torchlight, reflected it like a wolf's eyes might. He wasn't just the Nicholas I'd argued with since I was little, he wasn't even the Nicholas that had kissed me senseless yesterday; he was another Nicholas altogether. The hunter had risen to the surface.

I should probably be worrying about the fact that I was about to walk into the vampire courts instead of staring at his butt. Staring at his butt made me feel less like hyperventilating.

"Breathe," Nicholas murmured, sounding half-strained, half-comforting. "Your heart's not meant to skip beats like that."

I wiped my free hand on my pants, hoping the palm he was holding wasn't as sweaty. I'd changed into a pair of Solange's cargos, assuming they looked more like something a secret agent would wear than my velvet skirts and beaded scarves. There was clay all over the left leg. It made me feel like crying for some reason. I was trying so hard not to imagine the hundreds of horrible things that might have happened to my best friend. She had to be safe. Absolutely nothing else was acceptable. Nicholas's thumb made small soft circles over my knuckles. I released my pent-up breath. My eyes stopped burning. We could do this. We *had* to, it was that simple.

"I'm okay," I whispered.

"I—" He cut himself off, squeezed my hand once, hard. My heart stopped, then leaped into overdrive. I couldn't hear anything except the blood rushing in my ears and the drip of water, even though I was listening as hard as I possibly could. He sniffed once. I tensed all over; even my eyelids felt tight. He held up three fingers. Since he wasn't speaking, not even a whisper, I assumed it was vampires.

Footsteps were suddenly audible and they were incredibly close. I reached for one of my stakes, wondering suddenly if I was really going to be able to stick it into someone's chest. As a theory it worked fine; as an actual attempt to shove a hunk of whitethorn wood through bone and flesh and heart, I wasn't so sure. In any case, I didn't have the time to consider my options. Nicholas pushed me against the damp wall. His hand fisted in my hair and tugged my head until my neck was exposed. He ripped off the Drake cameo I'd forgotten to take off. His eyes met mine, his lips lifting slowly off his teeth. His canines were sharp, long, and gleaming like pearls. I wasn't quite as immune to his pheromones as I'd assumed. I was mesmerized, and he pressed even closer to me.

And then we weren't alone anymore.

I could tell he knew the moment the hall disgorged the three vampires, but he didn't turn or freeze or give himself away. He only dragged his mouth over the arch of my bare neck until I shivered. My crossbow was slung back, hanging behind me.

"Hey." One of them snickered.

Nicholas kept his back to them—risky, but not as risky as giving himself away as one of the Drake brothers. His teeth scraped my throat. I shivered again.

"Busy," he drawled at them. "Get your own."

"No time to have a drink," they replied. "Hunting the Drakes. Seen any?"

Nicholas shrugged one shoulder.

"At the farmhouse, usually. Second door around the corner will get you out into the woods." And straight into the eager, waiting arms of Hope's agents.

"Thanks."

He only grunted, nibbling my ear. My hair fell over his face, veiling his features. We stayed as we were until even he couldn't hear the receding footsteps anymore. He pushed away from me as if it was the hardest thing he'd ever done. His jaw was clenched so tightly, the muscles in his cheek jumped.

"That was close," he ground out.

I nodded, trying to catch my breath. "Thank God they were in such a hurry."

"That's not what I meant," he whispered.

"Oh." I stayed where I was, even as he leaned against the opposite wall, jerking his hand viciously through his hair. "Are you okay?"

"Let's just get this over with," he growled.

"How are we going to find your parents?" I asked as we started jogging down the corridor.

"If they're not already at the courts, they should be in the woods just outside. This way." He pushed open a grate in the ceiling and made a stirrup out of his linked hands for me to step up into. I leaped, he threw, and I landed half in the dirt with my legs dangling. I scrambled out of the way. He shot up out of the earth, landing in a graceful crouch. He tossed his hair off his face.

"Let's go."

The wind was warm, pushing its way between the leaves, but there were no other sounds—not a single cricket chirping or a rabbit dashing for safety. I walked as carefully as I could, trying not to break any twigs to give away our location. The mountain crouched over us, solid and filled with secrets. I used to worry about bears this far into the wild, not vampire queens.

We ran for a while, until I had to stop, panting, and rest against an elm tree. My lungs burned and sweat soaked my hair. I pressed a hand to my chest.

"Just a minute," I gasped. "Just a minute."

Nicholas looked around, nostrils flaring.

"Nothing," he said, his fists clenching. "I can't smell them anywhere—it's all Lady Natasha and her damned Araksaka." He slapped at a low-hanging branch. "Solange doesn't have any time left."

"I know," I said quietly. "But she's stronger than you think."

"Not during the bloodchange. She'll be out cold."

"Even then," I insisted stubbornly. "You don't know her like I do."

"Lucy." He looked beaten. "Listen, you have to face—"

"No," I interrupted fiercely. "*You* listen. We will find her. We will save her. Period. Okay?" I blinked back tears, fighting a bubble of hysteria in my throat. "Okay?"

He stepped closer, and I had to wipe my eyes so he wasn't blurry.

"Shh." He touched my cheek very gently. "Okay, Lucy. Okay."

I pushed away from the tree even though my legs still felt like jelly. "So we keep looking."

He looked at me for a long moment and then nodded. "If Mom's planning to attack the courts, she'll do it through the side entrance there. No one ever uses it anymore. If they're not there, we'll leave a message for them."

I armed my crossbow. He winced.

"Careful with that thing."

"Yeah, yeah."

We climbed through the brush, using tree roots as handholds, scattering pebbles underfoot no matter how carefully I stepped. The entrance was blocked with rocks.

They weren't there.

Nicholas didn't lose his temper again, only crouched and made marks on the rock with the edge of a broken stone. There were no marks already there, waiting for him to decipher. His parents hadn't been this way after all.

"And if your dad was the one with the plan?"

"Then he'll already be in there, talking treaties."

"They might still be looking for Solange, might have found her and brought her home."

"Maybe."

"So what do we do now?"

"Plan B."

I stared at him, the back of my neck prickling. "Plan B?"

He nodded grimly. "Royal guard, coming from the west."

"Shit." I fumbled for the set of handcuffs we'd found in the weapons room. We'd made sure to open the links in the chain that secured them together so he could break free if our plans went awry, which they already had. He held out his wrists and I snapped them shut. I, at least, got to keep all of my weapons, though he had made me hide my pink rhinestone stake. I added a swagger to my walk. I was pretty sure all Helios-Ra agents learned the swagger along with how to sharpen their weapons and the proper way to apply holy water.

"Why are you limping like that?" Nicholas demanded.

"I'm swaggering," I informed him.

"You look like you're wearing a diaper."

Charming. And I had a crush on this guy.

Wait.

I had a crush on this guy?

"Now what?" he asked. "You're making weird faces."

"Nothing," I said quickly. "Never mind." One crisis at a time.

Speaking of a crisis.

Two of Natasha's Araksaka came at us, quick as wasps. The insignia of Natasha's house was tattooed over the left side of their faces: three detailed raven feathers. One was a huge oiled man who belonged on the set of *Conan the Barbarian*. The other was a petite black-haired woman whose smile was feral enough to make my palms sweat again.

"Who are you?" she demanded.

"I'm here to collect the bounty," I announced, my voice cracking only slightly. I tossed my hair off my face in a way I hoped looked cool and nonchalant and not like a nervous tic, which it most definitely was. The woman sniffed, narrowed her eyes.

"Human."

"Go away, little girl," the man said brusquely. "You don't want to come in here."

The woman took a step closer. "Humans don't collect bounties," she snarled. "Helios."

I moved the crossbow slightly, still keeping it at the level of her chest. Moonlight glinted off the dented sun pendant around my neck. "I'm with Hope, actually."

Something flickered in their faces but I couldn't read it. She jerked her head in a nod for us to follow. I poked Nicholas in the shoulder with the crossbow.

"Move it," I ordered. He walked slowly in front of me and I tried not to look as if I was nervous enough to drop my crossbow and shoot myself in the foot. Which was a distinct possibility.

It took forever to climb down and around to the cave entrance. Two more guards waited at the door. They didn't say a word, barely glanced at us. Halfway down a damp tunnel, a woman with long curly hair stepped into view, and several more guards came up behind us. They bowed, but only quickly, so I guessed she wasn't Lady Natasha. I expected the queen of the vampire tribes might not pout so peevishly. But then I'd never met royalty, vampire or otherwise.

"Is this a Drake boy?" She sniffed once, disdainfully. "Pretty enough, I grant you, but hardly seems worth all the fuss."

"Juliana, go away," the female guard snapped impatiently.

Juliana frowned. "You should be more polite. I am the queen's sister, after all."

"Go away, *my lady*," the guard amended. "Lady Natasha's orders are to keep you safe."

"I hardly think these children are a danger to me," she said scornfully, but she eventually drifted away. The rest of the guards pressed behind me. The silence stretched, like a bowstring about to snap. I knew the rules: show no fear. And I couldn't just wait around until they decided to rip out my throat.

"Look, are we going to stand around here all night staring at each other? I want my reward."

"This way."

Actually, standing around was starting to have some appeal.

The damp cavern gave way to an arched stone hallway lit with oil lamps set into deep crevices. The dirt floor became flagstone layered with Persian rugs as we went deeper into the labyrinthine caves. The Araksaka fanned out, three in front, three in back. I felt like I was in the middle of a particularly tense vampire sandwich.

Shadowed figures coalesced in the dark openings to watch us pass. Eyes and teeth gleamed menacingly. By the time we reached the central cave, which was surprisingly tall, with jeweled stalactites, a crowd of pale-eyed vampires waited for us. Quartz glittered in the walls between hand-embroidered tapestries showing various events in vampire history and lore. There was a lot of red thread. The furniture was an eclectic mixture of antiques passed down through the centuries. It was mostly old wood, with a smooth patina of age, accented with a few modern pieces here and there.

I was trying really hard not to focus on the hissing. Even growing up around the Drakes wasn't quite enough to immunize me to that many vampires. The air was so thick with pheromones that adrenaline poured through my bloodstream. I felt a little drunk and edgy with it. More than one vampire licked his lips, staring at me like I was chocolate mousse cake. I lifted my crossbow threateningly. The vampires eased back, but only barely.

There were mirrors everywhere. There were massive ones in gilded frames, tall cheval glasses, small broken shards glued to the wall. And in the center of the cavern, there was a single throne made of whitethorn wood, the kind that makes the best stakes, carved into dozens of pale crows. Every feather was painstakingly detailed, and their obsidian eyes glittered in the torchlight. Sitting on the throne, smiling faintly, was Lady Natasha. She was beautiful, of course, and dramatic, with long, straight blond hair. Her bangs were cut straight over arched brows and pale blue eyes so light they appeared nearly translucent. She was slender and as white as a birch sapling.

"And what have we here?" she murmured, sultry as a long summer night. Her voice held back the ocean of tension as if it were a cup of water. "Hansel and Gretel, lost in the woods?"

Soft laughter draped over us like fur blankets. I locked my knees together so they wouldn't shake.

"I've come for the bounty," I announced. "I've captured a Drake."

"Have you now?" One of her guards handed her a glass goblet filled with blood. She took a dainty sip, dabbed at her lips with a square of lace. "And you are?"

"I'm with Hope."

"I see." She tilted her head. "Arrogant smirk, lovely cheekbones. Yes, this is definitely one of Liam's spawn."

"Go to hell," Nicholas spat.

"And Helena's spawn as well, clearly. Abominable manners."

"The bounty?" I asked, my brain racing frantically. We needed to leave this main hall with its crowds of vampires, but I didn't know how to get us out of there.

Lucy

And then it went from bad to worse.

Much, much worse.

Kieran Black stalked toward us, trailing guards. His face was all angles, his smile sharp and insolent. In his hands he held a wooden box inlaid with pearls. Before any of us could move or even speak, he flipped open the lid.

Inside, a heart dripped blood through the iron hinges.

"The heart of Solange Drake," he announced. "Your Majesty."

CHAPTER 23

◆

Lucy

Everything stopped.

I couldn't bring myself to look away from the red lump bleeding in the delicate box. The pearls went pink under the oozing blood. Nausea rolled in my stomach. I couldn't form a coherent thought, couldn't move, could barely breathe.

Not Solange. Not Solange.

Kieran stood like any good soldier, looking straight ahead, blood dripping at his feet. He was muddy and tired, his sleeves pushed up to display his Helios-Ra tattoo. I had never physically hated anyone in my entire life the way I hated him now.

"No," I finally choked out. "It's not possible."

"So many gifts," Lady Natasha murmured, rising gracefully to her feet.

And then, chaos.

Lucy

"My baby sister," Nicholas yelled, leaping into the air, fangs extended, snapping his handcuffs apart. He aimed at Kieran's throat, his eyes like silver coins. Lady Natasha raised an eyebrow, and it was as if she'd let out a battle yell. Araksaka closed in from all directions so quickly their feather tattoos seemed to flutter.

"Nicholas, behind you!" It wasn't enough to help him in any way, but it was just enough to give ourselves away entirely. I was hardly part of Hope's unit if I was trying to save my Drake captive. And I did try. I went to pull one of my stakes from its sheath, but it was as if I were moving in slow motion and everyone else was in fast-forward, like those nature documentaries where an orchid blooms and wilts in three seconds. Only we were trapped in a garden of vampires, blooming like deadly nightshade and belladonna and thirsty for our blood.

Nicholas didn't land as he'd planned, thrown off course by the flying granny boot of an Araksaka, which caught him full in the chest. Kieran went into a roll and came up several feet away, bloody heart rolling across the floor. I gagged as it came to a soggy halt near my left foot. I was shaking and choking on the bile in my throat and absolutely no match for the guards who grabbed me.

"Get off her." Nicholas struggled as he was hauled to his feet, nose bleeding sluggishly. Kieran wouldn't look at me. Lady Natasha flicked her hand.

"Such drama," she said, as if we were a dinner show that bored her.

For all I knew, we *were* the dinner show.

And dinner, for that matter.

"I haven't time for children," she said. "There are still preparations to be made for the ball tomorrow night." She patted a stool next to her throne. "Have a seat near me, dear boy." She smiled at Kieran, showing teeth like polished shells. "We have much to celebrate. Civil war has been averted, thanks in part to you."

"I only want the money."

I spat at him. I couldn't help it. I was immobilized between two Araksaka and there was nothing else I could do.

At the moment.

Because, karmic baggage or not, if I got through this alive, I was going to break more than his nose.

Lady Natasha sniffed with distaste. "Barbaric." She waved a hand. "Take them away, won't you? They're becoming tiresome."

Nicholas and I were dragged out of the plush hall. I was shorter than my captors and my feet dangled slightly off the ground. The stairs were narrow and damp, cut roughly out of the stone and leading into more damp and more darkness. One of them shoved me, and I stumbled down the last few steps, landing hard on my hip. I could hear Nicholas struggling, cursing.

"Lucy! Lucy, are you okay?"

"I'm fine," I forced out, once my breath returned. "Ouch!" I was hauled back up to my feet and none too gently. The stairs had led us down to dungeons. Actual dungeons, carved out of rock, with slick iron gates and the chitter of rats. "This is so not good," I muttered, fear making me mouthy as usual. "You can't seriously think you can keep us here. We have friends, you know, angry friends. And you're serving a paranoid selfish—*urk*." My tirade was cut abruptly short by a hand to my throat. I couldn't even swallow, couldn't breathe, could only feel my face turning purple. I tried to make a sound, scratched at the unbending fingers. The eyes that met mine were cold, flat. And then I was sailing backward into a cell, hitting the wall with enough force to make me see stars. I slumped, gasping. Nicholas was shoved into the only other cell, across from me.

"My family will come," he promised darkly.

"As it should be," the guard said. "The Drake clan will witness the final crowning of Lady Natasha, with none to usurp her throne."

"Solange didn't even want your stupid crown," I croaked through my bruised throat. "Or your throne."

"She was a threat, now she's not."

I opened my mouth to yell. I was angry and bereft and afraid and all of those things made my temper harder to control than usual. Nicholas's eyes flared at me warningly. He was right. I could swear and fume all I wanted, it wouldn't change anything. And I was already bruised all over, and we'd been here less than a half hour. I wasn't exactly a force to be reckoned with. I slumped against the wall and held my tears until the royal guard had filed out and we were alone with the cold drafts and the mildew. Sobs finally racked through me and I couldn't stop them. They were loud and ugly, not like movie tears, which always seem so delicate and fragile. My tears burned and stung and didn't make me feel the slightest bit better.

I'd known Solange all of my life. Sometimes I knew her better than I knew myself. She was solitary and clever and elegant even when she was adamant that was she was no such thing. She was special, and not just because she was the only vampire daughter.

She was loyal and had always been there for me, no matter what. She was the one who nursed me through countless ill-advised crushes; she was the one who snuck me ice cream when my parents discovered tofu desserts and wouldn't buy anything else. She was quiet and strong and artistic.

It was unthinkable that she was dead.

I gagged on more tears. It wasn't right. This wasn't how it was supposed to happen. We were supposed to be at her house, where she'd drink her first taste of blood at midnight tonight and wake up sixteen years old and dead—or reborn, technically, whatever. Not this. Never this.

"Lucy." Nicholas pressed against the iron bars. I had no idea how long he'd been saying my name. I was curled into a ball, my eyes swollen. I wiped my nose on my sleeve.

"Sorry," I said, blinking away the last of the tears. More hovered behind my lids, clutching at my throat, but I had to fight them back. It wasn't in me to just give up, even when I desperately wanted to. I couldn't force a smile, but at least I could sit up. Nicholas looked worried and wretched. "What are we going to do?" I asked.

His fists clenched around the bars.

"We're going to get out of here somehow. They're going to take us up to the hall for the ball. Lady Natasha wants to gloat and show the vampire clans that she's defeated the Drakes. It's posturing."

"I really hate her."

"I know."

"No, I mean, like, a lot."

"Me too."

"And Kieran, that rat." My voice caught. "I'm going to break his nose again. And the rest of him."

"I'll help."

"My mom's going to make me spend weekends at the ashram for the next ten years to cleanse me of all this violence if we survive."

"*When* we survive," he corrected. He was pale, almost misty in the flickering light of the single torch on the wall between us. Smoke hung near the low ceiling, darkening the stones. "Dawn's not far off," he said, frustrated. His eyes looked bruised, even from a distance. "I won't be able to stay awake much longer." He sat on the ground, leaned his head back on the wall. "I'm sorry I wasn't able to protect you."

"Right back at you."

He half smiled. "Don't shoot your mouth off while I'm asleep."

"I can't make any promises."

"My family *will* come," he said again.

I thought of Liam's grim face, of Helena's sword flashing.

"I can't wait."

CHAPTER 24

◆

Solange

I lay there for a long time. I could have been there hours, days, months; I'd lost track. There was only my breath becoming longer and deeper and slower. I felt like a dandelion gone to fluffy white seed, drifting on the wish of some petulant child. I hoped my family was safe, tucked into the old farmhouse. I'd miss its crooked halls and creaky floors and my little pottery shed with its views of the fields and the woods and the mountains beyond. I'd miss Nicholas nagging at me to be careful, Lucy arguing with everyone about everything, Kieran's quiet confidence.

At first I thought I'd imagined the faint clang.

But the voices were real, echoing down to my bed. I tried to move, to open my eyes, but nothing happened.

"This is the one," someone said. The voice was rough. "I can smell her."

"Aye, like bloodwine just waiting to be sipped."

The footsteps approached. I managed to pry one eye open, not enough that anyone would notice, just enough that the faint light showed me two men and a woman through the fringe of my lashes. Each of their faces was tattooed with the three raven feathers of the royal house.

Araksaka.

I tried harder to move, to scream, to kick out. It was as if I was barely in my body—it paid virtually no attention to my frantic commands.

"Not quite out yet, are you sweetheart?" I tried to fight but only dangled limply over his arms when he picked me up. His mouth was very near my neck. I shuddered violently. "Just a little taste."

"Michel, no." Someone plucked me away like an apple off a tree. "Lady Natasha would have your head," he said. "And more importantly, mine as well."

"But she smells so delicious."

"Put in your damn nose plugs—you know it's the bloodchange pheromones."

"Spoilsport."

"If you two are quite finished courting," the woman snapped, looking down as she climbed the rope back up to the forest floor. "We don't have much time."

My captor slung me over his shoulder and went up the rope, quick as a hummingbird. The light in the woods was faintly gray, the sky like a black pearl. I could feel the approach of dawn, the way I'd never actually felt it before. It was like a weight on my chest, like being wrapped in chains and dropped into the ocean.

The guards felt it just as keenly as I did, I could tell by the way they lowered their heads and ran faster than I'd ever seen a vampire run. The trees blurred into shadows, the leaves slapping at us faintly as we passed. Coyotes yipped hysterically from the valley behind us. The mountain loomed closer and closer, blocking out the shimmer of light on the horizon. The woman cursed. They ran faster. I hoped they crumbled into ashes, even if it meant I would too.

And then we were at the caves and they leaped inside as if their feet were on fire. The first spear of sunlight hurled from the sky, fell between the branches and struck the ground. It gilded the humus underfoot, the curling ferns, the white birch bark peeling into strips. The woman cursed again.

"Too damn close."

That would be my very last moment of sunlight. Ever. My skin itched all over. I was certain that if I'd been caught out there, I would have blistered as badly as the other vampires would have.

I was taken down a narrow tunnel and into a circular hall with rugs on the floor and tapestries on the walls. Torches burned and candles were scattered everywhere, like stars on a clear winter night. Ravens cawed from floor to ceiling in wrought-iron cages, eyes gleaming like jet beads. The few vampires there stopped what they were doing and followed us to a white throne, trailing behind us like the train of a wedding dress. Lady Natasha was on her feet, her face so pale it could have been carved out of moonstone. Even her hair seemed stunned, white as orchids. I might have enjoyed that brief moment of victory, if I hadn't seen Kieran beside her, equally pale. What was he still doing here? Our plan was falling apart around us and there wasn't a single thing I could do about it.

"Is that Solange Drake?" Lady Natasha's voice was cold enough to crack steel. I couldn't quite place her accent. It seemed vaguely French, vaguely Russian.

The guard still carrying me lowered himself to one knee.

"Yes, my lady. We found her in the woods."

"Did you now?" She turned her head a fraction of an inch toward Kieran. He was staring at me, so many emotions chasing across his face that I didn't have time to decipher them all.

Our plan hadn't worked after all.

Natasha gestured to a silver plate on which lay a roasted heart, swimming in a pond of blood. The pearl-studded iron box Kieran had taken from the chest before leaving me to go hunting sat nearby. "And what, pray tell, is this delicacy I was about to consume?"

Kieran didn't answer, didn't look away from me as I was released to tumble to the carpet.

"I asked you a question, boy." One backhand and Kieran was crashing into the table, scattering a vase of roses, a crystal bowl, and the silver plate. The heart hit the side of the throne and slid slowly down in a syrupy trail of blood. I would have gagged, but even my throat was too tired from the bloodchange to react. Kieran coughed, rubbing his chest as he pushed himself up into a sitting position.

"It's a deer heart," he replied without inflection.

"How very clever," she purred. One of the royal guards winced at the sound. She raised an eyebrow at the guard still on one knee.

"We've much to do apparently. The ball will go on as planned, and we'll set the Drake girl up on the dais so that everyone can watch her die, along with any threat to our unity."

"No." Kieran leaped to his feet.

She smiled at him.

"And you'll watch every moment of it, after which, I will pull your heart out of your puny rib cage and eat it. Seeing as I was denied my treat."

"Solange doesn't want your throne or Montmartre," Kieran insisted, crouching to put his back to a tapestry of a maiden drinking from a white unicorn, when two guards began closing in on him. "She doesn't want to be queen of the damn vampires."

"Don't be stupid." Lady Natasha paused, turned to the doorway. She sighed. "Now what? I don't recall inviting you."

"There's been a change of plans." Hope marched into the room, two agents behind her. Her eyes narrowed. "Kieran. What the hell are you doing here?"

Natasha lifted her chin.

"Kieran?" she repeated icily. "As in the son of Hart's brother? When you killed him you said you had everything under control."

Kieran froze. He looked as if he was going to choke on his fury.

"What?" He turned slowly toward Hope. "What did she just say?"

"Everything is under control, but I hardly expected you to invite a Helios agent into your court."

"He brought me a heart." Lady Natasha nodded toward me. I was still sprawled on the carpet. "Clearly not hers."

"Well, the Drakes are on to me now," Hope snapped.

"You," Kieran bit out, fists clenching.

Hope didn't look particularly concerned with the hatred pouring out of him.

"I'm doing what I have to for the Helios-Ra, and I guarantee it's more than your father or uncle could ever have accomplished. Lady Natasha understands that. We look after our own."

Kieran didn't bother with more debate; he launched himself at her. He didn't make it within two feet of her, of course, not with her men there and the Araksaka as well. He didn't have a chance. I doubt that mattered to him.

"Honestly, children these days." Natasha waved her hand, looking bored. "Take them away."

CHAPTER 25

◆

Lucy

Monday morning

I must have dozed off, even though the thought of it seemed impossible. The sound of the iron lock opening woke me up. I was on my feet before my eyes were even fully open. It was the *Conan* extra who had led us into the hall yesterday. His muscles were even bigger close up, but he looked a little haggard. I had no idea how long I'd slept, but Nicholas was out cold in his cell, didn't even stir at the sound of the iron gate swinging open on rusty hinges. I might have tried to dart around the guard but he was big enough to block the entire space and, anyway, where would I go? Up the stairs into the main hall?

He placed a jug of water on the floor. "You should clean up."

I frowned. "What? Why?" For some reason I thought his voice

sounded familiar, but I was pretty sure I would have remembered him if I'd seen him before.

"It's expected."

"Well, you can take your—"

"Stay down," he advised quietly. "And keep your mouth shut."

Was he actually trying to help me? The apple he tossed me nearly hit me in the face. I caught it mostly by reflex. Then I realized why I recognized his voice. He was the vampire who'd come to the window of the farmhouse and offered his allegiance.

He straightened at the sound of footsteps on the stairs. His expression went hard, blank. Two women came up behind him, not tattooed with the mark of Araksaka but not exactly friendly, either. They brought in a basket and a beautiful gown, all brocade and embroidered velvet with a square neckline and panniers and lace petticoats. It was burgundy with pale blue crystal beads and accents on the bodice and around the hem. The dress's hanger was placed on a hook intended for iron chains and other methods of torture.

Now I was really confused.

That the basket was filled with a silver-backed hairbrush, a hand mirror, a square of lavender soap, and vials of perfume didn't clear things up even a little.

"Um . . . what is all this stuff?"

The women eyed me critically.

"It should fit. The shoes look too small, you'll have to go barefoot."

"I'm supposed to wear that costume?" At any other time, I would have been thrilled to prance around in some old-fashioned gown dripping with ornamentation.

"You can't very well attend a ball in those dirty things, can you?" She sneered at my pants. "It would be an insult to our queen."

I felt staggered. I actually pressed a hand to my temple.

"Wait, it's an actual ball? Waltzing and canapés and glass slippers?" My very first ball and it was in honor of a lunatic murderer and would likely end with a vampire killing me. And I had to dress up for the pleasure?

"Don't get the dress dirty," one of them said.

"Why not?"

"Lady Natasha would be . . . displeased."

"This is totally surreal," I muttered after they'd left me alone with my very own ball gown. There was a zipper up the side, so at least I wasn't expected to contort myself around to do up my own laces. Hyacinth had always said the reason well-to-do ladies had maidservants was because none of the clothes were user-friendly. The gown was beautiful, embellished by hand, every minute detail perfectly done. And I didn't want to wear it, not one bit. I edged back as if were dipped in poison.

Instead of using the water in the jug to wash with, I drank every drop. I was thirsty and hungry enough that my stomach cramped around the apple I ate. I paced a while because I literally had no idea what else to do with myself. This was the last situation I'd ever expected to be in. I was at a complete loss.

"Nicholas," I called out. He was on his back, still as stone. "Nicholas," I tried again. Nothing. Not a flicker of an eyelash. I gave up and went back to pacing. After an hour of pacing, my calves were sore and I was feeling dizzy. I used the chamber pot, while I knew Nicholas was still asleep, and then decided to put the dress on when I realized that if the guards came down and I was still in Solange's cargos, they'd likely strip me down themselves. A white cotton slip dress went on first, followed by the panniers, which were basically two baskets hanging on a wide leather belt that went around my waist. It felt weird and bulky. The dress went on top and was heavier than it looked. The fabric was stiff and tight enough that I had no choice but to stand up straight. There was a blue velvet choker. I wished I still had the Drake family cameo; I'd attach it out of spite.

And it might give me courage.

Because I talked a good game, but the truth was, my knees were weak as water and I felt sick to my stomach. Panic was stealthy and it hunted me on soft, silent feet, not quite closing in but never going away, either.

So when Conan returned, I really thought that I was hallucinating.

Kieran was thrown into Nicholas's cell, his face bloody and bruised, his left arm hugged to his chest as if it was broken. But what really caught my attention was the body draped over Conan's huge arms, gently placed on the pallet beside me.

Solange.

CHAPTER 26

◆

Lucy

It was surprisingly difficult to crouch down by Solange's side, and not just because of the ridiculous dress. Her head lolled to one side as if even her neck was too tired to hold it up. I couldn't tell if she was breathing, and my hands shook as I leaned closer. I really didn't want to see a gaping hole in my best friend's chest. I wouldn't just dirty Lady Natasha's dress, I'd throw up all over it.

"It wasn't *her* heart," Kieran groaned from his cell. "It was a *deer* heart."

"Shut up," I shot back. "I don't know if I'm talking to you yet." I touched Solange's shoulder. She was cool and covered in mud. "Solange?"

"It's the bloodchange."

"I said shut up," I tossed over my shoulder. "I know what it is, she's my best friend, isn't she?" I narrowed my eyes. "And you look like shit."

"Arm's broken," he agreed. He looked gray, hollowed. "Hope killed my dad."

"I told you it wasn't the Drakes." I wrinkled my nose. I could hear my dad in my head, going on about compassion. "And I'm sorry. Not that I don't still want to wring your neck."

"I had to be believable, for all the good it did. Hope's up there. She gave me away."

"Want me to break her nose?"

"Hell, yes."

"I'll add it to my list."

"What are you and Nicholas doing here anyway?"

"Hope," I told him. "She escaped and sent her unit in to take over the farmhouse. Nicholas and I made it out. We were hoping to warn his parents off but we couldn't find them. And they're still out there looking for Solange."

"I'm sure they're here or near enough anyway. They don't strike me as the type to stay out of the action for long."

"That's true," I said, buoyed. I turned back to Solange. "Thank God, she's alive. When she wakes up I'm going to kill her." I brushed her hair back. "If you can hear me, Sol, you better come through this. I know you can do it. Your namby brothers did it, so you can, too." I draped my discarded sweater over her. "What the hell was she doing, anyway?" I asked Kieran.

"She was running away."

"No way."

"We found Hyacinth."

My heart dropped. "Is she . . . ?"

"She should survive, if they got her home quickly enough."

"Assuming there's still a home, of course. Hope's got it in her crosshairs."

He shifted, swore when he bumped his arm. I tossed him my belt since I wasn't sure he'd be able to get his own off. Nicholas was still lying in a heap in the corner.

"Here, set your arm."

"Thanks." Sweat beaded his forehead as he worked to wrap the belt around his shoulder. He looked like he knew what he was doing. "Do a lot of battlefield medicine, do you?"

"You've met the Drakes."

"Good point."

I watched him struggle and sighed irritably. "I guess I don't hate you after all."

"I tried to save her." He pulled the belt tight with his teeth. Lines of pain etched around his mouth. "She was supposed to be safe underground."

"Everything's such a mess," I mumbled.

"It's worse than you think."

"Of course it is." I rubbed my face. "I'm afraid to ask, I really am." At least my panic seemed to have desensitized itself.

"Lady Natasha wants to watch Solange die as the entertainment for her freakin' ball."

I ground my teeth. "Oh, I *don't* think so." I reached for the vial of Veronique's blood Logan had said she was wearing around her neck. I frowned, lifted her head to see if it had fallen behind her. "Where's the vial? Kieran, where is it?"

"She used it to save Hyacinth."

"What?" I let her head drop, none too gently. "It's the only thing that could have saved her." I slapped the ground. "You know what this means?" I asked grimly.

"What?"

"Lady Natasha might just get her wish."

◆

Monday evening

When Nicholas finally woke up, it wasn't pretty. He went from unconscious to hyperalert so fast I missed the transition.

"You bloody bastard." His eyes flashed as he stalked him. "You killed my sister!"

"Wait—," Kieran screamed when Nicholas grabbed his broken arm. He kicked out, aiming for Nicholas's knees. There was a grunt, more sounds of fists and feet hitting flesh.

"Nicholas!" I shouted through the bars. "Nicholas, stop it."

"He killed Solange."

"No, he didn't." Kieran was dangling off the ground, his face going purple. "Put him down."

"He has to pay."

"Nicholas Drake."

He didn't let go, but he did finally turn to look at me. I pointed to Solange, on her back on the pallet. He dropped Kieran so fast, Kieran stumbled.

"Solange? Solange!"

"She hasn't moved since they brought her here."

He finally grinned, looking like the Nicholas I remembered from the Christmas Eve he got his first bike. "She's not dead!" He frowned. "Why don't you look happier?"

"She gave her vial away."

"She gave her . . . son of a bitch."

I leaned my forehead on the cold bars.

"Today just sucks." I tried for a smile. "On the plus side, I get to see you prance around in tights."

Only his eyebrow moved, but it was enough. "I beg your pardon?"

I pointed to the pile of clothes on the ground by his foot. "Your formal wear."

He glanced at it, then back at me. "Nice dress. Can you breathe in that thing?"

I smoothed the front of my dress. "It would be much more fun to wear if it wasn't what I was going to be buried in."

"You are not going to be buried." He paused, lifted the clothes up suspiciously. "Vampires don't bury their victims," he added distractedly.

"Hey, looking for comfort here."

"Sorry." He shook out the doublet, complete with lace froth at the cuffs. "Logan would love this." He smirked at me. "No tights." He dropped everything. "I'm still not wearing this crap."

"They seemed rather adamant."

"She can kiss my—hey." He scowled at Kieran. "There's only one costume. How come you don't have dress up like some eighteenth-century jackass?"

Kieran was still cradling his arm, his hair damp with sweat.

He looked wan but still managed to smirk back. "I'm not a prince from the illustrious Drake family."

"Cut it out." Nicholas's ears actually went red. I was so going to tease him about that later. "I'm not a bloody prince."

"May as well be." Kieran shrugged his good shoulder. "Lady Natasha knows more than half her court would defect if Solange wanted them to. They're just waiting for a better offer."

"I'm still not wearing this." Nicholas plucked at the ribbon on the black velvet sleeve of the doublet

"Yeah, you are," I said cheerfully. "Or else they'll strip you naked when they come get us."

He glared at me for a long time and then pulled off his shirt, muttering vile curses the entire time. I caught a glimpse of bare chest, wondered if I should look away to give him privacy, then decided that it might be my last chance to see him with his shirt off. His arms were lean and sculpted, like a swimmer's.

"I didn't get to see you take your clothes off," he complained.

"That's what you get for sleeping all day," I quipped back. He went farther into the shadows to exchange his pants for the leather breeches. Too bad. When he emerged again, he looked pretty good even though it wasn't his style. And he was lucky there were no tights, after all. He tilted his head.

"You like it."

"Shut up." I blushed. I hated vampire extrasensory perception. It wasn't fair that he could hear my heartbeat or smell my skin or whatever.

"Girls are so weird."

Kieran snorted. "No kidding."

"Please, you two were fighting ten minutes ago, and now you're the best of friends?" I said witheringly. "*Guys* are weird." I turned back to Solange, touched her hand. "She's still not moving."

Nicholas and Kieran both went grim, quiet.

"She'll need blood," Nicholas finally said. "But I'm sure Bruno got hold of my parents by now, and they'll bring it with them. I doubt it's a secret Solange is here. Natasha does rather seem to want to make this as public as possible."

"Do we have a plan?"

"We fight like hell."

"Good plan."

◆

It wasn't long before the Araksaka filed down the stone steps to escort us to the hall. I wouldn't let go of Solange's hand, even when one of them lifted her up to slide an embroidered silver robe over her torn dress. She looked so fragile, with her dark hair and pale features. They marched us upstairs. They wore white silk shirts and heavy breeches, which should have made them look silly but instead made them seem even more fierce. One of them shoved me when I got in the way because I was still clinging to Solange. I stumbled.

"Hey, don't touch my girlfriend." Nicholas seethed.

"Girlfriend?" I blinked at him. He thought of me as his girlfriend? Then I shoved the guard back, before anyone could see me blushing. "I mean, get off of me."

The hall was beautiful, crowded with candles and lanterns hanging from the ceiling and even more mirrors everywhere. Apparently Lady Natasha really liked looking at herself. A long table held countless jugs of every description: silver inlaid with rubies, gold, carved mahogany, painted china. I knew every single one of them held blood. Musicians played in one corner, the soft notes of harp and piano and violin drifting around us.

Lady Natasha's courtiers were easy to recognize—they all wore raven feathers in their hair. The rest kept their allegiances more subtle; I didn't know the meanings behind most of the pendants and embroidered family crests. I didn't see London or anyone else from the Drake family. I did see yards of velvet and silk embroidered with gold thread, brocade gowns, elaborate wigs. I wouldn't have been entirely surprised if Marie Antoinette strolled by. They drifted and lolled and reclined gracefully on chaises and piles of cushions.

Solange was carried up to a dais draped with red sari fabric. In the middle was a glass bier on which she was stretched out. Her hand fell over the side and lay there limply. There were roses all around her. A raven flew down from a crevice in the ceiling and perched patiently at Solange's feet. Another raven landed, and another. Soon she was surrounded by huge black birds, all watching her expectantly. The old-fashioned grandfather clock read nearly midnight. When it rang its twelfth chime Solange would have to wake up then and there.

Or not at all.

"Welcome, welcome," Lady Natasha called from her white throne. We were herded toward her. She wore a white gown with sequined silk over her panniers. Her pale straight hair fell to her elbows, and on her head she wore a medieval horned crown hung with sheer veils that draped to the floor. She dripped diamonds;

they were around her neck, wrists, fingers, and even around her ankles beneath the sway of her bell skirt. Hope sat next to her in an evening gown and high-heeled sandals. And just when I thought it couldn't get much more surreal, Lady Natasha clapped her hands regally.

"Let the celebrations begin."

The crowd broke off into couples in the wide space of the hall, and they whirled in a waltz as the music swelled. They wore medieval dresses, Norse aprons, Tudor whale-boned corsets, Victorian dancing slippers, pin-striped suits from the 1920s, dashing pirate shirts, and velour frock coats. They circled in a kaleidoscope of colors and fabrics until the sheer press of them started to make me dizzy.

Solange lay still; even her chest was frozen, suspended in the bloodchange. Her lips went purple, as if they were bruised. The blue of her veins traced under her parchment skin, like rivers through a winter landscape.

"Her lips are turning blue," I whispered to Nicholas. He nodded grimly.

"She hasn't much time."

I'd never felt so helpless in my life. I could only stand there in the elegant ballroom inside the mountain and watch my best friend struggle not to die. She moved once, jerking as if electricity fired through her. Kieran took one step forward and was roughly shoved backward by one of the guards. Lady Natasha's laugh was light and pretty.

"Soon all this will be over," she said, preening.

"Sooner than you think."

CHAPTER 27

•

Lucy

We whirled, recognizing the voice. Liam stood in a white cloud, wearing silver nose plugs. He pointed to three guards rushing at him with axes.

"Sleep."

They crumpled, axes clattering to the ground.

Hypnos.

"You," Lady Natasha sneered. "You're too late. Your precious daughter has nearly slipped away completely. My throne is safe, this kingdom is safe."

"Let's see, shall we?" Helena asked, her swords flashing, her black braid hanging neatly down her back. Her sons flooded in behind them, joined by Hart and his agents. I'd never seen so many nose plugs and so much black army gear in my whole life.

The waltzing courtiers turned to a more violent dance. The

music was drowned out by the sounds of swords clashing. The tribes chose their sides, and the Drakes and Helios weren't nearly as outnumbered as I'd feared. The Araksaka convened around Lady Natasha—all but Conan. I did what he'd suggested earlier, and I stayed down. In fact, I crawled on my hands and knees through broken crockery toward the bier. The ravens stayed by Solange, cawing viciously. When one bent his head, about to poke into her eye, I picked up a crystal shard and whipped it at him. He squawked and flew off, offended, in a flurry of feathers. I wished I had my crossbow.

Helena was tumbling like some deranged acrobat, flinging knives and stakes as she went. She left a trail of dust and ash behind her. Helios agents scattered like beetles, blowing Hypnos to clear the vampires out of their way. It was like Sleeping Beauty's castle—ladies in fine dresses and gentlemen in complicated cravats all dropping to the Persian rugs, asleep. Crystal vases tumbled off tables; wooden chairs splintered under impact.

Hart's agents ignored Natasha's courtiers once they fell, preferring to attack Hope's rogue unit. Blood splattered the stones, stained the tapestries.

Liam strode toward the bier, his grim eyes never leaving his fading daughter. He took out three vampires without moving his glance away even once. One of Hope's men flew backward after a vicious punch, face bruising before he even hit the wall.

Nicholas rolled toward me, landing at my elbow. His eyes were fierce. He grabbed my chin and kissed me hard. It was over before I had time to react.

"Stay down," he ordered.

"Duh," I shot back, and returned the kiss, just as quick and just as hard before he dove away to gather stakes from a sleeping guard. He rose from a crouch and threw them like deadly confetti. They all moved so fast, it was like a watercolor painting, all blurs and smears. A woman dressed in red silk bared her fangs and hurled a sleek jet stake. Logan caught it before it imbedded itself in Nicholas's chest.

"Shame to ruin such a nice jacket," he said.

"Took your time getting here," Nicholas returned with a grin, whirling to meet the next advance. They fought back to back like a spinning top of fury.

Helena reached Lady Natasha with a feral grin. Lady Natasha lifted her chin haughtily but stepped behind one of her guards. Helena slashed at his raven tattoos relentlessly until it was just her and the queen. Their swords met, clashing like ice cracking in the sea.

Hart followed Hope down the tunnel when she made a dash for safety. The rest of the battle went on, both impossibly quick and dragging on forever.

I kept crawling around the bodies, ducking flying boots and weapons. I had to get to Solange. I reached the bier with only shallow scrapes and a bruise from the elbow of a clumsy Helios-Ra agent. I swatted at the ravens until they flew off, landing on nearby furniture and eyeing me malevolently. Solange was cold, so cold I snatched my fingers back. Her eyelids and fingertips were the same purple as her lips. She made strange wheezing sounds, as if she was trying to breathe but couldn't. Her mouth opened and closed, like a baby bird starving for its first meal.

And I had nothing to give her.

Which wasn't even our biggest problem.

"Natasha, darling, you always did know how to throw a proper party."

The fighting stopped. It was as if someone pressed a cosmic pause button. Everyone turned to stare at the vampire now standing just inside the cave, surrounded by warriors in brown leather tunics. He was smirking, his pale face striking under long black hair. I'd have thought he'd used Hypnos with the way people were reacting. He walked slowly forward, as if he had all the time in the world. His guard kept pace.

"Montmartre," Lady Natasha murmured, satisfied. "I knew you'd come."

Leander Montmartre and his Host. Lady Natasha was the only one who was pleased with this new development. She actually shook Helena off to smooth her hair back into place. The mirrors reflected her smug, chilling smile.

"Yes, darling, but you're looking a little haggard." His gray eyes tracked Solange's fitful breathing, her bruised-looking lips. "I've come for her, actually."

The smile turned to a snarl. "No."

"Of course." He sniffed the air as if it were laced with perfume. "No one else will do, surely you know that."

"She's a child. You love *me*."

"Love." He flicked a surprisingly smooth manicured hand. I would have expected it to have long nails crusted with blood, that's how menacing his aura was. "Don't be banal."

"You've let yourself be swayed by talk of prophecies and legacies. But I'll change that, you'll see. She's nearly dead."

"I'll have her, Natasha," he said coldly.

"You'll die first," she shot back. "Araksaka!"

At Natasha's command her tattooed guard swarmed forward to attack. She threw a whitethorn stake, fangs gleaming. Montmartre's Host bared their own teeth and leaped into the fray. The snarling and growling made the hair on my arms stand up. Vampires turned to ash all around Montmartre, as if he was standing in a dusty field on a windy day.

"A moment, if you please," he interrupted.

Again, the fighting stopped.

"There's no need to thin our numbers this way," he said pleasantly. "All I want is the girl."

"Stay the hell away from my daughter." Helena seethed. She flung her own stake, but one of the Hounds intercepted it before it could hit its mark.

"Your daughter needs me," Montmartre told her. "So you'd best mind your manners when you speak to me." He held up a chain with a glass vial encrusted with silver ivy leaves. "My Host were tracking in the woods and came across this most curious artifact." Every single one of Solange's brothers hissed. "I am assured this was once filled with Veronique's blood, for Solange here. There are only a few drops left, but it should be enough. It rather looks as if she needs it."

Solange was barely breathing, and she was so pale the blue of her veins made her look nearly violet.

She was dying.

Or about to turn into a *Hel-Blar*.

I wasn't sure which was worse.

"Hang on," I whispered. "Please, please hang on."

"I am prepared to let her have this," Montmartre continued, swinging the chain. The Drakes watched it, as if he were a hypnotist. "But I am going to need something in return."

"What is it you want?" Liam asked, standing close to Helena, his hand on her arm. She was straining not to explode.

"Why, I want the queen, of course."

"I'm the queen," Lady Natasha barked. Montmartre ignored her, which enraged her further. The whites of her eyes were slowly going red.

"You give me Solange, and I will give her life."

"No way," I croaked, though no one paid any attention to me.

Liam suddenly looked old, as if all of his years were hitting him at once. He nodded his head once.

"Dad, no!" Quinn advanced.

"She'll die," Liam said. "She doesn't have any time left. We have no options."

Montmartre gave a courtly bow and strode toward the bier, his Host at his side. Liam was jostled, trying to hold back his family.

"Trust me," he whispered.

I felt sick. Montmartre leaned down and picked Solange's unresponsive body up into his arms.

"No," Liam said furiously. "Now. You give it to her now where we can see."

"I don't recall offering that," he said. Solange looked so tiny against his chest.

"*Now.*"

"Montmartre," a new voice interrupted, sounding young but hard. "Weren't you going to invite us to the wedding?"

The girl looked about my age, but she was a vampire, so she could have been a hundred years old for all I knew. She had long black hair and wore a leather tunic and bone beads in her hair. There were tattoos on her hands and arms.

Cwn Mamau. The Hounds.

The Host snarled. The girl and her warriors snarled back. These were the vampires Montmartre had turned and who had then turned against him. The Host hated the Hounds on sight. Montmartre didn't look too pleased either. And for the first time, he looked faintly disconcerted.

"Isabeau. Go home, little girl."

"The Hounds do not support your claim to the throne," she told him very precisely, her accent French. She nodded a greeting to Liam and Helena. "I apologize for the delay." She turned back to Montmartre. "We will not be ruled by you."

"It hardly matters what you savage whelps want," he said, but his demeanor had changed. Even I could see it. He wasn't quite as confident. Fury and something else I couldn't read colored his movements. He flicked a glance at his Host. "Take her."

Another battle. The Hounds and the Host were evenly matched.

Which was all fine and good except that Solange didn't have this kind of time.

Blood splattered the floor along with the ashes. It was so fast and so feral, I had a hard time keeping track of what was going on. I did see Nicholas creeping forward, staying low. Then he disappeared into a blur and Montmartre's feet went out from under him. Solange tumbled from his grasp, landing half sprawled against the bier.

A Hound smashed his fist into Nicholas's face, then flipped him over two more Host fighting a Hound. He hurtled into a table and then lay still. I cried out.

"Human!" the Hound girl shouted before plucking the vial from the floor and throwing it. It flew toward me, its silver chain catching the light from the candles.

A hand caught it in midair.

Not my hand.

"Are you kidding me?" I screeched. It was Juliana, Natasha's bored sister, who'd flitted around us when we were first captured. She waggled the vial at me. I wanted to claw her eyes right out of her head. I launched myself at her. What I lacked in finesse I made up for with angry flailing and a stubborn need for vengeance. I was not going to lose Solange. Not again and not when her cure was so close.

I was no match for Juliana unfortunately. That was clear after the first punch to my face. The second I ducked, but I wasn't quick enough to avoid the third one, to my stomach. I staggered, nauseous and breathless. The vial swung tauntingly in front of me. I grabbed for it and missed.

And then Kieran was suddenly there, swinging with his good arm. The vial dropped next to his boot. Juliana reached for it and

I kicked her hard, right in the throat. She swung up snarling, fangs extended. Kieran was closer to the vial and couldn't fight her off with his broken arm.

"Go," I yelled at him. "Go, go, go."

He grabbed the vial and skidded to Solange's side just as I crashed into a delicate chair that had the good grace to break apart on impact. One of the legs, painted with pink rosebuds, broke off. At least I had a weapon now.

"I'm going to kill you, little girl!" Juliana yelled.

The chair leg didn't quite pierce her heart, but it was near enough to make her freeze, gasp, and clutch at her chest.

"Lucy!" The stake Nicholas tossed at me finished her off. Ash drifted at my feet, like mist. My first vampire kill. When I got home, I'd have to recite countless malas to appease my mother. And my churning stomach. But not right now; right now I could indulge in a moment of triumph. But only a moment.

Because it was just one of those days.

I hung over the back of a bench, trying to convince my severely bruised diaphragm that standing up really was a necessity. Kieran leaned over Solange, tipping the contents of the silver vial between her lips. Those precious drops ran down into her throat. Still, she didn't look particularly healed.

"Nicholas," I croaked. "It's not working."

He ducked a dagger with a rusted handle. "It stopped the sickness, but now she needs to feed." He threw an entire stool at an approaching Araksaka guard. "She needs human blood—it's better for the first time."

I was trying to drag myself over to the bier, but Kieran was already slicing a shallow cut across his forearm. He held it to Solange's mouth, urging her to drink, whispering.

"Drink," he begged her. "I can't lose you now, not after all this. Drink, damn it." For some reason, the way he spoke to her, gently and desperately, had tears burning on my cheeks.

Lady Natasha howled, her long pale hair flying behind her like a banner. Her dress was stained with blood. Several of the carved ravens on her throne had broken off. "Montmartre! You love me," she howled, even as she tried to fight off Helena.

Montmartre's Host weren't exactly losing the fight with the Hounds, but they weren't winning it either. Hunters, vampire rogues, half the royal court under Conan's direction, and the Drake family all stood against them. Montmartre cursed.

"Fall back," he ordered. The Host retreated instantly to form a circle around him. "She will be my queen," Montmartre promised before flicking his hand. The Host pressed against him and they retreated down one of the tunnels.

Lady Natasha, abandoned on all sides, turned her anger to Helena. Helena twirled a stake until she found a proper grip. The fight stretched on, two determined women with a penchant for ancient weaponry. It was a beautiful dance, in its way, flashing blades and flips through the air. But in the end, Helena's stake flew true. Lady Natasha blinked uncomprehendingly and then her empty dress fell in a delicate heap of fine silk, dusted with ash.

The noise and fury in the hall stopped so suddenly, it practically echoed. Even the Araksaka paused.

Each to a one, the vampires dropped to one knee in front of Helena.

Lucy

In lieu of rightful succession, killing the present monarch granted you the crown.

Nicholas limped up beside me and held on to my hand tightly. I squeezed his fingers, stepping back so that our sides were pressed together, feeling better with his cool skin against mine. Neither of us spoke. We didn't have to.

On the glass bier, Solange finally gasped once, then swallowed hungrily. When she opened her eyes and saw dozens of kneeling vampires in their best court finery, she groaned weakly, blood smeared on her lips.

"Oh God, I'm not a vampire queen, am I?"

EPILOGUE

♦

Solange

I met Lucy in town. She was determined to force me into a semblance of a normal life, and meeting for coffee every Thursday night was her current plan. She was waiting for me in the park. It hadn't even been a week since I'd turned, and I wasn't ready to face the temptation of a coffeehouse full of human hearts beating all around me. I could ignore the squirrels and the fox hiding in the far bushes.

Lucy was sitting on a bench with two paper cups and a plastic to-go container filled with what was left of a chocolate-covered cherry tart. She wiped crumbs off her hands.

"I'm still celebrating," she mumbled through a mouthful. "I won't be able to fit into my clothes if I keep this up." She eyed me critically. "You're wearing that?"

I frowned at my clay-stained pants. "So? I didn't know I had to dress up for you."

She eyed me again. "How are you feeling?"

"I'm *fine*. You're as bad as my brothers." I felt better than fine, actually. I felt strong and alert, my eyes amplified every spark of light from the moon, the stars, streetlights. It was a little distracting, I had to admit, to hear her heart beating and smell the warmth of her blood just under her skin. And disconcerting to know my brothers had been right: blood now tasted better than chocolate. In fact, I couldn't remember much from the night of the caves, just the taste of Kieran in my mouth. He'd left with his uncle before I could properly thank him.

"Any word from Kieran?" Lucy asked quietly as if she'd known I was thinking about him.

I shook my head, tried not to look like I cared. I had enough to occupy me, after all. My mom was the new queen, which meant the prophecy hadn't technically been fulfilled. We weren't sure what to think about that. And we were still replacing an entire wall of the farmhouse, which had been burned out by Hope's unit. The gardens were full of water and soot. Bruno needed stitches, and Hyacinth wouldn't leave her room or lift the black lace veil off her face. London disappeared down the tunnels again; no one knew to where. And I'd actually caught Nicholas sending roses to Lucy's house, and they were on the phone with each other all the time.

And Montmartre was still out there. He'd sent an engagement gift: a diamond ring.

I'd flushed it down the toilet.

So I was too busy to sit around thinking about Kieran Black.

"Oh, here." Lucy passed me a package tied with ribbon. "A

belated birthday present from my dad." She rolled her eyes when I pulled out a piece of carved deer antler on a leather tong. "When he heard about the deer heart, he said to tell you the deer is clearly your totem animal and should be honored."

I slipped it over my head as she guzzled the rest of her drink. Her eyes watered.

"Ouch, still hot." She stood up quickly.

I stared at her. "Where are you going? I just got here."

She grinned at me, her gaze flicking toward the sidewalk.

"You have a date."

I froze.

"Lucy Hamilton, what have you done?"

"Gotta go!" She darted out of the park before I could say anything else. I didn't have to look to know who it was standing there. I could smell him, taste him.

Kieran.

"Solange," he said softly. He looked good, even with the bruises on his jaw going yellow and the sling cradling his arm. He didn't smile, but the way he was looking at me made me feel warm all over. I stood up.

"Kieran." I didn't know what else to say.

So I leaned over and kissed him.

Blood
Feud

PROLOGUE

♦

England, 1795

If Isabeau St. Croix had known it was going to be her last Christmas Eve, she would have had a third helping of plum pudding.

As it was, she was avoiding the drawing rooms. She'd never imagined a parlor could be so crowded and stuffy, but when she'd mentioned it to Benoit, he'd only laughed and told her to wait for summer, when coal fog clogged the city.

"Don't think I don't see you there, *chou*," he remarked dryly. He was tall and thin with a dashing mustache. So many fine gentlemen had fled France during the Revolution that every fine house in London now boasted a French chef. Never mind that most of those chefs had never even learned to boil an egg at home. They certainly did well enough here. "*Mais non*, you are murdering my carrots." He shooed away one of his harried helpers.

Taking advantage of his momentary distraction, Isabeau shrank back into the shadows of the bustling kitchen. She ought to have known better. Benoit was determined to have her dancing in satin slippers, as any nobleman's daughter would. Not too long ago she would have begged for the chance. And before that she would have expected it.

Spending a year on the streets of Paris had changed her.

Silk dresses and pearl earbobs seemed decadent now, and the concerns of fashion and gossip ridiculous. Benoit despaired that she preferred his company to the opera. But she loved the crackling of the hearth, the heavy scents of baking bread and roasting meat. Tonight there were bowls of oysters, plates of foie gras, a turkey stuffed with chestnuts, almond cream, and tiny perfect pastries in the shape of suns and holly leaves.

Benoit was the only person she could truly talk to. Her uncle was kind enough, as was his wife, but he hadn't lived in France for nearly two decades. Benoit had lived in Paris during the storming of the Bastille. He knew. But he still wasn't going to let her hide out in the kitchen all night, no matter how she begged.

"One little slice of galette." He handed her a plate and a fork. It was a traditional Galette des Rois, served in every French house during the holidays. She took a greedy bite. The second mouthful revealed the hidden dry bean tucked into the cake. She sucked the filling off it and dropped it onto her plate.

"Voilà!" Benoit grinned. "I knew you would get the bean. Now you are queen for the night." He plucked the fork from her hand even though she protested. She hadn't finished scraping every grain of sugar off the silver tines. "And so you must dance until dawn. *Allez-y!*"

She slid off a wooden stool, knowing she couldn't avoid the festivities any longer. It would be rude of her, and she had every reason to be grateful to her uncle. It hadn't been easy for her to steal enough money for the passage to England and he could have turned her away when she reached his doorstep. He'd never even met her, after all; she was the daughter of his estranged brother. His dead estranged brother, who hadn't spoken to him since before Isabeau was born. And if it wasn't for her uncle Olivier, or Oliver St. Cross as he was known here, she'd be spending this Christmas the same as she'd spent the last: huddled under the eaves of a cafe hoping some *citoyen* might give in to the holiday spirit and buy her a meal. If not, she'd have nicked the coins from someone's pocket and bought it for herself. One learned to do as one must while living in the alleys of Paris during the Great Terror.

"*Allez, allez,*" Benoit urged her. "I insist you find some handsome young man to flirt with you."

She couldn't imagine any young man would notice her, even in the beautiful white silk gown she'd been given to wear. She still felt skinny and hungry and smudged with dirt and hadn't the vaguest notion how to dance anymore. She had confidence only in her abilities to steal food and to find the best rooftops on which to hide when the riots broke out.

She forced herself to leave the kitchen mostly because the thought of the dozens of guests upstairs terrified her so. Before Paris, she had lived on a grand family estate in the countryside.

The house had marble floors and silk settees and dusty vineyards where she could eat grapes until her fingers turned purple. But then her parents had been taken.

What was a Christmas ball to the threat of the guillotine?

She found her way to the drawing room, where the guests had gathered for the midnight supper. Her uncle had leaped at the chance to re-create his own favorite childhood memories of *Réveillon* under the guise of making his niece more comfortable. He wasn't fooling anyone. They could all see how thrilled he was to be serving tourtiere and champagne to his friends. He stood by the main hearth, which was draped with evergreen branches and white lilies from the hothouse. His waistcoat was holly-berry red, barely containing his cheerful girth.

"Ah, here she is," he said.

Isabeau concentrated on smiling, on not tripping on the hem of her gown and not wiping her sweaty palms on her skirts, on anything but the curious and pitying eyes tracking her progress. "My niece, Lady Isabeau St. Croix," her uncle announced. In Paris she had introduced herself as Citoyenne Isabeau. It was safer.

"Oh, my dear," an old woman fluttered at her, the ostrich feather in her hair bobbing sympathetically. "How awful. How perfectly awful."

"*Madame.*" She didn't know what else to say to that, so she curtsied.

"Those barbarians," she continued. "Never mind that now, you're quite safe here. We English know the natural order of things."

Another sentence she had no reply for. The woman seemed

genuine, though, and she smelled like peppermint oil. Her satin gloves were trimmed with red bows when she patted Isabeau's hand. "My nephew is around here somewhere, I'm certain he would love to partner you in a dance."

"*Merci, madame.*" She had every intention of hiding behind one of the giant evergreen displays before succumbing to any such fate.

The drawing room was even more beautiful than Isabeau could have imagined. She had helped set out the bowls of gilded pine cones and holly leaves dusted with silver and tied the ribbons around the pine boughs fastened to every window. But at night, with dozens of beeswax candles burning and the frigid winter wind pushing at the glass, it was magical. And just as stuffy as she had feared, thanks to the hot air laced with cloying perfumes and floral hair oils filling every corner of the room. She edged toward the doors leading out to the gardens.

The rosebushes and yew hedges were edged with a delicate frost, as if lace had been tossed everywhere. The moon was a soft glow behind thick clouds. She shivered a little when snow began to fall gently, but didn't go back inside. She could hear icy carriage wheels creaking from the road and the sounds of music from the room behind her. The snow made everything pale as a pearl. She smiled.

"With a smile like that, I forbid you ever to frown again."

She whirled at the voice, shoulders tensing. She'd only been living in the pampered townhouse for a little while and already she was losing her edge. She ought to have heard his footsteps, or at least the door opening.

"Forgive my intrusion," he said smoothly, bowing. "And my impertinence, seeing as we have yet to be properly introduced. But you could only be the mysterious Isabel St. Cross."

"Isabeau," she corrected him softly. She'd never known a man like him. He only looked to be in his twenties, but he carried himself with an elegance and a confidence of one much older. His eyes were gray, nearly colorless in the winter garden.

"Philip Marshall, Earl of Greyhaven, at your service." When he kissed the back of her hand, his touch was cool, as if he'd been standing in the snow too long. She was suddenly nervous and felt inexplicably trapped, like the time she'd been caught behind a fire set in the streets to keep the city guards at bay.

"I should return," she murmured. She was only eighteen years old, after all, and the only reason she'd been permitted to attend the ball was because it was Christmastime. It was probably unseemly for her to be outside unchaperoned, even if he was an earl. She couldn't remember. Her aunt had listed off so many rules, they were bleeding together. She'd known them all before the Revolution. Now she only knew she felt an odd desire to stand closer to him, and not just because she had forgotten her wrap inside.

He released her hand, arched an eyebrow. The faint light from the parlor glinted on the silver buttons of his brocade coat. "Surely a girl who survived the French mobs isn't afraid of me?"

She lifted her chin defensively.

"*Mais non, monsieur. Je n'ai pas peur.*" She had to concentrate to speak English; temper or distraction always slipped her back into French. "*Pardon.*" She shook her head, annoyed with her lapse. "I am not afraid."

"I'm glad to hear it," he approved. "Wine?" He handed her a glass she hadn't realized he was holding. Hadn't Benoit been pushing her to dance and flirt? Normal girls her age would be thrilled to be standing here with a handsome earl. She should drink and eat candied violets and dance until her satin slippers wore thin. She accepted the cup.

"*Merci, monsieur.*" The mulled wine was warm and laced with cinnamon and some other indefinable taste, like copper or liquorice. Or blood. She frowned inwardly. She was letting her misgivings make her silly.

"You are lovely," he said. "And I am so tired of these English roses, too meek to enjoy anything but the quadrille and weak lemonade. You are a welcome change, Miss Cross. A welcome change indeed."

She blushed. The wine was making her feel warm, befuddled. It was nice. Snowflakes landed on her eyelashes, dissolved instantly. They landed on her lips and she licked at them as if they were sugar. His silvery eyes glinted like animal eyes, like a fox in a henhouse.

"If this were a gothic novel," he drawled, "there would be ghosts and vampires, and you *would* be afraid."

She thought of the books she read late at night in the library, sensationalist novels like Ann Radcliffe's *Mysteries of Udolpho* and Burger's *Lenore,* all fraught with villains and undead creatures who roamed the nights with insatiable appetites.

"Don't be silly." She laughed. "I don't believe in vampires."

CHAPTER 1

◆

LOGAN

It had been a hell of a week.

Cleaning up after a psychotic vampire queen wasn't easy at the best of times. It was much worse when your mother was the one who'd dispatched the old queen, you and your brothers were suddenly princes, and your baby sister was being stalked by a centuries-old homicidal vampire.

Like I said, hell of a week.

At least we'd all survived, even Aunt Hyacinth, whose face was now so scarred she wouldn't lift the veil off her Victorian hat or leave her room. Helios-Ra vampire hunters did that to her—right before one of their new agents started dating my baby sister.

That's just weird.

Still, he saved her life less than two weeks ago, so we're willing to overlook a little making out.

As long as I never, ever have to know about it.

I mean, sure, Kieran's a good enough guy—but Solange is my only sister. Enough said.

"Quit brooding, Lord Byron." My brother Quinn smirked at me, shoving me with his shoulder. "There are no girls here to impress with your Prince of Darkness routine."

"As if." Quinn was the one who used the whole vampire mystique thing to get the girls. I just happened to like dressing in old frock coats and pirate shirts; that some girls liked it was incidental. Well, mostly.

"Any word yet on the Hound princess?" Quinn asked.

"Nothing yet." Dad had invited the reclusive Hound tribe to the table for negotiations now that Mom was the new vampire queen, ruler of all the disparate tribes. Sounds melodramatic and medieval, but that's a vampire for you.

"Think she's cute?"

"Aren't they all?"

Quinn grinned. "Mostly."

The royal caves behind us had been left in shambles after the battle that took out Lady Natasha. The dust of staked vampires was swept up and the shards of broken mirrors carted out in boxfuls. There were still at least a dozen left hanging on the wall. Lady Natasha had really liked looking at herself. Some of the ravens carved on her whitethorn throne were chipped, some decapitated. Everyone was busy with some task or another, cleaning, arranging, or just staring at my mother as she sat at the end of the hall scowling at my father, who wouldn't stop talking about peace treaties.

The tension vibrating the air was harder to clean out than the ashes of our dead.

Everyone was watching their backs: the old royalists loyal to Lady Natasha, the ones loyal to the House of Drake and my mother, and the ones caught in between. Lucy would have been running around with white sage chanting some Vedic mantra to cleanse our auras if she were here. But she was forbidden to come to the caves until the worst of the politics had been sorted out. She shouldn't have been staying with us either, but her parents' drive home was interrupted by their ancient van and some ancient part that fell out on the highway. They were stuck in a small town and Lucy was stuck with us. Humans were fragile at the best of times, and Solange's best friend didn't have the basic self-preservation of a gnat. If there was trouble, she always jumped right in feetfirst. If she hadn't started it in the first place, of course.

Between her and my sister, we had our hands full. Vampire politics paled in comparison.

"Now *she's* cute," Quinn murmured appreciatively as one of the courtiers dragged a box of what looked like the remains of a broken table. "I'll just go help her out. It's the princely thing to do."

"You're an ass," I told him fondly.

"You're just jealous because I'm so much prettier," he tossed out over his shoulder as he left to charm yet another girl.

He never reached her.

She straightened suddenly, stepping onto a footstool that gave her a good view of the length of the hall, and my parents in particular. She pulled a crossbow loaded with three wickedly pointed stakes out of the bag.

Not a broken table after all.

And no matter how prepared you are, or how careful, there's always an opening somewhere.

Mom taught us that.

The girl aimed and squeezed the trigger, barely making a sound. We might not even have noticed her at all if we hadn't been actively watching her. The stakes hissed out of the crossbow, hurtling through the air with deadly accuracy.

Or what would have been deadly accuracy had Quinn not been close enough to grab her leg and yank her off the stool.

The shot went wide, but not quite wide enough. She tumbled to the hand-embroidered rug, Quinn's fangs extending so fast they caught the lamplight. My own stung my gums, my lips lifting off the rest of my teeth.

I didn't have time to reach her or my parents.

I only had time enough to whip the dagger at my belt out into the trajectory of the stakes. It caught one and split it into two, the pieces biting into a huge wooden cupboard, the knife into the back of a chair. My nostrils burned.

Poison.

Everyone else seemed to be moving in slow motion. Guards turned, eyes widening, fangs flashing. Swords gleamed, lace ribbons fluttered, and boots clomped onto the wall as the best of them flipped out of the way of the other two stakes. A wire birdcage toppled, spilling the stubs of half-burned candles. Beeswax joined the sharp, sweet smell of the poison. One of the stakes caught a thin pale courtier in the shoulder when he failed to lean backward quickly enough. He yelled and even that sound seemed too slow and stretched out until it distorted. His blood splattered onto the tiles laid into the ground between the edges of the carpets.

The third stake went unerringly on its way, straight toward my mother's heart.

The girl smiled once, even as she fought to free herself from Quinn's grim hold.

Which just went to show how little she knew my mother.

My father whirled to put himself between her and the stake, as two of my other brothers, Marcus and Connor, somersaulted to his side to form a wider barrier.

Even as my mother leaped into the air and tumbled over their heads, refusing to use a shield made of her husband and sons.

She landed a little to the left and stuck out her arm, safely encased in a leather bracer, and knocked the stake right out of the air. It hit a tapestry and fell into a basket, looking innocuous. Guards closed in. There was so much snarling, the royal caves sounded more like cougar enclosures at the zoo. Mom fought her way free of her overeager guards as the girl was hauled away from Quinn.

"I want her alive!" Dad was shouting.

Too late.

The assassin-girl was clearly prepared, and knew enough not to be captured and questioned by the enemy. The inside of her vest was rigged with a slender hidden stake. She pulled a small piece of rope sewn into the armhole of her vest and smiled. There was a very small *thwack* sound and then she crumbled into ashes. Her clothes fell into a pile.

Dad swore, very loudly and very creatively.

Mom's fists clenched. "Quinn, Logan. With me. *Now*." She shot a glare at Marcus and Connor. "You too."

Mom did *not* like being saved by her children.

We followed her into a small private antechamber. Adrenaline was still coursing through me. Quinn's jaw was clenched so tightly he looked like a marble statue, pale and cold. I knew just how he felt.

We had a short reprieve as Dad cupped Mom's face and ran his hands down her neck, over her shoulders. "Helena, are you hurt?"

She waved that away. "I'm fine." She smiled briefly, then turned hard eyes on us. Each of us took a healthy step backward and not a single one of us felt any less manly for the wise retreat.

"I distinctly remember," she said softly, her long black braid swinging behind her as she crossed her arms over her chest, "after the events of last week, ordering you never to step between me and a weapon again."

"Mom," Quinn ground out. "Give me a break."

Her glare could have sizzled steak. "I will not have my sons killed by some third-rate assassin."

"And we won't have our mother killed by one either," I added.

She closed her eyes briefly. She looked less like an ancient Fury, pale as fire and just as angry, when she opened them again.

"Thank you, boys," she said finally. "I'm very proud of you. Don't ever do that again." She leaned against Dad. "You either, Liam."

"Shut up, dear," he said affectionately, kissing the top of her head. He looked at the guard standing in the doorway, under the string of small glass lanterns. The candles flickered. "Well?"

I recognized Sophie when she stepped forward. She had a mass of curly brown hair and scars on the side of her face from when she'd been human. No one knew how she'd gotten them. She bowed sharply. "The girl belonged to Montmartre. His insignia was stitched on the inside of her vest."

"And?"

"And that's all we know."

"That's not nearly enough," Helena snapped.

"I agree, Your Highness."

Helena sighed. "Don't 'Your Highness' me."

"Yes, Your Highness."

"Wait." Quinn frowned. "She had a tattoo."

"You're sure?" Mom asked. "Where?"

"Under her collarbone, above her left breast." To his credit, he didn't blush. Exactly.

Mom's eyes narrowed on his face. "You were looking down her shirt?"

Quinn swallowed. "No, ma'am."

"Mmm-hmmm. What was the tattoo?"

"A red rose with three daggers or stakes through it. I didn't get a very good look."

Dad frowned. "I don't know that insignia. I wonder if it's new?" He glanced at Sophie. "Find out. And double the patrols, and set another guard on my wife."

Sophie bowed and left the antechamber just as Mom started to bristle.

"Liam Drake, I can look after myself."

"Helena Drake, I love you, take the extra guard."

They glowered at each other. I knew Dad would win. Mom was vicious when cornered, but Dad had a way about him, like a snake hypnotizing his supper. His glower softened. "Please, love."

Her fangs lengthened with her annoyance. "Don't do that," she muttered, but we knew Dad would get his way. "Only until the coronation," she said finally, firmly.

Dad nodded. "Deal." He'd find some other argument come the coronation. The walkie-talkie on his belt burbled some garbled sentence. He pressed the button. "Repeat."

"You asked us to let you know when it was midnight."

Dad looked at his watch. "Right," he said to the rest of us. "The Hound delegation should be here any minute. Logan, you'll go meet them. If what we know about this Isabeau is true, she was turned just after the French Revolution. You'll be more familiar to her in that frock coat."

"Okay." I ignored my brothers' smirks out of long habit. They were strictly the jeans and T-shirt types. I couldn't help it if they had no style.

"The mountainside guards know to expect them, but no one else does," he added. "We didn't want the drama."

"All we get is drama." I rolled my eyes, leaving to make my way down to the main cave entrance. Dad's walkie-talkie warbled again. His voice went grim when he called out to me.

"Logan?"

"Yeah?"

"Run."

CHAPTER 2

•

Isabeau

I hadn't expected the ambush. And that's saying something.

I hadn't become a Hound princess in the year and a half since I'd been dug out of the ground because I was a trusting sort. If the French Revolution hadn't cured me of that, being bitten and abandoned by one of Montmartre's Host would have.

And I might have been taken by surprise, but I wasn't an idiot.

I was, however, armed to the teeth.

The guards outnumbered us. I'd only traveled with two others, Magda and Finn, since it was difficult to find a Hound who had the temper to deal with the vampire royal courts and the associated unrelenting arrogance. Magda's temperament was hardly stable, but she was beautiful and just, which mostly balanced everything else out. Finn was as serene as the cedar woods he loved so much.

And I was just me: lonely and vengeful but still as polite as the French lady I'd been raised to be. I was both eighteen years old and more than two hundred years old. As if this wasn't confusing enough, I'd been pulled out of the grave by a pack of witch's dogs.

Kala preferred *shamanka* to *witch*. Most of the princes and lordlings respected her and since she'd been the one to send me to the meeting, no one had argued or offered to take my place. I was her apprentice and that was enough for the others, even if I wasn't sure it was enough for me. I'd have been happier fading into the background, but I owed Kala my life, such as it was. She'd pulled me through the madness and made sure I didn't turn feral or fall prey to Montmartre. She claimed if I was strong enough to last two hundred years in a coffin, I was strong enough not to go savage too. I didn't remember the centuries in the cemetery, only brief images before I lost consciousness. But I definitely remembered the pain of being pulled out and reawakened. And it wasn't strength of character that had seen me through, or even Kala's considerable magic.

It was the need to find the Earl of Greyhaven and my thirst for revenge.

For the sake of outsiders, I'd been labeled a Hound "princess" even though we didn't have princesses or other royalty. It was a useful title though, since the new queen would be more apt to listen to me, even if they were probably expecting a savage girl with mud on her face who ate babies for dinner.

That was why Kala had sent me to the courts for the coronation of Helena Drake and her husband, Liam Drake; that and the fact that I and the other Hounds had kind of saved their daughter's life. Unfortunately Montmartre had gotten away, so I didn't consider the mission a complete success, even if everyone else seemed to.

I was here to represent the best of the Hounds, and I had a wolfhound puppy to present as a gift. Kala's wolfhounds were legendary; I had a full-grown one as a companion: Charlemagne.

And he was growling low in his throat, muscles bunched under his wiry gray fur.

"*La*," I murmured, pointing for him to stay behind me. I had no problem releasing him to attack, but only if I knew he wouldn't be hurt. And right now there was an arrow aimed at his throat.

"*Hounds.*" One of the guards sneered. I knew that half-disgusted, half-fearful tone intimately. We weren't exactly famous for our elegant table manners. It hardly mattered that half the rumors weren't true. We used them to our advantage. The more the others disdained us, the more they left us alone, which was all we really wanted in the first place. Let them worry about politics and hunters. We only wanted the caves and the quiet.

Well, most of us.

The puppy in the basket slung over my shoulder barked and I set him down. I drew the long slender sword strapped to my back, which the guards hadn't noticed yet. The moment I touched the hilt, both Magda and Finn sprung into action.

Learning to fight was no different than learning to waltz or dance the quadrille, in my opinion. It was all about the tension between you and your partner, about footwork and balance and timing.

And I preferred the long deadly sword to any silk ball gown I'd ever worn. I wasn't sure what that said about me, but I had bigger worries.

Like the polished mahogany stake flying through the air toward my heart.

I leaned back as far as I could. It passed over me, close enough that I could see the wood grain. Trust the damned royals to polish their stakes to a high gloss. We just sharpened sticks.

I popped back up again to crack my opponent on the side of the head with the hilt of my sword. I might have stabbed him into a pile of ash but Kala had warned us time and time again that we were here for negotiations.

Someone might try telling the guards that.

Magda took one out before I could stop her. It was hard to feel regret since he'd been about to snap her neck. Charlemagne whined with the need to jump into the fight.

"*Non*," I told him sharply. "We were invited!" I added, shouting as I cracked my boot into the guard's heel. He stumbled, dropping his stake.

"Stop!" Someone else hurled himself into the melee. Great, just what we needed.

He leaped between us, lace cuffs fluttering. He was pretty, like the boys I'd known at my uncle's parties, but not nearly as soft, even in his velvet frock coat. His fangs were extended, gleaming like opals. I didn't know who he was but the guards eased back, weapons raised respectfully even if they were still snarling.

"She killed Jonas," one of them spat.

"Because he was trying to kill me," Magda spat back unrepentantly.

The guard snarled. The boy turned to him, speaking blandly. "Don't you recognize them?" He pointed at me. "This girl saved your life not too long ago."

That hardly got the snarls to subside.

He looked about eighteen, same as Magda and me—though technically I was really 232 years old. Only Finn looked to be in his thirties, though he was nearly eight hundred years old. Kala had sent him to keep us level-headed. He wasn't really a Hound, just an ordinary vampire, but he'd been with us for so long that we treated him as if he was one of us, especially since he hated Montmartre as much as we did.

"My apologies," he added, bowing to us. "My mother's only been queen for a few days and everyone's still on high alert. Someone tried to assassinate her not ten minutes ago." He must be one of the legendary Drake brothers. There were seven of them and a single daughter who'd just been turned. "But you'll be safe," he hastened to assure us.

"I know." I did not need his protection. His eyes were as green as mine, like moss. I didn't like the way he was looking at me, as if I wore one of my old ball gowns instead of a leather tunic with chain mail over my heart.

"Isabeau," he said. "And Magda and Finn, I presume?" He nearly drawled each word. "I'm Logan Drake." His brown hair tumbled over his forehead, and the shape of his jaw and his narrow nose were distinctly aristocratic. He would have been more at home among the nobles of my time than this modern place. It made me both distrust him and feel oddly drawn to him. I straightened my spine. I wasn't here to admire pretty boys; I was here as Kala's emissary. It was inexcusable to be distracted, even for a moment.

"We're here for the coronation," I explained stiffly.

"It's not for another two weeks," another guard said.

Logan made a sound of frustration. "At ease, Jen," he said before offering us a charming smile. "If you'll follow me?"

I snapped my fingers and Charlemagne bounded forward to trot at my side. The basket full of wriggling puppy went over my shoulder again. They led us down a carved hall, the gray stone dipping low over our heads. Magda was scowling.

"These caves used to belong to us," she hissed.

"A hundred years ago," I hissed back. "You weren't even born then, never mind turned."

"So what? They still stole our home from us." Her long flowered skirt flowed around her ankles, the silver thread embroidery glinting in the torchlight.

"Lady Natasha stole the caves," Logan said, without turning to look at us.

"Are you planning on giving them back?" Magda snorted, before I could stop her. I pinched her arm. She jerked out of reach but didn't say anything else. Actually, she said a lot but she was grumbling, so we were able to pretend not to hear her.

The hall widened and finally brought us to a cavern dripping with stalagmites. Candles burned in silver candelabra and iron birdcages. There were numerous benches and a dais with the splintered remains of a white throne and dozens of cracked mirrors.

And vampires everywhere.

Conversations halted abruptly. They all turned to stare at us as if we were poisonous mushrooms suddenly growing in a manicured garden. They were pale and perfect, with gleaming teeth and hard eyes. I saw every manner of clothes, from leather to corsets to jeans. One of them wore a poncho such as Magda often wore. Finding comfort in the styles of one's human youth was common to all vampires. It was a similarity between us but it was hardly enough to outweigh the snarls and suspicious sneers.

Even Finn stiffened, and Magda was practically vibrating with the need to attack. Charlemagne's ears went back when he sensed the tension, thick and sticky as honey. Only Logan sauntered forward as if we were here for nothing more than tea and cake.

"I've brought our guests," he announced. No one could miss the inflection on the last word. And the warning. The conversations resumed, but mostly murmurs and whispers. No one wanted to miss the presentation between the queen and the Hound princess who helped save her daughter. I didn't see Solange anywhere. I put my shoulders back and swore to myself, yet again, that I wouldn't let Kala down.

Logan stopped in front of a slender, short woman with a long braid. I cast an envious glance at the daggers lined up neatly on her shoulder strap. The man next to her had wide shoulders and a calm smile.

"Mom, Dad, this is Isabeau St. Croix." Logan presented me with such a flourish, I nearly forgot myself and curtsied. He'd introduced me to them and not the other way around, subtly claiming that his parents had a higher social standing. I felt sure he'd done it on purpose but I was surprised someone born in this century would know those particular rules of etiquette. They hadn't survived the centuries, which meant I'd had to learn a whole new set of rules. As if it hadn't been tiresome enough the first time. "Isabeau, this is Queen Helena and King Liam Drake."

"Welcome," Liam said, his voice soothing and rich as brandy cream. I knew they were looking at my fangs. I had two sets, sharp and white as abalone shell. The more feral vampires went, the more fangs they grew. Even we avoided the *Hel-Blar*, who had a mouthful of razor teeth and blue-tinted skin. Before Montmartre, they had been rare. You could go your whole life without ever coming across one. They were mostly created by accident or ignorance, especially centuries ago when the bloodchange was even more of a mystery than it is today.

But now, because of Montmartre, they were like fire ants pouring out of an anthill; where there used to be one there was now a hundred. He'd been so eager to create his own personal army, he'd ravaged the old cobbled towns of Europe for hundreds of years, turning humans into vampires with indiscriminate greed.

That wasn't good enough for him though. He wanted his personal army to be the best, the strongest, and the most vicious.

He began leaving people half-turned under the earth to prove themselves, to survive the bloodchange alone. Those who didn't die, or go mad with hunger, were recruited to become part of his Host. The rest were abandoned as *Hel-Blar*.

And Hounds, or Cwn Mamau as we knew ourselves, didn't fit anywhere easily. We weren't regular vampires, we weren't *Hel-Blar*, and we most definitely weren't Host, as much as that fact irked Montmartre. We were a thorn in his side, seeking out the vampires he left underground and rehabilitating them before he could claim them for his own.

"A pleasure to meet you," I said politely. "Finn, Magda, may I present Helena and Liam Drake." Logan's mouth twitched slightly and I knew he'd caught what I'd done. Finn bowed slightly. Magda inclined her head stiffly. Her long brown hair and soft clothes made her look like a fairy princess but she was contrary by nature, and admitting to being nervous or inferior in a royal court, especially this one, was right out of the question. I laid the basket on the carpet and hoped our gift wouldn't relieve himself on the hand-embroidered roses. "I bring a gift from our shamanka, Kala."

Liam's smile was genuine when he bent down to help the puppy out of the basket. I watched Charlemagne carefully, who was studying Liam carefully. When Charlemagne didn't growl or tense, I relaxed as well. His instincts were sound. The puppy rolled over, barked, and then leaped to his feet, startled. Even Helena grinned. It softened her features considerably.

"Kala's witch dogs are legendary," she said.

"Yes, they are." I nodded proudly. I wasn't sure if she knew just how legendary they were. It was Kala's giant dogs that had scented me in the cemetery and dug me out with their claws. They'd been loyal to me ever since. And, truthfully, I preferred their company to those of my own kind. It was less complicated. "And Kala's not a witch, she's a shamanka."

"I beg your pardon. She says your gift for training them is just as legendary."

I tried not to blush; it was unseemly for a vampire. Still, Kala wasn't easy with her praises and I felt myself standing a little taller.

"You'll be our guest at the farmhouse." It wasn't a request. Even if it had been, there'd have been no polite way out of it. I wasn't sure which was worse, staying in these caves with those who clearly didn't want us here or staying in the house of the queen. She was making sure everyone knew we were under her protection but there was something else to it, I was sure. She didn't fully trust the Hounds, whatever her husband said about wanting treaties and reconciliation. This was a test.

"Of course." The amulets Kala had given me glinted in the soft light when I lifted my chin.

"Logan will take you there to rest. Your friends may remain here and acquaint themselves with the court."

Another test.

"Thank you." I ignored Magda's scowl; she'd been scowling since Kala first mentioned this visit. Finn bowed once and didn't say anything else, so I assumed he didn't have any serious objections. I wasn't yet used to the cavalier attitude to unchaperoned girls. True, I hadn't had a chaperone in Paris, but I'd been living in the alleyways pretending not to be a St. Croix. Anyway, we'd assumed they'd separate us; we'd have done the same if a group of royals or ancients had been invited to the caves. They might yet, if the treaties and negotiations went well. That gave me pause.

"I'll take you to the house." Logan smiled pleasantly at me. He didn't seem fazed by my extra set of fangs or the scars on my bare arms and the one on the left side of my throat. The few non-Hounds I'd met couldn't help but stare.

I hated being stared at.

I couldn't help but think Logan's eyes were knowing, as if he knew what I was thinking, when he motioned for me to precede him down the narrow cavern passageway curtained off with a tapestry of a moonlit forest. The embroidery was familiar. We'd hung similar tapestries in the château to keep out the drafts. Charlemagne padded softly by my side, alert but calm. I dug my fingers in his fur for strength when Logan wasn't looking.

"I take it from your accent that you're French?"

"*Oui.*" I didn't say anything else.

"Turn here. It's fastest," he explained, leading us down several more passageways and out into a clearing. He didn't pry but I could see the speculation in his quick glance. He'd ask more questions soon enough, he and his entire family. I tried to remind myself that I was Kala's emissary and strong enough to deal with the Drakes, royalty or not, ridiculously handsome or not. The moonlight glinted on the silver buttons of his frock coat. He really did look as if he belonged in a Victor Hugo novel, sipping claret wine by the fireside. "And this way we won't have to climb down the mountain."

The stars were thick overhead, visible only when the wind pushed at the cathedral ceiling of leaves and branches. The mountain was a black shadow hulking behind us. A wolf howled somewhere in the distance. Charlemagne threw back his head and opened his jaws to howl back. I snapped my fingers. "*Non*." I was nowhere near comfortable enough to have him give our location away. I had no way of knowing who else walked the woods with us. I found it hard to believe they would send the queen's young son out with a savage princess without some kind of guard.

"The house is through the woods. We can take the tunnels if you'd prefer or . . ."

"Or what?"

"Can you keep up?" His grin was charming.

"*Mais oui*." I was immediately on my guard. "I mean, of course."

"Great." He winked and then was gone. The leaves fluttered. Charlemagne whined once, excited. I felt the same way. I gave him the hand motion to release him and then we were both running through the woods, passing between huge oaks and maples, ducking under pine boughs, leaping over giant ferns. I'd never seen trees like these. I was used to the stately gardens and ancient vineyards of my childhood or, more recently, the Hounds' caves; not towering trees so tall I couldn't see their tops. Mists snaked at our ankles, drifted up to blow a cool breath around my waist. In the clear pockets, warm summer air pressed against me. My hair came loose of its pins and streamed behind me like a war banner. I would have laughed out loud if I hadn't been sure Logan would hear me and smirk. Somehow he'd known this would center me and calm me down again. I'd only been in the royal court for just under half an hour, scrutinized by barely a quarter of their numbers, and I was already itching for the seclusion of the caves and the uncomplicated company of Kala's wolfhounds. This was almost as good. I did laugh when Charlemagne charged through a river, splashing me unrepentantly.

Logan was still ahead. He was a blur and I was determined to catch up, if not pass him altogether. I knew his scent already, like the incense they used in church when I was a girl, underlaid with wine. Even under the thickness of the forest smells, of damp mud and decomposing vegetations and mushrooms, I could recognize it.

My boots barely touched the ground. A rabbit dove for safety into the bushes. His voice drifted back to me. "Come on, Mademoiselle St. Croix, nearly there."

I broke through a copse of thick evergreen and then I could see him, barely a yard ahead of me. I ran faster, feeling the burn in my legs, remembering how my heart might have pounded if I'd been able to move this fast as a human. We leaped out of the forest and into a field, landing at the same time in a puddle of mud hidden under a carpet of pine needles and wilted oak leaves. Only Charlemagne was smart enough to sail right over it.

Logan sighed. "These pants cost a fortune to dry clean." They were black, shiny like plastic or worn leather. These vampires worried about the strangest things.

The mud sucked at my boots when I stepped out onto the long grass. Barking erupted out of the farmhouse and I touched Charlemagne's head, whispering a command. His leg muscles quivered with the need to keep running, to meet the challenge, but he stayed by me. Logan shook his head.

"They weren't kidding when they said you had a way with dogs."

I shrugged. "We understand each other."

"He doesn't even have a collar."

"There's no need. He is not my servant, only my companion, and that is always his choice."

"Well, maybe he can teach our dogs some manners. Especially Mrs. Brown."

"Mrs. Brown?"

"Is a terror. And only about fifteen pounds of pug."

"Pug?" I echoed, interested despite myself. "I don't think I've ever seen one."

"Cross a small dog with a pig and you have a pug."

"Why would one do that?" I wondered.

"Lucy claims they're cute."

"Lucy is your . . . girlfriend?" Now why had I asked him that? I was suddenly too embarrassed to be proud that I'd remembered the modern English word for "girlfriend."

He slanted me a sidelong glance. "Lucy's my sister's best friend and pretty much like a second sister to me. She's the mouthy one, hard to miss."

"Oh."

"And you? Are you being married off to some Hound prince?"

"We don't have princes."

"But you have princesses?"

"Not really, but it is the nearest word to describe my position among my people."

"So will you marry for politics?"

I shook my head. "We rarely marry and never for politics. The bones lead us to our mates."

"The bones?"

"A ritual passed down through the centuries."

"And have the bones led you to anyone yet?"

"*Non.*" I had absolutely no intention of telling him the bones had told Kala I would find my mate in the royal courts. Or that she was rarely wrong in these matters. After all, her magic was so strong she had dreamwalked to find my tomb, projecting her spirit across the ocean to locate me with nothing more than an omen and a wisp of a dream. She could have ignored them to work her spells for some other, more personal purpose. Magic took as much as it gave, and one didn't just send one's spirit on such a far and dangerous journey without some cost.

So when Kala said my mate would be from the royal courts, she meant it.

And no Hound in the world would disbelieve her. It didn't bear thinking on. No other shamanka or shamanka's handmaiden had ever been joined with someone outside the tribe.

I'd rather be alone.

Besides, omens or not, I was here for another purpose.

"Hey, are you okay?" Logan reached out to touch my elbow, above a jagged scar from the mouth of one of the dogs that had pulled me out of my grave. I jerked back. He lifted an eyebrow.

"I am fine." I deliberately turned toward the farmhouse. The porch was wide with several chairs and a swing. Roses grew wild under the windows. The barking grew louder, punctuated with snarls. Logan looked concerned for the first time since he'd stopped a sword from cleaving my rib cage.

"The dogs have never met a Hound before," he said awkwardly. Even with my limited knowledge of him, I knew for a fact that he wasn't often awkward. It was endearing, more so than his charming smiles.

I climbed the stairs confidently. Dogs didn't hide their moods, didn't play games of manners or intrigue. Logan's hand was on the doorknob. "There's no need to worry," I assured him.

I felt better with three huge shaggy Bouviers charging at me. If Benoit were still alive, he'd have clicked his tongue at that. I didn't speak to the dogs, barely flicked them a glance. I just stood my ground and let them sniff me once before I snapped my fingers and pointed to the ground. Three furry backsides hit the marble floor.

Logan gaped at me. "Dude."

I gathered by his tone that he was impressed. When I was sure the Bouviers had accepted I was higher in the pack hierarchy, I let Charlemagne past me so they could meet.

The foyer was spacious, cluttered with boots and jackets and bags. The lamps and the overhead chandelier were lit. I tried not to stare. I was still half-awed by electricity. I might have woken up in the twenty-first century, but I still lived in a cave with amenities closer to the Middle Ages. I had recently allowed Magda to foist a cell phone on me but I still wasn't entirely sure how to work it properly. The first time it rang, I'd tried to stake it.

"Whoa." A girl interrupted my inspection. I assumed she was Lucy, as she was the only one with a heartbeat. I vaguely remembered her from the night Solange turned, staying close to her and trying to kick anyone who came too close. She'd hadn't been entirely successful, but she never gave up. "Did you give the dogs Hypnos or something?" she asked. She had brown hair cut to her chin and brown eyes behind dark glasses. She wore an excessive amount of silver and turquoise jewelry. There was a purse slung from her left shoulder to her right hip. It wasn't for a cell phone or lip gloss; rather it was stuffed full of stakes.

Two vampires followed her out of the living room; Solange, whom I'd last seen lying pale and dead in Montmartre's arms, and another one of her many brothers. They both stopped, watching me warily. It took Lucy a little longer. She glanced at them, then at me.

"What? What am I missing?" She sounded disgruntled. She tilted her head. "Hey, we know you. Isabel, right?"

"Isabeau," I corrected stiffly. I hated how polite and stilted I sounded. It was how I was raised but I knew enough to know it wasn't the way of modern people my age, vampire or not.

"Nice," she approved. "You don't look like an Isabel anyway. I'm Lucy, and that one's Nicholas. There's so many of them sometimes it's hard to keep track." She darted forward, arms out. I stumbled back, watching for a stake, knees bending into a fighting crouch. "Oh, sorry," she said. "I was just going to hug you for saving my best friend's life. I guess you're not the hugging type."

Logan sounded like he was choking back a laugh. Solange and Nicholas still hadn't said a word. Lucy turned to stare at them. "What is *wrong* with you two? She saved Solange's life." The irony that the human was more comfortable around me than the other vampires was not lost on me.

"I'm a Hound," I murmured.

Lucy shrugged. "You could sing boy band songs all day long and I wouldn't care." She shuddered. "You don't, do you?" That seemed to distress her more than the fact that the Hounds were rumored to be mad killers.

Logan rolled his eyes. "I don't think she's had a lot of exposure to boy bands, Lucy."

"But you do wear bone beads," she said, ignoring him and nodding at the beads hanging from the braids twisted at the nape of my hair. "Cool." She tilted her head. "You don't look crazy."

"You're like a runaway train," Logan groaned at her. "Can't you shut her up?" he asked his brother pleadingly.

"How?" Nicholas said somewhat helplessly.

"Kiss her, you idiot."

I happened to appreciate honesty, so it was impossible not to like her. She reminded me a little of Magda. "I guess you don't look crazy either," I told her.

Nicholas snorted. She jabbed him in the stomach with her elbow. "Be nice."

"You first." He rubbed his sternum. "Ouch."

Solange stepped forward. "I'm sorry," she said quietly. "You took me by surprise." She licked her lips. She still looked frail, for a vampire anyway. I wondered how she could resist the temptation of Lucy's heartbeat filling the house. "Thank you," she said. "I'm in your debt."

"We all are," Nicholas agreed.

"It's nothing." I looked away, embarrassed. "We have no love for Montmartre."

"Jerk," Lucy muttered. She stepped forward, breaking the uncomfortable silence by linking her arm through Solange's and then through mine, gingerly. Surprisingly, I let her. "Come on," she said cheerfully. "You guys can watch me eat chocolate."

The front door opened behind us.

"Solange, are you—"

He didn't finish his greeting.

Vampire hunter.

CHAPTER 3

•

Isabeau

I didn't think, I just reacted.

A Helios-Ra agent should not be able to breach the security of the Drake house now that they were the ruling family, especially when he had a broken arm. I might not consider them *my* ruling family particularly, but I wasn't about to let Solange get staked by a hunter after all the trouble we'd gone to to save her.

Shockingly, I was the only one who felt that way.

If I'd had a moment to let the group's reaction, or lack thereof, register, I might have wondered at it. They merely glanced at the intruder and were now positively aghast that I was flying through the air, double fangs bared.

I didn't like hunters.

This one was fast, I'd give him that. He slipped on the nose plugs that hung around his neck. It took him far less time to realize I was attacking than it had taken the others. The look of surprise on his face might have been comical if he hadn't been reaching for the release button on the Hypnos powder I knew was hidden in his sleeve. Once the secret was out about their new drug, it had spread like wildfire through the underground informants.

"No!" Solange yelled, but I wasn't sure whom she was shouting at.

I landed in front of the hunter before the Hypnos powder billowed in front of him, but only barely. I dropped into a crouch and rolled out of the way. I'd never actually experienced Hypnos, but I'd heard enough about it to want to avoid it. It had been created by the Helios-Ra as one more weapon in their arsenal in their fight against our kind.

Vampire pheromones could befuddle humans, could make them forget what they had seen or done, and could even make them succumb to us without the faintest threat of violence, if the vampire was strong enough. The Helios-Ra had grown tired of battles ending with their hunters wandering around perplexed and weaponless, or killed outright while they waited meekly for fang or knife. Certainly not all vampires were as civilized as the Drakes purported to be.

And now Hypnos was beginning to travel among the vampire tribes, making us vulnerable to one another in a way we had never been before. Pheromones didn't work on other vampires, but Hypnos, by all accounts, did.

I didn't have time to cover my nose and mouth. The powder

was so fine, like delicate confectioners' sugar on a poisoned pastry. I reached for a stake, fingers fumbling.

"Don't," the hunter snapped. "Don't move. Quiet."

I only took orders from Kala. I tried to leap to my feet but couldn't. The drug really was as nefarious as I'd heard. He had ordered me to stay where I was, and that was all I could do; I couldn't even move my mouth to speak. Even though every part of me screamed for release, every muscle ached with the pressure of it and my mind gibbered like a cornered badger, all teeth and claws and the need for violence.

But all I could do was lie there.

Charlemagne stood over me, growling, hackles raised. The Drake dogs growled in response but clearly hadn't yet decided who the enemy was.

Logan tried to approach me, moving slowly and warily. "Isabeau, don't panic."

Don't panic? *Don't panic?* I was virtually trapped inside my own body, unable to make it do what I wanted it to. I was at the mercy of royal vampires and a hunter.

I was an idiot.

I hadn't learned anything from Kala to protect myself in this situation mere hours after leaving the Hounds' caves. I probably deserved to die here in a puff of dust. But that would leave Greyhaven free, my first and second death utterly unavenged. Unacceptable. I actually growled, like the dogs, with my frantic need to be free.

"Isabeau, listen to me." Logan crouched to look at me since

Charlemagne wouldn't let him any closer. His eyes were very green, very intense. His jaw was tight. Behind him, Solange touched the hunter's arm, as if she worried for him. He took her hand in response.

This family made no sense.

"The effects will fade soon," Logan promised me soothingly, giving me his full attention. The light from the lamps made his cravat look like frozen snow. "You're not in any danger. I won't let anything happen to you."

I glared at him, then over his shoulder pointedly. He flicked his sister and her hunter a brief glance. "Kieran's a friend," he explained. "He won't hurt you either, I promise."

I wanted to tell him that I could look after myself.

But I couldn't.

I might never forgive any of them for seeing me this way.

"I'm sorry," Solange said to Kieran, then to me. "Really. He's not like the other Helios-Ra."

Kieran didn't look particularly flattered by that. He wore the unrelieved black of most hunters. He looked just like the other Helios-Ra to me. "Is she a Hound?" he asked, sounding stunned. His arm was encased in a soft cast.

"She's a guest," Logan snapped. Lucy crouched next to him, looking sympathetic. Charlemagne didn't move. A drop of his saliva hit my neck.

"I know it sucks, Isabeau," Lucy said. "Kieran did it to me two weeks ago."

"Shit," he muttered. "You guys had me tied to a chair."

Lucy waved her hand like that was hardly a good enough

excuse. "Whatever." She turned back to me. "You'll feel normal again in a few minutes. Promise." She really meant what she said, I could smell the truth of it on her even if I wasn't entirely convinced.

I couldn't stand the way they were all just staring at me. I knew what I must look like in my battle leathers and scars and double fangs and my angry dog by my side. I was proud of being Kala's handmaiden, of being a Hound, but the rest of the vampire tribes clearly didn't see us the same way.

"Let's give her some space," Logan said quietly, as if he knew what I was thinking. "I'll stay here. Why don't the rest of you wait in the living room."

"Are you sure?" Solange asked.

"I don't think she'll be too happy when she comes out of it," Kieran added doubtfully.

"Just go on," Logan nearly sighed.

When they left it was marginally less awful. I would have preferred to be completely alone. The thought of Logan seeing me at my weakest didn't thrill me. But still, there was a certain kind of comfort to his presence, which made no sense since we'd just met. Must be another effect of the Hypnos.

I tried to move again, but couldn't. I was able to speak though, which was a relief. It must be starting to fade. "Charlemagne," I croaked. "Ça va."

He sat on my foot, unconvinced but obedient. Logan stayed where he was.

"Do you want me to carry you upstairs to your room?" he asked.

"No," I said witheringly. I wasn't a delicate flower, I'd survived the Revolution and being buried for over two hundred years. I could handle ten more minutes lying on the floor. It had better not take longer than ten minutes. Though I couldn't remember exactly what it was like to lie in a coffin, I imagined it felt a little like this. I was glad I'd blocked it out, or lain comatose for centuries. Sweat gathered under my hair, cold on the back of my neck. It took a lot to make a vampire sweat. My expression must have been wild, because Logan cursed.

"This isn't how we meant to introduce you to our family. I hope you won't hold it against us for too long. The hunter is a little exuberant. He's not used to us yet either."

I snorted as control over my voice finally returned. "I can't believe a Helios-Ra hunter feels he can just walk through the front door."

"He and Solange have gotten . . . close."

"Does she have a death wish? We didn't save her to hand her over to the likes of them."

He shook his head, his tousled hair falling over his pale forehead. "He . . . loves her. Well, he's crushing on her anyway."

I didn't know the term but I understood its meaning well enough. I sighed. "I thought she'd be smarter."

He raised his eyebrows. "She's plenty smart." He looked thoughtful. "You don't believe in love then?"

"No." I wanted to look away, couldn't. "I don't know."

His smile was decidedly rakish. I'd seen its like on young aristocrats at my uncle's house. I tried to ignore it. I flexed my toes but wasn't able to do much more.

When the front door opened both Charlemagne and I tensed. I struggled to sit up, to reach for a weapon, any weapon. Logan rose and stood between me and the new arrivals. The four who burst in had to be his brothers, the physical similarities were too pronounced. Charlemagne growled, standing up again. They stopped mid-conversation, stared at the wild girl prostrate on the marbles.

I ground my teeth. This was hardly the way to foster respect for my tribe.

"Logan," one of them drawled. "Your technique's slipping if you need dogs to keep them from running away."

"Very funny, Quinn," Logan muttered. "This is Isabeau."

They froze each to a one, staring.

"Isabeau, my brothers: Quinn, Marcus, Connor, and Duncan. Sebastian's still at the caves."

"*Un plaisir,*" I said dryly. My Hounds training might not have prepared me to be gracious under any circumstance, but my aristocratic upbringing had.

"Nice to meet you." Connor blinked. "Why are you on the floor?"

"Hypnos," I said.

Quinn snorted. "Dude, Hypnos and dogs? I thought you were the one who was supposed to be good with the girls, Darcy?" I recognized the nickname; I'd read voraciously once I'd grown accustomed to my new body and appetites. I'd needed to grow accustomed to hundreds of years of history as well.

"Shut up," Logan said. "Kieran blew Hypnos on her."

Quinn bared his fangs. "Why the hell did he do that?"

"Well, to be fair, she did try to kick him in the head."

Quinn grinned at me. "I like you already."

I tried to push myself up again. I couldn't lie there for another second while they stared at me curiously. I was too anxious to be able to retract my double fangs. If I'd been human, I would have been hyperventilating by now. Logan glanced at me, cursed.

"I'm taking you upstairs," he muttered. "Call off your dog," he added, scooping me up into his arms. Charlemagne was right there, pressed at Logan's knee.

"Ça va," I whispered, even if I wasn't sure I entirely believed it. Charlemagne trotted by our side as Logan climbed the stairs, carrying me lightly and easily. I was mortified and grateful. The conflicting emotions didn't make the present situation any easier to handle.

"I know you said you didn't want me to do this," he whispered. "But it's better than all my brothers cracking jokes over your head, right?"

I nodded because I didn't trust my voice. The fact that I could move my head enough to agree with him was heartening. He noticed the small movement.

"Any minute now," he promised.

The second floor of the house smelled even more like smoke and water. The far wall was faintly scorched. He followed my gaze.

"Hope," he said succinctly.

Hope had led a rogue unit of the Helios-Ra who'd kidnapped Solange and tried to burn down her parents' farm. It had only been a week ago at most and the damage was still visible.

Logan took me down a hall and kicked a door open to a guest room. The windows had thick wooden shutters with strong iron locks on the inside. There was a narrow writing desk and a padded chair by a fireplace. The mahogany bed was huge and soft-looking, with a small discreet fridge by the end table. I knew it would be stocked with blood. I was still young enough to need to feed immediately upon waking, something all the Drake children must also be dealing with. It raised my opinion of their hosting capabilities so far, drastically.

Logan laid me gently down on the bed, leaning so close that I could see the flecks of darker green in his irises. I swallowed.

"I feel like I know you," he murmured. "Is that weird?"

I didn't know what to say. Charlemagne hopped up to lie next to me on the quilt, breaking the moment before I could find a reply. Logan stepped back.

"I'll leave you alone," he said. "When Lucy came out of the Hypnos she broke Nicholas's nose. I'd wager you have a stronger swing and I happen to like my nose exactly where it is. No one will disturb you," he added fiercely. "Come down whenever you're ready. I'll be waiting."

He bowed. "*Mademoiselle.*"

The door shut very quietly behind him. When I could hear by his footsteps that he was down the stairs and out of earshot, I allowed myself a very small sigh. Charlemagne tilted his head curiously.

"This isn't going at all according to plan," I told him.

CHAPTER 4

♦

LOGAN

My brothers are idiots.

Anyone can see that under the scars and the attitude, Isabeau is more fragile than she looks. And as a reclusive Hound princess, her first introduction to the royal family shouldn't be a dose of Hypnos and four idiots gawking at her.

If I'd managed not to gawk, they sure as hell could have. She was beautiful, fierce, and utterly unlike anyone I'd ever known.

It was really hard not to gawk.

Much better to pace outside her door with one of our Bouviers sitting at the top of the stairs watching me curiously.

"This sucks, Boudicca," I told her. "I don't think we inherited Dad's diplomacy."

She laid her chin on her paws. I could have sworn she rolled her eyes.

I hovered by Isabeau's door for another fifteen minutes until I started feeling like a stalker. Solange came down the hall from her room and met me at the staircase.

"She'll be fine, Logan."

"I know."

She tilted her head. "Did you change your shirt?"

"No."

"You totally did." She grinned. "Too bad your girlfriend tried to kill my boyfriend."

I snorted. "Too bad he dosed her with drugs. And she's not my girlfriend. I just met her. And lower your voice, would you?"

She raised an eyebrow. "I've never seen you like this."

"Shut up, princess." I mock-glowered at her. She narrowed her eyes at the term "princess."

"I will dye all your pirate shirts pink," she threatened.

I just grinned. "I'd still make them look good."

She paused on the landing, her expression turning serious. "Is it true an assassin tried to stake Mom?"

"Who told you that?"

She poked my shoulder. Hard.

"Ow," I said, rubbing the bruise. "What was that for?"

"For thinking I'm dumb and avoiding giving me an answer."

"I don't think you're dumb."

"Then stop trying to shield me, Logan."

"No."

She made a sound of frustration in the back of her throat.

I sighed. "Fine. Yes. Some girl tried to stake Mom. No one was hurt."

"Montmartre?"

"Yeah, she wore his insignia." I hated to admit it. Especially when her face went hard and her eyes flat. "But she staked herself before we could get any answers."

"Damn it." She slapped the wall, rattling the crystal chandelier above us. "He's trying to make me queen by killing Mom."

"Looks like," I admitted. I slung an arm over her shoulder. "But it's not going to happen."

She rubbed her arms as if she were cold. Vampires didn't really get cold, so it was more habit than necessity. "I hope you're right, Logan."

"I'm always right."

She chuckled, which is what I'd intended. "Careful, you'll be as vain as Quinn soon."

"No one's as vain as Quinn," Lucy said from the bottom of the stairs. She was carrying a mug of hot chocolate and a handful of cookies. Taking advantage of her stay with us, she was gorging herself on white sugar and junk food. She had more issues with her mom's tofu casserole than the fact that everyone currently around her drank blood.

"Where's everybody?" I asked. A fire popped in the hearth but the living room was empty. So was the kitchen.

"Fixing the wall outside," Lucy replied.

The north side of the farmhouse was a mess of scorched and water-damaged logs. The wraparound porch had taken the brunt of the attack when Hope busted out of the guest room and returned with the rest of her crazy rogue Helios-Ra agents. Bruno spent so much time in the home-improvement stores since then muttering his bewilderment at us on his cell phone that we'd started hearing "noises" in the woods so he'd stay home and patrol the perimeters. Hope had a lot to answer for. So did Montmartre. It really sucked that we hadn't gotten a chance to make them pay horribly and at great length. Defeating their plans didn't seem to be enough. A little vengeance might have been nice, regardless of what Dad said in his "rebuilding stronger" speeches. Truth be told, we were all just glad Solange had survived the bloodchange and the various attempts to abduct or kill her.

I was really glad not to be sixteen anymore.

Because being sixteen in our family just plain bites.

"I guess I should help them out," I said reluctantly. Manual labor was brutal on the wardrobe.

"Hell, yes, you should," Nicholas called out, emerging from the basement with an extra toolbox and a saw. Lucy grinned at him as he hauled the back door open.

"Tool belt," she said, licking hot chocolate off her lip. "Yum."

The wind shifted and I could smell the warm blood moving under her skin. We all could. Nicholas took a step back, looking vaguely pained.

She frowned at him. "What's the matter with you? You look nauseous."

"I'm fine," he said through his teeth. "Stay inside. It's not safe."

She rolled her eyes. "Quit fretting. It's perfectly safe, there's all of you and like a gazillion guards."

"That's not what I meant," he muttered, easing outside into the shadows to busy himself at a pile of cut logs. Tension made the tendons on the back of his neck strain. Lucy stared after him for a long moment before closing the door behind him.

I followed him, grabbing a stainless-steel thermos filled with blood from the cooler on the deck. I tossed it at him. He caught it and turned away to drink. It wasn't easy for a young vampire to resist the taste of fresh human blood. It was even more difficult when your new girlfriend was staying at your house while you struggled to tame the biting thirst. Now that Solange was newly turned, she had started to sit at the opposite end of the room and Lucy had been forced to move into one of the guest rooms, with a lock inside the door. We'd grown up with her and would never intentionally hurt her, but a young vampire was more animal than human in those waking moments after the sun went down. It was some sort of biological imperative. Our bodies forced us to drink what our brains would rebel against. Otherwise, we'd die.

"Hey, man, you're doing good," I told him quietly as he wiped his mouth with the back of his hand.

"She doesn't get it," he said. "Not really."

"She gets it more than anyone else ever could."

"Still."

"Yeah," I agreed. "Still."

Quinn, Connor, Marcus, and Duncan were ripping off the parts of the logs that were unsalvageable. I grabbed a hammer and tried not to be so aware of Isabeau inside the house.

Nicholas ran a hand through his hair, frustrated. "When did this all get so complicated?"

"Girls are always complicated," I told him. "You know that."

He half smiled. "Some more than others."

I thought of the scars on Isabeau's arms and the haunted look in her eye. "Got that right."

We got to work, mostly following Duncan's lead because he almost had a clue as to how to fix a wall. When we needed plaster for some reason I couldn't quite fathom, I went out to the garage to find some. On my way back, I paused, goose bumps suddenly lifting.

A noise in the woods.

Something quiet, subtle.

And unwelcome.

I couldn't alert my brothers without alerting whoever was lurking in the woods as well. I set down the bucket of plaster dust and doubled back toward the front door and woods on the other side of the lane. I peered into the shifting shadows of the rose-bushes and cedar trees. The faint moonlight glinted off the Jeep in the driveway. The lamps burned softly at the windows. I smelled roses, newly cut oak logs, blood, and lilies.

Lilies were never a good sign.

Montmartre smelled like lilies. And while I doubted he was loitering in the woods outside our farmhouse, I had no problem believing he'd sent minions to do his dirty work.

He was after Solange again, just as she'd said.

He wanted her to be queen, as the old prophecy claimed, and

more importantly, he wanted her to be *his* queen. He thought he could rule in her place, using her as a figurehead. And after tonight, he apparently thought if he took Mom out of the picture, Solange would fall in line.

He *so* didn't get Drake women.

And he really needed staking.

I was happy to oblige . . . if he would just stand still long enough.

CHAPTER 5

◆

Isabeau

When the Hypnos powder finally wore off, it was quick as summer lightning. I reared up as if I'd been jolted full of electricity. Charlemagne barked once and I laughed out loud. The ability to control my limbs again was intoxicating. I felt as giddy as a debutante at her first ball. Even the cell phone vibrating in my pocket didn't bother me.

"Magda." I grinned into the receiver. No one else would be calling me.

"Isabeau? Is that you?" Magda demanded.

"Of course, who else would it be?" I stretched to make sure I could. Then I did a backflip somersault.

"Are you giggling?" she asked incredulously. "What did they do to you?"

"Hypnos."

There was a pause, a choked cough. "And that's funny why?"

"It's not," I assured her. "But it's just worn off."

"Are you in trouble? What are they doing to you? Don't they know you're a princess, or whatever? I'm getting Finn."

"No!" I stopped her before she could get going. "I'm fine. It was an accident."

"Are you *sure*?" she pressed suspiciously. "They're not like us, Isabeau."

"I know," I said. "Believe me. Even their humans are odd." Even though I hadn't met many humans since I'd been pulled out of the grave, I was fairly certain Lucy was unique.

"They have humans there?"

"A girl. And some guards."

"Did you taste her?"

"I don't think they'd like that." I could just picture the look on Nicholas's face.

"Is the Hypnos as bad as they say?"

"Yes." There wasn't a moment of hesitation. "Worse even."

"Bastards."

"Keep your voice down," I told her. "We're supposed to be here as diplomats, remember?"

Magda snorted. "I'm not the diplomatic sort."

I snorted back, feeling better. "I know." Before she'd accepted me as a sister, Magda had been jealous of my closeness with her mentor, Kala. She'd tried to cut off my hair in a fit of pique. After I'd broken her fingers, she'd immediately warmed to me and had been fiercely loyal ever since.

"How is it over there?" I asked.

"The Drakes are all right, so far," she grudgingly admitted. "But most of these courtiers don't want us here."

"Should I come back?" I wondered, concerned.

"As much as I'd prefer it if you were here, we're fine. We'll see you tomorrow. I'll eavesdrop as much as I can until then."

"Good." She was exceedingly skilled at it. "I'll do what I can here."

"Watch your back."

"You too."

I slipped the phone back into my pocket and then searched the room for traps, cracks in the wooden shutter that might let in the sunlight, anything out of the ordinary. I even sniffed the blood in the fridge but it smelled fine. They would have thought me paranoid, but Hounds were accustomed to looking after themselves. Between Montmartre and his Host and the disdain of the rest of the vampire community, we couldn't afford to let our guard down.

And I couldn't sit in this room much longer. I had work to do.

"Come on," I told Charlemagne, pushing open the door. "Let's go."

I had planned to go back downstairs but changed my course when I heard Lucy's human heartbeat from the other end of the hall, around the corner. I found her standing at the window with Solange.

"Isabeau." Solange searched my face with worried eyes. "Are you feeling better?"

I nodded. "Where's your hunter?"

She flinched. "He went home. We thought it would be best." Her eyes went from worried to warning. "He's under Drake protection."

"So am I, or so I've been led to understand."

"Of course you are," Lucy said, her nose pressed to the window. "Misunderstanding. No big deal."

Solange quirked a half smile. "You might try complete sentences, Lucy."

"Can't. Busy."

I was curious despite myself. "What are you doing?"

"Drooling," Solange explained fondly.

"I totally am," Lucy admitted, unrepentant. "Just look at them."

Lucy moved over to give me space. She was watching five of the seven Drake boys repairing the outside wall of the farmhouse, under our window. I had to admit they made an impressive picture, handsome and pale and shirtless, muscles gleaming in the moonlight. I couldn't help but look for Logan, but he was walking away.

Solange leaned back against the wall, bored. "Are you done yet?"

"Hell no," Lucy said. She'd left nose prints on the glass. Nicholas smirked up at her. She blushed. "Ooops. Busted."

"I told you they could hear your heartbeat," Solange said. "Even from up here."

"I can't help it. Even if they all know they're pretty and are insufferably arrogant," she added louder. "Can they hear that?"

"Yes."

"Good." She glanced at me. "Yummy, right?"

"I'm sure Isabeau would rather recover, not ogle my brothers," Solange said. "You remember how stressed you were after the Hypnos?"

"Please," Lucy scoffed. "This is totally soothing."

When Lucy finally let herself be dragged away from the window, we went down to the main parlor. One of the windows was boarded up and the smell of smoke was thick here as well. Lucy chattered away, which was a blessing. Solange seemed as reserved as I was, and without the cheerful human it would have been awkward and uncomfortable.

"Your tattoos are gorgeous," she said. "I'm desperate to get one but Mom's making me wait until I turn eighteen." She made a face. "They pick the weirdest things to be strict about. I mean Mom's got three and Dad has one. Doesn't exactly seem fair, does it?"

My sleeveless tunic dress bared my arms, which ran dark with tattoos. It hadn't been easy to get them to stay permanent. I'd had to get them all redone three times. Vampire healing tended to push the ink and charcoal out.

"I've never seen work like that," she continued. "You didn't just walk into a tattoo parlor, did you?"

"No, Kala did these with charcoal and a needle." Most of them had been drawn in the ritual that dedicated me to her service. The first one they'd done before I'd fully awakened, after the dogs found me. It was a greyhound circling my upper left arm, catching his tail in his mouth, surrounded with Celtic knot work. All the Hounds had one just like it.

"Ouch." Lucy winced at the thought of the slow tattoo process. Most of the others were also dogs chasing one another up my arms, accentuated with vines. "Still, they're totally cool."

"You're not afraid of me." It wasn't a question but a statement. She looked surprised that I'd mentioned it.

"No. Should I be? You saved Solange."

"Even vampires are nervous around the Cwn Mamau," I pointed out. I wasn't sure why I was insisting she be scared of me. I just hadn't had a lot of experience with unconditional acceptance, not from the revolutionaries in Paris and certainly not from other vampires. I felt the need to poke at the odd experience, like a sore tooth.

"Because you wear bones and do weird rituals in caves and paint mud on your faces?" she asked, grinning. "Please, my parents do that all the time. They're totally into shamanistic rituals and dancing naked under the full moon."

"Explains everything, doesn't it?" Solange glanced at me with a shy smile, inviting me into the moment.

"She is . . . unique," I agreed.

"She's also right here," Lucy grumbled good-naturedly. "And even with my wimpy human hearing, I can hear you."

It was all very surreal. If my life had taken a different turn I might have taken for granted sitting with girlfriends in fine silk dresses drinking tea and eating petits fours. As it was, I'd never done this before. I wondered what Magda was doing right now, if she was touring the caves or arguing with a guard. I'd wager arguing with a guard.

"Can I give you a word of advice?" Lucy asked.

"I suppose so."

"You have a great French accent. If a guy asks you to wear a French maid's costume, kick him in the shin."

"Especially if it's one of my brothers," Solange agreed.

Charlemagne started to growl. I frowned at him, looking quickly around the room for the source of his alarm. I couldn't find a thing until there was a thump at the front door. We ran for the foyer, Lucy considerably slower behind us. Solange looked through the peephole, then reached for the handle.

"Another gift," she sighed. "Honestly, I thought once the worst of the bloodchange pheromones faded they'd go away."

At the front stoop lay a package wrapped in red foil paper, white rose petals scattered around it. She reached down to pick it up but I grabbed her arm.

"Don't," I said. "It's Montmartre. I can smell him on it." I nudged her back, reaching for my sword. "Go inside."

I didn't wait to see if she'd listened, only kicked the door shut in her face. I was climbing off the porch when a pale shadow was suddenly at my elbow.

I only narrowly avoided decapitating Logan. He bent out of the way of my blade, graceful as a dancer. His pretty face was grim.

"There's someone in the woods," he said.

"I know. Host," I added. I knew that smell, however faint— blood, lilies, and wine. Montmartre's personal army always smelled the same.

"Stay here," he ordered.

"I'm a Hound," I told him. "This is what I do. *You* stay here."

"Like hell."

"Then stay out of my way."

"Like hell," he repeated.

We moved like smoke between the cedars and maple trees lining the drive, toward the fields bordering the forest. I kept my sword lowered so the moonlight wouldn't flash off the blade and give us away. Charlemagne padded beside me, eager but silent. The trees towered over us in their mossy dresses, branches crowned with leaves and owls and sleeping hawks. The ground was soft underfoot, ferns touching our legs as we passed. Even the insects fell silent; not a single cricket or grasshopper gave away its position. Only the river sang quietly to herself in the distance.

Logan stopped, jerked his head to the right. I followed his gaze, nodded once to tell him I saw what he saw.

A single white rose petal, trampled into the mud.

For someone who wore lace cuffs when he wasn't bare chested, Logan knew how to track. The wind shifted and my nostrils flared. The smell of bloody lilies was stronger now, thick as incense. We followed it, splitting up in unspoken agreement around a copse of oak trees. Logan went left, I stayed right. This, at least, was something I was comfortable with. Tracking the Host was what I did. It sat easier on my skin than polite conversation and royal politics. I was almost looking forward to it.

There were two of them left, though it smelled as if there'd been more. They were quick, but not quick enough. Logan went ahead to block them off and I crept in behind them. One of them hissed.

"Do you hear—"

He didn't finish his question. Instead he spun on one foot to face me with a leer. I didn't waste time leering back, only leaped forward with my sword flashing.

"A Hound whelp," he spat. "A little far from home, aren't you?"

"No farther than you."

He swung out with a fist, confident of his strength. I danced backward, cocked an eyebrow in his direction.

"Serving Montmartre's made you fat and lazy," I taunted him. His face mottled with rage and he roared, attacking again. Anger made him clumsy and easy to avoid. I flitted around him like a hummingbird. Charlemagne stood to the side, waiting for a command.

Logan engaged his companion before they could join forces. "Quit playing with him and finish him," he grunted, ducking a dagger strike.

The Host who was trying his best to dismember me had a similar dagger, curved and nearly as long as a sword. There was no crossbow, no gun loaded with bullets filled with holy water. It was a favorite among the Host, stolen from fallen Helios-Ra agents. This one, though, was dressed for hunting and infiltrating, not battle. I noticed these details dispassionately, concentrating on staying light on my feet. Our movements grew faster, more vicious until we must have looked like a blur, just a succession of colors, like paint smears on a wet canvas. Logan dispatched his opponent, ash settling on the nearby ferns. He bent to pick something up out of the clothes left behind.

I parried a stab at my heart, the chain-mail patch sewn into my tunic jingling faintly. I aimed for his head, moving with deliberate and deceptive slowness. He blocked it, leaning back instinctively. I took advantage of his position and the momentum of my swing and jabbed at his lower leg. I caught him by surprise and he stumbled back, cursing. Blood seeped down his leg, splattered into the undergrowth. I moved in for the kill but he was gone, running through the woods. I probably could have caught up to him, could certainly follow the trail of blood droplets.

Which was the point.

Logan wiped blood from a cut on his arm, shaking his head.

"You're as good as they say you are," he said. "I'm surprised you didn't dust him."

"Better to give him a few minutes' head start."

"Why's that? Didn't your mother teach you it's rude to play with your food?"

"I wouldn't drink from him if I was starving. He's wounded and he'll go back to his pack. If we're lucky that cut won't heal until he's led us there."

Logan stared at me, then at the thick green undergrowth. Even slowed down, the Host would be moving fast enough not to leave footsteps. Not flying exactly, but certainly a speed-enhanced float, which was difficult to track.

Much more difficult than tracking a trail of blood, even in a forest thick with the scents and markings of various vampires and assorted animals. Logan whistled through his teeth.

"I'm definitely impressed." He reached for the phone in his

pocket. "Let me make a call and then let's get the bastard. What the hell did they want this time? Solange has already turned."

"Montmartre," I said flatly. "They were leaving a gift for your sister at the front door."

"Son of a bitch. Is this a Host symbol?" He showed me the small wooden disk he'd plucked up out of the ashes of his attacker. It was engraved with a rose and three daggers. "The assassin who tried to dust my mother tonight had a tattoo like this."

"I've never seen it before," I said.

"There's something else going on here, something we're missing." He spoke curtly into the phone and then tossed his hair out of his eyes. "Let's go."

"I can do this alone," I assured him. "I'm quite capable."

"Mmm-hmmm," he murmured noncommittally.

We went swiftly, but not so swiftly that we'd catch up before he'd had a chance to lead us anywhere interesting. It was uncomplicated work.

The surprise came in the form of a piece of fabric, pinned to a narrow birch tree, gleaming pale as snow. The silk was indigo, faded with age and encrusted with silver-thread embroidery. The delicate stitching showed a fleur-de-lys and the frayed end of a tattered ribbon.

I knew that scrap of cloth, knew it intimately.

I shivered, reaching for my sword again.

CHAPTER 6

•

France, 1788

Her mother's dressing room was Isabeau's favorite place in the entire château. She loved it even better than the dog pens and the stables, even more than the locked pantry where the cook kept the precious blocks of chocolate and jars of candied violets. She wasn't allowed in either room, so she tried very hard to be quiet and unobtrusive, perched on a blue silk stool as her mother's maids flitted in and out with various cosmetics and gowns.

Her mother, Amandine, sat at her table, applying rouge to her powdered cheeks. Her hair was pinned under an elaborate white wig laden with corkscrew curls and bluebirds made out of beads and real feathers. Isabeau had heard stories of Marie Antoinette's beauty and the stunning displays of her hairpieces, some with ships so tall she had to duck through doorways. Isabeau couldn't imagine the queen could have been any more beautiful than her mother was tonight. When she was old enough, she would wear ropes of pearls and sapphires in her hair as well, and silk-covered panniers under her gowns.

Amandine's underclothes were made of the finest white linen and silk, ornamented with tiny satin bows. The gown she had chosen for tonight's ball was indigo, like a summer sky at twilight. The buttons were made of pearls and the silver-thread embroidery paraded fleur-de-lys from hem to neckline. The St. Croix annual ball was famous throughout the countryside; aristocrats traveled from as far away as Paris to attend. At ten years old, Isabeau was too young to join in but finally old enough to escape her nurse's attentions. She had already staked out a perfect hiding spot, inside a painted armoire with a cracked keyhole. She'd be able to see all the fine gowns and the diamond cravat pins and the pet poodles on gold-chain leashes. She bounced a little in her excitement. Her mother's glance slid toward her and she stilled instantly.

"You're very pretty, *Maman*," she flattered.

"Thank you, *chouette*." Amandine smiled at her in the mirror, clasping a necklace with three tiers of diamonds, pearls, and a sapphire the size of a robin's egg. She took a sip of red wine, dabbing her lips delicately with a handkerchief.

"I think you'll be even prettier than the queen. And our house is so much better than Versailles."

Amandine looked amused. "Do you think so, *chouette?*"

"Everyone says so," Isabeau assured her proudly. "They say the nobles pee in the back staircases, *Maman!* We would never pee on the floor."

Amandine laughed. "You are quite right, Isabeau."

"Except for Sabot," she felt obliged to admit. "But he's only a puppy."

Amandine's head maidservant plucked the gown off the hanger. "Madame."

Amandine stood up to let another maid tie her panniers into place and secure her corset. The gown slipped over the top. Isabeau scuttled forward to lift the hem so it wouldn't catch on the edge of the vanity table. It was surprisingly heavy and she wondered how her mother could stand so tall under all that weight. Her wig tipped precariously to the side and she caught it with one manicured hand.

"Francine," she said. "We'll need more pins."

"*Oui, madame.*"

When the wig was secure again, Amandine turned to admire herself in the long cheval glass.

"Oh, *Maman,*" Isabeau breathed. "*Tu es si belle!*" When she was grown-up, she was going to wear lip color and a heart-shaped patch on her cheek, just like her mother.

Amandine smiled. "I remember watching your grandmother prepare for balls." She reached for a hair-ribbon-length piece of cloth just like her dress. "Here, *petite.* I didn't need this after all. You may keep it."

Isabeau took it with a wide surprised smile. "*Merci.*" She rubbed it against her cheek reverently. She followed her mother out through her bedchamber down the mahogany steps, staying behind the maids. Her father, Jean-Paul St. Croix, waited at the bottom of the staircase. The duke was perfectly arranged, from his rolled wig to the gold buckles on his heeled shoes.

"*Ma chere,*" he greeted Amandine. "Spectacular as always."

Isabeau kept close to the maids, sneaking behind a potted cypress tree when they abandoned her for other duties. She ran to the ballroom as fast as she could, ducking around footmen bearing jugs of wine and champagne, and servants carting gilded chairs and baskets of sugared fruit. She crept into the armoire, which usually stored excess table linens. Every single piece had been needed for the buffet tables at the back of the room and the more formal dining room across the hall, so the cupboard was empty. She fit perfectly inside once she'd drawn her knees up to her chest. She left the door open a sliver; it was even better than peering through the keyhole.

It didn't take long for the first guests to arrive. She could just imagine the beautiful carriages pulling up the limestone lane, drawn by magnificent horses with plumes in their manes. The footmen rushed through the ballroom, lighting the last of the candles and oil lamps. The crystal chandeliers glittered over tables laden with all manner of delicacies: strawberries, marzipan birds, sugared orange peels, roast goose, oysters, lavender biscuits, petits fours, and chocolate-glazed candies. Isabeau rubbed her stomach, which was growling at the sight of so many desserts. She'd missed her supper by hiding away from her nurse.

She forgot her hunger the very moment the guests began to

pour through the doors. The women laughed behind painted lace fans, the men bowed with sharp precision. She could smell the heavy perfume and eau de toilette mingling with the warm pâtés being circulated on silver platters. Champagne flowed like rivers at springtime. The orchestra began to play and the music filled every corner, even the dark space of the armoire. She imagined this was what angels' music must sound like, all pianoforte and harp and the soaring, ethereal voice of the opera singer.

Her parents joined the crowds just as the gaming tables began to fill up. Painted cards and coins changed hands. Someone's pet poodle growled at the singer. Isabeau felt her stomach clutch hungrily again and wondered if she dared escape her safe hiding spot. If she was caught not only would she be sent straight to bed, which would be mortifying enough, but she'd also never be able to use this armoire to hide in again. She chewed on her lower lip, considering. Finally the smell of all that food grew to be too heavy a temptation.

She eased the door open a few inches, waiting to see if she'd been noticed. A couple passed by, intertwined. They paused, kissing passionately. Isabeau made a disgusted face. The man looked as if he was trying to eat that lady's face. It didn't look comfortable at all. He should eat some supper if he was that hungry.

She slipped out, landing quietly to hide behind the woman's gown. Her panniers stuck out so far on either side of her, she was the width of three people. Neither she nor her companion noticed. They seemed to be breathing rather hard, as if they'd run a race around the garden. Isabeau abandoned them for the thick brocade curtains, pouncing from one window to another. Most of the guests were laughing too loudly, drinking strawberry-garnished champagne, and losing money with great shouts at the card tables. No one noticed her. It felt a little like being inside a kaleidoscope, swirling with colors and sounds and smells. It made her a little dizzy and she was glad for the relative safety of the buffet tables. She rolled under the first one she could reach, well hidden behind the floating white tablecloths.

From this angle, the gleaming parquet floor showed the scuff marks of fine shoes and beeswax drippings from the candles. She'd never seen so many silk slippers and silver buckles in her whole life. She couldn't wait to host parties of her own, just like this one.

She slipped her hand up the back of the table, where it was nearly against the wall, and took a blind handful. She'd been hoping for madeleines or a puff pastry filled with custard. The oyster was slimy and thick, though its shell was pretty enough. Perhaps she'd keep it on her desk and use it to display her treasures: a stone with a perfect hole through its center, a stalk of dried lavender, Sabot's baby canine.

The second handful was far more worth the risk of discovery. The cakes were light and smeared with icing and raspberries. They stained her fingertips red, like blood. She thought her teeth must be red too and she bared them like an animal, grinning. She'd have to remember this trick the next time she played with Joseph, one of the young stable boys. It would scare him silly and she would be avenged for the prank he'd played on her last month with that bucket of cold water.

She ate until she was full and sleepy and her teeth ached a little from all the sweets. She curled into a little ball and pillowed her cheek on her hands. One of the poodles sniffed his way toward her and lay down beside her, licking the last of the raspberry juice off her fingers. One by one, the little dogs found her, creeping under the tablecloth in their diamond collars to lick her face and snore themselves to sleep against her. Smiling, she fell asleep as well under her canine blanket, holding the ribbon of her mother's dress.

CHAPTER 7

◆

Isabeau

The Host led us through the woods at a comfortable pace. He was stumbling enough to leave a trail of broken branches and blood. He healed quickly though and by the time he stopped in a shadowed clearing, there was only the scent of blood remaining, and only very faintly. Logan nodded to a tangle of blackberry bushes. The thorns would pull and scratch but it offered the best protection; everything else was delicate feathery ferns. We crouched silently, waiting. I tried not to remember how my mother had loved blackberry tarts best of all, tried not to feel the scrap of worn silk burning in my pocket. I was grinding my teeth loud enough that Logan nudged me, frowning.

I tethered myself firmly to the present, focused on the mud under our feet, the thicket of leaves, the white flowers glowing on the border of the meadow, the Host standing in the tall grass. The gleaming marble and gilded scrollwork of the château of my youth faded slowly. Dusty grapes became ripe blackberries, piano music became the silence of crickets sensing predators nearby, lavender fields became a dark forest.

The Host wasn't alone for long, as two more joined him from the direction of the Drake farms.

"They got Nigel," one of them spat. He was pale enough to gleam in the moonlight, as if he'd been covered in crushed pearls.

"Got me too," the one we'd tracked muttered. "Isabeau stabbed me, the bitch. Ripped my damn shirt. Since when do the royal courts have Hound whelps for backup?"

"Everything's changing, Jones." The third Host shrugged pragmatically. "Was Montmartre's gift delivered?"

"Doorstep," Jones confirmed. "As ordered."

Logan's lips lifted off his protruding fangs but he didn't make a sound. I was impressed at his control. I'd assumed the Drake brothers were a wild, undisciplined lot, being royal and all. It would have been easy to forget by their fine manners that they'd been exiled from the royal court since Solange was born, and strongly discouraged from attending for at least a century before that. They all carried themselves with a certain flair and confidence.

Jones was fully healed now and pacing a rut in the ground. "Any word from Greyhaven?"

The name hit me so hard I flinched as if I'd been struck, then I went as still as a hungry lion spotting a gazelle. A red haze covered my eyes, as if I looked through a mist of blood. If I'd had a heart-beat, it would have been loud as a blacksmith's hammer on his anvil. Time seemed to go backward, speed up, and then stop altogether.

"He's with Montmartre, waiting for the right time."

"We've waited long enough, haven't we?" Jones grumbled.

"He wants everything to be perfect this time. No surprises." The first smirked. "Well, not for us anyway. The Drakes will be plenty surprised."

I knew they were still talking but their words barely registered. All I could hear was that one word.

Greyhaven.

Greyhaven.

My skull felt like a church bell, ringing the same sound over and over again.

I hissed, tensing to leap out of the bushes, my vengeance closer than it had ever been before. They knew where Greyhaven was, could lead me to him so I could kill him for murdering me.

I never made it out of my crouch.

Logan was on me, quick as a hornet. His hand pressed over my mouth, his eyes flaring a warning above me. He was close enough that I could have bitten him, if he hadn't had my jaws locked together. His body chained mine to the ground. He was stronger than I'd given him credit for, but I was faster and could have flipped him into the nearest tree.

Only the realization that I'd been about to give us away altogether made me pause.

Even Charlemagne was smart enough to stay quiet, though he was trembling with the need to protect me. I wanted the fight with

Jones, with all of them, even if it meant giving away our only tactical advantage: a mere hint of a plan whispered by a group of Host in the woods. It wasn't much, but it was certainly more than we'd had at the beginning of the evening.

And I didn't care. I would have thrown it all away for a chance at Greyhaven.

And Logan knew it.

He stayed where he was, stretched out as if he were protecting me from a rain of fiery arrows, a crumbling mountain, some unseen danger. But the danger wasn't anywhere but inside my chest, circling like a vulture.

It took every ounce of strength I could muster not to hurl him off me. I forced my body to soften infinitesimally, molding me into the undergrowth. Even at that small surrender, Logan didn't move. His scent was strong: anise, wine, a faint trace of mint. I knew I smelled like scalded wine and sugar to him—Kala told me I always smelled that way when I was furious beyond logic. The rage boiling on my skin didn't faze him. His fangs didn't retract; his face stayed mere inches from mine. Most vampires cowered away from a shamanka's handmaiden when she was in this state. Logan was too busy listening to the others to cower.

"Any nibbles from the old guard?"

"Yes, most of those loyal to Lady Natasha's memory fled when the Drake woman murdered her, but a few stayed behind for a more subtle attack. They'll join with us when it's time."

"Good. Let's get the hell out of here. The Drake boys are probably still out looking for us."

The Host took off between the trees, toward the mountain. Logan stayed where he was and we stared at each other for a long, strange moment. In the shadows, his eyes were the color of sugared limes. Lovely and distracting, but not *that* distracting.

When our enemies were far enough away, I heaved him off me with a sudden violent jerk.

I rose into a crouch, panting. My body might not need air but breathing remained a habit, especially in times of stress. Logan hit the trunk of a birch and twisted in the air to land on the balls of his feet right front of me.

We both crouched, fangs bared, muscles tensed for attack.

We might have stayed there for the rest of the night if it wasn't for Charlemagne, who whined once, confused. It was like a flame was blown out.

Logan stood, all feral grace and ironic smile. He looked as comfortable and pretty as a guest at one of my parents' balls, even shirtless. I was still panting, nearly nauseous from the swirl of emotions swamping my stomach: anticipation, anger, regret, humiliation. My mother's dress, Greyhaven. It was very nearly too much. I stood slowly, like an old woman. Charlemagne pressed his cold nose into the palm of my hand for comfort and I wasn't sure which of us needed the comfort more.

"Are you okay?" Logan asked quietly.

I nodded jerkily. "I'm sorry." I was accustomed to being lauded for my focus and control.

"What happened? Do you know that Greyhaven guy?"

"*Oui.*"

His eyes narrowed on my face. "Who is he? What did he do to you?"

"What makes you think he did anything?" I stepped out of the blackberry thicket, scenting the air for any trace of Host. We were alone.

Logan's expression was grim. "Isabeau, I saw the look on your face."

I shrugged one shoulder. "I'm fine now. We should return."

I turned to walk back through the trees but he grabbed my arm. "You nearly lost it back there."

I stiffened. It didn't make it any more palatable that he was right. "But I didn't."

"Next time, you could put my sister in danger with your temper."

I swallowed a hot retort. "It won't happen again."

"I know," he sighed, letting his hand drop. For some indiscernible reason, I felt its absence. It was as if I were cold now, and I never got cold.

I didn't know what it was about Logan that flustered me like this. I was going to have to find a way to stay away from him. He clearly wasn't good for me.

"I can see it's not in your nature to give like that. Would you tell me what he did to you, anyway? Please?"

I lifted my chin, refusing to be pitied.

"He's the one who turned me and then left me in a coffin underground for two centuries."

◆

We didn't speak again on our way back to the farmhouse. As far as diplomatic missions went, mine was already a disaster. I'd attacked a family friend, got doused with Hypnos, and nearly went mad with rage—all in one night.

No wonder I was so exhausted.

We'd barely been gone for half an hour, for all that it felt like days. Logan's brothers were all dressed and sitting in a grim half circle around the foil-wrapped package in the parlor. Solange was frowning at it, tapping her fingers on her knees. Lucy was asleep on the sofa, her head resting on Nicholas's leg. He'd draped an afghan over her, and she looked tiny and defenseless in a room of predators who couldn't help but hear the temptation of her heartbeat. She dozed on, utterly trusting.

"Did you get any of them?" Quinn snarled.

"Yeah, we tracked one, thanks to Isabeau," Logan replied wearily, dropping down to sit in a chair.

"And?"

"And we got minimal info and nothing we hadn't already guessed: traitors and surprise attacks."

"I can't believe the bastard got through our defenses." Quinn continued to seethe. He shot to his feet and prowled the room, his agitation rousing Lucy. She blinked blearily at him, then at Logan and me.

"You're back." She yawned. She glanced at Solange. "Quit staring at it so hard—you'll give yourself a migraine."

Solange pried her gaze away with visible effort, turning to me. "Is it safe to open it? I mean, Bruno scanned it and everything, so we know it's not a bomb or anthrax or whatever, but still. What do you think?"

"I would always rather know what I'm dealing with," I said.

Logan groaned. "You would so open the bomb every time, even when it's ticking right at you."

I wasn't entirely sure what he meant. I was still getting used to modern vernacular, and English at that, but Solange nodded fervently at me. "Exactly. These guys just want me to play Snow White singing in her little cottage while they do all the work."

Lucy snorted. "Snow White and the Seven Buttheads. You could give Disney a run for their money."

Nicholas poked her in the ribs. "I am not a singing dwarf!"

"No, you're a butthead. Weren't you paying attention?" She grinned and kissed him quickly.

"I'm opening it," Solange announced suddenly, grabbing the package.

Every single one of her brothers started to talk at once, voicing the same basic variation on two themes: "Don't" and "Let me." She ignored them and tore at the paper instead. The box underneath was plain white cardboard, the kind for transporting cakes. She bit her lip, pausing very briefly. Nicholas reached across to take it from her and she slapped his hand away without even looking at him. She lifted the lid, leaning backward slightly, as if she expected something to leap out of it like an evil jack-in-the-box. Her brothers did the opposite and all leaned in closer. Then we went as still as only vampires could go, prepared to attack, prepared for anything except what was actually in the box.

Lucy shuddered. "You guys are creeping me out. Quit it."

"That's it?" Solange asked, finally breaking the tableau. In the center of the box was a red velvet pillow displaying a small lump wrapped in red thread. It smelled strongly of rose water and cinnamon. My nose itched. "What is it?" she asked.

I knew exactly what it was.

"Isabeau?" Logan turned to look at me. I wondered what made him already so sensitive to my moods.

"It's a love spell," I said flatly.

"What?" Solange recoiled. "Ew. God. Do these things even work?"

"Sometimes."

Her eyes widened. "Seriously?" She stood up to put more distance between her and the box. "Why won't he just go away? I thought this would finally stop after my birthday."

"He doesn't stop, not ever," I said. As a Hound, I knew Montmartre and his Host better than anyone. "He has the patience of a snake and that's what makes him so dangerous, more so than his cruelty or strength or selfishness."

"Will he ever get it that I don't want to be queen and I sure as hell don't want to marry him?"

"No," I replied truthfully. "Not unless you tell him with the help of a stake through the heart."

She was pressing her back against the far wall; any farther and she'd be through the window and in the garden. "Um, is it my imagination, or do I feel funny?"

"It's possible." I stood up, sniffing at the charm. "It's very strong. Those are two apple seeds wrapped in red thread and a strand of your hair. He must have gotten it that night we stopped him in the caves. And that's a hummingbird heart it's all pierced into."

"What do we do?" The whites of her eyes were showing now, like a wild horse.

"Don't panic," Lucy said soothingly. "And what is it with you guys and disgusting hearts?"

"Lucy, I don't hate him right now! Not like I should!"

"I'll hate him enough for the two of us until we figure this out," she promised grimly.

"Let's burn it," Quinn said, reaching for the box and tossing it toward the dwindling fire in the hearth.

"No!" I cried out, leaping to catch it before it fell. The charm was pinned to the heart pillow, which I plucked out of the air. The box landed in the embers and caught almost instantly. Light flared into the room. Everyone stared at me. "Fire will only make it stronger," I explained. "Fire is passion."

"What about water?" Lucy asked. "My mom's always dunking stuff in water to purify it or cleanse it or whatever. She chants naked in the woods too."

Logan tilted his head, considering. I ignored him, grateful that vampires didn't blush easily. "No, not water either," I said coolly. "That would feed the emotion targeted by this spell: love."

Solange swallowed hard. "Can we do something fast? Please?"

"I need salt," I said, "two freezer bags, ice, and white thread."

Logan vanished and returned within moments with my supplies.

"Are you sure you know what to do?" Connor asked doubtfully. "Maybe we should ask around, do some more research? I could go online."

"I know what to do. This is what it means to be a Cwn Mamau handmaiden."

"I thought it was all about kicking Host ass."

"That too." I half smiled. "We are magic as much as we are aberration and genetic mutation." I dumped salt into both plastic freezer bags. "Surely, you've noticed as much?"

"I . . . guess."

I felt bad for them, to have so much knowledge and so little instinct. Magda had told me enough times that magic and prayer weren't relied upon in this century. It seemed a waste of tools to me. Anyone who had seen Kala work her magic would never think otherwise. I had nowhere near her experience but I knew I could handle a charm, even one bought by Montmartre. And there was no question he'd bought it off some witch—no one else would be able to make these bits of string and apple sing this way.

"Now what?" Logan asked.

The strand of Solange's hair was long, wrapped, and knotted in red thread. I worked it out carefully, tugging gently, patiently unwrapping even when Quinn came to stand behind me and scowl. Logan nudged him back a step.

I freed the hair and placed it between two ice cubes. I tied them into place with the white thread. "This will protect you," I murmured at Solange, concentrating on scenting the magic, as I'd been taught. I imagined the thread to be as impenetrable as a shield, as strong and sharp as a sword, as implacable as midwinter. "White represents protection and purification."

Solange nodded. "Okay. Use the whole spool, would you?"

Quinn growled. "Hurry."

I dropped the ice cubes in one of the bags and sealed it. I buried the apple seeds and the unraveled red thread and hummingbird heart in the salt of the second bag and added a layer of ice cubes to the top. I sealed that one as well.

"These need to be frozen."

Several hands stretched toward me. Solange was faster, though pale and tight around the mouth. "I'll do it," she said, her tone hard, brooking no argument.

She left and we could hear muttering and the slamming of the refrigerator door. Hard.

"In three days put them both in a jar of salt and sour wine and bury it at a crossroads," I advised her when she returned. "And don't let anyone see you do it."

"Can I spit on it?"

"By all means."

"Thank you, Isabeau. This is the second time you've stood between me and that horse's ass."

"*De rien.*" I yawned.

We hadn't noticed the dawn in our concentration. I'd been exhausted before working the charm; now I was beyond fatigue, though still pleased to have redeemed myself from my earlier mistake in the woods.

The others weren't faring any better, young enough not to be able to fight the lethargy that came with the sunrise. I felt weak as water, crumpling to lie on the carpet. Charlemagne curled at my head to protect my sleep. I saw Logan yawn as well and stretch out on the rug beside me. Nicholas was propped up on the couch, Connor slumped uncomfortably in a nearby chair. Only Marcus managed to crawl upstairs, but I had no idea if he'd made it to his bedroom. I was conscious just long enough to hear Lucy mutter.

"Vampires. Sure are the life of the party."

CHAPTER 8

•

Isabeau

I didn't know if other vampires had nightmares, but mine always came in that hazy place between dead sleep and sudden wakefulness.

It was the same dream every time.

It had been a full week since I'd last had it, the longest I'd gone yet. I'd never told anyone though I was pretty sure Kala suspected. She found me once, stuck in the loop of fear, wide-eyed and clammy, a crowd of dogs licking my face and trying to get me to move. Now it was strong enough to pull me out of sleep, even before twilight did.

Even though I didn't remember all that time trapped underground, the dream was always the same. I was inside the white satin-lined coffin, the fabric dirty and crawling with insects. Dirt crumbled through the cracks in the wood, and roots dangled like pale hair. I was wearing the silk gown I'd worn to my uncle's Christmas party but not the choker I'd made from the length of my mother's dress. That was as upsetting as being buried alive; I carried that indigo fleur-de-lys scrap with me everywhere, even in the alleys of Paris.

I scratched at the coffin and kicked my feet until my heels were bruised but I couldn't find my way out. I didn't even know if I was lying in a London cemetery or if I was in France. I couldn't smell anything but mud and rain, and the darkness that should have been complete seemed less than it was. I couldn't see clearly, of course, but I could catch the odd root, the pale white of parsnips, and the scuttle of blue-tinged beetles.

I screamed until I tasted blood in the back of my throat and still no one heard me.

And I wasn't hungry, not once.

The thirst, however, was maddening. It clawed at me like a burning desperate beast, raked across my throat, scorching all the way down into my belly. My veins felt withered in my arms. I was beyond weak, beyond alive, beyond dead. In a moment of clarity, I felt the wound of sharp teeth on my neck, felt a mouth suckling there until I was limp as a rag doll. And then the merest taste of blood smeared on my lips, which made me gag, or would have, if I'd had the strength. And it tasted like the wine Greyhaven had given me.

Greyhaven.

He let them bury me, even though he knew I'd had enough of his blood to taint me beyond any normal human death.

Greyhaven.

I wasn't strong enough to claw out of the earth, hadn't even realized it was what I was meant to do. It all seemed like some horrible accident, something out of a gothic novel. Earth filled my mouth, worms circled my wrists like bracelets, ants crawled through my hair.

Greyhaven.

And dogs howling, snuffling, digging with their claws.

That's when I woke up, every time.

The dogs were real enough; they'd been the ones who'd found me and pulled me out, even before Kala had pinpointed the right grave in Highgate Cemetery.

And Greyhaven's name was my first thought, was still my first thought when I reared out of that nightmare.

Charlemagne's nose lifted off my face when I stopped whimpering. I hated that sound, hated that it waited until I wasn't conscious enough to control it.

I was in a bed; someone must have moved us all out of the living room. The wooden shutters were bolted tight across the windows. I fell out of the bed and crawled to the fridge, yanking the door open. The light hurt my eyes and I groped blindly for a glass bottle filled with blood. The thirst was sharper in the evening, so sharp that I'd trained Charlemagne to defend himself against me if I spoke a certain word. The hunger wasn't easily leashed in our first nights. It still made me gulp the blood greedily, the way I'd eaten cake as a child, but I'd stopped actively worrying for Charlemagne's safety. This would be the same reason Lucy had grumbled earlier about being moved to a guest room with a double deadbolt lock on the inside and an alarm button connected to Bruno, the head of the Drake security detail. Newly turned vampires had little control over themselves upon waking.

When I'd drunk enough blood to have it gurgling in my belly, I straightened my leather tunic dress and left the relative safety of my bedroom. Solange and her brothers would sleep for another hour yet, so I made my way downstairs to let Charlemagne outside and check on the puppy.

"Isabeau."

I halted at the unfamiliar voice. A woman stood in silhouette against a tall arched window in the library overlooking the garden. Rosy sunlight fell into the room. I'd forgotten the glass in the house was specially treated; the wooden shutters in the bedrooms must be for added security and the comfort of concerned vampire guests. I certainly wouldn't have trusted a glass pane and lace curtains.

The woman turned, her face obscured behind a black veil attached to the velvet hat perched on her head. She wore an old-fashioned gown over a corset and fingerless lace gloves.

"Are you Hyacinth Drake?" I asked, courtesy pinning me in place. I'd heard Connor and Quinn talking about her. She was their aunt and had been injured by a Helios-Ra hunter. The holy water they used, charged with UV rays, had burned her face. It hadn't healed yet and no one was certain it would. Scars were rare on a vampire, but they were certainly possible. My bare arms were proof enough of that.

"Yes, I am. *Enchantee.*" She flicked a glance at the scars on my arms, then turned back to the window. That's when I realized she'd been watching Lucy running through the garden with the puppy, who was barking with hysterical glee. Lucy's laughter was nearly as loud. Charlemagne left eager nose prints on the glass door, then looked at me pathetically.

"Go on," I murmured, letting him out to join the melee. The puppy rolled over in the air in his excitement. Lucy laughed harder.

"Your scars don't bother you," she said. It wasn't a question, it was more of a flat statement. I shrugged.

"Not really." The half-moons and disjointed circles left by sharp teeth had faded to shiny pale skin, like mother-of-pearl. "I wear these proudly." I touched the puncture scars on my throat. "These I would burn off if I could." Since burning wouldn't help, Kala had tattooed that side of my neck with a fleur-de-lys.

"I was beautiful for so long," she murmured.

"Then you're still beautiful," I said bluntly.

"No pity from you, Isabeau," she said, and I could hear the faint smile in her voice. "I find that very refreshing."

"My people measure beauty by how quietly you can hunt," I explained. "And by how well you train a dog or how fast you run. We have tests to prove ourselves worthy and none of them have anything to do with the color of our hair or the shape of our nose."

"Then perhaps I should run away to live in the caves after all." Her tone changed, irony washing over the grief. "But I do so love my creature comforts."

Lucy was panting in the yard, wiping sweat off her face. The dogs raced around her like a merry-go-round. When she came toward the house, Hyacinth stepped back immediately.

"It was a pleasure meeting you," she said to me before disappearing into the depths of the house.

"Isabeau, you're up already," Lucy exclaimed, startled. The garden door shut behind her. She brought in the scents of summer rain, leaves, and fresh blood pumping under skin. I ground my back teeth together. "It's not even fully dark yet," she continued on heedlessly. The dogs milled at her feet.

"Sometimes, I wake early," I said. I had no intention of sharing my weaknesses and the violence of my nightmares. Like Hyacinth, I couldn't stomach pity.

Charlemagne blocked me suddenly at the sound of the front door opening and closing. I tensed. Lucy leaned back. "Wow, you're scary when you do that to your face."

"Get behind me."

"The other dogs aren't barking," she said quietly. "I don't think there's anything to worry about." A tattooed bald man in a leather vest marched into the room, jaw set grimly. I felt her stance soften immediately. "Bruno."

"Lassie." He met my eyes. "I want to talk to you."

"Bruno is the head of security," Lucy explained.

"But you're . . . human."

"Aye. Hunters like the daytime with most of the vamps lying around waiting to be staked. It evens up the fight." Though it was at odds with his expression, his Scottish accent put me at ease; the French and the Scots had often been allies. And I understood his bewildered frustration. His heart was practically pounding with aggravation. "We have the best security this side of presidents and kings, I want to know why in one bloody week a vampire faction and a Helios-Ra rogue unit have both managed to break through. It's bloody ridiculous."

"Montmartre doesn't care if his Host die. It's considered an honor, proof of loyalty," I told him. "I gather you would take it amiss if your people died."

"Yes."

"Montmartre just makes more Host. And last night they sent four with the purpose of only one making it to the front door. If they'd attacked outright, I don't know that they could have taken you by surprise."

He sighed. "You're right there, lassie. I was expecting a great deal of violence, not some ijit present." He shook his head. "Still, no excuses." He unrolled blue drawings of the farmhouse and the Drake thousand-acre compound with other assorted buildings. "Show me the weak point, would you?"

I went through the drawings, matching them with what I knew of the surrounding topography. "They would have moved from treetop to treetop. It's slower but stealthier."

"They came from above," he breathed out.

Bruno was smug by the time Solange and her brothers began to stir and trail downstairs.

"Are you ready?" Logan asked me. I nodded. Lucy scowled at Nicholas. He held up his hands defensively.

"Not my fault," he insisted. "Mom and Dad think you should stay out of the courts until after the coronation."

"That is so not fair," Lucy said. "It's not like I haven't already been there."

"Yeah, you were kidnapped by an evil vampire queen. Hello? Not exactly a point in your favor."

"When my parents come home next week I'm getting my dad to teach me how to ride his motorcycle and then I won't need a lift on your stinkin' bike anymore."

Nicholas grinned. "You think your dad's going to let you ride through the woods to hang out with a bunch of vampires in a cave?"

"He lets me hang out with *you*."

"Because I'm not the bad influence in this relationship."

She seemed to soften a little at the word "relationship." Then she immediately straightened her spine.

"I'm still annoyed," Lucy grumbled at him.

"You're cute too," he answered, unfazed. He leaned in and kissed her until she was nearly cross-eyed. Connor coughed.

"Dude, get a room."

Nicholas pulled away, grinning.

"Are they always like that?" I asked Logan as we left the farm-house.

"You should have seen them before they decided they liked each other."

◆

It was considerably easier to gain access to the royal courts this time around. The presence of five of the Drake brothers smoothed the way, even if it didn't completely erase the curious glances or suspicious, disgusted glares. It didn't bother me, but I noticed

Logan was glaring back at every single vampire who dared even to blink my way. It was kind of sweet, if unnecessary. He was close enough that his arm brushed mine.

"Isabeau!" Magda darted out from behind a cluster of bare birch trees in gold pots. She was wearing pink petticoats under an antique cream-colored skirt. She tucked her arm in mine, elbowing Logan away from me with a hiss. Magda did not share well. Logan didn't hiss back, he was too well brought up for that, but he did look as if he was considering it.

"Are you all right?" Magda asked, glaring at each of the brothers. Quinn smirked at her. She glowered more ferociously. "They didn't dose you with Hypnos again, did they?"

"No, of course not."

The courtiers drifted out of our way as we passed through the main hall, where they'd been hard at work. Since last night, the broken raven throne that belonged to the last queen had been carted out. There were fewer mirrors as well so that it didn't feel as if the crowd was twice its actual size. I felt better already.

"How was it here?" I asked her quietly.

"Fine, I guess. Finn is in his glory. He actually said three full sentences back to back."

I had to smile at that. Finn's long silences were legendary. "That's practically a monologue."

"I know." She scowled at a staring young vampire who didn't get out of her way fast enough. "I feel like we're some kind of circus show. Some guy asked to see my fangs. Can you believe that? And he asked me if we painted ourselves in mud."

Quinn chuckled from behind us. "That's called flirting."

She ignored him, even though it was bad form to ignore your host's children when on a diplomatic visit. It was worse form to attack their daughter's boyfriend, so I was in no position to criticize. I wondered yet again why Kala had sent me.

Everyone but Logan and Magda drifted away on their own errands. We went through several rooms, each more decadent than the last. One was decorated in red silk and velvet with gilded framed paintings on the wall. Logan made a face.

"Lady Natasha's tastes weren't exactly subtle," he said. "But we're keeping the paintings and we've started adding more. They're a lineage of ancient kings and queens and whatever."

There were dozens of portraits, framed and unframed, mostly oil but some watercolors and ink drawings. There were a few photographs near the end of the line. It was like being in a museum. I recognized some of the faces from legend and stories Kala had told us: the Amrita family, the Joiik family, Sebastian Cowan, who'd loved a hunter in the nineteenth century.

"That one's Veronique DuBois, our matriarch." Logan pointed to a small painting of a very dignified-looking woman in a medieval dress and wimple.

"Finn is drawing one of Kala," Magda added proudly, not to be outdone.

But I wasn't listening anymore.

On the end of the lowest row was an unframed oil painting of a familiar face. I knew the short black hair, the pale gray eyes, the smug smirk.

Philip Marshall, Earl of Greyhaven.

I took a step closer, feeling distant from everything except that face, as if I were underwater. The paint was still moist in one corner, gleaming wetly. This portrait had been done recently, hung before it was fully dried and cured.

I didn't know what to think of that. I felt my lips lift off my elongated fangs, felt a growl rumble in my chest. At first I thought it was Charlemagne. It took me a moment to realize the pained sound was coming from me. I curled my hands into fists, willed myself not to explode.

"Isabeau?" Logan stepped closer, concerned. "What is it?"

Magda insinuated herself between us, forcibly pushing Logan out of the way. "I'll take care of her," she told him darkly, putting a comforting hand on my shoulder.

"I'm fine," I murmured, barely recognizing my own voice. It was hoarse, but soft as water. I forced myself to turn my back on the wall of portraits, even though I felt Greyhaven's painted eyes boring into the back of my neck. I needed time to think. It was obvious to me, even without the warm tingle of the amulets around my throat, that something was going on.

"Let's go," I said, refusing to meet either of their gazes.

CHAPTER 9

♦

LOGAN

I led Isabeau toward the antechamber my parents had reserved for private meetings. She seemed paler, her fingers tightening in her dog's gray fur, as if searching for comfort. I didn't think she even knew she was doing it. But I'd noticed. Something in that portrait gallery had spooked her. But I knew however many times I asked her, she wouldn't answer me.

So I'd bide my time.

For now it was enough to deal with the image of Solange making out with Kieran in a dark corner of the hall, where they thought no one could see them. Between Solange and her hunter and Nicholas kissing Lucy, Isabeau was going to think we did nothing but grope and flirt.

Which sounded just fine to me, but I didn't think she'd oblige.

"Dude," I snapped as Kieran's hand strayed under the hem of Solange's shirt. The cast on his arm was sharply white against his black clothes. The fact that he'd hurt that arm saving Solange was the only reason I wasn't currently yanking him right off her. "That's my sister."

Solange peered over Kieran's shoulder. "Go away, Logan. You're just jealous because you have no one to kiss. Hi, Isabeau."

I could kill her. She was just getting me back for the princess comment from the night before. And Isabeau would scare easier than a doe in hunting season if she thought for one second I wanted to feel her lips under mine. I narrowed my eyes warningly at Solange. "Shouldn't you be at the meeting?"

Kieran pulled away, having the grace to flush just a little. I didn't like the tempo of his heartbeat, or the direction his blood was flowing. "I have to wait for my friend Hunter," he said. "This is her first time in vampire territory and I promised I wouldn't go in without her."

Solange kissed him one more time just to annoy me, and then went to the antechamber.

"I begged Mom and Dad for a cat," I muttered at her back. She tossed me a grin over her shoulder, hearing me perfectly, as I'd intended. I grinned back.

"Helios-Ra really are allowed in the royal caves," Isabeau murmured as we trailed after Solange. She and Kieran gave each other a wide berth.

"It's crazy." Magda shook her head.

I shrugged one shoulder. "My parents want to do things differently. Dad's big on treaties."

"And your mother?" Isabeau inquired.

"She's big on making grown men cry," I replied dryly.

Isabeau's smile was brief and crooked and practically had me drooling. "I like her already," she said. She let go of Charlemagne. "I could use a moment," she said softly. "Are we expected right away?"

I glanced at the pocket watch hanging from my black jeans. "We have a good half hour. I just said that about the meeting to get Kieran off my sister's face."

"Are they betrothed?"

I nearly choked. "I sure as hell hope not. They've only known each other a couple of weeks."

"Ah." She and Magda exchanged a girly glance I had absolutely no desire to decipher. I decided to pretend I hadn't even seen it.

"Did you want a tour of the caves?" I asked, to distract us all.

"*Oui*. If it's not too much trouble."

"Not at all." I held out my arm, the way they do in period-piece movies. It would have been smooth too, if Magda hadn't glowered and shoved her way between us.

"I'm coming too."

I'd have to console myself with the hope that I'd seen Isabeau soften, even hesitate, as if she might actually have taken my arm. It was suddenly very easy to picture her in a gown with petticoats and ringlets in her hair and diamonds at her throat. It was just as easy to picture Magda with horns and a pitchfork.

"Let's double back to the main hall and start from there." I led them back, avoiding the portrait gallery. The hall bustled with activity, guards at every passageway. I took the one on the left, behind a tapestry of the Drake family insignia. Madame Veronique had sent it to us the night after Mom killed Lady Natasha. It was hand-embroidered and at least half a century old, with the royal mark of a ruby-encrusted crown along the top edge. Veronique had made it herself, long before Solange was even born. Apparently she paid more attention to vampire politics and prophecies than she'd have everyone believe.

"This tunnel winds around through most of the rooms," I told them as we ducked into the narrow stone walkway. It was lit with candles in red glass globes hanging from nails in the ceiling and it had a simple dirt floor and damp walls. Magda looked at me suspiciously but I ignored her. "All these doors we're passing lead to guest chambers." I nodded to an iron grate locked over a thick oak door with heavy hinges. "Blood supply's in there," I explained. "In case of a siege. It was Mom's first request."

"*C'est bon*," Isabeau approved. "We have something similar in our caves."

"There's a bunch of council rooms down that way, and a weapons store currently undergoing inventory."

"It's lovely," Isabeau said politely. "But where are your sacred stories, your paintings? Blood has magic, surely you know that much?"

"We have tapestries," I said, but I didn't think that was what she meant.

"Is it true your mother took out Lady Natasha single-handedly?" Magda interrupted, as if she couldn't help herself.

"Yes," I said proudly. "Sort of. None of it would have gone down the way it did if Isabeau hadn't arrived, just in time."

"So you admit you owe us?"

"Magda, hush," Isabeau said. "We all want to stop Montmartre. He's too powerful as it is."

"And a pain in the ass," I agreed grimly. "Not to mention a cradle-robbing pervert. He's what, four hundred years older than Solange?"

Isabeau glanced away. "I am technically two hundred years older than you."

"Not the same thing," I said quickly. "*At all.*"

Damn. If I tried, maybe I could shove my other foot in my gigantic mouth. So much for smooth. Magda grinned from ear to ear. I had no idea how to reclaim that lost territory. "I think we can all agree you're nothing like Montmartre."

Isabeau inclined her head, a glint of humor in her green eyes. "I do not want the crown," she agreed. "No Cwn Mamau does."

And the crown was pretty much all Montmartre wanted.

Aside from my little sister.

The thought made me grind my teeth hard enough that the noise startled Charlemagne. I relaxed my jaw through force of willpower alone. Then I realized I'd led us into a dead-end chamber. I'd been so distracted by Isabeau's scent and the sound of her voice and the way her black hair swallowed the flickering light of a single candle, that I'd practically walked us into a wall.

Hard to believe, but before Isabeau I'd had a fair bit of skill with the whole flirting thing.

She turned on her heel and I noticed she was smiling, a true startled smile, as if she wasn't used to it. "Oh, Logan, *c'est magnifique.*"

Apparently she liked cave walls and the clinging damp of mildew.

And then I realized her fingertips were hovering an inch over a faded red ocher painting. It was so faint I'd never have noticed it. As it was, I could only really make out a handprint.

"What is it?" I asked.

"It's a Cwn Mamau sacred story," she explained. "It's older than anything I've ever seen."

"From before the royals stole the caves from us," Magda felt the need to add.

"Hey, I've only been royal for just over a week." I felt the equal need to defend myself.

"Shhh," Isabeau murmured gently, as if we were bickering children. "This is a holy place. Can't you feel it?"

I felt the quality of the silence, the weight of stone pressing all around us. And if I concentrated, the very faint lingering traces of some kind of incense.

"This handprint here is the mark of an ancient shamanka. And here, these lines represent the thirteen full moons in a year." She pointed out the drawing in such a way that I could actually see it clearly, see the faint lines solidifying, see the dance of torchlight from centuries earlier, smell cut cedar branches under our feet. A slight wave of vertigo had me tensing. I must have made some sound as I peered around, because she smiled that crooked smile again. "You see it now, don't you?"

I nodded, turning to take in the cave drawings and the story they told. "Are you doing this?" I asked, stunned. "And *how*?"

"Simple enough for a handmaiden," she replied. "I just had to find the thread of this shamanka's story, the energy she left trapped in the painting." She pointed to the outline of a handprint done in spatters of red. "That's her mark."

"So I'm not insane?"

"No," Isabeau replied, just as Magda snorted, "Yes."

"Watch," Isabeau urged us.

A woman who I assumed was the shamanka shimmered into view. She looked about Solange's age, but with several long blond braids and symbols on her face and arms in mud and some kind of blue dye. She wore a long necklace that looked like it was made of bones, crystals, and dog claws.

She scooped red ocher paint out of a clay bowl and smeared it on the walls. There was chanting but I couldn't see anyone other than half a dozen giant shaggy dogs at her feet, and what looked like a wolf. Incense smoke billowed out of a cairn of white pebbles.

Everything sped up until the paintings were abruptly finished. There were dogs who looked as if they were breathing and moving ever so slightly, as if wind ruffled their fur. There were vampires with blood on their chins and a red moon overhead. There was a human heart, a jug of blood, a woman with a giant pregnant belly filled with squirming puppies.

"Cwn Mamau," Isabeau explained in a reverent whisper. "The Hounds of the Mother."

There was a religious feel to the artwork, simple and primitive as it was. The painted dogs lifted their throats all at once and let out a plaintive ululating howl that lifted the hairs on the back of my neck.

And then everything went dark, except for a jagged scar of red light near the edge of the low ceiling, in the back corner. The ocher dog painted underneath it growled.

Isabeau drew her sword from its scabbard. The holy feeling inside the cave shattered instantly. I reached for my dagger even though I had no idea where the danger was coming from. I tried to step in front of Isabeau to shield her. She kicked my Achilles heel and I cursed.

"You'll get yourself skewered on my sword," she said distractedly, still staring up at the red light. It was throbbing now, like a broken tooth. There was something decidedly menacing about it.

"Isabeau, be careful," Magda said tightly as Isabeau approached it. I stayed at her side despite the half hiss she threw my way.

"What the hell is it?" I asked.

"A warning," she replied, lowering her sword slowly. "When I tapped into the energy of this place, I broke some sort of cloaking spell."

"Cloaking spell?" I echoed. "That doesn't sound good."

"It's a standard charm," she said, shrugging one shoulder. "You can buy them off any witch or spellsinger."

"Witches and spellsingers," I muttered. "I keep forgetting I woke up in some sort of a fairy tale."

She shook her head. "Vampires who don't believe in magic," she said. "I'll never understand you."

"I didn't say I didn't believe in it," I replied. "Just that I wasn't expecting so much damn proof." I didn't even like the feel of the light on my face. I took a step back. "So what the hell was it cloaking?"

"A very good question."

She poked it with her sword, as if she didn't want to touch it either. Charlemagne growled once. There was a groaning sound and a pebble dislodged, then another and another. A broken boulder the size of a watermelon tumbled and hit the ground in a puff of dust. The weird red light went out, like a torch in a windstorm.

But not before flashing on a narrow, half-completed opening.

"Son of a bitch," I muttered, grabbing the candle and holding it inside. The tunnel was long and dark and freshly dug through the limestone.

"Someone is planning an unannounced visit," Isabeau said grimly.

"Montmartre," I bit out.

"He is quite determined," Isabeau agreed. "He will have many plans."

I hefted the boulder back up and shoved it back into the tunnel, closing it off again.

"What are you doing?" Magda asked.

"I don't want them knowing we found their secret passageway until we've decided what to do about it," I replied, rubbing my hands together to get rid of the dust. Frock coats don't come cheap and I'd already ruined one hurtling through the woods being chased by bounty hunters and rogue Helios-Ra on Solange's birthday.

"Oh," Magda said, sounding reluctantly impressed. "Good point."

"We should go back," I said, waiting at the regular entrance for them to pass through it. I didn't want them turning their backs on the secret tunnel, even knowing it was empty. "The tour is officially over."

CHAPTER 10

•

Isabeau

Helena, Liam, Finn, and two others I didn't know were waiting for us in an antechamber off a cave filled with bookshelves with glass doors to protect against the inevitable damp. An oil lamp burned on a table. Guards nodded at us when we passed through the doorway. I barely noticed. I was trying hard to retain my composure, to be the strong, dependable handmaiden Kala had trained me to be. This work was important, even if I didn't feel suited for it. Even if the nightmare from earlier was circling in my brain again like carrion crows over a fresh corpse. Not to mention trying to decipher the unexpected dreamwalk with the cave paintings. Truthfully, I hadn't expected it to work quite so well with a vampire as untrained as Logan.

Liam rose when we entered. "Isabeau," he said warmly. Helena lifted her head from the piles of papers and books in front of her. Finn nodded to me once.

"Liam," I greeted him, my voice carefully blank.

"I trust you slept well?"

"Yes, thank you."

"I apologize for the unfortunate event with the Hypnos," he added soberly.

"As do I."

"And I thank you for ridding our woods of Host and breaking the spell against our daughter."

"You're welcome."

"We owe you for that," Helena agreed. She shoved the books away. "Now can we please dispense with this courtesy dance and get down to it?"

Liam glanced down at her ruefully. "Love."

She shot him an equally rueful look. "Sorry." She turned to me. "I hope you're not offended, Isabeau."

"Not at all," I assured her. In fact, I was rather relieved to hear her say it. I was starting to wonder if that was part of reason I'd been chosen: not necessarily because of who I was but because of who Helena Drake was. Anyone else, Magda included, would have bristled and assumed she didn't think Hounds worthy of the usual protocol. I understood she was too direct to bother with political games. It made me suddenly hopeful about the alliance between our tribes. We were sick to death of games and politics.

"I'm rather envious of you, actually," she added.

I blinked. "I beg your pardon?"

"I'd have loved to have chased a Host down last night. Instead it was all treaties and protocols and hyperactive guards." She shook her head. "I'm going out hunting tonight, Liam, so you'd best get everyone to just deal with it."

She didn't seem like any mother I'd ever known. My own had been more interested in lace and dancing until dawn.

Logan grinned. "I don't think queens are supposed to hunt, Mom."

"Then I'll take Isabeau with me." She quirked a dry smile in my direction. "Then it won't be hunting, it will be alliance improvements."

"We'll make a politician out of you yet," Liam said.

"There's no need to be insulting." She sat back in her chair, her long black braid falling behind her.

"Mom, we found a secret tunnel," Logan told her grimly. "Very new, off behind the empty caves on the other side of the weapons room."

Her eyes narrowed dangerously. "Another one?"

He blinked at her. "There's more of them?"

"Two that we've found so far," she replied. "Your father won't let me fill them with dynamite."

"I'd rather not have the entire compound fall on our heads," he said dryly. "I'll take care of it." He spoke into his cell phone at a discreet murmur just as one of the guards opened the door. Suddenly the room seemed too small and constricting. Hart, the leader of the Helios-Ra, strolled in with Kieran and a girl with long blond hair. Her shoulders were tight, her hand hovering over a stake at her belt. She wore the black cargos and shirt that virtually every other agent wore while on assignment. I looked for the vial of Hypnos powder they strapped inside their sleeves but I couldn't find it.

"Hart," Liam greeted the other man with an amiable handshake. "Glad you could make it."

The blond girl and I were the only ones who looked as if we didn't think this was entirely normal. Well, and Magda, of course. She pressed closer to me, second set of fangs protruding slightly. Hart was handsome, dressed in a simple gray button-down shirt and jeans instead of camo gear. There was a scar on his throat.

"You know Kieran, of course," he said. "This is Hunter Wild." He motioned to the blond girl. "The Wilds have been part of the league since the eleventh century."

"How do you do?" Liam murmured calmly. "Have a seat."

Hunter nodded stiffly, eyes wide. Kieran cleared his throat, nudging her into a chair next to him. The rest of the Drake brothers filed in, stealing the last bit of air and space left in the room. Hunter stared at them. Out of everyone in the room, the vampire hunter was the one I could relate to most right now. My eyes would have bugged out of my head too, if I'd let them. This kind of group gathered together peacefully was unprecedented, outside of the old families on the Council.

"We can do good work," Liam said quietly. "If we let ourselves. We've called the Council. They'll be here in two days. Meanwhile, Hart has already agreed to work with us."

"What, and just give up killing vampires?" Magda asked. "And you believe him?"

Hart half smiled. "We're all learning a little discretion is all. We have a common enemy, after all."

"Montmartre?" I asked. I hadn't thought Helios-Ra was particularly interested in vampire politics.

He shook his head. "No, the *Hel-Blar*. Something has them running brave. We've never intercepted so many calls to the police about strange people wearing blue paint. I think we can agree they need to be hunted."

Magda nodded reluctantly. She had no love for the *Hel-Blar*; none of us did. It was too easy for the Hounds to remember that we might have been like them, but for a little luck and a little hidden inner fortitude.

"We've been getting disturbing reports all evening as well," Helena said. "The *Hel-Blar* are everywhere suddenly."

Magda hissed. "They're like cockroaches."

"Only rather more deadly," Finn agreed.

"Is Montmartre behind this?" Hunter asked. "I didn't think he could control them. Isn't that the whole reason for their existence?"

"We don't know," Helena replied darkly. "I'd really like to feed him his own—"

"Darling," Liam cut her off smoothly.

"Well, I would," she insisted. "*Hel-Blar* or not, he needs to be dealt with."

"Agreed."

"We can stop Montmartre," I told them confidently. "We nearly had him last week. He's not invulnerable."

"That's the nicest thing anyone's said to me all night," Helena told me. "But tell me the truth, Isabeau, would the Hounds ally themselves with us?"

"We all want to stop the *Hel-Blar*," I assured her. "And Montmartre."

"And after he's been stopped?"

"The Hounds will recognize no one but our shamanka as our rightful leader," I said delicately. "We will never be part of the courts."

Helena raised an eyebrow. "I've got enough vampires. I don't need any more."

"Actually, that's reassuring," Finn murmured. "You might try stressing that point as often as you can when it comes to the Hounds. They're rather keen on the right to govern themselves. I think you can understand that, given their history."

"We don't bow to Montmartre or anyone else," Magda agreed fervently.

"Do you think our tribes would be able to form an alliance?" Liam asked. "One that recognizes everyone's autonomy."

"I think so." Despite my natural misgivings toward the royal courts and non-Hounds in general, I genuinely liked the Drakes. I believed they were trustworthy, even if I had no actual proof of it. It was something I felt in my gut. "There are many superstitions and rituals that are dear to our people," I said. "Some Hounds will never agree to work with you because you've not been initiated, but they won't go against Kala either."

Hunter was staring at Magda and me so intently that Kieran elbowed her.

"Sorry," she muttered.

"She's never seen Hounds," Kieran told us.

"I can speak for myself," Hunter snapped at him.

"Well, you're being rude."

I glanced at him. "At least she didn't greet me with a face full of Hypnos powder."

Kieran went red.

Quinn grinned, lounging back in his chair. "She's got you there."

"Children," Helena said, half sharply, half fondly.

Hart's cell phone warbled discreetly. He glanced at the display. "I'm sorry, I have to take this. Hart here." His jaw tightened. "When?" He glanced at Liam. "Another *Hel-Blar* sighting. This one right on the edge of town."

Liam cursed.

"We've got a unit deployed," Hart assured him.

Liam nodded to Sebastian. "Take a guard and see if you can help." Sebastian was out the door without a word.

"I'll go as well." Finn pushed to his feet. "We may as well all start working together right away. Besides, we have a certain expertise in this matter that no one else has."

"But you're not a Hound, right?" Hunter pointed out, honestly confused. "You don't have the tattoos or anything."

"No, but I've lived with them for nearly four hundred years," he told her before following Sebastian. It felt odd not to go with him but I knew I was needed here more, however much I might prefer to run off and bash a few *Hel-Blar*.

"Let's reconvene in half an hour," Liam suggested to the rest of us. "We can compare notes and take it from there."

"Come on, Buffy," Quinn drawled at Hunter. "I'll give you the tour."

I took the opportunity to leave the small room. I was used to caves, dark and secluded, but ours weren't filled to the brim with people. Logan and Magda followed me, as if I had a plan. We were on our way outside when I paused, frowning. I touched my fingertips to the jumble of amulets at my throat. They were warm and vibrating slightly, as if they felt an earthquake no one else did.

"Something's wrong," I whispered.

Magda and I both reached for our phones, which rang at exactly the same moment. I didn't bother to answer mine. The chain of my amulet broke and scattered the pendants across the rugs. The wolfhound tooth capped in silver and painted with a blue dye made from the woad plant broke in half. I looked up to meet Magda's wild expression.

"Kala's hurt," she confirmed. "The Host attacked our caves." She hissed. If she'd been a cat, her fur would have lifted straight into the air.

I felt oddly numb. "I have to go," I told Logan, scooping up the amulets and stuffing them into my pockets. Charlemagne was at my side before I spoke the command. The courtiers whispered to one another as we rushed past them and out the other side of the decorated hall. "We'll be back for the coronation."

Logan grabbed his jacket from a coat tree. "I'm coming with you."

I didn't have time to argue with him and I was oddly comforted by the fact that he would come with me. Even if I didn't need him.

And I didn't.

"Tell my parents we're going to the Hounds. Their shamanka's been injured," he tossed out to one of the stern-faced guards at the entrance.

Magda and I were already scrambling down the cliffside, scattering pebbles. Something tumbled out of Logan's pocket when he caught up to us. He picked it up, bewildered. "What the hell is this gross thing?"

He was holding a gray dog's paw, the nails curled in. It was wrapped in black thread and thorny rose stems without blossoms. I went cold all over.

"That's a death charm," I said. "A rare Cwn Mamau spell," I elaborated when he just stared at me.

"It's a dog's paw," he said very clearly, dropping it into the dirt. "That's disgusting. I thought you guys liked dogs."

"It wasn't killed for its foot," I told him. "When our dogs die, of natural causes," I pointed out, "or in an attack, we use them for spell work, after the burial rites."

"Yeah, still gross," he muttered.

"And see this?" I pointed out a flat bone disk painted with a wolfhound and a blue fleur-de-lys. "That's my personal mark. Someone's trying to frame me."

CHAPTER II

◆

Paris, 1793

"*Papa*, I don't understand," Isabeau pleaded. "Why do I have to wear this horrid dress? It itches." The dress in question was gray wool without a stitch of ornamentation. She could pass for a maid-servant or a village girl. Even her hair was tied back in an uncomplicated twist without a single pearl pin or diamond bauble.

"*Chouette*, it's not safe anymore," Jean-Paul answered.

She'd never seen him like this before. Nothing scared him, not Versailles, not wolves howling in the woods, not even the huge spiders that crawled into the château just before winter fell. She'd seen him fight a duel once, when she was supposed to be asleep in her bed. Now he looked haggard and tired and nearly gray with grief. Her mother sat weeping in the corner. She hadn't stopped crying in days. Her hair was losing its curl, her face unpowdered. Isabeau shivered.

"This is about the king, isn't it?" she whispered.

He slanted her a glance. "What do you know, *chouette?*"

"That the mob took Bastille, that Paris is no longer safe."

"It's not just Paris anymore," he said quietly, shoving another wheel of cheese into the leather pack in front of him. They were in the kitchen, huddled by the hearth. Her old nursemaid Martine stood by the door, spine sword-straight. She wore a brown woolen dress and her hair was scraped back under a cloth bonnet. Isabeau had never seen her look so plain before. She shivered again.

"They've gained in strength and numbers. They've set up the guillotine as a permanent gallows. And the king was executed yesterday. France truly has no royalty now."

She stared at him, shocked. "They killed the king?"

"Do you know what this means, Isabeau?"

She shook her head mutely.

"It means none of us is safe." He wrapped a thick cloak around her shoulders. "Here, keep this on. It's cold outside."

She tied the ribbons together tightly. "Where are we going?"

"We're going to my brother's house in London."

"England?" she repeated. Her mother wept harder, choking on her sobs. "But you haven't spoken to him in years."

She was interrupted by the shattering of broken glass coming from the front of the château. She whirled toward the sound. Her mother leaped to her feet, her hand clasped over her trembling mouth. Her father tensed. "*Merde.*

"There's no time." His eyes were determined, sharp as they found hers. "Isabeau, I need you to hide. Go with Martine, take your mother. You remember the broken stone I showed you?"

Isabeau nodded, her heart racing so fast it made her sick to her stomach.

"Pull it out and crawl inside. The passageway will take you out into the woods, by the lavender fields." More glass broke, and something hard thudded against the locked front door. She could hear shouting, faintly. "Do you understand, Isabeau?"

She forced herself to look at him. "*Oui, Papa.*" She understood perfectly well. She was sixteen years old and better equipped to protect them than her fragile mother.

"Then go! Go now!"

"*Non,*" Amandine shrieked, clutching his arm so tightly the fabric of his shirt tore under her frantic nails. The door splintered with such a loud sharp crack that it echoed throughout the château. Martine's face was wild as she grabbed Isabeau's shoulder.

"We have to go."

Footsteps crashed toward them. The mob shouted, knocked paintings off the wall, howled with hunger and frustration. The golden candlesticks in the hallway could have bought a winter's worth of food for an entire family. Never mind that there was scarcely any food to be had, bought or otherwise. January frost covered the fields and the orchards, and the summer crops had been thinner than usual due to weather and political upheaval.

Jean-Paul tried to tear Amandine's hand off him, to shove her toward Isabeau for safekeeping, but his wife was wild with terror and would not move. He wouldn't let her save him and he couldn't risk their daughter. They couldn't all get away, they'd be chased through the countryside, found.

"*Cherie*, please," he begged his wife. "Please, you have to go."

The mob was nearly on them. There was no time, no options left. He threw Martine a desperate glance. "Take Isabeau."

"*Papa, non*! We'll all go!" Isabeau struggled to convince him even as her mother fell completely apart in his arms.

Angry villagers poured into the kitchen in search of food, leaving a few others to vandalize and loot what they could.

"The duke!" a woman with gray hair shouted. She was so thin her ribs were visible beneath her threadbare chemise. Someone howled, more animal than human. The flames from a torch leaped to a tablecloth, catching instantly. The smell of burning fabric mixed with burning pine pitch.

Martine yanked Isabeau backward and out into the dark pre-dawn kitchen garden before she could struggle. They landed in the basil, crushing the dried shrubs under them as they rolled to the shadows under the decorative stone wall.

"*Vien*." Martine tugged on her hand. "*Je vous en prie*."

"My parents," Isabeau said through the tears clogging her throat. "We have to help them."

"It's too late for them."

"*Non*." But she could hear the shouting, the tearing of hands through the barrels of salted meats and baskets of dried apples. She could hear her mother's strange yelping, like a terrified cat, and her father's cursing as he struggled to shield her.

"Your father would never forgive either of us if we didn't get you to safety," Martine told her quietly, urgently. Isabeau knew she was right. Martine took advantage of her stunned pause to pull her off balance and drag her running into the edge of the woods. Torchlight gleamed from the kitchen window as more of the cloth caught fire. Smoke billowed out of the open door.

She watched her parents from the tall cradle of an oak tree. The mob dragged them to a farm cart and lashed them to the sides. Isabeau's father stared straight ahead, refusing to search for his daughter lest he give her away. Isabeau knew somehow that he could feel her there, up a tree, stuffing her fist in her mouth to keep from screaming out loud. Martine clung to the trunk beside her, her face wet with silent tears. The cart rolled away.

"I'll go to Paris," Isabeau swore. "And I'll find a way to save them."

◆

Isabeau waited until Martine was asleep before making her escape. They'd found an abandoned shepherd's hut; the wooden slats were pulling apart under the wind and there was snow in the corners, but it was better than the exposed January night. They risked a tiny fire, barely enough to warm their toes in their sturdy boots. Isabeau drew her knees up to her chest and let her thick cloak fall around her like a tent. She closed her eyes and pretended to drift off until she heard Martine snoring softly. She was shivering lightly and the gray in her hair seemed more pronounced, the lines around her eyes deeper. Isabeau couldn't stand the thought of leaving her behind, but she couldn't expect her old nursemaid to go with her.

Paris was a death trap.

But there was no possible way she could go anywhere else. Her parents were being dragged there even now. They would be paraded through the streets, condemned of some royalist crime, and executed.

She had to stop it.

And Martine would have to try and stop her.

So it was best all around if she left now, before it was even harder. Her eyes felt gritty and swollen, her stomach was on fire with nerves, but underneath it all she knew she was doing the right thing. She left Martine most of the coins her father had sewn into her cloak, keeping only enough to see her to the city. Martine would need it more than she did. She'd have to find passage to England or Spain, or a villager to take her in. Perhaps someone would marry her. She was plump and pretty and dedicated; she deserved to be loved and taken care of the way she'd taken care of Isabeau her entire life. It should have been Isabeau's job to find her nursemaid a new position, a new family to live with; or else beg her parents to keep her on until she was married and had babies of her own. None of that was likely now. Marriage was the furthest thing from anyone's mind. The king was dead, Marie Antoinette was imprisoned, and most of the aristocracy had been murdered or fled to make cream sauces and pastries for the English.

Isabeau was sixteen years old, and she was clever and resourceful and she would do whatever needed to be done. She would free her parents and then find a ship to take them somewhere, anywhere.

She pushed the door open, wincing at the cold wind that snaked inside, fluttering the last of the fire. Martine moaned and shifted uncomfortably. Isabeau shut the door quickly and waited pressed against the other side, listening for the sound of Martine's voice.

Satisfied that her nursemaid hadn't woken up, Isabeau crept away from the hut. The night was especially dark without a moon to light her way. She was alone in the frosty silence with only a light dusting of snow for company. She walked as fast as her cold feet would let her, stumbling over twigs, keeping to the forest on the edge of the road.

She walked the entire night and didn't stop even when dawn leaked through the clouds. Her feet and her calves ached and she wasn't convinced she'd ever get the feeling back in the tip of her nose. She kept walking through the pain, through the cold wind and the growling emptiness in her belly. She hid in the bushes when she heard the sound of wagon wheels, not trusting anyone enough to beg a lift on the back of a cart. She might blend with her wool cloak and simple gray dress, but she knew her accent was too cultured, too obviously aristocratic, and that alone might make her a target.

The closer she got to Paris, the more clogged the road became, mostly with people fleeing to the countryside. Only radicals and adventurers and madmen went toward the city these days. She pulled her hood over her hair and lowered her eyes, keeping to the trees. Eventually they thinned to ragged bushes and then to fields and then she was on the outskirts of the city and everything was cobblestones and gray roofs in the winter sunlight. She'd been walking for three days with very little sleep and only frozen creek water to melt and drink. Her head swam and she felt as if she had a fever: everything was too bright or too dull, too sharp or too soft.

She stopped long enough to buy a meal and a cup of strong coffee to fortify herself. She huddled in her cloak, trying not to stare at everyone and everything. Smaller houses crowded together gave way to buildings, towering high and made of stone the color of butter. The river Seine meandered through the city, past the Tuileries, where the king had once lived, before they'd cut off his head. Isabeau shivered. She couldn't think of it right now. If she gave in to the grief and the fear she might never move again.

She forced herself to her feet and followed the river. The water churned under a thick, broken layer of ice. She rubbed her hands together to warm them, being careful not to catch anyone's eye. Men swaggered in groups drinking coffee and distributing pamphlets while women with cockades pinned to their bonnets stood on the corners talking. Their faces were serious, fired with purpose. Isabeau could smell smoke lingering and saw piles of burned garbage from riots and the fighting that took over the streets at night. She'd heard her father speak of it more and more, especially last autumn, when so many had been massacred.

She'd heard the guillotine had been set up in one of the city squares but she didn't know where it was. Her parents hadn't been to their Paris house since the Christmas she was eleven. She remembered passing the opera house in the carriage and the snow falling in the streets. She could walk in circles and never find her way.

She finally noticed that the crowds seemed to be heading in the same direction. She paused behind a group of women with chapped hands, smoking under an unlit streetlight. Taking her courage in both hands she approached them slowly.

"*Pardon, madame?*"

One of the women whipped her head around to glare. "*Citoyenne,*" she corrected darkly.

Isabeau swallowed. "*Pardon, citoyenne.* Could you tell me how to find La Place de la Concorde?"

The woman nodded. "Visiting *la louisette,* are you?" When Isabeau looked at her blankly she elaborated. "The guillotine."

"Oh. Um, yes."

"Not from here, are you?"

Isabeau backed away a step, wondering if she should dart into the safety of the maze of alleyways. "Yes, I am."

The woman shook her head, not unkindly. "Down this street and turn right."

"Thank you."

"If you hurry, you'll catch the last execution. Just follow the crowds and the noise. Robespierre got himself a fat duke and duchess." Her companions nodded smugly. One of them spat in the gutter.

Isabeau's stomach dropped like a stone. She broke into a run, dodging cafe tables and barking dogs and carts trundling slowly in the street. She could hear a loud cheer from several streets over, even with the pounding of her pulse in her ears. The cobblestones were slicked with ice and she slipped, crashing into a pillar of a large building. She pushed herself up, looking wildly about. All the buildings looked the same, stone and tall windows, pillars and pavement. She gagged on her frantic breath. Another cheer sounded, louder this time. She ran again, following.

She made it into the cacophony of the square just as the guillotine fell, the blade gleaming in the sun. There was a pause of silence and then more shouts. The ground seemed to shake with all the noise and stamping feet. The pressure of the noise made her nauseous. She'd never seen so many people in her life. There were guards with bayonets, hundreds of *citoyens* and *citoyennes*, children, urchins and pickpockets, and rouge-cheeked prostitutes.

Isabeau pushed through the crowd, heedless of the feet she stepped on or the bored curses flung her way. She struggled against the wall of people toward the dais in the center of the square. It was warm with so many bodies and the fires lit in braziers. At the very front, sitting in a row by the tall strange machine that was the guillotine were the *tricoteuses*, the women who sat and knit as the heads fell in the basket in front of them. If they sat too close, blood splattered them. They'd long ago figured out the exact perfect distance. Isabeau could hear their needles clicking as she pushed between them.

Just in time for the blade to drop a second time.

Her father's head rolled into a large basket, landing lip to lip with the decapitated head of her mother. Their long hair tangled together. Blood seeped through the wicker, stained the wood of the dais.

Isabeau's shrieks were drowned out by the enthusiastic spectators. She screamed herself hoarse and then felt herself falling and didn't even try to stop her head from cracking on the cold cobblestones.

CHAPTER 12

◆

LOGAN

I wasn't about to let Isabeau go off without me.

I didn't care how long she'd known Magda, didn't even care that she was going back home to the tribe she loved. Her shield had cracked and I couldn't forget the glimpse I'd seen. And I hadn't been feeding her a cheap line when I'd told her I felt as if we already knew each other. Something in me recognized something in her.

But I wasn't stupid.

I knew she'd never admit to it—and not only because I was a Drake and royalty.

It still felt weird to think of myself as royalty. I was just one of many Drake boys with a handsome face and a smart mouth. I didn't stand out particularly; I didn't have Connor's knack for computers,

Quinn's right hook, or Marcus's gift for negotiation. I just dressed better.

"Can I assume you're not trying to kill me?" I asked as we ran on, leaving the dog's paw behind.

"I didn't make that charm," Isabeau said. "But I damn well want to know who's trying to muddy my name."

"And kill me," I reminded her dryly.

She looked remote and cool, but I could see the strain of worry under her polite mask. I'd never known anyone more self-contained than she was, running with her giant dog loping at her side, her sword strapped to her back. Magda sent me another glare, which I ignored. Someone materialized at my side.

"Jen, stay here," I told her. The last thing we needed was a hot-head like her barging into Hound territory. She was armed to the teeth, stakes lining the leather strap that fit tight between her breasts, and there were daggers on her belt.

"Someone has to watch your back," she said stubbornly.

"I'll be fine," I insisted, annoyed. It wasn't like I was Solange with some deranged vampire lusting after me, or a little kid. I could take care of myself. I was eighteen years old, for Christ's sake.

"You're royalty," she told me, following me out into the dark forest. "I'm a royal guard."

I sighed irritably. I didn't have time to charm her or to shake her loose.

"Fine," I snapped. "But we'll be guests of the Hounds, so don't pick a fight."

"As long as they don't start anything, I won't either."

"I need your promise."

Her blue eyes sparked. "You have it."

"Less talking," Isabeau called back to us. "More running."

She was shooting through the woods like a star, her skin pale and glowing faintly when the moonlight found its way through the thick leaves. She had no idea how beautiful she looked, even grim and deadly as she was right now.

And I probably shouldn't be watching her ass quite so carefully but I couldn't help myself.

The forest went quiet at our approach. Five vampires moving quickly will silence even the cicadas. An owl rustled in a tree overhead but didn't fly away. I didn't know what to expect in the Hounds' caves. No one had set foot there uninvited in nearly a century even when they were backup caves and not the main residence. I'd been hearing stories about the savage Hounds since I was little. Isabeau had been a surprise to all of us. So had Finn, come to think of it, since he wasn't technically a Hound at all. He'd *chosen* to ally himself with them and they'd let him. I wasn't sure which part was more rare.

We stayed close to the mountain, skirting the huge pine trees. The wind was warm, even here. August was nearly finished, soon the leaves would change colors and fall away. It made it harder to stay undetected in the forest, but not impossible.

"Do you smell something?" Magda asked suddenly, slowing to a stop and frowning. She sniffed the air like a suspicious cat. Her expression went flat. "Blood."

My nostrils flared. Definitely blood. A lot of it. Despite

the situation, my stomach grumbled. My fangs extended instinctively.

"And something else," I added, hearing a soft tinkling sound, like ice in a glass. "Did anybody hear that?"

Isabeau nodded grimly. I shifted to be closer to her, even though Magda tried to block me. She acted like I was a threat, like I was planning to stake Isabeau when she wasn't looking. As if I ever would, and as if Isabeau couldn't stop me. I don't know what it said about me that it kind of turned me on that she could probably kick my ass if she wanted to. She might look like a porcelain doll, but I knew from experience that she was tough as iron nails. I'd have to find a nicer way of telling her that. I didn't think she was used to compliments. I may as well start getting her comfortable with it, because I planned to compliment her a lot. Just as soon as she stopped looking at me like she was trying to figure out what I really wanted.

Which was her. Just her.

I nearly groaned out loud. Having an aunt who'd slept with Byron and insisted we read all the Romantic poets had evidently addled my brain. My brothers would never let me live it down if they found out I'd fallen in love with a Hound princess after a single night without even kissing her. Like I had any intention of telling them. You didn't survive five older brothers and a younger one by running your mouth off about stuff like that. Basic survival skill.

We crept around a copse of stunted oaks and into a narrow clearing. It was the same one where we'd eavesdropped on the wounded Host after Solange received Montmartre's "gift." That couldn't be a coincidence. I saw the flicker of recognition on Isabeau's face.

But we didn't have time to discuss it.

At first, none of us knew what to say. I'd never seen anything like it. The smell of blood was so strong I actually had to cover my nose until I got used to it. The muscles in the back of my neck tensed up.

The long grass was undisturbed, dotted with wildflowers. The moon made everything silver, as if it were wet. There were no bodies, no drained humans or animals, no sign of struggle.

Just open uncorked bottles everywhere, dangling from string and wire from the branches. The sound I'd heard was the clinking of glass touching glass when the breeze rattled the macabre wind chimes. There were dozens of them.

"What the hell is this?" Jen muttered.

Every single one, from green wine bottles to jam jars, were filled to the rim with blood. Fresh, warm blood. All of our fangs were out now, Isabeau's double ones, even Finn's ancient opal-sharp ones. I took a step closer to a juice bottle, swallowing thickly. I could all but taste it. Jen's hand slapped my arm, forcing me back.

"Could be poisoned," she said.

She was right. We all froze. Isabeau turned a slow circle on her heel.

"It smells familiar, but it's not poisoned," she said finally, a kind of horrified awe in her French voice.

"It's not?" I echoed.

She shook her head. "It's a trap," she said. "Like a bowl of sugar water to draw the bees away from the kitchen."

I frowned. "A trap for who? Us?"

"*Oui.*" She reached for her sword just as Charlemagne growled in the back of his throat.

Hel-Blar.

They were everywhere. We would have smelled them if it hadn't been for the blood-saturated air around us. They had a very distinctive stench: rot and mildew and mushrooms. Their blue-tinted skin made them look bruised. Every single tooth in their mouth was a fang, sharpened to a needle's edge. And their bite was contagious.

And they were coming at us through the trees like spring rivers rushing into the same lake, like deadly blue beetles on fallen fruit.

Hell if I was going to be some ripe piece of apple waiting to be eaten.

"Shit." I reached for one of my daggers. I hadn't stopped to grab a sword, which was stupid. I'd thought a dagger and a handful of stakes would be enough.

Really stupid.

There was no sense in running since there wasn't a clear path out of the meadow. We could hear them growling and hissing, spitting like rabid animals. It made my jaw clench tight. The blood wasn't just tempting them the way it tempted us, it was driving them mad.

"Someone wanted them to attack us," I snapped at the others. "Someone knew we'd be coming this way."

"Host," Isabeau agreed in a voice like winter in the steppes. "Whoever attacked Kala must have set this up."

I leaped toward her, landing behind her to guard her back before the *Hel-Blar* reached us. She shot me a half-surprised, half-grateful glance. The moon glinted on her sword and the chain mail sewn into the leather of her tunic, over her heart.

"Stay close," I told her.

She snorted. "I have a sword and you have a butter knife. Staying close is about your only option."

And then there really wasn't any more time for witty banter.

The unnerving sound the air made as it sliced around them made me understand the old superstitions about vampires turning into bats. I bared my fangs. I had every intention of plucking them right out of the sky if I had to. The first wave hit hard, but at least half of their numbers were distracted by the bottles swinging over our heads. They drained them, gulping frantically as if they were frat boys at a kegger. Blood ran down their chins, dripped into the flowers. It was only a very brief moment though and then they all wanted the kill and wouldn't be deterred by bottles of cow blood.

The fight was fast and feral. We had skill on our side but we were outnumbered. And the *Hel-Blar* had battle frenzy down to an art. I killed one before he could get too close, but lost my stake in the long grass. He was too far for me to reclaim my weapon without leaving Isabeau unguarded. I had two more stakes.

"Shit, don't be a martyr," Jen yelled at me through her teeth. She tossed me one of her swords. She still had one in her hand and one at her hip.

"Thanks!" I caught it, grinning. I felt better already. I leaped over the thrust of a rusty rapier.

"Royal plums for the picking," one of them sneered. An empty bottle crunched under his boot. "Is this the way you decorate for your fancy parties?"

So they hadn't been sent after all, only lured and manipulated without their knowledge.

That was something to think about.

A stake grazed my left shoulder, leaving a raw burn in its wake. Later.

"Damn it, Logan," Isabeau shouted. "Pay attention. *Franchement*," she added in French. I could tell by the tone that it wasn't a lover's endearment.

She swung hard and blocked the attack of a screeching *Hel-Blar*. His arm, now unattached, sailed through the air and landed with a thud. It was still clutching a long stake soaked in poison. I could smell it, like salt and iron and rust. I kicked it aside.

Jen had dispatched two of them and Magda was shrieking back at one like a psychotic banshee. She might look like a flower fairy but she had wicked good aim. Dust puffed in front of her and she turned to the next one. Jen was nearby, hacking away with deadly arrogance in every swing.

A *Hel-Blar* thrust her dagger at me. I kicked out, snapping her wrist. The knife tumbled and she howled, then leaped at my head. We sprawled on the ground. A bottle snapped from its tether and landed by my head. Blood seeped into the ground. The *Hel-Blar* bared her fangs. They gleamed like needles. I cracked my elbow under her jaw and she nearly bit her tongue off. Saliva hit my neck. I fought harder until I managed to get my leg up enough to dislodge her. She hit the tree beside us and my stake dug into her papery heart before she could recover. She crumpled.

I leaped to my feet. Later, I'd feel bad I'd had to kill her. Right now, my mother's training was too strong, stronger even than the gentlemanly courtesies the rest of my family had instilled. I might wear frock coats and recite poetry better than sports stats but I knew the rules: you fought, you survived. And *Hel-Blar* took no prisoners.

Jen was proof of that.

I had time only to turn and the *Hel-Blar* she'd been fighting took her legs out from under her and buried the sharpened end of a staff in her chest.

"Son of a bitch," I yelled, using Jen's borrowed sword to cleave his head right off his shoulders. Then I stabbed him in the heart, pushing through his rib cage. But Jen was reduced to gray ash in a cup of primrose petals and clothes patterned with the Drake crest. I couldn't even stop to mourn her or hate myself for being the reason she was here in the first place.

Isabeau was tiring. I could see it in the arc of her sword arm, still deadly but infinitesimally slower. Magda was limping, holding herself up on a stolen broadsword, her hair matted with blood. We couldn't keep this up much longer.

"We have to get out of here," I said to Isabeau. "Now. Up into the trees maybe."

"Charlemagne can't fly," she said, and I knew that was the end of that half-formed plan. Isabeau would never leave her dog. She'd lie down and get staked first.

"Fine," I said, grabbing Jen's sword from under her empty clothes and surreptitiously slipping a bottle of blood into my shirt. "Then we do it another way." I stepped out of the safe ring Isabeau, Magda, and I had formed. Isabeau hissed at me.

"What are you doing?"

"Saving your very cute ass," I hissed back. Then I smirked my most arrogant smirk at the *Hel-Blar.* "Did you know royal blood tastes sweetest?" I dragged the blade across the inside of my forearm, biting back a curse. In the movies, no one ever mentioned how much cutting yourself open really freaking *hurt.* I held up my arm, blood dripping down to my elbow and spattering over the ground. Most of the *Hel-Blar* paused, turning to stare at me hungrily.

For this to be a rescue mission and not a suicide mission I was going to have to move *fast.*

"Come and get it," I shouted at them before throwing myself into the shadows between the trees, away from Isabeau and the mountain caves. I heard her litany of curses, all in French and all at the top of her lungs. Most of the *Hel-Blar* followed me, driven by bloodlust. They weren't stupid exactly, just mindless when it came to feeding. Only a few stayed behind to fight the others, which I felt certain they could handle.

I made sure my blood dripped everywhere, leaving a trail a blind puppy without a sense of smell could follow. Damn waste of blood, too. The *Hel-Blar* moved so fast I could barely hear their footsteps. I could hear them skittering though, like insects. They were really good at tracking.

So I'd just have to be better at escaping.

I pushed my legs as fast as they would go, until the forest blurred into smears of green and black on either side. The stench of rot hung heavy in the warm air. When I was sure they were well and truly distracted by my flight, I bent my arm and pressed the inside against my bicep to stop the flow of blood. The cut was already tingling warmly, which meant it was healing. I didn't want to leave a trail anymore though; it was time to get the hell out of here.

I slowed down slightly, in the interest of precision. I tossed the bottle aside, making sure it rolled in the undergrowth, spilling its bloody contents. Then I went in the opposite direction. I zigzagged a little until I was sure I was out of sight of any of my pursuers and then scrambled up an oak tree. I swung into the next tree and the next before finding a large enough branch to stand on with some confidence. I peered down into the shadowy green, searching for blue-tinted skin and needle teeth.

There were at least three *Hel-Blar* moving through the tall ferns. Acorns and twigs crunched under their feet. They weren't trying to be quiet anymore. Their teeth flashed. One of them stopped, sniffed the air in a surprisingly delicate way.

"He's here."

I tightened my grip on my sword and shifted slightly. I could probably leap down and land right on his head if I timed it right.

Instead, he gurgled and turned to ash. A stake dropped into

the grass where he'd been standing. His companion whirled and also crumpled. Isabeau pushed through the bushes, stopped under my tree. She looked up at me, her face unreadable.

"Don't do that again."

CHAPTER 13

◆

LOGAN

I'd never seen so many dogs in my entire life.

Even though I hadn't known what to expect, this still wasn't it.

There were several cave entrances, the main one guarded by two Hounds with Rottweilers. The Rottweilers were happier to see me than the Hounds. They hissed at me but they bowed their heads to Isabeau with respect.

Inside was a wide opening leading to the back and several more doorways carved into the rock on either side. Some of these were barred with black iron gates, the kind you find in old wine caves in Europe.

"Private homes," Isabeau explained, her tone clipped. Her brow was furrowed with worry. She hurried down the main hall, down a few steps and then out onto a narrow rock ledge.

It was beautiful.

Everyone spoke of the reclusive Hounds as if they lived in holes and burrows in the ground, like badgers. But this main cavern was straight out of a Lord of the Rings movie set and it fit the name they called themselves, Cwn Mamau. Lit torches and fires kept the damp away and caught the amethyst and quartz imbedded in the walls, flickering like lightning bugs in a jar. Red ocher paintings of dogs and people with antlers and raised hands leaped in the torchlight. On our right, a waterfall fell like glass down into a pool of milky blue water. There were at least two dozen dogs, who all lifted their heads at our approach. We took the uneven stairs, which carved into a meandering trail. Isabeau practically leaped the last few steps, running to a woman lying on a bed of furs by the underground pond.

"Kala," she cried.

Kala was the infamous Hound shamanka who was rumored to have witch dogs and magical powers. She was also the closest thing Isabeau had to a queen, or a mother. Possibly both. The old woman had long white hair twisted into braids and dreadlocks and hung with beads made of bone carved into roses and skulls. She had blue tattoos in bold spiral patterns reaching from her left temple all the way down her arm and across her collarbone. Her eyes were so pale they were nearly colorless. There was blood on her teeth when she smiled.

"Isabeau."

Hounds floated toward us out of the fissures and nooks like moths converging on a flame. I kept my hand on my borrowed sword, but I didn't unsheathe it. I tried one of my most charming smiles.

Nothing.

I shifted so I wouldn't knock Isabeau off her feet if I needed to fight.

"Is this your young man?" Kala whispered hoarsely. Isabeau flicked me a glance.

"This is Logan Drake," she said. "Logan, this is Kala."

"Nice to meet you." My training was such that I could bow and keep a grip on my weapon at the same time.

Kala cackled. There was no other word for it.

"Told you the bones never lie," she said. I could have sworn Isabeau blushed. Magda looked at her sharply, then at me.

"What?" I asked.

"This is hardly the time," Isabeau murmured. "And it's not like that."

I didn't know what she was talking about but I very much doubted I would agree with her.

Isabeau smoothed a braid off Kala's cheek. "Where are you hurt? What's been done?"

Kala patted her arm. "I'll be fine. I've had blood and my ankle has already reset itself. You didn't have to come back."

"Yes, I did," Isabeau replied fiercely. "Who did this to you? Host?"

She sighed. "Yes. I went out to gather more mushrooms for the sacred tea and they ambushed me."

If she needed mushroom tea, I nearly said, she could have

bought some from anyone wandering the alleys in Violet Hill at night, and some of the farmsteads as well. Violet Hill was nothing if not a progressive hippie town.

"Did you go alone?" Isabeau frowned. "You know you should take someone with you. Kala, you're no good in a fight."

I was surprised to hear that. I'd assume the leader of such a ferocious tribe would be deadly with every weapon imaginable.

"Just because I'm a vampire doesn't mean I'm a warrior," Kala said to me. She clearly had other talents, like mind reading.

"Did you recognize any of them?" Magda asked.

Kala tried to sit up, settling instead against the back of a huge black dog of indeterminate breed. "No, there were a few of them. Their auras were strange and it distracted me. Dogs ran them off before I could get a good look. Hello, old boy," she added when Charlemagne licked the side of her face. "They could have staked me. They chose not to."

Isabeau sat back on her heels. "*Merde.*" She met my eyes grimly. I had to fight the urge to put my hand on her shoulder for comfort. She'd probably break my arm if I tried. Damned if that didn't make me like her even more. I was totally screwed. "If they didn't want to kill Kala, then they meant to create a distraction."

"And to get us out of the royal caves and in the path of that *Hel-Blar* trap."

"I don't like being yanked about like a marionette," Isabeau said darkly.

"I didn't think you would," I said dryly.

She rose to her feet. "Are you sure you're all right?" Isabeau asked Kala.

Kala nodded. "I'll be fine."

"Then I have to go and think," she said, mostly to herself, before stalking off, Charlemagne at her side as always.

Magda went to follow her but Kala stopped her. "Leave her be," she said, but she was looking at me.

"You stink of cow," Kala murmured to us. "What on earth have you been doing?"

"We were caught in a trap," Magda said bitterly. She raised her voice, turning to glare at me. "By his people."

Hounds all turned to me, baring their teeth. I was pitifully aware of my single set of fangs. I narrowed my eyes at Magda. I'd been raised to be nice to girls on principle but I still really wanted to kick her. I felt sure Byron or Shelley would have wanted to also.

"We didn't set the damn trap," I snapped. "Why would I go waltzing to a death trap if I knew it was there?"

"You weren't meant to be there at all," she said. "Your family could have set it without you knowing it."

"The Drakes didn't send the *Hel-Blar* after you." I seethed, my temper prickling. "We've treated you with every courtesy. I'm the one who was marked by some creepy-ass Hound spell."

It was funny how sharp silence could be, like a needle scraping against your skin.

Kala pushed herself up so she was sitting against a large rock painted with triple spirals.

"What mark, boy?"

"The dog paw," I told her. I was beginning to feel real concern. I hadn't had much time to think about it with the *Hel-Blar* attack and I kind of assumed it was just a scare tactic. I kept forgetting that this magic stuff might actually work.

Not a pleasant realization, actually.

"Do you have it on you?" Kala asked. Her eyes glittered, like ice breaking on a pond in spring.

"No."

"That will make it harder to break, but not impossible. Are you sure it was meant for you?"

"Isabeau said it had her mark on it."

"Are you accusing Isabeau?" Magda asked, incensed. "Do you see what royal loyalty is worth," she spat.

"I never accused Isabeau," I ground out. "I didn't even know it was her mark until she told me."

But she was already swinging her fist at me and it nearly collided. Disgusted surprise slowed my reflexes. She clipped my ear and I swung back and around. I didn't punch her, as punching girls, even crazy ones, wasn't cool. But I did trip her and I felt damn good about it.

"What the hell is your problem now?" I yelled at her.

"Isabeau is too good for you!" she yelled back. "And you'll take her away from us to live in your stupid royal house."

I was too stunned to duck the next blow. I barely felt it.

"I'm taking Isabeau home?" I echoed. "She forgot to tell me that part."

"Just like she forgot to tell *me* the bones said she'd find her mate in the royal family." She tried to snap my kneecap with her foot but I shoved her away.

"You're nuts," I told her. I couldn't deny I was intrigued though, couldn't deny I liked the idea of Isabeau promising herself to me and me to her. Even though I knew she was too prickly and independent to love me just because her shamanka told her to.

Still.

"Will you read the bones for me?" I asked Kala, ducking an empty urn Magda threw at my head. It broke into pieces against the wall. One of the dogs chased the shards, hoping for a treat. Kala wheezed a laugh.

"Come here, boy." She pulled a handful of painted bones out of a pouch at her belt. They looked like a cross between rune stones and spirals. I couldn't decipher them at all. She handed them to me. "Shake them in your cupped hands and then toss them on the ground between these two crystals." She thunked down two crystals.

"Kala, you're not well," Magda protested. "The royal pain can wait."

She had a point, much as I hated to admit it.

Kala only waved that away. "Throw!" she barked at me. I threw mostly out of reflex, the sharp whip of her voice startling me. Why were all the old ladies I knew so damn scary?

The bones tumbled and scattered on the dusty ground.

To Kala apparently they told a story. Some of the other Hounds edged closer, craning their heads for a better look. There were murmurs, a gasp. Magda scowled as if I'd just kicked a puppy. Kala nodded smugly.

"You see now? You all see. This is the boy."

I didn't see anything at all.

"You'll run with the dogs," she assured me, as if that was helpful. Then she coughed, bloody spittle on her lips.

"Leave her alone now," Magda snapped at me, gathering the stones up for Kala and turning her back to block me.

CHAPTER 14

◆

LOGAN

I found Isabeau sitting on a rocky outcrop under the stars and a stunted pine tree. I climbed up toward her, dislodging pebbles under my boots. There was a behemoth sitting on her left, all fur and immensity.

"What the hell is that?" I asked.

"It's a dog," she replied matter-of-factly.

"Isabeau, that's not a dog, that's a moose."

She half smiled. "He's an English mastiff. His name is Ox-Eye."

Ox-Eye lifted his head. I'd seen smaller horses.

"Ox-Eye because he's part ox?" I asked, lowering into a crouch beside her.

"No, like the daisy."

"You named this beast after a flower?"

She scratched his ear fondly. "He's rather gentle. *Très sympathique.*"

"Sure he is," I said doubtfully. She was rubbing a piece of faded silk between her thumb and forefinger. It was frayed at the edges. "Good luck charm?" I asked softly.

She paused, slipped the cloth into her sleeve. "Yes, I suppose so. I thought I lost it a long time ago."

"What is it, Isabeau?" I asked.

"What do you mean?"

"Isabeau." I didn't know how I knew exactly, but I was sure there was something else going on. She bit her lower lip, finally looking like an eighteen-year-old girl.

"I was wearing that good luck charm, as you call it, the day I died. The day I was turned and left for dead, I should say." She sounded angry, bitter, and fragile in a way I hadn't thought was possible for her. It made me want to find the bastard and rip his head right off his shoulders. "I haven't seen it since that night."

I frowned. "Where did you find it?"

"In the woods outside your house," she replied. "When we were tracking the Host."

"Shit."

"*Oui.* It was left for me."

"By?"

"Greyhaven. Or so I assume. I was wearing it the night he killed me."

I sat back. "That's why you lost it when they said his name in the woods last night."

"*Oui*," she said again, grimly. "He's back. And now I can finally kill him."

"Isabeau, he's what, three hundred years old? Four hundred?"

"So?"

"So, you're a newborn, however long he might have left you in your grave." I really, really wanted to rip his head off. "You're not strong enough yet."

"We're not like other vampires, Logan," she insisted coolly.

"Yeah, believe me, I get that." I raised an eyebrow in her direction. What, did she think I was an idiot?

"I couldn't find Greyhaven before. He's always been off on Montmartre business. I couldn't get close to him, didn't even know if he was on the same continent." She pulled out the indigo silk. "But now I know. Now I can track him."

"How? I know you're good, Isabeau, but he's one of Montmartre's top lieutenants. Even I've heard his name."

"There are rituals."

I jerked a hand through my hair. "I'll just bet there are."

"I have this now. I can smell him on it."

"But why? Just to taunt you? There's something else going on here."

"I know," she admitted. "But I won't figure it out by sitting here and waiting for him to make his next move. What I can do is take this back to where I found it and dreamwalk."

"Dreamwalk?"

"Like a trance. Similar to what you saw with the cave paintings."

"And where exactly did you find it?"

She winced. "In the meadow where they set the trap."

My mouth dropped open. "In the field with the *Hel-Blar* and the blood everywhere? That's where you're going to lie down and go into a trance?"

"*Oui.*"

"Wow. That's the worst idea I've ever heard. And I've known Lucy practically her whole life."

"You don't understand."

I snorted. "I totally understand. You're nuts."

She shrugged one shoulder, let it fall. "I'm handmaiden to the shamanka. This is what I do."

"Ever notice you only say that when you're about to do something reckless?" The soft light from the setting moon caught the shiny skin of her numerous scars. "Did he give you those?" I was surprised that my voice sounded more like a growl. Ox-Eye lifted his head curiously.

"*Non*, the dogs did this."

I stared at her. "Your own dogs attacked you?"

"No." She smiled for the first time, softening the tight lines in her face. "They rescued me. Kala's dogs pulled me out of the earth. I would never have been able to do it by myself. Greyhaven only slipped me enough blood to change me, not enough to revive me. I was unconscious for centuries in that coffin."

"In France?"

"No, I was buried in London, in my uncle's family plot."

"And Kala went to get you?"

"No, she never leaves the mountains or these woods. It's her power center and the dogs are her totem, you would say. For all of us."

The only reason I could follow what she was saying was because of Lucy and her New Age parents. Lucy talked about totems and auras and full moon rituals the way other people talked about ballet classes and summer barbecues.

"So who found you?"

"She sent Finn across the ocean with three of her most trusted dogs. They have a way of calling other dogs to them. Finn told me that by the time he found me in Highgate cemetery nearly twenty of the city's stray dogs were there too."

I could picture it: mists, the middle of the night in a posh ancient graveyard in turn-of-the-century London under torchlight, the sound of horses and carriages over the wall. She'd have been wearing some kind of corseted gown with pearls at her throat and elbow-length gloves.

She was totally made for me.

"So the dogs found me and dug me out. I remember the sound of their claws and their teeth closing over my arms. And the air, finally, real air I could breathe. That's when I realized I wasn't actually breathing and I wasn't waking up from some nightmare in my uncle's townhouse in 1795. It was over two hundred years later and nothing made sense." She shivered, her eyes distant.

I'd thought our bloodchange was bad, but we knew it was coming and our family had had centuries to adapt and prepare. We got sick, sure, and weak, and some of us came closer to actually dying for real than others; but usually a draft of blood and we were right as rain. Vampiric, but otherwise okay and still ourselves in our recognizable undead life. In fact, Connor's real worry had been that he was going to have to start dressing like me. I'd given him a black velvet frock coat for his birthday that year and hung it on the back of his door so that it was the first thing he saw when he woke up.

"Finn gave me blood to drink," Isabeau continued. "I thought he was insane. He had to force me and I was sick all over his boots. After an hour I was so thirsty I would have drunk a barrel of blood. He brought me here as soon as I was well enough to travel, on a ship with a windowless bedroom and a captain who didn't ask questions. As soon as I saw Kala, I knew I was finally home."

I whistled. "So it's not just a story told to scare the rest of us?"

She shook her head. I reached out and traced a fingertip over a half-moon scar above her elbow. I half expected her to break my hand, or at least jerk away. She just went still.

"Your aunt thinks her scars make her hideous."

I went still as well. "You talked to my aunt Hyacinth?" I gaped. "And by that I mean, Aunt Hyacinth actually talked to someone?"

"Yes. She seems . . . distraught."

"That's one word for it. She's barely been out of her room since those rogue Helios-Ra bastards doused her in holy water and left her for dead. She won't talk to any of us, and she absolutely won't lift her veil. Not even for Uncle Geoffrey, and he's practically a doctor. You should have seen her before the attack. She was unstoppable, afraid of no one, and a bear about courtesy and proper gentlemanly behavior."

"So that's where you get it from."

"What?"

"The way you dress, the way you can bow like this is still the eighteenth century."

"I suppose." I shrugged, sternly telling myself not to ask her if she liked it or hated it. I wasn't going to be that guy.

"If you had dug me out instead of Finn, I might not have realized right away that it wasn't still the eighteenth century."

Ordinarily, I'd take that as a great compliment; with her though, I just wasn't sure.

"Between our matriarch, Madame Veronique, and her medieval lessons and Aunt Hyacinth, I guess it was bound to rub off on one of us."

"You're different than your brothers," Isabeau insisted. "They don't live it the way you do. I could tell right away."

"You noticed all that in the few hours you saw them?" And I absolutely wasn't going to wonder who she'd thought was the cutest. Quinn had a way around girls, and it made them stupid. I suddenly wanted to punch him for it.

"No, it's kind of nice," she murmured, and suddenly Quinn's face was safe from my fist. "It's like the boys I knew in France."

I wasn't entirely thrilled with the word "boy."

"I didn't know I missed it," she continued, as if surprising herself.

I'd never wanted anything more than I wanted to kiss her. I

wanted it more than I lusted after Christina Ricci in *Sleepy Hollow*. And I'm all about the girls in corsets. Isabeau's long, thick black hair, straight as the waterfall in the caves underneath us, her green eyes and scarred arms and vicious parry with a sword. Hot. Every last bit of her.

I decided to take my own life in my hands and I leaned in slowly. I didn't rush, gave her plenty of time to pull away, but I was inexorably closing the distance between us. She smelled like rain and earth and wine. If she'd been in a goblet I would have drained it of every drop. I was a whisper away from her now and she still hadn't moved.

I wanted to bury my hands in her hair and draw her up against me but I thought she might not be ready for that. She was a little bit like a wild animal, untamed, unbroken, and as untethered as a hawk in the sky. I wouldn't want her to be anything else.

I slanted my lips over hers and it felt right, necessary. I kissed her deeply, slowly, as if we had all the time in the world. Her mouth opened and her tongue touched mine, hesitantly, sweetly. I had to clench my fists to keep from grabbing her. The kiss went darker, wilder—one of us made a small sound but I honestly didn't know which of us it was.

There was a tingle in the back of my head, a flush of burning heat over my entire body. I pulled away reluctantly. Her mouth quirked into one of her rare smiles.

"Dawn," she whispered.

I smoothed her swollen lower lip with my thumb. "Dawn," I agreed.

The forest was ever so slightly less dark than it had been, more gray than black.

"We should go inside," she said, both sets of fangs protruding slightly. It was cute as hell.

"Got someplace safe for me to sleep?" I asked.

She linked her fingers through mine.

"Yes."

CHAPTER 15

◆

LOGAN

"Have I mentioned that this is the worst idea ever?"

"A hundred times." Isabeau rolled her eyes. Charlemagne looked like he was considering it too.

"If I say it a hundred and one times will it convince you?"

"No." She ducked under a low-hanging branch. "You fret worse than my old nursemaid."

"I have a great deal of sympathy for your old nursemaid," I muttered. It was a beautiful night, warm and filled with stars and the songs of crickets and frogs. White flowers glowed in the grass. It was a night made for poetry. We should have been kissing. A lot.

Instead we were sneaking out of the caves to a blood-soaked clearing where we'd been ambushed not twenty-four hours earlier. Not exactly an ordinary date.

"It will be fine," she assured me, her long black hair swinging behind her. "It's just trancework, nothing to worry about."

"Really?" I answered dryly. "Is that why we snuck out and you wouldn't tell anyone what we're doing, not even Magda?"

"I don't want to worry them. And they wouldn't understand, anyway."

"*I* don't understand," I shot back.

"I know. But you're still here, you're still helping. You're not trying to stop me."

I shook my head. "I am so trying to stop you—I'm just doing a piss-poor job of it, apparently."

When I woke up next to Isabeau in her cave, her hand on my chest, I'd thought the night would go rather differently. I should have known better. There was nothing soft about Isabeau, not even in her sleep. Well, that wasn't precisely true. I'd seen a flash of her vulnerability, after all, a flash I didn't think she was even aware she possessed. She was all shamanka's handmaiden out of the caves, all warrior and duty. But this was her home and she was comfortable enough to shed a few of her hard outer layers.

Her room had been simple, nearly sparse. There was a futon covered in quilts and several dog beds in the corners, thick rugs, and a small oil painting of a French vineyard. There were no concert posters or a closet stuffed with dresses, just a hope chest for her clothes, another one for weapons, and a jewelry box filled with amulets and bone beads. Everything about her was different.

And she'd ruined me for regular girls.

Even now, as she stalked through the forest, hypervigilant for the stench of *Hel-Blar* or a sneak attack from the Host.

"We're close," she murmured.

"I know." I could feel the stinging in my nostrils, the penny-sharp tang of dried blood. Broken glass glittered in the undergrowth. Charlemagne sniffed his way around the clearing and then sat, tongue lolling out of the corner of his mouth. Clearly, we were alone. What a waste of a moonlit night.

She frowned at the ground. "Look, dog prints."

I followed her gaze to the trampled grass, the paw marks. "Charlemagne?"

"No, there are too many. And they're fresh."

I took a closer look. "Someone came back here after we left, just to add dog prints?" I rocked back on my heels, chilled. "To frame the Hounds for the attacks, same as the death charm in my pocket."

She nodded tersely. "Montmartre, probably."

"He doesn't want the treaties," I agreed. "He'd much prefer we fight each other than him." I sighed. "So, what now?"

She was walking the perimeter much as Charlemagne had, her head tilted, sniffing delicately. "Now for the ritual."

I frowned. "Are you sure about this? Montmartre could be anywhere. And I didn't even know magic was actually real before your trick with the love charm."

She shook her head, mystified. The bone beads in her hair clattered together. "I'll never understand how vampires could be so ignorant of the magic in their own veins, in their own bodies."

I shrugged uncomfortably.

"I can do this, Logan," she said confidently. "Kala trained me for this."

"What if something goes wrong? I can't exactly wave a magic wand over you. I'm not Harry Potter."

"Who?"

"Never mind," I said.

"All you have to do to pull me out is say my name three times. If that doesn't work, bury both my hands in the earth."

"I'm not even going to ask."

"It will ground me back into my body. Honestly, what does your family teach you?"

She pulled dried herbs out of a pouch hanging from her belt and scattered the mixture in the center of the meadow. I could smell mint, clove, peppercorn, and something unfamiliar. She'd put a new amulet around her neck: this one was tarnished silver and hung with tiny bells and garnet beads like frozen drops of blood. There were symbols etched around the edges.

Next she pulled what looked like tibia bones out of her pack and stuck them into the dirt. They were smooth and polished and painted with more symbols. One was wrapped in copper wire and pearls.

"Are those human?" I frowned. Vampires didn't leave bones behind, only ashes.

"Dog," she replied. "And wolf."

"Oh." I didn't know what else to say to that.

She lay down on her back between the bones, one at her head, one at her feet. The trees around us glimmered with broken bottles. Her arms were bare as usual, scars proudly displayed, chain mail draped over her heart. She closed her eyes, looking like a feral Sleeping Beauty.

I unsheathed my sword and paced slowly around her, listening so intently for sounds of another ambush that sweat gathered under my hair. She shifted, making herself more comfortable and murmured something too softly for me to hear.

She lay there for a long time, quietly and eerily still.

Just as I was beginning to think there was nothing more magical happening than a nap, every nerve ending tingled and the hairs on my arms stirred. It suddenly felt like I was entirely covered in static electricity.

I turned to Isabeau, sword swinging out protectively.

She was alone, safe. But I could have sworn a silver glow pushed out of her skin, making her shine. She didn't seem concerned; in fact she smiled, the corner of her mouth lifting slightly. I admit I was relieved. I wasn't exactly sure how to go about fighting an invisible enemy.

There were clearly gaps in the famous Drake education.

I could just imagine what Mom would have to say about that.

And then the grass around her flattened outward in a circle, as if pushed by a strong wind. When it hit me, I staggered back, hitting a tree. A bottle fell from a branch overhead and tipped blood into the grass. I straightened, cursing.

Isabeau stood up as well. She seemed to be glowing even more than before. It was a little distracting.

"I guess it didn't work," I told her.

She blinked at me. "Actually, it worked a little too well."

I was beginning to notice that everything around me seemed insubstantial, faded. And that I appeared to be glowing a little bit too, like those nature films about incandescent phloem under the surface of the sea. "I don't think I want to know what you mean by that."

"You're dreamwalking with me, Logan."

"Yup, that's what I didn't want to know."

She looked confused. "This has never happened before."

"Yeah, that's the opposite of comforting." I could see through my hand.

Not good.

I tried to clench my fingers tighter around the sword. Everything glittered around the edges, like the night sky was reaching down to touch everything. In fact, the sky seemed closer than it ought to be.

"Put that away," Isabeau told me. "It won't do you any good anyway. Weapons are useless when just a wayward thought can kill."

"Well, shit, that's just great."

"The best weapon's a mirror."

"Huh?" I was only half paying attention.

"So you can see a person's true face. Don't trust appearances here, Logan, any more than you would in your regular body."

"Okay, sure." The trees had a green glow, pulsing slowly like a heartbeat. In fact, everything seemed to have some kind of bright, candy-colored aura. "Did you slip some of that mushroom tea into my blood supply when I woke up?"

"No, this is perfectly normal," she assured me.

"Right," I countered dubiously.

"Well, not exactly normal," she amended. "I've never taken someone into a dreamwalk with me before."

"I feel totally weird," I told her, staring at my body, which was shooting off sparks.

"You'll get used to it. We should hurry though, it's not good to stay too long on your first journey."

"Why?"

"You might turn into a toad."

I gaped at her in horror, tried to stutter a reply but couldn't form the words. It took a full two minutes for me to realize she was joking. She actually chuckled out loud.

"Oh, sure, now you giggle like a girl. You have a sadistic sense of humor."

She grinned, unfazed. "You're not the first to say so."

I turned, saw myself leaning against the tree, lace cuffs spilling out of my sleeves, sword tip resting in a clump of violets. It was like the near-death experiences people talked about on all those psychic shows. Only I was already technically dead. I wasn't moving and my eyes were open, watching nothing. "Okay, that's just creepy."

"Don't look at yourself for too long," she suggested. "It'll make you queasy."

"I can see why." I turned away deliberately. "So now what?"

"Now we hunt for psychic traces, for anything that looks out of place, anything with an absence of light or a strange scent."

The blood from the bottle traps was a different color, like I was looking at a photographic negative. It was molten silver and it made everything else look darker, more translucent. Isabeau was crouched, sifting through the undergrowth with her fingers, plucking bits of broken glass as if they were petals off a flower. I tried not to be distracted by the way her eyes went green as mint leaves, by the way the stars seemed to leak light, by the hundreds of spiders and beetles and moths moving all around us.

She shoved to her feet, wiping her hands. "Nothing," she said, frustrated.

I paid closer attention to our surroundings, to the scents. I could smell mud and the river and pine needles and the humming off Isabeau's skin. And aside from the fact that everything looked like it was covered in glow-in-the-dark paint, it was all pretty normal. Footsteps, scuffs in the dirt, all the marks of our battle in the proper places.

Except.

I paused. The spot where Jen had disintegrated was dull, as if the shimmering light had dried to powder. I felt sick to my stomach.

"Isabeau."

She hurried over, startled at my tone. "What is it?" She stopped. "Oh. A violent death leaves psychic marks that can take years to fade," she said quietly.

"But she's not stuck here, right?" I asked sharply. "This is just residue?"

She nodded. "*Oui.*"

I released the breath I would have been holding if I'd still been able to breathe. "Okay. Good." She had a weird look on her face, her nostrils flaring. "Isabeau?"

"I didn't notice before," she murmured. If vampires could go green with nausea, she would have.

"What, damn it?"

"It wasn't just cow blood in the bottles," she said. "Montmartre's blood was in there as well. Just enough to be certain the *Hel-Blar* would follow the scent."

I frowned. "You know, that doesn't exactly make a lot of sense. Just once I'd like an answer, not more questions. We know Montmartre is after Solange, and he's making sure the rest of us don't negotiate a treaty. We can assume Greyhaven is doing his dirty work here, but that still doesn't explain why he has it in for you."

"I would really like to kill him," Isabeau said, as if she was asking for a second eclair at the local cafe.

I nodded at her amulets. "Um, you're sparking."

She looked down, blinking. The amulet was like the tooth that had broken when we'd heard about the attack on Kala. It was polished and capped with silver and small crystals that shot off a fountain of light, like a Fourth of July sparkler.

"*Bien*," she said, slipping the necklace off and wrapping the chain around her wrist so that the dog tooth dangled over her thumb. She stretched her arm out, watching it turn in circles, clockwise and then counterclockwise. I'd seen Lucy use a pendulum once in the same way, only she'd been trying to find out where her mother had hidden her birthday presents.

"There's something here," she said. "A connection I am missing." She stalked the perimeter with concentrated purpose, frowning into the grass, at the trees, spending extra time over the remains of the bottles. She stopped, swore fervently and fluently. It was all in French but there was no mistaking her tone. She dug a shard of green glass out of an exposed oak tree root.

"What is it?" I asked, grabbing for my sword, even though she'd assured me it was useless.

"I know this," she said, peeling the painted yellowed label with her thumbnail. Her eyes went dangerously watery, then brittle. "This is from my family vineyard."

I took a step toward her. "It's definitely personal," I said darkly.

"*Oui.*"

"Why?"

"I really don't know."

I hated how shattered she looked. "Greyhaven is playing you, trying to get under your skin."

"*Oui.*"

"Don't let him, Isabeau." I grabbed her shoulders, squeezed hard until she stopped staring at the wine bottle fragment and blinked up at me. "Don't you let that son of a bitch win."

There was a long moment when I wondered what she would do next. She was utterly unpredictable.

"You're right. He's doing this for a reason." Her chin tilted up and she was the Isabeau I'd first met: fierce, hard, and a little bit terrifying. "So I have to find out what that reason is."

"*We* have to find out," I corrected her, just as grimly. "You're not alone."

"Of course I am." She smiled wistfully, but she unclenched her fingers from the shard. Blood welled on her skin, but it was silver.

I'd assumed you couldn't be physically hurt when you were astral traveling or whatever the hell it was we were doing. It seemed only fair.

She frowned at the silvery blood. "*Non*," she squeaked. She dropped the shard, frantically wiped her hands clean, even wiped her fingers on her pants until they were raw.

"*Merde.*"

And then her eyes rolled back in her head and she crumpled.

CHAPTER 16

◆

Paris, 1793

After the food riots broke out, Isabeau took to the rooftops of Paris.

She'd scrambled up to the sturdy roof of a *fromagerie* to get away from the horde of starving Parisians and local villagers as they stormed the cobbled streets with bayonets, pitchforks, and torches. Her favorite *patisserie*, the one the revolutionaries never bothered with and whose owner often gave her stale croissants, burned to the ground in a matter of minutes. Thick black smoke filled the air; coughing and cursing filled the alleys. The fire traveled next door to the tooth puller and crept too close to a popular cafe. Buckets of water were hauled and passed hand to hand. Isabeau dropped back to the ground to help, pulling her collar up over her face. She wore the workmen trousers of the revolutionaries and a tricolor cockade on her hat. She'd put up her hair and tried to affect a lower voice when she spoke, which was rarely. She'd learned quickly that looking like a boy and spouting *"Fraternite"* whenever anyone asked her a direct question was the surest way to stay unnoticed and uninteresting. A girl with an aristocratic accent, soft hands, and long hair would never survive.

And her father had died so she could survive.

So she would survive.

However much she might want otherwise.

It was the end of February and the streets were slick with rain and cold, the smoke clinging in doorways. The fire raged, as hungry as the rioters. Isabeau crept closer, closed her eyes at the feel of the warmth on her face. She didn't move back until a rafter broke and hung over the alley, dropping burning wattle and wood. Her hands felt warm for the first time in a month. Even with the burn on her thumb it was worth it.

She was jostled aside. More water arced into the flames and they sputtered indignantly. It wasn't long before the *patisserie* was a pile of smoldering embers, the dark-haired owner yelling obscenities from across the street.

When the *gendarmes* arrived, Isabeau slunk away. It hadn't taken her long to learn to avoid anyone in power: police, a magistrate, even the night watchman who sat under a streetlight and drank wine until he fell asleep, snoring into his chest. The urchins liked to set spiders on his hair and run away giggling.

She hauled herself back up onto a nearby roof and flattened herself down, staying out of sight. She tucked her fingers into the frayed cuffs of her shirt. It was safe up here, quiet. There were only pigeons to contend with and the odd skinny cat. She could walk along the roofline from one end of town to the other, as long as she took care to avoid the poorer sections where the roof might give out altogether. She could eavesdrop on the revolutionaries shouting amiably at each other in the cafe and the beat of the drums from La Place de la Concorde when another prisoner was dragged up to the guillotine. She couldn't stand to watch the executions; just listening to the crowds chanting and those drums made her ill.

A few hours later when her stomach was grumbling louder than the quashed rioters, she slid down a spout and landed nimbly in an alley that stunk of urine and rose water. Once the sun went down, the prostitutes would lounge at the corner, winking at the men. She had an hour yet before it was dark enough that she had to find a rooftop.

She hunched her shoulders and kept her eyes on the ground as she turned onto the crowded pavement. Horses trundled past, their hooves clicking loudly on the stones. Someone had set a fire to blazing in a iron cauldron outside a cafe. She slowed her pace, casting a surreptitious glance at the abandoned plates for uneaten food. One of the servers glowered, flicking his fingers at her. She'd become an unwashed, faceless street urchin who drove away customers. It seemed like ages ago that she been choosing brocade for a new gown and wondering when she was going to be betrothed, and to whom and if he would be kind and still have all his own teeth. Now she smelled like dirt and mildewed roof shingles. She grimaced.

"Such a face on such a pretty girl."

Isabeau froze, then hunched her shoulders more.

"You'll never pass for a boy if you keep walking like that, *chouette*."

Isabeau turned her head slightly. The prostitute smiled at her. One of her teeth was missing and her cheeks were rouged enough to resemble apples.

"I don't know what you mean," Isabeau said as hoarsely as she could. She spit on the ground for good measure and only barely avoided her own foot.

"Better," the prostitute approved. "But you need to take bigger steps, as if you're ready to fight anyone who gets in your way."

"I don't want to fight," she protested, alarmed.

"And you won't have to if everyone thinks you want to."

"I'm not sure that makes sense."

She grinned. "Sense doesn't have a lot to do with being a man." Her bosom was dangerously close to spilling right out of her stained corset. Her long skirt was tucked up to her hip, showing stockings with several runs and a sturdy, sensible pair of boots. The contradiction made Isabeau blink. "My name's Cerise," the woman introduced herself.

"I'm . . . Arnaud."

"Not a bad name," Cerise said. "But you might do better with something more common, like Alain."

"Oh." She couldn't believe she was spitting and talking to a prostitute. The old Isabeau would have sniffed a lace handkerchief soaked in lavender oil to cover the scents of this place if she'd ridden by in her family carriage. She wouldn't even have noticed Cerise with her cold-chapped hands and frizzy hair. Isabeau shivered when the wind sliced around the corner.

"You need a coat."

She shrugged. "I'm all right." She clamped her back teeth together so they wouldn't chatter.

"Mmm-hmmm," Cerise said dryly. "If you follow the cart down to the river, that's where they dump the bodies after executions."

Isabeau swallowed thickly. Cerise patted her shoulder. "It's better than freezing to death."

Isabeau wasn't convinced, but she'd been raised to be polite. "Thank you," she replied cautiously.

"If you go now, you might catch it before it's picked clean."

Isabeau nodded and pulled her collar up to cover the back of her neck.

"And *cherie?*" Cerise called after her. "Stay away from the cafe at the end of the street. It's not safe for young girls *or* young boys."

"Thank you," she said again. This time it was more heartfelt.

She found herself walking down to the river, even though the thought of robbing a decapitated body made bile rise in the back of her throat. The truth was, she didn't have a single coin to her name and nothing worth selling aside from a scrap of silk from her mother's favorite gown. It probably wasn't enough to buy her a meal and she wouldn't have sold it regardless. It was all she had left of her parents, her home, and her real life.

She spotted the cart a few streets over, wheels creaking as it rumbled down toward the Seine. Most of the shopkeepers didn't even bother looking up from their work. Children and dogs chased after it singing a song Isabeau had never heard before. It sounded like an old lullaby but the words were obscene. The cart jerked over a broken cobblestone and an arm flopped over the side. Isabeau gagged but somehow kept walking. The rain started to fall fitfully, more like ice pellets than a gentle spring shower. It was still winter. She shivered violently, tried to tell herself that her shirt was thick enough to keep her warm, she just had to get used to the cold. She was soft, too accustomed to fireplaces and hot stew and mulled wine at any hour of the day or night.

The river moved sluggishly, as if it were too cold to do its work as well. She knew mill wheels would be creaking farther down the flow, in the villages. There'd been a wheel just like it near her parents' country house. Here the river was muddy and ordered with a broken stone wall.

Isabeau wasn't the only one easing out of the alleys as the cart stopped at the bank. She tried to tell herself to turn around and find herself a hidden rooftop where she could warm her hands in the smoke out of the chimney. Instead, she watched, frozen, as the two men began tossing severed heads into the river. Blood dripped into the dirt under the cart wheels. Bodies were rolled down into the gray water. There were half a dozen of them. Then the men got back up onto the cattle cart and urged the horse into a walk.

Isabeau leaped over the wall and crept along its broken stones like rotten teeth, keeping low. A head bobbed in the icy water, spinning to grimace at her with a grotesque leer. She stuffed her fist into her mouth to keep from screaming. She felt light-headed, as if she wasn't in her body. She watched herself approach a headless corpse caught on the bank and turn it over. It had been a man once, slender enough that his coat would fit her. It was dark gray and wool, already missing all its buttons. There was only a small tear in one shoulder and it was relatively free of blood. The scarf he was wearing had sopped most of it up.

She couldn't think of it. She could only keep moving, like a marionette, aware only of the frigid wind and the way her fingernails were turning blue with cold. The other bodies were being picked over by a gang of young boys and a girl no older than five who kept demanding something shiny. She had to be quick. She yanked and pulled until the coat was free, tears freezing in her eyelashes. She slipped it on and then ran back into the alleys, stopping only to retch in a dark corner before hauling herself up onto a roof.

The sun sank slowly, bleeding red and purple light over the city.

◆

By the time spring unfurled its tender green buds on all the treetops, Isabeau had learned the layout of the streets, and thanks to Cerise, which neighborhoods to avoid altogether, even in daylight. She'd found a jar of olives packed in oil and spinach leaves left over at the market. They were only a little bit trampled and reminded her of the spinach and garlic sauce Cook used to make for special occasions. She ate them with her fingers, crouched on the roof of a bookshop. She'd stopped seeing the bodies on the riverbank every time she closed her eyes and was grateful for the warmth of the coat when the rains started.

She saved the last few olives and tucked the jar in her pocket, swinging down to the ground. If there had been a carnival around, she liked to think she could have been an acrobat or a tightrope walker. She gave wide berth to a cafe known for its political squabbles and ducked under a creaking sign of an apothecary. The chain had snapped in last night's storm and the sign was swinging drunkenly, banging into the wooden frame around the window. She found Cerise leaning out of the window of the room she shared with five other prostitutes.

"Fancy a go, *citoyen*?" A thin woman with bruises on her arms smiled at her. Isabeau took a startled step backward.

"Never mind him, Francine," Cerise called down. "He's here for me."

"You get all the clean pretty ones." Francine pouted, wandering away.

Isabeau was embarrassed right down to her toes. Cerise laughed loudly.

"I forget how young you are sometimes," she said.

Isabeau made a face at her and used the sagging counter of a fishmonger's to boost herself up to Cerise's porch. It was more of a wooden ledge outside a broken window than an actual proper porch, but it did the trick.

"What did you bring me this time?" Cerise asked eagerly. Her roommates were snoring loudly in the darkened room behind them. She looked tired, the lines around her eyes were deeper. Isabeau sometimes forgot she was a couple of years younger than her own mother had been when she was born. Amandine had retained a kind of childlike innocence that Cerise had likely outgrown by the time she'd lost her last baby tooth.

"Here." Isabeau handed her the olives.

Cerise clutched it. "I haven't had olives in weeks."

"I've got something even better," Isabeau assured her, fishing out another treasure from her inside pocket, wrapped in old butcher's paper. She'd stolen it from the back garden of a fancy townhouse a street away from her parents' old house.

Cerise goggled when Isabeau pulled the paper back. "Are those . . . ?"

Isabeau nodded, sliding the bundle into Cerise's trembling fingers. "Strawberries."

"I've never had strawberries before."

"Eat them quickly or you'll have to share."

Cerise stuffed them into her mouth before her roommates could stir and ask about the sweet sugary smell. Her eyes closed as if she were eating chocolate mousse for the first time.

"Heavenly," she declared in a soft voice. Tiny seeds stuck between her teeth.

"I knew you'd like them." The sun was high overhead, hot for the first time since the autumn. Isabeau turned her face up to it. "I can't wait for summer."

"Marc told me to tell you that they're having a big rally in La Place de la Concorde today."

Isabeau looked at her hopefully. "How big a rally?"

"He said you could work it with your eyes closed. He's never seen anyone with fingers as nimble as yours." She waggled her eyebrows. "I wager he could think of better ways to occupy those dainty hands of yours."

"Cerise!" Isabeau lowered her voice. "You didn't tell him I'm a girl, did you?"

"No, *chouette*. He definitely thinks you're a boy."

"Then why would he be interested in . . ." She trailed off, confused.

Cerise laughed so hard she choked. "Never mind, I'll tell you later." She wiped her eyes. "How have you survived this long?"

"Because of you," Isabeau replied seriously.

Cerise wiped her eyes more vigorously. "You'll make me cry."

"Why did you help me, Cerise?" Isabeau had always wanted to ask but she hadn't wanted to frighten off the only friend she had. One didn't ask questions in the back alleys.

"I had a daughter once," Cerise replied, her voice so soft it was nearly drowned out by the squawk of pigeons pecking at the weeds at the side of the building. "She would have been about your age now."

"What happened to her?"

"She caught a fever one winter when she was still a baby. I couldn't afford medicine. When I broke the window of the apothecary to steal some, the *gendarmes* took me off to Bastille. She died before they let me out again."

Isabeau bit her lip. "I'm sorry."

Cerise nodded, touched the tiny glass drop earrings she never took off. "That's why I wear these."

"That's glass from the Bastille, isn't it?" It had become fashionable to wear rings and jewelry set with stones or glass from the Bastille, to commemorate the storming of the jail four years earlier.

She nodded fiercely. "Yes, I was never so happy as the day we pulled that prison apart." She swallowed harshly, shook her head. "Enough of that now, it doesn't do to live in the past." She squinted at the position of the sun. "You'd best hurry if you're going to make the square in time."

Isabeau hauled herself up onto the roof, poked her head back down.

"What do you want today, Cerise?" she asked, forcing a note of cheer into her voice.

"A ribbon for my corset," Cerise suggested, smiling again. It had become a game, to see what odd trinket Isabeau could find for her, once she'd finished working the crowd for more serious wares.

Isabeau hurried along the rooftops, following the sounds of the political rally. As promised, the square bulged with people, children, dogs, and cheese vendors hoping for a sale. The rain had washed the cobblestones and the streets clear, and the wind carried off the stench of so many unwashed bodies and the garbage in the alleys. There was a man at the podium dressed in the trousers favored by revolutionaries instead of the aristocratic knee breeches—thus the name "*sans-culottes.*" He had the tricolor cockade pinned to his hat, just as Isabeau did. Almost everyone in Paris wore one, even if they were secretly royalists. Everyone wanted to avoid unwanted attention. It was the only way to survive the riots and the National Guard and the *gendarmes* and revolutionaries.

He was yelling passionately about *Fraternite* and *Liberte* and state education for children. Isabeau didn't pay much attention to what he was saying. She wasn't here to join the cause, or even to fight against it. She was here solely for the coin she could lift from unattended pockets. She had a small stash tucked under the roof shingle of a ribbon shop that saw few customers these days. Soon, if the summer was kind to her, she would have enough to buy passage on a ship to England. If she went before winter, she could walk from the shore to London, to find her uncle's house. She was trying to convince Cerise to go with her but the other woman absolutely refused to leave France, and spat at the mention of England.

Isabeau used her high vantage point to scope out the movement of the crowd, where it clogged together and where it thinned out. Once she'd marked her best point of entry, she leaped down into an alley, scaring a cat and neatly avoiding a puddle of unidentified liquid. She strolled casually toward the main part of the square, looking for all the world as if she were paying close attention to the speeches. Someone handed her a flyer.

She let herself be jostled, stepped on a foot and apologized profusely. The man shrugged her off, checking his pockets. They were gratifyingly full and he forgot her instantly. The man next to him didn't think to check and she hid a smile, dropping the silver coin she'd filched from his coat. She'd hung her coat on a chimney and practiced for days until she could pick her own pockets without even disturbing the pigeons nesting above it. She was proud of herself, as proud as she'd been the day she'd played her first song at the piano without a single pause or mistake. Prouder even then when she'd earned the praises of her dancing master.

Anyone could learn to dance.

Picking pockets was a harder skill to learn and eminently more useful.

By the end of the square she'd amassed another silver coin, a copper chain with a broken clasp, a bag of walnuts, and a feather from a woman's bonnet. She'd have to find a red ribbon later. If she stayed any longer she increased the chances of being discovered. Greed would get her killed.

She spotted Marc leaning against a pillar, his dirty face half-hidden under a cap. He winked at her as she passed but otherwise made no sign that he knew her. She slipped him the copper chain as a thank-you, nicked a clump of radishes from a basket, and vanished onto the maze of shingles and broken chimneys above the city.

CHAPTER 17

◆

LOGAN

"What the hell was that?" I choked as we were tossed back into the clearing. We weren't in 1793 Paris anymore, but we weren't in our bodies yet either. We shimmered like ghosts over the grass, our bodies slumped several feet away. I couldn't get the image of Isabeau, abandoned and orphaned, clinging to rooftops.

"That's never happened before," Isabeau murmured, startled and embarrassed.

"You know, you keep saying that."

She swallowed, turning away slightly as if she was embarrassed to look at me. That was definitely new. "So now you know what I was."

I blinked. "Resourceful, clever, self-sufficient. Same as now."

She blinked back. "Logan, weren't you paying attention? I robbed corpses and picked pockets."

"You survived." There wasn't an ounce of censure in my voice, except maybe at the suggestion that I would think less of her.

"I was no better than Madame Tussaud," she said, disgusted.

"What does this have to do with wax museums?"

"I'm talking about Madame Tussaud, who made death masks. I read that she dug through the corpses of the guillotine victims to find decapitated heads for her masks. What are you talking about?"

"A tourist attraction. They make wax replicas of famous people. I guess it was named after your Madame Tussaud."

"This century is just odd," she muttered.

"This from a girl who survived the French Revolution."

"We're blue already," she murmured. That's when I noticed the glow we were emanating was brighter, slightly blue around the hazy edges. "We don't have much time left, we'll need to get back into our bodies before our spirits forget the way."

"I do feel kind of odd." Like the pull of my body was warring with the pull to just float away.

"Are you all right? I still need to get a connection to Montmartre." She kneeled and wiped her hands in the silver blood. "Which I can do, with this." Her palms were smeared with thick silver, like oil paint. Her teeth were clenched tight together as she dabbed the metallic blood on her forehead, between her eyebrows. She wavered, as if I were looking at her through heat lightning. She was going to vanish again and I wasn't touching her this time. Hell if I was going to stay behind and float. I grabbed her hand, the blood cool on my skin.

"Dangerous," she croaked, fading.

"Shut up," I croaked back, suddenly feeling a wicked jolt of vertigo. This wasn't like watching a memory out of her head, this was being pulled into a different place and not knowing where that place was. Everything was a bleary smear of colors, then black, then a painful thump on the head.

"Ouch, damn it."

We were in real time, pressed against the ceiling of a house, as if gravity had reversed itself. For all I knew, it had. She was practically vibrating with rage. I was trying not to throw up. Could disembodied spirits throw up? Best not to think about it.

"Look," she said, her voice nearly hollow with pain.

Below us was a lavish living room with a bar with a green marble countertop and bottles of blood lined up like vintage wines. A human woman wept in the corner, curled into a ball, blood staining her wrists and the inside crease of her elbows. Two guards were stationed at the main doorway in the Hosts' customary brown leather, and another two at the back door, which led out to a flagstone patio. In the center of the room, Montmartre reclined in a leather chair, looking like a dark prince out of some movie. His black hair was tied back, his eyes unnaturally pale. The last time I'd seen him he'd been trying to abduct my unconscious baby sister.

I cast Isabeau a sidelong glance, tried to keep my tone light. "If you keep grinding your teeth like that your fangs will break right off."

She wasn't smiling but at least she didn't look like someone was driving nails through her skull anymore.

"Can they hear us?" I asked.

She shook her head. "Only a witch or a shamanka could hear us now and they have neither down there."

"Finally, a bit of luck. Rat bastard," I hissed down at Montmartre. "Mangy dog of a scurvy goat."

"That doesn't even make sense," Isabeau murmured.

"Feels good though. Try it."

She narrowed her eyes at the top of Montmartre's perfectly groomed hair. "Balding donkey's ass. "

"Nice."

"Sniveling flea-bitten rabid monkey droppings."

"Clearly, you're a natural." I frowned. "Why is he glowing red?"

"You're seeing his aura," Isabeau explained. "It's easier to see when you're in this state. And that particular shade of red is unique to him. Do you see the guards there? Their auras are unique as well, but there's a tinge of red, on the outside." She was right. They looked like hazy jawbreaker candy, all layers of color. "It marks them as Montmartre's tribes."

"Wait, so we all have that?" I couldn't help but notice that Isabeau's aura and mine were the same shifting glimmer of blue-opal, all along the side of our bodies that were nearly touching.

"Yes."

"What color are the Drakes'?"

"Blue-gray, like the surface of a lake when a storm's coming. Lucy's is very, very pink, like cotton candy. The *Hel-Blar* have an absence of color, which makes my head hurt."

"This really doesn't get less weird, does it?"

The guards saluted and moved aside before she could reply.

Another man strode into the room, dressed in a ridiculously expensive designer suit. His hair was dark brown and artlessly styled, the kind of careless style you have to work really hard at. He wasn't very tall, too soft and aristocratic to look threatening, if it weren't for the sinister power that all but leaked out of his pores. I drifted closer to Isabeau. I felt the sudden need to protect her, floating delicately above two predators who'd already tried to kill her more than once. I didn't recognize the new vampire, but my mother hadn't raised an idiot.

"Greyhaven?" I whispered.

She nodded once, brokenly, like a doll with a wooden neck. I wanted to hold her even more than I wanted to get back into my body. Neither was an immediate option.

Greyhaven mixed blood and brandy into a glass and threw the contents back before speaking.

"The *Hel-Blar* are causing a nice distraction," he said. The sound of his voice had Isabeau jerking back as if he'd tried to stake her.

Montmartre didn't look particularly impressed. He looked exhausted actually, nearly gray with fatigue. Good.

"We got the package in through sheer luck," he said. "We don't have the time or the men to launch an attack on the Drake farm. We'd need the element of surprise and we can't get it, not now. And they won't let the blasted girl out."

They were talking about Solange. There was a weird growling sound I didn't realized was coming from my own throat until I nearly choked on it.

"She'll be at the coronation," Greyhaven assured him smoothly. "You can grab her then. And the crown."

"Yes, because that worked so well for me the last time," he said dryly.

"You worry too much."

"They'll be expecting us at the coronation," Montmartre said, rising to his feet. "We'll have to act faster than that. I can get the girl once I have the crown." He smiled and it sent a chill through me. "Get your men ready. We'll send in the human guards before sunset tomorrow and follow them."

"But . . ." Montmartre didn't see the odd look on Greyhaven's face, but I could see it clearly enough. And I had no idea how to interpret it; it was tense, hopeful, sad, angry, jealous, adoring. Too much, too fast for one expression. And it was washed over with a thin veneer of panic. Clearly Greyhaven wasn't the spontaneous sort. He didn't like having the plans changed.

Since those plans involved killing my family and marrying my little sister against her will, he could bite me.

"We have to warn them," I said to Isabeau. Suddenly, hovering like a waft of mist was extremely annoying. I was too angry and tense and worried to float; I wanted to feel the ground under my boots as I thundered through the woods to the royal caves. I wanted the hilt of a good sword in my hand, the smooth deadly grip of a stake. Now.

Greyhaven frowned lightly and peered suspiciously into the dark corners of the room.

"*Merde.*" Isabeau reached for me before I could reach for her.

Her fingers dug into my arm. "Think of your body," she whispered, her mouth so close to my ear it tickled the lobe. Greyhaven's head jerked up and then we were shimmering through another bout of vertigo. I had no idea if he'd seen us. I had no idea which way was up and which was down. I hurtled through the air for what felt like years and then landed in a lump right beside my body. I looked decidedly more peaceful than I felt.

Isabeau looked utterly shell-shocked, as if her astral limbs were heavy as stones. Her aura flickered, like a lightbulb about to burn out.

"Hey," I said gently, pushing to my feet. "Isabeau." She didn't blink, didn't look at me, didn't respond to her name. "Isabeau." She'd told me to say it three times to pull her back into her body. I didn't know if it worked when I wasn't exactly in my body either. "Isabeau."

Nope. Didn't work.

She stayed ethereal and still, like she'd swallowed the moon. I felt tired and disoriented.

"Isabeau, damn it."

She turned her face slowly toward me. "Logan."

"Shit. You scared me," I grumbled, feeling drunk. My aura looked wrong, faded.

"You should get back into your body," she said urgently. "Right now."

"Good idea." I smiled sluggishly. "Isabeau?"

"*Oui?*"

"How exactly do I do that, *ma belle?*" French classes had been a good idea after all, and not just because Madame Veronique demanded a rudimentary understanding. I could charm Isabeau in her native tongue. She smiled at me. I was sure I hadn't imagined it. Well, pretty sure.

"Just sit back into it, as if you were sitting in a chair."

"Okay." I touched her cheek, or tried to. Our auras touched, sparked. "You don't smile enough."

"Flirt with me later, Logan." She shoved me and I tumbled, falling backward and landing in my body. My arms and legs twitched, as if electricity coursed through me. I felt heavy and weird and tingled all over. Charlemagne nosed me roughly, leaving a wet cold smear on my neck. I sat up, grimacing. "Not the kiss I was hoping for, dog," I told him. He nudged me again and I froze. I'd heard it too that time. Footsteps, bodies moving with vampire speed between the trees.

Toward us.

Isabeau was lying too still, she wasn't back in her body yet.

Before they could spill into the clearing, I leaped into the air and landed in a crouch at her feet, stake in my hand. Charlemagne stood by her head.

He relaxed when the Hound warriors surrounded us.

I didn't.

Magda stepped forward, her face unreadable.

"Logan Drake, come with us."

"Like hell."

Isabeau still wasn't moving and I had to warn my parents, had to make sure Solange was safe.

"This is not a request." There were dogs at her feet, ears pricked, teeth bared.

I snarled. "Look, you're at the bottom of my list of priorities right now, Magda. Take a freaking number."

"You have been summoned by Kala."

"She can wait too."

Isabeau jerked once and then sat up abruptly. She blinked dazedly.

"Magda? What's going on?"

Magda tossed her long curls back over her shoulder. "He's been summoned for the rites."

"What?" Isabeau leaped to her feet, nearly knocking me onto my face. "No!"

I rose slowly. "What are you talking about?"

"It's not like that," Isabeau said pleadingly at the warriors.

"Kala read the bones again," one of them said. "He has to prove himself worthy of you, of the Hounds. He has to be strong enough to be one of us."

"You never told me," Magda added, sounding hurt.

Isabeau winced. "I know. But it doesn't mean he's the one. And anyway, we don't have time for this."

"You can't be handfasted without the rites," another warrior insisted. "He has to be initiated if he'd going to be your consort."

"Consort?" I echoed. I stared at her. "Consort? Seriously? That's what they meant?"

She blushed lightly. "One of our traditions," she said softly. She weaved on her feet, fatigue making dark bruises under her green eyes. "Kala predicted that I would promise myself to a vampire of the royal courts. To a Drake."

"And here I thought you didn't like me."

"It's not like that." She pushed her hair out of her face. "We have to warn the others," she said. "Kala's orders."

My fangs were out, my fists clenched. "Let me at least call my parents to warn them."

Isabeau looked crestfallen. "Phones won't work here, not after all the magic that's been done. It's why phones don't work in the caves either."

"Then send someone to somewhere where they do work," I ground out. I reached for her hands, remembered the thin girl stealing coins and eating stale crusts of bread, the woman I'd kissed just this morning as the sun rose like a candle set too close to lace curtains. "If I do this," I asked huskily, "I'm proving myself to you?"

She nodded almost shyly. "Yes, but—"

I cut her off, turning to the band of armed warriors.

"Let's go."

CHAPTER 18

◆

LOGAN

The march back to the caves was formal and irritating. At least Magda wasn't smirking at me anymore. Isabeau was bewildered and embarrassed. I probably should have been more concerned about my own welfare, but I was kind of glad to have a chance to prove myself to her. Even if it was the worst possible timing. And I'd been tested before, by Madame Veronique, who might prefer embroidery to warfare but was still remarkably intimidating.

Possibly I was underestimating this test.

Most of the torches had been doused inside the caverns; only a few candles were left burning along the edge of the milky lake. Kala already looked better, sitting on a worn stone, her amulets and bone beads clacking together when she shifted. Warriors lined the walls with their dogs. I could only see the glint of their eyes.

The ground was swept clean of pebbles and broken chunks of sta-lactites but sprinkled with what looked like salt and dried herbs.

"Logan Drake, do you come to the rites willingly?" Kala asked me, her voice echoing in a way that wasn't entirely a result of the caves.

I stripped off my jacket and my shirt. "These things aren't cheap," I muttered, folding them on a ledge. Someone sneered. I could just imagine what they must think of me in my pirate-style frock coat and steel-toe boots. It was easy to assume a guy who was comfortable wearing lace cuffs might not know a sword from a toothpick. I was used to it. And I knew how to use it to my advantage.

Isabeau swallowed, sent me a look I couldn't quite decipher. She opened her mouth with a warning but the man next to her clapped his hand over her mouth. I scowled.

"You know the rules," Kala told her sharply. "The bones and the dreams are not to be ignored."

"I'll be fine," I assured her. I raised an eyebrow at the Hounds still muscling her into silence. "Get off her." I couldn't believe she was allowing it. These traditions must run deeper than I'd thought. "Now."

He smirked and let his hand drop but didn't move away from her. Charlemagne didn't look as if he felt the need to bite the man's face off so I supposed I shouldn't either. It probably didn't bode well that a dog had better self-control when it came to Isabeau than I did.

Kala shook a seed rattle hung with dog teeth. The sound was

like rain on a tin rooftop. Six other Hounds lifted their own rattles and joined the prayer. Kala was chanting in a language that sounded like Sanskrit accented with guttural Viking-esque sounds. If I closed my eyes I could have been in some beautiful desert temple . . . or about to be ripped apart by a Viking Beserker in bear armor.

The song ended, the rattles trailing off into silence.

"Begin," Kala barked.

I tensed, half expecting vampires to rush at me howling. Nothing happened. There was the cold silence of the caves, the steady drip of water into the lake, the shifting of dogs. The unremarkable quiet moment was nearly worse than an out-and-out attack. That at least I had some vague idea how to handle. This was unnerving.

It was meant to be.

I lifted my chin arrogantly, standing with loose knees, ready to spring. I could take what they threw at me. And hell if I'd let them see me squirm and sweat.

And then I heard it.

The growl was low enough that I nearly felt it rumble in the ground under my feet.

The dog was that big.

He had the heavy bulk of Ox-Eye, with a generous dash of Doberman and Rottweiler. Drool plopped into the dust as his lips lifted off teeth that would have done a *Hel-Blar* proud. It was all muscle, not an ounce of soft puppy fat anywhere. And he was trained to fight and kill, with a leather collar armed with spikes to protect him from his prey. I'd heard they'd used dogs like this in the gladiator rings in ancient Rome and to hunt boar in the Middle Ages.

Knowing that hardly gave me an advantage though; just a shot of adrenaline in my veins.

I should have known they'd use dogs. And if I hurt it, even to save my own skin, they'd likely kill me for it anyway. The other dogs ringed around us in the dark growled in response.

Trial or trick?

Too late to regret my rash decision now.

I knew better than to back away or make eye contact. And I didn't have a handy drugged slab of steak with which to distract it. Just my own pitiful self.

This whole tribal negotiation thing just sucked.

Not to mention crushing on a girl who came from a tribe of bloodthirsty lunatics.

The dog paced toward me, head lowered threateningly, stalking me.

I wasn't going down like a damned gazelle. That would hardly prove my worth to Isabeau.

Very possibly this was the night my white-knight complex, as Solange put it, would get me killed. Someone had better write a poem about it. It was only fair.

I held my ground. There was nowhere for me to go at any rate, I was surrounded by warriors and their dogs. The light glimmered off the silver buttons of my coat on the ledge. If I was very lucky, I might be able to flip up and land on the narrow stone outcrop and climb out of reach. I looked back at the slavering war dog and bent my knees further, waiting. Everything else receded: Isabeau's carefully blank expression, the telltale way she clutched her hands together, the flickering light, the thunder of the waterfall. It was just me and the dog and the uneven stone.

I had one chance.

I carefully made eye contact and bared my fangs.

He didn't waste a single moment on barking or growling. His legs bunched up and he lunged at me, all teeth and wild eyes. His collar gleamed viciously. I bent, pushed off, and flung myself into a backflip that would have done any acrobat proud. I sailed gracefully through the air, nearly grinning.

The landing, however, wiped my smirk right off. The steel toe of my boot jammed into the wall. There wasn't enough room for my entire foot, and not enough of a handhold to keep me comfortably upright. The stone crumbled under my heel as I teetered, cursing. I slipped, dropped to the ground. The jagged rock tore at my arms, drawing thick rivulets of blood. I nearly lost a tooth bashing the side of my face.

No one was looking at me anyway.

There was a snap of teeth on air and another growl. Charlemagne sailed out of his position at Isabeau's feet and landed between me and the war dog. He landed with more power and grace than I'd shown. He snapped his teeth, growling. The war dog paused, lowered his ears, and promptly sat down, whining.

My mouth dropped open.

Kala inclined her head. "Very good," she said.

I wiped blood and grime off my hands. "What the hell just happened?"

"You passed the first trial," she said as if I was slow, as if this sort of thing was perfectly normal. "And, much more impressively, one of our own dogs claimed you as his own. That does not often happen."

I blinked sweat out of my eyes. Charlemagne's tongue lolled happily out of his mouth.

Kala sprinkled a handful of dried herbs and what looked like chalk into a small fire burning at the limestone bank of the white lake. "Ground-up bones of some of our most sacred dogs," she explained. She pointed to the hundreds of grottolike shrines that had been dug into the rock. They each held a candle or clay urns. "We keep them all close by, along with the ashes of our Mothers." I assumed "Mother" was another term for "shamanka."

And the smoke from the fire filled my nostrils and I stopped caring about semantics and powdered bones. The Hounds seemed to fade slightly into the background and Isabeau might as well have had a spotlight on her. She glowed like pearls and stars and moonlight. She was even more beautiful than usual, her long straight hair gleaming, her stance graceful, nearly coquettish. She wore a slinky dress of clinging satin in a deep burgundy, slit up one leg practically to her hip. Her slender leg emerged as she took a step forward. My mouth went dry. She wasn't wearing any jewelry, only those faded scars.

And she was smiling at me.

"Logan," she said softly, her green eyes glowing with amusement and heat as she approached me.

"Isabeau," I croaked. My voice cracked in a way it hadn't done since I was thirteen years old. I felt about as suave as I had then.

The fire crackled beside us, sending out curtains of scented smoke that lingered in the air between us and the others. We might have been entirely alone in the caves, in the whole world even.

She stopped when she was close enough to lick me without leaning forward.

Which she did.

She kissed me so thoroughly the war dog could have snuck up behind me and chomped on my leg and I wouldn't have noticed. She tasted sweet, like mulled wine and spices. Her tongue touched mine and I pulled her so close against my chest there was no room between us even for the billowing smoke. She nipped at me playfully and then she was soft and pliant in my arms, clinging to me and sighing my name.

It took a moment for coherent thought to hit me.

Isabeau would never sigh and cling like that, never run her hand under my shirt, along the waistline of my trousers with her entire tribe watching.

Not Isabeau.

It still required a supreme application of will to enable me to pull away. She was barely an inch from me, our noses practically touched. She licked her lower lip. I lost my train of thought. *Shit, man up, Drake*, I told myself.

She nuzzled my ear until shivers touched my spine.

"Logan, let's leave this place," she murmured. "Leave the Hounds and the Drakes and all of the politics. It could be just you and me. Alone."

There was probably a really good reason why I shouldn't agree with her and let her lead me out of the caves. As soon as the blood returned to my brain, I'd remember what it was.

She nibbled on my earlobe and I knew I was in trouble. Serious trouble. Vampire megalomaniacs and civil wars had nothing on this girl.

"Come with me, Logan."

It was physically painful to pull away. The smoke seemed thicker, it clung to her hair and stuck in my throat.

She ran a silver awl needle across the delicate skin of her inner wrist. I could see the blue rivers of her veins. Warm fragrant blood pooled on her winter-cool skin, across her arm to drip on the ground. She held up her red wrist.

"Drink, Logan. I want you to."

Self-control around fresh blood was never exactly easy for a very young vampire. I knew if I hadn't drunk my fill earlier that evening I'd have been utterly lost. Isabeau and blood were just too much to resist when put together. As it was I had to clench my back molars, trying to stop my fangs from protruding. I was only half successful.

She smiled, licked a drop of blood from her fingertip.

"I'm offering, Logan."

I snarled when my fangs won the battle with my gums and clenched jaw. I grabbed her elbow and dragged her toward the lake.

She giggled.

Definitely not the real Isabeau.

The smoke followed us. Her blood trailed pink ribbons in the milky water.

"What are you doing?" she asked nervously. She shifted, bared her leg invitingly.

But I'd already remembered what she'd told me earlier, when we were in spirit form. The trio of fat candles flickering on my left sent just enough light skittering on the pearly surface of the lake. I jerked her a little closer, angling her so I could see her reflection.

The lake might not be an actual mirror, but it was close enough.

I saw the smoke in the vague shape of a woman. It was the first time I'd come this close to the old myth of vampires not having a reflection.

I let go of her with a stifled curse, jerking back so quickly I would have spun her off her feet if she'd been real. I was alone suddenly in the smoke, grinding my heel in the dirt as I turned to glare at the Hounds. They weren't standing in the shadows anymore.

Kala didn't smile but she looked faintly pleased. "Last test," she murmured.

"Which is what exactly?" I asked suspiciously.

"Trial by combat."

I nearly sighed. "Of course it is," I muttered, unsurprised. I might have been more worried if I hadn't been defending myself against six brothers my whole life. And if I didn't have a mother who thought she was a ninja.

"Morgan." Kala motioned a woman out of the crowd. She looked barely sixteen, wearing a gray velvet dress that fell to her bare feet. Her hair hung to her knees in three fat braids, all clattering with bone beads, some painted blue, some gold. She was graceful, dainty, small as a ballet dancer.

I wasn't fooled.

Especially when she leaped at me, without even a warning battle shriek—even the telltale sound of her sword scraping its scabbard as she pulled it free was nonexistent. I wasn't going to be able to dance my way out of this one. I went low, rolling under her feet before she landed. When I flipped back up into a standing position she was already spinning to face me.

I had to leap backward so the tip of her sword didn't take my nose right off. The bracelets around her wrist jingled prettily. Since I happened to like my face where it was, I turned into my lean and kicked out. I got her in the solar plexus but not with enough force to actually cause any damage. She'd anticipated me and was fast enough to avoid the full punch of my heel. She grabbed my boot as it passed and yanked hard. I fell back, smashing my elbow and shoulder into the uneven rock. The flames of the candles by my head trembled.

This was ritual to the Hounds; they didn't holler or clap, only chanted and shook the occasional rattle.

It was both annoying and creepy.

When she came at me again, I stuck out my leg and tried to trip her. She stumbled but didn't fall. It did give me enough of a pause to get back up though. I flicked my hair out of my eyes. Blood smeared over my back from the rocks, dripping down my arm. Double and triple sets of fangs extended all around me. Morgan's nostrils flared.

And then there was just no escaping her attack.

She jabbed at me like a hornet, her sword drawing blood at my wrist, arm, chest, thigh. I fought her off as long as I could, landing a few blows but nothing definitive enough to win me the fight. And then, somehow, I was sailing through the air. I landed at Isabeau's feet, her boot digging into my ribs.

So much for proving myself to her.

The tip of Morgan's sword, already stained with my blood, rested on my Adam's apple. I froze and tried not to swallow. It seemed to take forever before Morgan stepped back, sheathed her sword, and glided away. I swallowed convulsively. Isabeau crouched down, half smiling.

"That was brilliant."

It almost made my total humiliation bearable. I pushed up out of my sprawl. "Did you miss the part where she kicked my ass?"

She shrugged one shoulder. "Morgan always wins. She's our champion."

I frowned. "I don't get it."

"It wasn't about winning. Only two Hounds have beaten her in the last one hundred and fifty years."

"Then what the hell was it about?" I held up my hand. "You know what, never mind. I don't think I care."

Kala approached us. "Well done, Logan Drake. We now consider you a brother."

"Yeah? Cool."

She handed me my shirt and jacket, and a leather thong with a dog's tooth wrapped in copper wire. "This was one of Charlemagne's baby teeth. It marks you as one of us and has magic worked into it."

I slipped it over my head as the Hounds traded rattles for drums. The bruises around my right eye pulsed. "Thanks." The drumbeats echoed all around us and a fire was lit in the center of the cave.

"Ordinarily we would celebrate and dance until dawn." Kala lowered her voice. "But I understand you have matters to attend to?"

I nodded. "I'm sorry."

Isabeau turned to me. "Yes, we should go." She slanted me a glance as we climbed the rough-hewn steps to the balcony-type ledge. "Logan?"

"Yes?" I pulled my clothes back on even though the fabric stuck to my wounds. So much for trying to keep them clean.

"How did you know it wasn't really me?"

"Are you kidding? Your eyeballs could be on fire and you wouldn't bat your lashes at me like that."

(HAPTER 19

◆

LOGAN

We reached the ledge when the barking started.

At first it sounded like it was coming from far away, echoing down the stone passageways. Once it reached the main cavern the other dogs joined the chorus, barking, growling, howling. The hairs on my arms stood up. The Hounds went on high alert instantly, reaching for weapons. I strained to hear beyond the dogs' frantic singing. Kala clapped her hands and spoke a one-word command, sharp as broken glass. I'd have shut up too if I were a dog. Hell, I'd have shut up anyway.

Isabeau tilted her head. I heard a faint thump, three long, one short, as if something was hitting a pipe. It clanged toward us, so shrill I thought the water of the lake might have rippled slightly.

"Attack," Isabeau said, mostly for my benefit. I expected

everyone else there knew exactly what those series of sounds had meant. All I wanted was to get out and warn my family about Montmartre's attack. "A warning for battle and—" She stopped, clearly stunned to hear two more short clangs. "And to hide," she elaborated finally, as if such a thing had never occurred to any of them before.

I hated to think what could make the entire pack of Hounds, on their own territory and with their war dogs, blanch.

I wasn't eager to hang around and find out.

Discretion was definitely the better part of valor sometimes—plus, someone had to save Isabeau from herself.

I knew for a fact that she would jump into the fray, regardless of the danger. I was frankly amazed she hadn't gotten herself killed already.

Morgan was standing guard over Kala, ushering the shamanka toward a narrow crevice in one of the far walls, hung with cobwebs. Most of the dogs went with them. Isabeau snapped her fingers and pointed for Charlemagne to join them. A few of the more ferocious ones stayed behind with the Hounds. The efficient way they stepped into battle formation would have brought tears of joy to my mother's eyes.

A shriek echoed toward us. I whipped one of my daggers into my hand. Isabeau lifted her sword grimly. I heard scuffling, grunting, and then a Hound trailing blood from a head wound stumbled onto the ledge. I nearly skewered him. The fact that he collapsed at my feet saved his life and the future of the alliance between our tribes.

"*Hel-Blar*," he gurgled, choking. "Dozens of them."

"Shit," I said as Isabeau and I stared at each other wide-eyed. I went cold all over. "It's misdirection."

"What do you mean?" she asked as Hounds scrambled up to wait on either side of the tunnel. Someone dragged their wounded compatriot out of the way so he wouldn't be trampled once the fighting began.

"It's Montmartre," I said. "It has to be. He wants to discredit our tribes to each other to make sure none of you come to our aid." I went even colder, if that was possible. I wouldn't have been entirely surprised if ice had formed in my mouth. "He's going for the royal courts tonight," I said. "Now. They've moved up the attack and this is how he's going to keep the Hounds out of the way."

Her hands curled into fists. "Greyhaven might have sensed me at Montmartre's. He would know my spirit signature. He'd have reacted accordingly."

"I have to get out. I have to get to my family."

She nodded. "I know."

"Show me the nearest passageway."

"This way." She led me to the other side of the water and shimmied down a rope, swinging onto another ledge behind the curtain of white water. When the thick rope swung back, I grabbed it and followed her. The ledge was slippery and the thunder of the waterfall shook through my bones. Isabeau fumbled for a flashlight and switched it on, sending the beam bouncing down a tunnel that was really no more than a crack in the rock.

"Parts of it are so dark not even we can see," she explained, handing me another flashlight with a strap to fit it over my head.

She was fitting her own, like a headband. The light blinded me from seeing her expression. "You shouldn't go alone," she said. The clash of swords floated down, barely audible.

I stared at her briefly. "You're coming with me?" I hadn't expected that, wouldn't have imagined for a single moment that she'd leave the Hounds to help me. She turned away to face the passageway, light swinging.

"I expect I'll do more good with you than I would here. Kala didn't ask me to join her, which means she wants me to safeguard the alliance. Why else would she have insisted on your initiation so soon after meeting you?"

I didn't really have time to talk her out of it. "Thank you," I murmured as we wedged ourselves into the damp tunnel, rock scraping each of my shoulders. I turned sideways. There was still barely room to maneuver. I really hoped this crevice led in the right direction. They all looked the same from the outside. I really didn't relish the thought of getting stuck and starving to death inside a mountain. Hardly an effective way to stop Montmartre.

We crept along slowly, too slowly for both our tastes but there wasn't anything we could do about it. There was no way to move faster since the tunnel seemed to be getting even more narrow instead of widening up to the sky.

"I hope you know what you're doing," I muttered as I scraped another layer of skin off the side of my neck and the back of my hand. The flashlight speared Isabeau's back, the fall of her dark hair, pale glimpses of skin. She turned her head slightly, reached up to flick the light off.

"We're nearly there. If we keep these on we'll give ourselves away."

I shut mine off as well. After a moment of blinking away the sudden change in light I could differentiate all the shades of black and gray. If I'd still been human, it would have been unrelieved pitch-black. I could smell a change in the air too. It was still cold and damp but every so often a warm breath of leaves and mud snuck its way in. It wasn't long before I could hear the wind.

We stumbled out into a very small cave that opened up to the glimmer of stars and the shifting of branches from a stunted tree near the opening. The outcrop was relatively narrow, we'd have to climb our way down. I reached for my cell phone.

"I should call my parents. Can I get reception here?"

Isabeau nodded. "You should be able to. It's not reliable but at least it shouldn't be blocked by magic this far away from the main cavern."

The faceplate of my phone was cracked and it wouldn't turn on at all. "That just figures," I said, frustrated. "I wasn't sure I believed in magic before, but I totally believe in curses now." I stuffed it back into my pocket, disgusted. "I must have landed on it when Morgan was kicking my ass. It's useless." Kind of like I was starting to be. It was doing nothing for my mood.

Isabeau handed me her phone. "Here, try mine."

"Thanks." I dialed quickly, listening with growing agitation as it rang and rang. I tried my mother's number, my dad's, Sebastian's. No one answered. That was virtually unheard of unless they were hunting or fighting. Someone always answered. "This is not good," I said, dialing the farmhouse.

Solange answered on the second ring. "Hello?"

"Sol? What's going on? Why isn't anyone answering their phones?"

There was a long pause and when she spoke again her voice squeaked. "Logan?"

"Yeah, who else?" I answered, irritated.

"Logan!" she shouted so loudly and suddenly I nearly dropped the phone.

"What are you yelling for? And, ouch." Isabeau looked at me questioningly and I shrugged. I couldn't explain my family at the best of times.

"You're alive! Oh my God."

"Of course I'm—"

"Nicholas! It's Logan. He's okay. I don't kn—hey, you're such a pain in my—stop it!"

They were clearly fighting over the phone. Solange won. I could hear Nicholas shouting: "You kicked me!"

"Oh, Logan, I am so happy to hear your voice." Her own voice wobbled a little, as if she were crying.

"Hey," I said. "I'm okay. Don't cry, Sol. I'm fine."

"Okay." She sniffled once. "Where the hell have you been?"

I had to angle the phone away from my ear again when she got shrill. "I'm at the caves with Isabeau. I told one of the guards to let you know. Jen came with me . . ." I paused. "She didn't make it."

"What happened?"

"We got attacked by *Hel-Blar*. Kind of like we are right now, so I can't exactly chat."

"Logan, everyone thinks you're dead. That guard never told us anything except that he found a death charm with your scent on it and Isabeau's mark. Dad's been trying to stop Mom from attacking the Hounds. Finn's been calming her down."

"Shit. Listen, I really can't talk. Montmartre has been setting the *Hel-Blar* on all of us. It's misdirection. He wants us to fight among ourselves so we can't fight him. He's probably at the courts right now. Can you get hold of Kieran? If neither Mom or Dad are answering their phones we're going to need help. And fast."

"I'll call him now."

"Good. Tell him I'll meet him there."

"You'll meet us all there."

"Stay home, Solange. I mean it."

"I'm glad you're alive but bite me, Logan. I mean it."

"Montmartre wants *you*."

"Duh. But if misdirection has worked so well for him, we can make it work for us too."

"I'm not using my baby sister as bait. Not after what happened on your birthday. He almost had you, Sol. If it hadn't been for Isabeau and the Hounds . . ."

"See you soon. Bye, Logan."

"Wait, you can't—argh! She hung up on me. Brat."

"You can't expect her to sit at home when her family is being threatened."

I glanced at Isabeau thoughtfully. "Maybe you could go sit with her. Protect her."

She snorted. "You're very transparent, Logan."

"Please?"

"*Non. Absolument pas.*"

I would have argued a great deal longer if something heavy hadn't struck the side of my head, sending me teetering on the edge of the outcrop. I stumbled back, blood dripping into my eyes. Pain lanced through my skull. Isabeau whirled, sword in hand, but we were too late. *Hel-Blar* dropped down from the cliffside above us and others climbed up from below. Their skin was an odd shade of blue in the darkness, their teeth like bone needles. The stench of rot was suddenly overpowering. Isabeau gagged, swore in French.

We fought like cats suddenly dunked in cold water. There was virtually no thought, it was instinct and a feral need to survive. I wasn't moving as quickly as I should have been. The head wound was tripping me up, making my arms feel uncoordinated and heavy. I kicked out, threw a stake with poor aim but enough anger to catapult the *Hel-Blar* off the side of the mountain. Isabeau pressed her back to mine, cutting off a blue arm, a blue hand.

"We're outnumbered," I slurred. "And I'm wounded. Run."

"You're not a white knight and I'm not a damsel in distress."

She was so stubborn I hissed. "Look around, Isabeau. This definitely qualifies as distress. Now, run, damn it. I'm only holding you back."

"Shut up and fight, Logan."

Every girl I knew was entirely insane.

Unfortunately, Isabeau probably couldn't have run even if she'd agreed to it. The only escape was launching ourselves right off the cliff and we'd need to get past three salivating *Hel-Blar* to do even that. My head felt like a rotten pumpkin, oozing and not entirely containable in its casing. We managed to take out one of the *Hel-Blar* and he puffed into mushroom-colored ash, but his demise only served to enrage his already unstable companions.

I stumbled, dizzy, and when I fell to one knee, another rock came down on my head. There was a burst of fire and shooting stars and then nothing.

◆

I didn't know how long I'd been unconscious.

It couldn't have been a full day, since my head still throbbed, though at least it didn't feel torn open. The scratches and gouges and bruises had all faded. My hands and feet tingled, mostly because they were locked in place with chains. I pulled and yanked. They rattled alarmingly but didn't budge.

"Isabeau," I hissed. "Isabeau!"

"I'm here," she said. "Behind you."

Her voice had relief flooding my system like champagne. I could've gotten drunk on the feeling.

"Thank God. Are you hurt?" I tried to turn, couldn't quite manage it from where I was lashed to the chair. Fury and pain replaced the relief and had me tensing every muscle until my jaw threatened to pop. I tested the chains again.

"It's no use, Logan," she said softly. "I've tried."

If I turned slightly I could see the side of her face and neck in a heavy mirror hanging on the wall beside us. There were bruises on her throat and over her cheekbone. We were in a small room with chains on the wall and several heavy wooden chairs. A window was hung with a thick curtain but I had no doubt it was regular glass, not enough to keep sunlight from weakening us. I was young enough that if they left me in the sun for a few hours, I'd pass out and let them stake me without a single twitch of a fight. I kicked at the floor with my boot, disgusted. Then I frowned.

"Since when do *Hel-Blar* have Persian rugs? Or leave their victims unbitten?"

"They don't."

I stared at her reflection in horror. "Are you telling me one of them bit you?" Adrenaline jerked through me. A *Hel-Blar* kiss could turn even an ancient vampire. Their blood infected our own and made us as mad and vicious as they were.

"No," Isabeau assured me before I lost my cool completely. "I'm only saying that Montmartre has better control of them then we'd thought."

"Hypnos," I muttered. "Bet you anything it's because of that damned drug."

She shivered.

"I won't let them take you." Big words from a guy covered in his own dried blood. I must be ridiculous to her. I'd failed her, damn it. I should've been able to protect her.

"Montmartre never leaves a Hound unmarked. We're proof that he's not infallible, that he can't control everything. He fears us and tells himself that fear is hate."

"We've stopped him before. We'll stop him again. For good this time." Hell if I was going to let him run around threatening the people I loved for the next hundred years.

"Noble words," an amused voice interrupted us from the door-way. I didn't recognize him but I saw all the blood drain from

Isabeau's face, saw an almost animal-like pain twist her features. For a moment she looked like the young girl I'd seen struggling to survive in the alleys of the Great Terror. That fear was brief, quickly covered by a burning thirst for vengeance.

Which could only mean one thing.

It wasn't Montmartre after all.

It was Greyhaven.

CHAPTER 20

◆

London, 1794

It took Isabeau nearly a year to save, steal, and weasel enough money to buy passage to England. Even then, she hardly knew what she was going to do when she set foot in London. She had her uncle's name, her father's assurance that he was selfish and arrogant, and two pennies left to her name. Cerise had refused to accompany her on the grounds that England was full of the English.

And the London docks were unlike anything she'd ever seen before. London was unlike anything she'd ever seen before, far removed from the familiar alleys of Paris. It was gray and blue and black, soot-stained and sitting under a fog of indeterminate color that made her cough.

"You'll get used to it soon enough, lad," the old man she'd sat beside for most of the journey cackled at her, jabbing his bony elbow into her ribs. Even though she'd kept her disguise as a boy, she'd thought it prudent not to appear to be traveling alone, even if she hardly expected an old man with rotting teeth to protect her. Sometimes, it was the illusion that counted.

But now that she stood on the wharf, being jostled by surly merchants and sailors eager for the nearest pub and prostitute, she felt more uncertain than she thought. She'd been saving up for this moment for so long, had held it up as torchlight in the dark nights to see her through.

The reality was somewhat daunting.

Wagons trundled by, children in dirty, torn clothes waded into the mud of the Thames for abandoned goods that might fetch a pretty price streetside. Voices and horse hooves and smoke from countless chimneys made a soup of sound and smell that had her holding her nose.

"Do you know where society lives?" she asked her elderly companion.

"Lookin' for the fancy, are you? They don't take kindly to urchins and pickpockets, my lad."

"I wasn't—"

He harrumphed. "I was young once, my boy. No need to worry I'll give you away." He nodded to the west end of the sprawling city. "Mayfair is where polite society resides and best of luck to you."

"Thank you." She handed him one of her pennies. He bit into it to check its worth and then slipped it into his pocket with more nimble fingers than she might have given him credit for. They were gnarled and bent but fast all the same.

"Mind the watchmen, lad," he said in parting before tottering away. He paused long enough to make eyes at a buxom fishwife with a stained apron. She laughed and went back to shouting about mackerel and eel.

Isabeau huddled into her jacket and lifted her chin determinedly. If you looked like prey, the world treated you as such. She walked easily and confidently, strolling westward as if she knew exactly where she was going, as if she'd lived here all her life. No one had to know that her heart was thundering so quickly she felt ill and the muscles in the back of her neck were so tight she'd have a splitting headache by nightfall. All they had to see was a young boy with a quick step and a clever eye who was able to take care of himself.

She walked for a couple of hours, trying to count right and left turns so she wouldn't be hopelessly lost. There were girls with baskets of violets and oranges for sale, muffins and baked potatoes and shops with towers of candies decorated with powdered sugar, hats with plumes dyed yellow and pink and green, ribbons of every description, lemon ices, books, anything anyone could ever conceive of buying was available. There were no scorched stones or broken windows from riots, no smell of fires or radicals shouting on every corner. It was utterly alien, decadent, and soft. But she couldn't afford to let her guard down just yet, if ever.

She began to notice the state of carriages improving; the streets were cleaner with boys waiting with brooms to clear a path through the horse droppings for a coin. The houses grew larger, the smells less pungent. Trees clustered in back gardens. When she came across the huge park, she stopped abruptly. She'd missed lawns of grass and thick oak trees and flowers everywhere. She hadn't realized how much she'd missed it until now. At least she knew where she would sleep tonight if she couldn't find her uncle. The thought bolstered her.

"Here now, mind yourself," a gentleman snapped, nearly walking into her immobile form. She snapped her jaw shut. She ducked her face into the shadows under the brim of her cap and stepped aside to let him pass.

She tore her gaze away from the horses and their well-clad riders picking their way into the park and followed the ornate carriages that trundled past. A vast majority of them were headed in the same direction and she took that as a good sign. It was still early morning; they wouldn't be off to balls and parties or shopping for new gowns. She didn't think the English aristocracy was that different from the French; mornings were for long breakfasts, correspondence, and resting after the excesses of the night before. More than a few of the carriage occupants were probably on their way home and hadn't even been to bed yet.

The houses became palatial, with gleaming brass door knockers and giant urns overflowing with every kind of flower. Maids walked small pet dogs on leashes and the occasional cat. Delivery boys, fish carts, and muffin sellers made their way to and from back doors. She stopped a rag man.

"St. Croix house?" she asked in halting English.

"Eh, Frenchie? Speak up?" He cupped his hand to his ear, barely stopping as he pulled his cart past. She helped him maneuver it over a protruding cobblestone.

"St. Croix?" she repeated.

"You mean St. Cross? House at the end of the street with the blue door." He waved in its direction and continued on his way without a backward glance. Her heart started to race again. Part of her wanted to run toward it, another part briefly considered running in the opposite direction. She would never let that part win. She forced herself to pick up her pace, though she did pause at the end of the walkway to catch her breath.

The townhouse loomed over her, several stories high, with a freshly painted blue door and brocade curtains in every window. Carriages rumbled behind her. An oak sapling dropped acorns on the street and sidewalk. Roses bloomed in copper urns. A lane led along the house to the back, where the gardens and stables and servant entrances were located.

She climbed the steps, which were swept clean of even a single petal. The door knocker was in the shape of a lion with a cross in its mouth. Isabeau ran her fingers over her family crest before letting it fall with a thud against the door. It swung open and a man with thick gray hair looked down his nose at her. His black jacket was perfectly pressed, his cravat immaculate.

"*Oncle* Olivier?" she asked tentatively. She'd never met him before but she'd expected he'd have some family resemblance, her father's cheekbones perhaps, or the famous St. Croix green eyes. This man was taller than any of her relatives and sniffed disdainfully.

"Lord St. Cross does not receive muddy boys who smell like you do," he informed her. "Off with you." He went to shut the door. She shoved her foot against it.

"*Attend, s'il te plaît!*" Her cap dislodged in her agitation, letting her hair spill out. She knew she must look half wild with her babbling in another language and her pleading, watery eyes. "*Non! Monsieur!*"

"If you go to the back door Cook will feed you, child. And then on your way." He shoved the door shut. She yanked at the handle but it was locked. She bit back tears of frustration. Weeping wasn't going to help her. She'd just have to find another way in.

The butler had pointed to the lane along the house. She tromped along it, gathering mud on her boots. A light rain began to fall, further muddying the lane. One of the windows was partially open, the curtains billowing in the wind. She looked around to make sure no one was watching her before diving into the rosebushes to get a better look. Thorns scraped the back of her hands and pulled at her hair. Stupid roses. Petals fell over her, cloying as perfume under the warm rain.

The parlor had several chairs with embroidered cushions and a pianoforte in one corner. The ceiling was painted with cherubs. She shuddered. How was a person supposed to relax with fat floating babies staring at the top of her head all day long? Between the angels and the gilded candlesticks and shell-encrusted lamps, the room was hideously overly decorated.

But at least it was empty.

She pushed the window open a little more and then shoved her leg through the opening, hugging the sill as she squirmed her way inside. She could smell lemon wax and more roses. The house was remarkably quiet for one so large. She wondered if she had any cousins banished to the attic nursery. No dog came to greet her, no cat slunk out from under the table. Her heart resumed its regular pace.

She went out into the hallway, wondering where her uncle might be. If he was awake he'd surely be in his study. That was where her father had spent most of his time when he wasn't on horseback or escorting her mother to some soiree. Even the hall was beautiful, with framed paintings, gilded sconces, marble-topped tables, and urns of flowers. She had to fight the urge to slip a small silver snuffbox into her pocket.

She turned a corner and walked straight into the butler.

He yelped but was much faster than she'd anticipated and hauled her off her feet by the sleeve of her coat before she could dart out of his reach. Her instinct was to run and hide but that was hardly going to get her what she wanted. The butler shook her.

"I'm calling the magistrate. We don't take kindly to intruders here in England. I don't care if you *are* a girl!"

Isabeau did the only thing she could think of.

She opened her mouth and screamed at the top of her lungs.

"Mon oncle! Mon oncle!"

The butler recoiled at her impressive volume. The chandelier overhead rattled. Footmen came thundering toward them. A door burst open, slamming into the wall.

"What the devil is going on here?" The voice had only the faintest traces of a French accent. The man wore a gray silk waistcoat straining subtly over his belly. His graying hair was swept off his high forehead.

"I beg your pardon, your lordship," the butler wheezed. "I caught an intruder."

"*Mais non, arrête.*" Isabeau struggled to get out of his grasp. She blew her hair out of her face. "It's me," she said. "Isabeau St. Croix. Your niece."

"My niece?" he echoed in English.

Silence circled around them, thick as smoke. Her uncle blinked at her. The butler blinked at her uncle. The footmen blinked at all of them. A woman she assumed to be her aunt made a strangled gasp from another doorway. She wore a lace cap and a morning dress trimmed with silk ribbon rosettes.

"Your lordship?" The butler was no longer sure if he was apprehending a criminal or hauling an earl's niece about by the scruff of the neck.

"Let her go," Lord St. Cross said. "Let me get a look at her."

Isabeau straightened her rumpled and stained coat. Her uncle stared at her for another long moment before he clapped his hands together.

"By God, it is her!"

"Are you certain?" his wife asked, her fingers fluttering at her throat. "You've never met her."

"I haven't, but I'd know those eyes anywhere. Just like Jean-Paul." He shook his head. "Remarkable. Where is he?"

Isabeau swallowed. "He's dead."

Olivier's mouth trembled in shock. He went pale as butter. "*Non,*" he slipped into French. "How?"

"Guillotine."

His wife fanned herself furiously.

"And your mother?" he asked quietly.

"Same." She swallowed hard. She couldn't lose her composure now. She'd fought too hard for her father's sake to be the strong girl who survived. Her uncle's warm palm settled on her shoulder.

"Oh, my dear child."

His wife lowered her hands from where they'd been trembling at her mouth. "My Lord, look at her, she's terribly thin."

"You are rather scrawny, my girl. We'll send for tea. Bring extra biscuits," he told the nearest footman. "Our cook is French. We'll have him make your favorite for supper."

"Come by the fire," his wife urged kindly, leading her into the parlor. "I'll ring for a bath after your tea."

Isabeau followed, slightly dazed. She'd expected more of a fight. She felt off center, thin as dandelion fluff. She was shown to a deep comfortable chair by the hearth. The fire snapped cheerfully. Warmth made her cheeks red, her eyelids heavy. It was a far cry from the fires in the metal bins on street corners, or the flames from piles of broken wooden furniture used as barricades.

"She's in shock, I think," her uncle murmured. He shook his head. "Poor Jean-Paul."

"Oh, those terrible French."

"Careful, love. You married one," he teased her.

"Don't be ridiculous. You barely even have an accent anymore. Only a fondness for that awful pâté."

Isabeau pinched her leg to keep from dozing off. "Father was planning to bring us here. Before we were caught."

"Don't worry, my dear, we'll take care of you."

"You are nothing like he said," she blurted out, bewildered.

He chuckled. "No, I imagine not. We never did see each other plainly, even as children." He sighed. "Lady St. Cross and I weren't able to have a family of our own."

"Oliver, really," Lady St. Cross murmured, flushing. "What a thing to say."

He patted her knee, his arm big enough to knock her over, but she just smiled at him. He turned to Isabeau. "What I mean is, it will be nice to have a young lady in the house."

"Oh yes," Lady St. Cross exclaimed. "We'll take you to all the balls, my dear. We'll need gowns, of course, and the dancing master, a lady's maid to do your hair." Her eyes shone with enthusiasm. Isabeau wasn't sure whether she should be nervous.

"Don't fret," her uncle said jovially when Lady St. Cross was distracted by the arrival of the tea cart. "You survived the Terror, you'll survive being a debutante."

CHAPTER 21

•

Isabeau

Greyhaven.

The last time I'd seen him was at the Christmas ball, his frock coat immaculate, his smile charming. I had no experience with men like him, had given in to the magic of the night and one glass too many of champagne. I thought I'd seen all sorts of monsters in my eighteen years: prisoners, rebels, cruel power-hungry guards, pimps, and earls with too much money.

But how did you defend yourself against a monster you had never imagined could actually exist?

He'd tainted my first real moments of comfort, of trusting the first happiness I felt since the mob had stormed my family château.

I wanted to kill him all over again.

I struggled against my restraints, heedless of the raw gashes I was digging into my skin, of my blood smearing the iron manacles. Logan was saying something but I couldn't understand him over the roar in my ears. It was as if my head was being held underwater.

Greyhaven sounded just as cultured and smooth as he had two hundred years ago. The scars on my arms ached. "One of the Drake princelings," he said pleasantly to Logan. Logan didn't reply. "Rumor has it our girl here has murdered you."

Logan sneered. "Are you going to fix that oversight?" He didn't sound afraid, only faintly bored.

I was starting to be able to concentrate again. Blood pooled in my hands. My fangs stung my gums, hyperextended.

"Certainly not. You're worth far more to me as a hostage. These little revolutions aren't easy to bankroll, you understand."

"I'll pay double what you get for me if you let Isabeau go right now."

Greyhaven laughed. "You're eighteen years old, Logan, and hardly a self-made billionaire. You can't afford her, even were I inclined to give her up."

Logan yanked at his chains. If he pulled any harder, he'd dislocate his own shoulder.

"Logan, don't," I said. My voice was dry, as if I hadn't spoken in years.

"Ah." Greyhaven turned toward me. I tried not to move, not to flinch, or to lean closer snapping my fangs. If I reacted now, it would only give him pleasure.

And he would never get a single moment of pleasure from me.

"Isabeau St. Croix," he said, "you've certainly caused me no end of trouble."

I hadn't seen him since that night in my uncle's garden. I had no idea what he meant by that.

"What does Montmartre want with me?" I asked, even though I knew the answer. The same thing I wanted with Greyhaven: revenge. I'd foiled his plans to kidnap Solange Drake and had taken down his Host. And I was a Hound, something that was an affront to his sense of power and entitlement.

Even if he killed me—again—I wouldn't be sorry for it.

Greyhaven folded his arms, leaning negligently against the wallpaper, as if we were still at that ball. "This isn't about Montmartre, it's about you."

"What? He isn't attacking the courts?" Logan asked.

"Yes." Greyhaven smiled. "He is. And probably wondering where I am. But I just had to stop in to see you." He approached me slowly. I lifted my chin defiantly. "I had to know if you remembered me."

"Hard to forget my murderer," I spat. "You left me in that coffin for two hundred years."

"Yes, regrettable. If I had any idea just how strong you were, I'd have made more of an effort to retrieve you." He flicked a dismissive glance at my leather tunic and tall boots. "Though you dressed much better in 1795."

I snarled. "Why did you bring me here? Just to amuse yourself?"

Greyhaven shook his head sorrowfully. "It would have been

better if you hadn't remembered me. Now it's messy, and I can't abide a mess. I never could."

I was confused. All my dreams of finding Greyhaven involved my driving a stake through his gray, withered heart, not partaking in annoying chatter.

"You did all this just to test my memory?" I asked, perplexed. "The ribbon from my mother's dress," I added slowly. "The painting in the courts, the wine bottle. *That's* why?"

"Indeed."

"Not Montmartre?"

"He ordered the traps, certainly. He's not fond of you. But I did the work, as usual," he emphasized. "So why not use it to my own purpose?"

"You're stalking her, you git?" Logan, snorted, disgusted. I knew what he was trying to do. He wanted to make Greyhaven angry enough to take his focus off me. "Pathetic, don't you think? Especially for the Host."

His lips lifted off his face but he didn't look away from me.

He had more control than Logan gave him credit for.

Not especially heartening, actually.

At any rate, I wouldn't beg for Logan's life. Greyhaven was perverse enough to kill him just to watch me suffer. Better that Logan was worth something to his greed.

"This isn't easy for me, you know," he said conversationally, nearly apologetically. "You were my first. I consider myself your father."

"I had a father." I hissed through my teeth, every word like a flung dagger. "You're not him."

He waved that away. "I gave you life eternal."

"You gave me death."

"Semantics."

A red haze filled my eyes. Anger soaked through me like a monsoon. I tasted blood in my mouth from where I bit my tongue.

"I can't have you giving me away," he continued, sliding a lacquered black stake out of the inside pocket of his pinstriped jacket.

"Get away from her!" Logan shouted, chains rattling frantically. "Me for her! Me for her, damn it!"

I felt nearly mesmerized by Greyhaven's version of our story, as if he were talking about someone else. Emotional shock. I'd felt like this the first night in my uncle's house, touching the books, the thick blankets, eating too much at supper. Like everything was finally right, but nothing made sense. I felt removed.

But I could still hear him, could watch dispassionately as he approached, nearly close enough to kick; but not quite yet.

"I've taken great pains, planned, and been patient for over a century now. When I first joined, the Host was strong, organized, powerful. I climbed the ranks, paid my dues. And still Montmartre denies me my own fledglings. As if he could stop me forever. I deserve my own army, my own Host."

"How many have you done this to?" Logan demanded, horrified, as he realized what Greyhaven was really saying. "You're making *Hel-Blar*."

"I admit I tried. But *Hel-Blar* are weak castoffs and mistakes. Now I've chosen better. I'm smart enough not to repeat Montmartre's mistakes."

"Smart? Is that what we're calling it now?"

"You bore me, little boy. And you won't sway me with temper. But if you don't stop your childish tantrums, I'll gag you." He flicked the stake at Logan and it bit through his sleeve at his shoulder, pinning him to his chair.

"Now where were we?" Greyhaven still hadn't actually looked away from me, not for a moment. I might have shivered if I wasn't floating inside my own head, bewildered by memories and fury. "I'm sorry I didn't come back for you, Isabeau. Forgive me?"

That startled me out of my daze. He had to be joking. My answer was a string of curse words I'd learned from Cerise. The air should have blistered.

"I just can't have you giving me away. Not when I'm so close. If Montmartre finds out before I'm fully prepared . . ." He trailed off with a delicate shudder. "Well, as I said, I prefer things to be neat and tidy. The battle will be on my terms and the Host my own to command." He withdrew another stake, pointed at me. "You can say your prayers, if you like. You *were* always my favorite. You never forget your first."

When he was close enough that I could smell his expensive cologne and see the grain in the lacquered wood of his stake, Logan managed to hook his foot around the rung of the stool next to him. He jerked his foot with an audible snap and the stool whipped over his head. It caught Greyhaven in the back of his knees. He stumbled, fury making his face bone-pale. A small wooden disk engraved with a rose and three daggers fell out of his pocket. Just like the one we'd found in the woods the night Solange received the love charm. He hadn't been lying then. He really did have his own men.

I kicked him as hard as I could.

Logan gave a wholly undignified whoop of joy. He sounded like a child opening presents on Christmas Eve. I kicked again. My only goal was to make it as difficult for Greyhaven as possible.

"I was prepared to offer you a quick, honorable death," he said. "But now you'll both suffer."

There was a stake in his hand again but before he could follow through on his promise, the door slammed opened on its hinges.

"Greyhaven, quit playing with your new pet. You're needed."

Greyhaven turned to slant the new arrival a seething glance. "Can't you see I'm busy, Lars?"

"This can wait," Lars assured him, his voice cool, quiet. "Montmartre can't. You'll give us all away because you can never delay yourself a little gratification. The battle's begun and his lieutenant is lecturing little girls. It doesn't look good."

Greyhaven tensed his jaw until it looked as if it might crack. Then he smiled at me. "Only a momentary reprieve, I assure you," he said darkly. "Watch the doors," he told the guards before storming out, the door slamming behind him and Lars.

"That was too damn close," Logan muttered. "This is our only chance. Sounds like most of the Host are at the courts." He stood up. The chains hung from the ceiling, not quite long enough for him to lower his arms. He tugged, then swung with his entire body weight. Nothing.

I stood as well, inspected the locks on my manacles. "I might be able to pick these," I said. "But I need a pin of some kind." I was going to start wearing hair pins again just as soon as I got out of here.

We searched the room: fireplace utensils, cushions, lamps, a stack of magazines. Nothing useful.

"Are you wearing a bra?" Logan asked suddenly.

I frowned at him. "What?"

"A bra," he repeated. "Are you wearing one?"

"Yes."

"Can you get it off?"

"I suppose so. But how is that going to help?"

"The underwire comes right out. You can use that."

I really was beginning to like him more than I ought to.

I tried to maneuver my hands behind my back. My muscles screamed after a few minutes. I was undead, not boneless.

"I can't reach," I said finally.

"Turn around. Let me try." He rolled his eyes at my expression. "I'm not trying to cop a feel before I die, though the idea has merit." He stretched, swore. "Can't reach either. Stand on the chair."

I climbed up onto the seat, trying not to feel ridiculous. His hands grazed my back.

"Hold still," he said as if he was concentrating harder than he'd ever concentrated in his entire life. His vampire pheromones were suddenly stronger, flooding the room with the smell of anise and incense. It had no effect on me, of course, but it smelled nice. He made quick work of the lacing on the back of my tunic, exposing my bare back. His fingertips were cool and gentle on my skin. He reached for the clasp, had it apart in seconds.

"You're rather good at that," I remarked dryly.

He pushed my tunic down over my shoulder to reach the strap. I felt warm suddenly, tingly. I had to remind myself we were locked up, chained, and about to be killed. I heard him swallow. And then his mouth was on the back of my neck. He pressed a hot kiss there, searing through me.

Then he stepped back abruptly.

"Can you reach it now?" he asked hoarsely.

I nodded mutely and didn't turn around. I couldn't look at him just yet. I knew my face was red; my fingers trembled. My knees felt soft as I climbed off the chair. I reached into the armhole of my sleeveless tunic and pulled the bra strap down and then did the same on the other side. A quick shimmy and the bra slid out, dangling from my hand. It was white lace, a gift from Magda. And for some reason having it out where Logan could see it like that made me blush harder.

I used my fangs to bite a hole into the fabric and then I slid the thin steel wire out of one of the cups. Logan was watching me intently, his cheekbones ruddy. I wasn't the only one blushing over a scrap of lace. Somehow that made me feel better.

I inserted the end of the wire into the lock of the manacle on my right wrist and jiggled it gently, tilting my head to better hear the scrape of metal on metal. When I heard the delicate, barely audible snick, I smiled faintly. Another twist and the manacle opened. I slid my hand out and repeated the procedure on the other lock.

"Sweet," he said. "You'll have to teach me that trick."

The guards were still quiet on the other side of the door, but we didn't have much time. I hurried over and picked the locks to free him as well.

"Are you coming?" Logan grabbed Greyhaven's discarded stake off the rug and then looked over his shoulder when I didn't move. "Are you okay?"

"I'm fine, Logan," I answered calmly.

"Well, I'm not," he muttered. "We have to get the hell out of here."

"He's not after you, you have nothing to worry about."

He sucked in his breath, to express emotion rather than for need of oxygen. When he spoke, his voice was a little husky. "I'm not worried about me."

I didn't know what to do with this concern, with the way he looked at me, as if I mattered. I needed to stay strong, focused, cold. I couldn't afford to let him get in my way. I was too close now. I spent too long waiting for my chance.

And when Greyhaven came back in to kill me properly, I'd have that chance.

I couldn't regret not having the opportunity to explore the connection I felt with Logan.

And I did feel it.

In a few short nights, he'd broken through some of my defenses, had made me long for things that were impossible.

He was a romantic, charming, and loving.

And convincing.

I knew if I said a single word about the way he made me feel he'd spare no quarter in convincing me that we had a chance. But his kind of life just didn't have room for someone like me, no matter what Kala's oracle bones had said. His family was civilized. I was proud to be a Hound, but there was no denying we were a different vampire breed: wild, primal, superstitious. Not to mention disdained and feared by the other vampires.

And though Logan had passed his tests, had been initiated as a Hound, I couldn't know yet if he truly understood what that meant.

Just like he couldn't know that making Greyhaven pay had been the only thing to see me through my first days as a vampire.

How was I supposed to give that up, now that it was within my grasp?

"I have to stay," I finally said tonelessly. "You should go though."

"Don't be stupid. I'm not leaving without you," he argued. "And if you don't come with me, my parents—hell, my entire family— could die. You know Montmartre and you know how to sneak into the court caves. I *need* you, Isabeau."

"I can't," I said brokenly. "I have to kill Greyhaven. *I have to.*" He was asking too much from me.

"If you stay, you'll die. He'll kill *you.*"

"Probably."

"So, what—I'm supposed to let you commit suicide?"

"It has nothing to do with you, Logan."

"Coward," he raged at me, the charming young man vanishing. The predator in him, usually disguised in lace and old-fashioned clothes, broke free.

Instead of being afraid, I leaned in closer to him subconsciously.

"I can't," I whispered again, jerking back.

"You have to," he insisted hotly. "You're a survivor. I saw what you lived through, so you can damn well live through this too. Survive Greyhaven, Isabeau. Please."

"You don't understand."

"I get it. And it's stupid. Now, I'm getting out of here and I hope you'll choose to fight instead of giving up." His eyes flared with green fire. "The Isabeau I know wouldn't give up. Not now. Not when her tribe is out there fighting."

He was right.

Insufferable, but right.

"Your choice," he said finally.

CHAPTER 22

•

Isabeau

My choice was to stay and get my vengeance—and likely die.

Or fight and only possibly die.

Logan made it sound so simple.

"I've only known you three days," I said. "And you're asking me to choose you."

He speared me with a glance. "I'm not asking you to feel for me the way I feel for you. I'm just asking you to choose *you*. Not Greyhaven."

I wasn't as strong as I'd thought. Because part of me really wanted to stay. It was easier, tidier, and hurt less.

Tidier.

Greyhaven thought like that.

Not me.

But if I wasn't the girl who brought down Greyhaven, who was I? I'd built my new life, my new identity, on that one single goal. But this was a battle of a different sort, one I couldn't win with a sword or a magic charm. Otherwise he'd keep winning, without even realizing it. I'd survived him once, but I'd carried him around and let him hurt me over and over again. And that part was on me.

And it was the only part of this whole mess, of the emotions and needs bubbling inside the cauldron of my chest, that I could control.

So I'd damn well control it.

"*Je viens*," I said tightly. When he looked at me blankly, I repeated myself in English. "I'm coming." Something broke inside and there was pain and sorrow and then, surprisingly, lightness. Ironically, it was as if I could breathe again.

Logan stepped close to me and slid his hand through my hair, cupping the back of my head, bone beads dangling against his fingers. He didn't kiss me but he looked at me with such a fiery kind of joy that I felt scalded all over.

And naked.

"Let's hurry," he said huskily. "So I can kiss you for an hour or two."

It was surprisingly good incentive.

"The window," I said as he stepped back. "It sounds as if most of the Host are busy with Montmartre. We couldn't ask for a better chance."

We quietly dragged a chair to the door and very carefully tilted it so it was shoved tight between the handle and the floor. We moved with studied caution since the guards would have hearing as good as ours. When no one raised the alarm we carried a table and set it under the window, then climbed up on top. I could just reach it. Logan nudged me out of the way and stuck his head outside, looking right then left.

"Clear," he mouthed before hauling himself up and out. He stayed low in the grass, reaching down to pull me out. We lay side by side for a long moment, just listening. The night was innocuous, crickets and frogs and an owl somewhere in the forest. I looked up, noting the stars.

"We're east of the courts," I told him. "They'll have guards posted just inside the trees."

"Can we outrun them?"

"Maybe."

"We're mounting a rescue without weapons," he muttered. "They stripped us bare."

"I know." I was very aware of the empty scabbard strapped to my back and the bare loops on my belt. They'd even taken the dagger hidden in my boot.

"Are you ready?"

I nodded, smiling grimly. I had enough pent-up frustration that taking on Host guards seemed like a calming pastime. Nearly as good as a bubble bath.

We managed to crawl to the lilac hedge before we noticed anyone at all. The house was quiet, windows casting squares of yellow light on the lawns. There was a carriage house behind the main building but it was dark. We were pressed in the mud, waiting for the wind to shift the leaves. Moonlight caught the metal zipper on a Host vampire's jacket. He was leaning against a tree, bored. I reached up to snap off a branch of the lilac. It wasn't exactly a sophisticated weapon but it was marginally better than my bare hands.

Logan touched my wrist, jerked his head toward the backyard, where the pool wafted chlorine fumes to tickle our noses. I had to press my tongue to the roof of my mouth to stifle a sneeze. Two more guards came toward us, from behind the pool shed.

We froze, hunched in the roots. They turned right, following a flagstone path that curved away from us. We waited a little longer before easing out of the hedge, rolling to a circle of birch trees. It was the last bit of cover between us and the forest. The guard yawned, shifted against the maple, startling a bird asleep near enough to notice a predator shifting.

Logan picked up a large stone, hefted it in his hand.

"Ready?" he murmured in my ear so low it was more of a tickle than an actual sound. I nodded, shifting into a crouch. He tossed the stone low but far enough so that it dropped into the bushes to the left of the guard. The leaves rustled.

The guard leaped into action, hurling himself toward the sound. We threw ourselves into a run, heading into the edge of the woods on his far right while he was momentarily distracted.

He wasn't the problem.

A shout came from the house, closely followed by a bright spotlight suddenly swinging across the lawn, bright as sunlight. Every blade of grass stood in sharp relief, the peeling bark of the birches, the blue ripple of the pool water.

Us.

"Hell," Logan muttered, tugging my hand. "Run!"

My feet barely touched the ground. Judging by the voices, there weren't many Host left behind, as we'd thought.

But certainly enough to kill us.

I stopped, spinning around, splintered branch held high. Logan skidded in the dirt.

"Are you *smiling?*" he asked incredulously.

"Just a little bit."

"Okay, well, could you run and smile at the same time?" The guards thundered out of the house, racing through the gardens, toward the forest and the fields behind the carriage house.

"I'd rather fight."

"Yeah, I get that." He shoved me, forcing me into a backward stumble. "Let's run anyway."

"There!" someone yelled. "I see them."

Logan kept pushing me until I had to run or trip over my own feet. We leaped a fallen trunk, blossoming mushrooms and moss. Branches slapped at us, catching in my hair. Leaves rained down on us. We darted around trees, zigzagging to make our trail harder to follow. We ran, splitting up at a clearing and rejoining on the other side, further muddying our trail. A rabbit darted out of our way and then we were truly in the dark secret of the forest.

Safe.

I was perversely disappointed.

Logan shot me a knowing grin. "Cheer up. You can hack someone to bits soon enough." He shook his head when I brightened, heartened.

I was even more heartened when I heard a plaintive dog howl. I paused, the abrupt switch from all-out running to dead stop making me briefly dizzy. When Logan realized I was no longer keeping pace, he doubled back. I held up my hand before he could say anything, listening harder. The howl came again, trailing at the end.

I knew that howl.

Grinning and watery-eyed at the same time, I stuck my thumb and forefinger in my mouth and whistled. It pierced the forest, shrill enough to leave Logan wincing.

"My ears are bleeding. Thanks for that," he said. "And so much for stealthy."

"We left the Host miles back," I assured him, whistling again. A series of yips answered. And then barking from across the river. A different howl from the mountainside.

It wasn't long before Charlemagne came running at me from between the trees. He leaped on me, tongue lolling happily. He wiped it across my cheek, tail wagging furiously. He gave Logan a swipe in greeting and then leaned so joyfully against me, I staggered under his weight.

"Good boy." I scratched his ears, then ran a hand over his fur, searching for wounds. He was unmarked.

More dogs came at us from all directions until we were surrounded. Logan raised his eyebrows, impressed. There were six aside from Charlemagne, three of them massive, trained Rottweiler war dogs.

"Finally," Logan remarked. "We have weapons again. Except that one looks like it wants to chew on my leg."

"He probably does," I said cheerfully, snapping my fingers to get the dog's attention.

Logan led the pack to where he'd arranged to meet his brothers and sister. Dogs sniffed ahead of us, ran behind us, and ran along either side.

I felt more like myself than I had in a long time.

CHAPTER 23

◆

LOGAN

Solange, Nicholas, Connor, and Quinn were waiting for us. Connor was pacing; Quinn was crouched in the ferns. He rose when he spotted us, and Solange came running. The dogs milled around our feet.

"Logan!" She hugged me so tightly I grunted, extricating myself after tugging affectionately on her hair.

"I'm fine, brat. *Oof,*" I mumbled, tripping over one of the eager dogs.

"I told you the Drake boys are harder to kill than that." Quinn smirked and clapped me on the shoulder. Nicholas and Connor did the same. They turned to Isabeau cautiously.

"Isabeau," Solange said politely.

I bumped her with my shoulder. "She didn't murder me, as you can see, so chill out."

Solange looked a little sheepish. "Sorry."

"I understand," Isabeau said quietly. "Could I borrow someone's phone?"

Solange handed hers over and Isabeau dialed quickly. "Magda? Are you all right? Kala?"

I could hear Magda's reply. "Kala's fine. We set some of the dogs loose to find you."

"I know. We found each other. Did you get rid of the *Hel-Blar*?" Isabeau asked.

We eavesdropped without pretense.

"Yes, but only just," Magda replied. "And we haven't had a chance to go back to the caves and make sure none are nesting."

"Listen, Montmartre's making his move tonight, right now, against the Drakes. We have to stop him."

"Why?" Magda snapped. Isabeau glanced my way, wincing. "What do I care about the royal courts? And we have enough problems of our own tonight, if you hadn't noticed."

"Believe me, I noticed," Isabeau shot back. "And if you want to know why, it's because we're next."

"Fine," she grumbled.

"I'll keep you posted." Isabeau clicked off.

"Where's Lucy?" I asked the others.

"At the farmhouse," Nicholas said with grim satisfaction.

"How'd you manage that?"

"She's in a closet." Solange rolled her eyes.

I stared at Nicholas. "You locked your girlfriend in a closet? Smooth."

"She's going to eviscerate him," Quinn said cheerfully.

"Yeah, well, she'll be alive to do it," Nicholas said. "And that's all I care about right now."

"What about the others? Mom and Dad at the courts?"

Connor shook his head. "No, and they never made it home. It's nearly sunrise, so they must have gotten caught in between. Sebastian and Marcus are with them."

I checked my pocket watch. "They can't have been ambushed that long ago. They'll still be alive. They have to be." I looked at Solange. "Did you call Kieran?"

"Yeah, but the Helios-Ra can't help us."

"Why the hell not? What's the point of dating a hunter if you can't use him?"

"They've got their hands full," Connor explained. "*Hel-Blar* are close enough to town to cause a serious problem."

"Greyhaven," I said, disgusted.

"What does he have to do with it?"

"He's been making vamps on the sly," I answered. "I guarantee most of them went feral. The ones who didn't are helping him plan a coup to oust Montmartre, while the others are being used as misdirection."

"Shit," Quinn said. "Bastard."

"You have no idea." I looked at Isabeau, but her expression was carefully blank. "So now the problem is, how do we find Mom and Dad in time?"

"I can help with that," Isabeau said confidently, "but I need something of theirs. A piece of clothing would be ideal."

"Magic?"

She shook her head, half smiling. "Dogs."

"Oh. Right."

Solange and my brothers looked at one another and shook their heads. "We've got nothing on us and no time to go home and get it," Quinn said.

"Wait." Solange opened her pack. "I have something that belonged to Montmartre. It was left at the property line in the woods. We found it on the way here." She pulled out a slender, delicate silver crown, dripping with diamonds and rubies. She made a face. "He doesn't go for the subtle metaphor, does he?"

"He gave you a tiara?" I grimaced. "Tacky."

"I know, right?"

"It's perfect," Isabeau said, plucking it out of her hands. "Gwynn," she called over one of the hounds. He was huge, taller than Charlemagne with a distinctly regal bearing. He padded over to her and she held out the crown. "Scent," Isabeau demanded. Obediently, he sniffed the ornate filigrees, the egg-sized rubies and seed pearls. "Good boy. Now find Montmartre!"

He *woofed* once and fit his nose to the ground, smelling through the undergrowth. Isabeau made sure the other dogs received the same instructions, giving them a good thorough scent of the crown. "Find Montmartre!" she repeated.

"Your dogs have a 'find Montmartre' command?" I asked.

"Yes," she answered with a dark smile. "You forget how much we dislike him."

We trailed after the dogs and it wasn't long before Gwynn lifted a paw and then resumed his sniffing, more fiercely this time.

"He's got the scent," Isabeau murmured.

"Good. Let's go kick some ass," Quinn said, withdrawing a stake from the leather strap across his chest.

"Hey, give me one of those." I took one from Connor as well and handed it to Isabeau. She'd tossed the broken lilac branch into the bushes earlier.

"Wait," Isabeau said repressively as we jogged after the dogs. "We need a plan."

"We find them, kill the bastards, rescue our parents," Quinn explained.

"You can't just run in there and hope Montmartre trips on his own stake," Isabeau said. "He's really good at this sort of thing. He's been doing it for centuries and we . . . haven't. And there's only six of us, and most of us are newborn. Once the sun comes up, he can keep fighting. We can't."

"We only need to distract him," Solange insisted. "Give Mom and Dad and the others a chance to fight back."

"That's something," Isabeau agreed. "But it's not enough. We've got the dogs," she said as we picked up speed. "I'll call the Hounds with directions once we know where they are and they might be able to get to us in time."

"We can't wait," Quinn argued.

"I know that. We can't just barge in either," she insisted. "But maybe we can use one of their own tricks against them. How's your balance?"

We looked at her like she'd lost her mind.

"Our balance? We're not joining the circus here."

"Just listen. We send the dogs in and then we follow, but from up high. If we can move from tree to tree, we'll have an advantage and the element of surprise."

"I haven't swung from a trapeze lately," Quinn said dryly, but he was grinning. "But I'll damn well learn fast. You're sneaky and vicious, Isabeau," he added. "I think I like you."

"I think they're heading to the clearing off the fens." Connor frowned down at the GPS on his phone. "I'm sending the coordinates to everyone we know right now."

"Send them to Magda too." Isabeau rattled off her number. Two soft short whistles had the dogs moving more silently, ears perked.

"Nearly there," Connor said.

"Let's climb," she suggested. Quinn and Nicholas went wide, circling to the other side of the clearing. I could smell the Host and their victims now, the forest drenched in pheromones and blood-lust. Fangs extended all around. Isabeau's hadn't retracted since we'd been ambushed. She shimmied up an elm tree, startling a squirrel into a hole in the trunk. She moved lightly along a high branch, dropping down onto a nearby oak branch and hopping up to another elm.

We used a curtain of leaves to hide as we assessed the situation down below. An outer circle of Host guards in their brown leather patrolled with crossbows. We had managed to avoid their notice so far. There were more just inside the clearing and a clump of them in the center where Montmartre stood, an arrow pointed at Mom's chest. Dad was snarling, on his knees, a sword tip grazing his jug-ular. Blood dripped from a gash on his temple. Sebastian and

Marcus stood very still. Montmartre was smiling pleasantly. Greyhaven waited behind him impatiently. I wished I had a crossbow of my own.

But that would have to wait.

"*Merde*," Isabeau snapped. "You're not the only Drake with a martyr complex."

Solange strolled into the meadow, muffled curses shivering in the treetops as Nicholas, Quinn, and Connor struggled not to give themselves away. Only Isabeau's hand on my arm stopped me from launching out of the tree.

"Montmartre," Solange called out, swinging the crown from her fingertips, the faint moonlight glimmering on the diamonds. "Let's make a trade."

CHAPTER 24

•

Isabeau

Montmartre looked up, smile widening. "Solange, darling. So glad to see you've recovered."

Helena closed her eyes briefly. "Solange, no."

"Stay the hell away from my daughter," Liam added, seething. Montmartre flicked his hand dismissively. Solange took another step forward, out of the protection of the sheltering trees.

"Little idiot." Logan seethed. "The last time she gave herself up for us, she nearly got killed."

"I knew you'd come to your senses," Montmartre told her pleasantly, his long hair hanging down his back.

"If you let my family go unharmed," she said, fisting her hands to hide the trembling of her fingers, "I'll stay with you."

"The hell you will," Logan yelled, finally swinging into the clearing. His brothers followed suit, like deranged monkeys. I barely had time to whistle the dogs into an attack.

Every single one of the Drake brothers was insane.

We had no idea if the Hounds were close enough to help us; we had barely enough weapons between us and a traitor below.

What was a lady to do?

I leaped into the fray, of course.

I staked a guard as I landed and she plumed into dust. I caught her sword before it fell in the grass with her empty clothes. I drove the bottle shard smeared with Montmartre's blood into the ground. The *Hel-Blar* would follow its scent to us. They would make things worse, no doubt about that, but they'd attack Montmartre and the Host at least as much as they'd attack us.

The Host didn't hesitate, didn't even wait for orders. Helena didn't hesitate either. The very second Montmartre glanced at her daughter, she kicked the crossbow out of his hand. She couldn't do much more than that; there were too many of them. Liam roared to his feet, Sebastian and Marcus spun to fight their captors. The dogs growled and bit their way through the Host. Nicholas and Connor were fighting back-to-back and Quinn was flipping his way to Solange's side. Greyhaven was in the middle of it all with wildflowers incongruously around his knees. I saw him open his cell phone and bark a terse command into it. There were too many battle sounds to hear him properly but I could read his lips. *It's time.*

He was calling his men for the coup.

And then suddenly that was the least of our worries.

The smell of mushrooms hit us first, and one of the dogs let out a howl-growl that warned of the *Hel-Blar*.

And then they were everywhere, like blue beetles eating through everything in their path.

Calling them had seemed like a good idea at the time.

Well, not precisely a good idea, so much as the only one we had.

But it wasn't enough.

Not nearly.

I fought my way toward Logan, using sword and stake. Charlemagne stayed close, savaging the knee of a Host who got too close. He stayed down, clutching his leg. I jumped over him, staked another Host, and got stabbed in the left arm for my troubles.

"Logan," I called.

His eyes narrowed on my wound. "You're hurt, damn it."

I shrugged, causing more blood to trickle down my forearm. He ducked a stake, grabbed me, and knocked me down as an arrow grazed over our heads.

"I need to dreamwalk," I told him.

"What, *now?*"

"We can't win, not like this."

"Damn," he said, but I knew he agreed with me. "There." He pointed to a thick nest of ferns. I rolled into them, lying still until the fronds draped over me. I wasn't completely hidden but it was the best we could reasonably expect. Charlemagne stood over my head. Logan stood at my feet.

"Hurry up," he grunted, staking a *Hel-Blar* that snapped his jaws at us.

I closed my eyes, which was an act of will in itself; lying still and vulnerable like this while a battle raged around me was the hardest thing I'd done, nearly as difficult as abandoning my vengeance.

I took three deep breaths, counted them slowly, focused intently on the sensation of air my lungs didn't need; it was the ritual of it that mattered. I chanted the ancient words, then sat up, leaving my body behind lying scarred and eerily still in the ferns.

Blood soaked silver over the grass, ashes gathered on wildflower petals and the exposed roots of knobbly oak trees. The Drakes had only brought three guards with them when they'd left the caves for home and two of them had already been turned to dust. The third was howling, her pale skin and hair practically glowing.

Montmartre stalked toward Solange. Connor tried to block him and was tossed into Nicholas. They both landed hard, nearly knocking Marcus down in the process. Solange, wildeyed, threw her last stake. It went wide and only clipped Montmartre's collar. She flung the crown at his head, it was all she had left.

"For the last time, I don't want the damn crown," she yelled.

"You can stop all this fighting," he said. "If you come with me now."

"Don't you dare, Solange Rose," Helena bellowed. "He can't control the *Hel-Blar* and he sure as hell doesn't keep his word."

"And haven't we been through this before?" Quinn grunted, punching his fist into a Host eyeball. "You couldn't have her last week and you can't have her now."

We were running out of time.

I floated over the meadow and forced the energy of my glowing spirit out into the air, visualized it turning to mist and clinging to the Host and the *Hel-Blar*, choking Greyhaven with a glitter of sunlight. I visualized it so hard even my astral body dripped sweat. I was using my own energy, pushing and pushing until I was sick with exhaustion and fog snaked into the clearing. I sent it toward our enemies, gritting my astral teeth at the pain lancing through both my bodies. I'd never been able to sustain the mist for long periods of time before—it was too advanced, too draining. No help for it.

"What the hell is this?" Greyhaven batted at the mist as it clung to him. It wasn't thick enough yet, he could still see the others. For this to work properly, soon we would see the Host but they wouldn't see us.

At least Montmartre's advance on Solange had been delayed, not just by the strange mist, but also by the *Hel-Blar*, maddened by his scent. Logan was tiring but he refused to give in. I knew he'd protect me until he was dust. I had no intention of letting that happen. I had to get back into my body, and soon.

But first I needed to create just a little more mist. The light cord linking my spirit to myself dimmed and I knew the longer I stayed incorporeal and using this much magical energy, the more I risked being stranded like this forever. I added just a little more mist and was talking myself into making a little more when I noticed the glitter of fireflies between the branches and all around us.

Not fireflies.

Hounds.

To my spirit-sight they came through the trees like sparks of light, like firecrackers exploding.

But it was too early to celebrate.

Because from the other direction, I could see the red-tinged sparks that were Greyhaven's men's auras, also closing in. I couldn't separate magical vision from ordinary vision in this state. Auras shifted and glowed and sparked, like a watercolor wash over a charcoal sketch.

"Incoming!" Liam shouted grimly. "Who the hell are these guys?"

"Greyhaven's trying a hostile takeover," Logan shouted.

"What, *now*?"

The Host still loyal to Montmartre were stunned into pausing, seeing some of their brothers turn to help the newcomers against them. The unexpected coup rattled them.

It was just enough of an advantage for our side. We might not all die horribly after all.

I saw the exact moment when Greyhaven noticed Logan, when he saw my arm hanging limp out of the ferns.

He was faster than I was.

He flung a stake at Logan and caught him just next to his heart. Logan stumbled, pain twisting his pretty face. Blood seeped through his fingers, staining his shirt. He'd be mad about the damage to his clothes later.

If he survived the night.

He'd damn well better survive, since he'd forced me to.

I flung myself at my body but I was so tired, it was like moving through honey. I didn't realize I was screaming until Magda looked up.

Greyhaven had reached Logan, who was fumbling with wet fingers for a stake. The one in his chest was still there, stuck in bone and muscle. Charlemagne growled, lips quivering. Greyhaven bared his own fangs and reached out, quick as a wasp, to shove at the stake already piercing Logan. He drove it deeper. Logan screamed. Greyhaven backhanded him hard enough to knock him off his feet. Logan shook his head, groaning, and tried to crawl between Greyhaven and my defenseless body.

And I could only hover uselessly, too slow to stop Greyhaven from killing me again.

And Logan.

That thought alone was enough to galvanize me into action.

But it was too late. Greyhaven's sword flashed as he kicked the ferns aside, exposing me completely. Charlemagne sprung but Greyhaven was a blur of tailored suit and sword.

If he hurt my dog I'd find a way to kill him twice.

Magda was faster than all of us.

Her sword blocked Greyhaven's just as it cut through a lacy frond, skimming the chain mail over my heart.

"She's my kill," Greyhaven spat.

"Go to hell."

Her eyes met mine as I floated above them. And then she drove her sword through Greyhaven's heart, twisted, and stepped back.

Greyhaven had time to look surprised and then he broke apart into ashes. One of his men howled.

Logan crawled to my side, yanking the stake out of his flesh with a savage curse.

The Hounds descended at the same time and at some signal from Finn, they fell into formation, dispatching Host and *Hel-Blar*, and Greyhaven's men, all stumbling blindly in the mist. The Host had the added difficulty of fighting their own turncoat brothers. I tried to pull some of the mist away from the Hounds and the Drakes but I was too weak.

"Retreat!" Liam shouted at his family. "That's an order!"

Montmartre flung orders but his Host were too far away to help him. He bumped into Helena, mostly by chance, just as she was drawing her arm back to stake a *Hel-Blar*. He caught her hand and jerked his other arm around her throat, fangs descending. She was caught by surprise, twisted at a strange angle, half-obscured by mist. Everyone was too busy, too wounded, or too far to help her.

Except Solange.

She elbowed Montmartre in the ear, hard enough to snap his head to the side. He turned, snarling. But she was already scooping the discarded crown out of the ash-covered grass.

Solange drove the broken spokes through his back, right over his heart. It wasn't enough to pierce his heart entirely, snapping off in his shoulder. Helena spun him around and finished the job, shoving a stake through his chest.

He howled and disintegrated, leaving mother and daughter staring at each other with dusty boots.

Quinn gave a bark of triumphant laughter and Magda spun like a mad fairy, flinging stakes from her hands. The Host, seeing their leader dispatched, stumbled, looking for escape.

And I still wasn't inside my body.

I'd stayed too long.

The mist was thinning, the battle was breaking apart, and I hovered over myself as if a pane of glass barred my return. The veins under my skin looked too pronounced, my cheekbones too harsh. My scars were like satin. I was disoriented, dizzy.

I wasn't strong enough to control the magic.

It was controlling me.

The sun rose, sending arrows of light between the trees. The *Hel-Blar* howled, seeking shelter. The Host dispersed. Logan scooped me up, running through the ferns. Birds began their morning song. The sky turned the color of opal. Liam pushed his family forward as Helena dove for a wooden door hidden under the brush. Sebastian was carrying Solange, who, being the youngest, had already passed out. My spirit followed behind them, too slow, watching my body get carried farther out of reach.

The Drakes dropped into the tunnel, one by one. Logan handed me down to one of his brothers as blood still seeped from his wound. I felt his mouth brush my ear.

"Isabeau." He sounded frantic, furious. "Isabeau," he said again. "Isabeau!"

He'd remembered what I'd told him about repeating a name to return a spirit to its body.

I'd have kissed him if I could have.

I landed so suddenly and so violently that I twitched uncontrollably, eyes rolling back in my head.

EPILOGUE

◆

LOGAN

The next night I found Isabeau sitting on the roof of the farmhouse, watching the stars come out over the forest. She still wore her tunic dress, a little torn at the hem but wiped clean of mud. I couldn't help but remember the vision of her running along the roofs of Paris in her stolen coat. I stretched out next to her on the shingles that still retained the heat of the day. She wouldn't look at me, as if she didn't quite know how to be around me. I was going to take that as a good sign.

"How are you feeling?" I asked. Her veins were still unnaturally blue, her eyes red; side effects of nearly burning herself up with magic.

"Ça va," she replied. "Thank you," she added, so formally she actually winced afterward.

I smiled a little. "That was some trick with the mist."

She nodded. "There is so much we don't know yet about our magic. I wasn't sure I could work that spell. I certainly couldn't unwork it once I'd started. I'd have been trapped in spirit form if it weren't for you."

"Are you sorry you didn't get to kill Greyhaven yourself?" I asked quietly.

She considered that and finally shook her head slowly. "No. I guess that doesn't make me much of a warrior, does it?"

"I wouldn't say that." I snorted. "Dogs and magic mists are a hell of a battle strategy." I reached for her hand, weaving my fingers through hers. "You're still staying for the coronation?"

"*Oui.*"

I looked at her. She sighed a little. "How do you do that?"

"Do what?"

"No one else in the world has ever seen me the way you have, not even Kala. You saw what I was. Before." I knew she was remembering those rooftops too. "And yet you still look at me as if I matter, as if I'm somehow precious."

"You *are* precious," I insisted. "Stubborn and secretive and independent to a fault, but precious."

"Oh."

I thought she might be blushing. "I love you, Isabeau."

She was definitely blushing now. She blinked at me. I just stared back patiently. "Come on, the bones said we're meant for each other," I reminded her.

"Who told you that?"

"Magda. She doesn't hate me quite as much as she used to."

"Oh."

I smiled. "Don't be scared, Isabeau."

"I'm not scared," she insisted indignantly.

"Oh, please. One little 'I love you' has you all freaked out. No sword or stake or slavering dog-beast can get you that pale and stiff."

She seemed to fight a short battle inside herself, one I could only watch. I didn't have the weapons to help her. Only she had them.

"You have a point, I suppose." She unfisted her hands. "And what is a warrior but someone who faces her fears and defeats them?" She swallowed. "*Je . . .*" She swallowed again. "*Je t'aime.*"

I'd never known the kind of bone-deep satisfaction I knew right then and there. I lifted our joined hands to my mouth, kissing her knuckles.

"That wasn't so hard, was it?" I asked hoarsely.

She smiled. "I suppose not."

She lay back down next to me, our sides touching, her hair fluttering over my arm, smelling like leaves and berries. We lay under the stars for a long time.

"Will you visit me in the caves?" she whispered finally. "After the ceremonies and the council meetings are through?"

"Of course."

"Even though everyone will disapprove?"

I pushed up on my elbow. Her eyes were so green they nearly glowed. "I couldn't care less what everyone else thinks." I lowered my head, my mouth hovering over hers. "Besides . . . ," I grinned slowly. "Think of it as intertribal negotiations."

She touched my jaw, smiling back, softly, lightly. "As handmaiden, it *is* my duty to foster a good relationship between the Cwn Mamau and the royal family."

"Exactly." I closed the last inch between us and kissed her.

And when she kissed me back we weren't a prince and a handmaiden, weren't Drake and Hound, weren't anything or anyone but Logan and Isabeau. Together.

Out
for Blood

CHAPTER 1

•

Hunter

Tuesday evening

Shakespeare said, "What's in a name?"

Well, my name's Hunter Wild, so I say: *a lot*.

For instance, you can tell by my name that our family takes our status as vampire hunters very seriously. Good thing I'm an only child—if I'd had brothers or sisters, they might have been named Slayer or Killer. We'd sound like a heavy metal band.

Hard to believe, in reality, we're one of the oldest and most esteemed families in the Helios-Ra. When you're born into the Wild family, no one asks you what you want to be when you grow up. The answer is obvious: a vampire hunter.

Period.

No ifs, ands, or buts. No deviations of any kind.

One size fits all.

"I hate these stupid cargo pants," my roommate Chloe muttered, as she did at the start of every single school year. Classes didn't start for another week, but most of us moved into the dorm early so we could spend that extra time working out and getting ready. Chloe and I have been friends since our first day at the academy, when we were both terrified. Now we're eighteen, about to start our last year, and, frankly, just as terrified. But at least we finally get to be roommates. You only get to make rooming requests in twelfth grade, otherwise they throw you in with people as badly matched as they can find, just to see how you deal with the stress.

Have I mentioned I'm really glad this is our last year?

Even if the room will probably smell like nail polish and vanilla perfume all year. Chloe already had her bare feet propped up on her desk, applying a second coat of silver glitter over the purple polish on her toenails. She was, most emphatically, not wearing her regulation cargos.

I was, but only because my grandfather dropped me off this morning, and he's nothing if not old-school. He's still muttering about our friend Spencer, who has long blond dreads and wears hemp necklaces with turquoise beads. Grandpa can't fathom how Spencer's allowed to get away with it, why there's a newfangled (his word) paranormal division, or why a boy wouldn't want a buzz cut. Truth is, Spencer is such a genius when it comes to occult history, the teachers are perfectly willing to turn a blind eye. Besides, cargos are technically regulation wear only for drills and training and actual fieldwork. And Grandpa still doesn't understand why I won't cut off my hair like any warrior worth her salt.

I totally earned this long hair.

I had to pass several combat scenarios without anyone being able to grab it as a handhold to use against me. Nothing else would extract a promise from Grandpa not to shave my head in my sleep. I think he forgets that I'm not G.I. Joe.

Or that I like looking like a normal girl sometimes, with long blond hair and lip gloss, and not just a hunter who kills vampires every night. Under my steel-toe combat boots my nails are pink. But I'd never tell him that. It would give him a heart attack.

He'd still be out there on patrols if the Helios-Ra doctors hadn't banned him from active duty last year because of the arthritis in his neck and shoulder. He might be built like a bull but he just doesn't have the same flexibility and strength that he used to. He is, however, perfectly capable of being a guest expert at some of the academy fight-training classes. He just loves beating down sixteen-year-old boys who think they're faster and better than he is. Nothing makes him happier, not even my very-nearly straight As last year. The first time Spencer met him, he told me Grandpa was Wild-West-gunslinger scary. It's a pretty good description actually—he even has the squint lines from shooting long-range UV guns and crossbows. And the recent treaty negotiations with certain ancient vampire families are giving him palpitations. In his day, blah blah blah. He still doesn't know Kieran took me into the royal caves last week to meet with the new ruling vampire family, the Drakes. And I'm so totally not telling him until I have to.

Grandpa might be old-school, but I'm not.

I like archery and martial arts, don't get me wrong, and I definitely feel good about fighting the Hel-Blar. They are the worst of the worst kind of vampire: mindless, feral, and always looking for blood. The more violently procured the better. They're faintly blue, which is creepier than it sounds, and they smell like rotting mushrooms.

Needless to say, mushrooms don't get served a lot in the caf.

But I like all the history stuff too, and the research and working with vampire families. I don't think it should be a kill-them-all-and-let-God-sort-it-out situation. I love Grandpa—he took care of me when my parents both died during a botched takedown of a *Hel-Blar* nest—but sometimes he sounds like a bigot. It can be a little embarrassing. Vampires are vampires are vampires to him. If he found out Kieran was dating the sixteen-year-old Drake vampire daughter, he'd freak right out. He thinks of Kieran as an honorary grandson and would totally marry us off to each other if we showed the slightest inclination. Hell, he tries to pair us up anyway, and he's about as subtle as a brick. Kieran's like a brother to me though, and I know he feels the same way about me. I might be willing to sacrifice a lot for the Helios-Ra, but who I date is not one of those things.

Unfortunately Grandpa's not exactly known for giving up. The thing is, neither am I. The infamous goat-stubborn streak runs strong in every Wild, and I'm no exception.

"Would you please change into something decent? Just looking at those cargos is giving me hives." Chloe grimaced at me before going back to blowing on her wet nail polish. She was wearing a short sundress with lace-up sandals and earrings that swung down practically to her shoulders. Her dark hair was a wild mass of curls as usual, her brown eyes carefully lined with purple to match her clothes. She'd already unpacked every stitch of her wardrobe and hung it all neatly in our miniscule closet. It was the only spot of neatness I'd see all year. I'd bug her about her stuff everywhere, and she'd make fun of me for making my bed every morning. I couldn't wait. I'd missed her over the summer. E-mails and texting just aren't the same, no matter what she says.

"I don't mind the cargos," I told her, shrugging.

"Please, I've seen what few clothes you have and they're all pretty and lacy."

"Not a lot of call for lace camisoles in survivalist training and drills," I pointed out.

"Well, since I don't intend to set foot in that smelly old gym until I absolutely have to, I demand you wear something pretty." She grinned at me. "I took you to dinner, didn't I?"

"We went to the caf for mac and cheese," I shot back, also grinning. "And you're not my type."

"Please, you should be so lucky."

A knock at the door interrupted us. Spencer poked his head in. His dreads were even longer and more blond, nearly white. He'd spent most of the summer at the beach, as usual. "I am so stoked to finally be on the ground floor," he said by way of a greeting. "I'm never climbing those stairs again."

"Tell me about it," Chloe agreed.

The dorm was an old Victorian five-story mansion. Ninth graders lived in the converted attic and had to climb the narrow, steep servant stairs several times a day. Every year we were promoted, we descended a floor. Our window now overlooked the pond behind the house and the single cranky swan that lived there.

"That bird's looking at me again," I said. He'd nearly taken a finger my very first day at the academy when I tried to feed him the bagel I'd saved from lunch.

Spencer sat on the edge of my bed, rolling his eyes. "It's dark out, genius."

"I know he's out there," I insisted. "Just waiting for me."

"You can take out a vampire, you can take out a pretty white bird."

"I guess. You don't know how shifty those swans are." I wrinkled my nose and sat on the end of my bed, resting against the pillow. "But speaking of vampires—"

"Aren't we always?" Chloe said. "Just once I'd like to talk about boys and fashion and Hugh Jackman's abs."

"Hello? Like you ever talk about anything else?" Spencer groaned. "I need more guy friends."

I nudged him with my boot. "Guys would never have been able to put in a good word for you with Francesca last year," I told him.

"Yeah, but she broke my heart."

"Give me a break. *You* dumped *her*."

"Because there's only room in my heart for you two lunatics."

I threw a pillow at his head.

"What she said," Chloe agreed, since she couldn't reach her own pillow.

"And anyway, if you were hanging out burping and scratching

with other guys you wouldn't hear about my visit to the vampire royal caves last week."

"We don't burp and scratch," he turned to eye me balefully. "And *what?*"

Even Chloe put down her nail polish. "Seriously?"

"Kieran took me," I said, a little smugly. It was rare that I was the one with the story to tell. Usually I was too busy trying to get Chloe and Spencer out of trouble to get into any of my own.

"Dude," Spencer whistled appreciatively. "How did you get that past your grandfather?"

"I didn't exactly tell him," I admitted. "I said I was going out for extra credit."

"Finally." Chloe pretended to wipe away a tear of pride. "She's sneaking around and flat-out lying. Our little girl."

Spencer and I both ignored her.

"So what was it like?" he asked eagerly. "Tell me everything. Any rituals? Secret vampire magic?"

"Sorry, nothing for your thesis," I told him. "But a princess from the Hounds tribe was there."

"Get out," Spencer stared at me. "You are the luckiest. What was she like?"

"Quiet, intense, French." Like the other Hounds, she'd had two sets of fangs. "She had amulets around her neck."

"Can you draw them for me?" he asked immediately.

"I could try."

"You two are *boring.*" Chloe huffed out a sigh. "Quit studying— we haven't even started classes yet. Tell me about the Drake brothers. Are they as yummy as everyone says?"

"Totally." I didn't even have to think about that one. "It was like being in a room full of Johnny Depps. One of them even kind of dressed like a pirate."

Chloe gave a trembling, reverent sigh. Then she narrowed her eyes at me. "Don't you dare leave me behind next time."

"I think it was a one-time thing. Hart was there and everything." Hart was the new leader of the Helios-Ra and Kieran's uncle. "It was mostly treaty talk. I still don't know why I was invited."

"Because you're good at that stuff," Chloe declared loyally. "Idiot," she added, less loyally.

I hadn't felt particularly skilled, more like the bumbling teenager at a table full of adults. I'd had to remind myself more than once that I'd been invited, that I wasn't obviously useless or an outsider.

Especially when Quinn Drake smirked at me.

All the Drake brothers were ridiculously gorgeous, but he had that smoldering charm down to an art. The kind you only read about in books. I'd always thought it would be annoying in real life.

So not.

Although the fact that he called me "Buffy" all night was less fun.

"You have a funny look on your face," Chloe said.

"I do not." I jerked my errant thoughts away from Quinn. "This is just my face."

"Please, you never turn that color. You're blushing, Hunter Wild."

"Am not." Quinn wasn't my type anyway. Not that I knew what

my type was. Still. I was sure pretty boys who knew they were pretty weren't it.

I was spared further prodding and poking when the lights suddenly went out.

The emergency blue floor light by the door and under the window blinked on. Spencer and I jumped to our feet. The windows locked themselves automatically. Iron bars lowered and clanged shut.

"No! Not now!" Chloe exclaimed, blowing harder on her toes. "They're going to smear."

"Isn't it too early for a drill?" I frowned, trying to see out to the pond and the fields leading to the forest all around us. It was dark enough that only the glimmer of water showed and the half-moon over the main house where Headmistress Bellwood lived. "I mean, half the students aren't even here yet."

"Chloe's the one who's supposed to know this stuff," Spencer said pointedly.

"I haven't had time! I just got here!" She swung her feet to the floor and balanced on her heels, wriggling her toes. Usually she hacked into the schedules and found out when the drills were happening so we'd have some warning. She was disgruntled, scowling fiercely. "This sucks."

"Maybe it's not a drill?" Spencer asked. "Maybe this one's real?"

"It's totally a drill. And I'm registering a complaint," Chloe grumbled, slinging her pack over her shoulder. She didn't go anywhere without her laptop or some kind of high-tech device. "I'm still on summer vacation, damn it. This is so unfair."

"Glad I didn't change out of these," I told her, pulling a flashlight out of one of my cargo pants' many pockets.

"If you spout some 'be prepared' school motto shit, I am so going to kick you."

"Like you'd risk your nail polish," I said with a snort, pushing the door open. "Let's just go."

CHAPTER 2

•

Hunter

There were students in the hallway, grumbling as they tried the front door.

"Locked." Jason sighed, turning to face us. He'd had a crush on Spencer for two years but Spencer had a crush on Francesca. Or had, anyway, but I seriously doubted he'd switch teams entirely.

"Everything's locked," Jason said. He was wearing flannel pajama bottoms and a white T-shirt. Chloe nearly purred at him even though it was a lost cause.

"Blue light over here," someone called out from the other side of the common room.

Spencer groaned. "So it's a speed drill?"

"Looks like," I agreed.

We followed the rest of the students heading down the hall to the basement door. Good thing it wasn't a stealth test, since it sounded like a herd of elephants thundering down the stairs.

"I hate this hole," Chloe said as we reached the damp basement. She shook her phone. "Nothing ever works down here."

"I think that's the point."

"Well, it's stupid. This whole school's stupid."

Spencer and I just rolled our eyes at each other. Being deprived of Internet access always set Chloe into a snit. It was her forte, after all, and she hated not coming in first.

The trapdoor leading into the secret tunnel was already open. There were sounds of fighting up ahead and very little light. The objective was to get through the tunnel, up a ladder, and onto the lawn. No one elbowed or tripped each other; it was too early in the year. Come midterms and exams there'd be insurrections and mutinies down here.

I heard a squeak from behind us and whirled toward the sound, reaching for the stake at my belt. There was always a stake at my belt. Grandpa never asked me the usual questions growing up like, "Did you brush your teeth?" and "Have you eaten any vegetables today?" It was always, "Got your stake?"

But I wasn't dealing with a vampire or a training dummy. Just a ninth-grade student who was pressed against the wall, crying. She looked about thirteen and there was blood on her nose.

"Hunter, are you coming or what?" Spencer asked.

"I'll catch up," I waved them ahead and ducked under one of the rigged dummies that swung from the ceiling, shrieking. The girl cried harder, trembling.

"Hey, it's okay," I said as she stared at me. "I'm Hunter. What's your name?"

"L-Lia," she stuttered. Her glasses were foggy from the combination of tears and damp underground air.

"Is this your first day?"

She nodded mutely.

"Well, don't worry, Lia, it gets better. Where's your floor monitor?" I asked her. She was way too young to be dealing with this. I couldn't believe her floor monitor hadn't bothered to keep an eye on her. When I found out who she was, I was so going to give her an earful.

"I don't know." Her stake was lying useless at her feet. "I want to go home."

"I know. Let's just get out of here first, okay?"

"Okay." She pushed away from the wall and then jumped a foot in the air when a bloodcurdling shriek ululated down the hall, followed by eerie hissing.

"Never mind that," I told her. "They add all the sound effects to train you not to get distracted. You read about it in the handbook, right?"

She swallowed. "Yeah. It's worse than I thought."

"You get used to it. Look, we need to run down this hall toward the ladder and climb up to get outside. There's going to be dummies swinging at you with red lights over their hearts. Just aim your stake at the light, okay? Think of it like one of those Halloween haunted houses."

"I hate those," she said, but sounded annoyed now, not nearly as scared. She scooped up her stake, holding it so tightly her knuckles must have hurt.

"Ready?"

She nodded.

"Go!"

I took the lead so she wouldn't panic again. The first "vampire" came at me from the left and I aimed for the red light. The second came from the right; the third and fourth dropped from the ceiling together. I let one get away to give Lia a chance to stab at it. It was nothing if not a good way to release frustration. It caught her in the shoulder but she managed to jab the red light.

"I got one!" She squealed. "Did you see?"

"Behind you," I yelled, throwing my stake to catch the one swinging from behind her. The red light blinked out and the dummy came to a sudden stop, inches away from Lia's already sore nose.

"Okay, that was cool," she squeaked, apparently over her little meltdown. The adrenaline was doing its work—I could see it in the tremble of her fingers and the slightly manic gleam in her eyes. It was better than panic.

"Nearly there," I told her over another recording of a grating shriek. "Go, go, go!"

We ran as fast as we could.

"Jump that one." I leaped over a dummy crawling out of a trapdoor. The tunnel was empty of other students but I could see a faint light up ahead. "Nearly there."

When we reached the ladder I pushed her in front of me. She scrambled up like a monkey. She had good balance if nothing else.

I was the last one out.

Two teachers and all of the students waited in a clump, watching for us. Lia's face was streaked with dirt and dried tears and her lip was swollen, but at least she was smiling.

"Well, well, Miss Wild." Mr. York held up his stopwatch with the most condescending sneer he could muster. "Apparently you've gotten rusty over the summer. What will your grandfather say to hear a Wild came in dead last?" He was enjoying this way too much. It was no secret that Mr. York hated my family, and Grandpa in particular. He'd been on my case since my first day at the academy. Chloe pulled a hideous grimace behind his back.

"It's my f-fault, sir," Lia stammered. "Hunter stopped to help me out."

"Did she now? Well, admirable as that may be, this is a speed test." He made a mark on his clipboard.

I really wanted to stake that clipboard.

"I hardly think Hunter should be penalized for showing group loyalty," Ms. Dailey interrupted. "We are teaching them loyalty and courage, aren't we? As well as speed?"

"Be that as it may, this test is timed. Rules are rules."

"Her floor monitor should have been looking out for her," I muttered.

"What was that, Miss Wild?" Mr. York asked.

"Nothing, sir."

"I distinctly heard *something*, Miss Wild. Students, quiet down please. Miss Wild is having trouble being heard."

God, he was a pain in my ass.

"I was only wondering where her floor monitor was." First day and I was getting reamed out for helping someone. This just sucked.

He frowned at his clipboard. "Courtney Jones."

I had to stifle a groan. Of course it would be Courtney. We'd been roommates in tenth grade and frankly, I don't think either of us was over it yet. To say we didn't get along and had nothing in common was a gross understatement. She was so in league with the nasty swan.

Courtney stepped forward, smiling winningly. "Yes, Mr. York?"

Kiss-ass.

"Is this student on your floor?"

"Yes, Mr. York."

"And did you leave her behind?"

"*No*, Mr. York." She sounded stunned and deeply grieved. Mr. York, of course, totally fell for it. At least Ms. Dailey pursed her lips. It was a small victory but the only one I was probably going to get. "Lia was right behind me, sir. She told me she was fine."

Lia was blinking like a fish suddenly hauled out of a lake. "I—"

"I see," Mr. York said, tapping his lips with his pen as if he was deep in thought. I shifted from foot to foot. Spencer shot me a commiserating wince. I winced back.

"Seeing as you are so concerned with the ninth graders' welfare, you will be Courtney's assistant. You can be in charge of all their delicate sensibilities and making sure they get through drills." Which, loosely translated, meant Courtney would get her big single room on the fourth floor and "floor monitor" on her transcripts but I would be doing all the actual work. And she'd get to boss me around. She smirked at me.

"Do you have a problem with that, Miss Wild?" Mr. York snapped.

"No, sir." I sighed. I refused to slump, even though I really wanted to. I was so not going to let him see how much he'd just screwed up my last year for me. I didn't know anything about taking care of ninth graders—or Niners, as we called them. And my course load was already approximately the size of an Egyptian pyramid. The big one.

"Good. You're dismissed," he barked at everyone before stalking across the lawn toward the teachers' apartments. Ms. Dailey patted my shoulder before following him. Courtney sneered at me and flounced away.

"I'm sorry, Hunter," Lia said, looking like she was about to burst into tears again.

"Don't worry about it," I told her.

"I didn't mean to get you in trouble," she said. "But I'm really glad you're one of our floor monitors now." She lowered her voice. "Courtney's a bitch."

I laughed despite myself. "Yes. Yes, she is."

Chloe and Spencer descended, all inflamed with righteous indignation on my behalf. Chloe shook her head. "I guess York still has it in for you. Jerk."

"That was totally unfair," Spencer agreed. "You should see the headmistress."

"No way," I said. The only teacher worse than Mr. York was Headmistress Bellwood. "She'd only tell me I was whining anyway."

"I guess. She's not exactly big with the warm and fuzzy."

Chloe slung her arm through mine. "Come on, we'll go drink hot chocolate and watch some old *Supernatural* episodes on DVD. Dean Winchester always cheers you up."

"I thought our last year was supposed to be fun," I said, kicking at dandelions as we skirted the gardens toward the now-unlocked front door.

From the direction of the pond, the swan honked mockingly.

◆

No one felt like staying up very late after that. We watched a couple of episodes and then went to our rooms. The halls were quiet. Chloe marched to her desk and turned on her computer with a determined click and set her laptop next to it. The screens flickered to life, pooling pale light over the carpet.

"I thought you were tired," I told her.

"I'm already behind," she said. "They got us by surprise. And York smirked at me like he knew. I'm so going to get him for that. And for ragging on you all the time." She cracked her knuckles. "And it starts now."

"You were the one complaining that it was too early to study."

"I changed my mind. I'm going to ace this year and then shove it up his nose." Mr. York, along with being the proverbial thorn in my side, was also one of the combat teachers. Chloe was quick and fierce on a computer but she wasn't quite as good in hand-to-hand fights. He'd only barely passed her last year.

I left her to stew. I didn't want to talk about York. It would make me grind my teeth. I didn't know anything about being a floor monitor. My jaw clenched. If I was going to relax at all, I was going to need what was in the trunk under my bed. Watching TV had helped settled my mood some, and so had Chloe's stash of chocolate macaroons, but this required the big guns. No matter how much Chloe was going to make fun of me. I pulled it out, hoping she was too buried in her work.

No such luck.

"Are those romance novels?"

I shot her a look through my hair, which was falling over my face. "Yes. And shut up."

"I didn't know you read romance novels."

"Shut up."

She turned on her wheeled desk chair. "You told me last year that you kept your stakes and stuff in there."

I pulled a book out, wondering if I should even bother trying to hide the cheesy cover. Chloe was a pitbull. "I also told my grandfather I kept my tampons in here."

"I am totally digging this new side of you."

Since she wasn't making as much fun of me as I'd thought, I stopped scowling. "I know it's silly, but I like them. They don't make me think too hard and there's always a happy ending."

"Lend me one."

"Seriously?" I asked.

"Totally. That one with the cleavage and the guy with the mullet."

I snorted. "That's all of them. The hair is rather unfortunate."

"How about that one?"

"Can't go wrong with a duke." I tossed it to her.

"Are there naughty parts?"

"Not in that one."

She tossed it back. I laughed and handed her a new one. It was five hundred pages of Victorian historical intrigue. She stared at it. "This is bigger than half the stuff on our lit class syllabus."

"Probably better researched too."

She put it next to her laptop and went back to the mysterious things she did on the Internet. I could check my e-mail and navigate some basic blog sites but that was about it. She could probably hack into government sites if we gave her enough time.

I read until she finally went to asleep and my cell phone vibrated. It was two in the morning. I flipped it open and read the text waiting for me from Kieran.

Get dressed and meet me outside.

CHAPTER 3

•

QUINN

Connor didn't bother knocking, just opened the door and stuck his head into my room. He was pale, and not because he spent most of his time at his computer. Vampires didn't tan well and the Drakes were no exception. "Quinn, it's time."

I wiped blood off my lower lip and tossed the glass bottle in the blue recycling box sitting under a poster of Megan Fox. Connor and I were both turned three years ago on our sixteenth birthday. As twins, we shared the same blue eyes and dark brown hair and the same uncanny ability to know what the other was thinking. We'd also shared the sickness, the struggle to survive, and the searing bloodlust when we woke that first day as vampires.

Now we shared the same bloodlust every time the sun set, but it was starting to get a little better, just as Dad had promised it would. He didn't lock my bedroom door from the outside anymore.

"Better hurry, Dad's got that look on his face," Connor warned me as we ran down the stairs from the top floor of the house that we shared with our five brothers. Our sister, Solange, had a room on the second floor, which was most definitely locked—from the inside and outside—when she went to bed every single morning. She'd only turned a couple of weeks ago and our delicate, serene baby sister turned feral at the last ray of sunlight. Her best friend, Lucy, was staying in one of the guest rooms, as far away from Solange's bedroom as physically possible. We made her promise to engage the dead bolt, and Mom set two of the farm dogs to guard her every night at dusk. Just in case.

She shouldn't have been living in our house at all while Solange was so volatile. It was dangerous and, frankly, stupid. All of us could smell the sweet hot rush of the blood in her veins. It was like living inside a bakery, constantly surrounded by tempting pastries and cakes with chocolate frosting. Nicholas had a will of iron. I don't know how he did it, resisting the tender flesh on her neck every time she hugged him or he smelled her hair. My fangs poked out of my gums just a little whenever she was nearby.

I was not good at resisting girls.

Still, Lucy had practically grown up here, and since she was dating my brother she was thoroughly off-limits. And she was stuck with us for at least another week since her parents were out of town, even though vampire politics, which were messy at best, had just exploded all over us.

"Mom deserves a little pomp and circumstance, don't you think?" I asked, keeping my voice low as we passed Aunt Hyacinth's room. I wondered if she'd finally venture out of the house for the coronation. "I mean, it's not every day a vampire queen gets crowned."

"You know Mom prefers it low-key. And anyway, I like to think we're too smart to attempt a *third* elaborate ceremony."

Connor was right. Mom was pronounced queen after killing the last self-proclaimed queen Lady Natasha—to stop her from killing Solange over an ancient prophecy that foretold Solange's birth and her own rise to the throne. Now everyone was trying to kill both Mom *and* Solange. Not exactly an improvement. No one holds a grudge like a centuries-old vampire. You'd think they'd learn to lighten up eventually.

"Hell of a lot of fuss over a thankless job," I said. "Controlling vampire tribes is like herding cats. Into a bathtub. Blindfolded." I tossed my hair off my shoulder and winked at Solange, who was sitting on the bottom step, looking miserable. "Maybe we just need a king. Someone charming and handsome like me."

She flashed me a grin. "Your head's too fat for a crown."

Connor snorted and continued down the hall into the living room. I sat next to Solange. "What's up? Sitting alone in the dark is too gothic for you. Leave that sort of thing to Logan."

"I just hate this whole stupid thing," she muttered. "If one more person tries to kill someone I love over that damn prophecy, I swear I'll go postal."

I put an arm over her tense shoulders. "It'll be fine. Montmartre's dead. And you know we'll protect you."

She speared me with a glare that could have fried the hair off my head. "That right there, Quinn Drake, is exactly what I mean. Protect yourself, not me."

I rolled my eyes. "Hello? Big brother. Occupational hazard."

"Well, get over it," she grumbled. "I seriously can't take much more. I won't have your blood on my hands. It's bad enough Aunt Hyacinth nearly died."

"But she didn't die. Drakes are harder to kill than that." She'd been seriously burned by Helios-Ra holy water, though. It ate away at her face like acid and now she refused to lift the heavy black veils she wore hanging from her little Victorian hats. "Why aren't you in there with everyone else?"

She shrugged. "No reason."

"Liar."

She shrugged again.

I frowned. "Spill it, Solange."

"I'm fine, Quinn." She sent me an ironic grin. "I can protect *you* too, you know. Annoying, isn't it?"

"Very."

She hugged me briefly. "I don't mean to sound ungrateful. I'm just worried."

I noticed the dark smudges under her eyes. Her fangs were out and her gums looked a little raw, as if she'd been clenching her jaw. "And you're hungry," I said quietly.

She looked away. "I'm okay."

"Solange, are you drinking enough? You're looking kinda skinny."

"I'm drinking plenty. I just woke up and I'm . . ." She swallowed, fists clenching. "How do you get used to it? It's like this itch crawling inside me and there's no way to scratch it. You guys made this look easy. I think it's worse than the bloodchange. At least

I was unconscious through most of that. But now the lights hurt, everyone sounds like they're yelling. And Lucy." She looked like she might cry.

"What about her?"

"Lucy smells like food." She nearly gagged saying it.

I kept my smile light and didn't let her see anything but her reckless big brother who loved a good fight and a pretty girl and not necessarily in that order.

"Sol, all that's normal. Lucy smelled good before I turned and now she smells even better. But I haven't tried to eat her face and neither will you."

"She's not safe in this house."

"Safer than out there," I argued, even though I agreed with her. "Look, you used to eat hamburgers."

She blinked, confused. "So?"

"So, did you ever walk through one of the farms at a field party and suddenly try to eat a cow?"

"Um, no." Her chuckle was watery but it was better than nothing. "And, ew."

"Exactly. You can crave blood and not eat your best friend."

"You make it sound so normal. And I'm totally telling Lucy you compared her to a cow." She jerked a hand through her hair. "Between Lucy and Kieran I feel . . . dangerous."

I shrugged, trying not to scowl at the thought of Kieran and my little sister. "You should talk to Nicholas. He's looking as squigee as you are."

"Squigee? I'm squigee?" She poked me. "I don't know what that is but I am prepared to feel insulted."

"Nah, no need to be insulted. You got the Drake cheekbones like me. Saves you every time."

"Okay, no more whining," she announced decisively, faking a bright smile. "I'm getting on my own nerves. Let's go make Mom a queen."

"Yeah, because her self-esteem's so fragile otherwise," I said drily as we pushed to our feet. "She needs the boost of a crown."

"I heard that, Quinn Drake."

I winced. Vampire mothers had unfair advantages. "Love you, Mom!"

She stalked out of the living room trailing the rest of the family like the train of a dress. Her hair was in a severe braid as usual, her mouth stern. But her eyes were bright. "That's how you used to try to get out of trouble when you were little."

I grinned. "Does it still work?" She sighed, giving in to a smile. I winked at Solange. "See? Don't underestimate the cheekbones."

"Let's go." Bruno, the head of Drake security, opened the front door. The porch light made his neck tattoos look faded. He had so many weapons stashed under his coat it was a wonder he could move at all.

Dad stood very close to Mom, eyeing each of us. "We're going the long way. The rest of you go east and circle around to meet us there. Protect your sister."

Solange went red. Lucy squeezed her hand sympathetically. Solange swallowed hard and shifted a step away. Lucy frowned, looking confused and hurt. The door shut behind our parents, Uncle Geoffrey, and Bruno.

"Where's Aunt Hyacinth?" I asked.

"She's not in her rooms," Lucy said. "I knocked. I wanted to borrow one of her lace shawls."

"She will be there," Isabeau murmured in her heavy French accent. She was a Hounds princess and the reason Logan looked extra fancy in a new velvet frock coat. He couldn't stop looking at her, as if he was afraid she might drift away. There were scars on her arms and she had her dog with her as usual. He was a huge Irish wolfhound, the top of his shaggy head reaching nearly to her waist.

"Everyone ready?" Sebastian asked calmly. He was the eldest and usually traveled with our parents. It was a mark of how worried they were that he was with us instead. We got into formation, circling Solange and Lucy, guiding them outside and across the driveway to the fields leading to the woods.

"I feel like I'm in the witness protection program," Lucy whispered. "You guys need suits and dark glasses."

"I'm not wearing a suit even for you, sweetheart," I whispered back.

"You're no fun."

As the silence stretched uncomfortably, she started to hum the theme song to *Mission: Impossible* under her breath.

Solange smothered a startled laugh. "Are you nuts?"

"Your brothers need to meditate. They're all stressed out and their chi is bunching up. That can't be comfortable."

"I don't even know what that means," Nicholas hissed at her. "But there's this whole stealth thing we're going for. You're not helping."

Lucy grinned at Solange. "He's so cute when he tries to be all Alpha male."

"This is serious, Lucy."

She reached and pulled a piece of his hair. "I know that. But we're barely off the driveway."

"If you don't stop talking I will hide all of your chocolate," Nicholas promised. Lucy stuck her tongue out but she stopped chattering.

The forest was heavy with the sounds of scurrying animals and insects boring through trees and the ever-present wind slinking through the pine boughs. We crossed the narrow river, using a fallen oak trunk covered in moss. Everyone but Lucy moved so fast that we seemed to blur a little around the edges. She was panting for breath by the time we stopped in a meadow. "I'm going to need to take up jogging or something," she gasped. "For that alone, I hate you."

We let her rest for a few minutes and then continued toward the meeting spot. We didn't expect trouble since the ceremony had only been announced to a very few select individuals soon after sunset. No advance warning made it harder for our enemies to find us and disrupt the ceremony. Isabeau found the guiding mark in a tree and pointed to her left. We followed her into another meadow, ringed with pine trees. The crickets stopped singing.

We were the first ones to arrive. It took another half hour before the other council members showed up with their attendants. The Raktapa Council was secretive to the extreme and they didn't travel light, not even to a clandestine coronation. There were family banners and bodyguards and a lot of suspicious regal glares. The Amrita family favored caftans and saris. The Joiik were descendants of some ancient Viking vampire and were blond, pale as sunlight on armor. And we often looked like we belonged in some bizarre medieval-Victorian costume party. Of all of us there that night, only my brothers and Solange and I wore clothes from this century. Except for Logan, of course. He wore his usual eighteenth-century frock coat. And Lucy just looked like a confused time traveler, as always. Or like a little girl who'd just gone through her mother's dress-up trunk.

Mom and Dad would be here soon. Hart wasn't far either; I could hear the growl of his motorcycle on the other side of the grove. It was unprecedented for the leader of the Helios-Ra to be invited to a vampire coronation. We were making history in more ways than one tonight. The best part was that Aunt Hyacinth had joined us. She came out of the pine trees, still swathed in black lace veils, but at least she was here.

Lucy leaned into Nicholas, holding his hand. Logan and Isabeau were quiet but standing very close.

My brothers had the right idea.

We had time to kill, might as well have a little fun.

I caught the eye of a vampire girl from the Joiik entourage. She had long red hair and she smiled at me, flashing a provocative peek of fang. And a lot of cleavage. I grinned.

"Call me when it's about to start," I told Connor, following her into the woods.

CHAPTER 4

◆

Hunter

Tuesday night

Kieran was waiting for me behind the oak tree by the lane.

"What's going on?" I asked, yawning. I'd pulled my hair back in a messy ponytail and threw my cargo pants back on with the tank top I slept in.

"We're going on a field trip," he said smugly.

I blinked. "What, *now?*"

"Yeah, so hurry up." The teachers' main house was dark except for one of the upper bedrooms. The dining hall was deserted. Head-mistress Bellwood's house was farther down the driveway and dark as well. "It's a long walk."

"Why can't we take one of the bikes? There's dozens of them in the garage." The forest was so thick and there were so many fields that motorbikes were the easiest mode of transportation most of the time. On our own two feet, we'd never outrun a vampire in a million years. Bikes gave us a fighting chance.

"Kinda hard with this," he lifted his arm, wrapped in a soft cast. He'd hurt it last week helping to take down the old vampire queen, Lady Natasha. He had all the fun. "And you know they monitor the fuel gauges in those things."

I raised my eyebrows. "So the teachers don't know about this little side trip."

"No."

"Kieran, I'm already in trouble."

He snorted. "You're never in trouble."

"York."

He winced. "Bummer. Well, forget him. Hart himself gave permission to have you there."

"Seriously?"

"Yeah, so let's go already," he said impatiently. "It's at least an hour's walk from here."

"Where the hell are we going?" I muttered as we cut through the field and into the woods. The mosquitoes swarmed almost instantly. I slapped them away. This had better be worth it.

"Vampire coronation," he answered.

Totally worth it.

"What? Really? How did you get me clearance?"

"Hart asked for you. You shouldn't sound so shocked; you were at the meeting last week. You did good, kid."

"Kid? You're barely a year older than me."

"But I'm wise, little sister."

"Just get us there, Obi-Wan."

The moon poured out enough light to make the grass silver. The mosquitoes got worse the farther in we hiked and I didn't care one bit. We were going to a vampire coronation.

Grandpa would have been horrified.

I was thrilled.

There hadn't been one for over a hundred years. The last "queen," Lady Natasha, had been tolerated, not officially crowned. When her lover, Montmartre, discarded her and set his sights on Solange Drake, Lady Natasha had gone crazy and tried to kill Solange. Everyone knew she was the first girl born to the Drake family in eight hundred years and prophesied to be the next queen. Only, she didn't want to be queen—though that was hardly enough to stop Montmartre. He'd tried to abduct and marry her to take her power, but he'd been foiled by the Drakes and Isabeau St. Croix, the Hound princess I'd met at the treaty talks. And Kieran, of course, who was Solange's boyfriend now and wore his broken arm proudly. With Montmartre finally dead, the Host, minions who had acted as his personal army, had scattered. It gave the Helios-Ra an advantage.

The hundreds of *Hel-Blar* that Greyhaven, Montmartre's lieutenant, had created and left to run savage took that advantage away again.

There were so many of them that they were starting to close in on Violet Hill and other small towns in the area. The school now required twelfth-grade students to help on patrols until the problem was dealt with.

We walked for almost an hour until we reached a clearing with several parked motorcycles, all black. Helios-Ra agents. Hart and his group must have arrived already.

"Are we late?" I wished I was wearing proper clothes. I looked completely rumpled. I wasn't sure what one wore to a vampire coronation, but I had a feeling cargos and a tank top weren't it. I didn't even have my jacket with the vials of Hypnos set in the sleeves. Hypnos was a fairly new drug we carried in powdered form in little pen-shaped devices. Anyone who inhaled it, vampires included, were hypnotized for a short time into doing whatever they were told. It helped balance the odds since humans were susceptible to vampire glamour. Chloe's mom was a biochemist and had helped develop the newest version of Hypnos.

Of which I had none tonight.

"I'm not prepared." I showed him my bare wrists. No Hypnos, no daggers, nothing.

"You won't need anything," he assured me. "Besides, I know for a fact that you have no less than three stakes on you right now, and those boots have blades in the soles."

"Still."

"We don't have time to go back." He nudged me gently into a jog, flipping open his cell phone to use the GPS. "We're not far. The coordinates came in just before I got you."

"It's not at the caves with all the pomp and ceremony?"

"No way. After two botched assassination attempts in a single week, the Drakes decided on a secret coronation."

"That is so cool." And I still couldn't believe I'd been invited. "Will the council be there?"

"Representatives from each ancient family, yeah."

The Raktapa Council were formed of the three most ancient and powerful vampire families. The Helios-Ra had a similar council.

"Who else? The Hounds?"

"Yeah, Isabeau, the princess you met last week."

"That is so cool." I nearly bounced on my toes. "Thanks for coming to get me."

"Just don't tell Caleb it was me."

"As if I'm telling Grandpa at all."

"Good plan."

The concept of treaties between the peaceful vampire families, the Helios-Ra, and the Hounds was exciting to me. As exciting as firearms and surprise nest-takedowns was to Grandpa. And we'd almost lost the chance at an alliance entirely when Hope, one of the higher-ups, had sent her own rogue unit to attack the Drakes. She'd nearly taken down the entire society with her, putting any future hope of diplomacy in serious danger. I really admired Hart and what he was trying to do. Especially since Hope had killed his brother and partner, Kieran's father, in order to rule with Hart. Grandpa, of course, wasn't exactly full of admiration for the treaty. Big surprise. I hated to disobey him even when I knew he was wrong. So if he didn't know about it, he couldn't forbid me to be a part of it and I wouldn't have to lie and do it anyway.

"Can't we go any faster?" I urged, nearly plucking the GPS out of Kieran's hand. This was better than prom.

He swatted me away. "Cut it out."

"Can you believe we're doing this?" I shook my head. "I thought you were usually on Grandpa's side with this stuff."

"Yeah, then I met a girl."

I smirked. "I totally love that."

"Yeah, yeah. It also helped to learn that vampires didn't kill my father."

We stepped around a copse of elm trees and came face-to-face with a vampire, armed to his pointy fang-teeth. Instinct had me reach for my stake. He was wrestler-huge and bone-pale.

"We got the call," Kieran said, stepping in front of me. He stomped on my foot while he was at it. I fell back, but only a little. I might be thrilled to be here but I was still in training. I didn't smile prettily at vampires in the middle of the night in the middle of the woods. I was no Little Red Riding Hood.

"Password?"

Kieran glanced down at his phone's display and read off a word in a language I'd never heard before. It sounded old.

The guard nodded. "Go ahead. Turn right at the cedars and go straight through into the pine forest."

"Thanks."

It felt weird to turn my back on a vampire. I must have more of Grandpa in me than I thought.

The red pines towered above us, the ground a carpet of fallen needles and not much else. In the center, Helena Drake and her husband, Liam, waited, along with most of their sons, Isabeau, Lucy, and a bald human bodyguard. Hart was on Liam's left, with three more hunters. The Raktapa families were there, each with a guard holding up a banner painted with their family insignia. The Drake banner was a dragon entwined with ivy and Latin words I couldn't read. There were other vampires as well, nearly a dozen of them.

I didn't see Quinn.

Not that I was looking for him.

And not that his twin, Connor, wasn't standing right next to Solange, looking exactly like him. Except that Connor's hair was shorter.

Still.

I followed Kieran to Hart's side. He kept sending Solange sidelong glances. She smiled, pale as a pearl. Her fangs were very sharp but delicate. Treaties were all well and good in theory but something else entirely when a vampire was flashing fangs at someone you considered to be your brother. I wondered if I should worry about him.

"Hunter." Hart smiled at me. "Glad you could make it."

"Thank you, sir." I tried not to flutter and went overboard into formal cadet stance. He was the head of the entire society and he knew my name and he'd asked for me specifically.

"At ease," he said. "You're here to witness history, not do battle," he added.

"Yes, sir."

"We're nearly ready," Liam called out pointedly.

Quinn sauntered out of the woods, a vampire girl on his arm. They were both grinning and it was totally obvious what they'd been doing. He was just as gorgeous as I remembered, his long hair falling nearly to his shoulders, his eyes so blue they didn't seem real. The girl giggled.

I refused to stare. Mostly.

It wasn't my fault if I could still see him out of my peripheral vision. It was a hunter's duty to be aware of her surroundings.

Even if those surroundings included a beautiful vampire with a charming smile who liked to flirt with anything that had boobs.

Except for me, apparently.

I did *not* just think that.

Luckily the ceremony began before I embarrassed myself completely. I was also exceedingly grateful that vampires couldn't read minds.

Quinn was only smirking at me because he smirked at everybody.

Helena stepped forward, flanked in a semicircle by Liam and Hart on one side, the Council representatives and Isabeau on the other. The rest of us stepped back to form a loose clump of bystanders who eyed each other cautiously. We'd all lost family members to each other at some point in our history. You didn't automatically forget that.

"Weapons down," Helena said grimly.

The reaction was equally grim. No one wanted to be the first to relinquish any weapon, not in this crowd. Glances flickered back and forth, mouths tightened, hands curled into fists. No one moved.

Until Solange lifted her chin and pulled three stakes from her belt, holding them up so that everyone could see. Then she dropped them in the grass.

Silence. The kind you can only get when you're surrounded by vampires. It made my shoulders tense.

Helena was the next to disarm herself. She had a small arsenal on the ground by the time she was done. Everyone else followed their lead until we stood in a circle of discarded stakes, swords, daggers, crossbows, and Helios-Ra UV guns.

The coronation was simple and quick; there were too many *Hel-Blar* in the area and too many unproven loyalties. I imagined the more traditional version was longer and full of grand speeches and costumes. This one was as impressive in its own way. At least, I thought so. The pine trees were solemn, silent witnesses and the wind was warm and smelled of wet earth, tossing the boughs aside to show us glimpses of the stars. A wolf howled in the distance. Fireflies glimmered all around us.

Liam's voice was warm as whiskey and just as strong. "Do you acknowledge Helena Drake as the queen of the vampire tribes by right of conquest?"

One by one the representatives knelt, saying "aye." The council members wore elaborate gowns and suits. Isabeau didn't kneel, but she inclined her head respectfully. The Hounds offered fealty to no one but their Shamanka. Spencer would have given his left arm to meet that Shamanka but she wasn't here. Apparently she never left her caves. Hart nodded as well.

I tried not to look as awed as I felt. Helena stepped forward. Her hair was in a long black braid down her back and she wore a sleeveless black dress with a wide belt that normally hung with daggers and stakes. Her boots made me drool. I was sure she could have concealed at least four different kinds of knives in them. I *so* had to get myself a pair.

"I promise to stand between the tribes and danger, to foster autonomy and respect between the families, the councils, and the society. I promise to be your queen until such time as my daughter might choose to relieve me."

"Oh, Mom, not you too," I distinctly heard Solange mutter. Kieran reached for her hand. She leaned into him. A few of the vampires stared at them. Someone hissed and was elbowed into silence.

Helena dropped to one knee after everyone else had risen again. "I serve the tribes."

Liam unwrapped a velvet bundle, producing a slender silver circlet. It was set with three huge rubies and smaller pearls. Liam crowned his wife, looking proud. Isabeau tilted her head faintly, frowning thoughtfully at the crown.

There was a round of applause and silver pendants were handed out to the assembled group. They looked kind of like Catholic saint medallions, only they were imprinted with the Drake insignia on one side and the royal symbol on the other—a ruby-encrusted crown and sword. I slipped mine into my pocket. I couldn't wait to get back to the dorm where I could properly admire it.

The way another vampire, a different girl this time, was admiring Quinn.

There was no doubt he was a player, and there was no doubt none of his girlfriends minded. I turned away, waiting for Kieran and Solange to finish their discreet snuggling. The council was already leaving, to spread the word of the coronation. I shivered lightly in my tank top as the night cooled.

"Hey, Buffy."

I froze.

Quinn.

I turned slowly on my heel. "My name's Hunter."

"I know." He grinned. He was wearing his medallion around his neck on a silver chain. "But you've got the whole Buffy thing going. Though I think you might be cuter."

I was *not* going to giggle. I wasn't that kind of girl.

And hunters didn't giggle at vampires.

It was an unspoken rule.

"You're cold," he murmured when goosebumps lifted on my arms. I was really glad I *was* cold and didn't have to wonder if his presence was making me shivery and ridiculous. He stepped closer to me, blocking the wind. Pretty much blocking everything. "Better?" he asked casually, the way Spencer talked to me. Still, he was really close.

"Oh my God, Quinn," Lucy interrupted, causing us both to jump. "Could you stop flirting for three seconds and come *on?*"

CHAPTER 5

◆

Hunter

Wednesday Morning

Chloe was far too cheerful.

"Am not," she insisted, sipping root beer out of a straw as loudly as she could to annoy me. "You're just grumpy."

It was possible she was right. I hadn't even realized I'd spoken out loud.

I hadn't gotten back until four o'clock in the morning and it was only eight thirty now. We didn't get up this early even when we had classes, because they ran from 1:00 to 4:00 P.M. and again from 8:00 P.M. to midnight. We had to be used to late hours in our line of work. And Chloe was usually the last one out of bed, grumbling the entire time. I didn't know how or why she'd become a morning person over the summer but I suspected it was just to bug me.

I pulled my pillow over my head. "Too early."

"Just taking my vitamins," she said.

"You don't take vitamins."

"I do now. Mom gave them to me after my last report card. And these gross protein shakes, which I conveniently forgot to pack." She slurped more root beer. Loudly.

"Don't make me stake you." I revealed just enough of one eyeball to glare at her menacingly.

She grinned. "Morning to you too, sunshine. Want a vitamin?"

"Who are you, evil pod person, and what have you done with Chloe?" I was too tired even to yawn. My eyes felt glued shut. I snuggled deeper into my warm blankets. Chloe finally finished her root beer and went back to her computers. The tapping of the keyboard lulled me to sleep.

For about five minutes. Until the phone rang.

I threw a stake at it.

The receiver clattered to the ground and Chloe jumped, knocking her chair over. She whirled around, pointing at me accusingly. "You scared the crap out of me."

I wasn't too tired to grin. "Sorry."

"You will be, Wild." She tossed the receiver back into the cradle. The academy was too cheap to spring for cordless phones like every other modern facility on the face of the planet. My cell phone trilled, vibrating across the surface of my night table. I grabbed it, frowning at the display.

I sat straight up in my bed, swearing.

"Who is it?" Chloe asked.

"Bellwood."

Chloe's eyes widened. "About last night? York already nailed you for being a good person."

I swallowed, flicking my phone on.

"Hello?" I sounded hesitant, even to my own ears.

"Ms. Wild?"

"Yes."

"This is Headmistress Bellwood. You will come to my office, please."

"I . . . what's this about?"

"Don't play games, Miss Wild, I haven't the time. You left school property last night, after the drill."

"Uh . . ." I just stared helplessly at Chloe while the headmistress continued to lecture me in that stern, dry voice of hers.

"I will expect you in five minutes."

"Yes, ma'am."

I hung up and closed my eyes briefly. Grandpa was going to kill me.

"What happened?" Chloe asked.

"She wants to see me."

"That's never good."

"Tell me about it." I kicked free of my blankets, grabbing for my cargos and a T-shirt with the Helios-Ra High School logo printed on the front.

"You can't be getting busted that hard for helping a Niner? Before school even starts?"

"No. For sneaking off campus last night."

"For sneaking—*what*? Hunter Wild, you went and had fun without me?" She sounded both stunned and hurt.

"Of course not." I hastily tied my hair back. "I'll tell you all about it later. I gotta go."

"*You* snuck out." She shook her head as I hurried out the door. "And *I'm* the pod person?"

◆

I ran all the way to the main building where classes were held. Headmistress Bellwood's office was on the ground floor overlooking a rose garden she rarely stopped to enjoy. The school felt hollow and eerie without the usual scuffle of shoes or locker doors slamming.

And almost as creepy was the headmistress, who belonged in a Victorian gothic novel, scaring the children in an orphanage. Her hair was pulled back tightly, without a single strand daring to escape. She wore the same black suit she always wore and the same pearl earrings. If she'd had glasses, she would have been glaring at me over their rims. At least I was in proper school attire, but I hadn't had time to brush my teeth or wash my face.

"Ms. Wild, have a seat," she said when she saw me hovering in the doorway.

I swallowed and stepped inside her office, which was scrupulously neat, as expected. There were no mementos on her oak desk, no family photographs—even though I knew she had two daughters.

But she did have York cluttering up her office.

He'd been standing in the corner by the window and file cabinet, no doubt hiding to take me by surprise. I stopped in the middle of the room, standing at attention. Mostly so I wouldn't give in to the temptation to throw something at his head.

"The headmistress asked you to sit down," he said.

I sat down.

She put her pen down and looked at me, abandoning her paperwork. "I should tell you, Ms. Wild, that we installed new surveillance cameras on campus over the summer."

I was so totally busted.

And it was worth it. I'd been to a vampire coronation. Surely that was worth a lecture and some detention. I schooled my expression so that I looked properly chastised. If York thought for one second that I wasn't suffering enough, he'd try harder to have me punished.

"You were caught on video sneaking off school property in the middle of the night. I hardly need to tell you this kind of behavior is inappropriate. What do you have to say for yourself?"

"Uh . . ." *Hart, who is technically your boss, invited me to see Helena Drake get crowned in the woods?* Headmistress Bellwood would never believe me. And I wasn't entirely sure if it had been a clandestine assignment. I hadn't thought to ask, and no one had said. I'd have to call Kieran. "I—"

"You're not going to tell me that you were running laps or practicing drills, are you?" she interrupted drily. "Because I can assure you, there isn't a single excuse you could give me that I haven't heard before or that would exonerate you."

Damn it, and I totally had one.

"Yes, ma'am."

"Ms. Wild, I am very disappointed in you. You have been a model student these last three years. I would hate for that to change," she added pointedly. If her tone had been a weapon, it would have been a fencing rapier that drew blood with barely a scratch. York's would have been a cudgel.

"Yes, ma'am." I tried not to squirm or fidget.

She leaned back in her chair. "Two months' detention, one month of kitchen duty, and three demerits."

Crap.

"Three?" I gaped. We were allowed five per year; the sixth got us expelled. I'd never even had one. York looked smug.

"And we'll have to call your grandfather, of course," he added.

Double crap.

"But . . ." I had no idea how to talk my way out of this one. I wasn't prepared. Another rule broken. I was *always* prepared.

So not fair.

"You may go."

I stood up and went to the door, avoiding eye contact with York. It would just piss me off even more to see him looking so pleased. He really did hate me. Weren't teachers supposed to like everyone? Or at least fake it?

"Oh, Ms. Wild," the headmistress stopped me at the door, one step away from freedom.

"Yes, ma'am?"

"I don't want to see you here again."

"No, ma'am."

I dialed Kieran's cell the minute I was outside. The last of August's sweltering heat pressed all around me. I was sweating by the time I reached the barn, which had been converted into the school gym. I got his voice mail. I swore for a good long minute before adding, "Was last night a covert op? Because I want my demerit points wiped. And you suck as an undercover agent. Didn't you know there were new cameras?" And then I swore some more.

I stomped through the locker room, pulling on my workout clothes with enough force to stretch the fabric. The locker door had a satisfying slam and metallic reverberation when I kicked it shut. I was going to kick the stuffing right out of my favorite punching bag. Twice.

Except that Chloe was already using it.

"Okay, now you're just freaking me out," I said, stopping to watch her roundhouse kick. It was still a little sloppy, lacking power. Her thick curls were damp and tied back in a messy knot. Her gym shorts and sneakers were brand new.

"If you're on York's radar, then so am I," she grunted. "And if I fail his class this year my mom will kill me. Over and over again."

I went to the bag next to hers. I stretched for a few minutes and then taped my hands.

"So are you doing time or what?" she asked, trying an uppercut. The bag swung back and nearly batted her across the room.

"Two months' detention, kitchen cleanup, and demerits."

She paused. "You got demerits?" The bag swung again, hitting her in the hip and shoulder. She stumbled. "You've never gotten a demerit."

"I know," I said grimly. "If you let your hip pivot just a little when you do that punch, it'll be stronger. And use your first two knuckles for your jab."

I flicked on the ancient stereo in the corner with the toe of my shoe and turned up the volume until the windows rattled slightly. We stood side by side and punched and kicked the punching bags for a good half hour without talking. My lungs were burning and my face felt red and sweaty when I finally stopped. Chloe was bent over, panting and gagging. I handed her a bottle of water.

"Thanks," she croaked.

"You're overdoing it," I croaked back. "I've never seen you work out that hard."

She wiped her face with a towel and shrugged. "Then I guess I'm due. I can't fail the year, Hunter."

"You're not going to," I assured her. I'd never heard her this worried. She did so well in all of her computer classes and was already assigned to the Tech department. Her combat skills wouldn't hold her back from any of that.

She sighed. "You know I'm not very good at this stuff."

I finished my water and threw the bottle into the recycling bin. "Well, I am, so no worries. Listen, we can practice together. It'll be fine."

"Yeah?" she asked hopefully.

"Of course."

She grinned, looking slightly less panicked. Then she hiccuped and grimaced. "Good, 'cause that protein powder tastes like crap. Mom sent me a new tub." She scowled. "And if it makes me fat, I'm wiping her hard drive."

CHAPTER 6

◆

QUINN

Thursday evening

"God, Quinn, how many freaking girls' phone numbers do you have on this thing?" Connor shook his head, scrolling through my cell phone address book.

I shrugged, grinning. "I can't help it if I'm irresistible." Sitting on the edge of his bed, I leaned back against the wall. Moonlight filtered through the open window. The wind tasted like pine needles and smoke. "You'd get more girls if you ever actually left your computer."

He didn't even look up. "If I didn't spend so much time on that computer, you'd never get your phone working again. Or your laptop. I keep telling you not to open e-mail attachments from people you don't know."

"She was really hot."

"And now your computer's down."

I grimaced. "And my phone. Is that a virus too?"

"No, genius. It's just so crammed full of texts from girls sending you smiley faces and x's and o's that it's clogged up and buggy."

"Can you unbug it?"

Now he did look at me, all affronted techie. "Of course I can debug it. Question is, can you stop getting girls' phone numbers?"

"Hell, no. And why would I want to?"

He did whatever it was he did, hitting buttons, muttering curses, taking the innards of any technological implement personally until it bowed to his will. And then he grinned smugly, reaching for one of the bottles of blood in the bar fridge by his bed. He opened one for himself and then tossed me one, along with my phone.

"There. It'll work but it won't be completely reliable until you delete some of those contacts."

I scrolled through the names regretfully. "You're cruel, man."

"I prefer Evil Genius." He turned back to his computer.

"You should have more fun, twin of mine," I suggested.

"Or you could have *less* fun and leave some for the rest of us."

"There's no such thing." I left him to his machinations and went downstairs, trying to remember who Karin was and why she'd sent me a sonnet about my hair. The lamps were dim, the dogs snoring in the foyer. The front door opened and Logan and Isabeau came in, Isabeau's wolfhound trotting at her side.

I waved at them but didn't stop. I could hear someone's heartbeat in the back corner where the library joined the living room and the kitchen. It was going a little too fast for my liking.

I went straight into the living room, narrowing my eyes at Solange's back. Her arms were twined around Kieran's neck. His hands were a little too clever.

"Black, don't make me kill you," I told him pleasantly. He jumped and pulled back, his ears going red. Solange sighed.

"Thanks, Quinn," she said. "Way to ruin the moment."

"I try," I said, unrepentant.

"Someday, I'll actually get to kiss you without one of my nosy annoying brothers barging in," she whispered to Kieran.

"Don't count on it," Logan said as he and Isabeau followed me. Kieran's phone rang inside his jacket. He looked relieved to answer it.

"You kiss girls all the time," Solange pointed out to me. Lately the only girl Logan kissed was Isabeau.

"Flattery will get you nowhere." I made myself more comfortable.

"You're not going away, are you?"

"Nope."

Solange folded her arms. "Lucy and Nicholas are making out in the solarium. Go bug them."

"But I like bugging *you*."

"*Quinn*."

"Solange, look at your eyes," I said softly, too softly for Kieran to hear me. She frowned, then glanced into the art nouveau mirror on one of the shelves. A bronze woman in a flowing dress held up the reflection of Solange's pupils, ringed in red. The dark pupils all but swallowed up her usually blue irises. She froze, shooting me a horrified look. Her fingers trembled slightly when she reached up to touch the tips of her fangs. They were completely extended, in full hunger mode.

She tilted her head down and stepped into the shadows.

"I have to go," she told Kieran abruptly, and then bolted upstairs before he could answer. He flicked his phone off and frowned at me.

"Is she okay?"

"She'll be fine." She just needed more blood and less human temptation. The hunger wasn't easily explained, or easily controlled. Kieran would know that as a vampire hunter. But as her boyfriend, I wasn't sure how much he really got it. He took a step, as if he was about to follow her. "Just leave her be," I advised him quietly as Isabeau moved up the stairs, light as smoke.

He didn't look convinced but he nodded once. "I have to go anyway. Duty calls."

"Yeah? Who are we staking?" There was only a faint sarcastic edge to my voice. He was a vampire hunter, after all. And I was a vampire.

"*Hel-Blar*," he replied, heading toward the front door. "Got an all-call alarm. They're getting a little too close to town tonight."

"Yeah?" I grabbed my coat, even though I rarely felt the cold. I had stakes and various supplies in the inside pocket. There was a dagger strapped around my ankle, under the ragged bottom of my jeans. "Sounds like fun," I said, showing my fangs. "Let's go."

◆

We were in the woods when the smell hit: mushrooms and mildew and wet, ancient decay.

Hel-Blar.

"Incoming," I warned Kieran. He flipped a UV gun out of its hidden holster. I filled my hands with stakes, nostrils flaring as I tried to pinpoint which direction the stench was coming from. It was so thick and gag-inducing that it seemed to be everywhere. Kieran slipped on a pair of nose plugs. I knew what that meant and it had nothing to do with the miasma of rotting mushrooms and stagnant pond water.

"If you hit me with any of that Hypnos, I really will kill you," I said darkly.

He didn't have time to answer.

We were surrounded.

I didn't know what they looked like to Kieran's human eyes, but to me, even in the dark, they were bruise-blue and gangrene-black and utterly unnatural. Their teeth were all fangs, all contagious saliva, all feral, savage hunger. They even fed off other vampires, which no other vamp did. It wasn't nutritious like straight human or animal blood. It was about the kill, not the feeding.

And it was just rude.

I staked the first one after he swung down from a tree and knocked Kieran off his feet. He howled, jarring his wounded arm. The *Hel-Blar* burst into a cloud of blue-tinged dust that made us both gag. Kieran rolled to his feet. I was already leaping for another *Hel-Blar.*

There were four more that I could see, or hear, scuttling through the undergrowth. There was a pop from Kieran's gun and the bullet capsule of UV-injected water dug into a *Hel-Blar* chest and exploded. He screamed, smoked as if there was fire burning him from the inside out, and then he disintegrated.

I ducked a stake, then a fist. I kicked my boot into a chin, threw a stake with hard-won accuracy. We trained for years to be able to do that. I was grinning as I came out of a lightning spin. I was covered in ashes—I even had to shake them out of my hair. And the air stank, positively putrid with rot.

But at least this was simple.

I knew who the bad guys were and I knew how to dispatch them. It wasn't politics or assassination attempts or abductions.

In short, it was the best night I'd had all bloody month.

The fight was short and brutal. One of them got away but since neither Kieran nor I were bitten or dead, I counted it a success.

Kieran cradled his injured arm gingerly. "Bastard nearly broke it again," he said.

"Bastard's under your boots now," I told him cheerfully. I'd learned long ago you had to block out the rush of regrets that followed the adrenaline dip after a fight. Otherwise the loop of thoughts could pull you under. Did you just kill someone? Or was it a monster, plain and simple? Did that make you a monster? Was it murder if you were defending yourself? Was it a war and were we just soldiers trying to survive?

I preferred the adrenaline rush.

Kieran frowned, looking around. Then he checked the GPS on his phone. "We're near the school."

"Yeah?" I was grateful for the distraction. "I don't suppose they wear uniforms? Mini kilts? Knee-high socks?"

Kieran half smiled. "Is that all you think about?"

"If I'm lucky," I answered grimly as we started to walk. The wind off the mountains was cold and fresh, cleaning out the stench of *Hel-Blar* from my nostrils. I inhaled deeply. I didn't breathe exactly. My body didn't require it, but it was an ingrained habit. And inhaling helped us recognize and catalog scents. I still wasn't sure how the whole vampirism thing worked. Uncle Geoffrey called it biology, Isabeau called it magic. I just knew I was faster, stronger, and virtually immortal.

It didn't suck.

Well, so to speak.

Just around the time I could smell the warmth of many human bodies gathered in close quarters, I smelled something else.

The first was seductive and actually made my stomach growl, the way humans might feel after smelling a grilled cheese sandwich. The second made my head spin.

Blood.

So much blood, my fangs elongated past their usual battle-length. My gums ached. My throat ached. My veins ached. Hunger slid through me, weakening me like poison. And there was only one antidote.

Blood.

Kieran grimaced. "Do you smell that?"

I nodded and tried not to drool on myself. I had to clear my throat before I could speak properly. "Animal," I said. "And . . . something else."

"What, like hunters?"

I tracked the aroma, licking my lips only slightly.

Then we saw them.

"Not exactly," I said, hunger fading. The bloodlust still had my nostrils twitching but I wasn't thinking about a liquid supper anymore.

Animals hung from the trees and lay in a pool of clotting blood on the edge of the woods, their scent leaking into the field. There were three rabbits, a badger, two raccoons, and a small heap of mice.

"What the hell?" Kieran asked, disgusted and confused. "Who did this? And why? They're not drained."

"Not a vampire then," I said through my clenched teeth. "We don't waste blood." Because you never knew when your next meal might be. "Give me those nose plugs."

He handed a pair over. I shoved them in and waited for the red haze to stop licking at my every sense.

"Whoever did that added human blood to the mix." The lights of the school were gold, glimmering like honey. "Which means there'll be more *Hel-Blar* around here before you know it."

Kieran went pale, paler than any vampire.

"I have to check on Hunter," he said, breaking into a run.

I didn't want to admit how cold I got, or how fast I followed him, until the trees were a blur of green around me and I left him behind altogether.

CHAPTER 7

◆

Hunter

Jenna found me after dinner. I was crossing the lawn, wondering where Chloe was. She hadn't been in the dining room and she was already up and out by the time I woke up. She'd also been awake way later than me, tapping away at her computers. She was determined to break the school Web codes that controlled schedules, private files, and surveillance cameras. The latter might be useful actually. But she also wanted to be a martial arts expert, crack shot sniper, and kickboxing queen.

"Wild! Hey, Wild!"

I turned to see Jenna jogging my way, cutting across the grass from the track field. Her red hair was bright as ever, as if she were about to catch fire. We'd been friends since crossbow practice in tenth grade.

"Hey," I said. "Have a good summer?"

"Yeah, pretty good." She grinned at me. "Heard you got busted already."

"York." York liked her though, so she didn't have the same issues I had.

"And you snuck out," she continued. "I'm so proud."

"Why does everyone keep saying that?" I wondered out loud.

"Because you're unfairly gorgeous, blond, smart, athletic, and a straight-A student." She grimaced. "Wait. Why am I friends with you again?"

"Give me a break," I said, then smirked. "And by the way, all my demerits were wiped." I couldn't help but gloat just a little even if I couldn't elaborate that Hart himself had called the head-mistress to absolve me. "York was speechless for fully three whole minutes and then he looked like he'd bitten into a rotten egg."

"Man, I wish I could have seen that." York might treat her well, but she was still a loyal friend and didn't like the way he singled me out all the time.

"It was pretty sweet," I admitted. "I should have taken a picture." I had a miniature camera located in the school pin on my shirt. All graduating students had them. Actually, even Niners had them, but they were expected to acquire them on their own, usually through outright theft. I guess it wasn't technically theft since the teachers hid them around. In our last year they handed us the newest and highest-quality cameras in our orientation packets.

"Speaking of your hotness and athleticism," Jenna said.

I paused, raised my eyebrows. "What, already?"

"Come on," she nudged me, the freckles on her nose and cheeks incongruous against the bloodthirsty gleam in her eye. "You can't tell me you haven't missed it."

I shrugged. "Maybe a little. But why am I always the bait?"

"Because of all those disgusting good qualities of yours I just listed."

"Uh-huh."

"It's true," she insisted.

"Please, *you* could be the bait." She was just as good a combat student as I was.

"And deny you the chance to wear something pretty?"

I couldn't deny it was an incentive. Grandpa encouraged civilian clothes only for practical, don't-be-obvious reasons, and he didn't exactly endorse cute dresses and strappy sandals. And I was better at hand-to-hand combat. Jenna's expertise was her aim, both with a crossbow and a handgun. We didn't use regular bullets, of course, since they didn't do much against a vampire. We used bullet-shaped vials of what we called holy water, basically UV-infused bullets.

"When?" I asked, giving in just like she knew I would.

"Saturday night, meet at the van at eleven."

"Wait," I stopped her before she could jog away. It was vaguely inhuman how much she loved to jog. "Did you clear it? York's just dying for an excuse to bust me again."

"Yeah, I got Dailey's signature." She waved and picked up her pace, heading back to the track. I continued across the lawns to the dorms. Hart might have gotten me out of detention and demerits, but there was one thing he couldn't save me from.

Floor monitor duties. And being Courtney's assistant.

I think I preferred demerits.

I couldn't put it off any longer. Well, just a little bit longer but only because I wanted to swing by my room and grab an elastic band. It was so muggy and hot, my hair was sticking to the back of my neck.

When I opened the door, a rubber ball full of pink glitter hurtled toward my head.

I ducked and it missed my nose, but not by much.

"What the hell, Chloe?" I said just as she yelled, "Get the hell out!"

She looked up from her computer, paused. "Oops. Didn't know it was you."

"Who else would it be?" I kicked the ball back inside. It rolled toward her, bumping against her foot. I grabbed an elastic band from my desk and tied my hair back.

"Your little Niners have been coming by all morning," she said grimly.

I winced. "Seriously?"

"Yes." She speared me with a look. "It's annoying. I didn't like Niners when I *was* one. They're either needy or macho or both."

"I'll fix it," I promised, holding up a hand to curtail a long rant. She had that look on her face. She got her temper from her father, who was one of those temperamental chefs who threw pasta and entire chickens when a meal didn't go as planned. His assistants quit on a regular basis. I'd seen grizzly old vampire hunters with fewer battle scars.

"I'm staking the next pimply faced thirteen-year-old who knocks on that door," she told me.

"I'll go right now," I said. "Have another vitamin."

"Ha-ha," she grumbled, turning her attention back to her keyboard. I hurried out before she remembered I was there. Spencer was coming out of the small kitchen, a cup of coffee in his hand. He wore a chunk of turquoise on a braided hemp necklace.

"Did she throw stuff at you?" he asked, nodding toward my door.

"Rubber ball. You?"

"Xena action figure."

"That's never a good sign."

"I know. She loves that thing." He frowned. "She's all stressed out. I've never seen her like this."

"She'll calm down. York spooked her with that drill. She's afraid she's going to fail the year."

"Like she couldn't break into his computer and change her grades if she wanted to."

"Yeah, but her mom's on her case too."

"That woman is terrifyingly efficient. I like your grandpa better, even if he could snap my neck without breaking a sweat."

"Yeah, he's the best," I said proudly.

Spencer snorted noncommittally, then threw his arm across my torso to stop me so abruptly that I stumbled.

"*Ooof.* What is *wrong* with you?"

"Sorry," he said sheepishly.

"And why are you staring at my boobs, perv?"

"Is that the medallion you told us about? From the coronation."

I glanced down. The silver pendant on its long chain had fallen out of my shirt.

Spencer looked positively greedy. "Can I see it?"

For some reason I didn't want to take it off. I held it up but kept it around my neck. "It's not magic, Spencer, just a symbol."

"That's half of what magic is," he said. "Symbology." He ran his finger over the insignias. "I'd love to do some tests on this."

I batted his hand away. "Forget it. It'll come back melted or smelling like cheese."

"One time," he muttered. "One time I misread a spell and I'll never live it down."

"You smelled like cheese for a month."

"Believe me, I remember. I still can't eat grilled cheese sandwiches."

Satisfied that he was distracted from trying to steal my necklace, I looked up the long staircase and squared my shoulders. "Here goes nothing."

"You'll do fine." He snorted. "And pretty much no matter what you'll do, you'll be better than Courtney."

That was comforting, at least.

Still, there seemed to be fewer stairs than usual. I reached the top floor distressingly fast. It smelled like popcorn. The common room looked the same, but there were plants in the windows. That was new. Homey.

"Courtney put those there," Lia said, when she saw me looking at them. She looked more cheerful today, less like she was about to have a panic attack. She still looked really young though. "Hi."

"Hi," I said back. "You okay?"

She looked embarrassed. "Yeah. Sorry about that. I totally lost it yesterday."

"It happens to all of us," I assured her.

"I bet it's never happened to you."

She was right. But that was only because I'd been five years old when Grandpa had started my training. When I'd thought there were monsters under the bed, he taught me how to do a proper sweep to get rid of them.

"So are you settled in?" I asked, changing the subject.

"Pretty much."

"And you know not to use the last shower stall in the back?"

Her eyes widened. "Why not? It's the cleanest one."

"Let me put it this way: magic gone wonky plus a cranky ghost makes for ice-cold water. Or sometimes blood instead of water."

"Okay. Gross."

"Yeah, that's why no one ever uses it. But they never put that stuff in the orientation manual."

She shivered.

"Don't let it get to you." I smiled. "By this time next month you'll know every corner of this place." I went toward the bulletin board, smiling at the two girls sprawled on the couch watching television. "Also, don't eat the meatloaf."

"I'm thirteen, I'm not an idiot."

I laughed. "Okay, then." I scrawled a note on a piece of paper and tacked it to the board. "Can you do me a favor and spread the word for me? Ask the girls not to bug my roommate or she'll send viruses to their computers."

Lia blanched. "She can do that?"

"Yup."

"Cool."

"She's just as likely to throw something at you though. Anyway, I'll come up here once a week . . . say Thursdays after dinner, if anyone needs to talk to me." Not that I expected they would, since they had Courtney, who was actually supposed to be doing this, and what did I know about this stuff?

"Are you the new monitor?" one of the girls asked.

I nodded. "I guess so."

"She's my *assistant*." Courtney sneered from the doorway to her room, which was decorated from floor to ceiling in purple. Her hair was in perfect hazel-brown waves to her shoulders, her eyes expertly lined and smudged with silver eye shadow. Her dress was really pretty, with lace layered over silk. I coveted it instantly.

Which just made me cranky.

"Courtney," I said evenly, counting to ten.

"You're not the floor monitor," she said defensively. "You're my lackey. Your job is to do what I tell you to."

"You wouldn't need an assistant if you'd done your job properly in the first place," I shot back. Like hell I was going to let her make me her minion.

She narrowed her eyes at me. "Excuse me, but it's not my fault one of them was too slow. She had to pass the entrance exams like everyone else. She should've been fine."

"She's thirteen," I said softly, since I knew everyone around us was eavesdropping.

Courtney blinked. "She is?" She frowned and flipped her hair over her shoulder. "Whatever," she added, her cheeks pink. "York says I'm in charge."

"He would," I said under my breath.

"And if you don't do your job, I'm supposed to tell him about it."

"Fine," I said through my teeth. "I already posted my hours so chill, already."

"My family's just as good as yours," she snapped suddenly.

It was my turn to blink at her. "Okay." I didn't know what else to say to that.

"I mean it."

"I'm sure you do."

I was so glad we weren't roommates anymore. I'd rather have Chloe throwing stuff at my head any day. I heard one of the doors creak open. "You, in room 403!" I snapped. "Always check for creaky hinges before you try to listen in on someone. It's a dead giveaway." There was a gasp and the door slammed shut, followed by stifled giggles. I rolled my eyes. "So's that," I muttered.

"Look, I don't need your help," Courtney insisted hotly.

"You need some kind of help," I said, turning on my heel and going back downstairs. I was on the landing when my phone vibrated in my pocket as a text message came through.

Hel-Blar attack. All 12th-grade students
to town line rendezvous.

I took the rest of the steps at a dead run.

Spencer was already in my room when I got there. Chloe was shoving a stake through one of her belt loops. She looked excited. She never looked excited about drills and outright runs.

"You got the message?" Spencer flicked me a glance.

I nodded, reaching for my jacket. I secured the tear-gas pen, altered to hold Hypnos powder, in my cuff. "*Hel-Blar* on the outskirts of town again?" I asked. "That's twice in one week."

"And enough of them this time to call us all in," Spencer added grimly as we thundered down the hall. The front door was already open. A cluster of Niners stood on the stairs watching the dorms empty of twelfth-grade students, armed to the teeth.

Courtney shoved past them, stakes lined up on her designer leather belt. "Hunter," she smirked at me. "Someone has to stay behind and babysit the girls, as you so kindly pointed out."

I did not like where this was going.

"So you stay," I replied tersely. "You're the floor monitor."

"You're my assistant," she strode past me. "So assist."

I grabbed her elbow. "You said you didn't need help, remember?"

She shrugged me off. "Let go. You're the one who was all worried about them." She jerked her head toward the lane, visible through the open door. "There goes York. Should we ask him?"

Crap.

"Why do you have to be such a bitch, Courtney?" Chloe snapped. "Is it your superpower or something?"

"Shut up." She flounced out, hurrying to catch up with York.

"Sucks," Spencer said. "Want me to stay?"

I shook my head. "Sounds like they need you." My teeth were clenched so tight it was hard to speak.

Chloe made a face. "Sorry," she said, shutting the door behind them.

I was left standing in the foyer under the dusty chandelier, covered in stakes, with night-vision goggles pushed up on my head like a headband.

Talk about being all dressed up with no place to go.

The Niners were whispering excitedly to themselves, a few brave ones coming down to press their noses to the windows. Jason, who was the boys' ninth-grade monitor, turned to me sympathetically. "You're having a hell of a year so far, aren't you?"

I had to grin, even if it was only faintly. "Maybe I should have Spencer check me for curses."

"Wouldn't hurt," he said before turning to the nervous students. "Everyone back upstairs. Now."

They went reluctantly, but they went.

"Did you tell them their common room windows have a better view of the vans leaving campus?" I asked, remembering how we used to sneak out of bed and cram ourselves into the window seats, jockeying for the best position to watch the official runs and middle-of-the-night drills in the woods.

"No way," Jason said. "I might lose my spot." He slung an arm over my tight shoulders. "Come on, Wild, let's go watch reruns of *Warriors* on the History Channel and wait up like little old ladies left out of all the fun."

I let him lead me up the creaky old staircase, dragging my feet a little.

"I can't believe I'm missing the first real vamp takedown of the semester," I said glumly.

The chandelier flickered once and then all the lights went out.

I whirled just in time to see a shadow pass by one of the front windows.

"Or not," I amended.

CHAPTER 8

◆

Hunter

Jason was already upstairs when the first *Hel-Blar* crashed into the foyer, shattering the glass. I was still on the landing and the only one properly armed.

"Go!" I yelled up to Jason. "Trip the alarms."

He hesitated.

"Just go!" I insisted before leaping off the landing. I grabbed the chandelier and used it to swing forward, gaining enough momentum to catch the *Hel-Blar* in the chest with my heels. He was swept off his feet just as the chandelier chain snapped and dumped me in the center of the foyer. The crystal beads rained down on our heads, skittering into the broken glass from the window. The *Hel-Blar* didn't stay sprawled on the ground for long. The smell of wet mushrooms was overpowering. He snapped his teeth at me, all pointed and needle-sharp. I shoved a stake through his chest and he crumbled into ash, leaving behind an empty pile of clothes.

I didn't exactly have time to pat myself on the back.

Several more *Hel-Blar* came racing out of the woods, like blue beetles. There were thumps upstairs, a shouted curse. They must be on the roof as well. The tenth and eleventh graders would have already barricaded themselves in their rooms or else gone for the secret passageways leading outside when Jason turned on their silent alarms. I should get back upstairs and help him corral the Niners. I kicked the ash off my boots and took the stairs two at a time, slipping in a pair of nose plugs.

It didn't make sense. Vampires didn't attack the academy as a rule, at least not in the last few decades, and the *Hel-Blar* never had even before then; why would they bother now? They didn't have a leader or political aims, just an overwhelming hunger that usually chose the path of least resistance.

Another beast came through the broken window and raced up the stairs behind me. I barely heard him, only felt the press of air full of rotting vegetation and copper. There was blood on his chin.

I went low because he expected me to jump and leap out of his way. Instead, I dropped and swept my leg out, catching him in the ankles with the steel toe of my boots. I activated the tear-gas pen in my sleeve because he was moving too fast for the blade in my boot to be useful. Hypnos wafted out in a puff of white powder, like confectioners' sugar. He was already leaning over me, his saliva dripping onto my shoulder, by the time I could bark out an order and be relatively confident there was enough Hypnos in his face to do the trick.

"Drop!"

He collapsed on top of me like a load of bricks.

I wiggled out from beneath him before his teeth could accidentally graze my neck. There was nothing more contagious than the kiss of a *Hel-Blar*, no matter how doped up he was. His pupils were dilated, ringed with a tiny sliver of pale gray. His skin was tattoo-blue and mottled.

Grandpa would have told me to stake him then and there. He was *Hel-Blar*, after all, the most vicious of the vicious. But I couldn't just take out a will-less, unarmed opponent, even if he was dangerous, even if it was tactically sound. It just felt wrong.

I shoved him away, making sure to use enough force to crack a few ribs. I might have more scruples than my grandfather, but I wasn't soft. And I didn't want him staying here to jump back into the fight after the Hypnos wore off.

"Go back to your nest," I snapped. "And stay there. Don't hurt anyone on the way."

"I will kill you, little girl—"

"And shut up," I added.

He stumbled down the steps, making weird growling sounds in the back of his throat.

I knew the precise moment Jason reached the main alarm switch. The altered tanning-bed bulbs set all around the dormitory, from windowsills to garden landscaping lights, seared through the darkness. It was high-powered UV light with the same toxic effect on vampires as sunlight. It wouldn't make them burst into flames like movie vampires, which would have been a hell of a tactical advantage. But it would at least weaken them considerably. And it should convince any other vampires coming this way to turn back.

I met Jason on the third floor, trailing students heading for the secret passageway door.

"You all right?" he asked.

I nodded. "Two down."

"This is unbelievable," he snarled. "They're coming down from the roof too. There are at least three upstairs."

"I saw that many coming in through the back," an eleventh-grade girl, still in her pink pajamas, offered. "From the gardens."

"What the hell is going on?" I shoved my hair back into its ponytail.

"It does seem rather sophisticated for the *Hel-Blar*," Jason muttered as we rounded the corner and came up against the wooden panel door. "Let's go," he called out to the other students. "I'll take point."

"But they're outside too," one of the ninth-grade boys said.

"We can't stay here," I told him. "Anyway, the tunnel leads far enough away, near the road and the van parked under the willow trees."

"That broken-down, rusted old thing?"

"It only looks broken down," I said grimly. "And there are two more vans hidden deeper in the woods. Now move."

"Don't argue, Joshua," Lia said, shoving him to get him going. Her hands were trembling and her hairline was damp with sweat, but she was keeping it together. I turned my back to them, watching for *Hel-Blar*. We could hear their footsteps creaking through the ceiling. The old wooden floorboards were meant to be creaky like that, to teach us how to move quietly and give us fair warning if someone was sneaking around.

The light pouring through the windows was almost blinding. It should weaken them, but if they were in a battle frenzy they could still do a considerable amount of damage before they realized they should retreat. The secret passageway door slammed open. I was still guarding the rear so I had to look over my shoulder when I heard Kieran's terse voice.

"Exit's blocked," he said.

"Crap," I muttered. "Sophie, take my position," I said, turning to stare at Kieran. He was in regulation cargos, a strap of stakes over his good shoulder. "What are you doing here?"

"Talk later."

"Bet your ass," I muttered. "And what do you mean the exit's blocked?"

"Dead end, Buffy," Quinn said, coming out of the passageway behind Kieran. He looked just as gorgeous as ever, even covered in dust. His hair was loose, his eyes blue as fire.

I gaped at him. "What the hell are you doing here?"

"We came to rescue you." He grinned at me as if we were alone at a candlelit dinner, his fangs gleaming like ivory daggers.

"You do realize you're in a *vampire hunter* school, right?"

"He's a vampire!" The eleventh-grade floor monitor flung a stake at Quinn. Quinn snarled, leaning to the right until his torso was practically parallel to the floor. The stake thudded into the wall.

"Stand down!" I yelled as Kieran stepped in front of Quinn. "He's a Drake! And an ally."

There was a startled pause, then grumbling and frantic whispers.

"You know him?" Jason stared at me as if I'd just grown an extra head.

"Kieran, you're fraternizing with the enemy now?" Sophie snapped.

"He's a vampire," Simon muttered. He was in eleventh grade now and already covered in scars. And he was built like a big blond Viking. "What are we waiting for?"

"He's a Drake," I repeated. "And Hart's signed a treaty with them so stand the hell down or I will put you down."

"It's not right, is all I'm saying. In case you two haven't noticed, we kill vampires. Kind of under attack right now."

Kieran snorted. "I'm not going to let you kill my girlfriend's brother, so get over it."

"You really *are* dating a vampire?" Sophie goggled at him. "Dude."

I stood very pointedly next to Kieran, blocking Quinn. He was close enough that I could feel the coolness of his body, the noticeable absence of his breath on the back of my neck. It should have creeped me out. I was kind of surprised that it didn't.

"Look, could we debate the bigotry of this organization at some other time?" I bit out. "Quinn's not our problem right now. As Simon pointed out, the *Hel-Blar* are." I lifted my chin, glaring down at everyone. "And Kieran outranks us all, so shut up and follow orders or I'm handing out demerits."

"Can you do that now?" Kieran whispered at me.

"I have no idea," I hissed back.

"Okay, listen up, people," Kieran raised his voice so that it was all gravelly and impressive. I wasn't particularly impressed since we'd grown up together and I'd force-fed him mud pies when we were little, but it seemed to work on everyone else. Lia actually sighed.

Only a thirteen-year-old vampire hunter would get a crush in the middle of a vampire attack.

I was a little bit proud of her actually.

"The tunnel exit is no good," Kieran continued. "We had to barricade it behind us and set fires to keep the *Hel-Blar* from using it. Someone's tipped them off about it. That's not our concern right now. Our only goal is to take as many out as possible and stay alive in the process. Don't be a hero or I'll have Hunter take you down. That said, the lights should keep the worst of them away. In the meantime, I want everyone bunkered in the tenth-grade common room. It's the easiest one to defend and the windows are barred." That had less to do with protection and more to do with a prank Kieran and his friends had apparently pulled in tenth grade.

"What are you waiting for?" Kieran shouted as the *Hel-Blar* came down the stairs. "Go! Monitors on perimeter," he added, though they were well trained enough to do it anyway. I stayed where I was.

"Hunter, go," Kieran said, drawing a stake.

"Give me a break." I took out my own stake and stepped aside just enough to keep Quinn out of my way and vice versa. "Your arm's busted. You need me."

Kieran didn't have the time to argue with me. He couldn't have changed my mind anyway. He was the closest thing to a brother I had and I wasn't about to leave him behind. Not when the other students were plenty well protected now. And while I trusted that Quinn was a good fighter, he was dangerously cocky too.

Three *Hel-Blar* came from the top floor and another two from our right. Quinn laughed before throwing himself at them. He actually laughed.

"Is he insane?" I asked, flinging a stake at one of the *Hel-Blar* on the right.

"Pretty much. Duck!"

I ducked. Kieran's stake whizzed over my head and pinned the second vampire to the wall. Another stake finished him off. I held my breath until the ash settled. Breathing in dead vampire dust is just as gross as it sounds.

We'd dispatched them all when Quinn turned back to us, grinning. "That was fun."

"You're—" I cut myself off as the shadow of a smaller, more cunningly hidden *Hel-Blar* dropped from the ceiling ledge. She landed behind Quinn, every fang exposed. "Quinn, down!"

Quinn dropped into a crouch, revealing a stake in each hand. Before he could spin and jab up with his weapons, I threw a pepper egg. He blinked at it with the kind of astonishment that would have been funny in any other circumstance. The black-painted egg-shaped container was thin and made to break on impact. When it struck the last *Hel-Blar* in the face, it splashed a combination of ground glass, cayenne pepper, and Hypnos into her face. She recoiled, screeching and clawing at her red, watering eyes. One of Quinn's stakes pierced her heart and finished the job.

We joined Kieran on the next landing and stood there for a long moment. The only sound was Kieran and I panting. The house was quiet.

"I think that was the last of them," Kieran said finally. "I'll go up and do a sweep. You guys watch the front and back doors."

I led Quinn down to the end of the staircase. I stood on the last step, able to see not only the front door but right through the broken windows to the lawn. He stood next to me on the ground, facing the other direction, toward the back door. My one step advantage made us almost the same height. Our shoulders touched, the banister between our bodies. Adrenaline was still flooding through me, making me feel inexplicably like giggling.

"You guys throw eggs now?" Quinn asked, raising an eyebrow. "What the hell's that about?"

"It's a ninja thing," I shrugged. "We've only started using it recently. One of our history teachers is into that stuff."

"You're kinda scary, Buffy." He winked, then looked suddenly thoughtful.

"What?" I asked.

"I was just wondering if you'd consider teaching Lucy some moves."

"Lucy? Your sister's best friend?"

He nodded. "She needs some extra tricks up her sleeve. Our family is proving to be a bit of a liability and she's only human." He flicked me a glance. "No offense."

"None taken," I returned drily.

"You know what I mean. She's vulnerable. And her parents will be back soon and she'll go home. We're just a little worried."

He smelled like smoke and incense. I probably shouldn't be noticing that. What was wrong with me? I wasn't usually the type to get all flustered over a good-looking guy. Even a *really* good-looking guy who kind of resembled Orlando Bloom. Plus, he saw me as a fellow soldier. I'd been fighting next to guys long enough to know the look. I tried not to sigh. It would have been a totally inappropriate reaction. I was a hunter. I was supposed to be cool under pressure.

"So, would you?" he asked again.

"What?" I gave myself a mental shake. "I guess it would be okay, if the headmistress approves."

"Do you always do what you're told?" he drawled.

I snorted. Flustered or not, I was still me. "That's what story-book villains always say to the girls to get them to do something stupid."

There was a pause before he chuckled, as if the sound surprised him. "I'll just take that as a yes."

"I'm sure you usually do."

His grin widened and he nudged my shoulder companionably. "I like you, kid."

I tried not to groan out loud. I was as bad as Lia.

I had totally developed a crush during a vampire raid.

And he saw me the same way Kieran saw me—as a little sister.

I didn't exactly have time to analyze the fact that I was crushing on a vampire.

Besides, anyone with eyeballs would crush on Quinn Drake.

Right now I was far too busy running up the stairs toward the screaming. Quinn was at my heels, cursing. "Hunter, wait. Let me go ahead."

"Not a chance." I ran faster. He was quicker, of course, being a vampire and all. In fact, he was practically a blur of color streaking past me. It didn't seem fair. I worked my ass off to be as fast as I could, I ran, I practically lived at the gym most mornings, and I had to put up with York. All Quinn had to do was die.

Not exactly a viable option for me.

CHAPTER 9

•

QUINN

When I got to the common room, where the screaming had originated, it was quiet again. I waited for Hunter to catch up.

"So not fair," she muttered, gasping for breath.

Kieran stepped into the hallway, grim-mouthed. "Man down. Well, boy, anyway."

"Is it bad? What happened?" Hunter brushed past him to see for herself.

The room was bright considering all the light reflecting through the windows. It was getting warm, too. Definite drawback to those UV bulbs; the students might be sunburned by morning. While they'd no doubt trade a peeling nose and heat blisters over getting eaten by a *Hel-Blar*, I, however, was feeling like I might cook right through. Sunlight wasn't good for us. I wouldn't burst into flame or anything dramatic like that, but I'd get weak and pass out.

In a school full of vampire hunters.

No thanks.

I put on my sunglasses and flicked up the collar of my shirt. The back of my neck already felt tender. In the center of the room, the students were huddled around a couch where a very skinny student was moaning. There was blood soaking his white T-shirt. I tried not to lick my lips. I didn't think it would go over well.

"Will," Hunter said. "Shit. Was he . . . ?" She trailed off, wincing. His shoulder looked bad, his shirt torn.

"He wasn't bitten," Kieran went to stand beside her.

I stayed by the door, watching the shadows in the hall and trying not to be distracted by the scent of so many humans in one room. If my stomach growled they'd probably stake me before I could explain it was an involuntary reaction. They craved donuts, I craved blood. It was just one of those things.

"The screaming came from the girl who found him. The blood's from when he tripped and fell on his own knife."

I snorted. They were shish kebabing themselves for us now. They may as well offer themselves up on silver platters. Hunter shot me a look, as if she knew what I was thinking. I just shot her back a crooked grin. She wasn't likely to apologize for accessorizing with stakes and I wasn't going to apologize for my fangs.

"*Hel-Blar* tried to drink from him," Kieran continued tersely. "Apparently got a mouthful before Will got away."

Her eyes widened. "Crap. Will he turn? Are there marks?"

"I don't think so. But no one can tell me for sure if there was any saliva or blood exchange. It was just a convenience feeding."

"So he needs the infirmary," Hunter said.

"There are some teachers on campus," Kieran assured us. "But they've got their hands full."

"I'll take him," she offered right away.

Kieran frowned. "Hunter, campus is crawling with *Hel-Blar*."

"Duh. And you have to stay here. You're the one with the actual rank; the rest of us are just students. Plus, you've only got one good arm."

"Shit," he grumbled. He knew she was right. "I don't like it. It's dangerous."

I didn't like it either.

"Blah, blah, blah," Hunter cut him off. "Are you going to hold my hand every time we're out in the field?"

"There's gratitude for you," Kieran said.

She kissed his cheek. I was oddly glad it looked like the kind of kiss Solange might give me. Sister to brother. "I love you, stupid."

"You too, idiot."

"So get out of my way already." She had to shove him. "Give him some space," she told the others, trying to get through the clump of horrified students. "You'll be fine, Will."

"That's a lot of blood," someone said dubiously.

"Which is why I'm taking him to the infirmary." She hooked her arm under his shoulder and helped him up. He was clammy and pale and looked surprisingly heavy for someone so lanky. And he was about a foot taller than she was, which didn't help matters.

"I've got him," I murmured, coming up to support his other

side. Will jerked away wild-eyed, and then gagged on a sound of pain when his shoulder bled more profusely at the sudden movement.

"Easy," Hunter said gently. "He's just helping."

I couldn't stop my fangs from biting through my gums. I clamped my lips together. I was glad my eyes were hidden behind sunglasses. I knew they'd look too blue and too pale in this weird light.

"Vampire," Will croaked.

"Want to lose your arm?" Hunter asked him sharply. He shook his head, gulping. "Then shut up and let him help you."

"Yes, ma'am." He nearly saluted.

Kieran moved aside to let us out the door. "Watch her back," he told me.

I snorted. "I let you grope my little sister and I haven't broken your other arm for it yet. You can trust *your* little sister with me."

Hunter paused. She skewered each of us with a stare. Someone in the room started to sweat, she was that good. I could have kissed her right then and there.

"First—*ew*. Second—I can look after myself. If you guys want to do the macho knight-in-shining-armor thing, do it on your own time. And find yourself another damsel in distress, because I'm not her."

We exchanged a glance, then looked at her. Kieran sighed. "Just be careful, Hunter."

"I'm always careful."

"Uh-huh."

She stumbled a little. "Look, Will's leaving a puddle of blood on the floor and he's not getting any lighter. Stop worrying and let's do this already."

At that moment the phone in the common room, all of the phones in the dorm, and every cell phone in every pocket rang.

The sound was sudden and shrill enough to make everyone jump. I jerked back slightly as it pierced my sensitive hearing. Hunter nearly dropped Will. I caught him and hefted him easily over my shoulder in a fireman's hold.

"What the hell is that?" I snapped as Hunter checked her phone. The text and voice mail icons flashed.

"It's the first all-clear," Hunter explained as she read the message. "We're still in lockdown but the immediate attack should be over."

Kieran nodded. "Go on then. And try not to accidentally stake a prof making the rounds."

She made a face. It was cute as hell. "How was I supposed to know she wasn't a vampire? And that was four years ago. I'd barely been here a month," she grumbled.

I carried Will down the stairs. Hunter went ahead. She pushed the front door open and slipped out first to make sure it was safe. I could have told her not to bother. I couldn't smell a fresh waft of mildew and mushrooms so I knew there was no *Hel-Blar* in the immediate vicinity.

The lights outlined everything in pale yellow, like a movie special effect. Every leaf was delineated, every blade of grass. On the edge of the gardens there was a blackness soothing to my eyes. They were actually watering under the force of so many UV bulbs.

She led me down the path from the dorm to one of the main

buildings. The lower floor was the infirmary—I could tell by the sheer blinding force of the white paint on the walls and the faint underlying odor of antiseptic.

Will moaned again.

"Nearly there," Hunter promised. "Theo'll fix you up in no time. You know he's really good with stitches."

"That *Hel-Blar* bitch stank. And she had white spiky hair. D-Don't want to turn into that," he stammered. "Gran would . . . kill . . . me."

We exchanged a grim look over his head. It was hard to know if he'd been speaking metaphorically or not. You never could tell in hunter families. Or vampire families for that matter.

"You won't," Hunter said with a confidence I could tell she didn't really feel. "They have meds now, to stop the change. If they catch it early enough, it has a pretty good success rate."

"How good?" I asked softly.

"Fifty-six percent success rate, according to the files Chloe hacked into last year," she replied, barely above a whisper. I wouldn't have heard her at all if it wasn't for my excellent hearing.

"More pills," Will babbled, delirious with pain and fear. "Those new vitamins taste like ass."

Hunter chuckled. "That's what Chloe says. You must be taking the same kind."

He didn't answer, having passed out on us. Luckily we were on the walkway to the infirmary door. A nurse met us halfway. His black eyes were curious and concerned and they didn't change, not even when they landed on my fangs. I was impressed.

"Uh . . . vampire?" he asked.

Hunter nodded. "He's a Drake."

"Well, I'm not going to bow to His Fangness, if that's what you're implying." His scrubs were the color of seaweed and he wore them like armor.

"Like I'm that stupid, Theo," Hunter shot back, half grinning. Theo was obviously someone she liked. I decided I wasn't jealous. I didn't do jealous, not with girls.

"Will here needs stitches and antibiotics or whatever," she said as they wrestled Will through the door and onto the nearest cot. The fluorescent lights made me squint.

Theo took one look at Will and forgot about me entirely. He pried Will's eyelids open and shone a light into them, frowning at the messy wound.

"Knife?" he asked.

"Yeah," Hunter replied.

"You guys stab yourselves a lot?" I asked.

Theo's mouth quirked. "You'd be surprised."

"*Hel-Blar* got him too," Hunter added.

Theo didn't stop his ministrations, not even for a moment. But I heard his heart accelerate. "Explain."

"He got the wound before a *Hel-Blar* found him but she apparently lapped at the blood."

"Shit. Not good." He called out for another nurse. "Bite too?" He looked for teeth marks.

Hunter shrugged apologetically. "No one's sure."

"All right, let us do our work," he turned away, shouting orders at his assistants even as he cut through the rest of Will's shirt. Needles slid under skin. Hunter looked away, swallowing.

"Don't tell me blood makes you nauseous," I said, amused. I moved closer, ready to catch her if she fainted.

"Not blood," she shuddered. "Needles."

"Then why don't we get out of here?" I suggested. "You can't do anything else for him but Kieran could probably use you. And I'm feeling a little exposed here with all these lights."

She nodded, following me back outside. "I wonder how the others are doing in town."

"Montmartre and Greyhaven sure left a mess behind," I agreed. "Bastards."

"Who's Greyhaven?" Hunter asked.

"One of Montmartre's lackeys. His first lieutenant, actually. He made his own *Hel-Blar* on the sly, trying to create his own personal army, like Montmartre's Host."

"Oh, great, 'cause that's just what we need," she said drily.

"One of the Hounds staked him," I assured her. "One of Isabeau's friends."

The Hounds were a superstitious and solitary tribe of vampires, many of them having been turned by Montmartre but rescued from the grave before he could recruit them. They had old magic the rest of the world had forgotten about centuries ago.

We walked in an easy companionable silence, even though she still held a stake in her hand and I still had my fangs out. I was the first to hear the faint hiss. I stopped suddenly, turning my head slowly.

"There," I murmured before vaulting into the lilac bushes bordering the dirt path. Hunter caught up to me just as I was snarling over a lump in the grass on the other side of the bushes. The

Hel-Blar was female, lying on her back, hissing weakly. There was blood on her mouth, and her bloodshot eyes were wild. Her skin was mottled blue, nearly gray. Her hair was in short bleached-white spikes.

"She's the one who attacked Will!" Hunter exclaimed. She stepped closer, stake raised.

The *Hel-Blar* started to convulse, blood and saliva frothing at the corner of her lips. She flailed and hissed. I stepped partly in front of Hunter. We both stared at her, speechless, when she screeched and then disintegrated.

We didn't say anything for a long moment.

"What in the hell was that?" I finally broke the silence.

"I have no idea," she answered. "I didn't even touch her!"

"Vampires don't just disintegrate like that—not without a pointy stick or lots of sunlight." And we hadn't been close enough to hurt her. If I didn't know better, I'd have sworn she'd been sick in some way, or poisoned.

But that was impossible.

Before we could decide what to do, flashlights sliced across us. Hunters and two professors ran at us from either direction.

"Stand down," one of them ordered. "We'll take it from here."

"She's gone." Hunter blinked as one of them crouched to gather the ashes. "We didn't touch her. She just . . . fell apart. Like she was sick or something." She shook her head. "I know that sounds crazy."

I didn't say anything but I bent my knees slightly, in case I needed to leap out of the path of a crossbow bolt or a stake. You never could tell with hunters. Some of them were jumpy.

"Back to your room, Wild," one of the profs snapped at Hunter. "And Agent Black is waiting to escort you off the premises, Mr. Drake," she said to me, clearly not pleased to even acknowledge my presence. I could smell the fear on her skin, like a perfume.

"He helped us," Hunter pointed out, frowning, "while the rest of you were elsewhere."

I admit I got a charge out of watching her defend me. I hadn't expected that. Kieran had told me enough about her family that it was frankly surprising she hadn't tried to stake me yet, out of principle.

The professor stood to block our view of what they were doing. "*Now*, Miss Wild. That's an order."

Hunter looked like she wanted to argue but she just nodded sharply, turned on her heel, and walked away, tugging my hand so I'd follow.

"Something's not right," I said when we were out of earshot.

"I know," she agreed grimly as we stepped onto a lawn bustling with students, teachers, and the occasional hunter in full gear. The predator in me rose to the surface. It was a struggle not to growl out loud. Kieran came to get me, nodding at Hunter to move toward the dorm before she could say anything else.

"What the hell, Kieran?" I barked.

"Not here," he barked back.

CHAPTER 10

◆

Hunter

Friday afternoon

No one would tell us anything, even the next day.

The most information I could get was out of Theo, and he would tell me only that Will was critical but hadn't turned or died as of yet. It wasn't much to go on.

It didn't help that Chloe wouldn't stop complaining.

"It's so not fair," she said again as I wiped the sweat off my face and began my cool-down stretches. We were in the gym, which was nearly full. The attacks last night had all the students eager to train again, even though those of us left behind at the school had seen the most action. Which was what had Chloe in a snit. Her face was nearly purple.

"Take it easy," I told her. "You're going to give yourself a heart attack if you keep pushing like that."

She drained her water bottle and wiped her mouth. "I feel fine, and I had my checkup yesterday to prove it. So there." Students had to get a physical exam at the beginning of each school year.

"Well, you're the very flattering color of raw hamburger," I corrected. "Not a good look for you."

"I just need to take another vitamin," she panted, shaking out what looked like a yellow horse pill from a bottle she pulled out of her bag. It had her mother's name printed on it: Dr. Cheng.

"How do those not make you gag?" I asked her.

She shrugged. "You get used to it. Not that you'd need to."

"Not this again."

"Well, it's true," she insisted. "You're a natural athlete. *And* you get straight As."

"So do you!"

"I suck at the combat stuff."

"You don't suck," I said, pulling the elastic out of my hair. I was getting tired of defending myself when I hadn't done anything wrong. She was so prickly this year. I couldn't imagine how stressed she was going to be when classes actually started. It was kind of making me wish we weren't sharing a room. "But you are getting on my nerves."

"Not all of us are getting commendations for saving lives," she said. It sounded suspiciously like whining. "You kicked ass last night and all I saw was the back of a *Hel-Blar* head as it turned to ash. And I wasn't even the one who staked him."

"You're pouting because you didn't get to kill anything?" I asked her, astounded. "Seriously?"

"You don't get it."

"Got that right."

She shoved her stuff into her bag. "Everything's easy for you."

I blinked at her. "Are you high? Have you not been paying attention the last couple of days?"

"You came out smelling like roses every time."

"And that's a bad thing?" I couldn't believe her. "Shit, Chloe. What's *wrong* with you? You're my friend. You should be glad I didn't get slammed with all those demerits York tried to give me."

"I *am* glad."

"No, you're not. You're ragging on me because I got attacked by vampires and you didn't."

"I'm just tired. *God*."

"Then get some sleep," I shot back, annoyed. "And get a grip."

"You're not perfect, you know."

I stared at her. "When did I ever say I was?"

She scowled. "You act it."

"I do not."

"Yes, you do. You're good at everything."

"You're nuts." I slung my gym bag over my shoulder and stalked away before I said something I might not be able to take back. I couldn't believe the way she'd talked to me, the way she'd looked at me—like I was making her life miserable. I'd never seen her like that. She was still muttering to herself when I slammed the door behind me. I didn't even bother changing, just went outside in my gym shorts and tank top. I didn't want to be near her for a second longer than I had to right now. We never fought, not like this. We bickered over stupid stuff during exams, but so did everyone. This was something else. I knew her mother was being even harder on her than usual, but how was that my fault?

"Hunter! Did you want to—whoa." Jenna raised her eyebrows when I swung around. She was coming from the cafeteria with a basket and Spencer and Jason behind her. "Scary face."

"Sorry." I sighed, trying to shake off my mood. It wasn't fair to take it out on them, especially after getting mad at Chloe for doing the very same thing to me.

"You okay?" Spencer asked.

"I'm fine," I grumbled. "Chloe needs therapy though."

He snorted. "Tell me something I don't know."

Jenna held up her basket. "Picnic time. You in?"

"Always," I answered, following them off the path toward one of the back fields bordering the woods. We did this every time we needed a little privacy from possible surveillance cameras, bugged phones, and teachers in general. It wasn't easy to hide in a school that trained you in spy maneuvers and combat. Campus was full of bugs and hidden cameras. Sitting in the middle of a field was our favorite way to trade information. The potato salad wasn't a bad incentive either.

We spread out a blanket and dug into the food right away. We sat shoulder to shoulder, angled out so that we could see in all directions and no one could sneak up on us.

"So what's the scoop?" I asked, wiping mayo off my top lip. "Any word on Will?"

"Nothing new," Jason said. "He's stable enough but they're still waiting to see which way he goes."

"It was weird." I frowned. "Really weird, the way that *Hel-Blar* just disintegrated."

"Something's up," Jenna agreed, her red hair caught back in a messy braid. Her sneakers had little stars all over them.

"The Niner boys are whispering about some kind of pill that will make them stronger," Jason said, shaking his head. "I totally don't want to narc but, man, I'm going to have to if I can't figure out where they're getting it from."

I went cold.

"Wait. What?"

"They're saying it's some kind of vitamin that makes you stronger."

"Will mentioned something about taking vitamins," I said quietly. I looked at Spencer pointedly. "And Chloe's taking all these vitamins and protein powders."

He frowned. "But her mom gave her those. She's a doctor and a biochemist."

"True."

Jenna tilted her head. "If they really are vitamins, who cares? I mean, I'm taking vitamin C right now. My roommate's got that flu and I really don't want to catch it. If they need to think it makes them better fighters, where's the harm? It's not like they're on steroids."

"I guess." I wasn't sure why, but I wasn't convinced.

"But we all agree we need to find out what's going on, right?" Jason asked. "I mean, with the *Hel-Blar* and all the secrecy and some of the teachers being all weird?"

Spencer lay on his back, soaking in the sun and abandoning

his watch. No one was paying attention to us anyway. It was too nice a day.

"We'll figure it out," he said yawning. His dreads spread out around him like honey-pale snakes. "We always do."

◆

I didn't see Chloe for the rest of the day. But when I went back to our room Friday evening after dinner there was a note on my pillow. It was in her handwriting and read, *Sorry. I think I have a wicked case of PMS.* She'd left a chocolate bar and a new romance novel as a peace offering. I wasn't mad anymore, but I was still worried.

So I did what any vampire hunter would do.

I snooped.

I felt bad going through her stuff but I couldn't help myself. It was no use booting up her computer and going through her files; some of that encryption stuff may as well have been in ancient Babylonian for all that I understood it. Her gym bag was by her bed though, the zipper half open. I could see the white plastic cap on the bottle with the prescription sticker poking out. I plucked it out of the bag, along with the second bottle I found underneath it. That one was a popular brand of protein powder. I looked inside and sniffed it but it seemed innocuous enough. Not that I really knew what I was looking for.

The second label described the contents as a multivitamin and it had Chloe's name on it and her mom's. They looked normal and even had the regular gross vitamin smell.

I should let this go. I was being ridiculous.

But it didn't stop me from pocketing one of the vitamins in case I needed to get it analyzed later.

I was probably just being paranoid. It happened sometimes to hunters. And PMS could totally account for Chloe's weird mood swings and sudden obsession with working out and combat practice. Still, I kept searching.

I didn't find anything, though—just her normal assortment of nail polishes and data sticks and computer parts, and her secret bottle of peach schnapps in the back of her closet in her left rain boot. She hid a bottle there every year.

I was being a paranoid idiot.

I closed the closet door with a determined snap. I had enough to worry about with Courtney and the Niners and Will to be rifling through my friend's stuff.

Like the fact that Quinn was waiting for me in the clearing in the woods right this very moment.

The sun had fully set while I was rummaging through Chloe's things, which meant Quinn was out there with Kieran and Lucy. Kieran had gotten permission for me to train Lucy as long as we did it out of sight of the school and kept it quiet. It wasn't a precedent they wanted to set, and there was something about insurance as well. Whatever. I didn't want an audience. I felt self-conscious enough knowing Quinn would be there.

I took the bag of supplies I'd packed earlier and ducked out of the dormitory, cutting through the gardens to the woods. I avoided the squares of light falling over the grass from the infirmary. The woods were quiet and warm, thick with the smell of pines and the yellow lilies from the edge of the pond. I followed the glow of light on the other side of the pine grove to the clearing where Kieran had already set up a perimeter of lanterns.

I paused at the sound of a footfall behind me. "You're not supposed to be here."

"You're not the boss of me," Spencer returned good naturedly. "And we're not getting left out of another night of your stealthy fun."

Chloe was beside him, smiling hesitantly. "Okay?"

I wrinkled my nose. "Okay. As long as I can kick your ass in the name of training."

"Deal," Chloe slung her arm through mine. "I want to get a look at one of the famous Drake brothers." She lowered her voice. "I really am sorry I snapped at you."

"I know." *And I'm sorry I went through your stuff*, I thought. But I didn't say it.

Quinn, Lucy, and Kieran were waiting for us in the meadow. Quinn was leaning against a tree, looking dangerous and hot.

"Yummy," Chloe murmured to me. Quinn flashed us a grin. I fought a blush.

"Vampire hearing, remember?" I murmured back.

She shrugged, grinning back. I tried not to feel jealous of the way he winked at her. I turned my attention deliberately to Lucy. She was wearing an embroidered peasant top with jean shorts and Doc Marten boots. Her hair was in a straight bob, her glasses dark-rimmed.

"I'm so going to learn to kick your ass." She smirked at Quinn. "And your brother's."

"Where is Nicholas?" Kieran asked.

"He's locked in a closet," Lucy said with grim satisfaction. After a moment of stunned silence, Quinn snorted out a laugh.

"You locked your boyfriend in a closet?" I asked.

"Cool," Chloe approved. The rhinestones on her earrings caught the blue lantern light.

Lucy shrugged. "Serves him right. He locked me in there last week."

Kieran rolled his eyes. "He was trying to save your life."

"Whatever. Don't make me lock you in there too." She rubbed her hands together excitedly. "Come on, Hunter. Show me some stuff."

"Yeah, Buffy," Quinn grinned amiably at me, pushing away from the tree as we stepped farther into the clearing. "Show us your moves."

Lucy shoved him gently toward me. "Use him as your vampire dummy."

"Hey now."

"This was your idea," she told him. "You're the one who wanted me armed and dangerous."

"What the hell was I thinking?"

She kissed his cheek, as if he really was her big brother, then turned to me expectantly.

"First, I need to see your style," I said.

"Steamroller," Kieran said blandly.

She narrowed her eyes at him. "Can I practice on him?"

I swept my arm out in invitation, grinning. "Be my guest."

She danced back and forth like a boxer, but she was all grace and little technique.

"Just run at him," I suggested.

She lowered her head and charged him like a demented bull. Kieran waited until the last possible second before stepping out of the way, smirking. Lucy stopped herself, but only barely. Another step and she would have brained herself on a tree. She whirled.

"Damn it!" She pointed at Kieran and Quinn. "Don't you dare laugh."

Quinn pressed his lips shut with exaggerated care.

"It's okay," I said. "Take a swing at him now."

Kieran backed up so fast he nearly tripped over his own feet. "No way. She already punched me in the face once."

"Me too," Quinn said. "She has really good aim."

"Good. I can work with that," I replied. "Kieran, pretend to attack her."

He looked dubious but complied. When he grabbed Lucy's shoulder, she turned into a wildcat. She flared, kicked, bit. I was pretty sure I even heard her hiss. After a few minutes, Kieran was scratched and bruised and she was panting and red-faced.

"Not bad," I told her. "But you'll wear yourself out long before you do any actual damage."

She thumped her chest. "I'm starting to get that," she huffed. "I think my heart just exploded."

"We should probably stick to stealth and escape. I can show you how to inflict the maximum amount of damage with minimum force, which will buy you time to run away."

Quinn pinned Lucy with a fierce and knowing glance. "But you actually have to run away, brat."

She made a face. "Yeah, yeah."

"Show me your aim." I handed her three rocks and pointed to

a slim birch. She tossed her hair back off her face, took a deep breath, and launched them. She hit the trunk dead center every time. Spencer whistled through his teeth, impressed. Chloe looked like she was ready to start taking notes.

"Is it true Hope tried to recruit you?" she asked.

"Yeah," Lucy grumbled. "As if I would turncoat for some cheesy comic-book league." She paused, winced. "Oops. Sorry."

I shrugged. "Hope wasn't true Helios-Ra." Never mind that Grandpa had been rather sympathetic to her ultimate goals. Since Lucy had proven herself with her aim and the turn in conversation was making everyone uncomfortable, I showed her our altered ninja eggs.

She blinked. "I'm going to throw Silly Putty at vampires?"

When I explained what was in them, her eyes shone.

"Okay, these I officially love." She proved her point by juggling them, ending with a bow and a flourish. "Let's see you do that, 007," she teased Kieran.

"You should get yourself some Hypnos," I suggested. "I can't give you any because it's against school rules. But if you get some, I can give you an old tear-gas pen you can fill up and tuck in your sleeve. And I have a bunch of eggs without the Hypnos."

"Uncle Geoffrey probably has a stash of the stuff by now," Quinn told her. "Not that I approve," he said to me.

I wasn't the least bit apologetic. "You have pheromones, we have Hypnos. Call it even."

"We're not the ones selling our weapon on the black market and taking unfair advantage. We only use our glamour to protect ourselves."

"First, we don't sell it." I raised an eyebrow. "And second, are you really trying to tell me you've never used your pheromones to steal a kiss?"

"I steal them the old-fashioned way," he said. "With charm."

"Lucy, aim for the big swelled head when you throw those eggs," I said.

"I usually do." She grinned.

"You should also get a staff or a walking stick, something you can attach a blade to or sharpen to a point. It'll keep your attacker out of biting range."

Quinn kicked up a long stick with his boot, throwing it to me.

"Show me," he said as I caught it. I twirled it once. I admit I was showing off a little. If he was going to insist on seeing me as one of the guys and a fellow soldier, I was damn well going to out-soldier him.

"Come on, Buffy," he urged, pale eyes twinkling.

"Any time, Lestat," I shot back.

We circled each other in a slow, predatory dance. It was easy to forget we had an audience. His blue eyes were sharp and hot, like the heart of a candle's flame. It could warm me or burn me clean through.

"No Hypnos," he murmured.

"No pheromones," I countered, though I didn't know how much actual control he had over that sort of thing.

He was quick, of course. Vampires always were. But we'd been trained to focus on that blur of movement, on the displacement of air, on the tiny meticulous details that might just save our lives.

When he came at me I had to convince my reflexes that I

wasn't actually allowed to stake him. The first part of him that was close enough to un-blur was his fangs. They were mesmerizing, but not so mesmerizing that I didn't swing out and catch him in the sternum with the end of my stick. I could tell by the flare of his grin that he felt the impact. I'd never met anyone who enjoyed a skirmish quite so much. Even Grandpa saw it as duty before pleasure. With Quinn, it was almost like he was flirting with me.

I couldn't be sure if he was going to lean in to tear out my jugular or kiss me senseless.

Instead, he kicked out and tripped me, but when I fell backward his hand was at my back to catch me. My left arm crossed between us, fist pressed over his heart to prove my point. I might have staked him in that moment, if the situation were different.

But I might not have been alive to do it.

His fangs rested tenderly on the inside of my throat. The length of our bodies pressed close together. I felt the coolness of his skin and wondered if the heat of mine felt like a burn to him. It was the first time I could actually understand the seduction and the allure of baring your throat to a predator. It had always seemed like madness to me, or the result of reading too many novels. It still did. But there was the barest sway of my body toward him.

His hair swung out to briefly curtain our faces. There was something in his expression that I couldn't entirely decipher.

And then he stepped back abruptly, his familiar smirk erasing that mysterious warmth I'd glimpsed.

Chloe was the first break the silence. She let out a shaky breath.

"Is it suddenly hot out here, or what?"

CHAPTER II

◆

Hunter

Saturday morning

When I woke up the next morning, Chloe was still sitting at her desk and frowning at her computer. I couldn't imagine how she couldn't have a wicked headache. Her shoulders were hunched, the monitor's glare was annoyingly bright, and there were three empty cans of a sugary energy drink on the floor by her chair. Her usually perfect hair was decidedly frizzy, pinned in a knot on top of her head. This was not the Chloe I was used to, perfectly polished and fashionable even in her pajamas. She was also tapping her foot incessantly, like a woodpecker too frantic to realize it was hitting metal, not wood.

I sat up, blinking blearily. The light was pale at the windows, barely light at all. The forest was still dark, as if it was as sleepy as I was. "Chloe?"

"Just a minute." Her fingers clattered over the keyboard. She didn't look up. Something about her, the frenetic energy or the slightly manic way she was chewing her lip, made my stomach nervous. When she suddenly shoved away from her desk, cursing, I jumped.

"Damn it," she seethed. "I really thought I cracked it that time." She glanced at me, at the window. "What time is it?"

I turned the clock radio around so its bright numbers could glow red judgment at her. "5:34."

"Ew."

Now that was more like the Chloe I knew.

"Why'd you pull an all-nighter?" I asked, trying not to sound worried. "It's not like you have homework due. School hasn't even started yet. And it's way too early for classes anyway. Or for normal humans to function."

"I didn't mean to. I just got on a roll with the security codes. Well, I thought I was on a roll, anyway. I'm so handing this in as my independent study." She rubbed her red-rimmed eyes. "I feel like shit."

"They have this new cure for that," I said drily. "It's called sleep."

"Ha-ha."

"Are you gonna crash now or what?" I insisted. I could pull the plug on her computer but she'd probably scratch my eyes out. And it was too early for a catfight. She yawned and crawled into her bed. She was asleep before she'd even answered me.

I decided to take advantage of the early hour and the still dormitory. It was so rarely quiet and today was Saturday. All the students who weren't already here would start arriving after breakfast. Courtney would almost certainly pawn off some of her less glamorous duties on me, and then tonight we were going into town for vampire bait night.

So if I was going to follow through on the possibly illegal idea I'd had last night before falling asleep, now was my best chance.

I grabbed my knapsack and stuffed it with supplies as Chloe began to snore. I didn't bother changing out of my pajamas since I planned to go right back to sleep as soon as humanly possible, but I did stop by the bathroom. There was just enough light from the windows to make the hall gray instead of black. I stayed on the edge of the staircase so it wouldn't creak, skipping the third and eleventh steps altogether.

As much as my grandfather was strict and full of hunter pride, he'd given me awesome toys over the years—mostly old weapons, crossbows, and surveillance equipment.

It was the latter I was planning to put to good use.

I didn't have Chloe's knack, and I could hardly ask for her help. After that *Hel-Blar* woman died and Will mentioned vitamins, I knew something was up—I just had no idea what. We needed more information on this so-called vitamin, but I didn't know anyone in the science department I trusted enough to test the pills I'd pocketed. Chloe's mom helped devise Hypnos, and apparently she had a hand in the vitamins too, but that kind of chemistry or biology or whatever was way beyond my scope.

But I did know someone who might able to help me.

Quinn.

If Kieran trusted him, surely that meant I could too.

Even if he was a vampire.

And I was a hunter.

When had life become so freaking complicated?

For the part of this mess where I was essentially accusing higher-ups in the league and my friend's mother besides, I was on my own. I wouldn't even tell Kieran about that right now. He was already walking a thin line by dating Solange and allying himself with the Drakes. Not only would they have him under some kind of surveillance, but he didn't need extra flack for my unproven theories.

And anyway, it was far more likely that if the vitamin was making Chloe act weird, it was because she was taking it too often. Maybe she was even allergic to it.

There were too many questions that didn't make sense and not nearly enough answers.

So I was bugging the eleventh-grade common room.

Also, I was going to have to steal a sample of Will's blood from the infirmary.

I had no idea if this sort of thing could get me expelled or if I could plead extra credit. I hoped I never had to find out. It was worth the risk, though. This is where Will would hang out when they finally released him from the infirmary.

I only had three reliable microphones and just one of them had a motion sensor. I hid one under the couch, tucked behind the ugly brown fringe and a gross lump of gum no one was likely to want to breach. Another one I slid inside the removable drawer handle on the bottom left of the dresser under the bulletin board. I figured those would be the two most likely places students would gather to talk. There was no point in tapping the communal phone; they only used it to call home when they were out of minutes on their cell phones.

I could hear the faint sounds of someone padding down the hall toward the bathrooms. I had just enough time to duck behind the coat tree, still thick with discarded and lost clothes from last year. The student ambled past, scratching parts of his anatomy I didn't need to know about.

I unscrewed the knob on the top of the coat rack and dropped my last microphone into the pole. Luckily the microphone was an old-fashioned one from WWII and fit into a ballpoint pen–like casing. Unluckily, it dropped straight to the bottom, where I might never get to fish it out again. I couldn't risk trying to shake it loose now either. Cursing, I ran all the way back to my room.

I slipped under the sheets, the muggy August morning already too humid for blankets. Chloe was still snoring. I rubbed the coronation medallion I wore around my neck and hoped I knew what the hell I was doing.

This had every indication of going horribly wrong.

Into the breach, then.

I lay there, staring at the ceiling, and wondered what exactly I was going to say to Quinn.

◆

"You're late," Courtney snapped at me later that morning.

"I'm not late because I didn't have an appointment," I replied.

And I was late because I'd been at the infirmary, stealing a test tube of blood. Theo wouldn't let me in to visit Will, but he left me alone in the waiting room after wheeling the cart of blood samples into one of the examination rooms to await pick-up. All I'd had to do was reach around the curtain. The only difficult part was making sure I had the right sample. Apparently there were a lot of students with the weird flu that was going around because there were a lot of tubes in the tray. The thought of that many needles had me cringing.

So did the fact that I'd stolen a vial of Chloe's blood as well. But at least they hadn't reached the end of the alphabet yet for the yearly checkups, so I was off the hook with needles for another week at least.

"Just stand over here." She actually snapped her fingers and pointed behind her.

I stared at her. "Woof." I was glad I'd worn my favorite pair of pink cargos. She'd coveted them since we'd roomed together last year. Small, petty revenges were all I was likely to get.

And about a hundred demerits for poking her eyes out if she kept glaring at me like I was some disgusting substance she'd just stepped in.

She sniffed and ignored me. Fine by me.

The staircase was packed full of wide-eyed students and parents lugging suitcases. The dorm felt like a beehive, vibrating with sound and energy. There'd be stings by the end of the day, no doubt. Lia was hovering in the common room, trying to get a look at her roommate before having to introduce herself. Courtney smiled at all the parents and introduced herself politely and pretended I didn't exist. She wiped her hands with alcohol sanitizer after every hand she shook. Another student had been carted off to the infirmary with a high fever this morning.

I slipped my cell phone out of my pocket and texted Kieran to get Quinn's phone number. I texted him quickly and tried not to obsess over every word.

Need to ask you a favor. Can you come by the school Sunday night? Meadow, midnight. Don't tell Kieran. Hunter.

It wasn't like I was asking him out or anything. I was only asking for a professional courtesy. I shouldn't worry about whether or not I sounded too formal or curt or if he'd think I had a crush on him.

Because I didn't.

Mostly.

It was only natural to be curious about Quinn. He was a vampire, for crying out loud, and a Drake. He was becoming a friend of Kieran's too, so that made him a friend of mine.

And so what if he was gorgeous.

Lots of guys were gorgeous.

Of course, he was the first one to make me feel like blushing when I so much as thought his name. Like right now. Damn it.

"Oh, hello, Hunter." One of Grandpa's friends smiled at me, effectively distracting me from my mental freak-out.

"Mr. Sagasaki." I smiled back. His hair had a lot more white in it than the last time I'd seen him. He hadn't made it to our family barbecue this year, which is when I usually saw him and his son, who was standing beside him, a full foot taller than last year.

"Oh, call me Louis, honey. You're practically family." Mr. Saga-saki grinned. "I used to change your diapers, after all."

At the sound of his name, several heads turned. Courtney's eyes widened and she stood straighter, smoothing her hair back. Louis was a hunter with the kind of reputation it took decades to build. He had a record seventy-two vampire kills and had once taken out a *Hel-Blar* nest all by himself, two doors down from a grade-school ballet recital. I wasn't sure about that part of the rumor but I knew he was good. He had the scars and the faded tattoo on his upper arm to prove it.

"Mr. Sagasaki. It's a pleasure to meet you," Courtney held out her hand. "My name is Courtney and I'm the girls' ninth-grade floor monitor."

He shook her hand. "This here's my son, Martin."

"Hey, Hunter," Martin said, trying to hide his relief at seeing a familiar face. It probably wasn't cool for a fourteen-year-old boy to appear the least bit nervous about his first day at the academy. It hadn't been cool for me as a thirteen-year-old girl either, but Grandpa got me into classes a year early out of sheer stubborn pride that I could do better than anyone else.

"Hey," I said. "Still a mean shot with that crossbow?"

He nodded proudly. Over his head, his dad winked at me.

"Glad he's in good hands, Hunter," he said, urging his son forward so they could unclog the traffic jam of people trying to move around them. "You too, Kelly."

"It's Courtney," she corrected, but he was already out of earshot. She glowered at me. "I'm the floor monitor. You shouldn't hog people like that. It's rude."

I rolled my eyes. "I'm not going to ignore a family friend because you're insecure."

This was possibly part of the reason why she hated me so much. I just couldn't let her weird bragging and overcompensating go by unremarked. I went back to checking my phone before I could say anything else.

No reply text from Quinn.

Maybe he wouldn't answer. Maybe he was busy with his tongue in some girl's mouth.

Maybe I was an idiot.

It was noon, the hottest, brightest part of the day. He was a vampire. Duh.

I slipped my phone back into my pocket and vowed never to mention to anyone that a straight-A vampire-hunter student had momentarily forgotten that vampires didn't waltz about in broad daylight.

Talk about being off my game.

I went back to standing at attention and tried to look like someone you'd trust your thirteen-year-old kid's safety to, someone my grandfather would be proud of.

Not like someone daydreaming about a vampire.

CHAPTER 12

•

QUINN

Saturday evening

I couldn't stop thinking about Hunter.

If I'd been any one of my brothers, I would have mocked myself mercilessly.

Because she wasn't just human, she was a hunter. I suddenly had way more sympathy for what Solange was going through. Although, at least Hunter didn't smell like food to me. Mostly.

But she did smell damn good regardless.

I wondered if she'd gotten into trouble for wandering around campus with a vampire. Or if that boy we'd taken to the infirmary had turned and now there was one more *Hel-Blar* that needed to be put down. If they kept attacking like this, it wouldn't be long before the residents of Violet Hill began to wonder what kind of creatures lived in the mountains and the forests on the edge of town. Soon it wouldn't be safe for anyone to go out at night—but try telling that to the college students and the wilderness freaks.

There were stories already, and stories were never good. We relied on secrecy, and the common belief that vampires don't exist, to keep us safe. But the current pop culture obsession with all things vampire wasn't helping us any. We really had to get a handle on this *Hel-Blar* infestation, and fast. Mom was sending out patrols, and Kieran said the Helios-Ra were scouting as well.

I couldn't help but wonder if Hunter would be recruited for one of those patrols. She was good enough. I'd seen that for myself. And Hart had called her into the meeting at the caves last week and to the coronation. That said something.

I hadn't quite been able to ask Kieran if she had a boyfriend.

The question throbbed like a broken tooth, impossible to ignore, impossible not to poke, just to see if it still hurt.

I never did this.

I liked girls—human or vampire. I liked them a lot, but I never wondered what they were doing or if I'd hear from them. Because I always heard from them, usually more than I liked. I treated them all well, don't get me wrong. You couldn't be raised by my mother and not treat girls with a hell of a lot of respect. But they knew up front that I wasn't looking for strings, just a good time for everyone involved.

And none of the humans knew I was a vampire. I wasn't stupid.

Well, except for that one time.

But that was a long time ago. It wasn't even worth mentioning.

Besides, Hunter was different. She was strong and brave and sexy. I loved the way she looked at me, just slightly suspicious, as if she was thinking about kicking my ass. That shouldn't be hot, but it was. And I was just itching to convince her to unbraid all that blonde hair. She'd look killer with it down.

Damn it, I was thinking about her again. About her *hair*.

"Shit," I muttered. If I wasn't careful I'd start writing sonnets too, like Karin had written for me. "I have to get out of here."

◆

The royal caves were a good distraction, because if you lowered your guard for a moment, you could get your head chopped off.

Right now that sounded perfect.

I nodded at the guards at the main entrance and strolled into the caverns. They were lit with torches, the tunnel opening into several larger chambers. The largest one was the Great Hall, which suited the Drake family's very medieval tendencies. Just look at our only surviving matriarch, Veronique Dubois. She was even scarier than Mom was, and she could embroider your funeral shroud by hand. It was easy to accept Mom as a queen, or Veronique. Dad had that monarch thing going for him too. I had a harder time picturing the rest of us as royal princes. Connor didn't like people, vampire or otherwise. He just wanted to be left alone with his computers. Logan dressed like a pirate. And I knew more about pick-up lines than I did vampire politics—and I didn't have any great desire to learn more about it.

But I did have a great desire to stop vampire assassins from attacking my mom and my sister. So I'd man up and study vampire politics and show my face in court and pretend I knew what the hell was going on.

Anyway, it was better than mooning over Hunter Wild.

The Great Hall was drafty, the oil lamp lights flickering. It was saved from being damp and unwelcoming by the piles of thick rugs underfoot and the tapestries hanging from iron rods. Veronique had sent a huge banner embroidered with the Drake family crest and the royal vampire crest, which now hung behind a wooden table ringed with chairs. The chairs each had thick wooden backs, to protect against stakes, arrows, and daggers. Dad was all about treaties and diplomacy. Mom was all about the attack. Between the two of them they might actually be able to control the chaotic vampire tribes, at least for a little while.

Vampire tribes tended to be independent at best and belligerently autonomous at worst. Ruling them was mostly about making sure no one wiped each other out in such a public manner that we'd all be discovered. Prosaic but true.

"Quinn." Sebastian raised his eyebrows. "You walked right by that girl. What's wrong?"

"I did?" I looked over my shoulder. A vampire with short brown hair and beauty mark at the side of her mouth winked at me. I winked back. Then I turned back to Sebastian, horrified. "I didn't even see her."

"You're off your game."

"Shh, keep it down, will you?" I straightened my shirt. "I have a reputation. I'm going back. She's cute."

"Forget it. She flirts with everyone."

"So?" I grinned.

"Just come on. Mom and Dad are in the back room. And we can't handle any more disgruntled exes."

"My exes are never disgruntled." That was a point of pride actually. "Any more packages for Solange?" Solange's bloodchange pheromones, coupled with the old prophecy, had sent more vampires than we could count into a frenzy. They sent her gifts, stalked her, and generally acted like asses.

"Twelve letters, three packages, and a box of puppies."

I winced. "Puppies?"

"They're fine. Isabeau took them all."

"Good. Who eats puppies?" I shook my head.

"Yeah, Isabeau swore in French. A lot."

"Hot."

"Yeah, Logan nearly went cross-eyed."

"So where are they now?"

"Isabeau's gone back to the Hounds and Logan's studying up."

"He's studying?" I shuddered. "For what? Girlfriends give exams now?"

"He's an honorary Hound, remember," Sebastian reminded me as we passed two more guards and entered the private family room. Logan had gone through the ritual initiation of the Hounds, something that was rarely offered to anyone not already connected to the reclusive tribe. "So he wants to know more about them. Connor downloaded stuff from some ancient library in Rome."

"Do they know he hacked their system yet?"

"Hell no," Connor replied from where he was trying to fix Mom's laptop. "I'm just that good. Though even I can't get wireless down here."

"So what's going on?" I asked. "Dad looks like he's about to break into song. It's kind of scary actually." A grown man shouldn't wear that kind of goofy grin. Especially when he was my father.

"We just got word that a Blood Moon is being called for November."

"Seriously?" No wonder Dad looked so happy. Blood Moons were only very rarely called, and no one knew who exactly called them. It was essentially a week-long festival with the main night reserved for tribal leaders to talk treaties and various vampire issues. The last one had been nearly a hundred years ago. "Why now? 'Cause of Mom?"

Sebastian nodded. "And the *Hel-Blar.* They're becoming a real problem, and not just here in Violet Hill."

"Any word on why they swarmed the Helios-Ra school?" I asked.

Connor shook his head. "Nothing yet."

"Well, it sure as hell wasn't an accident. And you didn't see that *Hel-Blar* disintegrate. It was weird."

"We're looking into it," Dad called over to us. "And I mentioned it to Hart."

"Good. There are a lot of kids in that school."

Sebastian raised an eyebrow. "Not every day I hear you worrying about hunters."

I shrugged.

Connor snorted.

"Shut up," I told him. Sometimes the twin connection was a pain in the ass. I hadn't said a word to him about Hunter, but he already knew I was into her.

If the royal courts and all their melodrama weren't enough to stop me from thinking about her, I'd just have to think of something else.

"I'll check out the scene in town."

"Hot date?"

"Working on it."

CHAPTER 13

◆

Hunter

Saturday night

I know it's not very secret agent of me, but I really, *really* love dressing up.

Even if it's just to flitter around like dumb horror-movie vampire bait.

I love choosing a dress, shaving my legs, and painting my toes. I love pretty sandals with little heels, though I couldn't exactly wear them tonight. I'd never get a good kick in with those, and I wouldn't be able to outrun a raccoon. So I wore a pair of low-top Converse sneakers with my sundress. It was blue, with lace at the hem and spaghetti straps, which Grandpa thought were trampy because my shoulders were bare. I added a matching chunky turquoise necklace and pink lipstick.

Chloe grinned at me from where she sat on the edge of her bed. Against all odds, she was ready before me. And she wasn't wearing any jewelry or makeup. Just jeans and a tight T-shirt. Her hair was in a simple braid. I barely recognized her.

"You look great."

I twirled once. "If a vampire muddies this dress, I'm kicking ass."

"I'll help." Her eyes shone. I'd never seen her so happy to fight before. She usually preferred flirting with locals at the club over the actual work of bait-nights. Maybe she'd just changed over the summer and I was being paranoid. I really hoped so.

"Where are your weapons?" She tilted her head curiously.

I held up my purse. "In here. And I've got a stake strapped to my thigh."

"Ooh." She waggled her eyebrows. "Sexy."

"Yeah, yeah."

At the bottom of the stairs outside our room were clusters of whispering Niners. They stared at us like we were movie stars.

"Creepy much?" Chloe muttered at them.

Lia was the only one brave enough to step out of the pack. "Is it true you guys go to town and lure vampires out of clubs?"

I nodded.

"That is so *cool*," she breathed. "Can we do that?"

"You're not allowed off campus at night until you're sixteen," I said as we shut the front door behind us. We hurried down the lane to the garages, passing students out for a walk or a jog on the track and others lying in the grass by the pond and catching up with each other. Night had just barely settled over the school, making the old buildings look somehow quaint and old-fashioned. I wouldn't have been surprised to see the ghost of a Victorian gentleman or a pioneer woman churning butter on the porch of the headmistress's house. Jenna, Spencer, and Jason were waiting by the old van we'd booked for the night. It was unassumingly gray, clunky, and hideous. And it beat walking to town, hands down.

"Get in," Jenna said, sliding into the front seat before anyone else could. She loved driving almost as much as she loved shooting stuff.

"Shotgun!" Chloe yelled. She always got shotgun because she made mixes for the half-hour drive to town. I climbed in the back with Spencer and Jason.

"So where are we going?" Spencer asked as Jenna pulled out, scattering gravel. "The Blue Cat?"

"The Blue Cat shut down last month," Jason told him, raising his voice over the loud music that filled the van.

"What about Conspiracy Theory?" Jenna asked. Everyone nodded. Conspiracy wasn't a dance club like the Blue Cat had been, but it was a funky cafe in an old three-story house with live bands on the weekends. It'd be the most popular spot now—mostly because none of the other clubs let in minors as easily as Conspiracy Theory did.

I rolled my window down, enjoying the cool breeze that smelled like cedar and grass, flatly refusing to check my phone one more time. I had a life; I was busy taking out bloodthirsty vampires to make the neighborhood safe again. I didn't have time to wait around for Quinn Drake to deign to honor me with a reply.

The forest and mountains gave way to fields and farms and then the tiny town of Violet Hill, tucked into the edge of the lake. It was mostly art galleries and old bookstores and organic cafes. There were probably more crystal shops in the village than in all of San Francisco. Every July there was an art festival and people drew on the streets with chalk. There were farmers' markets and a pioneer museum. I loved it, even though Grandpa thought it was run by a bunch of, and I quote, "pot-smoking hippies." He could overlook that though, since it was a convenient crossroads for several vampire tribes, both civilized and *Hel-Blar*.

There were other creatures too, according to Spencer, but I'd never seen any of them. He was convinced there were werewolves, but even his professors in the Paranormal Department wouldn't give him a straight answer. I kept telling him that probably meant one of *them* was a werewolf. You never could tell at our school.

Jenna drove too fast, as always, so we made it to the main street in twenty minutes. Violet Lake looked like a dark blob of ink on the edge of the paper-white stones. We parked down the street from the coffeehouse and walked up through the abandoned factory district. All half a block of it. Violet Hill was nothing if not quaint.

"That's the one," Chloe said confidently, nodding to the old glass factory. Broken shards still glittered on the pavement, even though it had closed ten years ago. It was wide enough to maneuver in with some cover, so we wouldn't draw the attention of any late-night pedestrians. They mostly went in the other direction toward the taxi stand or the bus stop.

The lawn outside the cafe was littered with smokers, the music from the jazz-rock band pouring out of the open door. We eased through the crowds and claimed the torn velvet couch in the very back where the light was dim and the floors were sticky with spilled drinks. Candles burned everywhere in jam jars, and twinkly lights were wrapped around the bar counter. The buzz of the espresso machine was a constant vibration under the music.

I took everyone's drink orders since I was the bait. I was the one who had to prance around being all obvious and dumb. I giggled.

"Better," Spencer approved. "You sound less like you ate an angry helium balloon."

I made a face at him before making my way through the crowd toward the counter. I eyed the patrons unobtrusively. The three guys at the pool table were trying to look like predators, all suave and cool, but they were harmless. The girl in the back corner flirting with a guy in a leather coat was on my radar. She looked hungry and I didn't know if it was for attention or blood. The two at the table under the window were underage and desperately trying not to look it. The waitstaff looked harried and didn't have time to care who was drinking illegally and who wasn't. Besides, it was Violet Hill, possibly the most liberal, free-thinking town on the planet. Drinking was no big deal. Fur coats and pesticides on the other hand . . .

The bar was actually a series of old wooden doors hinged together. The one at the end had belonged to a saloon at the turn of the century. There were two bartenders and a press of thirsty people waving money and shouting orders over the band. I fluttered my eyelashes and leaned on the bar, making sure my cleavage, such as it was, was visible. Part 1 of the plan required I be seen.

"A shot of Kahlua, please," I ordered. I made sure my voice was a little too loud. I leaned farther over, catching the eye of two guys who were staring at me. The one on the left might possibly be vampiric. It was kind of hard to tell. I worked up an annoying giggle.

He raised his glass to me and eased out of the line, leaving a gap and a better view of the people on his other side.

I choked on the giggle.

"What the hell are you doing here?" I scowled at Quinn.

It was just my luck that he was lounging there with a pretty girl on each arm. No wonder he hadn't answered my text message.

And worse, he would catch Part 2 of the plan, in which I was soon going to make an ass of myself, and he'd miss Part 3, in which I redeemed myself by kicking actual ass.

"Buffy." He grinned, eyes flaring when he took in my short dress and daring neckline. I forced myself not to blush or fidget. I lifted my chin, daring him to make a single comment.

"Your name's Buffy?" The girl on his left sneered.

The other girl pinched her. "Don't be rude." She smiled at me apologetically.

Quinn didn't look away from me once during the whole exchange. I raised an eyebrow.

"Shouldn't you be tucked away safely in your little bed?" he asked.

"Shouldn't you be wearing a red velvet jacket and talking with a bad European accent?" I shot back.

"Are you really from Europe?" the first girl asked, misunderstanding. She ran her finger along his collar. "Do you live in a castle?"

I snorted and turned away, taking my shot glass off the sticky counter. Quinn's hand closed lightly around my wrist.

"You're not legal," he said, nodding at the Kahlua.

"My ID says differently," I assured him with a bland smile. I wasn't about to tell him that the drink was just for show. I needed to appear drunk. *Appear* being the operative word, because a drunk hunter was a dead hunter.

He leaned in, tucking my hair behind my ear and whispering so that only I could hear. His girlfriends frowned. Three guys and a girl near the band seemed suddenly interested in us.

"Where do you keep a stake in a dress like that?"

I angled my head to whisper back, half smiling. "Strapped to my thigh."

He drew back sharply, blue eyes burning. I smirked and flounced away. I could feel him watching me the entire way back to my table. The others had gotten their Cokes already and they drank them slowly, looking relaxed. Only I knew each of them had stakes inside their jackets, Hypnos in their sleeves, and blades in the soles of their boots.

I tossed back my shot with a flourish. I could hardly convince a vampire I was drunk if he couldn't smell alcohol on my breath.

Spencer frowned at me. "You know how you get when you drink," he said loudly.

I shrugged, laughed. "I'm just having fun. You should try it sometime." Under my breath I added, "The group by the stage, possibly two guys who went up to the second floor." I reached for the whiskey sour he'd left on the table, surreptitiously spilling most of it on the table.

"How many shots have you had?" Jason demanded.

"Just the one. Don't be such a spoilsport. *God*." I stumbled, just a little. Jason opened my purse and took out the three shot glasses I'd slipped in there before leaving. He made a big production of tossing them on the table and looking disgusted. I just laughed and prayed Quinn was too far away, too distracted by the pretty girls throwing themselves at him, to notice me.

"You promised you wouldn't drink," Chloe said.

"You guys are *lame*," I said, too loudly. A few heads turned our way. Chloe hid a gleam of satisfaction behind a fake worried scowl. I twirled away. "I'm going to dance if you're all going to be such boring old ladies."

This was the part I hated the most: dancing by myself like an idiot.

But it worked every time.

I twirled and shook my hips and giggled when I tripped into someone leaning against the amps. He caught me easily, smiling. His hands were cold, his eyes a pale hazel.

Vampire.

"I'm so sorry," I simpered at him.

"That's okay," he replied, still holding onto my arm. He was good, I'd give him that. His expression was open and guileless. He successfully avoided the silky menace that was always such a dead giveaway. With his blond hair and white T-shirt he looked like a local college student, the athletic sort with lots of interesting arm muscles and strong shoulders. Just the type a drunk underage high school student would flirt with.

I hated flirting.

"Thanks for catching me," I said, stepping closer. "My name's Amber."

"Of course it is." I pretended not to understand what he meant by that. "It's a very pretty name."

Ha.

"Your friends appear to be ditching you," he added. His own friends pressed closer. I turned my head to see Chloe and the others leaving.

I pouted. "They're no fun."

He was still holding on to my elbow. "We were just leaving too. They're shutting the doors in half an hour but there's a party down the street." He drew his hand down my arm. "Want to come with us, Amber?"

Gotcha, you undead bastards.

I bit my lip, tilted my head. "I don't even know your name."

"It's Matthew." He nodded to his friends. "That's Nigel, Paul, Sam, and Belinda."

There were a lot of teeth suddenly gleaming at me. The smiles were calculating. Amber, fictional though she might be, would have found them charming and fun. So I smiled back.

"Okay, I guess." The music pulsed between us. "Is it far?"

"Not at all." His hand moved to my lower back, pressing me forward and out the door. I had just enough time to glance at the bar. Quinn was gone.

Outside, the wind had cooled. Litter skittered along the curb.

Matthew led us down the street, toward the dark alleys, away from the pubs and restaurants, just as we'd planned. I hesitated.

"Come on," he said. "I thought you wanted to have some fun."

Nigel laughed. "Yeah, Amber, don't wimp out on us now."

I shrugged and let them convince me. The others would be positioned around the old glass factory. Jenna would likely be on a rooftop somewhere. We turned a corner, effectively shielding us from the parts of town still inhabited to the stretch of abandoned warehouses. Our footsteps echoed. The streetlights were dim.

Amber was an idiot.

But Chloe was a bigger idiot.

Chloe knew the plan.

It was her bloody idea in the first place to corner the vampires on the other side of the glass factory where there was an abandoned parking lot full of weeds, a broken-down wall for cover, and nothing else.

Not, I repeat, *not* by the road where anyone might drive by. It was unlikely, true, but still possible.

And yet there she was, hollering like a lunatic and launching herself at us.

I didn't know where the others were, beyond *not here* and not close enough to be of any immediate help. What had Spencer been thinking, to let her run off on her own?

She managed to knock Nigel off his feet, at least. She'd improved in the last week, but not enough to take on five vampires and survive, even with my help. I took advantage of the brief moment of surprise when the vampires whirled to see what crazy animal had pounced on their friend. I stepped back and liberated the stake from my thigh holster. Matthew glanced at me and licked his lips.

"Well, now, Amber," he said as his fangs protruded from his gums. "Aren't you suddenly more interesting."

I didn't waste my breath answering him. The other four circled Chloe, showing their own fangs.

If we lived through this, I was so going to kill her.

I only had the one stake. If I used it on Matthew, it left Chloe unprotected. And she was already on her knees, a hole ripped in her jeans, blood on her lip. She used her wrist harness to send a stake through Nigel's heart. He crumbled into ash. Go, Chloe.

Of course, now the rest of them were really pissed.

And I couldn't reach her.

Our teachers were always going on about how vampires would chase you if you ran away; the predator in them found it hard to resist the hunt.

I really hoped they were right about that.

As backup plans went, this one kind of sucked.

I turned and ran, pausing only to shoot Matthew the most taunting smirk I could manage. Because teasing an angry vampire is always such a good idea.

I ran fast.

Matthew, of course, was faster. Much, much faster. And so were his friends.

On the plus side, it left Chloe only one vampire to deal with, and he was fairly small.

On the minus side, it left me three.

I didn't make it to the glass factory parking lot, but I was close enough that a good yell should alert the others, if there wasn't a cold pale hand currently squeezing my trachea. I gagged on a breath, eyes burning. I clawed at the hand out of instinct, even though I knew it wouldn't do me any good. When I started to see spots, my training kicked back in.

I had a perfectly good stake.

I shoved it through Matthew's chest as hard as I could. My vision was gray and watery and lack of oxygen was becoming a serious issue. I didn't quite get his heart; I was an inch or so shy on the left. But at least it hurt him enough that he released me with a yell. Blood welled around the stake, still sticking out of his rib cage, while I heaved air into my screaming lungs. I also turned to deliver a kick to his wound with the heel of my shoe. He didn't turn to dust but he stumbled out of reach. And then Belinda had me by the hair, wrapping it around her wrist and yanking savagely.

I could all but hear Grandpa's grumble of disapproval.

Why did a certain kind of girl always go for the hair?

My neck muscles stretched near to breaking, my head angled painfully to the side, exposing my jugular. Saliva dripped on my arm and onto the ground. She was drooling. Gross.

"That wasn't very nice," Matthew said, approaching me. He plucked the stake out of his flesh as if it were a thorn off a rose-bush. Red petals of blood scattered around him. Belinda held me steady for him, giving into the temptation of my blood by nipping me once. It was no worse than a bee sting but I recoiled, going cold down to my bones. She licked at the tiny puncture marks as if I was bleeding ice cream.

"Ew," I tried to elbow her. "Get off me."

I couldn't see how Chloe was doing, couldn't even hear her. I could only see Matthew's sharp teeth and the way he twirled the bloody stake over his knuckles, like a street juggler. Even his polo shirt was suddenly menacing.

"Ever wonder how it feels to get one of these in the heart?" he asked pleasantly.

I tried to shrink back, even as Belinda forced me forward. I crushed her instep. She didn't let me go but she did swear viciously, which I enjoyed.

Where the hell was everyone?

"It seems only fair," Matthew continued. "A bit of karma, if you will." He twirled the stake again. "Shall we see how long you scream?"

"Are you ever going to shut up?" I snapped, fear and irritation filling me in equal measures. "This isn't your monologue, Hamlet. It's the battle scene, in case you've forgotten."

His eyes narrowed so fast they nearly sparked. They were the color of honey on fire. One of the others growled like an animal, low in his throat. It made all the hairs on my arms stand straight up.

I was going to die for making fun of Shakespeare.

My English Lit professor would be so proud.

And then Matthew was screaming.

The stake clattered at my feet but I couldn't reach it. I used Belinda's iron grip to secure a pivot that knocked Sam off both his feet as he came at me. Out of the corner of my eye, I saw Matthew hit the ground, broken glass grinding under his weight. There was a blur of movement and then the shadow coalesced into a dark shirt, pale skin, and blue eyes like burning gasoline.

Quinn.

I had no idea where he'd come from and I didn't have time to wonder about it. Belinda was clacking her teeth at me.

"I said"—I elbowed her in the nose, hearing bone snap—"get"—I used the side of my hand to chop at her wrist—"off!" And then I dropped, pulling her off balance so that she stumbled. I used the momentum of a roll to toss her over. I managed to stretch just enough to reach the stake. I blocked Belinda's second attack, mostly by happy accident. I twisted the stake and shoved it as hard as I could. She went to ash and drifted over the dirty pavement.

Matthew howled. He reared up furiously, slashing at Quinn with a penknife. I threw a rock at his head and kicked back to trip Paul before he could make a grab for me. Quinn leaned so far back his hair brushed the ground. He went into the turn completely and landed beside me.

"Back-to-back," he ordered, but I was already pressing my shoulder blades against his. Standard hand-to-hand combat stance.

He was grinning.

I rolled my eyes. "How is this fun for you?"

He shrugged one shoulder. "Not ash yet."

"I can fix that," Matthew hissed.

"You're right," Quinn said conversationally to me, as if we weren't currently outnumbered and fighting for our lives. "This one just won't shut up." Quinn's punch was so fast I heard the crack of one of Matthew's fangs against Quinn's knuckle. I didn't see it but the sound was unique. "Let me help you with that."

"You broke my tooth!" Matthew spat blood, the whites of his eyes going red with rage. It was just distracting enough that I missed

Paul's fist, until it caught my cheekbone. Pain bloomed over my face. I'd have a wicked bruise by morning. I stumbled back, bumping Quinn's arm. He flicked a glance over his shoulder.

"Shit," he said."Your face."

"Ow." I agreed.

"Where the hell are your friends?"

"I don't know." But at least all the vampires were attacking us, not Chloe. Right now I wanted to kill her myself. I fumbled for the silver whistle around my neck, hanging next to the Drake coronation medallion. I only wore it on bait-nights. It looked like a little silver pendant but it was much more useful. I blew into it and the shrill whistle pierced the night.

"I don't even want to know," Quinn muttered, moving so fast he was a dark shadowy blur like ink spilled in the shape of a man. He was fighting off all three vampires as best he could, circling me protectively like dark fog.

"Let me help," I shouted.

"You're hurt."

"I'm *fine*." I insisted. The day one little punch, vampiric or not, took me out of an entire fight was the night I was no longer a Wild. "Let me in," I adjusted the hold on my stake, slippery with Matthew's blood. My throat hurt from being strangled, my face hurt from being punched, and we were surrounded.

And I was kind of having fun.

Probably not a good sign.

CHAPTER 14

◆

Hunter

"On your right," Quinn barked, materializing on my other side. I jabbed the stake to my right and caught flesh and bone, but not heart. Still, Paul stumbled and slowed down enough that I could see him clearly now, even in the dim light of a single faded streetlight. I jabbed again, hit closer to the heart.

And then everyone else was there in answer to my whistle. Jenna's wicked aim took out Sam with a crossbow arrow. Jason stood back, holding Chloe, who clutched her side. I saw Spencer pop his vial of Hypnos and knew what he was about to do.

I took a deep breath, whirled, and grabbed Quinn, jerking him toward me. His eyes widened. My mouth closed over his just as Spencer tossed the Hypnos. It was everywhere, like confectioners' sugar on a cupcake.

"Vampires stop!" he yelled.

I kissed Quinn harder, making sure he wasn't inhaling any of the powder. He kissed me back, returning the favor.

His mouth was just as delicious as I'd imagined it would be. Not that I'd been thinking clearly about it. Not that I was capable of thinking right at that moment anyway.

His lips were cool, as if he'd been eating ice cream. His hands gripped my arms, holding me tight against his chest. His tongue touched mine, lightly, then deeper, until even my knees felt weak. I kissed him back. I wasn't going to pull away and be the only one feeling soft as water. He made a sound in the back of his throat, like a groan or a purr.

It made me feel stronger than if I'd been fully armed.

His eyes opened, the pupils wide and very black. It was a long hot moment before I realized the sounds of battle had faded altogether, and not just because of the kiss. I pulled away, taking a deep breath. I knew I was blushing, knew Quinn could feel the warmth of my blood rushing to the surface of my skin. I took another breath.

Everyone was staring at us.

"Dude," Spencer said.

I cleared my throat, taking a big step away from Quinn. I couldn't look at him. I didn't want to know yet if he was smirking. Matthew and Paul, the only two remaining vampires were slumped at our feet, glaring at us with furious pale eyes. Jenna stood over them, crossbow at the ready.

"Hypnos is going to wear off soon," she warned.

I pushed my hair off my face. "We need to tie them up." My voice was only a little squeaky.

"What for?" Quinn asked. "Stake them."

We all stared at him. "They're prisoners of war," I said.

"They're vampires."

"So are you."

"So I know what I'm talking about."

I shook my head. "You can't be serious."

"You haven't seen your face, Hunter," he said coldly.

No, but I could feel it. The bruise was already throbbing under my eye and across my left cheekbone.

"We can't just kill them in cold blood," I insisted as the heat of battle faded. "We're not assassins."

"Then I'll do it."

I stepped between him and the vampires. "Don't."

"He has a point," Jason said quietly.

"Hello? Killing a prisoner of war? Do you know how much detention that would be?" I swung around to stare at him. And now that they were immobilized, we'd have to stake them when they couldn't fight back. Maybe I was being stupid, but it felt wrong this way. It was different in battle.

"Whatever we do, we have to do it fast," Jenna interrupted us. "Like in the next three minutes."

"We have enough rope to tie them up and call the mobile unit. They'll come get them and lock them up."

"Your puny knots won't hold them," Quinn said as I flipped open my cell phone and hit speed dial.

"Then your vampire ones will." I gave him a dry glance, waiting for the call to go through. "So get tying."

Jenna handed him the rope hanging from her belt. Quinn sighed after a moment and took it. "This is a bad idea," he muttered, yanking hard on the rope.

"I'm with you," Jason muttered back.

"Chloe needs a medic," I said after I'd given our coordinates to the agent on the other line. I slipped the phone back in my purse. "So why don't you guys take her back and I'll stay here and wait for the unit."

"It's just a flesh wound," she tried to joke. "Ow. Stupid vampire speed. Used my own knife against me."

"You shouldn't have snuck off on us," Spencer said flatly to Chloe. "And you're not staying here alone," he told me firmly.

"I'll stay," Quinn said quietly.

I turned back to him, surprised. "You don't have to. This is what we're trained for, remember?"

"I'm staying." He raised an eyebrow. "You need me."

I opened my mouth to argue, just on principle, but Spencer cut in. "He's right." He tossed me an extra vial of Hypnos from his belt. "Just in case."

"Chloe's starting to bleed on my new shoes," Jenna interjected. "So let's go already."

I bit my lip. "Should I go with you?" I asked her. "Are you okay?"

She was a little pale but she looked more mad than in pain. "I'm fine. I'm sure I just need a couple of stitches."

"And a smack on the head," Jenna told her. "You *knew* the plan."

"Can you yell at me later?"

"Count on it. We were in position. We almost didn't get here in time."

They hurried off, still bickering. The night was silent and a hundred shades of blue and gray. The streetlight made the shattered glass look as if some of the stars had fallen from the sky, littering the pavement. It was almost pretty.

You know, except for the two vampires currently tied up and wanting to kill me, the other vampire scowling at me, and the throbbing of my face.

I shook my head. "Grandpa would just love this."

Quinn looked at me quizzically.

"The fact that a vampire is helping me babysit two other vampires," I explained.

"Not a fan of the alliance?" he mocked.

"Um, no."

"This bunch was hunting tourists all summer," he said. "The papers were full of animal attacks on hikers, but animals don't bite throats and drink blood. And now they've moved on to high school girls and college students. Not all bad vampires are conveniently blue," he added, referring to the *Hel-Blar*.

"I didn't say I wanted to buy them cake," I defended myself. "I just don't want to murder them either."

"They'd have murdered you."

"All the more reason to not do what they'd do."

His grin was crooked. "You must drive your grandfather crazy."

I half grinned back. "Probably. And, ironically, he'd agree with you. He'd want me to stake them as well."

"I like him already."

"He'd want me to stake you too."

"That's just because he's never met me. I can be very charming."

"I bet you can. The girls at the cafe seemed to think so anyway." Now *why* had I said that? He gave me his usual insufferable smirk. I was spared his reply when he tilted his head.

"Two cars, from the north."

"That'd be the unit. Maybe you should go."

"I'm not leaving you here."

"I just meant the League might have questions, might . . . you know. Vampire. Car full of vampire hunters. You do the math."

"You're worried about me," he said softly, stepping closer. I was suddenly very aware of my short sundress and my bare shoulders.

"It's only polite," I replied. "And I want something from you."

"That sounds promising." He dipped his head toward mine. "And that kiss wasn't polite."

I swallowed. "I was saving you from the Hypnos."

"Remind me to thank you later."

There was the sound of engines approaching, loudly enough that I even could hear them. "Please just go."

"Let me take you home," he murmured. "I'll hide if you tell them you've got a way home already."

I met his eyes, could see the glitter of them even in the darkness. "Why?"

His mouth brushed my ear, sending shivers over my scalp and down my neck.

"Because you want to."

The worst of it was, Quinn was right.

I did want to be alone with him.

Luckily the two vehicles stuffed with stern Helios-Ra agents screeching around the corner were rather distracting. Quinn was somewhere in the dark shadows of the warehouse district and I was standing alone with two bound vampires at my feet. I probably looked fairly impressive, especially for a student.

I just felt confused.

"Hunter Wild?" the extremely competent-looking woman asked as she slid out of the passenger seat of the first SUV. She had nose plugs loose around her neck and a phone earpiece wrapped around her left ear.

I nodded. "Yes, that's me."

"Your call came in," her companion added. He was very tall, with incredibly white teeth and a nose that had clearly been broken repeatedly and tilted drastically to the left. He would have looked scary to anyone else, especially with the scar tissue on his neck. To me, he just looked like family.

"Brandon." I grinned. "Nice to see you."

He grinned back and nodded to the vampires. "Nice job, kid."

"I had help," I hastened to explain. "There were five or six of us. The rest took Chloe back to school for stitches. I'm just the last on cleanup."

"That would be us, actually," the woman said, waving the others out to grab the vampires. "Good work, Wild. I see your family reputation isn't just hype."

"Thanks." I shrugged one shoulder. I wanted to tell them Quinn had helped us but I wasn't sure if that would just make everything more complicated. They'd definitely take me back to school themselves if they knew he was still lurking around. It was best to pass on the info to Kieran to pass on to Hart. "So what's going to happen to them?" I asked as the vampires were tossed into the back of the van.

"Don't worry about that," she said grimly. "We know Matthew. We've been trying to find his nest for weeks now."

I swallowed. I really hoped I hadn't just handed prisoners of war over to an execution squad. "Brandon?"

"Don't worry about it, kid. It'll be fine." Which wasn't exactly an answer. He held the door open. "Hop in, we'll take you home."

"That's okay," I said, lying through my teeth. "We took one of the bikes and I should get it back. It's just on Honeychurch Street." Which was around the corner, near the cafe. I really hoped Quinn hadn't been lying when he said he'd get me back. I didn't have enough cash to call a taxi and I wasn't looking forward to the hour-and-a-half walk in the dark back to school.

"Are you sure?"

I nodded, trying to smile like everything was normal. He gave me a friendly salute.

"All right, get gone then. We'll keep an eye on you until you reach the corner. Movie theater'll be letting out the late show. You should be fine." He winked. "Anyway, you got the bad guys already."

"I guess so." I walked away, casting glances out of the corner of my eye to see if I could spot Quinn. There were only squat gray buildings with broken windows and tall weeds growing between the cracks in the pavement. A raccoon waddled behind a garbage can.

The Helios-Ra SUV and the van idled until I reached the corner and waved, before turning onto Blitt Street. Sure enough, there were loads of people coming out of the theater and out of Conspiracy, which was closing its doors. I eased back into the mouth of the alley between a bookstore and an occult shop with crystals glimmering in the display window. Even closed down for the night it smelled strongly of Nag Champa incense. Spencer hung out here all the time, digging through herbs and stones and bronze statues, all in the pursuit of secret spells and magic amulets. I wondered, not for the first time, if the proprietor had any idea how many of her customers were undercover vampire hunters.

I also wondered where Quinn had gone off to.

I flicked my hair back and tapped my foot impatiently. Five more minutes and then I'd have to find my own way. I couldn't wait all night. Not when it was Quinn we were talking about. He might have seen some cute girl and would spend the next hour flirting with her and forget all about me.

"In case I haven't mentioned it yet, you clean up good, Wild."

Or not.

I turned to see him drop down off a fire escape behind me. It was at least three floors up but he landed as gracefully as a cat, looking just as smug as one.

"Show off," I said blandly.

He shrugged one shoulder. "I don't believe in hiding who I am."

"Um, isn't that kind of a requirement when you're a vampire?"

"In general, yes. But you already know I'm a vampire, so why pretend otherwise? I won't lie to you, Hunter."

Damn, he was good at that smoldering thing.

My insides quivered a little, despite myself. Maybe I'd been reading too many romance novels lately.

"Come on," he said softly. "I'll take you home."

It felt weirdly normal to cross the street with him, like all the other couples heading for their cars. We must have looked like we'd been on a date, especially when he led me to his black convertible Mustang and opened the passenger door for me. The seats were soft leather and all the chrome shone as if it had been recently polished. There wasn't a speck of dust or a single piece of trash on the floor mats.

"Nice car," I said, mostly to fill the sudden silence.

"Yeah, it was my aunt's car back in the day. She's a pack rat, thank God."

I had to laugh. "Only a Drake would pack-rat a car, like a memento."

"You should see some of the stuff she keeps." He shuddered. I couldn't help but be curious.

"Like what?"

"Finger bones."

"Um . . . ew."

"You want ew? She keeps them in an old Cadbury box. Try being seven years old and thinking you found the jackpot secret stash of chocolate. Talk about a rude awakening." He shook his head, throwing his car into reverse and backing away from the curb. "Put me off chocolate for a good year and a half."

The wind was warm on my face and lifted my hair every which way. It'd be a mess of tangles by the end of the ride but I didn't care. It felt nice to sit in a car with a boy. I could almost pretend it was that simple.

"Did you ever find out whose fingers they were?"

He shot me an incredulous look. "You don't ask Aunt Ruby questions."

"Why, is she mean or something?"

"No, just insane." He said it nonchalantly, without judgment. It was just fact.

"Oh."

"Hunters killed her family."

"Vampires killed mine," I pointed out defensively.

His voice softened. "I wasn't accusing you, Hunter."

I winced. He had saved my life tonight. I shouldn't be snapping at him. "Sorry."

He shrugged. "No big deal. It's weird, isn't it?"

"What is?"

"Treaties and all that. It's like we woke up one morning and we weren't supposed to be enemies anymore. It'll take some getting used to."

"True," I said. "I think it's really cool though."

"Unfortunately, not everyone agrees."

I thought of my grandfather and what he would do if he could see me now. "I know. But it's worth protecting."

"Yes," he said, and something about the way he was looking at me made me think he was talking specifically about me. "It is."

That was crazy though, wasn't it? I was just a hunter to him, one of the guys. But he hadn't called me Buffy since the cafe. He'd actually used my real name. Did that mean anything? *Get a grip, Wild,* I told myself. *He was also making out with at least two different girls not three hours ago.*

He slowed the car before we reached the turnoff for the school. He pulled into the undergrowth and turned the engine off, killing the lights. We were well-hidden by the grass and low-hanging tree branches. Fireflies winked at us from the field across the street. There wasn't a single other person, human or vampire, anywhere. Even the stars hid themselves behind thin clouds, as if to give us privacy.

"I got your text while I was waiting for you. You have a favor to ask me?" he said, turning to face me. Even in the darkness, his cheekbones were strong, his face pale. His teeth gleamed, looking slightly too sharp even with his fangs retracted.

"So you did get it?" I asked, suddenly babbling. "I wasn't sure. I mean, sometimes we don't get very good reception at school. But I guess you know that, living on a farm and all." *Shut up, shut up, shut up.*

He smiled slowly. "Hunter, are you nervous?"

"Shut up."

"Are you going to ask me to prom?" he teased.

"Shut up," I repeated, choking on a horrified laugh.

He grinned. "I look pretty good in a tux."

I rolled my eyes, suddenly comfortable again. "And you're so refreshingly modest."

"It's a curse," he agreed cheerfully. Then his eyes went from silver rain to stormy lake. "And you're still wearing the coronation medallion."

I felt like I'd been caught mooning over his photograph. I tucked the pendant back into my dress. I wiped my damp palms on my lap. "Can I trust you with school secrets?"

"Helios-Ra secrets? Cool." He leaned back, satisfied.

I bit my lip. "Never mind. This was a bad idea."

He touched my hand. "I'm kidding. What is it?"

I hoped I wasn't about to make a really big mistake. He felt trustworthy though, even with the charming smirks and the fangs. I pulled the vitamin I'd stolen from Chloe's bag out of my purse. It was in a little plastic bag, the kind you get when you buy jewelry. "I need to have this analyzed," I explained quietly.

"You must have labs here at school."

"We do. But I don't know anyone well enough to trust them with it."

"But you trust me."

"Yes." Even if it didn't make any sense.

He took the pill, frowned at it. "Looks like a vitamin."

"I'm really hoping that's all it is."

"But you think it's something else?"

I nodded. "Chloe's taking them and she's been weird and moody."

His eyebrows rose. "Steroids?"

"Maybe. She's obsessed with taking them and working out and getting strong, so it's possible. And that guy Will? The one we took to the infirmary? He said something about vitamins too, remember?"

"Huh. How is he anyway?"

"Nothing definitive yet. And no one will tell us anything about that *Hel-Blar* woman who disintegrated. There's definitely some weird shit going on."

"Yeah, that wasn't normal," Quinn agreed. "I'll see if my brother Marcus can analyze this. He's good with that sort of thing. I'd ask my uncle, the biology teacher, but he'd have way too many questions." He slipped my only piece of evidence into his pocket.

"Can you analyze this too?" I asked, pulling the blood samples out of my purse. I was the kind of girl who carried blood in her purse and daggers in her boots.

Maybe I should see the school counselor.

I felt nervous but relieved at the same time as he pocketed the samples. A totally uncharacteristic giggle stuck in my throat. I might finally get some answers after all. I touched his wrist and it was cool under my fingertips. "Thank you."

He paused, eyes narrowing. "You're not taking this stuff too, are you?" he asked sharply.

"No way." He leaned closer, sniffing along my collarbone and under my jaw. "What are you doing?" I whispered.

"Just checking," he answered, somewhat hoarsely.

"Checking what?" My pulse fluttered.

"We can usually smell drugs in a human's bloodstream. We can definitely taste it."

"I told you I'm not on anything."

"I know. You smell like . . . raspberries . . . and limes."

"Is that . . . good?"

I felt him smile against my skin. "Yes."

"Oh." I swallowed. It was getting difficult to form a coherent sentence. "So, you could sniff Chloe? Or Will? And know if something was wrong."

"Maybe. I'd rather breathe *you* in, though."

Yup, he was really, *really* good at this.

I actually felt like I was melting, like I was on fire, like I'd swallowed those fireflies.

He pulled back just enough to look at me, as if I was a puzzle that needed solving, or a candy he wasn't sure he was allowed to eat.

Bad analogy.

His fangs lengthened, but only a little. I wouldn't even have noticed if I wasn't used to watching for things like that. And it didn't make me nervous for some reason. I wasn't scared, and not just because I had a purse full of small sharp weapons. There was something between us suddenly, and it wasn't merely a secret unraveling.

It was something else, something more forbidden, more mysterious, more delicious.

I closed the tiny gap between us, swaying toward him as if he was a magnet. Our eyes connected, held. His pupils dilated, irises lightened. I smiled.

"You're not the only one who wants a taste," I said.

And then he was kissing me, or I was kissing him. We were just suddenly in each other's arms, like lightning—not there, then just suddenly there. Everywhere. His mouth was wicked, his tongue bold. I couldn't get enough. I tingled all over. His hand dug into my hair, cradled the back of my neck. He pulled me closer. The muscles of his arms were sinewy under my palms.

I'd never felt like this before.

He was a vampire and I didn't care.

I was a hunter and I didn't care.

I could barely catch my breath and I didn't care.

I just wanted more.

And then the car could barely contain us and his elbow accidentally hit the horn. The sudden noise cut through the warm summer night and we jumped, pulling apart. I was light-headed, disoriented. My lips felt warm, swollen.

He smiled ruefully, forcing himself to release me. "Guess that's my cue to take you home."

"I'd better walk from here," I murmured. "Surveillance cameras."

"Text me when you get in," he said. "I'll wait right here until you do."

"Okay." I was pretty dazed, surprised that I could stand up properly. I was really glad he looked just as bewildered.

"Good night, Hunter."

CHAPTER 15

◆

QUINN

I grinned all the way home.

I'd bailed on two hot girls, nearly been staked, and had to hide from a car full of vampire hunters in full battle gear.

Totally worth it.

Nicholas was on the front porch when I pulled the car up the driveway. He shielded his eyes from the glare of the headlights, fangs gleaming.

"How was your date?" he asked as I slammed the car door shut.

"Which one?"

"Show-off."

"With great hotness comes great responsibility," I answered. I was still grinning.

"Up for patrol, pretty boy?"

"Always." I was still wired from the fight and the kiss. Kicking *Hel-Blar* ass sounded like the perfect way to end the evening.

"There's a pack in the hall closet," Nicholas told me. I went in and grabbed it along with a handheld crossbow, stuffed into the sleeve of an old coat no one ever wore. It was my favorite, and I had the worst time hiding it from Lucy. I slung the pack over my shoulder and went back outside.

There were still some scorch marks at the end of the porch and a soggy plank that would rot through if we didn't replace it soon. Hope's rogue Helios-Ra unit had done some serious damage when they'd tried to blast their way through the house. We hadn't finished all the repairs yet but at least we'd patched up the big gaping hole in the wall.

I tied my hair back and loaded the crossbow. An unloaded crossbow would be about as useful as a spoon. Mom could have been an undead boy scout with all her "Be Prepared" speeches. "Let's go."

On the farm and in the thick woods around the mountains where we patrolled, we didn't have to hold back. We could move as fast as we wanted and not worry that we might appear blurry to human eyes. There was freedom in that, and exhilaration.

I hadn't been lying when I told Hunter I didn't believe in hiding who and what I was. I also didn't believe in moping about because I happened to be undead.

In my opinion, being a vampire kicked ass.

And undead was better than dead.

Okay, when I was human, the thought of drinking blood had me worried I was in for a lifetime of an eat-your-

Brussels-sprouts-they're-good-for-you diet. But once I'd changed, so had my taste buds. Why turn your nose up at what kept you alive? Or, not dead? Whatever.

The only drawback, as far as I could see, was that it was easier to score a cheeseburger than a pint of blood. And I missed the whole sunlight thing, but I got over that pretty quickly. It made me feel like crap now anyway. Duncan was the one who moaned about daylight and not being able to taste coffee anymore.

I just counted myself lucky that girls thought vamps were cool, even if they never actually realized I was a vampire. Pheromones had their uses.

The irony that I wasn't crushing on one of those girls, but on the type that *killed* vampires, wasn't lost on me.

But I wasn't going to let it ruin my night. Or the taste of her, still on my lips.

"You're actually strutting," Nicholas muttered.

"Just a little. It's good for the soul." I ducked under a low-hanging branch. The smells of damp earth and cold wind and cedar was thick as smoke. "Finally got rid of that Matthew vampire and his gang." We hadn't had a lot of time to deal with him what with Solange dying at her own birthday party. And anyway, the Drakes weren't vampire police. We just tried to take care of our own backyard. I wasn't joking when I told Hunter not all bad vampires are easily recognizable.

"Are they dust?"

"Not all of them. Hunter and her friends were there. She called in some Helios-Ra cleanup crew to take them into custody."

"And they just left you there?" he asked incredulously.

"Like I hung around to shake hands."

The forest was dark and full of shifting shadows but we could see just fine. Another perk to vampirism: really great night vision. I saw the leaves shifting, the outline of tree branches and ferns and the path glowing as if the moon were full over head. Everything seemed to glitter, just a little, around the edges. An owl called from some pine bough, searching for unwary mice. The owl would have to find new hunting grounds or go hungry tonight. Vampires tend to scare small animals into hiding.

Nicholas paused, sniffed. His expression went flat. "Hel-Blar," he mouthed.

I nodded, catching a whiff of boiled mushrooms and mildew. If the Hel-Blar ever got their shit together and figured out how to cover their stench, they'd really be a force to be reckoned with.

I took point, steadying the crossbow. Nicholas walked backward behind me, a stake in each hand. There was no one I trusted at my back more than one of my brothers.

The Hel-Blar came in a wave, three of them swinging down from a branch, bursting out of a thicket, and leaping out from behind a thick elm tree. A crossbow bolt hit the first one in the chest, piercing his rib cage and his heart. He screeched and crumbled into a gray dust. The next one crashed into me, knocking my crossbow into a patch of primroses. Nicholas was occupied shoving a stake, only half-stuck, into the last one.

"Drakes," my Hel-Blar laughed at his companion. "Even better."

His many fangs clicked at me hungrily and the sound was like bones breaking. I leaped back out of the way, avoiding the drip of his saliva. No one knew how contagious it really was. And this guy didn't look like he was about to conveniently disintegrate, like the woman at the high school. Whatever sickness she'd had clearly wasn't widespread through the *Hel-Blar*.

He followed my backward bend, clinging like a barnacle. I used momentum against him, falling into the undergrowth and flipping him over my head. He landed in a crouch, snarling over his shoulder. His veins were nearly black under his blue skin. There was fresh blood under his fingernails.

I didn't bother scrambling to my feet; I just rolled toward my discarded crossbow. The first bolt missed, biting into a birch tree and sending papery bark into the air.

"Nick, you okay?" I yelled. He grunted what I thought was a "yes." I loosed another bolt and it missed the heart again, but at least it sliced through his shoulder. He hissed in pain.

Good.

Except now he had an open bleeding wound that might contaminate Nicholas or me.

Bad.

And now my *Hel-Blar* was closing in and staying just in front of Nicholas so that if I used my crossbow I risked shooting my own brother. I was usually a pretty good shot but there were just too many variables. I exchanged my crossbow for the stake inside my coat and launched myself into the fray, hollering.

I don't care what Mom says about the advantage of surprise; a good battle yell can sometimes make the difference between winning or losing.

The *Hel-Blar* yelled back and then we were grappling again, trying to see who could cause the most damage. He didn't have a weapon. They mostly used their numerous fangs and the threat of their poisoned blood. I shoved the stake toward his chest and he blocked it, trying to shove it back. I held on with a viselike grip, my fangs burning through my gums, my fingers cramping around the stake. Out of the corner of my eye I saw a cloud of ash and heard Nicholas cough. *Hel-Blar* ashes were nasty.

I kneed the *Hel-Blar* in the groin and then used my free arm to drive my elbow into the back of his neck. Already doubled over, he staggered and folded further.

Right into my upraised stake.

The force of his flailing body drove me to my knees, and then I was alone with the ashes drifting into the grass and the blood-stained stake. I dropped it, scrubbing my palms clean in a pile of fallen leaves.

"Three down." I pushed to my feet. "Not bad." I dusted my shirt off, grimacing. "But I'm going to smell like soggy mushrooms for the rest of the night."

"Did that seem kind of easy to you?" Nicholas wondered out loud.

"Easy? Are you smelling the smell?"

"Seriously. Didn't they seem tired to you?"

I frowned. "I guess they could have fought harder. It's not like they laid down and died for us like that chick at the school though."

A flock of birds winged into the sky in the near distance, inter-rupting us with their excited squawking. We exchanged a knowing glance, breaking into a run. Nothing tired out the *Hel-Blar* like fight-ing or feasting. And both would disturb a flock of sleeping birds.

We ran harder. The wind pushed at my face with cool fingers. Our feet barely touched the ground, broke no twigs, made no sound to betray our presence.

What gave us away was the shocked sound both Nicholas and I made, abandoning all of our training in two choked curses.

It was hard to stay stealthy when you stumbled across your baby sister, ankle-deep in a mountain stream, red-pupiled, fangs flashing, and stakes flying from her fingertips.

Hel-Blar clicked their jaws at her from both banks, blue-tinged as poison beetles. She looked our way. Either she didn't have the time to recognize us or we'd really pissed her off.

One stake whistled toward us, then another.

"Solange, no!" I yelled.

Nicholas was too busy running forward, heedless of the stake aimed at his heart.

Because Lucy lay at Solange's feet, sprawled over the black river pebbles, her blood leaking like red ribbons into the water.

CHAPTER 16

◆

Hunter

Later Saturday night

I texted Quinn on my way to the infirmary to let him know I was safely on campus. Chloe was standing right inside the door, a bandage under her T-shirt and another one on her forearm. She was pale and her pupils were dilated but otherwise she seemed all right.

"I feel good," she said, weaving on her feet. Her smile went decidedly goofy. "Theo's nice."

"Theo gave you painkillers." I was relieved to see she was fine.

"Yup. Better than vitamins. Better than *candy*." She sounded shocked. And she was slurring her speech.

"Sit down before you fall on your face." I nudged her gently into a chair.

She poked her bandage. "Do I have a ghost arm now? Can't feel it."

"Stop that," I told her. "Or it'll hurt like hell tomorrow."

"'Kay."

"If you start drooling I'm taking pictures."

"'Kay."

I was grinning at her when the shouting started. I leaped forward just as the curtain to the back examination rooms swung open. Will thundered toward me. I was surprised enough just to stand there and stare at him. He was faintly blue, his eyes bloodshot. It didn't really register at first. Theo and Jenna were behind him and so was Spencer, holding a cloth to his neck. The cloth was rapidly turning red, almost as rapidly as he was turning white.

"Stake him!" Theo shouted at me. There was a long hypodermic needle in his hand. "Stake him now, Hunter!"

"What?" I had the stake in my hand. I was close enough to reach him. I was also frozen. "Are you kidding?"

"Now!" All three of them yelled in unison. It was enough to get me moving. So was Will, lunging at me, saliva dripping off his fangs. When did he grow fangs? There was mottled bruising on his neck and two festering puncture wounds. Jenna threw a tube of antibiotic ointment, hitting the alarm button on the wall. Help was coming.

But not fast enough.

"Shit!" I yelled, because I had to yell something. Will was wearing one of those hospital paper gowns, with the same tousled hair as always, the same earnest face. He was the class sweetheart for every class, even if they weren't in his year. He was nice to everyone. He wouldn't hurt a fly, which made vampire hunting problematic. But his parents wouldn't hear of him dropping out. So he did the best he could and immersed himself in the Science Department, where there was less actual fighting.

He was the one who asked the shy girls hiding in the corner to dance at school functions.

And now he was the one hissing at me.

Definitely not Will anymore.

"Shit!" I hollered again as his fist cracked against my shoulder. It didn't reach my face because I'd leaped sideways, but not quite fast enough. There was blood on his mouth. And blood on Spencer's throat and hemp T-shirt.

Every ounce of training snapped to attention inside me.

I went with my sideways lunge and then spun around so I came up behind Will. He was in the classic newborn *Hel-Blar* frenzy, which I'd read about but never actually seen in person. Their thirst for blood was primal and vicious and unstoppable. The moment I'd left his line of vision, he'd focused on Chloe, who was weaker. She was slouched in the hard plastic chair, giggling.

"You smell like old socks," she told him pleasantly, before shaking her head. "No, like mushrooms." She looked concerned. "That's bad, right? I can't remember why that's bad."

She was still babbling to herself when he lunged for her and I lunged for him. My stake went through his skin where his hospital gown gaped open. I angled it away from his shoulder blade and then pushed with as much strength as I had, still shouting profanities. Because cursing was better than thinking about what I was doing.

Staking a friend.

He yelped, tried to spin around to grab at the stake. He managed half a spin, just enough to meet my eyes before he crumbled into ashes on the shiny linoleum floor. Theo was the first to reach me. His hands were on my shoulders.

"Did he bite you? Are you hurt? Hunter?"

I didn't drop my stake, because I'd been taught never to drop my weapon, but my fingers felt weak, my palms sweaty. I thought I might throw up.

"Hunter, are you hurt?"

I shook my head, gagged.

"Hey!" Theo shook me. "You can't go into shock right now."

I blinked, vision going back to normal. The gray spots floated away. "I'm okay," I answered hoarsely. "What the hell just happened?"

Jenna handed me a paper cup of water. "You just saved all our asses."

I drank, mostly because I didn't know what else to do with myself. "I didn't save Will."

"You saved Chloe," she said quietly.

"And no one could have saved Will," Theo added. He went to Spencer, who was leaning against the wall, eyes glassy and hair damp with sweat.

"He bit you," I said flatly.

Spencer nodded weakly. "I'm okay."

"I've already given him his first antibiotic injection," Theo said, lifting Spencer's eyelids to check his pupils.

"That didn't help Will," I said quietly, trying not feel the panic swelling inside me.

"Will's bite was worse," Theo said. Spencer winced when he applied more pressure on his wound. "He barely grazed him. Still, you're all going to have to get out of here. He needs to be quarantined."

"What? No!" Jenna exclaimed. "You just said he'd be fine."

He hadn't actually said that, but I didn't point it out.

"Procedure," Theo bit out tersely, swinging his shoulder under Spencer's arm to help him to a cot. Chloe started to snore in her chair.

I was really glad Quinn had agreed to help me analyze that pill. Something clearly had to be done. And fast.

I crouched by Spencer, waiting until he looked at me. I made sure there wasn't a single ounce of doubt or worry in my expression. "You are going to be fine."

He nodded jerkily.

"I mean it, Spencer," I insisted. "Don't make me beat you up."

"You can't take me." He tried to grin. "Even like this." He dropped his voice to a whisper. "I never took any pill, Hunter. Not like Will."

"I know." I reached out to touch his dreads but Theo's hand snapped around my wrist.

"No contact," he said. "You know the rules."

I did know the rules. And I had about two minutes before the infirmary was swarming with people and we were hauled bodily away.

"We'll fix this," I told Spencer confidently. Jenna hovered behind me looking grim, even though she tried to smile at Spencer. "I've already got us some help. We'll know something soon."

"You'll beat this thing," Jenna added fiercely just as the first response to the alarm barreled through the front door. We stepped back. If we were all quarantined we'd never get Spencer the help he needed.

There were two security guards and Ms. Dailey behind the first response team. She assessed the situation at a glance, taking in every detail, right down to the dust on my sneakers. She used her cell phone to call for another nurse and the head doctor for Spencer. She sent him and Theo and a guard into one of the back rooms. They'd probably tie him to the bed, like they had with Will. I tried not to think about it.

"What happened?" she asked us. "Hunter?"

"I staked Will," I answered. My voice sounded weird, even to me.

Spencer cried out from the back room and I winced. The guard swore. There was the sound of a scuffle and Spencer moaning. "I'm fine. I'm not *Hel-Blar*. I'm not *Hel-Blar*."

"Hold him down," Theo snapped. "He needs another dose."

Jenna and I swallowed miserably. My eyes burned.

"Hunter staked Will?" Ms. Dailey prodded.

"Will turned," Jenna said dully. "Just like that. Theo was giving him his meds, checking his blood pressure while we tried to get

Chloe to stop licking the tongue depressors like they were lollipop sticks and then he just . . . turned. Ripped the restraints right off the bed frame."

"And he bit Spencer?"

"Kind of," Jenna said. "It happened so fast, we all tried to stop him. I don't know if it's fang damage or the scalpel he grabbed off the counter."

Ms. Dailey's expression was hard but not judging. "And then what happened?"

"Will got free, went for Hunter, then Chloe. Hunter dusted him," Jenna said. "She saved Chloe's life. And whoever else Will might have come across if he'd gotten out of the infirmary."

"I see." Ms. Dailey looked at me for a long moment. "Hunter, you're green. Why don't you go on back to the dorm. We'll look at the security camera footage and then discuss this further in the morning."

I nodded mutely.

"Make sure Hunter has some hot tea," she added to Jenna. "And . . . why is Chloe drooling on herself?"

"She had stitches. Theo gave her something."

"Right. You'll have to get her back to her room then. She can't stay here right now."

Chloe didn't even wake up. Her head just lolled from side to side as we hoisted her up and dragged her out. The last security guard eyed us suspiciously. We didn't speak on the way to the dorm, not until we laid Chloe out on her bed.

Jason knocked on the door and poked his head in. "I had to check on my floor," he said, coming in to sit on my desk chair. "Chloe looks all right . . . ," he trailed off. "But you two don't. What happened?"

"Will turned," I explained. "And Spencer was bitten. Maybe."

He paled. "What?"

"He's in quarantine."

"But he'll be okay." Jason swallowed. "Tell me he'll be okay."

"Damn right he will," Jenna said, low and determined.

"And Will?" Jason asked, looking as stricken as we felt. "What will happen to him?"

"Nothing." I replied. I sat on the edge of my bed, feeling kind of numb but not numb enough. "I staked him."

After a stunned moment, Jason came to sit next to me. "It's not your fault," he said firmly.

"You did what you had to do," Jenna agreed. "Even though it sucks monkeys."

"He was sixteen. And he was nice."

"I know. But he was a student at a Helios-Ra school. He knew what he signed on for."

"He didn't even want to be here."

"And that's not your fault either," Jason pointed out, trying to comfort me. I wasn't entirely convinced I should be comforted. I'd just killed a friend of mine, after all. I should be painfully uncomfortable.

I must have said it out loud because Jenna shook her head. "That *Hel-Blar* woman killed Will. You saved him."

"Hello? I staked him."

"Yeah, and do you think he would have wanted us to let him

become a monster? The same guy who refused to let the maintenance crew kill the squirrels in the attic?"

"I guess not. Still."

"Yeah," Jenna sighed. "Still. You did good, Hunter, even if it doesn't feel like it."

"It feels like ass." I rubbed my eyes hard so the tears wouldn't drop. "School assembly on Monday is going to be a funeral too," I remarked.

"Won't be the first time." Jenna was the color of milk in the faint light of the lamp. "I know what we need."

She went straight to Chloe's secret schnapps in the closet. Jason and I slid down to sit on the floor with Jenna as she opened the bottle and passed it around. I took a sip and the overly sweet peach liqueur ran down my throat.

"Disgusting," Jason spluttered.

"Totally is," Jenna agreed. "Quit hogging it."

"No more for me, you guys." I waved away the bottle and lay on my back, staring up at the ugly beige ceiling. The continuous loop in my head of Will as he crumpled was exactly what I deserved. I shouldn't try to forget it or dull it with alcohol. Or the fact that Spencer might possibly be fighting for his life right now. And it was a battle we couldn't help him with. We didn't have his back. It felt awful. And I should feel awful.

"Hey, eighteen is the legal age in Quebec." Jenna waved the half-empty bottle at me and the liqueur sloshed over the edge. I wiped it off my cheek. She giggled. "Oops. Sorry."

"We're not *in* Quebec." And it was an automatic suspension if you were caught drinking on campus.

"Still. You're gonna make a really good hunter," she added. "Like, really. You know?"

"You will too."

"No, it's different," she insisted. She nudged Jason with her foot. "Isn't it different? It's different."

"Yup." He nodded enthusiastically. "Hunter's a hunter!"

"Ha!" Jenna laughed so loud she startled herself and fell over. Jason and I looked at each other, looked at her, and then laughed so hard we were panting for breath. Chloe groaned.

"What's going—hey," she mumbled groggily. "That's my schnapps."

"Spencer got bitten by Will and then Hunter staked Will," Jenna told her, trying to look serious but just going cross-eyed instead.

Chloe blinked. "Shit." She held her hand out for the bottle. "Gimmee." She fished a pill out of her pocket and swallowed it down with the alcohol.

"Dude, what is that?" Jason gaped at her. "A horse pill?"

"It's a vitamin," she informed him loftily.

"Not you too," he groaned. "All the Niners are suddenly obsessed with vitamins and protein powder. There's some rumor going around that it'll make them strong."

I rolled over to frown at Chloe. "I thought you took one already today. And you shouldn't drink when you're on pain meds."

"I'm doubling up now." She propped herself on her elbow and took another mouthful. "I'm injured. I need my strength."

"Does it make you pee fluorescent yellow?" Jenna asked. "Vitamins always give me Day-Glo pee."

Chloe shook her head and eyed the bottle. "You guys owe me twenty bucks."

"Twenty bucks! No way does that nasty crap cost twenty bucks."

"It's a delivery charge." She grinned and then winced. "Ouch."

"Don't lean on your stitches like that," Jason offered helpfully.

"Duh."

"I hope Spencer's okay." I reached for my cell and texted Kieran and Quinn to tell them what had happened. I hiccuped on a sob that snuck up on me.

Jenna blinked at me. "Nuh-uh," she said, making a grab for the bottle. "Nasty peach booze, stat!"

I made a face. "No way. I'll throw up."

Jason shifted over a foot. "Not on me."

I lay back down. The sound of my friends giggling helped a little.

But not as much as what suddenly occurred to me.

I sat straight up.

"I have a plan," I announced.

CHAPTER 17

•

Hunter

"Did you hear me?" I repeated louder. "I said I have a plan."

Everybody groaned except for Jason, who was already snoring. I nearly stepped on his head when I stood up. "Let's go!"

He jerked awake. "Mmfwha?"

Jenna helped him up. "Hunter's on a mission."

"It's four o'clock in the morning," he groused.

"Chloe, come on," I insisted from the doorway.

She opened one eye. "I am injured."

"You have stitches," I said, unconvinced. "Come on, already. You'll miss all the fun and then you'll bitch about it for the rest of the year."

"That is true," she agreed, finally getting up. She clutched the bottle to her chest. They moved in an exaggerated slow huddle across the carpet, stopped when they realized we were still in our room, and then burst into muffled giggles. The fact that Jenna sounded like a hyena made us all laugh even harder. My stomach hurt. It was a nice change from my brain.

I just couldn't think about what I'd done or worry about Spencer all night. I'd go mental. This was better. This was a goal. This was action.

Chloe was the last into the hall. She tripped over the threshold as the door slammed shut behind her. "Shhh!" she practically yelled. Jenna slapped her hand over Chloe's mouth to shush her, then pulled away squeaking.

"Did you just *lick* me? Gross."

"Teach you to grab my face."

This was going to be a disaster.

"Cut it out," Jason tossed over his shoulder. "I feel like we're back in kindergarten. Let's go." He stopped in the foyer, under the remnants of the broken chandelier. "Um, Hunter?"

"Yeah?"

"Where are we going exactly?"

"Eleventh-grade floor," I mouthed. "And watch the cameras."

We hurried up the steps, avoiding the creaky stairs, the corner with the camera, the loose floorboard. The common room was empty and all the doors were shut tight. Everyone sane was asleep.

"Anyone know which one's Will's room?" I asked.

Jason stared at me. "Great, you've got a dozen demerits so now you want us to get them too?"

I lifted my chin. "I'm going to find out what's going on. You can go back to bed if you want."

Jenna snorted so loud she coughed. "Forget it," she added. "I want in." She poked Jason hard in the shoulder. "And so do you."

"Yeah, all right," he muttered. He grabbed the bottle from Chloe. "I need to be drunker." He swallowed, crossed his eyes. "Nope. Bad idea." He tripped over nothing. He hadn't even taken a step. "He was in room 209, the one at the end by the back staircase."

"That was obliging of him," I whispered back, cheered.

"Obliging? Who talks like that?" Chloe shook her head. She was right. I'd been reading too many romance novels. But now probably wasn't the time to wonder about it. "You're getting weird, Wild."

"You're already weird, Cheng."

She slung her good arm over my shoulder. "That's why we're such good friends."

After shooting her a grin, I touched the door. "Anyone know if Will's roommate is here yet?"

There were a lot of shrugs.

"You check," Chloe suggested. "You're our fearless leader."

I stuck my tongue out at her, which was terribly leader-like of me. But she was right, though. This was my stupid idea so I should take point. I turned the doorknob slowly but pushed the door open an inch in one quick motion. If you went too slowly, which was the temptation, it actually had more of a squeak. The room was dark. I couldn't hear any snoring but that was hardly conclusive proof.

I took a step inside. The others giggled behind me. I shot them a look over my shoulder. There was a hush and then more giggling. They'd wake up the entire floor if we didn't hurry. I took another step inside and hit the Indiglo light on my watch, cupping my hand over the light. I needed just enough to see if the beds were empty, not so much that it might wake up any roommate.

The beds were empty. I let out a breath I hadn't realized I'd been holding.

"Clear," I whispered. They tiptoed inside with such exaggerated care that I snorted out a laugh. "This isn't a slapstick movie."

Jason shut the door behind him and flicked the light on. We blinked at each other for a moment, waiting for our eyes to adjust. The room looked like any other room—two beds, two desks, two chairs. There was no roommate. There were also no posters on the wall, no books on the shelves, no clothes on the floor.

It was empty.

Will had only just turned. Half the staff wouldn't even know about it yet. None of the students would either.

"Okay, that's weird." Jenna turned a circle on her heel.

"Are you sure this is the right room?" I asked.

Jason frowned. "Yeah. I came down here to give him back a video game I borrowed at the end of last year. He was already unpacked and everything."

"So his roommate hadn't arrived yet?"

"No, not yet."

"All right, so maybe they didn't put anyone in this room because he was in the infirmary and it'd be weird." I looked under the bed, which was swept clean. "But that doesn't explain why they'd get all his stuff out before he was even out of quarantine." I rubbed my arms, suddenly chilled. "Unless they knew he wouldn't recover?"

"Educated guess," Chloe said. "It's possible. We all know *Hel-Blar* venom is nasty stuff."

"So what do we do now?" Jason asked, perplexed. "What were you looking for?"

"I'm not even sure," I admitted. "It's just that the *Hel-Blar* who got him mysteriously turned to ash. And Will mysteriously mentioned something about a vitamin. That's too many mysteries." I wouldn't look at Chloe even when she hissed out a disgruntled breath. I went over to the desk and opened all the drawers. "Nothing."

"Closets are empty," Jenna confirmed.

I did finally look at Chloe.

She narrowed her eyes. "Why are you looking at me like that?"

She was going to be pissed at me for asking. No help for it. "You've been hiding your vitamins, haven't you?"

She frowned. "What?" She backed up a step. "You saw me take one like an hour ago."

Jenna and Jason watched us as if we were a tennis match.

"Why would she hide vitamins?" Jason wondered.

"Because I've been bugging her about them," I said, not glancing away from Chloe. She shifted from foot to foot. It was her nervous tic so I knew my guess had been right. "So if you were Will, where would you hide your vitamins in this room?"

"I don't know." She shrugged.

"Chloe, please. This is important."

She gave a long, suffering sigh. "Okay, but you have to get off my case."

Not a chance.

She surveyed the room thoughtfully. The first place she looked was the desk drawers, feeling for a false bottom. Nothing. We helped her check under the mattress, but there was nothing there but dust.

"This is stupid," she muttered.

But I really felt like we were onto something.

She sat on the edge of the bed and checked under the lip of the night table.

Nothing.

Jenna and Jason were starting to shoot me weird looks.

Chloe lifted the lamp and stuck her finger inside the iron stand. She pulled out a small plastic bag with little white pills.

"Damn," Jason whistled.

Chloe and I met each other's grim gaze.

"These don't look anything like my vitamins," she said quietly.

CHAPTER 18

•

QUINN

I hit the ground just as the stake sliced past me. I grabbed for Nicholas's ankle and he slammed into the dirt, kicking me off before he'd even landed. The second stake landed in a willow tree. The *Hel-Blar* paused. Lucy didn't move.

"Lucy!" Nicholas was back on his feet before I could grab him again. I went for the nearest *Hel-Blar*, cracking my fist across his face, taking care not to get too close to his mouth. His answering punch nearly dislocated my shoulder.

So the *Hel-Blar* from earlier tonight had been tired because Solange had been kicking their asses.

Small consolation.

I broke a kneecap and used my last stake until there was dust on my boots. Nicholas flipped into the air, somersaulting over an attacking *Hel-Blar*, and landed in the river, blood-tinted water arcing up around him and splashing us. A human wouldn't have noticed it in the darkness but it had the rest of us distracted, thirsty. One of the *Hel-Blar* licked his lips, studded with puncture marks from his fangs.

And then the frenzy hit.

The hissing was nearly loud enough to ripple the surface of the slow-moving river. Lucy became the focus of such gut-burning hunger, I wondered why it didn't wake her up. She still wasn't moving. I didn't know how badly she was hurt. And there wasn't time to wonder about it. I ran downstream and leaped over the water, coming back around to block access to Lucy from the other side. Solange, Nicholas, and I formed a ring around her, like petals to her blood-soaked center. Then Nicholas fell to his knees, shouting her name. She stirred once, faintly.

"Incoming!" I yelled at him. He knew better than to stay there, distracted and vulnerable. He finally rose to his feet, his eyes searing hot enough to have one *Hel-Blar* stumbling in his tracks. The rest just laughed.

"If she's dead, you're dead," he promised darkly. He smiled. "Wait, you're dead anyway."

I'd worry about that smile later. Right now I had two crazed siblings to deal with. And no more stakes.

"Shit, give me your pack," I said to Nicholas. He tossed it to me over Lucy's body. Solange looked at her and bit back a sob. Her fangs elongated farther until I thought they'd fall right out of her head. Her flying roundhouse cracked a *Hel-Blar* neck. The woman fell, snarling, facefirst into the water. Solange turned her over and staked her in one move. There was blood on her clothes and I wasn't sure how much was hers, Lucy's, or various *Hel-Blars'*.

This was turning into a hell of a night.

To human eyes, the fight probably looked quick, colors smearing with the speed of our movements. Inside the fight, it felt like forever. Lucy needed help and she needed it now.

Try telling that to the *Hel-Blar* currently trying to chew on my face.

"Ow, son of a bitch!" He'd nearly taken a fang off. I hated to admit it but I'd been fighting vampires all night and dawn wasn't far off. It was taking its toll. I kicked, I punched, I staked. The thick *Hel-Blar* ashes resembled a mist on the river. Solange took a blow to the kneecap and stumbled, going down. She flipped to her feet before either Nicholas or I could reach her. The last two *Hel-Blar* ran, scuttling off between the trees. Nicholas scooped Lucy up into his arms, pink water dripping from her hair.

Sunrise trembled on the horizon.

Solange was still snarling, the whites of her eyes now completely red.

She didn't look right.

"Solange," I said, trying to catch her attention. "Solange, focus."

She hissed. The dark sky lightened to a pale gray, glimmering like a pearl. I felt the weariness of the dawn start to tug at my bones. Nicholas's jaw clenched so tight I could see the muscles spasms from here.

"She's still bleeding," he ground out.

Solange licked her lips, stumbled back a step, howled. We both flinched.

"Get Lucy help," I told him. "She can't spend the night in one of the safe houses and you can't wait for me to talk Solange down." The safe houses were actually more like underground bomb shelters hidden throughout the forest in case any of us got caught far from home at sunrise. Some linked to the tunnels connecting our farmhouse to various parts of the area; others locked up tight, impenetrable. We had no way of knowing if Lucy could wait until sunset for medical attention. Nicholas hesitated, glancing at Solange, who was growling low in her throat.

"Just go," I said, approaching Solange as if she were a wild beast. It wasn't far off from the truth. Her internal tethers were new, untested. Fragile. She was strong, already stronger than anyone else so newly turned. But she might not be strong enough to completely control her inner vampire. It wasn't an exact science. I just had to stop her from giving in entirely, and sunlight would do the rest. Assuming I could get her to safety before it dropped her like a stone in a deep pond. We were nothing if not susceptible.

Nicholas looked wrecked, cradling Lucy against his chest. Her arm dropped limply. She'd never done anything limp in her life. Fear for her nibbled at me. Nicholas broke into a run so sudden, the air displaced all around him. Fallen leaves whirled at my feet. Solange took a step, following the scent of blood.

"Stop me," she pleaded, even as she pulled a dagger from her boot. She suddenly looked so much like Mom, I felt disoriented.

"I'm trying," I whispered, holding up one hand. "Solange, you're okay."

She laughed but there was no humor in it. "Quinn, we both know I'm not okay." She swallowed, as if it was the hardest thing she'd ever done. She squinted at the sky. "God, it's burning inside me. Did this happen to you? I don't remember you guys being like this." Her hair was damp. It took a lot to make a vampire sweat. We didn't exactly run hot, temperature-wise.

"You'll be okay," I said soothingly.

"I can still smell the blood," she said softly, as if she was talking about chocolate cake. She inhaled, nostrils flaring. "I have to follow it."

"Wait." I blocked her way. "Just wait a minute."

"No."

She shoved me and then vaulted over my flailing limbs, taking off between the pine trees.

Damn it, I was *not* going to be outdone by my baby sister.

We raced through the forest, the sun burning at our heels. I didn't even know if she was racing to Lucy's blood, to the safety of the farm, or just away from me. I only knew I had to stop her.

There's one sure way to stop a vampire.

Blood.

I had to make myself an easier target than a wounded human.

I reached into my pocket, leaping over a fallen moss-draped tree trunk. I still had the test tubes of blood Hunter had given me. It wasn't much but it might be enough to stop Solange, to give her the strength to find her control again.

I stopped running, acorns and needles crunching under my feet. I popped the lid off one of the glass tubes and flicked a few drops out. Hunter's friend's name was on the label: Chloe.

"Solange," I called out. "Can you smell that? I've got fresh blood here for you."

"What is that?" she asked. I couldn't see her but at least she'd stopped running.

"It's human blood, Sol," I said tauntingly. "It's better than animal blood. Don't you want a sip?" I felt like a freaking drug dealer. This night was not exactly going according to plan. I waved the tube, trying not to react to the scent myself. My fangs elongated a little and saliva filled my mouth. We avoided human blood. It was so easy to become addicted. "Just imagine how it tastes."

She came around an oak, the leaves hanging over her head like a crown. She was as pale and slender as a shaft of moonlight. She moved slowly toward me, feral and predatory.

I waggled the tube. "Come on, Sol. I know you want it."

The sun steadily pushed its way over the horizon. I could see it in the fatigue in Solange's face, under the hunger. And I could feel it in my bones, turning them to water. I struggled against it. This was definitely the worst part of being a young vampire. If we got caught out here we'd be vulnerable. If the sunlight didn't weaken us to the point of death, something else would come along and finish the job. A well-meaning hiker who'd take us to the hospital where lab tests would prove disconcerting, or else an anti-treaty Helios-Ra hunter who knew exactly how to dispatch us. Or even a human loyal to a vampire family who didn't particularly care for the Drakes.

I had to hurry.

I circled around so that I was in the lead and then headed toward the farmhouse.

"Come and get it," I told her grimly.

We were on Drake land when she caught up to me.

"Give it to me!" Her nails scraped into my hand. She grabbed the tube and licked the glass rim, tilting it for a greedy mouthful. There wasn't much in there but she gulped at it like it was water and she'd been lost in the desert for a year.

Then she spat the whole mouthful out without swallowing.

"Gross. What the hell's in there? Tastes like medicine." She grimaced, throwing the tube at my head. I caught it and slipped it back into my pocket. There was just enough blood left to smear the inside of the tube, like stained glass. One thing was for sure—Chloe's vitamins were definitely not vitamins.

"There's blood at the house," I told her. "We're nearly there."

I grabbed her wrist and dragged her toward the squares of lamplight. We reached the house just as the light sent spears of fire between the branches. Solange was asleep on her feet, sliding onto the porch floor like a silk scarf. The lethargy was so sudden, so deep that I was limping when I fell, dragging her through the door.

CHAPTER 19

◆

Hunter

Sunday afternoon

The next day came entirely too soon. Will was still dead, we didn't know if Spencer would get better, and now my head felt like I'd landed on it repeatedly during the night even though I hadn't gotten drunk.

All in all, not exactly an improvement.

Chloe made a weird sound, like a grunt, as she pulled her pillow over her head. "I hate my life," she added.

"I hate your schnapps," I said, squinting at the alarm clock's digital numbers: 2:03 P.M. It felt way earlier. "It makes you snore like a horse."

"Karma," Chloe maintained from the depths of her covers. "That's what you get for stealing."

I snorted. "You steal chocolate from me all the time."

She poked one eye out from her pillow. "You know about that?"

"Well, duh," I said. I shuffled from the hall to the bathroom. It felt as if I hadn't gotten any sleep at all. There were way too many students running around, unpacking and reconnecting with friends they hadn't seen all summer. Someone squealed.

"Can we stake her?" Jenna begged, coming out of one the stalls and wiping her mouth. She stood at the mirror looking miserable. Even her freckles looked miserable. Then she winced at her choice of words. "Sorry." She filled the sink with cold water.

"Any word from Spencer?" I asked.

"None." Jenna shook her head, then moaned at the movement. "But as soon as I'm sure my head won't crack right open, let's go see Theo."

"Okay." I finally caught a glimpse of myself in the mirror. "Gack!"

Never mind the haggard combination of my too-pale complexion and dark smudges of fatigue; there was also a mottled bruise under my cheekbone from last night's fight. I poked it gingerly, hissed out a breath. Jenna toweled her face, finally looked at me, and winced.

"That looks painful."

"I guess I should learn to duck faster." I poked at it again and sighed. "At least he didn't give me a black eye."

"How's Chloe?"

"Same. Seen Jason yet?" Someone let one of the bathroom stall doors slam shut and Jenna clutched her head and whimpered. "Ow! That's it," she said, shuffling down the hall like an old lady—or an asylum patient. "I'm calling Jason. I hope the phone rings right in his ear. He's so not escaping this hangover."

Simon walked past us, eating a sandwich. I didn't know him personally but Jenna had been crushing on him from afar for two full years. She tried to smile at him.

Instead she threw up on his shoes.

"What the hell, man?" He leaped back, crashing into the wall. "Gross."

Jenna turned bright red and ran all the way back to her room.

I felt sure she was never going to drink again. Simon just stood in the hall. "What is wrong with the girls at this school?" he muttered.

I eventually wove my way around suitcases and went back to my room. Chloe was still a lump of disgruntled blankets.

"Are you dead?" I asked.

"Zombie," she answered. "Don't tell my Supernatural Creatures prof. She'll try to decapitate me." She pulled her blanket over her face. "On second thought, decapitation sounds soothing. Hook me up."

"Try aspirin first," I suggested, handing her the bottle after shaking two out for myself. I downed an entire bottle of water and felt marginally more human. Still, I didn't want to do anything but lie there and feel pathetic.

I definitely didn't want to answer the door.

"If that's another one of your Niners . . ." Chloe's threat trailed off menacingly, as if she couldn't think of anything bad enough to inflict on whoever dared knock on our door.

The second knock had us both snarling. I swung the door open, scowling. "What already?"

Ms. Dailey stood on the other side, eyebrow raised drily.

"Oh, um, Ms. Dailey." I flushed. Chloe smothered a snort of laughter.

"Hunter." Ms. Dailey smiled knowingly. "May I come in?"

I stepped aside to let her pass. "Is Spencer okay?" I couldn't think of another reason why she'd be here in our dorm room. My heart fell into stomach.

"Spencer's condition is unchanged," she assured me. "And he is receiving the best care possible. His parents are on their way here to the school today."

"Oh." So he was sick enough that his parents had been called. We'd known that already, of course, but this just made it feel more awful. More final. "Can we see him?"

"You know that's not possible," she told us gently and glanced at Chloe, who finally sat up, her curly hair looking like a bird's nest squashed on one side of her head. "He's in quarantine." She pursed her lips. "Which is why I won't be commenting on your obvious hangover, Chloe. After last night, I suppose you all deserve a break." She speared her with a stern glare that had Chloe squirming. "I won't tell the headmistress about this, but you're on kitchen duty until Christmas break. And if anything like this ever happens again, you'll be expelled. Understand me?"

"Yes, ma'am," Chloe murmured. It was pretty cool of Dailey not to bust her.

"Good." She turned to me. "Now, Hunter, there is something I'd like to discuss with you."

I tried to make my brain work. "Yes?"

"I am starting my own student group. The Guild will recruit the best of the best to help take out the new *Hel-Blar* and other threats. I'd like to formally extend an invitation for you to join us. You've exhibited leadership, team spirit, courage, loyalty, and resourcefulness time and time again and you ought to be rewarded for it. And I'm very proud of you for resisting whatever party was going on here last night. We could use you."

"Thank you!" I finally exclaimed after a stunned silence. This was way better than floor monitor duties. And Grandpa would puff up his chest with pride and brag to all his friends. I grinned.

"We'll expect you every Sunday afternoon for training and Tuesday evenings after supper for weekly orientation." She shook her head at Chloe. "Drink lots of water" was her parting advice before letting the door shut behind her. Loudly.

I tuned to Chloe, beaming. "Can you believe it? Cool."

She did *not* look happy for me.

She swung out of bed, glowering. "Figures."

I narrowed my eyes, some of my happiness congealing in my chest. "And by that you mean, congratulations?"

"I mean, I'm tired of the elitist nepotism of this school."

My mouth dropped open. "What the hell, Chloe? I work my ass off."

"And I don't?"

I was really sick of this argument.

"Well, it's not actually about you for one second," I told her. "It's about me."

"It's *always* about you."

I rolled my eyes. "I'm so over your pity party. Green's not a good color on you."

"Shut up." She stalked toward me, her hands clenched into fists. "You don't know what you're talking about."

I stood my ground. "I know exactly what I'm talking about so back off, Chloe. I mean it." I couldn't believe one of my best friends was all up in my face like that. It was totally surreal. "I really hope that this is a side effect from your dumb-ass vitamins," I told her grimly. "Even so, it's getting tired."

"God, get off my case, already," Chloe shouted, and shoved me. I stumbled back a step, shocked.

"You did not just do that." I shoved her back before I could stop myself.

"So what if I did? Going to tattle on me to your new Guild friends?" She shoved me again, or would have if I hadn't jerked my shoulder back. The momentum tripped her up, which infuriated her all the more. Frankly, I was past caring.

Especially when she hauled off and punched me.

The ensuing silence was cold and sudden, like a bucket of water. I'd managed to duck enough that her fist glanced my chin and shoulder but didn't do too much damage. Still, I felt the throb on my jaw. She stared at me, eyes watering, cheeks red with fury.

I really wanted to punch her back.

Before I could give in to some idiot catfight, I turned on my heel and stormed out of the room.

◆

Sunday night

"Are you telling me Chloe actually punched you?" Jenna stared at me. She whistled through her teeth. "Dude. That is messed up."

"I know," I agreed grimly. We were walking across the quad toward the infirmary. I hadn't seen Chloe all day, not since our fight. Definitely for the best. I shoved my hands in my pockets. "I'm tired of getting punched in the face."

"I can't believe you didn't punch her back. You are a better woman than I am." She shook her head.

"Remind me of that when my jaw goes purple to match the rest of my bruises." At least it was only a dull ache; she hadn't cracked a tooth or bruised the bone. I'd have been mad at myself if she'd managed to get the best of me, even hungover and doped up on those weird vitamins.

"You two weren't the only ones fighting," Jenna told me.

"What? Who else?"

"Two eleventh graders went at it over the last box of cereal in the common room."

"Seriously?"

"Yeah, one of them needed two stitches. And someone got carted off to the infirmary. Some kind of flu."

I hunched my shoulders. "Jenna, we have to figure this out. It doesn't add up."

"We will."

I wished I had her confidence. I felt as if we were going backward; everything was making less sense, not more. And it was starting to piss me off.

The safety lights blazed along the path and we could hear someone beating on the punching bags from the open window of the upstairs gym. Music poured out of the dorm behind us. It was familiar, homey.

Worth protecting.

We went straight to the infirmary, blinking at the bright fluorescent lights. The minute he saw us, Theo jumped up from his chair and blocked us.

"No way, girls."

We both scowled.

"Theo, come on," Jenna finally wheedled when he didn't move. "Be a pal."

"Not a toe past quarantine, kid."

"Kid? You're what, twenty-five?"

"Yeah, old enough to know better."

"We just want to see Spencer," I said.

"I know what you want. Forget it." His expression softened. "Look, I know it's hard. But he's in quarantine for a reason. You won't help him by getting locked up in quarantine yourselves, or getting demerits or expelled. You know the headmistress doesn't mess around with this stuff." He raised an eyebrow. "And you could get me fired as well."

"Guilt trip," Jenna muttered.

"Damn straight."

I knew we wouldn't change his mind, but all the same, I had to try.

"Theo, he shouldn't be alone. He's our friend," I said.

"He's not alone," Theo said just as Spencer's mother came out from behind the curtain blocking the quarantine rooms. Her eyes were red, her cheeks so pale under her tan that they looked paper-thin. The rest of her was the same, from her sun-bleached blond hair to her sandals and silver toe rings. Spencer got his love of surfing and the ocean from his mom and his supernatural obsessions from his dad. She saw me and her lips wobbled. I stared, horrified. If she cried, I didn't know what I'd do. Just because I'm a girl doesn't mean I do public displays of emotion. Luckily she clenched her jaw and tried to smile.

"Oh, Hunter, come here, sweetie." She hugged me hard. She smelled like salt and coconut oil. It was comforting.

"How is he?" I asked when she let go and squeezed Jenna's hand.

"He's strong," she said, her voice breaking. It wasn't really an answer. I shifted from one foot to the other. I felt guilty and I didn't know why. The clock on the wall ticked too loudly. "I have to get back to him."

She wasn't allowed in quarantine either, only on this side of the window. Once a day she was allowed in a full medical suit to go inside and hold his hand and talk to him. We'd studied the procedure in class last year.

The reality was so much worse.

"I miss him already," I said miserably as Jenna and I shuffled back outside. It was Sunday night; everyone was in a frenzy of last-minute unpacking and organizing and pretending school didn't start tomorrow.

"Me too," Jenna said. She kicked at a garbage can. "I wish there was more we could do."

And then it hit me.

"There is."

She turned to eye me. "What? What are you talking about?"

I stopped, nodding slowly. "I bugged the eleventh-grade common room after Will was bitten," I said. "I forgot."

"You forgot you bugged a room?" Jenna goggled. "Dude, you're fierce. And I totally love you right now."

"We might not find anything," I quickly added.

"But at least we'll be doing something. No wonder Dailey tapped you for her Guild."

"Didn't she ask you?"

Jenna shrugged. "No."

"She totally will," I said, utterly convinced. "No one handles a crossbow like you do."

"Thanks." She tugged on my hand, dragging me after her as if we were heading for a giant mountain of Ed Westwick–shaped chocolate. "Now let's go! I want to listen to those recordings of yours."

"Slow down." I tugged back. "If we go in there like a stampeding herd, people will notice. We're going for subtle right now." I scowled. "And everyone's staring at me as it is."

"I know," Jenna said, slowing her pace and relaxing her shoulders, as if we were just hanging out, strolling back to our rooms. "Everyone's heard about Will by now."

I nodded, my throat clenching. The dorm was buzzing with activity as students tried to put off going to bed. Morning meant school had officially started. We climbed the stairs and hung around the eleventh-grade common room but it was packed. If we stayed any longer people would start to wonder. There was no way to get in and get the microphones without giving ourselves away.

"Damn it," Jenna muttered. "It's like eleven o'clock. Don't they sleep?"

"Apparently not." We turned away, going back down to our own floor. "I'll sneak up tonight after everyone's in bed," I assured her.

She looked deflated. "Okay."

We couldn't stop from pausing outside of Spencer's room. The door was open a crack and we could see his roommate's desk, piled with books and hand-whittled stakes. There was already clothes on the floor and an Angelina Jolie poster on the wall.

But Spencer's side of the room was bare.

His surfing posters were gone, along with the old surfboard he usually hung over the bed. I kicked the door open, Jenna crowding in behind me.

"What the hell?" His roommate, John, jerked back. When he recognized us, his face went red. "Oh. Sorry."

"Where's Spencer's stuff?" I demanded. His bookcase was cleared of his supernatural encyclopedias and boxes of charms and spell bags. Even his jar of sea salt was gone, which he always kept on his nightstand because every protective spell he researched called for it. I marched over to his dresser and yanked it open.

Empty. Not even a single turquoise bead to prove Spencer had ever been here. Fury and something darker, more debilitating gnawed at me, fraying my temper. "John, where's his stuff?" I barely recognized my own voice.

John stood up, pity making him shuffle awkwardly. "They packed it up today. Didn't they tell you?"

"No. They did not."

"Who packed it?" Jenna snapped. She was vibrating with anger as well. Between the two of us we could have powered a nuclear reactor. John wisely took a step backward.

"A couple of the guards." He held up his hands beseechingly. "Look, I don't know."

"Well, they can damn well unpack it," I seethed. "Because he's going to be fine."

"Yeah? I mean, yeah, of course," he hastened to add. "Of course, he is."

I had to turn away from the bare mattress. It was making my eyes burn. It should have been heaped with Spencer's Mexican blankets.

"Don't let anyone move in here," I told John, whirling to glare at him. He swallowed, his Adam's apple bobbing.

"I don't really—" He swallowed again when Jenna added her glare to mine. "Of course. I won't."

Out in the hall, Jenna and I exchanged bleak glances. I knew she was remembering Will's room, stripped of his belongings long before I'd had to stake him. I shivered. Jenna looked like she wanted to throw up.

"We're going to fix this," I told her grimly. She nodded just as grimly.

"Damn right we are."

◆

I waited until I was sure everyone was asleep. I paused in my doorway to listen, and again at the bottom of the stairs, and once more on the landing outside the eleventh-grade common room. I didn't hear anything and saw no one except Chloe asleep on the couch in our common room, her laptop half open on the floor next to her. I didn't wake her up to go with me. I honestly didn't know if I could trust her. She'd feel the same way about me if she knew I'd gone through her stuff. I wasn't sure how we'd gotten here. It was a long way from counting the days until we could be roommates to punching each other.

But I couldn't worry about that right now.

Spencer was my only concern. He didn't have much time and we didn't have much information. I hadn't been lying to Jenna when I told her there was no guarantee my microphones had recorded anything worth listening to. But I could hope.

I could hope really hard.

The common room was finally deserted, the smell of barbecue potato chips lingering in the air. I crept forward, stepping as softly as I could. I retrieved the microphone from under the couch first, taking care not to stick my finger in the wads of old gum. Next, I plucked the one from the dresser. The one inside the coat rack was going to be decidedly trickier.

I stood in front of it, frowning as I ran through my options. I could tip it over and shake the microphone loose, but those old coat racks weighed a ton. There was a good chance the bottom would slide out and hit the floor. I didn't have a magnet to lure it up the pole either. If Chloe and I were still talking to each other, she probably could have rigged up something. She was good at that sort of thing. I unscrewed the top and stood on my tiptoes to look down the length of it. Darkness and dust. I took the small penlight from my pocket and switched it on, keeping the light angled down the pole. If it flashed into a window, one of the guards outside might see it and come to investigate. It didn't do me much good anyway. It only served to glint off the microphone pen casing and prove that it was far out of my reach.

I shook it once, rattling it. I'd have to abandon it until I had a better plan and hope the other ones had recorded something useful. I hated to do it. It galled my stubborn streak.

But I had bigger problems.

Such as the cool pale hand that suddenly clamped over my mouth, jerking my body backward against a hard chest.

CHAPTER 20

◆

Hunter

I jabbed my elbow back as quick as I could but he was already dancing away. My heel caught his instep hard enough for him to make a sound. And then he tugged and whirled me around, backing me into the wall. His hand was still over my mouth. I hooked my foot around his ankle and shoved. He staggered back and went down, slipping on the area rug. He took me with him, yanking so that I landed on top of him. He sprawled with uncanny silence, not even rattling the furniture when he landed. Blue eyes laughed at me.

"Quinn," I snapped, finally recognizing him. I whacked him. Hard. "What the hell are you doing? I could have staked you, you idiot."

He grinned. "I'm quicker than you are."

"Shut up, you are not." Okay, so he was. But only because he had supernatural abilities. If he'd been a normal human guy, I could have taken him. I could still take him. I just needed a few more weapons to do it.

"I didn't think you lived on this floor."

"How do you know where my room is?" I asked. "And what are you even doing here? You do realize this is a school for vampire hunters, right? Why do I have to keep reminding you of that?"

He smirked. "I have a pass." He was telling the truth. I hadn't noticed it yet but there was a discreet metal button, like the ones you get at museums, pinned to the collar of his T-shirt. The shirt was almost the exact blue of his eyes. The pin was contraband. It allowed the bearer to be on campus without a mess of security coming down on his or her head. It almost certainly had never been worn by a vampire before.

"Where did you get that?" I demanded.

"Off Kieran."

"Kieran gave you a campus free-access pass?" I repeated dubiously.

"Not so much 'gave' as left his knapsack out while he was kissing my sister."

"So you stole it."

"Did I mention he was kissing my *baby* sister?"

All the talk about kissing was making it hard not to look at his mouth. Or to pretend I didn't know exactly how his lips felt on mine.

He frowned suddenly, his fingers on my chin, his expression going hard as steel. "What happened to your face this time?"

I wrinkled my nose. Great. I'd forgotten I was bruised and

probably looked like a mottled grape. "Chloe punched me. Well, she tried to."

"*Chloe* punched you?"

"Yes," I grumbled.

"Well, I can't punch her back." He sounded disgruntled. "She's a girl."

I blinked. "I didn't ask you to."

"That's what guys do," he muttered. "When someone hurts a girl. Especially you."

I wasn't sure what he meant by that but I felt kind of warm and jittery inside, like I'd had too much hot chocolate.

And then I realized I was still lying on top of him.

We were pressed together, close enough that my breath ruffled his long hair. He had the kind of beauty that almost burns, as if he belonged in a Pre-Raphaelite painting of a poet or a mythic doomed lover. He was that gorgeous.

He raised his eyebrow, the trademark smirk getting more pronounced.

And he was a vampire. Which meant he could hear the sound of my heartbeat accelerating while I stared at him and thought about how pretty he was.

Crap.

Totally unfair advantage.

I pushed up on my palms to launch myself off him before I embarrassed myself completely and irrevocably.

"Hey." He watched me back away as if he was dangerous. He looked entirely too pleased with himself. "Where are you going?"

"To bed." Double crap. What if he thought that was an

invitation? Was it an invitation? And when, exactly, had I lost my mind? "Uh, I meant to my room. Where my bed is. And—shit." I forced myself to stop babbling.

He rose into a crouch, looking feral and predatory. "Do I make you nervous, Hunter?"

I stopped, glaring at him. "Excuse me, I know seventeen painful ways to kill you. You don't make me nervous."

"I know seventeen different ways to kiss you."

I ignored the flare of heat in my chest and focused on the fact that it was clearly a line. I tossed my hair off my shoulder. "I'm not one of your groupies."

"Good," he said, suddenly serious. He didn't bother denying that he had groupies. That made me like him even more.

I was in so much trouble.

"Look, Quinn, what are you really doing here? Do you have info on that pill I gave you?"

"Not yet. But I got your text about Will," he replied, straightening. He only towered over me a little. "And I thought you could use some company."

"You came for me?" Yup. So much trouble.

He nodded, touching my hair and tangling his long fingers in the ends, as if it was a fire and he was as cold as he was winter-pale. "What are you doing up here?"

"Retrieving personal property," I explained, mesmerized by the feel of his hand as he tugged me a little closer, winding my hair around his wrist like a golden rope.

"From the coat rack?" he whispered, puzzled. He must have seen me staring at it.

I nodded, wondering why my voice felt like it had faded away completely. I cleared my throat. "Yes, but it's stuck in the bottom."

"Allow me." He let me go so abruptly I stumbled back a little. He lifted the coat rack and turned it upside down, as if it weighed no more than a broom. The microphone tumbled out and I caught it before it hit the ground. He grinned, shaking his head. "Your personal property is surveillance equipment?"

I shrugged, slipping it into my pocket. "Thanks."

"You're welcome."

I peered out of the doorway, making sure it was clear before I started to creep back down the stairs. I paused on the landing. Quinn was right behind me.

"Where are you going?" I asked.

"I'm going with you."

"I don't remember inviting you," I said drily.

"That's a vampire myth," he shot back just as drily. "I don't need to be invited. I would have thought they taught you that here." He winked. I rolled my eyes. He followed me and I let him. Gladly. The truth was, I didn't think I wanted to be alone just yet. I was wired and exhausted and worried.

And I liked having him around. He was distracting. In a good way.

He paused, nodding to Chloe, who was still sound asleep on the common room sofa. "Want me to pull her hair?"

I grinned, shaking my head. He took a step forward.

"What are you doing?" I grabbed his arm.

"I'm going to sniff her."

I blinked. "I'm sorry, what?"

"You're worried about those vitamins, right? I might be able to smell them in her blood and I *might* be able to tell if they're messing her up."

"They're definitely messing her up," I muttered, touching the bruise on my jaw. "But go ahead. That could help. Just don't wake her up."

"Hello? Give me a little credit. Vampire stealth, remember?"

"Vampire arrogance, you mean."

"That too."

It went against a lifetime of training to crush on a vampire and, worse, to watch him skulk toward one of my friends. My hands actually twitched. But I stayed where I was. I trusted Quinn Drake, despite the fact that I was the latest in a long line of vampire hunters.

He was graceful as moonlight, fluid and pale as he draped over Chloe. She slept on peacefully, utterly unaware. Not exactly proof of the effectiveness of our education. Then again, right now, neither was I. Quinn was a dark silhouette out of any standard vampire horror movie, leaning over, teeth gleaming. And I just waited trustingly, patiently, hopefully.

Grandpa would pop a blood vessel if he could see me now.

I pushed that out of my mind and watched as Quinn's nose hovered along the line of Chloe's neck, sniffing as if she was a fine wine. His fangs lengthened. I tensed, took a step, stopped. He inhaled, or whatever passed as a smell-seeking inhalation for the undead, and then recoiled sharply.

He didn't speak as he approached, just jerked his head down the hall toward my room. Later, I'd have to ask him how he knew that was my room. Right now, I just wanted to know why he was wiping his nose as if he'd snorted pepper. I shut the door quietly behind him. The single lamp lit on my desk cast his face into shadows.

"Well?" I demanded.

"Those aren't vitamins," he said.

"I *knew* it!" I winced nervously. "What are they?"

"I don't know," he admitted. "There are vitamins in there—they have a very distinctive smell. But there's something else too."

I wiped my damp palms on my pants. "She'll never believe me. When can you get the lab results from your brother?"

"Maybe tomorrow. I'll make him hurry."

"God, her *mom* gave her those." I rubbed my arms, suddenly cold. "And she's hidden a whole stash of them somewhere so I can't even flush them. Well, maybe something here will convince her."

"Is that why you bugged that room upstairs?"

I nodded. "I thought Will was going to get better. And that whatever he was into, some of his friends might know about it. I don't know. But students keep getting this weird flu that doesn't get better. Something's just off."

I fumbled the microphones out of my pocket and switched the first one on. The quality wasn't very good; the scratchiness of the background was louder than the voices, but it was better than nothing. I'd set the motion sensor recorder to switch on and off throughout the evenings and late at night. I figured there was less chance of people whispering in the common room at lunchtime when anyone might hear them. It was mostly complaints about classes and people leaving milk out of the fridge in the kitchenette. I listened for about a half hour, fast-forwarding where I could.

Quinn leaned against my door, patient in a way I hadn't thought he was capable of being. He was usually teasing or taunting or eager for a fight. I was seeing another part of his personality, quiet and thoughtful but just as intense.

"Nothing," I said, dejected. "I guess it was a stupid idea."

"Wait." He pushed away from the wall. "Let me hear that one again." I handed it to him, showing him how to rewind. He held it up to his ear. "It's faint but . . ." He listened harder and I suddenly envied him his supernatural senses. I'd never envied a vampire before. I was too fond of sunlight and spaghetti and ice cream.

"Got it," he said, his eyes flaring triumphantly. He rewound again and repeated what he heard for my benefit. *"Are you sure this stuff works? Shut up, you moron, someone will hear you. It's pretty steep for a bunch of vitamins. I told you, they're better than vitamins— watch it. Leave it, we'll never get behind that TV. It weighs a ton."*

I shot to my feet. "They dropped some!"

He nodded smugly but stopped me from reaching for the doorknob. "Let me go."

"What? Why?"

"For one thing, I can move an ancient TV that weighs a ton without making much noise."

"Oh. Good point." Use the tools you've got. It was a hunter motto. And it made sense, even if my tool, in this case, was a vampire.

He was only gone long enough for me to notice the flashing light on my answering machine and to press play. Grandpa's gravelly whiskey-and-cigar-smoke voice rumbled out of the speaker. For some reason it made me feel like crying. I missed his confidence and certainty. It was in short supply right now. Even if I cringed at the actual words he was saying.

"Hunter, honey, I got a call from the school. Heard you did good. I know it's hard, but you did what you had to do. That's what hunters do and that's what Wilds do. And you saved your friend's life, the way I hear it. Your headmistress was making noise about seeing the school psychologist but I told her you don't need that quackery. You be strong. You're a good girl. I don't want you going soft over a *Hel-Blar*. Vampires need killing, you know that."

My bedroom door shut with a soft click. Quinn raised an eyebrow at me. I winced, knowing he'd heard every word of my grandpa's message.

"He means well," I said defensively.

"Okay," Quinn replied with deceptive nonchalance.

"He raised me the only way he knew how."

"Okay," he said again.

I frowned. I didn't know why I was justifying Grandpa. He was a good man. So was Quinn. One wasn't mutually exclusive of the other.

My head was starting to hurt.

"Did you find it?" I asked, changing the subject.

He nodded, sitting next to me and holding out his hand, palm up. The white pill looked innocuous. Hard to imagine that something so small was making such a big mess.

"It doesn't look like Chloe's vitamins," I said, confused. "Hers are huge and yellow."

"I know," he said grimly. "These aren't vitamins."

I blinked. "Wait. So there's *two* kinds of pills making the rounds now? What the hell is *wrong* with people?" I sat back, disgusted. "It does explain why we keep running in circles."

Quinn was staring at the pill as if it were a coiled cobra that might strike at any time. His nostrils twitched, his jaw clenched.

"Okay, what?" I asked uncertainly.

"This thing's poison," he answered through his teeth.

"Seriously? Is that what made Will sick? Not just *Hel-Blar*?"

"It's toxic to humans," Quinn explained. "But it's absolutely fatal to vampires."

The silence felt charged, like a battery about to explode. I grabbed the pill off his hand, as if it might start leaking acid. He shook his head once. "It's only fatal if ingested."

"So people are taking vampire drugs now? Along with some weird vitamin? That doesn't make any sense." I wrapped the pill inside a tissue. "Can you get your brother to analyze this too?"

"Hell, yes," he said, putting the little package in his pocket. "I want to know what this is. I've smelled it before."

"Where?"

"That's the thing, I don't know. I can't remember." He sounded annoyed with himself.

I scooted back to lean against the wall, the blankets twisting under my legs. "Spencer wasn't taking drugs or vitamins or any of that stuff. He barely takes aspirin."

"Spencer was bitten by a *Hel-Blar*," Quinn said, also moving back to sit next to me. "He's not a mystery."

"Then why is his stuff all gone from his room?"

"It is?" Quinn looked surprised. "Is he that sick?"

"Theo says Spencer's badly off, but stable. The meds are helping him more than they helped Will. But his room's empty, just like Will's was. And there's that flu everyone's worried about."

Quinn whistled through his teeth. "Look, obviously I've never really trusted the Helios-Ra, and maybe I've lived in Violet Hill too long, but this has 'conspiracy' written all over it."

"I know. And I won't let what happened to Will happen to Spencer." My throat burned. "I had to stake him," I added in a very small voice. "I *had* to."

"I know," he said softly, sliding his arm around my waist and tucking me into his side as if he was trying to protect me. It was kind of sweet. I let myself lean into him. "He was *Hel-Blar*," he added. "He wasn't Will anymore."

"Everyone keeps saying that."

"Because it's true." His hand stroked my back up and down, softly, soothingly.

"It doesn't feel like that. It feels like a betrayal. I couldn't help him, Quinn. I've never felt so helpless."

"Hunter, the last thing you are is helpless." He sounded so sure. I couldn't stop the first tear from falling.

"I don't want Spencer to die."

"He won't die." His lips were in my hair.

"You don't know that."

"I know about bloodchanges, Hunter. And Spencer is strong and healthy. He has a better chance than most."

I wanted to trust the little bubble of hope in my stomach, but I couldn't.

"Will didn't even recognize me," I said brokenly. "And it happened so fast. Why did he have to attack Chloe? Why did I have to be the one to stake him?" More tears fell and I didn't try to stop them this time. I cried because I couldn't not cry anymore. Quinn just held me, not saying a word. His hand cradled the back of my neck, running through my hair. I sobbed and trembled and sobbed some more until I felt weak and dehydrated. And a little bit lighter.

I sat up. Quinn's shirt was wet. "Sorry," I said hoarsely.

"Don't be." He touched my face, lightly skimming over my bruises so that I barely felt his fingertips. I wiped my nose on my sleeve, feeling well enough not to want to look like a disgusting mess.

"Thanks," I murmured.

He leaned in, closing the distance between us. His eyes stayed on mine. I didn't think, I just leaned in too. I kissed him first and his hands closed around my shoulders, pulling me closer. I slid my tongue along his, feeling warmth tingle throughout my body, melting the ice that had been creeping inside of me. He kissed me so thoroughly I felt naked, even though not a single button was undone. We were fully clothed and I had blades in the soles of my shoes and a stake in a harness in the small of my back but I'd never felt more exposed, or vulnerable. Still, I wasn't scared. I wanted more.

It became a kind of duel fought with lips and tongues to see who could make the other feel more, need more. I made small noises in the back of my throat. His arms were lean and strong under my hands and his hair fell to curtain our faces, smelling like mint shampoo. We tried to get closer to each other but it wasn't physically possible. We didn't care. We were so determined, nothing else mattered.

Until we tumbled right off the bed and landed in a lump on the floor.

"Ow," Quinn muttered. He rubbed his elbow. My shoulder shook. "Hunter. It's okay. Are you hurt? Hunter?" He sounded horrified.

I was laughing too hard to answer. He tipped my face up, saw the soundless chortle, heard the wheeze as I tried to haul in a breath. His answering grin was quick, followed a chuckle of his own. And another.

And then we were laughing so hard we had to hold on to each other. I wheezed. It felt nearly as good as Quinn's very wicked kisses. I'd been afraid it would feel like a betrayal of my friend who was lying in a hospital bed or my friend who was about to lie under the earth, but instead it felt like breathing again after being underwater for too long. Keeping the ability to laugh might be the only thing that would get my balance back. I couldn't fight for them, couldn't find out what was really going on, if I was crushed under sorrow and guilt and misery, which I could easily give in to if I let myself. But I couldn't risk that. I had to kick ass. All sorts of ass.

Starting now.

I eased back, holding my aching stomach. I tasted copper in my mouth. "Ouch, I think I bit my tongue," I said, wiping the tip of my tongue on my hand and seeing blood. "Yup. Gross."

Quinn went very still.

I was an idiot.

I'd let myself forget what Quinn really was.

I think, maybe, he'd forgotten a little too.

And now I was kneeling on the floor with blood in my mouth and there was no forgetting for either of us.

"Quinn?" I said softly. I didn't move.

It was just my luck that I finally got what I thought might be a real boyfriend, and now I might have to stake him.

Quinn was even paler than usual, crouched in front of me, his lips lifting off his fangs, which protruded as far as they could. I barely breathed. There were so many conflicting emotions chasing across his features, I hardly knew how to read them all. Most prominently I saw fear, violent restraint, desire, hunger. He swallowed and the movement rippled his throat. He looked like he was in pain.

And then he smiled.

And I knew real fear for the first time.

There was nothing more unpredictable than a young vampire. Nothing stronger or faster either. Or more hypnotizing. Speaking of hypnotizing, my vial of Hypnos was sitting on top of my pack at the other end of the room, where it did me no good at all.

I looked away from Quinn's burning eyes, from the flash of fang.

"Quinn," I repeated, sternly this time, like a cross librarian.

He flinched. Agony sharpened his smile into a humorless smirk.

"Hunter, run," he begged.

I lifted my chin. "No," I said, even though adrenaline was pumping through me like a sudden monsoon in the jungle of my insides. I was flooded with biological chemicals that made me want to bare my teeth back at Quinn like some caged panther.

"Please run," he pleaded again, but even as I shifted my weight, barely moving, he was on me.

His hand clamped around my wrist and he jerked me up as he surged to his feet. I was practically plastered to his chest, even as I leaned back as far as I could. Only my head and neck and shoulders had any freedom of movement, and I felt like one of those half-swooning pale girls in a Victorian novel.

Not a particularly nice feeling, as it turns out.

Quinn struggled but the animal inside him was at the surface, scenting blood and prey. No one knew what beast slept inside the vampire; all we knew was that it had sharp teeth and an insatiable appetite.

And I had no intention of being someone's supper, no matter how well they kissed.

Quinn lifted my hand to his mouth, closing his lips over the side of my thumb. His tongue moved over my skin, licking at the smear of blood. I would never admit this to anyone at any time, but it made my knees weak. It should have grossed me out. I was sure my heart was pounding because I was afraid. Not because of the way he was looking up at me, his eyes the blue of the hottest part of a flame, the part that burns the most.

"You taste like . . . raspberries."

I swallowed. "No, I don't."

"You do." He was staring at my mouth now. I clamped my lips together. The tiny cut on my tongue throbbed. It felt like a beacon, only it was calling the ship toward the rocky shoreline instead of safely away. I ran my tongue over my teeth, trying to get rid of the blood.

"I can get that for you," he purred.

I jerked back but I was still trapped in the cage of his arms. I narrowed my eyes. "Quinn Drake, stop it right now."

"But I don't want to," he drawled. "I want more."

"I don't want to dust you."

"I just want a little taste."

"You've had one," I pointed out.

"Not nearly enough. I'm greedy for you."

I didn't say anything, only stomped down suddenly, aiming for his instep. He easily spread his feet just as suddenly and leaned back against the wall, securing me between his legs.

"Damn it, Quinn."

"When you get mad like that, your blood smells even sweeter."

"Then you're about to go into sugar shock."

"Let's see, shall we?"

He kissed me, crowding out all the alarm bells ringing in my head. I kissed him back, hoping to distract him from his thirst. His mouth was gentle when I expected it to be predatory. He was dangerous like water, soft and smooth, even as it filled up your lungs, relentlessly stealing your breath away.

My head tilted and I wasn't sure if it was the pressure of his mouth on my jaw or my own movement. My throat was exposed and his fangs scraped the tender skin there, but he never pierced my neck. He didn't drink from me until I collapsed, didn't drain me until I was too weak to fight back, didn't let the beast win. He went against everything I was ever taught.

The longer we kissed, the more his hold loosened. He finally let me go, shoving himself farther against the wall.

"You should have staked me," he said. He looked as if he'd been in a battle, as if he should be carrying a stained sword and a battered shield. "I have to get out of here." He yanked the door open like it was rope and he was dangling from a cliff top.

"Wait."

"I have to go!" He snarled and the door slammed shut behind him.

CHAPTER 21

•

QUINN

Later Sunday night

When I got home, Lucy was lying on the couch saying the same thing she'd been saying when I left.

"I'm *fine*."

Solange was wearing sunglasses and sitting on a chair as far away as she could and still be in the same room, looking like she was about to throw up.

"Stop it." Lucy threw a pillow at her. Solange didn't move, and it hit her in the chest. Lucy snorted. "Nice vampire reflexes you got there."

Nicholas came in holding a painted tray with a steaming mug. Lucy sat up, glaring at him.

"No way."

He blinked at her. "What?"

"I am not drinking one more cup of chamomile tea. You can't make me." She folded her arms over her chest.

"You have a head wound."

"Yeah, and it hasn't affected my taste buds." She rolled her eyes. "Anyway, I have three tiny stitches. That's hardly a real head wound. They always look worse than they really are. Your uncle said so."

"You didn't see yourself passed out in the river," he said stubbornly. "We thought . . ." He trailed off.

Lucy's expression gentled slightly. "I'm okay, Nicholas. Promise. A little headache now, that's all."

"Are you sure?"

"For the hundredth time, yes." She looked sheepish. "I passed out when I saw the blood. It just took me by surprise."

I leaned in the doorway, feeling as if I couldn't catch my breath. I could still taste Hunter's blood on my tongue, like candy. I shuddered.

Lucy looked at me, then at Nicholas, who was hovering with a worried scowl, and then at Solange, who was sitting with her knees up to her chest. She let out a disgruntled sigh. "What is *wrong* with you guys?"

Nicholas and Solange exploded at the same time.

"You nearly died!" Nicholas shouted.

"I could have eaten you!" Solange added.

Silence throbbed for a long moment before Lucy rubbed her face. "You're both dumb. And way overdramatic." They just stared at her, clearly expecting a different reaction. There were smudges under her eyes but otherwise she looked fine. Uncle G. had checked her out. He had a couple of medical degrees stashed away, another benefit of a long life span. "Nicholas, stop worrying. I've been hurt worse in gym class. Solange, you like blood. Duh." She pushed three layers of afghans off her lap. "Hello? Vampire."

"You don't understand."

Lucy glowered. "Don't you dare pull that crap on me, Solange Drake. You might be a vampire but I've known you practically our whole lives. I totally understand. Give me some credit." She turned suddenly, jabbing a finger in my direction. "And you look weird."

I felt weird. Hunter just did that to me. But even she would understand the danger in being the only human in a room full of monsters. Lucy was stubbornly oblivious.

"I'm fine," I said with a dry smile. "Drink your chamomile tea."

"Only if it magically turns into hot chocolate." Lucy smirked suddenly. "You're all dressed up."

"Am not. I just naturally look good."

She grinned. "You went to see Hunter Wild, didn't you? That is so much more fun to talk about than my stupid stitches and Solange's meltdown."

"I did not have a meltdown," Solange protested.

"Please, you totally did." Lucy smiled briefly. "And I love you for it. But cut it out already." She waggled her eyebrows at me. The light reflected off her dark-rimmed glasses. "Did you kiss her?" She stopped. "Of *course* you kissed her. How was it?"

"I'm not a girl, Lucy. I don't want to braid your hair and talk about kissing."

Solange stared at me, sniffing the air delicately. She looked confused. "Did you bite her?"

"No, I didn't bite her," I answered, a little more roughly than I'd intended. "Instead of talking about me, why don't we talk about what the hell were you doing out in the woods in the first place?"

"Yeah," Nicholas agreed silkily. "Let's talk about that." He nudged Lucy into a chair. When he reached for the teacup, she narrowed her eyes at him.

"I will pour that on your head."

He didn't look particularly worried. "I'll tell Mom you're not resting."

Her mouth gaped open. "Dirty pool."

"Hell, yeah."

At least no one was talking about my love life anymore. "Solange, seriously," I said. "What the hell?"

"I just needed to get out," she said quietly. "With the abductions and the assassination attempts and the bloodchange, forgive me for feeling a little overwhelmed." She lifted her sunglasses. "And look at my eyes." Her pupils were still ringed in red, the whites bloodshot. They hadn't changed back.

"Ouch," Lucy winced. "Do they have vampire Visine for that?"

Solange didn't smile. "Anyway, you guys patrol all the time," she told Nicholas and me.

"Not alone!" he shot back.

"She wasn't alone," Lucy interrupted. "I was with her." She smiled sheepishly. "I followed her," she admitted.

"Why?" I asked.

"I don't know. I guess I was worried. But I knew she needed

some time alone so I didn't want to bug her." She shrugged one shoulder. "Montmartre's dead. And so's Greyhaven, and he was Montmartre's lieutenant or whatever, so I figured we were okay. It's not like the Host could have regrouped that fast."

"Did you conveniently forget about all the *Hel-Blar?*" Nicholas asked them with disgust. They both shrugged. He looked like his head was going to explode. My little brother had his hands full with those two. I just wanted to lie in a dark room and try not to replay every moment of that kiss.

You know, before I fanged out on the girl.

The *vampire hunter* girl.

I groaned, turning to stomp up the stairs. I didn't need super-sensitive vampire senses to know Lucy was chasing me.

"Oh no way, Quinn. No headache is going to keep me from getting the dirt."

She was as unshakable as a gnat. I couldn't help but shoot a grin at her over my shoulder. "I had no idea you were so kinky."

She flicked me. "If you want to save your brother's and your sister's undead lives, you will distract me right now."

"What, calling you a perv isn't distracting enough?"

She tilted her head. "I have photos of your superhero phase. I'm sure Hunter would love to see the one of you in the Batman tights and cape from that Halloween when you were ten."

"Remind me never to piss you off," I said.

"It's a basic life skill," she agreed cheerfully. "But an important one." She perched on the edge of my bed. "So spill, Casanova."

"Dream on."

She pouted. "I'm injured, remember?"

"Oh, so *now* you play the injured card."

She grinned unrepentantly, popping back to her feet. She'd never been any good at sitting still. "Why are you still all fangy?"

I ran my tongue over my fangs, being careful not to slice it open. I had no intention of telling her I'd had the urge to turn Hunter into a wineglass and drink her down like red wine. "Only you would reduce centuries of the mythical undead to 'fangy.'"

"I call 'em like I see 'em, fangboy." She paused at the window, frowning slightly. "There she goes," she said quietly.

"Who, Solange?"

She nodded. "She's going to hide in her pottery shed. I'm worried about her, Quinn."

"Why?"

She gnawed on her lower lip. "Because she's being weird. She told Kieran not to come over tonight."

"That's not weird."

"No, it's the way she said it." She sighed. "And my parents are coming back home the day after tomorrow, and I'm worried you guys are going to try and freeze me out. You know," she made sarcastic air quotes, "for my own good."

"We wouldn't," I lied. We totally would. We were a dangerous family to know right now. In fact, kissing Hunter and then actually tasting her blood had stirred my inner vampire closer to the surface. Even Lucy smelled good right now, and I was as used to her scent as to any of my siblings'. It rarely bothered me.

It was bothering me now.

"Lucy, I'm glad you're okay. If you do something stupid like

CHAPTER 22

◆

Hunter

Monday afternoon

I didn't hear from him for the rest of the night. Not a single text or phone message. Even so, I'd released some of the toxic knot of fear and worry clutching my insides, and I felt better prepared to do whatever I might need to do.

Which was convenient, since the first assembly of the school year was just as bad as I'd thought it would be.

It was after lunch and we were all gathered in the auditorium, which was in actuality an old wooden schoolhouse from the turn of the century, outfitted with salvaged church pews, also wooden. Hunters have always preferred everything to be made of wood— it's easier to splinter off a piece to use as a makeshift weapon that way. The first thing my grandfather did when he bought his house

that again, I'll kill you myself." I smiled to soften

go away. I'm tired."

She glowered at me. "You're not tired. You're try

of me."

I shoved her gently toward the door. Her neck was b

clean with antiseptic, but I thought I could still smell

blood from the stitches under her bandage. "Well, then tak

She turned and shoved her foot against the bottom of th

"Right there, Quinn. That's what I mean. You guys are all fi

like old ladies. It's like you're more afraid of vampires than I ar

"That's cause we're smarter than you are," I pointed out. "A

worried."

"Well, suck it up," she said crossly. "Because you're not gettin

rid of me that easily."

was rip off the aluminum siding and replace everything with board-and-batten.

There were rows and rows of windows and the thick, rippled glass diffused the sunlight into every corner of the building. It followed me into the room. There was no hope of hiding. Students whirled in their seats, staring at me as I passed, whispering loudly to each other. Luckily Jenna and Jason were close enough to the back that I wasn't on display for very long. I could see Chloe off to one side but she turned back to stare at the front, ignoring me.

I slid onto a polished pew to sit next to Jenna. She leaned forward and flicked the ear of a girl who wasn't even pretending not to stare.

"Ow," she squealed. She added a glare before shifting to sit properly.

Jenna folded her arms smugly. I sat with a straight back, my boots polished, my cargo pockets filled with regulation weapons and supplies. I couldn't avoid looking at the table near the first pew with Will's class picture from last year and a candle burning on either side. He was smiling earnestly. I tried not to remember him baring his fangs at me, trying to rip through my throat for my jugular. Or the feel of his skin and flesh and heart under the impact of my stake.

Jason leaned over from Jenna's other side. "Any word on Spencer?"

I shook my head. "I went over this morning but Theo said nothing's changed."

"That's not necessarily a bad thing," he pointed out.

"Chloe's still not talking to you?" Jenna asked.

"Guess not."

When Headmistress Bellwood strode across the stage, the heels of her sensible shoes clacking like gunshots, we all sat up straighter. The chatter died instantly. Even the first-year students knew enough to be afraid of her. The rest of the teachers filed in behind her. Mr. York was last, his whistle around his neck as always. I swore he slept with it on. He once blew it in Chloe's ear so loudly she was deaf for three days.

Headmistress Bellwood didn't need a microphone; her stern, crisp voice found you wherever you were. "Welcome to a new year at the Helios-Ra High School. You are embarking on a new journey and creating bonds with fellow hunters that will last a lifetime. Some of you will be discovering new talents and eventually choosing a department of the League in which to serve. The departments include standard Hunting, Paranormal Studies, Science, and Technology. What we do here is prepare you to hunt vampires and join the Academy college for further study in your chosen field."

I was only half listening. We'd heard variations of this speech several times over the years. And I was too busy talking myself out of checking for text messages from Quinn. He was unconscious in his bed; he could hardly have sent me a message.

Every time I thought about that kiss, my lips tingled, my belly grew warm, my knees went soft.

He was dangerous on so many levels.

"You will all be expected to model the virtues of this fine school: Diligence, Duty, and Daring," Headmistress Bellwood continued.

"I will not tolerate rebellion, recklessness, or arrogance. All of those qualities will get you killed and are, therefore, unacceptable. Those of you joining us for the first time will refer to the handbook for rules and regulations. Those of you returning are expected to remember those rules and follow them. I am certain you will all have an educational and enjoyable year. I look forwarding to meeting each and every one of our new students." Each and every one of those new students shuddered. "I am sure you've all noticed the memorial to one of our eleventh-grade students, Will Stevenson. I am saddened to report that he was infected with the *Hel-Blar* virus and did not survive." Everyone but Chloe was sneaking me glances. I lifted my chin, my expression blank. "Please pay your respects to his memory and take from this tragedy the necessity of always being on your guard."

Ms. Kali, one of the Paranormal Studies professors, descended the steps leading off the stage and went to stand behind the memorial. We all stood. The Niners exchanged confused glances before scrambling to follow suit. They'd never attended a student memorial before, but this would almost certainly not be their last. Ms. Kali's voice would have done an opera singer proud. She sang the traditional Helios-Ra mourning song, passed down through the centuries. Fallen hunters were usually buried with rose thorns, salt, and a mouthful of dried garlic. Garlic didn't actually have an effect on vampires, but the custom had started long before anyone realized that. Hunters who weren't cremated had a whitethorn stake driven through their dead hearts, another ancient precaution. Will had crumbled to ashes, so no one would be burying him in the local hunter graveyard. But the song was sung and a marker with his name would be added to the memorial garden behind the race track on the other side of the pond.

I was glad I'd shed my tears last night. It made it easier to get through the rest of the assembly with the weeping girls who'd had crushes on Will, the solemn faces of the teachers, the song raising goose bumps on our arms, the sunlight hitting Will's framed photo.

"Ninth graders will go to orientation on the south lawn," Headmistress Bellwood announced when the memorial was over. "The rest of you will pick up your schedules and get to your classes. On a final note, you've heard of the particularly virulent flu making the rounds. Two more students were hospitalized today, so I urge you to wash your hands and take extra care."

Students filed out, whispering respectfully at first, then chattering loudly and shouting to each other as they poured through the double doors onto the pebbled lane.

"Flu, my ass," Jenna murmured out of the corner of her mouth.

"Well, it's not like the school is ever big on full disclosure," Jason pointed out. "We're supposed to shut up and follow the rules."

"Yeah," I agreed. "Anyone else starting to find that really irritating?"

"I'm not loving it," Jenna confirmed. "Look, I gotta get to archery practice. I'm assisting in a demo for the Niners."

"See you at dinner," Jason called out after her. He frowned at me for a long moment. "When was the last time you actually slept?"

I shrugged. "I got a few hours last night."

"You look like hell."

I had to smile. "You know, if you ever decide to date girls, I have to tell you that's no way to compliment us."

"I'm serious, Hunter."

"So am I." I nudged him. "I'm fine, honest." I didn't tell him that making out with Quinn after sobbing through his shirt had done me a world of good. Quinn was hot enough that Jason would want details, and I wasn't the detail-sharing type. "I promise I'll grab a nap before dinner, okay?"

"Okay," he grudgingly agreed. "I'll see you later."

Classes went the way they always did on the first day. It was mostly roll call and a brief description of what we'd be expected to learn over the year. Ms. Dailey sent us away early; York made us run laps. I slept a little, mostly because I'd promised Jason, and then we had dinner and went to our respective rooms to start on assigned reading. Chloe wasn't around but there were clothes on her bed. I couldn't concentrate, so I went outside to sit on one of the stone walls around the decorative gardens by the front of the main buildings to watch the sun set.

The sky went sapphire, then indigo, and flared orange along the tree line. The stars came out one by one, clustered overhead in patterns I could never remember. I'd made up my own when I was ten: Dracula, a stake, a heart, a crossbow, a sun. I found them now as the crickets began their evening choir in the long grass at the edge of the woods. The harvest moon rose like a fat pumpkin growing in the fertile field of the sky.

Lights went on in the gym and the dormitory. I could hear the muffled sound of music from behind thick windows, the wind in the oak tree behind me, and the spit of gravel as a van roared up the path, lights out, hidden in the long weeds at the edge of the woods.

"Hunter," Kieran called grimly. "We found something."

CHAPTER 23

◆

Hunter

Monday evening

I crossed over to the driver's side, trampling wild chicory flowers under my boots. Kieran's face was solemn and tense, fingers tight around the steering wheel.

"What's going on?" I frowned up at him.

"We've got trouble," he answered, tone clipped. "And we can't talk about it here."

"Is it about the vit—"

"Not here," he cut me off, eyes widening in warning. He was right. There were cameras and microphones all over the place. We were probably being overly cautious since we were in the middle of a field, but something about his expression had me double-checking my pockets for stakes. "Get Chloe."

My stomach dropped. Clearly this was bad news. "Chloe and I aren't exactly talking right now."

I could read the desperation in Kieran's face. "Do whatever you have to do," he said tightly. "Knock her over the head and hog-tie her if you have to."

Gee, I can't imagine why one of my oldest friends wasn't talking to me.

"Does campus security know you're here?"

He nodded. "I told them it was covert ops and to ignore anything I do."

My eyebrows rose. "Seriously? Hart's in on this?" He was the only one with the kind of power to order that kind of covert op.

"No."

I paused, turned back. "No?"

"So we have to get out of here before I get busted."

"Shit, Kieran."

"I know. So hurry up."

I was so going to get expelled on the first day of classes. And then Grandpa would kill me.

I fished my cell phone out of my pocket and dialed Chloe's number. She answered on the third ring. "Hello?"

"Chloe, I have to talk to you."

"I'm busy."

"It's important." There was a long pause. I could hear her breathing, labored and short. She must be working out again. I started walking toward the gym, pointing at it so Kieran would know where to meet us. "Chloe?" I tried to think about what would get her outside with minimal yelling and fighting. I didn't think we could afford to attract that kind of attention, covert ops pass or not. "Look, Dailey wanted me to talk to you about her guild. We can't be overheard."

"Really?" She sounded startled and then pleased. I might have felt guilty if my jaw wasn't still bruised from her sloppy punch. "I'm at the gym. I'll be right down."

"Meet you there. Side door." I clicked off and cut across the lawn to the entrance tucked behind a wall and a copse of birch trees. It was dark and deserted enough that we might not get caught. She must have run down the stairs. She was still in her shorts and T-shirt, her hair in a ponytail. Her face was damp with sweat. She pushed the door open and looked at me warily.

"So?" she asked. "Does she want me to join the guild or what?" Kieran edged the van around the corner, blocking us from any passersby. She frowned. "What's going on?"

"I'm not sure yet," I admitted. "But Kieran has big news. He wants us to go with him."

"Where? And why me—" She cut herself off with a huff of impatience. "Is this about the vitamins? God, Hunter, you're, like, totally obsessed."

"Just get in," Kieran muttered, leaning out slightly. "We don't have all night."

"I'm not going anywhere with you psychos," she said, sneering.

I glanced at Kieran. "How serious is this?"

"*Very* serious," he assured me, hitting the button so the van door slid open. "'Spider-Man' serious." "Spider-Man" had been our code word since we were eight, used only in times of great danger. Chloe was turning away, disgusted. I didn't have a lot of options.

I did the only thing I could think of. I grabbed her shoulder and swung her back around toward us.

And then I punched her.

She staggered back, screeching. Not exactly covert ops. "Shit," she clutched her face. "Shit, are you nuts?"

I hadn't punched her hard enough to actually knock her out. She did look a little dazed though, so I took advantage of her momentary disorientation and shoved her into the van. She cursed as I slammed the door shut and Kieran locked it. I ran around the other side and got into the passenger side.

"I hope to hell you know what you're doing," I told him darkly, rubbing my sore knuckles.

"Oh, I'm sorry," Chloe snapped from the backseat. "Did I hurt your knuckles with *my face?*"

"No more than I hurt yours with mine," I shot back.

"Is that what this is? Revenge?"

"Chloe, don't be stupid," I said as Kieran shot the van into drive. We rumbled down the lane and out onto the road.

"Let me out!" Chloe was yanking at the handle and screaming at the top of her lungs. If she got any louder my ears would bleed. She kept yelling, a wordless high-pitched sound meant to make our eyeballs explode.

When we were far enough away from the school, Kieran slammed on the brakes. Chloe hurtled forward, nearly breaking her nose on the back of his seat. She swallowed another shriek.

"Put your seatbelt on," he demanded sharply, using the tone of an agent used to being obeyed. It was actually something he'd learned from his father. It wasn't common knowledge, but Kieran was only a graduate and not actually a full-fledged agent. He needed to do two years at the college for that, but he'd decided to take the year off to find his father's murderer. The profs had thought he was wasting his talents, that grief was warping him. But he'd been right. His father *had* been murdered—and by one of our own, no less. Hope was out of the picture now, but the damage was done. Still, Kieran had grown up a lot in the last few months. He wasn't the same guy who'd poured corn syrup dyed with red food coloring all over the cafeteria floor to freak the new students out. People still talked about that prank. Especially since a notorious bully fainted at the sight of it.

Chloe snapped her seatbelt into place, sulking. "Where are we going?"

"To the Drakes'."

We both stared at him, then at each other.

"Are you serious?" I asked. "We're going to Quinn's?"

"I get to see the famous Drake compound?" Chloe looked impressed despite herself. "I think you're both messed up, but it's totally worth it if I get to see that house." She kicked the back of his seat. Hard. "But I'm still telling Bellwood."

"Fine," he replied, unconcerned. "But first you'll shut up and listen to what we have to say to you."

I half turned in my seat to face him. "What *do* we have to say to her?" I still didn't know why exactly we'd just kidnapped Chloe.

"Marcus analyzed the vitamin you gave Quinn," he shot me a dry glance. "The vitamin you should have given *me*, I might add."

"He was right there, it was easier."

"Yeah, about that."

Chloe leaned forward. "Hello? Kidnap victim here. Focus." She scowled at me. "And you totally stole from me."

"Yup." I wasn't the least bit sorry about it anymore either.

"It's not a vitamin, Chloe," Kieran told her seriously.

She rolled her eyes. "Whatever. My mom gave them to me, Einstein. I think she'd know."

"Chloe, your mom's a biochemist," I said quietly.

"And a doctor, so shut up."

"She helped create Hypnos."

"So?"

"So," Kieran interjected, "it's not a vitamin, not completely. It's an anabolic steroid."

"I *knew* it," I muttered.

Chloe gaped at both of us. "You don't know what you're talking about."

"Here's proof." Kieran tossed her a folder with printed biological breakdown of her pills. "I need you to read that. When we get to the Drakes', you can go online on a safe computer shielded from the League and do your own research."

"Like the League can crack my computer security."

"All the same."

She ignored him and started flipping violently through the pages. I could tell the exact moment she really began to read and process the information. She went pale. When she looked up again, fear and anger and denial battled over her features. "Well, so what?" she snapped, as if either Kieran or I had spoken. "So she gave me steroids. They've made me stronger and faster. How is that a bad thing?"

I plucked the paper out of her hands and skimmed it until I had answer for her. "Have you grown a mustache yet?"

She blinked at me horrified. "*What?*"

"It says here that's one of the side effects. So's going bald."

She patted her hair a little frantically. It was one of her vanities. "I'm fine."

"You'll get acne too," I continued ruthlessly. I wanted my friend back. "And aggression and mood swings." I angled my head so she'd see the bruise on my jaw. "I think we can safely say you have both of those."

She winced. "I . . ."

"High blood pressure, liver damage, heart attacks, sterility, stunting your growth . . . do you want me to read on?"

She shook her head mutely. "But they were helping me," she finally said in a small voice. "I feel stronger."

"Chloe, they're bad for you."

"But . . ."

"Mustache," I repeated.

She swallowed. "Nothing's worth that."

She sat back and stared blankly out of the window. I didn't know what else to say, so I put the folder away. The trees and fields were dark, broken occasionally by the glint of moonlight or a cluster of stars through the leaves. The mountains loomed in the distance. Kieran drove for over half an hour before he turned into what looked like a field. There were tire marks in the grass but nothing else to mark it as anything but another field. Guards were discreet shadows. I caught the faint glimmer of light on a walkie-talkie. Kieran drove for another ten minutes before the tracks turned into a real lane leading to an old farmhouse.

It was impressive in its size. The logs looked like entire trees; the porch was wide and wrapped all the way around one side. The house itself was comfortably worn, like an antique. There were cedar hedges and oak trees and lamplight at the windows. Chloe let out an excited breath, briefly distracted from her own predicament.

"Wow," she said.

I slid out of the van and just stared for a moment. This was where countless vampires had been made, where blood was sipped like wine, where humans walked a dangerous path, where hunters had no doubt died.

This was where Quinn had grown up.

I thought I saw a shadow move in one of the upstairs dormer windows but I couldn't be sure. Even though I knew I was technically safe here, that there were treaties and friendships protecting me, I was still glad to have pockets full of stakes and Hypnos powder secured under my sleeve.

The front door swung open. I recognized Solange as she came down the porch steps, pale as a birch sapling, graceful as a white bird. The last time I'd seen her she'd been dressed for the Drake coronation. Now she wore old jeans and sunglasses. She smiled softly at Kieran.

He smiled back, taking her hand. "Thanks for letting us do this here."

"Mom and Dad are at the caves, so we should have most of the night." She turned to us. "Hunter, hi. And you're Chloe?"

Chloe nodded meekly. I'd never seen her so demure.

"What's the matter with you?" I hissed at her as we followed Kieran and Solange inside.

"She's royalty!"

"And a vampire, remember?"

"Oh yeah." Chloe paused. "Nope, princess trumps vampire."

"Does not."

"*So* does."

This was the real Chloe. The glimpse was enough to make me feel hopeful and confident. Even the foyer had her ogling again. I'd never been inside a vampire's house before either. The marble floors and crystal chandeliers were impressive, but I preferred the fire snapping in the hearth in the living room off to the right, and the worn sofas.

Somewhere, Grandpa was having a seizure.

I wouldn't have expected it to be so comfortable and, well, normal. I knew better than to rely on stereotypes, but thought I'd see at least one red satin dressing gown and maybe a coffin or two.

All I saw were shaggy gray bears barreling at us from all directions.

"Jesus." I stumbled back, fumbling for a stake. Kieran stopped my hand.

"Dogs," he murmured.

My heart leaped uncomfortably. I let out a nervous giggle. "I really thought those were bears."

"Bouviers," Solange explained, snapping her fingers once.

"Friends," she said, and the enormous dogs sat obediently, tongues lolling. A wolfhound puppy with legs like stilts slid across the hardwood floor leading from the kitchen, nearly kneecapping me. I grinned and crouched down to pat his head.

Lucy laughed, following him at a more sedate pace, a bandage under her hair. There was a peach in her hand. "Hey, Hunter."

"Hey." It was still startling to see a human girl so very comfortable in a vampire's house. She dropped down into a chair, throwing her legs over the arm and swinging her feet. Nicholas Drake sat across from her, watching her bite into the peach. It seemed intimate somehow, private. I looked away, wondering why I felt like blushing.

"I need to call my mom," Chloe said.

"Kitchen's free," Solange offered.

"Thanks." She paused in the doorway, cell phone in her hand. "Hunter, come with me?"

I followed, joining her at a harvest table with ladderback chairs. The kitchen was spotless. I couldn't help but look for a jug of blood. Chloe's foot tapped nervously as she waited for her mom to pick up.

"Mom?" she said. "I know you're in the lab, this will only take a minute." She paused. "Those vitamins you gave me are making me feel funny." She met my gaze bitterly. "Yes, I'm sure. Yes, I'm taking the right dose. I don't want to." She listened for a long moment. She was going to tap her foot right off her leg at this rate. "But . . . I know . . . but . . . Mom? *Mom?* Hello? Damn it!"

She turned off her phone and put it back into her pocket. "She's hiding something," she said with grim certainty. Her chair scraped the floor when she stood up. "Kieran," she called out. He came to the door, Solange at his side.

"Is there a computer I can use?"

He looked at Solange and she nodded. "Connor's got a few in his room," she answered. "I'll show you."

She led us up a wide staircase. "What are you going to do?" I asked Chloe.

"I'm going to break into my mom's files and find out exactly what's going on."

"Good," I said earnestly. "About time."

Solange took us up to the third floor, which had a sitting room and rows and rows of doors. With seven brothers all living up here, it kind of looked like a floor on our dorm. Solange knocked on a door and pushed inside. Quinn looked up from his computer.

"Quinn, where have you—" I stopped, confused. "You're not Quinn." He had the same features, but his hair was short and he didn't have that lazy smirk.

"His room's next door." Connor smiled. "And he'd tell you he's prettier, but I'm smarter."

I shook my head. "Twins," I finally clued in. "Sorry, I'd forgotten."

Chloe let out a reverent sigh. "Nice system," she said. She took inventory and spat out a bunch of technological jargon that had no resemblance to English as far as I could tell. "Sweet." She finally came back to words I understood. She cracked her knuckles. "Which one can I use?"

As she made herself comfortable in front of a computer on a desk made of a wooden door on blocks, I looked around.

"Where's Quinn?" I asked when I couldn't pretend not to care for a second longer. I did *not* like the look Kieran and Connor exchanged. "What?"

They both winced but wouldn't answer me. Dread was a ball in my belly.

Solange was the one to answer. I tried not to react to the tips of her fangs poking out under her top lip. "Quinn's hiding."

I blinked. "He's *hiding*? From what?"

"From you."

My mouth dropped open. Then my eyes narrowed, remembering the way he'd begged me to run away last night, the way he'd licked a drop of blood off my hand, the way he'd ignored my text message.

"Well, that's just stupid."

CHAPTER 24

•

QUINN

I knew Hunter was in the house even before she started pounding on my bedroom door. I could smell her, taste her.

"Quinn Drake, I know you're in there." She knocked again, harder this time.

"Hunter, go away," I said darkly.

"Like hell. I know what you're doing. So just stop it."

Silence.

I could feel her anger radiating through the door. She turned the knob but it only opened a couple of inches. The chain lock went taut at the top.

She craned her neck, glared at me through the small opening, and took a step back.

And then she kicked my door in.

Was it any wonder I was falling for her?

The chain ripped out of the wall, the snap of wood reverberating down the hall. She stepped through the doorway, glowering.

I shook my head, refusing to let her see how happy I was to see her. "I can't believe you just did that."

"I can't believe you're hiding from me."

"Hunter, you're not Wonder Woman, for Christ's sake. You're a good hunter, no doubt about it, but you're human. You're fragile."

"If you call me fragile again, I will personally break off your fangs and wear them as earrings."

I stalked toward her. "But you *are* fragile," I insisted, my hands closing around her shoulders before she could even see me move. I knew that to her I was a blur of pale skin and long dark hair and the glow of unnatural blue eyes. I pressed her against the wall, slamming the door with my boot at the same time. We were alone.

And I was just as pissed off as she was.

I had to make her understand. Even if she hated me for it. "You don't like to admit it, but I'm stronger than you are, and faster." I was so close that her legs, her hips, and her chest touched mine. Every time she took a ragged breath, it pushed her closer to me. "And I've tasted you now." I leaned in, lips moving over her throat, aching to taste her again. She might have been the canary to my smug cat. She'd hate that. "And I can never forget your blood on my tongue."

"I know what you're doing." Her voice was endearingly breathy. She swallowed.

"I'm just making my point." I said.

"You're being an ass." But she tilted her head so I could

continue nibbling. Centuries of her hunter ancestors rolled over in their graves.

"I could kill you, Hunter."

"Mmm-hmmm. I could kill you right back."

"This isn't a joke."

I seized her mouth, and for a long, hot moment there were no more words, no more warnings. Just tongues and tastes and lips seeking lips. I fisted my hand in her hair and hers hooked into my belt loops. And, as usual, it was over far too soon.

I pulled back abruptly, violent need and control twisting inside me. "I won't risk you."

Her eyes narrowed into slits. "You're trying to protect me," she seethed.

"And that's a bad thing?" I just didn't get her sometimes.

She drilled her finger into my chest. "When you make decisions for me, yeah, you're damn right it is."

"I'm just trying to do the right thing. I'm a vampire."

"Duh."

"And you're not."

"Again: duh."

"I could hurt you. I could lose control." I claimed her finger, my grip cool and utterly unbreakable. She'd have better luck snapping her own wrist in half than breaking my hold.

"If you were anyone else, I'd have kneecapped you by now." She poked me hard. "So give me break," she said. "You make out with girls all the time."

"They're not you," I replied quietly.

"Kieran's human," she pointed out. "And Solange is even

younger than you. She turned barely two weeks ago. Should I be worried about him?"

"I don't know."

"And Lucy?"

"I don't know."

She pulled back just enough to meet my troubled gaze. "Do you like me, Quinn?"

"It's not that simple."

"Yes it is. Answer the question." She looked horrified. "Shit. Unless this isn't about protecting me but about not wanting to see me again. Am I just another girl to you? Shit," she said again, going red. "I have to get out of here."

"Yes," I finally said, so softly it was a wonder she heard me at all. "Yes, Hunter, I like you." She released the breath she'd been holding. "I like you a lot."

I heard her heart lurch back into a proper rhythm.

And then she smacked me really hard in the shoulder.

"Ouch, way to ruin the moment," I muttered.

"You . . . ," she sputtered.

I tipped her chin up. "You didn't really doubt me, did you?"

"Hello? You locked yourself in your room to get away from me."

"Only to protect you," I defended myself. "I'm sorry."

"Don't you ever do that to me again."

"It won't be easy, you know. Despite how Solange and Kieran and Nicholas and Lucy make it look, this isn't simple. It might even be dangerous."

"You know I can look after myself."

"I know."

"And I'm way more terrified of my grandfather's reaction than your puny fangs."

"You're hard on the ego," I complained, but I was smiling again for the first time since I'd run out of her dorm room. "Your grandfather's an old man."

"Who could kick your ass."

"I've got moves, Buffy."

"I've seen your moves, Lestat," she teased, kissing me. I gathered her closer, hands roaming down her back and over her hips.

"You're not just a vampire, you know," she whispered. "You're the guy who let me cry all over you, when I never cry. Nothing makes sense right now—people at school are dying, my roommate's on some kind of hunter steroid—but you make sense. Somehow, you make sense."

Yup. I was totally, completely, and irrevocably into this girl.

A thump on the door had us both jumping.

"Hey, get off my sister," Kieran barked from the other side.

"Get lost, Black," I called out. "And she's not your sister."

"May as well be."

"Well, you stop kissing Solange and I'll stop kissing Hunter."

Silence. I smirked. Hunter pulled away, rolling her eyes.

"Hey, where are you going?" I murmured. "We're not done making up."

"We're in crisis mode out there," she answered, reluctantly taking another step back.

"It's always crisis mode in this house," I said with disgust.

"Still. We should go help."

I huffed a mock melodramatic sigh. "This is that Helios-Ra duty thing, isn't it?"

"Afraid so."

CHAPTER 25

◆

Hunter

Monday night

In the room next door, Chloe looked exhausted. She'd pulled her hair out of its ponytail and it was a mess of tangled curls. Solange and Kieran were sitting on the edge of Connor's bed and Connor was at his desk, tapping away at another computer. It was amazing how much he and Quinn looked alike. Quinn nudged me as if he knew what I was thinking.

"I'm cuter," he informed me loftily.

Connor shot me a knowing grin over his shoulder. Chloe scrubbed her face.

"Find anything?" I asked her.

She leaned back in her chair. "I don't really know. I mean, I got into my mom's files. Her passwords have always been pathetic."

"And?"

"And it's definitely a steroid, but that's it. There's nothing else sinister about it." She shook her head. "Except, why in the world would she slip me steroids? It's just weird."

"She didn't make lab notes or anything?"

"Nothing remotely helpful. Although she referred to a 'Trojan Horse' a couple of times. Nearly gave Connor and me a heart attack. I so don't need some hacker computer virus right now. But it's not that—we scanned all the machines to check. So it must be code for something else. I'll figure it out." She grimaced. "Maybe not tonight, but I'll definitely figure it out."

I glanced at my watch. "Yeah, we should head back. Just in case Kieran got busted. I really can't take any more demerits and detention this year. If York sneers at me one more time I might just lose it."

"What about the second pill we found," Quinn asked. "Did Marcus figure out what it is?"

"Should know by tomorrow night." Connor shrugged. "The Academy is basically a high school, you know. It could just be an upper or caffeine pill."

"Maybe," I said doubtfully. There were just too many coincidences and variables.

And secrets. Definitely too many secrets.

At the front door, Kieran kissed Solange good-bye. I cleared my throat at him obnoxiously until he glowered at me, but if I didn't set a precedent right now, he'd be interrupting all of my makeout sessions.

"I'll call you," he whispered to her before heading out to the van. He pulled my hair as he passed me. Chloe was already in the backseat, her knees pulled up to her chest. Quinn grabbed my arm as I was reaching for the front door handle. He twirled me backward into his arms and dipped me, like they do in those old-fashioned black-and-white movies. And then he kissed me cross-eyed.

"See you soon." Even his whisper felt like a kiss. I somehow managed to get into the van and buckle myself in. Quinn slapped the side of the van and Kieran pulled away, spitting gravel.

"Wow," Chloe murmured. "That was some kiss. I need a vampire boyfriend."

I grinned. "He has a lot of brothers."

"And every single one of them is yummy," Chloe agreed.

After that, we rode back mostly in silence, trying to process what we'd found out tonight. It wasn't dawn yet but the sky looked more gray than black, like ashes covering a red ember. The memory of Quinn's kiss kept interfering with my concentration.

Kieran groaned. "I don't trust that smile."

"Yup," Chloe reiterated as Kieran pulled up onto campus. "I definitely need a Drake brother of my very own."

Chloe might be making jokes but I knew she was freaked out. I'd have been freaking out too, if I'd just confirmed my own mother was drugging me. But it was late and we were tired and we both just wanted to fall into bed.

Hard to do that when the mattresses were half off their frames and most of our stuff was strewn about as if a mini hurricane had come in through the window.

We both stood and stared.

"Someone tossed our room!" Chloe shouted, incensed. She ran straight to her computers, running her hands over the wires and checking the plugs like a mother checking a small child for broken bones. "I'll kill them," she muttered. "I'll kill them."

The closet doors were open, spilling cargo pants and school sweatshirts and all my pretty dresses. A tube of toothpaste was on the floor by my foot. My books were everywhere, my organized stakes and daggers were scattered. My jewelry box was upside down and silver chains, turquoise pendants, and bracelets spilled out in a tangle.

"Whoever did this wasn't robbing us," I said flatly, untangling a necklace from the nearby lampshade. "They were looking for something."

Chloe finally looked up from her computers, reassured that no one had tampered with them. She scowled.

"Who the hell would do that? And what the hell were they looking for?" She nearly choked on her own words, staring horrified at the open bottles of aspirin and cold tablets spilling out like confetti. We looked at each other grimly. "Someone was looking for my vitamins," she stated dully, as if she couldn't quite believe it. She held up her Xena action figure, arm bent and marked with a footprint. "Someone who is going to die horribly when I find them."

I shoved my mattress back into position and then dropped on top of it. I was suddenly so tired I could barely stand up. "Who else knew you were taking vitamins?"

Chloe shrugged, wincing. "Anyone who heard us fighting or me bitching about it afterward. A few people asked me for some when they saw me finally do a good roundhouse kick at the gym. I guess they figured it was a magic pill. With the flu and *Hel-Blar* attacks and everything, everyone wants an edge."

"Steroids don't make you finally get a roundhouse," I told her. "Practice does that."

"Yeah, but the steroids made me stronger." She rubbed her palms on her legs, as if they were sweating. "And I'm really suddenly wanting another vitamin right now." She swallowed. "Does that make me an addict?" She stared at me frantically.

"No," I assured her sternly. Chloe's flare for dramatics could create a whole problem where there was none. Sometimes you had to cut her off at the pass. "It makes you a person who got used to taking vitamins, so try taking actual vitamins."

"Huh. That actually makes sense."

"And you might want to go talk to Theo. He'd know what to do."

"Okay." She took a deep breath, then another one. "Okay." She picked one of her bras off the floor. "I'm still killing whoever did this. And I'm doing it before the steroid strength wears off."

"Deal. I'll help you." My trunk poked out from under the bed, bursting with romance novels. I shoved it back under.

"Hunter?"

"Yeah?"

"Thanks for the whole steroid thing." She picked up the compact mirror left on her pillow and stared at her upper lip.

"You don't have a mustache," I assured her.

"I could kill my mom for that. She nearly gave me a beard and a bald spot."

I snorted a laugh, then tried to cover it up with a cough. She shot me a look but I could tell she was trying not to laugh too.

"It's not funny," she insisted.

"Of course not," I squeaked, choking on a giggle.

"I could have looked like the wolfman!" she added. "Or my grandma!"

We laughed until we were crying. Fatigue and relief and tension made us slightly hysterical. We finally wheezed ourselves out and calmed down.

"We should get some sleep," I croaked. "We have class in a few hours."

"God," Chloe groaned. "I have to face York. How fast am I going to get all weak and puny, do you think?"

"You were never puny." I yanked my blanket over me. I couldn't be bothered to change into my pajamas or to clean up the clothes piled messily around me. One of my boots was stuck under my pillow. I tossed it aside. "You're just better with tech than with your fists. It's no big deal."

I was almost asleep when there was a timid scratching at the door.

"Are you kidding?" Chloe mumbled. "Do we have mice? I can't deal with mice right now." The scratch turned into a hesitant knock. I groaned and stumbled out of bed. "What now?"

Lia stood on the other side in pajamas with pink lollipops all over them. Her eyes were red and watery.

"Lia, what's the matter?" I looked over her shoulder and down the hall, half expecting a *Hel-Blar* to jump out of the shadows. It was just that kind of night.

"It's my roommate," she sobbed. "She's really sick. I don't know what to do."

I blinked blearily. "Did you tell Courtney?"

Lia shook her head, biting her lip.

"Why not? That's her job. She'll get one of the nurses."

"No, *you* have to come. You can't tell anyone."

"What? Why?"

Chloe pushed in behind me. "Do you know what time it is?" she barked.

I grabbed Lia's arm because she looked like she was going to run away. "Lia, what's really going on?"

"Savannah's sick."

"And?"

She swallowed. I waited, refusing to let go. "Lia, if you want my help you have to be honest with me."

Her lower lip quivered and I felt like a monster, but I stood my ground. When Lia finally spoke, it all came out in a rush of words that took a moment to sift through. "I don't want to get in trouble and I promised her I wouldn't tell but her lips are going blue and she's breathing funny and I just don't know what to do."

"Okay, calm down," I said softly, as if she were a wild bird and I had a handful of bread crumbs. "What's the big secret?"

Lia reached into her pocket and took out three little white pills. "She's been taking these."

It was the same white pill Quinn and I had found in the common room.

I plucked one from her hand, growing cold all over. It was like an arctic wind was pushing through me, filling my lungs and freezing the blood in my veins.

"Chloe," I croaked. "Look."

Two letters were stamped in the center of the pill.

"TH."

Trojan Horse.

◆

Chloe and I bolted up the stairs, Lia hurrying after us. I called Theo from my cell and by the time we got up to Lia's room, three of Savannah's friends were hovering outside the door, worrying. Too many students had gotten sick already and too many of those had died for anyone to dismiss this as a simple flu, like the teachers were trying to tell us. The last thing we needed right now, though, was more attention and panic. Especially if Chloe and I had just discovered some sort of conspiracy, like I thought we had. We'd need witnesses eventually if we blew this thing wide open, but not right now.

"Is she going to die?" one of Niners asked bluntly.

"No," I answered and pushed inside the room, shutting the door firmly.

Savannah lay in her bed, moaning. Her skin was clammy and damp with perspiration. She was hot to the touch and her eyes, when she pried them open, were bloodshot. Chloe hissed out a breath. We exchanged a bleak glance.

"Savannah." I lowered my voice when she jerked at the sound. "It's okay, we're here to help. Savannah, this is very important. Can you tell me where you got those pills?"

"I don't want to get anyone in trouble," Savannah mumbled through dry, cracked lips.

"You won't," I assured her. "We just need to know where you got them."

"I bought them," she coughed. "I was only supposed to take one a day but I took three. They were supposed to make me stronger."

Chloe frowned. "Like steroids?"

Savannah nodded weakly. Chloe stared at me. "Hunter, these aren't the pills I was taking. Mine were yellow and huge."

"I know," I answered, frowning back. "People don't know there's two different pills, I guess. Who told you they'd make you stronger?" I asked Savannah.

She glanced away, coughed again. I handed her the glass of water on her nightstand. "You won't get in trouble," I told her.

"Some guy was selling them out of the eleventh-grade common room," she answered finally. She swallowed the water but her throat constricted violently, as if she was sipping from a glass of razor blades. She whimpered. "I don't feel good."

"There's a nurse on the way. He'll make you better."

"I'm scared." She clutched my hand. Her grip was pathetically weak and damp.

I didn't know what to say. Chloe didn't know either because she just sat there. "You'll be okay." I said it again for lack of something more convincing. "You'll be okay."

She closed her eyes, lips wobbling.

"I mean it, Savannah," I snapped, terrified she was about to slip into a coma. She had to stay awake. She half opened her eyes. I smiled encouragingly. "Just stay with me. Okay? Stay with me."

"I'll try."

Courtney and Lia rushed into the room. I'd never been so glad to see Courtney as I was right then. She had pillow creases on her cheek and she was blinking furiously as if she couldn't focus. When she finally did, she gasped. She looked scared.

"Not again."

I nodded gloomily. "Theo's on his way."

Lia shifted from one foot to the other. "She's going to be okay, isn't she?"

"Of course she is."

"She looks kind of gray."

Courtney took a deep breath and forced herself to stop staring at Savannah. She touched Lia's shoulder. "Lia, why don't you get her a cold wet cloth? And tell everyone else to go to their rooms and stay there."

"Okay."

We sat around Savannah's bed in a silent vigil, listening to the harsh rattle of her breath. I couldn't help but think of Spencer lying in quarantine. Chloe squeezed my hand, her eyes wet with tears.

"I know," she said quietly. "But Spencer's strong. And he didn't . . . you know."

She was right, Spencer was an accident of time and place. He wasn't the type to take pills. He was going to be fine.

The three of us leaped to our feet when Theo came through the door. He looked capable and confident and I could have kissed him. He lifted Savannah's wrist to feel her pulse.

"Is she lucid?" he asked.

"She was," I confirmed.

"How long has she been like this?"

"I don't know. Not too long, I don't think. Her roommate came to get me just before I called you."

"Okay." He lifted her eyelids, felt her forehead. "We're taking her to the infirmary."

Another nurse wheeled a stretcher into the room. One of the doctors and a security guard pushed in behind her. The doctor's mouth thinned when she saw Savannah.

"Let's move quickly," she ordered.

The room emptied in minutes and the guard stood in front of the door, arms folded. Lia blinked at him.

"But my stuff's in there," she said.

"The doctor said she wanted the room sealed off now, just to make sure it's not contagious," Courtney explained. "Come on, we'll find another bed for you."

Courtney led her away as Chloe and I hurried after the others. Students in pajamas gathered on each floor, craning their heads to see what was going on. Floor monitors tried to shoo them back. York barreled into the building and marched past us, blowing his whistle, practically right in my ear. "Everyone back to bed! NOW!"

The sound of scurrying feet echoed on every floor.

By the front door, I grabbed Theo's arm. "Wait," I said. "She took these." I handed him one of the white pills. He scowled at it. "What are they?"

"I don't know yet."

He shook his head, slipping them into his pocket. "This year just sucks."

CHAPTER 26

•

Hunter

Tuesday night

Most of Tuesday went by in a blur. I slept through all my early classes, but none of my teachers said anything. Everyone was subdued and solemn. Campus felt as if it were covered in ashes.

I loved this place and I loved the League. I'd been raised to think the League was better than Christmas and Halloween candy and birthday presents. And now I suddenly felt like a six-year-old finding out there was no such thing as Santa Claus. I didn't know what to think; I just knew it felt awful.

I went to the infirmary after dinner with Chloe and Jenna, even though Jason had already been and told us they weren't letting anyone in the door, especially with Savannah sick as well. Theo wasn't there so we were stopped at the threshold. The doctor shook her head sternly at us. We might have tried to argue with her, but we could hear Spencer's mom sobbing from behind the curtain so we slunk away. We kept to our schedule because there wasn't anything else to do.

Then I went to the gym that Dailey had reserved for her first Guild meeting. I wasn't really sure what to expect, but I was looking forward to being distracted, to have something else to fill up my brain. There wasn't the usual chatter as we waited for her to arrive. It was mostly twelfth-grade students with a sprinkling of others from the eleventh and tenth grades. There were no Niners at all. We all smiled questioningly at each other, but no one had any answers.

"Good, you're all here." Ms. Dailey strode in with a welcoming nod. "We have a lot of work to do, so let's get started."

One of the students raised his hand. "Um, Ms. Dailey?"

"Yes, Justin?"

"What exactly are we starting?"

She chuckled. "I've handpicked you all as the best this school has to offer. You're all honor students or well on your way to becoming such. And now, you'll be even better." She smiled at us. "We'll cover fighting, of course, and weaponry and tactics, but also stealth and technology and other, newer ways to win the fight. It's no secret that recently *Hel-Blar* have been crawling all over campus, Violet Hill, and even surrounding villages. If we're to contain this new threat, the League will need more help. And my Guild will be first on call, before any other student group. I'm excited to get started."

She gave us a list of books we needed to take out from the

library and the password for the private Web site she was putting together for us. I left feeling better than I had all day. I had a purpose again, and options. And confidence in the Helios-Ra, despite recent evidence to the contrary. I waited until everyone else had cleared out.

"Yes, Hunter, what is it?" Ms. Dailey asked when she noticed I was still hovering nearby.

"Could I talk to you for a minute?" I asked awkwardly. "It's . . . private."

"Certainly." She frowned worriedly. "What's wrong?"

"It's about all the sick students."

"Oh, Hunter, that's not for you to worry about. You're a strong, healthy girl."

"It's not that. It's . . ." I hoped I was doing the right thing. I was pretty sure Ms. Dailey would hear me out and not drag me to the headmistress or the school shrink. "There's some kind of pill going around," I told her. "I think it's making people sick."

She looked startled. "Drugs? Already?"

I blinked. "What do you mean already?"

"It's only the first week of school. Usually the pills don't start circulating until mid-terms." She shook her head.

I smiled uneasily. "I don't think this is that kind of pill."

"Oh?"

"I don't have the chemical breakdown yet, but this one's dangerous. Really dangerous. And . . . vampires don't like it."

"Vampires?" she sighed. "Hunter, what have gotten yourself into?"

"Nothing good," I admitted. "Will you help me?"

"After the speech I just gave everyone? Of course I will."

Relief flooded through me and I had to swallow a nervous giggle. "Thank you, Ms. Dailey! The pills are little and white and have 'TH' stamped on them. Savannah was taking them just before she got sick and I think Will was too."

White lines bracketed her mouth. "We'll get to the bottom of this, Hunter." She flicked the gym lights off. "Now let's not say another word about it until I can do some research of my own. The walls have ears."

I nearly skipped down the stairs. She winked at me before turning down the lane toward the teachers' residence, heels clacking. Teachers like Ms. Dailey were rare. I hadn't forgotten how she'd stood up for me when York busted me at the first drill. If it came to it, at least we now had someone on the faculty we could trust.

Bolstered, I was grinning when Quinn popped out of the edge of the woods and scared the breath right out me. I leaped into the air, shrieking.

So much for Dailey's training.

Quinn laughed so hard he bent right over. I laughed too and pulled his ponytail. "Shut up."

"Hunter, you're adorable."

"Excuse me, I am fierce and kick-ass."

"That too." He took my hand, his thumb rubbing over my palm. "And you're cute in your workout shorts."

I was suddenly aware of all my bare leg. I absolutely refused to blush. His grin widened.

"What are you doing here?" I asked him.

His hand moved comfortingly over my wrist and up my arm. "I'm here to take you on a date."

I blinked. "A date?" I repeated as if it was a foreign word I'd never heard before.

"You know, where we go out, hold hands, cast longing glances at each other? It's tradition. You might have heard of it."

"But I have class."

"Class?" Now he was looking at me as if I was speaking a different language. "But it's ten o'clock at night."

"We have classes until midnight." I smiled pointedly. "The thing about vampires is that they kind of like the night. It's tradition. You might have heard of it?"

"Oh, smart mouth." He grinned back. "Sexy."

He prowled forward, maneuvering me against the trunk of a tall pine tree. The branches started dozens of feet above us, spreading out branches like a green parasol. The ground was soft, carpeted in rust-colored needles.

"Can you ditch?" Quinn asked temptingly. "I've been up to my eyeballs in prep for the Blood Moon. All very political and hush-hush. You'd love it."

I shook my head. "I'm sorry, I can't."

"Can you be late?" he pressed.

"Well, I am interested in compromise between our people."

"My people are grateful." He captured my mouth with his. The kiss started slowly, turning deep and hot within moments. I was in a cocoon of feeling, of warm tingles, pale skin, and tree bark. Electricity ran between us. I half believed that if I opened my eyes I'd see sparks and forks of lightning licking at us.

Further in the woods, ferns shifted. There were stars, crickets singing, an early autumn breeze, and a handsome young vampire kissing me.

It would have been perfect if my grandfather hadn't interrupted us.

"Hunter Agnes Wild!"

Quinn, oblivious to the danger, pulled back, laughing. "Your middle name's Agnes?"

"After her great-grandmother," Grandpa roared. I winced, stepping around Quinn to shield him.

"Hi, Grandpa. What are you doing here?"

"I'm a guest lecturer," he barked. "And what exactly are you doing, missy?" He glared at Quinn. I counted under my breath, one, two— Grandpa choked on another roar. "Vampire!"

Three. He must be really flustered at finding me making out to have needed three full seconds to register the unnatural stillness and paleness of Quinn. Not to mention his fangs, delicately dimpling his lips, brought out by our kissing. I shifted another step in front of him.

"Grandpa—"

"Hunter, stake him and let's get to class," he said impatiently.

I swallowed. "I'm not staking him."

He raised an eyebrow disapprovingly. "Not prepared? Here, take one of mine." He tossed me one of his stakes. I caught it out of instinct.

"Grandpa."

"What are you waiting for?" He glared at Quinn. "And what's wrong with this one that he's just standing there?"

"Grandpa." I sighed. "This is Quinn Drake. Quinn, my grandfather, Caleb Wild."

"Vampire," Grandpa spat again.

Quinn smirked. "Old man."

I closed my eyes. This was going well. My boyfriend was an idiot and my grandfather was going to rip him into bloody pieces. Grandpa was built like a bull. And the only reason he hadn't staked Quinn yet was because I was standing directly in the way. I was also pressing my shoulder back into Quinn, forcing him to stay where he was. Who knew dating was so dangerous?

"Hunter Wild, you get away from him right now."

"No." He goggled, turning so red so fast I thought he might be having a heart attack. "No, sir," I added to appease him.

"I would never hurt her," Quinn said, his smirk fading. "You have my word on that."

"The word of a vampire? Pah."

"The word of a Drake."

Grandpa spit. Quinn growled. I slapped a hand on his chest.

"You can't bite my grandpa." I tossed a look over my shoulder. "And you can't stake my boyfriend."

Grandpa went gray. "Boyfriend?"

I cringed. "Quinn, you should go."

"I'm not leaving you alone," he protested.

"Please." I pushed at his chest. "Please just go. I'll call you when I can."

He searched my face for a long moment before touching my hair briefly. "Fine. I won't be far."

"I know," I said, relieved he wasn't going to fight me on this. I had my hands full as it was. When I turned back to Grandpa, Quinn was already gone, leaving behind shifting leaves and the fleeting touch of his lips on mine.

"Please just listen," I started as my grandfather struggled not to explode.

"I don't want to hear it," he ground out. "You'll stop all contact with that boy, with all of the enemy, and we'll pretend this never happened. Let's go."

"Grandpa, no."

"You're trying my patience, girl."

"I'm sorry," I said miserably. "But I have to do what I think is right. Quinn's not the bad guy here. He might be cocky, but he's also honorable and brave and loyal. He saved my life."

"He's one of *them*." He looked older suddenly, as if all his years pressed down on him at once. "You're my little hunter. Even when you were small you could hit a target with your stakes at thirty paces. You're gifted."

"I'm still a hunter," I insisted. "Nothing's changed, not really."

"Everything's changed!" he shouted. "You're part of the Helios-Ra! The Wilds have been members for as long as I can remember. We kill vampires. It's what we do."

"I'm still Helios-Ra."

"But you're not a Wild," he snapped. "Not if you behave like this."

It felt as if he'd slapped me. "What? Grandpa, don't. I know you're upset but don't."

He pointed a finger at me. "You owe the League your loyalty."

"It has my loyalty, but not my blind obedience. And anyway,

the League has a treaty with the Drakes, remember? Plus, someone's drugging students, Grandpa, someone in our precious League."

"Don't be ridiculous."

"I have proof. Students are getting sick all over. Chloe's own mother was giving her steroids. Have you heard about some operation called the Trojan Horse?"

I was so relieved at his honest bewilderment that I could have wept.

"What are you going on about?" he demanded. "Hunter, leave League business alone. Leave it to the adults."

"I can't."

"And stop seeing that . . . thing."

"I can't do that either."

"Your mother would be ashamed."

"I'm ashamed too."

"As you should be."

"Of your bigotry, Grandpa," I finished quietly. "You know I love you, but I'm not you. You can't force me to be. I agree with the treaties. I *like* what Hart's doing with the League."

"You're young."

"So? That doesn't make me stupid. You didn't raise me to be stupid. You raised me to be strong and independent and clever. Can't you trust that?"

"I don't even know you anymore, girl. How can I trust someone who willingly fraternizes with monsters?"

I took his big callous hand in mine. "It's not that simple. But it's still me. I'm still *me*."

"I love you, girl," he said gruffly. "You know I do. Now stop this nonsense. We have class."

He'd raised me. He was the only family I had left. And he looked at me as if he couldn't stand the sight of me. The only reason I didn't let the tears fall was because it would have convinced him right then and there that I was no longer his granddaughter. I tilted my chin, straightened my shoulders.

And I let him lead me toward the gym where the Niners waited for a demonstration from one of the League's most celebrated hunters.

Kieran was waiting for us outside the main gym. His hair was caught back in a ponytail, his cargos were perfectly regulation. He still wore his cast. Grandpa clapped him on his good shoulder.

"Glad you're here, Black. Maybe you can talk some sense into my granddaughter."

I waited stone-faced. Kieran looked wary.

"What do you mean, Caleb?"

"She's dating a vampire!" he exploded.

Kieran winced. "Oh."

Grandpa's eyes narrowed to slits. "You knew about this?"

"Uh . . . yes, sir."

I sighed. "Grandpa, leave him alone."

"He's supposed to look out for you."

"I do!" Kieran sounded offended. "You should be proud of her. Hart requested her presence personally at the Drake coronation."

I closed my eyes briefly. We were doomed.

"You went to a vampire ceremony?" Grandpa asked evenly.

"He didn't know?" Kieran asked.

"No, he didn't."

"Sorry."

Grandpa vibrated with rage. "I will not tolerate this kind of behavior in my family!"

"It's different now," Kieran tried to assuage him. "I'm dating Solange Drake. They're a good family."

Grandpa went red, then purple. Kieran took a step back. I whacked Grandpa between the shoulder blades.

"Grandpa, breathe!"

His breath was strangled but at least he didn't keel over. Before he could shout the rafters down, the door swung open and York eyed us all with the barest politeness. Grandpa glared at him.

"What?" he barked.

"We're waiting for your demonstration," York barked back.

Grandpa jerked his thumb at Kieran, ordering him inside. I winced sympathetically. Helping Grandpa with fight scenarios when he was in a temper never ended well. I followed, because skipping it would have started another lecture on family responsibility. The Niners looked eager and nervous, chattering among themselves. Lia waved at me.

Grandpa threw a ninja egg at a short boy with glasses before York even blew his whistle.

A pepper cloud had everyone in the immediate vicinity coughing and sneezing.

"First lesson," Grandpa growled. "Be aware of your surroundings."

The boy's face was bright red as he wiped his streaming eyes with the sleeve of his shirt. Everyone else stood at immediate attention, silently cowed. York looked reluctantly impressed.

"This is Caleb Wild," he introduced belatedly. "Mr. Wild has been a hunter for decades. This is his assistant Kieran Black, nephew of Hart Black." Excited glances were exchanged when Kieran's last name was recognized, but the only sound was the pepper victim choking on a cough. Grandpa cut an impressive figure, pacing in front of the cadets, his white hair cut short, his muscled arms scarred. His boots clomped, ringing like an iron bell. Students trembled.

"You've all been given a sacred duty to protect the world against vampires. And every single one of you is capable of winning that fight. You!" The girl next to Lia staggered back a step.

"Yes, sir?"

"What's your skill?"

"I . . . can throw."

"Good. You!"

"Um . . ."

"Figure it out. You!"

"I'm fast."

The students were still terrified, but they started to stand with more pride in themselves as hunters. Grandpa was good at that.

"It doesn't matter how small you are," he continued. "Or whether you're a boy or a girl, or what your last name is. What matters is the League and the amount of fight in you. Even if you're wounded, you can still make a difference. To demonstrate this, Kieran and I are going to spar."

"And I'm going to die," Kieran muttered so only I could hear.

Students broke from their stiff rows and circled the mat in the center of the room. The mirrors surrounding the walls showed their eager faces; the windows showed nothing but shadows.

"The first point I'll make is that if you're wounded, you stay out of the fight. You run the hell away if you can, so you don't endanger the mission or your team. If you can't run away, you damn well win. Understand me?"

"Yes, sir!" The chorus reverberated with enthusiasm.

"And you follow orders, hear me?"

I knew that was for me.

"Yes, sir!"

I didn't say anything. I had no intention of obeying.

"How would you fight me?" he demanded of Kieran.

Kieran already had a stake in his hand.

"Good. But you missed and I have you by the throat. Now what?"

Kieran gurgled since now Grandpa really did have him by the throat. "Another stake."

"And?"

Kieran swept out with his foot, hitting Grandpa's ankles. Grandpa staggered, stumbled. I hissed out a breath when he nearly fell over. Kieran didn't react and I didn't move. If we betrayed a single ounce of concern, Grandpa's pride would be wounded. In fact, he was grinning for the first time that night.

"That's my boy."

Kieran turned his back, glancing at the students. "And then I run," he said, to illustrate the earlier point.

Grandpa leaped to his feet. The floor shook. He grabbed Kieran's ponytail, jerking him to a stop. In his other hand, he held one of the daggers from his belt. I didn't have time to say a word, only to squeak.

The blade cut through Kieran's ponytail.

His hair drifted to the floor and he whirled, bug-eyed with shock. Everyone else gasped. Grandpa looked smug.

"If you have a weakness like a broken arm, you rid yourself of all other weaknesses," he said, sliding his knife back into his scabbard. "If you don't learn anything else, learn this. Weakness is not allowed."

His faded eyes pinned me where I stood.

◆

Grandpa left without saying another word to me. Kieran paused only long enough to squeeze my arm.

"I'll talk to him," he promised severely, holding his ponytail in his fist.

I nodded mutely and stalked back to the dorm, boiling with anger and hurt and guilt. Chloe was sitting cross-legged in the middle of her bed. She looked up when I stormed in.

"Let's figure out this TH thing," I said before she could ask me about my mood. I just didn't want to talk about it. I wouldn't know where to start. "So we know someone's selling the stuff at school and we know it's a recognized Helios-Ra drug. Well, sort of recognized," I amended. "It must be secret or it wouldn't have been hidden so deeply in the files, right?"

"Definitely. We could get your number-one fan Lia to try to score some. See if we flush out the dealer?"

I wrinkled my nose. "I guess. But I'd rather not endanger her like that. And anyway, I'm thinking since the dealer's a student he or she is just a small fish in a big pond."

"Probably."

"Okay, so then let's make a list of the students who have gotten sick. There was that first guy—I don't know his name."

"And then Will. Or was that just a *Hel-Blar* thing?"

"He mentioned he was taking vitamins, so let's add him to the list. Speaking of vitamins, have you talked to your mom yet?"

She grimaced. "No. She's been at the lab and I know she won't talk to me until she's at home. Jeanine after Will," she added. I added her to the list.

"Spencer," I said quietly. "Though I don't actually think he's part of it."

"Me neither. Jonas and James. Those ninth-grade twins, the really short ones?"

"Right. And then Savannah."

"She was short too."

"What, so the drug is for short people?"

She rolled her eyes. "I guess not."

I paused, frowning. "Actually . . ."

She blinked. "What do you mean, actually? You think the school's taking out short people? That's just weird."

"No, listen. What do they all have in common?"

"They're mostly Niners? And short."

"Will was in eleventh grade and tall," I argued. "But gentle." I raised my eyebrows. "All these students would have been considered weaker. Short, skinny, not into fighting." I leaned forward while details fell into place. "And who picks on those kinds of people on a regular basis?"

"Bullies?" Chloe's mouth dropped open. "York." She slapped her bedspread. "That must be why my mom's been feeding me steroids all summer. I would have been one of the weak ones without it! I found the info buried in her files just before you got here. She knew about it. She reads all the lab notes, but she didn't want to pull a society-wide alarm before proper tests were conducted. You know how she is about research. Damn it, Mom."

"So York's been making sure the weaker students get the TH?"

"Looks like."

I met her shocked eyes grimly. "So how do we take him down?"

CHAPTER 27

•

QUINN

Later Tuesday night

I got a text just before dawn. Marcus finally had results from the blood samples Hunter had given me.

He also had Solange sitting on a bench, looking shell-shocked.

Her eyes were red but it was the kind of red you get from too much crying. When I burst through the door of the barn Uncle Geoffrey used for his scientific experiments, she looked away, lower lip wobbling.

Solange's lower lip never wobbled.

Marcus looked like he was about to start running. Crying girls made him nervous, even when it was his little sister. Or maybe especially when it was his little sister.

"Hey, Sol," I said quietly, crouching down in front of her. There were acres of Bunsen burners and glass beakers on the counter behind her. Light sparkled on scrupulously clean equipment that looked like it belonged in a science-fiction movie. If Uncle Geoffrey ever wanted a gig as a mad scientist, he was well on his way.

"Quinn, go away," she said miserably, picking at the dried clay on her pants. She'd probably made a hundred pots on her pottery wheel in the short couple of weeks since she'd turned.

"Not a chance," I said gently. "What's going on?"

"Nothing. I just came to talk to Uncle Geoffrey."

"Okay, so what's the problem?"

She shrugged, keeping her head down and refusing to look at me. I glanced at Marcus. He shrugged too, then patted her shoulder.

"Solange, it's nothing to be embarrassed about," he said. I got the impression he'd said that a few hundred times in the last hour. "It's biological. Like acne."

She made a weird sound in the back of her throat. I closed my eyes briefly. "Nice," I said. "Tell a sixteen-year-old girl everything's fine because it's like pimples. And by the way? What the hell's going on?" I stared at her. "Where's Uncle Geoffrey?"

"He's gone to talk to Mom and Dad."

"Why? Are you sick?" Dread was heavy and metallic in my stomach, like iron.

"Yes!" she exclaimed at the same time Marcus muttered, "No."

Solange pursed her lips. "It's . . ." She finally huffed a sigh and then squared her shoulders. She tilted her chin up. "It's this." She lifted her lips off her teeth. Her fangs were out.

All six of them.

I blinked and counted again. Her regular canine teeth fangs were out, with two more on either side. The second pair were like the original and the third were very small, barely noticeable. Her gums were inflamed and raw.

Drakes didn't grow more than one set of fangs. It was a mark of our ancient blood, of our more civilized form of vampirism. There was some snobbery in the courts—the more fangs you had, the more feral you were. Isabeau had two sets and she flashed them proudly, but she was unique, even among vampires. The *Hel-Blar* had nothing *but* fangs. No wonder Solange was freaked out.

She thought she was turning into a monster.

She swallowed hard, trying not to cry. Marcus patted her shoulder harder.

"Don't cry." He was begging.

"What did Uncle Geoffrey say?" I asked softly.

"That I was special," she snorted, a flash of her regular self. "Special," she repeated. "God."

"Ouch." I winced sympathetically.

She hugged herself, as if she were cold. "Quinn, what if this means I'm not finished with the bloodchange? What . . . what if I turn into a *Hel-Blar* or something?"

I stood up, glowering. "You are *not* turning into a *Hel-Blar*."

"You don't know that."

"I do too. For one thing, you're not blue. And you don't smell like moldy dirt."

"I'm serious."

"So am I."

"Uncle Geoffrey said you'd be fine," Marcus reminded her.

"He said he *thought* I'd be fine. He also said he's never heard of this happening in our family. In any of the old families."

"It's just because you're a girl. You know, the first in hundreds of years and all that. Your change is a little different. That's all."

She poked at her new fangs. "The royal courts are going to have a field day with this, especially at the Blood Moon. The feral princess." She groaned. "Someone's going to write a song."

"Probably. But think of how much harder you can bite them when they do."

Her laugh was watery, but it was a laugh. "True." She stood up. "I'm tired. I'm going home."

"Wait for me," Marcus and I both said together.

Marcus pulled folded computer printouts from his pocket. "Your sample analysis."

I grabbed it, skimming the charts and graphs. I'd skipped the majority of Uncle Geoffrey's science lectures. That was the summer most of the girls my age in town miraculously grew boobs. I had fond memories of that summer. None of them involved anything that might help me decipher the blood analysis. I looked up, disgusted. "What the hell does this say? I don't speak geek."

Marcus snorted. "Careful, little brother, or I won't translate."

"Just tell me what it says."

"That your girlfriend was right." He paused, clearly waiting for me to react to the term "girlfriend." I didn't. I'd take Hunter any way I could get her. If I had to start using words like "girlfriend" and turning down other dates, I'd do it. "It's not vitamins in the blood," Marcus continued. "Those pills are a steroid."

"Yeah, we knew that. Her friend's already off those."

"They're not the real problem," Marcus said.

"This just gets better and better. Hit me."

"The second sample, from that kid who died?"

"Yeah?"

He looked grim. "He was poisoned."

I went cold. Hunter said people at her school were falling sick all over the place.

"And the poison wasn't just meant for him." Marcus's fangs flashed. "It was meant for us."

CHAPTER 28

◆

Hunter

Wednesday night

"Got something!" When Chloe's computer beeped the next night, she dove across the room, elbowing Jason in the gut.

He rubbed his sternum. "The hell, Chloe?"

"I hooked it up to beep when it cracked the TH file password," she said excitedly.

"I thought you didn't want to do that on campus, where they might tamper with the connection?" Jenna asked as we crowded around the back of her chair.

Chloe waved that off. "I put in a few more security shields and a red herring or two. We should be fine. Besides, we're running out of time and I've mostly been concentrating on my mom's files."

"So what've you got?" I pressed, bewildered by the gibberish on the screen. "What did you find?"

"Another file hidden in my mom's notes—labeled TH." Chloe bounced in her chair. I knew that bounce. She was onto something. "I want it." She chewed on her lower lip as the screen flashed. "Different password." She hit a few more keys. "This would be easier if I had my mom's actual computer. I could dust her keyboard." She tapped her foot impatiently. "Come on. Come on, I said!" It took a few more minutes but she finally grinned. "Gotcha, you sneaky bastard."

We all leaned in to read.

"That's some kind of chemical breakdown, isn't it?" Jason frowned. "For medications, or something."

I skimmed the page, nodding. "Looks like. Here's a list of side effects."

"The steroid?" Chloe asked in a small voice.

I shook my head. "No. Just the TH. And . . . holy shit. Holy shit, we were right. It *is* meant for poor fighters. It says right here that it should only be given to weak hunters who aren't expected to survive vampire attacks." I felt sick to my stomach. "It goes through their bloodstream and makes it poisonous to *Hel-Blar*, to any vampires." I remembered the blond *Hel-Blar* who'd disintegrated right in front of me after biting Will. "The League is sabotaging its own hunters to poison *Hel-Blar*." My head was spinning.

No one said anything for a long moment.

"That's just . . ." Jenna shook her head, unable to find a word heinous enough to describe what we'd just discovered.

"There has to be some mistake," Jason said doubtfully.

I marched over to my supplies and started shoving stakes in my pockets and checking microphones and night goggles. They turned slowly, staring at me.

"Hunter?" Chloe asked, as if she was afraid I was about to lose it. "What are you doing?"

"We're taking York down," I said forcefully. "Right now."

"Um, we're going to beat up a teacher? That seems like a really bad idea."

"We're not going to beat him up. Give me a break. We're just going to nail him for passing out that disgusting pill, and then we're going to dismantle the entire League if it comes to it."

Because sometimes you had to betray the League in order to safeguard it. Sometimes you had to break the rules. Sometimes duty was hard and uncomfortable and burned inside your chest. Grandpa taught me that last part well enough.

"How exactly are we going to do that?" Jenna asked. She held up her hands, palms out. "I'm all for a little payback, but I'm hunter enough to know better than to fight a battle I can't win."

"I have every intention of winning."

"I get that, I really do."

I tied my hair back in a braid, tucking it under my collar. "We use the same plan we had before," I explained. "For now. Jason is going to nose around and see if he can't get someone to sell him drugs."

Jason winced. "I feel like I'm in one of those after-school specials. If I get branded a narc, I'm blaming you."

I ignored him. "I'm going to e-mail this file to Kieran and have him give it to Hart. And then Jenna and I are going to switch off shifts staking out York when he's not in class."

"Am I going to need a fake nose and a trench coat?"

"And Chloe's going to ask York for after-school training help and act all clumsy and weak."

She sighed. "I guess I should be used to that."

"Are we ready?" I asked, sounding like a drill sergeant. "We need evidence and we need it soon."

"Sir! Yes, sir!" Chloe shouted with a mock salute.

I made a face at her. "Let's just go. Last class ends in an hour."

◆

I took the first shift, creeping around the pond to perch on a boulder at the edge of the woods, where I had a good view of the teachers' residence. If York left the building for any reason, I'd be able to see him and follow him. I felt a little like a detective in the old movies Grandpa loved so much.

Thinking about Grandpa just made me feel worse.

Helios-Ra and our duty to our hunter ancestors was the glue that had held us together after my parents were killed. I barely remembered them, but I remembered Grandpa dressing up like Van Helsing one Halloween and scaring all the little kids dressed as vampires. He'd taught me how to clean a wound properly, how to look for patterns in the movements of leaves and litter that betrayed a nearby vampire moving too quickly for human eyesight. He gave me my first stake. There'd been tears in his eyes last year when he got my report card. He'd always been proud of me.

Not anymore.

And I'd always been proud of the Helios-Ra.

Not anymore.

The difference was, I intended to do something about it. I wanted to be proud of the League again. And proud of myself. I wanted to make it right.

Making it right was surprisingly boring.

I sat on that rock for two hours, until my legs cramped and I'd nearly staked a chipmunk and a raccoon and traumatized a bunny.

All the rooms in the teachers' hall stayed dark. Even the motion lights stayed dark outside in the garden, where the animals liked to overturn the compost bin. The windows reflected the trees, the moon, the sky. Chloe was long since in bed, and Jenna wouldn't relieve me for another two hours.

I was staring so hard at the residence that when Ms. Dailey spoke softly behind me, I fell right off the rock.

I leaped back to my feet, going red. "Ms. Dailey!"

"At ease." She smiled gently. "Hunter, what are you doing out here?"

"I . . . uh . . . I couldn't sleep." I wondered why she was out here so late.

"Are you worrying about our little problem?"

I nodded. "We found out it's even worse than we thought," I explained in a rush. "It's some kind of weapon against vampires that uses students as carriers. It's sick."

She tilted her head. "Ingenious, actually."

I blinked at her. "Sorry?"

"I had such high hopes for you, dear girl. You've always been particularly talented. A little too clever, clearly, and now, sadly, misguided as well."

"Misguided?" I echoed. "What are you talking about?"

"You didn't think that scene with your grandfather wouldn't be all over school, did you? As well as your unfortunate and disgusting affiliation with that vampire."

I took a step back. Her expression was still pleasant but she didn't sound like the Ms. Dailey I knew at all. The instinct to run vibrated through me.

Before I could take a single step, she pulled a syringe from behind her back.

She stabbed me right in the arm with it.

I swore and jerked back but the needle was stuck in my muscle, pumping its clear liquid into my veins. I scratched at her face, managing to get her blood under my nails before the dizziness assaulted me. I stumbled.

"What did you do to me?" I panicked. My tongue felt swollen; my feet felt as if they were on backward. I stumbled again and fell to my knees. She watched me dispassionately.

"I'm rather grateful you chose to hide yourself away here, where no one will hear you. Very considerate of you."

My fingers shook as I yanked the needle out of my arm. It tumbled into the grass. "What is this stuff?"

"I think you know, a smart girl like you. It's a rather potent overdose of TH. I'm afraid you left me no other choice."

"What? No!" I clawed at my skin. My veins felt as if they were getting warmer, as if all of me was burning up. My breaths became shallow and short. "It was York. *York*."

She laughed lightly. "He's far too pedantic for this sort of genius."

"But he picks on all the weak students." I was beginning to slur. I felt like I was hit by the worst case of the worst flu ever.

"Caught that, did you? Yes, his temper made my work much easier. I knew exactly who the worst students were, as they made him the angriest. He was so scared for them, you see. He wanted them to get stronger and be able to protect themselves." She circled me, waving her hand to dismiss him. "This is much better. If they are going to die by a vampire's hand, they may as well become weapons in themselves. A sacrifice for the League. And so eager to comply when they think it's a secret pill to make them stronger. It takes a while for them to weaken, and by then—think of the vampires they might infect. Especially if they're like you, Hunter."

"I don't see . . . you . . . sacrificing yourself," I spat. I tried to turn over but I was too heavy. The effort had me gasping.

"There's no use struggling. I gave you quite a high dose. You might survive it. I hope you do, at least for a little while. Then you can take out that Drake brat as well."

She wanted Quinn to drink from me and die.

"Go to hell," I croaked.

Dailey pursed her lips. "To think I picked you for the next Guild leader. I had such hopes after the *Hel-Blar* attack, and after you staked Will."

"You're crazy." I had to call Theo. I fumbled for my cell phone but my hands weren't working properly. I couldn't scream either. I couldn't get enough air into my lungs.

"I'm just doing what must be done. With all these treaties and the *Hel-Blar* infestation, we're losing our focus." She was lecturing me as if we were in class. "I had to test you all, to see who was worthy to be a member of my Guild. I set blood traps for the *Hel-Blar* and they came like rats to cheese."

"You got the *Hel-Blar* to attack the school?" She'd had me totally fooled. York hadn't been the culprit. He was actually the good guy—even though he was a jerk. Dailey was the psycho. I'd had to stake Will because of her. Spencer was sick because of her, at least indirectly. I was drugged and poisoned and crumpled on the ground because of her.

I really, really hated her.

I would have spat at her if I hadn't been so thirsty and dehydrated, burning up with fever.

And I was apparently hallucinating too.

"Get the hell away from her," Quinn snarled, leaping to stand in front of me in a blur of pale skin, long dark hair, and sharp fangs. Dailey took a step back, startled.

"You're too late," she said. "I've already dosed her. It's in her blood."

"What's in her blood?"

I squirmed, as if fire ants crawled under my skin. "Quinn," I panted. "Call Theo and get out of here. She's nuts."

Instead, he punched her. Her nose cracked and she howled. Quinn patted through my pockets.

"What are you doing?"

"I know you must have rope somewhere . . . got it." He turned away for a brief instant, leaving trails of light and color like a smeared oil painting. He tied Dailey up and was kneeling at my side before I took another labored breath. His fangs extended farther, gleaming.

"You can't bite a teacher," I whispered through dry lips.

"I'm not going to," he assured me. "I'm biting you."

CHAPTER 29

◆

Hunter

He didn't understand.

If he drank my blood, it would kill him.

I struggled fruitlessly as his mouth descended on my arm, closing around the puncture hole the needle had made.

"No," I moaned. "No."

His fangs bit deep and I cried out. The blood burning my veins rushed toward the sucking of his mouth. I tried to pull away but he anchored me down, holding me still. The grass was cool and prickly under me.

"Don't," I begged, tears stinging my eyes. "It'll kill you."

He lifted his head, eyes blazing.

"It's killing *you*," he said harshly, spitting out a mouthful of my blood. A welt formed at the side of his lip. It looked painful. He went back to the wound, drawing my poisoned blood out of my veins and into his mouth. He spat more into the grass. He kept sucking the poison out and spitting as fast as he could, the way you would a snakebite. The ceiling of stars and cedar branches overhead whirled.

I was fading.

If I closed my eyes the pain would stop, Quinn would stop. He'd be safe.

My eyelids were heavy and I let them close.

EPILOGUE

♦

Hunter

Friday night

When I woke up I was in the infirmary.

The lights were too bright, washing everything out as I blinked furiously, eyes stinging. I was exhausted. I tried to move, moaning when it proved to be too much work. My arm was bruised and burning.

"She's awake!" Quinn was at my side first, holding my hand. He was paler than usual, nearly gray. The blue of his eyes was paler, the shadows underneath darker. "You scared the hell out of me." He kissed my forehead.

"You're alive."

"So to speak."

"Am I . . . am I a vampire?"

"No, you're just a stubborn know-it-all who thinks she can do everything by herself," he answered tenderly. "You didn't drink my blood, remember?"

"Don't hog her," Chloe said, brushing him aside with a grin. He leaned over enough to let her in but didn't let go of my hand. Jenna and Jason and Kieran stood on my other side.

"What happened?" I asked. My throat felt singed. I reached for some water and Quinn grabbed the cup so quickly he spilled half of it down his arm and into my hair. I drank the rest gratefully, greedily.

"You've been out for two days. You had to have blood transfusions," he explained.

"Are you okay?" I asked.

"I was sick as a dog there for a while, but I'm fine."

"Dailey?" I asked.

"Under house arrest until you're well enough to testify against her," Kieran answered. "Don't worry about it now."

"She tried to kill me," I said, affronted. "And Quinn. And she poisoned Will and the others."

"Hart's handling it personally," Kieran assured me.

"Bellwood's furious," Chloe added cheerfully. "It's like the stick up her butt caught fire!"

"Dailey's not going anywhere," Kieran added.

"Damn right she's not," I muttered. I patted myself down, searching for my left cargo pocket but finding only a paper hospital gown. I craned my neck. "Where are my pants?"

"Your stuff's here." Chloe plucked up my pile of clothes from a shelf behind me. She dropped the pants on my lap. I smiled even though it cracked my dry lips. I pulled a microphone out of the pocket.

"I recorded everything she said," I told them smugly. The effort made me cough. "It was meant for York. I guess I owe him an apology."

"He doesn't have to know we ever suspected him," Chloe protested. "He's been a jerk to you. And he yelled at me in class just this morning." She frowned. "He freaked Mom out in my report card last year. He said the usual stuff about me not living up to my potential, but since she'd just heard about the TH, she kind of panicked. She hadn't figured out who was in charge of it, so she snuck me those steroids, just in case. To make sure I was off the TH radar. She was trying to protect me in her own weird way. Mothers."

"Anyway, don't worry about that stuff." Jason patted my hand. "Just get better."

"She'll get better as soon as you all get to class," Theo interrupted, elbowing them aside.

"Wait," Jenna said, eyes glowing. "One more thing."

She and Jason shifted over. Spencer grinned weakly at me from the next bed. His dreads spread out over his pillow.

"Spence!" I squealed. "I would so hug you right now if my head didn't weigh seven hundred pounds."

"Ditto."

"You're better! You're out of quarantine!"

"Also, a vampire."

I tried to sit up. The room wobbled. I lay back down with a thump. "*What?*"

"Turns out your Quinn here accidentally discovered the antidote to TH in humans," Theo said. "Vampire blood."

"Okay, I haven't been in chem or bio class in a while but . . . huh?"

"Spencer got a transfusion too," Theo explained. "For one thing, Will transmitted some of the TH poison to Spencer, and we had to get that right out of him. That's what was stumping us—before Quinn's help. If he hadn't sucked it out of your veins, we might not have done enough transfusions with Spencer. Even so, the medications didn't cure his *Hel-Blar* infection. We had to give him even more blood so he wouldn't go feral. The doctor might get an award for that, actually. If she doesn't get kicked out of the League for technically creating a vampire, that is."

"I guess that means I graduate early," Spencer said.

"I'm just glad you're okay."

Theo cleared his throat menacingly. Chloe, Jenna, and Jason left but Quinn and Kieran stayed behind. Theo took my pulse and had me follow his flashlight with my eyes.

"Looking much better. How are you feeling?"

"Like a truck hit me and a bear ate my arm." My stomach growled. "And I think I'm starving."

"That's what I like to hear. I'll get some food sent over." He eyed Quinn and Kieran malevolently. "Five more minutes and you both get lost. Don't make me tell you again." He smiled at me. "Doctor will be in to check on you soon."

"They're talking about giving you a medal." Kieran grinned.

I winced. "No, thanks."

"You'll at least be the valedictorian."

I saw some daisies in a basket on the side table. "Who are those from?"

"Your grandpa," Kieran replied. "He's a stubborn know-it-all too."

"Is he here?"

He shook his head. "He won't come, Hunter."

I swallowed, trying not to let my lips wobble. "He's still mad."

"I'll talk to him," Quinn offered.

"No!" Kieran and I burst out together.

"He'll just try and stake you," I explained apologetically. "You can't rush him."

Theo glowered from the doorway. "Out!"

Quinn kissed me lightly. "I'll be back tomorrow night."

Spencer and I were left alone with the ticking and beeping of the machines and the tubes pushing liquid nutrients and medications into our bodies. There was enough blood being fed into Spencer via those tubes that I wasn't in danger, not the way I would have been if I'd been lying around with any other newly turned vampire. He touched his fangs and then jerked his hand away.

"Vampires are in now," I said quietly. "Don't you read? All the girls will be hot for you."

He tried to smile. "And I don't have to study for any exams this year like the rest of you. I guess I'm officially a dropout now."

"Oh, Spencer. It'll be okay. Things are changing."

"Yeah, I leave you alone for a week and you start making out with vampires."

"I told you," I teased, making my voice bubbly and high. "They're like totally trendy!"

"Dude."

"But you can't hide away and brood and go all melancholy. That's so yesterday. Plus, I'll kick your ass."

After a long moment he spoke again. "I'm going to miss the sun."

"I know." I turned my head. "We'd miss you more if you were dead."

He scrubbed a hand over his face. "Thanks."

"Besides, just think, now you can go hang out with the Hounds and ask them all sorts of magic questions."

He brightened instantly. "True."

I shot him a watery grin when Theo wheeled my supper tray in. "And I don't have to share my chocolate pudding with you ever again."

◆

Spencer was discharged the next night.

I didn't know where he'd gone, but Quinn promised to help him with the transition to his new undead life. I wasn't allowed to leave the infirmary for a full week, and even then it was only after promising that I'd take it easy and wouldn't even look at the gym for at least two more weeks—and then only with a doctor's permission. The doctor whom Grandpa would still talk to since he refused to talk to me. I'd called him twice and each time the conversation was the same.

"Are you still seeing him?

"Yes."

And then he'd hang up on me.

But I wouldn't let that ruin everything else. I was alive. Quinn was alive. Spencer was . . . a vampire but at least he wasn't completely dead. Savannah and the twins were recovering, though slowly. Dailey was being held by the League disciplinary committee pending a full investigation. And Hart had called me personally to invite me to form a Black Lodge of carefully selected students, apparently the first at the school in at least three decades. It was a subgroup within the League that no one knew about except its members and the head of the Helios-Ra. None of the teachers even knew, except for the headmistress. We'd be like a secret roving band of spy-warriors. I couldn't wait.

"Now, that's a dangerous smile," Quinn murmured, his voice tickling my ear. His arms wrapped around my waist and pulled me back against his chest. I leaned into him, my smile turning even more wicked.

"What are we doing out here?" I asked. I'd gotten a text to meet him out by the pond.

"Same thing I'm always doing: trying to get a proper date out of you."

"Who knew you were so traditional?" I turned, teasing.

"Who knew you were such a rebel?" He slid his arm lightly over my bandage and clasped my hand. The stitches from his bite would come out tomorrow. There'd be a scar, but I didn't mind so much. He tugged me through the field, tall grass brushing against my knees.

He led me into a copse of birch saplings. He'd spread a blanket on the ground and lit candles in glass jam jars. He even hung a few lanterns from the branches and they hovered like fireflies. It was beautiful.

"We're having a picnic," he announced.

"But you don't eat."

He shrugged. "But you do."

We sat down and he handed me a thermos of hot chocolate. There were baskets of chocolate chip cookies, a cherry-chocolate cake, sugar-dusted strawberries, and a tower of macaroons.

I grinned. "Finally, real food."

I ate until the sugar buzzed through my veins. Quinn lounged beside me, the candles pouring honey light over his pale cheekbones. He licked chocolate frosting off my finger, grinning darkly. He was everything my grandfather feared: reckless, wild, predatory.

And he was mine.

ALYXANDRA HARVEY studied creative writing and literature at York University and has had her poetry published in magazines. She likes medieval dresses and tattoos and has been accused of being born in the wrong century—except that she really likes running water, women's rights, and ice cream. Alyx lives in an old Victorian farmhouse in Ontario, Canada, with her husband, three dogs, and a few resident ghosts.

www.alyxandraharvey.com
www.thedrakechronicles.com

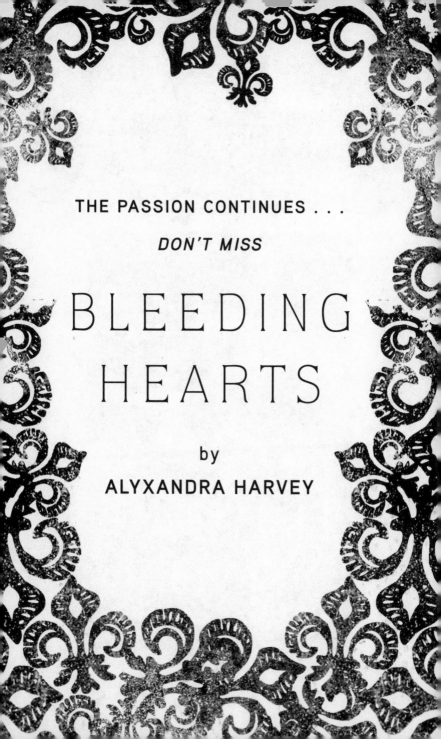

THE PASSION CONTINUES . . .

DON'T MISS

BLEEDING HEARTS

by

ALYXANDRA HARVEY

Don't miss
Alyxandra Harvey's darkly romantic,
spine-chilling ghost story

Violet doesn't believe in ghosts . . .
but they believe in her

HAUNTING
VIOLET

ALYXANDRA HARVEY

WALKER